THE GREAT TRAITOR

BOOK TWO OF THE *GALAXY ON FIRE* SERIES

JOSEPH KASSABIAN

KYANITE
Publishing

The Great Traitor

Copyright © 2020 by Kyanite Publishing LLC

For permission requests, please contact the publisher, Kyanite Publishing LLC, via e-mail, with subject "Attention: Permissions Coordinator," at the e-mail address below:

info@kyanitepublishing.com

Paperback ISBN: 978-1-952152-09-2
eBook ISBN: 978-1-952152-08-5
Hardcover ISBN: 978-1-952152-10-8

Cover design by Kyanite Publishing LLC
Editing by Sam Hendricks

https://kyanitepublishing.com

Books by Joseph Kassabian

Hooligans of Kandahar

The Galaxy on Fire Series

Citizen of Earth

The Great Traitor

The Consul
(Forthcoming)

THE GREAT

TRAITOR

CHAPTER ONE

Vincent sat down on a large wooden chair, his joints and the wood both sounding in protest. On the desk in front of him were several different black data displays. He had been ignoring his work again. Arai would be pissed. He clicked on the first display and white text glowed up from the receiver.

It was a large roll of names with a header that read: *Gumi Report for the 20th day cycle, formerly May 2146.* The Elysian humans, the hundreds of thousands who had escaped the killing fields of Grawluck and found refuge on the Fidayi Clan planet of Elysian, had still not quite figured out how to use the Mawr Calendar. Instead, they had just decided to stick with what they knew. It required a bit of translation, but it worked for the most part. Unfortunately, as Vincent was the only fluent Mawr-speaking human on the planet, it only added extra work for him.

The Fidayi Clan were considered the Free Mawr and Rhai of the galaxy. When the Anarchs, the giant armored alien race that chaired the Alliance, forced the Mawr and Rhai to join them in their galaxy-wide crusade, only a few Clans of the Mawr rejected them—one of which was Arai's Father' Clan, the Fidayi. Their resistance got them nothing more than a destroyed home world and their race being scattered into the stars. The other surviving Clans quickly joined the Alliance to save their race from utter destruction. It was those Clans that Vincent had fought against with the Earth Defense Forces in a futile last stand on The Hilltop.

The Clans that continued to resist reformed the Fidayi Clan on the planet of Elysian. The Rhai and the Mawr that had refused to kneel before the Anarchs flocked to their new Warlord Arai. Ever since, she has been a giant thorn in the side of the Alliance military juggernaut and to a lesser extent, the Central Committee.

Just below the header was a list of about one hundred different names. All of them had been arrested. This was hardly a new problem. In the year since the fall of Earth the refugee human population had done little to move on. Made up of mostly young soldiers of the Earth Defense Forces with little experience living a normal life, let alone accepting the fact that almost everyone they had never known or loved was now dead, meant they did little more than drink and fight one another.

This was why Arai decided that the human race was a big enough part of the Clan to warrant government representation, or Consul. Each race of the Clan had a Consul representing them and they came together to form the *Hamagumar*, or *the Gathering* in Earth Standard. The Gathering, headed by the Warlord, was the governing body for the entire Clan. Unfortunately for Vincent, she had appointed him to be that Consul.

Since Arai spent the majority of her time locked away with her military leaders, busy trying to fight a war against the

2

powerful Alliance, she only knew one human she could trust. So the most important and powerful job that he would ever hold in his life was given to him by default. He tried not to think about that too much.

That was how Vincent, a nineteen-year-old Defense Force Traitor, who had at one point been sentenced to death and nearly hung with a repurposed utility chain, became the sole leader of nearly one million humans. For reasons that were not entirely known to him, when Arai nominated him for the position, he was approved by the other Consuls without a single objection. He still had a hard time not laughing when he saw the name placard on his large desk. *Vincent Solaris – Office of the Human Consul.*

It had been six months since the office was created and Vincent was still unsure what impact it actually had. Humans, for the most part, were still distrustful of the Mawr and Rhai – the two dominate alien races of the Fidayi Clan – and Vincent was sure they held the same feelings towards the humans. It didn't help that Arai had shot down Vincent's idea of putting humans into the ranks of the Clan military or police to help get a handle on unemployment or crime. Her refusal meant that the only interaction that the two communities had was when the Clan's police, called the *Gumi,* popped their head into the Human Quarter and began arresting people.

Vincent clicked on another data display. The Mawr language's harsh symbols glowed out in front of his tired, bloodshot eyes. *Notices of Death,* the title read. Under it was a thankfully short list of humans that had been found dead the night before. The Mawr were an unsympathetic race. Vincent vividly remembered them leaving their suffering wounded on the field of battle. So, it didn't surprise him that they didn't bother to list how or why anyone died. The list he was given was only to help update the local census.

Vincent set the display down and rubbed his eyes. He dug a hand into the pocket of his grey uniform top and found a pack of cigarettes. He took one out and lit it, then blew out a large cloud of smoke and coughed roughly. He wasn't sure where the human traders were getting these cigarettes – the pack had no brand labels of any kind – but Vincent could have sworn they were getting worse. His office door swung open.

"Consul's closed," Vincent grunted without looking up. He had been swamped with so many angry people trying to get out of charges brought on them by the Gumi, or trying to find work, that he had stopped answering the door. And because the Clan leveed fines that equaled hours of manual labor, Vincent could hardly blame the poor ex-soldiers from trying to dodge punishment. Many attempted to bribe the local Gumi officers only to find the Clan did not see value in currency like humans did.

"Put that shit down and come out to the bar." Vincent looked up from the display to see Fiona Olympus. The pale-skinned, bright-eyed, mean-as-a-snake Martian girl that had somehow become his girlfriend. She was wearing a pair of baggy grey surplus Defense Force pants and a plain white shirt. Her pale arms, chest, and neck were covered in small black tattoos common amongst Martian gangers. They had only grown in number since they had moved to Elysian. Vincent wondered how she always managed to look stunningly beautiful, regardless of whatever rags she was wearing.

"If I keep putting off all this crap Arai will have my ass," Vincent muttered. He tapped an ash from the end of his cigarette.

"I already laid claim to that ass. She can't have it." Fiona's lips curled into a smirk. "You've been up here for days. You have to come out into the sunlight eventually."

"Fine." Vincent pushed the chair away from his desk and stood up, bracing himself for balance. Ever since the battle on Ryklar when his legs were torn to shreds by an Alliance rocket, his knees had a tendency to seize up on him. He winced as pain shot down through his feet.

"Forgetting something?" Fiona raised an eyebrow. On his desk sat a leather shoulder holster that held his Riten. A Riten was a hand-crafted, eight-shot wheel gun that held deep spiritual meaning to the Mawr. Being given one bordered on being given a religious sacrament. Both of them had been gifted one, specially made so it could be safely fired by a human hand, for accidently stumbling their way through heroics while fighting alongside the Clan. He grabbed the holster and threw it over his shoulder.

The Riten, while it had served him well through countless battles the year before, had become burdensome in the calm of Elysian. It was as heavy as a full-sized battle rifle and even though it had been tuned down in power, Vincent was sure it was going to break his wrist any time he was forced to use it. While the Human Quarter of Elysian was probably one of the rougher parts of the planet, Vincent was never worried about his safety. The main reason for that was his sworn bodyguard.

Zinvor walked into the room from where he had been standing guard outside. His flawless, jet black armor made it almost seem like he was wearing a shadow. The deadly Mawr Warrior, the brother of the Clan Warlord herself, was all the protection Vincent thought he would ever need. Any other Mawr would get sick of guard duty, but Zinvor wasn't allowed to.

Since he had left the Fidayi Clan to help Vincent, he was sentenced to be what the Mawr called a *Tsarra*: one doomed to serve only one mission. After the completion of that mission he was to die, and only then would his honor as a warrior be restored. Arai had ordered him to bring Vincent and Fiona home to Earth, and since Earth no longer existed, he technically had no mission. It was the kind of grey zone the Mawr traditions had obviously never prepared for. So now, Zinvor had fallen into the role of Consul bodyguard.

"Are you ready to depart, Sir Consul?" Zinvor grunted. While his Earth Standard was still harsh and emotionless, it was much better than before. When they first met, he reminded Vincent of a caveman from some old Earth movie.

"I keep telling you to stop calling me that," Vincent groaned.

"The Hamagumar has given you a title," Zinvor replied. "One worthy of respect."

Fiona laughed. "Look at that, you have one person who respects your office."

"And he's not even a *person,*" said Vincent.

*　　　*　　　*

The group exited the Consul's Office. The Office was a huge building. A large brown stone façade stretched up into the cloudy grey sky, completely devoid of windows. An aversion that the Rhai held that Vincent never quite figured out. Vincent shared the building with the Rhai Consul. Though it was hardly an equal partnership. The strange, skinny, high pitched speaking Rhai controlled the greater part of the office. Dozens of them worked there, running in and out all day carrying orders from the Fidayi's main Government building.

They walked down the cracked stairs that led to the bustling streets of the Government Quarter of Elysian. Crowds Mawr in flashy dress armor with ornate banners hanging off their pauldrons and rows of medals stuck to their chest plates, and

Rhai wearing pure white robes pushed and shoved passed one another.

Most of the Rhai didn't walk, they skated by a few inched above the ground on small circular platforms that hummed with power as they passed by. According to Zinvor the small platforms could only hold up the slight frames of the Rhai, which doomed Vincent to walk everywhere. The few Aero cars and Utility Transports that the humans managed to bring with them to Elysian had long ago ran out of fuel or had broken down.

The Government Quarter, by far the nicest and newest part of the sprawling city, was still slapdash and piece meal. Vincent could clearly tell which building was made by Mawr, and which was made by Rhai. The Mawr construction was mostly short, squat buildings made from large mud or stone bricks. The Mawr were born and bred Warriors, not builders and it showed in their construction. The bricks were mostly uneven, and it wasn't unheard of for a freshly constructed building to already have cracks in the foundation within a few weeks.

The Rhai's buildings were large, flawless alloy towers without windows or any feature at all. They jutted up from Elysian's cracked and broken streets like obelisks in neat orderly rows. Sky bridges as wide as highways would connect one metal tower to another, creating an entire other civilization that existed above street level. If the Mawr building happened to be an important one it would also be connected to the city's second level as a courtesy.

The busy government workers paid no attention to the small group of humans in their midst. Though every Mawr Warrior rendered a quick bow in the direction of Zinvor. He would acknowledge them with a curt nod. Zinvor had once explained to Vincent that they weren't giving any honors to him, but to the black Tsarra armor and what it represented, he just happened to be a vessel for it.

Traditionally Elysian had no street signs or traffic direction. Cargo vehicles, pedestrians and pack animals all fought for space on the roads while ships clogged the air above them. When the humans moved in, they quickly began placing signs in various areas to help them get around the city's confusing labyrinthian streets and alleyways. Up ahead was one such sign, staked into the ground and in rough handwriting it read *Human Quarter.* Unsurprisingly, next to the alleyway that lead into the quarter stood two Rhai Gumi. They wore long, white armored dresses with Yellow sashes, the color of the current Clan Warlord. They didn't carry the normal Rhai battle rifle, instead they carried a stun baton on one hip and a small laser pistol on the other. They turned and bowed to Vincent as he approached.

They walked past the two Gumi and down the dark alley. The Gumi rarely ventured into the Human Quarter unless they had some numbers with them, the reason for that was right in front of them. Several humans, cloaked in long black dress coats flanked the ally. They had rifles slung over their shoulders and eyed the group menacingly. They turned and blocked off the alley as they approached.

"Oh fuck off you guys, you know it's the Consul," Fiona hissed at them.

"You know there's a toll for coming into the quarter. We don't care about your fake title," an older looking man with sergeant's stripes on his collars said. Vincent sighed.

"And you know we aren't paying you a damn thing," Vincent said. The two soldiers moved to take their rifles off of their shoulders.

"I'd rethink that," Fiona said. "You're outnumbered."

"You two aren't even soldiers. Worthless Traitors," spat the other soldier. Most of his fellow humans on Elysian hated his guts, which was something Vincent had grown to accept.

Regardless of how many times he had explained what really happened in the weapons facility on Grawluck no one believed him. It turned out almost no one was willing to believe that a lowly soldier, one who had been sentenced to service in the Earth Defense Force as punishment for a crime, had been working with Aliens to try to save Earth. More people in the quarter knew him as "Traitor" rather than "Vincent".

"I'm not arguing my soldiering abilities. But we have him." Vincent thumbed over his shoulder where the short, thick, and incredibly angry looking face of Zinvor poked out from in between Fiona and him. The humans of Elysian had an independent streak in them, but the stories of the Mawr's battlefield acumen were well known. The two soldiers gave each other looks that said they were suddenly unsure of their post.

"You can go this one time. But you owe us," the sergeant said, his voice waiving.

"We don't owe you shit. Come at us again I'll skin ya," Fiona spat at them as the group walked past. Zinvor eyed them up and down as they did, his mitt-like hand wrapped around the butt of his Riten. The soldiers avoided his gaze.

"We really need to get a handle on these Black Coats." Fiona frowned. The *Black Coats*, as they have come to be called, were Defense Force soldiers who had completely rejected living with the Clan. They acted as their own police and shadow government within the Quarter, extorting anyone who was trying to make a living and beating anyone who tried to stand up against them. Instead of the normal EDF uniform, which had become normal human dress on Elysian, they chose the black dress uniform overcoat, which gave them their nickname.

Unlike Vincent and Fiona, the vast majority of the Black Coats were enlisted EDF soldiers and officers. Meaning they were loyalists to the Central Committee of Earth, back when that was a thing. The Central Committee of Earth ruled all facets of United Humanity's everyday life from the smallest district on Earth to the capital of Titan, a million miles away. All of that was destroyed in the blink of an eye and the Central Committee turned to dust when the Anarchs let loose with their plasma weapons.

Ever since the Black Coats held themselves up to be the last standard bearers of true human morals and ethics. Anyone who worked with the Clan was considered below them or a race traitor and subject to their iron fisted rule. They looked down on sentenced soldiers like Vincent and Fiona like they were the scum of the human race. The fact that the sentenced soldiers happened to assimilate into their new lives on Elysian only furthered the Black Coat's cause.

"What do you want to do about them?" Asked Vincent. "They have more power than I do."

"You don't have *any* power," Fiona said.

"Like I said, they have more power than I do."

"Let's see how much power they have when Arai sends a Cohort through here and wipes them out." Fiona frowned, lighting a cigarette. A Cohort was a battle formation of the Clan that numbered about two-thousand Warriors. It was truly a terrifying fighting force to behold. Vincent was still sure he had survived through only dumb luck when he came face to face with the Alliance sworn Mawr Warriors on Ryklar.

"I'm sure that would make Arai even more popular," said Vincent.

"Running a planet isn't a popularity contest. Maybe if you could figure that out your position would be worth something," Fiona said.

"I only have the power that Arai lets me have. She shot down my idea of humans joining the Gumi or the Military again, so I got nothing."

"You ever think she doesn't want the Consul to have any power in the first place? That she just created the office to make the humans feel like they're important on Elysian?"

"I don't think she's that cunning politically. And besides, she failed miserably if that was her goal because everyone hates me. And the Rhai have a Consul too. They have plenty of power."

"Because the Rhai actually do something." Fiona laughed. "They run the navy, man their tanks and artillery, and fix all of their machines. What the hell do we do?" Vincent tried to think of a retort, but she was right. In the year since the humans who fought on Grawluck had settled on Elysian they had been little more than a thorn in the side of the already strained Clan. Fiona saw him straining hard to think of a response.

"Zinvor, do you think she would do that?" Fiona asked.

"I would never underestimate my sister in a fight. Politics is just a battle without the glory," Zinvor grunted.

Vincent sighed. "Well, shit."

*   *   *

The layout of the Human Quarter was much different than the rest of the city. The roads were little more than dirt tracks and the beating Elysian sun was almost completely occluded by the vast network of Rhai pathways that branched over the area, connecting their towers. The elevated pathways placed the Quarter in a near constant state of dusk. The heavy foot traffic kicked up dirt from the roads created a never ceasing, choking cloud of dust that enveloped the area.

Vincent hated the Quarter. It was a dirty, miserable, hell hole. It smelled like packs of unwashed humanity, dust, and shit. He remembered from Ethics schools, reading about how Earth was before the Central Committee. When millions of people lived in shanty towns made out of little more than tin huts and tents. What he saw in front of him reminded him of the pictures from his schoolbooks. For every stone and brick Mawr building there were a dozen made out of tin, wood, or anything else the humans could scrape together during their limited time on the planet. Many people were living in their EDF issue tents.

Arai had insisted that Vincent and Fiona take a house with her in the Government Quarter, but he had turned it down. Thinking it would be better to living with the people he was supposed to be in charge of. Fiona had found them a one room apartment above the local bar. It was one of the few stable buildings in the quarter and was chosen because it was one of the few structures in the area that could withstand gunfire. Vincent seriously regretted not listening to Arai.

He was sure Fiona only liked the arraignment because it reminded her of her home on Mars. Mars was once a normal, functioning settlement of United Humanity until one failed revolution after another turned it into little more than a third world, backwater planet. Fiona had never known a normal Mars. Instead, what she did know was a violent life on the streets of Olympus running guns and drugs for a gang. The Quarter reminded her of home.

The bustling main drag of the quarter was full of rickety stalls or carts all trying to sell something. The salesmen hawked their wares loudly targeting the people who looked like they might actually be able to afford something. A human with a regular job in the quarter was pretty rare. Vincent was the only human on the entire planet with a salaried position in the Government, so he always tried to buy something whenever he could to spread the money around.

Most people fell into smuggling rings ran by the Black Coats. The Black Coats controlled all of the human owned ships that were still able to travel through space. While the Clan had taken all of the military craft, they left all of the cargo ships to the planet's new populace in an attempt to build some kind of trade with the other surviving human settlements. The Black Coats had taken control of the fleet through less than favorable methods and with it controlled most of the Quarter's unconventional economy.

What had surprised Vincent was the Black Coat's total disregard for the hundreds of thousands of Sentenced Soldiers. They refused to employ them in any way, even through smuggling, despite the fact they were by definition, criminals. This gave the sentenced soldiers little prospects for work in the quarter and forced them to look elsewhere. Vincent had noticed a growing number of humans working as hired muscle for Rhai traders.

The group finally pushed passed the growing throngs of salesmen and came up to a large, handmade sign that read *The Eagle and Bar*. The name was a clever riff of the old Central Committee flag name *The Eagle and Star*. On the cracked brick façade of the dilapidated building was a bad painting of the old flag: A large, fierce looking eagle, but instead of holding a single white star in its talons there was a bottle of whiskey. The bar, above which was Vincent and Fiona's small apartment, was the only bar in the Quarter where sentenced soldiers could have a drink without being hassled by Black Coats.

Vincent pushed open the swinging doors and walked inside. The bar was crowded with loud, drinking patrons. Smoke hung heavy in the air from countless cigarettes, and it stung Vincent's eyes as he walked through it. The walls were covered in various different insignia from the EDF units the patrons had once served in. Though, the Eagle and Bar had one thing no other EDF bar would have: pictures of patrons on the wall, the crimes for which they were sentenced to EDF service for written underneath.

Private Jonas Enroth. 175th Infantry Regiment.
Crime: Grand Theft Auto. 3rd Strike.
Sentence: 16 years.

Staff Sergeant Justin Stevens. 110th Supply Regiment.
Crime: Manslaughter.
Sentence: Life with the possibility of release after 40 years.

On another wall were pictures of the Martian soldiers. Pale skinned humans with bright blue eyes and almost white-blonde hair. The photos showed their grinning faces, many of which were giving enthusiastic middle fingers to the camera. The first picture on the wall was Fiona's.

Private First-Class Fiona Olympus. 175th Infantry Regiment.
Crime: Martian, first born.
Sentence: Whole Life Tariff.

A whole life tariff. The punishment that the Central Committee had levied against the people of Mars after numerous bloody and ultimately pointless rebellions against Earth's rule. They had decreed after the last rebellion that every first-born child would be turned over to the Earth Defense Forces on their seventeenth birthday to begin their sentence.

Fiona had told him that it turned the first child of every family into little more than an unwanted nuisance. The family knew that regardless of how they were raised, or how well they did in school, their life was in essence already over from the time they were born. She said they would be registered at the local draft office and then discarded into the streets to fend for themselves. Many never even survived long enough to be drafted.

He wondered, how exactly the EDF managed discipline for the Martians in its ranks. They couldn't exactly punish them to further time in uniform. That's when he saw another picture several rows down from Fiona's. The man it showed had deep scars on his face and was missing an eye. His pale bald head was covered in small black tattoos.

Condemned Sergeant Anton Tharsis. 10th Penal Squadron.
Crime: Martian, First born.
    Insubordination.
    Sexual Incontinence.
    Assault on a superior officer.
    Attempted Murder.
Sentence: Whole Life Tariff. Thirty years of service in Penal Squadron before possibility of being returned to Regiment of the Line.

"What the hell is sexual incontinence?" Vincent asked.
Fiona smirked. "He likes guys."
"Oh."
"What you worms call *Sexual Incontinence* is a pretty normal part of Martian culture."

"And the Penal Squadron?" he asked.

"It's where they stick the screw ups. They really only use those formations if they know there's an offensive coming up. They charge bunkers or minefields. Clear the way for regular soldiers." Fiona held two fingers up in the direction of the bartender. The bartender nodded and began to poor a dark liquid into two glasses. "The first wave on the Alliance's trenches on Grawluck were probably those poor bastards. It's pretty much a death sentence."

"Lovely," Vincent said. He thought he had stopped being surprised by the depravity and brutality of the Central Committee, but he was still shocked from time to time. Pieces of information like that made him a little happy they were unable to stop the Anarch's plasma weapons.

He tried to drown those thoughts out by paying attention to the music that was pumping out over the speakers of the bar. It was some heartbreaking song about a man leaving his family behind to fight the Alliance. Some genius communications soldier had managed to set up a receiver that picked up various radio broadcasts from Titan, the nearest human settlement, though the quality was spotty at best. It was better than the other musical entertainment options that they had on Elysian. You can only sing along to so many army drinking songs before they get old.

The group was seated at the corner of the room. Vincent was never sure why, but whenever they had gone out drinking Fiona insisted that she face the door, with her back to the wall. He chalked it up to her growing up on the streets of Olympus. Not that Zinvor was any better. Whenever he would sit down, he would unholster his massive Riten and set it on the table. The first few times they had come into the bar he had scared the hell out of people, but since they had since grown used to their only Mawr customer.

The bartender brought over the two glasses of dark brown liquor. Unlike the other cups in the bar: mugs and shot glasses made out of clay, he had brought them two real glasses. The glasses were chipped and dirty, but it was a small sign of respect some of the Sentenced Soldiers had towards the Office of the Consul.

Vincent could hardly blame them for being the ones that had slowly gravitated towards their strange new form of government. Their old one had forced them into slavery and in some cases almost certain death. He had no doubt that some of the sentenced soldiers that showed Vincent and Fiona respect were murders, rapist, or worse. But he knew from first-hand experience that the vast majority of the sentenced were like him: guilty of nothing more than a small violation of the *Central Committee Code of Ethics.* The tome of rules that had once governed every facet of their life.

Or, in thousands of cases on Elysian, they were guilty of simply being born on the wrong planet. The level of respect in some cases was unsettling to Vincent. While some of the sentenced were glad to see the Committee fall, others, mostly Martians, not only believed the Black Coat's lie that he had personally used the Anarch plasma weapons to destroy the Earth, but that was exactly why they liked him. Fiona didn't do him any favors by boasting that she had helped.

They clinked their glasses together and slammed the shot back. The liquor burned all the way down but was satisfying after such a long day stuck in his office. Vincent wasn't sure what the smugglers were bringing back to Elysian, but he was certain fine liquor wasn't on the checklist.

"Ugh, that tastes like chemistry." Vincent coughed.

"Yeah, the good stuff." Fiona smiled. She held up two more fingers and the bartender rushed back over. Vincent reached into the pocket of his jacket and produced three metal coins, called Bits, the legal tender on Elysian. The bartender waved him off.

"Sorry Boss, you know your drinks are always on the house." The bartender was an older soldier with deep set wrinkles. His left sleeve was empty and pinned up to his shoulder. Someone had told Vincent the man had lost his arm on Grawluck to an Anarch cannon at close range.

"It's a tip then." Vincent smiled. The man grabbed the bits and placed them in his pocket.

"Thanks, Boss," he said smiling. "Does your um…" He looked at Zinvor. "Friend? Want anything?"

While Zinvor had always been incredibly friendly to Fiona and Vincent, he almost never spoke to other humans and like most Mawr, showed little to no emotions other than anger. Most were afraid to address him directly.

"The biggest mug of beer you have please," Vincent said. The bartender nodded and walked off. As far as Vincent could tell, the Mawr couldn't get drunk. Not that it was from a lack of trying. At more than one night out Fiona had talked Zinvor into drinking shot after shot of horrible rotgut liquor and it never even phased him. The only part of a normal human diet he seemed to enjoy was beer.

As soon as the frothy mug of beer was set down in front of him Zinvor was on it. His thick fingers wouldn't fit around the handle, so he had to pick up the mug in both hands. He guzzled down the drink as some spilled down his face and his black armor. Fiona laughed, everyone else who was watching eyed her like she was crazy daring for laughing at a Mawr Warrior.

"So what do you think of these rumors about Lunar City?" Fiona asked in a hush.

"What rumors?" Vincent asked.

"Oh, sorry I know you're locked in your ivory tower all day and don't have time for us everyday folk," she mocked.

"Yes, clearly my status as one of the rich and powerful has made me naïve of my people's plight," he said sarcastically. Fiona laughed.

"Nox and the other smugglers are saying a new Central Committee formed in Lunar City. Trying to reform the old government." Nox, the strange Rhai ally they had made through their journey. Though he ended up saving Fiona and Vincent's life on Ryklar, he had never become friends with them. It didn't help that only hours after saving their lives he tried selling them to an Alliance bounty Hunter. Ever since the battle on Grawluck he had been one of millions of ship pilots that left Elysian every day to run goods, both legal and illegal, between here and Alliance or human space.

"Wait, Lunar City got hit with a plasma weapon too. Shouldn't the moon be destroyed?" Vincent asked.

"Kind of." Fiona slammed down her glass and wiped her face.

"What do you mean? I saw the fire on the Moon from Earth. It definitely got attacked," Vincent said.

"Oh sure, Lunar City is wrecked. Looks like a bomb went off from what I hear, but from the sounds of it, it was a near miss and blew up in the atmosphere or something. Torched a district or two." She paused fighting back a laugh. "It's certainly faring better than Earth is these days." Fiona laughed. Vincent was suddenly curious what a dead planet looked like.

"Hmm." Vincent thought. "Arai would probably want to hear about this."

"You think?"

"She hates them as much as we do. They stabbed the Clan in the back. If they would have gotten those weapons on Grawluck Elysian would probably be nothing but a memory. "

"Doesn't she have enough to worry about with the Alliance?" Fiona asked. "They sound more dangerous than a bunch of Committee Aristocrats trying to scrape together a government from their summer homes."

"Yeah." Vincent rubbed his temples. Suddenly the loud music was giving him a headache. "She doesn't talk to me about it much anymore."

"You should tell her," Zinvor said. They both looked over at him, almost forgetting he was there. "A Mawr remembers traitors."

"I'll bring up the rumors in the next meeting then. If I'm even allowed to talk," Vincent said.

"So what do you even do there?" Fiona said, fighting back laughter.

"Mostly listen to the Cohort Leaders bitch and complain about the war effort. Every single one of them has some stupid breakthrough strategy that Arai just *has* to listen too. None of them ever go anywhere and when they fail, they blame everyone but themselves."

"Anyone talking about some kind of peace effort?" Fiona asked.

"I don't think they know what that word means. Or the hatred goes so deep at this point the war is over when someone is completely destroyed."

"Can't argue with that," Fiona said. "I'd like to piss on the ashes of the Anarch home world."

"Yes!" grunted Zinvor. "Piss on the demons!"

"That's the spirit!" Fiona cheered and ordered more drinks.

*　　*　　*

The night ended, as it always did, back in their small apartment above the bar. It was a disgusting, unkempt place that had little more than a salvaged EDF as its furnishing. Vincent rolled over and looked at Fiona. He could help but smile whenever he looked at her. He remembered growing up and watching horrible romance movies with his family. In them whenever the dashing hero saw their women asleep, even after a night of drunken sex like they had just had, they were always unblemished angels. Even in the fits of love not a single hair would be out of place.

Fiona lay, an empty wine bottle near her hand and drool pooling around her face. Her legs were splayed out at awkward angles and took up most of the bed, forcing Vincent to sleep on the edge. Small black tattoos covered her naked body from her feet to her neck. They were interspersed with scars from battles she had never told him about. He didn't bother asking, just like she didn't ask him about the family he had lost when the Earth went up in flames. At some point they had subconsciously decided the first day of their new lives began the day they had met aboard the *ESS Victory* and that was all that mattered.

Vincent stood up, his mouth feeling like a desert. He found a dented metal canteen that still had some water it in and took a drink. His throat was thick from a long night of matching shots of liquor with Fiona and the room temperature water tasted amazing.

He sighed and looked at himself in a small, polished plate of metal that served as their mirror. Though he had been off the campaign trail for more than a year his body and still not filled back out to what it looked like on Earth. His face, once cleanly shaved per EDF regulation, had become overgrown with a thick brown beard and his wavy brown hair had grown down to his neck. He pulled his hair back and tied it up with a small band.

"I really wish you'd cut that pony tail off. It's hideous," Fiona groaned, waking up.

"It's not a ponytail," Vincent said.

"Yeah?" Fiona smiled, fumbling with a pack of cigarettes and a lighter. "What would you call that if I had it?"

Vincent frowned because she was right. Fiona was never one to care for fashion or style and cut her hair herself without even using the mirror. She had mixed results. Currently she had something resembling an uneven bob. "Find me someone who can cut hair and I'll get it done," he said.

"I keep telling you I'll cut it," she said.

"I didn't run away from the EDF to end up with a shaved head again." Vincent laughed.

"I could try a mohawk."

"And the ponytail remains."

"What are you even doing this early?" she asked.

"It's not early, you're just lazy. But today is the Gathering," Vincent said. He looked over at his Warrior armor. Only ordained Warriors of the Clans are given Ritens and Armor, each of them hand-made once one has proven themselves on the field of battle. Arai had gifted a set to Fiona and Vincent—the only non-Mawrs to ever have the honor—and it had served them well ever since.

In the underground tunnels of Grawluck when the traitorous Rostov had shot him at nearly point-blank range it was the Mawr's painstakingly hand-woven armor that had saved his life. Now, with no more battles to fight, it had turned into something of a ceremonial uniform for whenever he had to attend the Gatherings. His armor was a deep blue color, dedicated to the oceans of Earth according to Arai. Oceans that no longer existed as far as he knew.

From the armor's left pauldron hung two scrolls of cloth – The Clan's version of military ribbons. One was brown, Arai said it was supposed to represent the muddy fields of Grawluck, set over the brown background was a sword crossed with a Riten. The other scroll was yellow with two crossed rifles. He and Fiona were the only two people with that ribbon. It represented the slaughter of an entire EDF army on Ryklar. An entire army minus them anyway.

On the right side of the armor's chest piece was an embroidered golden phoenix. The phoenix was Fiona's idea, meant to symbolize the death of Earth and the rebirth of humanity on Elysian. Arai liked the idea and made it the official symbol of Vincent's new office.

The other two additions to the armor were meant to be a joke: two corporal pins stuck to the armor's leather neck guard. Fiona thought it would be hilarious to rub it in the Black Coats face that the newly appointed Consul was little more than a squad leader once upon a time. It didn't make him any new fans amongst them.

"Don't they just ignore you there? Why bother," Fiona complained.

"Not always. I'm going to push my idea for human inclusion. Eventually they'll listen to it."

"You mean the Gumi?" Fiona laughed. "You can't be serious."

"That's kind of my goal" Vincent smiled. "There's no way the other Cohort leaders would ever agree to an armed human formation. Not yet anyway. In comparison, a human division of the Gumi doesn't sound so crazy." Fiona raised an eyebrow.

"You're getting good at this politics thing, aren't you?" she asked.

"I've had Nox bring me a ton of books from Titan. It turns out being a politician is mostly just lying to people's faces whilst smiling," Vincent said, beginning to strap on his armor. "Are you going to come?"

"Pfft." Fiona ashed her cigarette into an empty beer bottle. "You already know the answer to that." Fiona hadn't made one meeting in six months. She was supposed to act as an official of the Consul's Office but never cared to actually work. The most Vincent had seen her do was take a swing at a Black Coat who had gotten too close to him one time.

"I'd figure I would ask," Vincent said, buckling the holster for his Riten around his waist.

"Enjoy licking the government's boot." She waved him off.

"Love you too, Dear." He laughed and she smiled and blew him a kiss.

* * *

Vincent stepped outside of the door to the external stairwell and saw Zinvor standing guard, his jet-black armor and dark, rough skin made him look like a boulder's shadow. No matter how many times Vincent had told him they didn't need a bodyguard he wouldn't listen. Vincent wasn't entirely sure when the Tsarra slept or if he did at all.

"You're late," Zinvor grunted.

"Yeah, yeah," Vincent dismissed. "We still have time."

The two walked down the creaking stairs and out into the street. It was still early, so the normal crowds of people were considerably thinner. Groups of Black Coats milled about, searching through vendor's carts, for what Vincent had no idea. It was then when Vincent saw something that made his heart leap in his chest:

The Eagle and Star flag. The Central Committee's flag. A flag Vincent hoped to never see again. There it hung, flapping in the dusty breeze from a newly erected flagpole near the entrance of the Quarter. The old flag had been strictly taboo after the EDF's betrayal of the Clan on Grawluck. Though never officially banned, to see it hanging in reverence worried Vincent.

"That's not good," Vincent said quietly.

"Traitors," Zinvor grumbled. They approached the tunnel that led out of the Quarter and Vincent saw another new addition. Above the tunnel was painted *THE CHAIRMAN LIVES* in thick black letters.

"That's definitely not good," Vincent said. The two Black Coats eyed him with intense hatred as they walked through the tunnel.

If Vincent thought that the Government Quarter was busy before, the amount of chaos going through the streets on the day of a Gathering was something else entirely. With the exception of Vincent's office, every Consul, Government Cohort, and Official had a small army of aides that accompanied them whenever they came to visit Arai on Elysian when she called for them.

Elysian was the unofficial capital of the Clans' small, but growing, Galactic Confederation. Vincent thought of it as more of a Fiefdom. The Clan leaders acted almost completely independently of the Gathering's rule unless she called them into her service. If a Cohort Leader managed to wrest control of a planet or Moon away from the Alliance, it was effectively theirs to own and rule as they saw fit.

Occasionally, a Cohort Leader would think that they were strong enough to defy the Gathering's summons or openly refuse an order from the Warlord. Vincent only knew of one such thing happening. A year before when Arai ordered all of her Cohorts to invade the Alliance Fortress world of Grawluck with assistance of the former Earth Central Committee. One Cohort Leader, a commander of hundreds of tanks, hated the idea of working with the humans and refused to dispatch his forces.

Only a few weeks after the battle Arai had him dragged before her during a Gathering, had him stripped of his ceremonial armor and Riten and had them destroyed in front of him. As Arai is not only the Warlord, but the Consul of Mawr, she had the power to demote him. Afterwards she submitted an execution order to be voted on by the Gathering which passed unanimously. It was the first time Vincent had voted at a Gathering. She executed him herself in front of everyone. He voted in favor of the Warrior's death.

It was a stark reminder that though Arai had only ever been helpful and friendly to Vincent, she was never to be crossed.

The two began to climb the stairs to the main Government building on Elysian, and in true Mawr form, it was nothing impressive. The Mawr had an aversion to anything that could be considered opulent and as such the Gathering was held in a simple one-story auditorium. It could not have been more different than the massive citadel-like buildings that made up the local committee buildings back on Earth that could stretch upwards of one hundred stories or more.

The Gathering Hall was a squat, windowless box of a building. It sat atop of a large sweeping stairway made of brown stone. Lining the stairs were the fluttering banners of the various Cohorts of the Clan. Rhai skyscrapers watched over the entire area, clumped together like a towering metal forest.

On either side of the stairs were Mawr Warriors lined in what Vincent assumed must have been their version of a parade. Each Cohort was easily set apart from one another by different colors of armor, some brighter than others. All of them stood ramrod straight as the chaotic flood of government workers pushed passed them. They all bowed as Vincent and Zinvor walked by.

The double doors at the top of the stairs were crowned with a large red banner that showed the Clan standard: A curved sword crossing a Riten. On either side of the doors two Mawr Warriors bowed to Zinvor and opened the doors for them to enter. On the inside the Warriors took on a much more intimidating stance.

Instead of standing rigid and impressive, the Warriors were all holding rifles in their hands. Their armor, instead of being flawlessly shined and adorned like Vincent's, hung heavy with ammunition bandoliers. Their armor was a dull yellow, most of the color faded with use, the color of the Warlord's own Cohort.

Vincent had seen this at every Gathering thus far. No other Cohorts would be allowed into the hall, regardless of the standing of the other Cohort Leaders. He knew it was Arai flexing her muscle against anyone else who thought the Gathering was a good place to try to question her authority. Once, Vincent was intimidated by such a show of force, now it was just another part of Clan politics.

The middle of the auditorium was a large, low, round table surrounded by an array of cushions. All around the table Rhai and Mawr leaders of various Cohorts and government offices were seated. They were all engaged in various side conversations filling the hall with a dull roar of hushed whispers. Vincent took his seat next to the Rhai Consul. As always, he was the only human at the table.

"Good Morning Consul Solaris," the Rhai Consul greeted him in the Mawr's guttural language. No matter how much time Vincent sunk into the Rhai's native tongue he could never get a grasp on it. To make things easier for him, all official Clan functions were conducted in the Mawr's language.

"Good morning Consul Nyxos," Vincent responded.

"Do you have much on the agenda today?" Nyxos asked, eyeing the data display that Vincent had placed on the table. Vincent had become known in the Gathering for not saying, or doing, much of anything. In order to build some good will with the Warlord, he tended to vote for whatever she did. His Rhai counterpart could always flex his race's commerce or space fleet muscle if the time came. As far as political powerplays went, Vincent had nothing.

"Not as much as you I'm sure." Vincent smiled. Through his months of dealing with Clan politics he had learned how to subtlety take a swing at someone. Not that he was a petty person, but Vincent knew that Nyxos saw the humans as an upstart challenger to the old order and he wasn't alone.

Vincent had quickly learned once Arai had invited him to the Gathering as a representative for his race that it would be an uphill battle to prove his people's usefulness to the Clan. He was sure the Rhai had done the same thing generations before. He just hadn't counted on the Rhai themselves becoming an obstacle in the way.

"I see your aide did not come again," Nyxos said, talking about Fiona.

"I don't need that much help with my work. I see others aren't so capable." At that dig, the Rhai glared at him with wide, dark eyes.

Arai entered the room and everyone at the table rose to their feet. Arai was, like most of her kind, short and stocky. Her thick arms were intertwined cords of muscle. Her bright yellow armor was resplendent with countless scrolls and ribbons, most of which Vincent had never heard the story behind. Around her wide waist hung a large Riten, nearly the size of a human carbine. Almost every inch of her bare skin that showed was covered in a tapestry of scars from untold amounts of warfare.

"Be seated," she growled. The Gathering sunk back into their cushions. "Greetings to my off-world brethren who made the journey here, despite all that is happening." She said it like anyone at the table had an option. "Who shall speak first?" A Mawr in deep red armor stood up quickly. A Warrior behind him stepped forward and announced:

"Cohort Leader Grigos, my Warlord." The Warrior in yellow armor bowed to Arai. Arai nodded to Grigos to speak.

"My Warlord. My Cohort's campaign on the outer worlds of Farsiris are going according to plan. The Alliance has been contained and their ability to launch attacks degraded greatly."

"Very good Grigos." Arai nodded. "And your Cohort's ability to press the attack?"

"Err." Grigos stumbled. "We are unable at this time to force the Alliance from their positions." The table erupted into conversation. Arai pounded on the table, her thick fist commanding them all to be quiet.

"Why is that Grigos?" she asked calmly.

"I—" Grigos began, but Arai cut him off.

"Do not give me excuses," she demanded.

"I have no excuse, My Warlord." Grigos bowed.

Arai glared at him. "Leader Flyos!" she grunted at another Warrior at the far end of the table. A smaller Mawr in brown armor shot to their feet.

"Yes, My Warlord."

"How are your holdings?"

"My Warlord," Flyos started. "The Alliances forces have pushed my Cohort off of our outposts in the Belt of Nyx." Vincent saw anger well up in Arai's face. Flyos must has as well because he quickly tried to turn the conversation positive. "But our forces withdrawal was orderly and losses minimal. A counterattack is in the works."

"Can no one at this table give me something positive?" Arai roared. She had still not sat down, instead she was leaning over the table like she was ready to pounce on the next speaker. Vincent looked around and no one looked willing to speak. He decided in was now or never.

"I do, Ma'am," he answered, climbing to his feet. The table fell silent and the Mawr in the yellow armor stepped forward and announced Vincent.

"Consul Solaris of the human race!" their voice boomed.

Though his Mawr was nearly fluent at this point, in times of stress he always found himself going back to old human honorifics. Arai didn't seem to care.

"Consul Solaris. What do you have?"

"Well Ma'am, I have a large population of trained personal that would want to help with the running and maintaining of Elysian's public order." Vincent clicked on his data display.

"And why should the population of Elysian welcome Humans as enforcers of the peace?" Nyxos asked.

"Because, you welcomed me," Vincent shot back. "If you weren't going to welcome my people as equal members of the effort against the Alliance, I don't know why I am here."

"What are you asking Vincent?" Arai asked, her voice calming.

"The people of the Human Quarter hate the Gumi." Vincent shook his head. "Because they just see a bunch of aliens trying to force them into doing things your way. On the flip side they can't support the fight against the Alliance because you won't let them."

Another uproar of conversation started. Vincent tried to cut it off, raising his voice into almost a yell. "How would you feel if someone wouldn't let you fight the Alliance after they killed everyone you knew and loved?" The sidebar conversations died off slowly, their attention turning towards Vincent. "Because that's what you're asking of the nearly one million humans that live on this planet right now."

"And what of these *Black Coats?*" asked the Gumi Cohort Leader named Kassaj. They were rail thin, even for a Rhai, and their skin was the color of rust. Their armored robes were the pearl white of the Cohort they commanded. The Gumi Leader reminded him of the Ethics Police back on Earth. "If create a Human Cohort and it is populated by criminals loyal to that *Chairman* of yours..."

"I don't have a Chairman," Vincent cut him off. A little too much anger seethed into his words.

"That is enough on this subject," Arai said, cutting the two of them off. "Consul Solaris, we will talk further about this at a different time." That was the first time his ideas had not been outrightly refused. Vincent was suddenly lost for words.

"Err, thank you Warlord." He nodded.

The rest of the meeting went on as they normally did, with each Cohort Leader trying to one-up the other on the progress of any given campaign their Warriors were off fighting. Vincent had a hard time following it all. He was no military mastermind, and his knowledge of active Clan combat operations as sorely lacking for someone in such a supposedly powerful position. At one point two Cohort Leaders challenged each other to one on one combat on the stairs out front and were nearly out of the door before Arai stopped them. Vincent was suddenly curious how a personal challenge to Cohort Leader Kassaj would go over.

CHAPTER TWO

Gunfire tore through the still night sending Vincent and Fiona diving from their bed and onto the dusty floor of their apartment.

"You okay?" Fiona called out over the unbreaking chatter of automatic weapons fire.

"Yeah!" Vincent yelled. "You?"

"I'm Good!" she said. The window over their bed-The only window in the apartment- exploded and shards of broken glass cascaded down on their heads. Zinvor burst through their door and ran over to them at a crouch.

"What the hell is going on out there?" Vincent yelled at him.

"Black Coats!" Zinvor said. He ran over to the counter and tossed them their armor, one piece at a time. Vincent awkwardly fumbled, trying to slide on his pants while lying on his back in an attempt to stay low and out of the way of the wild gunfire. Fiona quickly tossed on her rust-red colored chest piece without tightening down the straps on her sides.

"How much time do we have before they get into the apartment?" Vincent asked, unholstering his Riten and thumbing back it's hammer.

"No." Zinvor shook his head. "The fight is in the street."

"What?" Vincent asked, confused. He had been certain that one day, though he had no idea when, a squad of Black Coats was finally going to try to kill him. He thought for sure this was it. "What do you mean?" Fiona peaked her head out of the broken window.

"There's a damn firefight going on near the tunnel!" she said.

"Who are they shooting at?" he asked.

"Fuck if I know." She shrugged. "You hear that?" she asked. "It's tapering off." She was right, the steady drum of automatic fire was slowly dying off into spaced out single shots.

"Sounds like somebody's dead."

"Let's go take a look," Fiona said, slowly making her way to the door, keeping her head down.

"Wait!" Vincent yelled out, but she ignored him. She peaked out of the door and looked back at him.

"Shit!" she whispered. "They are dragging people through the street!" Vincent saw out of the corner of his eye that Zinvor and unholstered his Riten.

"Wait!" Vincent said again. "Not yet!"

Just as soon as the gunfire had broken the silent night, the calm had returned. The shooting was now replaced with men shouting and cursing at one another. Vincent had crawled up next to Fiona by the door to take in the scene below.

Five Black Coats had shoved three cowering people against the side of the building across from the bar. It was obvious to Vincent that one of them was wounded and his blood turned the street a dark crimson.

"Look!" Fiona pointed over by the tunnel. Under the large, *THE CHAIRMAN LIVES* sign, two dead bodies lay slumped against a wall. A single point-blank shot between their eyes had made their faces unrecognizable.

"Shit," Vincent said. "Who do you think they are?"

"Maybe smugglers?" Zinvor asked. "Would not be the first people that they have killed for owning them money."

"Trash taking out trash," Fiona spat. Vincent wasn't so sure. "Maybe."

Before anymore debate could be had on the subject the Black Coats leveled their rifles and fired into the cowering men. The brown brick façade of the building they were leaning against exploded with debris and blood as the bullets punched straight through their victims. One of the laughing Black Coats pulled a rag out of his jacket pocket and knelt down next to the still quivering bodies. He dabbed the rag in the pooling blood and painted a large star on the wall above the corpses.

CHAPTER THREE

Neither Vincent nor Fiona slept that night. Instead they sat in silence against the walls of their empty apartment, their Ritens held ready in their hands. Zinvor took his place once again by the door. Slowly the feeling that the Black Coats were making their move against him lessened.

The Black Coats had done a lot of outright criminal activity in the past including murder, but never anything like that. That single star, what was once called *The Light of the Chairman* had topped the flag of humanity. Seeing it drawn above such a massacre gave Vincent plenty to be worried about.

"I don't know what I should do," Vincent mumbled.

"Tell Arai," Fiona said. "She seems like a woman who has crushed a few rebellions in her day."

"Arai is technically leading a rebellion."

"Doesn't matter. The fact is those assholes went from charging people tolls to get into the Quarter to executing people in the streets. You have to show them who's really in charge around here," Fiona said. "This doesn't look like some gang shit—it looks like some Ethics Police shit." Vincent swallowed hard, even the mention of the State Ethics Police still gave him nightmares.

"I think they know they are the ones who are really in charge," Vincent said.

"Well with that attitude they sure will." Fiona smirked. "Ugh, I need a drink after all of this."

"It's 10 o'clock in the morning." Vincent raised an eyebrow. He wasn't even sure why he said anything, Fiona would routinely drink around the clock with few signs of real drunkenness. It was a source of pride for her.

"I didn't ask you for the time." She glared, standing up. She holstered her Riten and started for the door. "You coming?"

"I guess. I could use some Kaff before I go into the office," he said.

The group made their way to the bottom of the stairs to see a crowd of onlookers surrounding the corpses in the street. Black Coats stood on either side of the scene, rags covering their faces. The stench of the rotting bodies permeated the air and small black insects buzzed around the bloated dead. Vincent's nose wrinkled as the smell burned its way up through his nostrils.

"Ugh, why isn't anyone cleaning this up?" he said.

"It's a message." Fiona frowned, covering her nose with her arm. "Notice the guards?"

"Oh I see them, but what's the message?"

"Don't fuck with us?" Fiona said.

They walked through the doors of the Eagle and Bar and found it oddly crowded for the hour.

"The usual ma'am?" called out the bartender, and Fiona nodded.

"Just a cup of Kaff for me." Vincent smiled. The bartender quickly went to work. At their normal corner table sat a familiar Rhai. As skinny as always and wearing the normal Rhai fighter's uniform of a thin armor mesh dress.

"Nox?" Vincent asked, the Rhai turned from his drink and nodded.

"Hello, Vincent," they answered completely monotone.

"What are you doing here?" Since the battle on Grawluck Nox had gone back to their old ways of leading smugglers into forbidden space, whether it be Alliance controlled or otherwise. The thousands of pilots had kept Elysian's economy functioning, abet very disorganized, during the war. It had made him incredibly busy and months would pass in between meetings with them.

"I thought I would bring you something from Titan." Nox reached into a satchel he was carrying and set a bottle of Whiskey on the table.

"For the first time since I met you, I'm actually glad to see you." Fiona smiled and sat down next to him. Nox struggled to scoot away the best they could but Fiona wrapped an arm around their waif thin shoulders. "Bring anything for me?"

"Yes." Nox rummaged around in their bag again and brought out a carton of Cigarettes. A cartoon Fox was displayed on the front, running through a field. *Red Fox* was printed on the carton.

"You really do the know the way to a girl's heart!" she beamed.

"I do not know human surgery, but I can attempt..." Nox began but Fiona cut them off with a stern head shake. They had learned through their travels with Nox that the Rhai do not understand sarcasm, humor, or any sort of nuance of speech.

When they were being spoken to everything Nox heard was taken quite literally.

Even though Nox had begun their relationship by attempting to sell Fiona and him to the Alliance for untold riches, they had turned into a close friend during the strife of the year before. Though cowardly and risk adverse, Nox had dove into combat on more than one occasion to save Vincent's life, even if they had lacked any skill at fighting.

"So how is it going out there?" Vincent asked, sitting down across from Fiona and Nox.

"Not good," Nox said. "Titan space is safe, and they welcome the trade, but anything outside of that is dangerous."

"What is going on outside of Titan space?" Vincent asked.

"Unknown," Nox said. "Humans in Earth Defense Force flagged craft are attacking any craft that stray too far outside of Titan."

"So, you never made it to Mars?" asked Fiona. Since the fall of Earth Fiona had wondered what had become of her home. While they could pirate radio signals from Titan, no one had managed to find any news of human space beyond it. Other than rumors of course.

"No. Making it that deep into human space is unlikely. I am sorry Fiona."

"It's alright. Without the Committee there to control them I'm sure they're doing fine." Fiona smiled.

"Or devolved back into gang warfare." Vincent laughed. The human settlement on Mars had always been defined by conflict. Whether it be against the Central Committee or one another, Vincent was unsure if a time of peace had ever visited the red planet.

"Like I said, they're doing fine." At that, the bartender approached the table balancing a tray on his one good hand. He set down a scuffed and dented tray and slid the drinks across the table. Vincent was handed a small ceramic mug of a steaming hot brown liquid.

"I can't believe you still drink that crap." Fiona frowned. Kaff was an Earthian drink, served almost boiling hot. It was used by just about anyone who needed a jolt of energy. The drink tasted bitter unless some sweetener was added, which Vincent did in generous heaps. Out of all other humans, only Earthians seemed to be able to stomach the drink. The particular type he was drinking was popular amongst the former EDF soldiers and was a part of their daily rations while out on campaign. It was an instant brown powder that came in an airtight package that could just be dumped into any water the soldier had handy.

"So, you think Martians stole a bunch of EDF ships are raiding people?" Vincent asked.

"I could see that happening. But it would be kind of hard," Fiona said, drinking from her concoction of liquor and an unknown mixer. Her face twisted at the taste of it.

"Why would this be difficult?" Nox asked. "From your information it seems very likely."

"Because the EDF would never train Martians to be pilots," Fiona said. "Crewmen on the huge battle cruisers doing menial work, sure, but actually teach them to fly? Not in a million years. They never wanted to risk any future Martian uprising being able to match their air power."

"Very forward thinking of them," Vincent said.

"Yep, not to mention pilots are officers. Martians have been banned from Officer's Academy since the 2nd Rebellion. Keep us as ground pounders or laborers. The assholes."

"Have any Martians simply taught themselves how to fly? It would seem prudent for their needs," Nox said. Fiona sighed.

"Sure, but they never get enough time to practice before they get shot down. I doubt a couple Gangers who got their hands on a Reaper are fighting off anyone in deep space."

"If it's not the Martians who is it?" Vincent asked, taking a deep drink from his cup.

"Unknown," Nox said.

"Yeah, you've said that," Fiona grunted.

"Maybe humans from the Moon?" Zinvor said, Vincent glanced over at the Warrior, always a little surprised when he joined the conversation.

"Maybe. It would make sense with all of the rumors," he said.

"That would also mean even if the Committee did put itself back together, Titan isn't joining them," Fiona pointed out.

"Let's hope those rumors are just that," Vincent said. "I think if they did put themselves together, they would let it be known you know? The committee was never one for subtlety."

"True," Fiona said.

"If there is a committee presence in Human space, we have not yet seen it," Nox added. "Let us hope it stays that way."

"I can fucking drink to that. I'd piss on the ashes of that damn Chairman," Fiona spat. She glanced over at Vincent. "Shame about all those innocents and all."

"No need." Vincent waved her off. "I understand."

"We should be going soon," Zinvor butted in. Vincent drained the rest of his cup and set it down.

"You have another meeting?" Fiona asked.

"Yeah. After the Gathering Arai told me she wanted to meet alone. Not really sure why. Though I'm glad that asshole Gumi Leader won't be there. The prick."

"Yes." Nox nodded. "They are known to us for being very stern."

"I think that counts as an insult for them." Fiona laughed. "Good luck Consul, sir." She mocked a salute as he stood up.

"I hate you sometimes," Vincent said.

Fiona smirked. "I hate you too babe."

The crowd outside of the bar had thinned. At some point someone had finally taken the bodies away, leaving nothing other than dried pools of blood turned brown on the street. The Star was still there, dark brown and smudged on the wall of the general store. The crowd turned and looked at Vincent as he surveyed the scene and murmurs spread through the group. The eyes staring at Vincent showed him shades of fear and anger. They were looking at him. They were expecting *something.*

"I...uhh."

"You're supposed to be Consul!" screamed a voice in the crowd.

"What are you going to do about this?" screamed another.

"I—" Vincent tried to begin again.

"You're useless!" yelled a man. "I might as well pay the damn Black Coats!"

Vincent wasn't sure what to say. He tried to say *anything,* but his throat thickened, and his voice failed him. Zinvor began to push him through the increasingly agitated crowd and towards the tunnel where two Black Coats watched with smiles plastered across their faces.

At that moment more than any other Vincent wished he had power. Real power. The power to send the police, or the military into the Quarter to crush the Black Coats. He wanted to line the streets with their corpses. He wanted to instill the same fear into them has they had put into the people who were hiding in the bar. He cursed Arai for making him so powerless.

He tried to push those thoughts from his mind as he entered Arai's auditorium. The large, low table was empty. Data displays, maps, and scraps of food littered the table. The signs of a late night of campaign planning, he assumed. More meetings Vincent wasn't included in. What good was a military planner that had no military. At the rear of the open room was a door guarded by two yellow-armored Mawr Warriors. They bowed slightly to Vincent and opened the door as he approached.

Inside was Arai's office. It looked nothing like what a Human would consider the office of a powerful Political and Military leader. The room was empty minus a small pillow and table in the center where Arai sat, reading from a small display. In the corner was a thin bedroll that was badly worn and tattered with age.

"Greetings Vincent." Arai looked up from her reading. Vincent had no doubt she was reading her *Affirmations*. Or the deeply philosophical poetry that the Mawr that formed the central dogma of the Mawr religion. When he had first joined the Clan on Elysian Arai ensured he got a copy of it. He was surprised to find the religious text of a race he has assumed were little more than rough, blood-thirsty, barbarians full of excerpts on the beauty of sunsets and how to properly arrange flowers. Fiona said she had lost respect for them after reading it.

"Good morning Arai." Vincent bowed. She motioned for him to sit down next to her on the floor. She finished reading the passage she was in the middle of, clearly in no rush to start the meeting. "Um, out of curiosity why did you call me here?" She set the data slate down and looked at him.

"I forget how rushed you humans can be. I apologize."

"Sorry, there was...an incident last night. I didn't get any sleep."

"An incident? I did not hear of anything."

"You wouldn't have. The Gumi tends not to report the murder of humans," Vincent said, with maybe a little too much venom in his tone.

"Murder?" Arai asked, her voice showing concern. "Was it these *Black Coats*?"

"Yeah," he said. "They took a couple people out in the street and executed them."

"This is concerning Vincent." She scratched her wide jaw. Vincent felt the anger rise up in him.

"To be Honest Arai, you seem unwell too." Vincent nodded down at her display. Vincent knew she wasn't one to be alone; Arai was almost always surrounded by charts and maps planning new operations. Even when she was reading her Affirmations, she tended to have a few of her higher-ranking Warriors with her.

"You are preceptive Vincent." She nodded. "Things are not well in the Campaign against the Alliance."

"What's going on?" he asked.

"We have fully pushed them from the Elysian system, effectively carving out a small domain for ourselves, which has been a pleasant reprieve from their incursions. Unfortunately, we all know we do not have them beaten."

"What about the campaign for the Rhai home cluster?" Vincent asked. During the hours long meetings, the Gathering had planned a full-scale invasion of the Rhai home cluster. Their cluster named *Lumos* was made of several small worlds linked closely together. While the rest of the Cohort Leaders wanted to charge headlong at the Anarch's home world, which even Vincent knew would be a suicidal attack, Arai was smarter. She knew if the Clan managed to wrest control of Lumos from the Anarchs the Rhai would most likely join their side, tipping the odds in their favor for the first time.

"It has ground to a total standstill," Arai said. "The Alliance's defenses are nearly flawless. As much as we are costing them for holding their line we are being sapped as well." Vincent saw a small moment of weakness in Arai and as much as it hurt him to do so, he knew he had to take advantage of it.

"Arai, can I be honest with you? Like we used to be with each other before you made me Consul?"

"Of course." Arai nodded. "you always can be honest with me Vincent."

"You have a totally unused army sitting right here on Elysian and you refuse to use it."

"What do you mean?" she asked.

"The entire human population on Elysian are trained fighters. Sure, they aren't Mawr Warriors, but you saw on Grawluck that an EDF army can hold its own against the Alliance. You've fought side by side with Fiona and me. You know what humans can do," Vincent said, determined.

"I am unsure about this Vincent," she said.

"Think of it like this Arai: What did you want to do when the Anarchs' burnt your planet to a husk? There is almost a million humans sitting on their ass in the Quarter that would do anything to get revenge on the people who destroyed everything they loved. I'm just asking for you to give them a chance."

"The Cohort Leaders are unsure of your people Vincent. It was not that long ago that the Committee stabbed us in the back and nearly destroyed us all. The humans you want me to arm are the same ones who fought us."

"They tried to kill me too, Arai. They were just following orders. I told you what the EDF did to their own who stepped out of line. You've all witnessed it firsthand." Vincent remembered back to the muddy killing fields of Grawluck when he was sure he was about to die. Though, it seemed at this point in his life he had lost track of how many times he had nearly died in the last two years. He and Fiona were in the grasp of the bloodthirsty Colonel Rostov and about to be executed until Zinvor rushed in to save them at the last minute.

"And what about these *Black Coats?*" Her voice cut deep with hatred. "I've heard rumors about them."

"Trust me, most of us hate them too." His voice dropped. "There is something you don't know about humans, Arai. We are weak." He sagged.

"Explain," she grunted.

"The Black Coats are disgusting pieces of garbage, but they remind people of home. Of what we all just lost. Ever since we've been here, we haven't started a new life. We haven't created a new home. Everyone is just trying to hold on to what they used to know from Earth. Or from the Committee. The Black Coats remind everyone of that stiff, guiding hand ready to smash them if they step out of line, even if it's just a little bit. It's all they know."

"Hmm," Arai thought.

"You can give them something new," Vincent said, his voice rising. "Earth is dead, the Committee with it. We are the Humans of Elysian now and we need to create our own home, our own way of life, our own traditions, our new identity. Otherwise they will never put all of that behind them."

"You put me in a tough place Vincent," Arai said. "Though I suppose I did the same to you by making you Consul."

"You did." He nodded.

"What do you think will happen to these Black Coats?" she asked.

"They'll give up when they see people leaving their side when they're given other options."

"And if they don't?"

"I will kill every single last one of them." Arai thought for a moment, scratching her wide set jaw. After a moment she sighed, clearly admitting defeat.

"I'll give you what you want," she said slowly.

"What?" Vincent said shocked. "Really?"

"Yes. I will give you ample time to build an experimental Human Cohort for the Clan. Your people can also present themselves to Cohort Leader Nyxos for service in the ranks of the Gumi. Forward your reports to the Cohort of Armaments so they can be outfitted in due course."

"Thank you, Arai." Vincent smiled. He thought he had a decent argument, but he never actually thought Arai would agree with him. Maybe she really did respect him.

"Consul—Cohort Leader Solaris." Arai addressed him sternly, adding on his new title. "Remember one thing: The Clan does not accept failure from its military leaders."

The meaning of her warning was clear, his failure would mean his death.

CHAPTER FOUR

"I can't believe she's giving you a fucking army." Fiona laughed slamming down her empty glass on the bar table.

"Keep it down!" Vincent hissed. "I can't let the Black Coats find out before I get the ball rolling."

"And how are you going to do that?" Fiona asked.

"I...have no idea." His voice dropped. "Do I just put posters up or something?"

"Do you plan on commanding it yourself?" she asked.

"What!" Vincent exclaimed. "hell no. I'm not trying to get everyone killed."

"Well there's your answer. Find some officers who aren't loyal to the Black Coats."

"How the hell am I going to find sentenced officers? I've never even heard of one."

"I'll ask around. I made some contacts that might know something," she said nonchalantly.

"You made contacts?"

"Yeah, some of us haven't spent the last year locked up in an office playing politician you know." She smirked. The bartender quickly filled her glass back up without asking. Vincent, like always, tipped him several Bits. Bits were the official Clan currency. Though, the value of the currency had never matter much because the Clan's central economy was planned via the Public Works Cohort. The Bartender looked over his shoulder suspiciously and bent down to get closer to Vincent.

"I hear you're reforming the army," he whispered. His breath smelled like stale cigarettes and whiskey.

"How did you know that?" Vincent asked, shocked.

"Well, you're not exactly being very quiet about it, sir." It was then for the first time, with him only a few inches from his face, Vincent noticed one of the man's eyes was a very convincing fake. It was a dull brown and didn't move with his other one.

"Shit." Vincent sighed. "This is why official business shouldn't be carried out at the damn Bar," he spat at Fiona, she rolled her eyes and shrugged.

"Don't worry sir, I was Sentenced too, back when I was a whole person." The bartender held up the tied-off shirt that covered what used to be his left arm. "I wish I could join and fight those damn Tin Cans again." He cursed. *Tin Can* had become the human's slang term for the Anarchs.

"So..." Vincent thought and realized somehow, he had never learned the man's name after all this time. He really was bad at being Consul.

"Blackwell, sir. Formerly Staff Sergeant Blackwell, 16th Armored Regiment," Blackwell said.

"...Blackwell, how would you like to be a staff sergeant again?" Vincent asked.

"Uh, what do you mean, sir?" Blackwell asked, his eyebrow raised. "Can't do a lot of fighting like this."

"Not fighting. I need someone who can find people who not only want to fight the Alliance...maybe the Black Coats too," Vincent said. "I don't know anyone other than you and her, and no one knows more soldiers than a bartender. I'll make you my official recruiter."

"I would love to, sir, but what about the bar?" he asked.

"For every person you can bring me I'll pay you Two hundred Bits. You should be able to afford to hire someone to tend the bar while you're out," Vincent said. He wasn't sure how he was going to get that much money, he assumed there was some kind of form he could fill out to get the Clan to pay for it.

"Shit, can I get 100 bits per head too?" Fiona laughed.

"No, you just get to enjoy my love and affection." Vincent smiled at her.

"Man, I'm getting ripped off." She made a fake pouting face. Blackwell, ignoring Fiona's joke straightened up, stiff as a rod, and rendered parade perfect salute. Vincent waved off Blackwell's gesture.

"I'm not an officer. Shit, I was just a corporal until the damn Earth got blown up." Vincent smiled and sipped his drink. It burned down his throat and he coughed to recover from its harshness.

"Um, what should I call you then, sir?" Blackwell asked.

"Vincent works fine." He smiled. "I need people as fast as possible, but try to find officers first so there's some kind of organization. It's not going to take the Black Coats long to catch onto what we're doing. I'm working with the Warlord to get us some weapons, so we have to at least lay low until then." Blackwell nodded and turned to another bar patron, slapping him on the shoulder. It was a young woman with sandy blonde hair tied up in an EDF-standard bun.

"Bars yours until I get back," he ordered. She nodded and broke off her conversation, then took Blackwell's spot behind the bar. Blackwell turned back to Vincent and Fiona. "I'll get right on it, Consul Vincent." He saluted again and walked out of the bar. Vincent noticed a pronounced limp as Blackwell exited.

"Your recruiter has seen better days," Fiona said, her eyebrow raised.

"Haven't we all? Besides, he is one more soldier than I had ten minutes ago."

"That was a good idea. Very pragmatic of you." She nodded, sipping on her drink. Vincent smiled.

"Did you just give me a compliment?" he laughed. It was a joke, but not by much. Fiona's never-ending jokes on Vincent's behalf bordered on cruel at times. Fiona liked to call it "ball busting."

"What can I say, you're making me soft these days." She smirked. She finished her drink and waved to the new bartender for another. She quickly grew upset as the new girl didn't notice her hand. "But if you stole the only good bartender, you're going to have a damn revolution on your hands, not an army."

CHAPTER FIVE

"Unbelievable!" growled a Mawr Cohort Leader. They were wearing either brown or dark red armor, it was so badly repaired Vincent couldn't be sure. Their stone-like face was cut deep by countless scars and one of their normally black eyes was dead and milky white. The Council table was raging with angry debate after Arai had announced the creation of a Human Cohort. Vincent had narrowly dodged a flying gauntlet thrown his way moments before.

"We were good enough to be blindly thrown into the meat grinder on Grawluck, but not good enough to fix the bullshit you got yourself stuck in on Lumos?" Vincent yelled back. The battle plan that Arai had come up with during the invasion of Grawluck was centered on keeping the EDF in the dark about the true defenses the Alliance had on the planet. It would leave the Committee leadership distracted while Vincent and the Clan attempted to destroy the Alliance's planet killing weapons they had aimed at Earth. Trick or no trick, the EDF had managed to force their way through thousands of Alliance soldiers and had made a good account of themselves.

Unfortunately, the Committee knew about the weapons the whole time, but not that they were being aimed at Earth. They betrayed the Clan, and in turn caused the surprise attack on the weapon to fail and the subsequent destruction of Earth. Vincent didn't want to take the side of the now-defunct EDF, but the Clan knew they could fight.

"The means to an end!" Yelled a Rhai Cohort Leader who sat next to Vincent. Vincent's face turned red and he gritted his teeth.

"Were the Rhai once nothing more but a means to an end?" he shot back.

"You watch your tongue, human!" The Rhai hissed rising to his feet. Vincent stood up to meet the Cohort Leader. The Rhai stood, it's frail looking, bird-like chest puffed out and scrolls fluttering from its wispy, chain armor. Vincent cocked his arm back and delivered a vicious left hook to the side of its face. The Cohort Leader spun onto to the table, sending stacks of paper and data displays flying.

"Anyone else?" Vincent screamed. Rhai all along the table rose to their feet, protesting. "I'll take every single one of you skinny assholes!" Vincent seethed with rage. He noticed several of the Mawr were laughing and pounding on the table with their meaty fists, cheering him on. The Rhai Consul remained silent, their thin arms folded tightly across their chest.

"They took our homes the same as you!" Vincent yelled at the cheering Mawr. "Who are you to not allow us to fight them?" Vincent's words slowly rippled through the Gathering and the cheering died down to hushed whispers. "We don't have the technology that the Rhai have, and we aren't as strong as the Mawr, but goddamnit there's a million trained soldiers out there screaming for revenge! Are you going to tell them no?" Dozens of Mawr Cohort Leaders exchanged looks and slowly turned back to Vincent.

Arai, seated at the head of the table, slowly began to pound her fist against the table. A slow, repeating *thump, thump, thump*. The rest of the Warriors seated at the table took up her chorus of pounding. Eventually they were joined by the Rhai Leaders who Vincent hadn't just assaulted.

"It is settled!" Arai commanded. "In accordance with human tradition and the tradition of the Fidayi Clan as the second Warlord of the Fidayi Clan I declare the creation of the First Human Cohort and appoint Consul Solaris as it's Cohort Leader." Arai rose to her feet. "May Paterazm smile upon the glory of the Fidayi Clan forever strengthened by our comrades of the human race." Paterazm, Vincent thought. The same faceless war god of the Mawr that Zinvor was doomed to die for as a Tsarra. Ironic now that Arai was calling on it to honor him, though Vincent had cursed the Mawr's god countless times for his friend's punishment.

The rest of the Gathering slowly got to their feet in reverence of Arai or the utterance of Paterazm's name, Vincent wasn't sure which. Arai left her spot at the head of the table and walked down to where Vincent was standing. He turned to face her. She was nearly two feet shorter than him, normal for a Mawr. Though she was double his size in width, her armor strained to contain the thick chords of muscle that made the Mawr deadly and feared warriors.

From a pocket Arai produced a small silver medal. On it was stamped the symbol of a Riten crossing a dagger. It's rough workmanship, showing dents, scratches, and wear were normal for anything the Mawr made. She reached up and pinned the medal to his chest, next to the large burning phoenix. He couldn't help but notice that she pinned it on crooked. The pin matched the same being worn by the rest of the Cohort Leaders. When he looked down at Arai's armored chest, crowded with ribbons, he saw the same pin, though hers was the same dull yellow color as her armor.

"With this," Arai began. "You are no different than any military leader in the Clan," she said, though Vincent knew that no one at the table actually felt that way, even Arai. He knew he, and whatever version of an army he could scrape together from the dregs of the Quarter, would have to fight to proves themselves. The Leaders at the table pounded the table in unison once again, their expressions were hostile. They were simply obeying Arai's command, not paying homage to Vincent's position.

He would prove them wrong. He had too. It wasn't like he had much of a choice.

*   *   *

When Vincent and Zinvor entered through the tunnel what he saw stopped him in his tracks.

"Oh shit," he swore.

In the marketplace several Black Coats, armed with rifles, were gathered together. Their leader, an older officer wearing captain's bars on his collar, was holding a crumpled piece of paper in his fist and shaking in the face of Blackwell. Behind Blackwell was a dozen men and women armed with clubs, knives, and a few rifles or pistols. Curiously, Fiona was standing by the entrance of the bar, uninvolved, drinking from a glass and watching the scene unfold in front of her.

"Fiona!" Vincent yelled at her and she made her way over to them.

"Man, did you miss some shit," Fiona said, a smirk spreading across her face.

"What happened?" he asked. He looked over at the two sides concerned. They were screaming at each other in a show of barely contained violence. Blackwell was poking the Black Coat captain in the chest with his one good hand.

"Blackwell started putting up recruitment posters and the Black Coats seem to have taken offense."

"Well it looks like he was at least partially successful," he said.

"And they are already itching for a fight." Fiona smiled. "I like it."

"I don't. We aren't ready for this crap yet," Vincent said, and began walking towards the argument. He wasn't sure what he was going to do, but starting a civil war in the middle of the streets was probably a bad start to the army.

"So, what are you going to do?" Fiona asked.

"I don't know. Tell them to not start shooting people in the streets maybe. I am supposed to be in charge."

"I guess this is when we find out if you are or not," Fiona said. "This should be good." She smirked.

"One of these days you'll actually believe in me about something."

"One day."

As Vincent approached the Black Coat captain, he gave him a look of pure hatred. He turned and tossed the crumpled paper at Vincent's face. It fluttered down, and he caught it. Vincent unfolded it and saw the poster Blackwell had managed to put together. A triumphant looking EDF Soldier was bayonetting a crude drawing of an Anarch, which was very obviously drawn by someone who had never seen one in person. Above the combat scene it read "EDF Reborn! Rejoin today and fight with the Consul to avenge Earth!"

"What is the meaning of this?" The captain screamed in his face.

"I thought they taught you how to read in Officer's Academy?" Vincent answered.

"An army led by a Traitor and a slave to the toads. Disgusting!" *Toads* had become the go to racial slur for the Mawr.

"An army to avenge what happened to our home!" Vincent screamed back.

"What *you* did to our home!" The captain seethed with rage and took a step closer. Vincent noticed the captain's hand was on his sidearm. A small black pistol nestled in a hip holster restrained by a small safety latch.

"Just like a damn Black Coat to just repeat what someone else told him. Can't think for yourself, can you? What are you and your fashionable friends here doing to fight the Anarchs?" The safety latch of the captain's holster was flipped off by his thumb. "Just like I thought, absolutely nothing! You try to rule over us like petty kings and run away from the real threat. Just like the Committee did." Vincent fought back a smile, proud of himself as his dig at the Committee's expense clearly struck a chord.

"You dare mock the Committee in my presence?" Spit flew from the captain's snarling mouth.

"I'd piss on the Committee if they weren't turned to ash. Fuck you and fuck the Chairman's rotting corpse!" Fiona spat at the captain from behind Vincent. She always did have a way with words. Her insults seemed to throw the captain over the edge. He attempted to draw his sidearm as fast as he could, but it wasn't fast enough. A deafening *boom* silenced any arguments between the two sides.

A wisp of smoke curled up from the barrel of Zinvor's Riten. The close-range shot had cleaved a grotesque trench through the

Captain's head and sent his peaked black hat spinning to the dirt. Vincent winced as the remains of the captain's head splashed across his face and chest.

"Shit," Vincent cursed. He had walked into the middle of this to stop them from fighting and only succeeded in getting a Black Coat officer shot in the face. Another gun shot rang out, this time from a Black Coat. A young woman with red hair on Blackwell's side crumpled to the ground, holding her stomach.

"Open fire!" Screamed Blackwell. He had a pistol in his good hand and began to bang away on its trigger. The Black Coats fumbled trying to bring their rifles up to bare. That few seconds of delay was all the new army recruits needed to set upon them with their handheld tools. Soon, the flurry of hand to hand combat filled the Quarter.

Vincent unholstered his Riten and fired a shot into the Black Coat who had shot the young woman. His chest tore open and he fell to the ground. Fiona and Zinvor joined in on either side of him, hammering round after round into the panicking masses of Black Coats. A Black Coat sergeant's head was caved in by a dark-skinned man armed with a shovel.

A young Black Coat wearing corporal's chevrons attempted to get order of the situation, yelling for a retreat. His soldiers couldn't hear his voice over the din of combat, and it grew increasingly harder to hear when a Martian girl with a knife stabbed him in the side of the neck. The sudden outbreak of violence was too much for the Black Coats who had become so used to not having people fight back. They were soon running from the fight, leaving their wounded behind.

Vincent remembered while aboard the *ESS Victory* undergoing EDF basic training and reading from a large volume of rules and regulations a section titled *Rules of Land Warfare*. It specifically forbid shooting at a retreating foe, considering it dishonorable to shoot another soldier in the back. Vincent's ragtag group of recruits had apparently either forgot that rule or decided to ignore it outright. They whooped and hollered in celebration as the few recruits who were armed with guns dropped several of the retreating Black Coats as they fled.

The dust and smoke settled on the killing grounds and Vincent began to look around at the carnage. He saw at least four of his would-be recruits on the ground, not moving. Another was badly wounded. A thin, older looking man had his right leg reduced to tattered chunks of meat, the victim of a close-range shotgun blast. The redheaded girl wasn't making an attempt to hold in her guts any longer. The inequity of the two sides weapons had been made very clear.

Two wounded Black Coats writhed on the ground holding their various wounds next to three of their dead comrades. Recruits armed with clubs, knives, and other repurposed weapons poked and prodded the men on the ground. Vincent felt disgust rise in his throat as he saw the recruits laughing and kicking the wounded.

"That's enough!" he spat. "Leave the wounded alone!" Anger welled up inside of him. This was exactly what he was trying to avoid. "Blackwell!" he hissed. "What the hell happened?" Vincent's nose burned with the scent of gunpowder.

"You see Sir, Myself and the new recruits were hanging up these posters when those bastards showed up." Blackwell stuffed his pistol between his stump and armpit. Using his good hand, he reached down into his pocket and pulled out another magazine of ammunition and reloaded his pistol. It was a maneuver that had obviously been learned through practice.

"And?"

"They ordered us to disperse and take our posters with us. I informed them we were working under the orders of the Consul.

They didn't like that very much, sir, and we weren't about to back down from a challenge." Vincent looked around at the dead and wounded.

"I can see that."

"And when your bodyguard shot that captain, we had to act. They weren't going to just walk away from that," Blackwell said. He wasn't wrong. Once Zinvor dropped their commander any hope they had of avoiding a fight was gone.

"Thank you for acting quickly, Blackwell. I was a bit...surprised." Vincent glanced back at Zinvor who was meticulously reloading his Riten from the shells on his belt. "Gathered the wounded, theirs too, and get back to the bar."

"Their wounded, sir? But—"

"I don't intend to be as ruthless as they are. Do you?" Vincent raised an eyebrow. "And besides, they might be useful."

"Yes, sir." Blackwell nodded. He turned and began yelling commands at his gathering of recruits and they scrambled to obey them.

Vincent rubbed his eyes and tried to get his bearings straight. How did he go from being a powerless figurehead to commanding a group of soldiers into killing people in the streets? He wasn't sure if the people in the street were obeying him or fueled by hatred of the Black Coats in the moment.

"What now, *sir?*" Fiona asked sarcastically.

"I have no fucking clue." He sighed. "Try to find a way out of starting a damn civil war in the Elysian ghetto. You just had to shoot that guy in the face didn't you, Zinvor?"

"Yes," he said matter-of-factly. "He was going to shoot you. He was too slow."

"Ugh, *I know,*" Vincent whined. He couldn't help but think how much easier his life would have been if the captain would have been successful.

Fiona smirked. "This calls for a drink."

"Weird, I could have thought this calls for panicking. Lot of panicking." Vincent laughed nervously.

"I'll leave that to you. You do it so well," Fiona said, putting her arm around him as they walked towards the bar.

CHAPTER SIX

Vincent was afraid the collective rage of the bar patrons would overpower whatever small amount of authority his orders had, and the wounded Black Coats would be torn to shreds. Blackwell had hidden the men in the Eagle and Bar's basement stockroom, away from prying eyes. It was a good idea as the stockroom was already under a watchful eye for any thieves or soldiers looking to steal a drink. Zinvor standing guard in front of the stockroom door scared off anyone else.

An angry looking Black Coat sat on the floor of the bar's stockroom floor. He was surrounded on all sides by crates of Titanian beer, jugs of homemade liquor, and boxes of EDF rations. The man had to be in his mid-thirties or at least prematurely aged by a life of military service. He wore the stripes of a sergeant on the collars dirty black coat, Vincent could see several ribbons on his chest, one of which denoted service on Mars. The bandage he had wrapped around his forehead was red with blood, some of which had begun to drip down into his eyes.

The sergeant, it turned out, had been on the wrong end of a crowbar wielded by a short blonde woman.

"Good morning, Sergeant," Vincent began. The man frowned at his greeting.

"You're going to hang for this," he growled.

"Maybe." Vincent sat down on a chair that Blackwell had set up for him opposite of the prisoner. "At this rate that seems way more likely, actually."

"Did you come to finally shoot me?" the sergeant asked. "Just get it over with."

"Not at all." He shook his head. "I just have some questions."

"I'm not telling you shit."

"I'm not asking about intelligence or anything. I know you wouldn't tell me, you being a respectable non-commissioned officer and all." Vincent lit a cigarette and offered the sergeant one. He hesitantly took it. "As soon as you're healed enough, I just want you to pass a message for me."

"You're going to release us?" he asked. The other wounded man was much worse off than the sergeant. The Black Coat had been shot in the stomach and it took all the effort of every self-described medic that Blackwell could find to keep him alive just this long. He wasn't going to make it much longer without getting to a Doctor.

"That is the idea. The faster you can go, the more likely your friend is to make it." Vincent motioned over to the soldier who lay, unmoving, on a cot. "You see, us lowly criminals don't have access to medical supplies or Doctors like your people. We just have to make do with what we have. Unfortunately for your friend, what we have won't be enough for him." Vincent watched as the sergeant thought for a moment. He knew no sergeant would leave one of his own men to die if he could help it.

"What message do you want me to pass?"

"Here's the thing. For all of the fancy coats and strong arming no one really knows who is in charge of you people."

"For a good reason."

"Yeah, I'm sure," Vincent said. "I want you to tell them that I want to talk. It might not look like it from what happened out there, but the last thing I want to do is burn the Quarter down in some war against you."

"The General would never agree to that. He would never agree to anything with *you.*" The anger in the sergeant's voice was palpable.

"That isn't for you to decide, Sergeant. The faster you pass the message the faster your friend gets to some real medical care."

"And if I refuse to do your bidding *traitor?*" The sergeant tapped ash off of the end of his cigarette.

"Then I might lift my order about not hurting you two." He blew smoke out of his nose. Vincent leaned forward and poked the sergeant's Martian Service Ribbon. "I bet I know a few Martians who would love to get their hand on you." He leaned back. "Or Maybe I let Fiona decide your fates." The sergeant's eyes went wide. Fiona's reputation for ruthlessness was useful from time to time. "She has been in deep discussion with the others about how long you would hold up under torture. I think they may have placed bets on it. Either way, I wouldn't risk it." Vincent stubbed out his cigarette on the windowsill. "So, we have a deal?"

"Yes!" The sergeant blurted out. "Yeah, just keep that woman away from me." He glanced over at Fiona who was leaning against the Stockroom door, picking her nails with a knife. "But I can't guarantee that the General will let me live long enough to deliver a response once he finds out I agreed to this."

"See to it that he does. Your friend won't be released until I hear back from you and a meeting is set up." Vincent handed the sergeant a folded note which he took and slowly placed in the pocket of his great coat. "I won't kill a wounded man, Sergeant. But I know a few people who will."

"You just signed your own death warrant, Traitor," the sergeant said.

Vincent smiled. "If only you knew how many times I've heard that."

"I can't believe you're just letting him go." Fiona slammed down her drink on the table. It landed with a *crack* next to her Riten which she had out and ready. With this she was hardly alone. Ever since the attack the Bar had been on edge. Nearly every patron had a gun, knife, or some other weapon resting on the table next to their drink, waiting for the Black Coats to come get their revenge.

"Means to an end," Vincent said taking a sip of steaming Kaff.

"Like you're going to put a lid on all of this?" she asked. "You can't have a sit down with them like you're some kind of diplomat. They're not an army or a government, no matter how much they want to pretend that they are."

"They would probably say the same about me." He raised an eyebrow. "What are they then?"

"A gang. You know how we deal with gangs back home?" She eyed her Riten.

"I can imagine," he said. "but look around. The two dozen *soldiers* I have here" He said with maybe a little too much sarcasm "Don't even have enough weapons to go around. You can't expect us to go to war."

"So, you're going to play nice until we can beat them?"

"In a perfect world they would see the errors of their ways and join us," Vincent said. The look on Fiona's face was one of disbelief. "Or at the very least avoid an all-out civil war. For some reason I feel like Arai would be pretty pissed at me if I brought that shit to her front door." He remembered her dire warning: Fail and die.

"We should plan for both instances," Fiona said.

"Wait, since when do you make plans?" Vincent asked. The whole time he had known her he had to restrain her more times than he could count from running headlong into battle without thinking. More often than not he ended up in the middle of it all trying to catch her.

"Their forcing my hand." The new bartender, the woman chosen by Blackwell, came by and refilled her glass. Fiona gave her a dirty look.

"Forcing your hand?" Vincent laughed "and why do you hate her so much?"

"She's slow." Fiona frowned.

"She seems to move at an adequate speed," Zinvor said, sipping from his large mug of beer.

"Okay fine," Fiona said. "She keeps eyeing you. I don't like it when girls eye my property like that." Vincent exploded with laughter, nearly spilling his drink. Fiona slammed her drink down in anger. "Why are you laughing?"

"You of all people are jealous?" he laughed. "I'm not even going to get into the *property* thing."

"I'm just saying if she makes a move on you, I'm going to knife her."

"You don't see the look of terror in her eyes whenever she brings you a drink? She probably pees a little every time you throw that look at her," Vincent said.

"Good," she growled.

"You never explained what you meant when you said they were forcing your hand," Vincent said.

"Forcing me to be like you," she complained. "Boring and political." Vincent laughed and drained the rest of his Kaff.

"So, Zinvor, part of this plan requires your help," he said. Zinvor looked up from his mug. "Do you trust Nox?"

"I have never trusted Nox," he said flatly. "I do not know why you would think that."

"You didn't trust them after all that time together?" asked Fiona.

"Never," he repeated.

"Shit," Vincent said. "Well, Nox trusts you more than me. I need them to get their hands on weapons. Rifles, machine guns, pointy sticks, anything. I'm going to talk to Arai and see how long it is going to take for the Clan to outfit us, but if this deal with the Black Coats goes south we are going to need guns a lot sooner than the Clan can bring them."

"This I can do." Zinvor stood up, beer in hand. "If I go, she cannot leave your side." He nodded to Fiona. Fiona sarcastically put her hand over her heart.

"On my honor I promise my exalted Tsarra." She smirked. Zinvor and the Mawr at large, did not understand human sarcasm. Instead of getting the joke, he bowed low to them and pushed through the growing crowd in the bar towards the exit.

"Damn there are a lot of people in here," Vincent said, looking around. The Eagle and Bar had always been a busy place. Not because it was an overly nice bar or that the food was good. It was just the only bar operating in the Quarter that would serve Sentenced soldiers. No one was coming here for the hospitality.

"Your new recruits no doubt," Fiona said. "Looks like your plan is working." Vincent smiled, momentarily proud of himself. "Either that or you just attracted all of the people in the Quarter who want a chance to take a shot at the Black Coats."

"I'll take that," he said. "I'm not exactly in the position to be choosey on who I allow to enlist."

"Any idea how much money you owe Blackwell now?" she asked. Vincent looked around and shrugged.

"Significantly more than I have to give, I'm sure," he said, and they laughed together.

* * *

The atmosphere in the bar turned from one of tension and fear into one of a celebration as the night grew longer and the drinks flowed freer. Vincent had kept out of it, and no one attempted to drag him in. He wasn't sure if they thought he was above their station as Consul or just because they didn't like him.

Fiona was in the middle of it all, going shot for shot with Blackwell and then again with a rail-thin young man wearing lieutenant's bars on his collars. Several soldiers began joining each other, arm in arm and singing old EDF war songs—omitting any part that mentioned the Chairman.

"Arise, children of the Fatherland, the day of glory has arrived!
Against us, tyranny's bloody standard has been raised,
Do you hear in the countryside
The roars of those ferocious soldiers?
They're coming right into your arms
to cut the throats of your sons, your women!"

He grimaced at the violent lyrics. He had to wonder why the veteran soldiers thought that these were songs to be sung in celebration.

"Hey!" Shouted a drunk Blackwell. The old staff sergeant was red faced and swaying back at forth. "Raise one up for the

Consul! May Consul Solaris bring us the Great Victory we were once promised!"

The crowd broke into a roar. Glasses of beer, liquor, and wine were held up high, their contents sloshing down onto the cheering soldiers. Nobody seemed to notice. More than one rifle was thrust up in the air.

"Death to the Anarchs!" Blackwell yelled and again the crowd went wild.

"Death to the Alliance!" yelled another soldier, who was greeted with a roar.

"Death to the fucking Black Coats!" Fiona slurred, and to Vincent's internal horror she got the loudest of the cheers. The bartender rushed through the crowds carrying a tray with several glasses on it and put it down in front of Vincent. A soldier fired a rifle into the ceiling of the bar and the cheers only got louder.

"These are shots people have bought for you, sir." She smiled.

"Oh, tell them—" Vincent started.

"Sir, in all due respect you should probably drink them."

"Ugh, fine." Vincent took the four shots off of the tray and put them on the table, smelling the first one. It reminded him of a backroom chemical lab gone astray. He tipped it back into his mouth and winced as it burned down his throat. The crowd was watching him in expectation as he did his shots. He held up the empty shot glass to a roaring applause and fought back laughter as Fiona stared daggers at the poor bartender who was just trying to do her job.

After a few shots, Vincent loosened up. His mind abandoned the endless worries he had been constantly dwelling on ever since war had erupted in the marketplace. Fiona wrapped her arms around him and forced him to drunkenly dance with her. They swayed around the bar cutting in between other couples who had parred off for a slow song that had begun to play on the pirated radio station.

"Your army might be bullshit but at least they know how to party." She smiled up at him.

"Yeah." He smiled and kissed her. He stared down into her deep blue eyes and felt lost in them. She always had a way to take his mind off anything that troubled him with just a glance. He didn't notice at first when the music turned to static and died out. They stopped dancing and glanced upwards at the hissing speakers in confusion.

"Good morning Union of Titan! We interrupt your normally scheduled programming for some Breaking News!" Called an optimistic voice through the speakers.

"Ah, man," complained a slightly overweight soldier. "Your signal is picking up the local news." The crowd groaned.

"It'll pass," Blackwell said. "This normally only lasts a few minutes."

"The Ministry of Foreign Affairs made an announcement," the Newscaster said. "Foreign Minister Talon has said he had received an official notice of summons from the Central Committee of United Humanity, now based in Lunar City. The Central Committee proclaimed the ascension of the six-hundredth Chairman of Unified Humanity and demanded all Humanity once again kneel before his glory." The bar erupted into angry chatter.

"Be quiet!" Fiona yelled at them. The News Caster continued.

"Prime Minster Addler was quoted as saying "The people of the Union of Titan have mandated through plebiscite that they are an independent and righteous people free of the chains of any Committee or Chairman and thus it will remain. We will not kneel before anyone's glory other than our own." The radio hissed with static again and fell silent. The bar erupted with panicked conversation. Vincent could feel dozens of eyes burning into him, waiting for an answer. They were waiting for an answer that he didn't have.

"Shit," Fiona cursed. "What now?"

"Does this change anything?" he asked her.

"I don't know, probably?" she said. "I would imagine more than one person in here is going to change their mind now."

"Damnit." He pulled away from her. "I need to tell Arai. This could go bad."

"What about the Black Coats?" she asked. "This is going to make them go crazy."

"Goddamnit." He hadn't thought of them. She was right of course. Even before they had proof of a living Central Committee and Chairman, they were trying to impose their beliefs on the Quarter and attempting to police the area with the old laws. "Blackwell!" he yelled. The drunken staff sergeant stumbled over to where he was standing and saluted.

"Get whatever weapons you can and start digging in around this place." Vincent thought for a second. "And put some soldiers on the entry tunnel into the Quarter. If shit goes south, we might need a way out into the Government Quarter. I have to go talk to the Warlord."

"Yes, sir!" he obeyed. "But sir, you cannot be allowed to leave without a proper guard. Not with the current threats."

Vincent waved him off. "I have Fiona, I'll be fine."

"Sir, with all due respect, we know how well she can fight, but without your alien bodyguard I am worried for your safety."

Vincent had to admit, he always did feel a bit invincible whenever Zinvor was nearby. "Fine, but don't sacrifice a lot on my behalf. If the Black Coats come after you here while I'm gone, you're going to need everything you can get."

"Yes, sir. Take Privates Smith and Huang." He motioned over to two young men who had been standing guard over the bar's front door. If it weren't for the minimum age of recruitment in the EDF being seventeen, Vincent could have been convinced they were hardly fifteen. They wore ill fitting, dirty and worn grey uniforms with standard issue EDF rifles slung over their shoulders. "They have proven themselves to be reliable."

"They look like they should still be on their mom's tit," scoffed Fiona. Vincent ignored her.

"I'm just going down the street, Blackwell, don't be so high strung about it. Take care of yourselves here. You two ready?"

"Yes, sir!" The two privates chirped together.

"Oh boy." Fiona sighed. "They really are a serious lot, aren't they?"

"Well, I would hope so since they are supposed to keep me from dying."

"I wouldn't put my money on it." Fiona eyed the two young soldiers. "Did you two do any fighting on Grawluck?"

They exchanged panicked looks.

"Err, no ma'am," answered Huang, pushing his thick black glasses up his nose. "I was held in reserve and Smith was a supply clerk."

"Well isn't that wonderful. A supply clerk?" Fiona laughed derisively.

"I went to the same basic training as anyone else ma'am," Smith said with an edge in his voice. "I can fight."

"Well let's hope we don't find that out any time soon, eh?" Vincent smiled. "Keep your heads up just in case. I don't want to get caught unaware."

"Yes, sir!" they piped again.

The area outside of the Bar swarmed with activity. The previously partying soldiers were building fortifications out of anything they could get their hands on. The hours of drinking had made the quality of their work questionable at best. The soldiers themselves looked as likely to vomit into a sandbag than actually fill it with sand.

The Quarter entrance, once in firm Black Coat control, was now manned by two grey jacketed soldiers. They rendered Vincent a salute as he neared. One soldier had a pistol stuffed into a coat pocket while the other had a type of rifle Vincent had never seen before. Judging by it's rough looking construction he assumed it was something they had gotten from the Mawr market.

"Good evening, sir!" greeted the young woman. Her words were heavily slurred, and she swayed a bit as she attempted to stand.

"How is everything out here?" Vincent asked.

"They haven't had the balls to come out and challenge us since they got chased off earlier, sir."

"Make sure it stays that way."

"Of course, sir!"

The group walked past them and into the tunnel.

"They're certainly optimistic," Fiona said.

"They're drunk," Vincent responded. "That probably helps."

"True, though they don't seem to be handling it well."

"Not everyone can handle their booze like you."

"I consider it a skill."

"I'll make sure I put that on the new army's training schedule." He laughed.

At this time of night, the Government Quarter was almost entirely empty. A few Gumi officers stood around bored on guard duty, but the area was devoid of the normal constant hustle and bustle of a Gathering. Even the street merchants had taken the night off.

The idle officers hardly noticed when the group approached them. One of them, baring the shoulder insignia of a Gumi equivalent of a major straightened up and snapped into a quick bow when they saw him.

"Great evening, Consul," stuttered the major in a language he clearly still did not quite have a hold on. Vincent returned the major's bow with a Human salute, even if it was a bit lazy and loose.

"Aren't you important now?" Fiona said sarcastically.

"They kind of have no choice now."

"You look a little happy about that," Fiona said.

"For how little they think of humans making them bow to me does feel pretty damn good." Vincent smiled. The Rhai had a huge superiority complex, for what reason Vincent could never figure out. They were subjugated by the Anarchs without a fight and the few free settlements they had were rescued by the Clan. Granted, the Clan allowed each race virtually unlimited freedom, it wasn't as if the Rhai had saved themselves. They could level all kinds of accurate insults about humanity, but at least their home world went down with a fight.

He assumed because humans were new to the Clan the Rhai thought they could try to enforce their will over them as a kind of big brother. Vincent decided as soon as Arai made him a Cohort Leader, he would do everything in his power to ensure that didn't happen. Knocking out that Cohort Leader in the middle of the Gathering probably helped.

Smith and Huang pushed open the double doors to reveal a darkened chamber. The low table was empty for all except Arai and a Rhai that Vincent had never seen before. Arai looked up from a Data display, obviously surprised to see Vincent and his group of humans standing there.

"Vincent?" she asked.

"Sorry I didn't mean to interrupt anything. But there's something you need to know," he said.

"Of course, have a seat." She motioned to a cushion next to her. The Rhai standing next to Vincent skin was a deep black color, something he had never seen before. Instead of the normal chain linked dress of armor the Rhai wore, it wore a shimmering cloak of black.

"Greetings, Solaris," the Rhai said.

"Hi. I don't believe we have met..." Vincent said.

"Apologies. I am Cohort Leader Pharos."

"He is the Clan's master of spies," Arai added.

"The more literal human translation would be Cohort Leader of Special Activities," Pharos corrected. The title sounded ominous.

"That explains why you're never at the Gatherings," Vincent said.

"Yes. It is the intelligence he gathers that allows our meetings to take place." Arai nodded. "What is it you had to share with us Vincent?"

"Oh right." He had almost forgot. "Word from Titan..."

"You have spies in the Union of Titan?" Arai cut in, obviously surprised.

"No, not quite." Vincent scratched his thick beard.

"We pirate their radio broadcasts in the bar," Fiona added.

"I see..." Arai said. Vincent was sure the fact he did not have intelligence assets on a faraway planet disappointed her.

"Regardless, the state news of Titan said that the Central Committee has definitely reformed. They are demanding the surviving human settlements' fealty."

"Impossible," Pharos said. "The government perished with Earth."

"It's not hard for them to do," Vincent pointed out. "The Lunar settlement was always used as a vacation spot for high-ranking Committee members. A place they could live in luxury away from the prying eyes of the plebs. I always heard rumors when I was a kid that the Chairman actually ruled from there, not Earth."

"That makes the Alliance strike on the Moon make a lot more sense." Pharos stroked its thin face. "A decapitation strike to make humanity surrender rather than destroy them outright. The second strike was when it became clear they would not surrender."

"But if one strike destroyed Earth, how did the Moon survive?" Fiona asked.

"Maybe it wasn't a decapitation strike," Pharos thought out loud. "Maybe instead it was a warning shot. It is what they did to my kind. One look at the power of their weapons and the Central Governing Council surrendered. I assume they expected the same of the Humans."

Vincent sighed. "Well, either way it appears the Alliance failed twice."

"What of Titan and Mars then?" Arai asked.

"Well, the news broadcast said Titan's Prime Minister was refusing the Committee's orders," Vincent said. "Something about them being independent now."

"And I'd put money on the fact that Mars is a warzone again," Fiona said.

"Why is that?" Arai asked.

"It's in our blood." Fiona laughed. "Once word got around that the Chairman got turned to dust every Martian with a pulse would rise against the EDF garrison."

"Interesting," Arai said.

"If what they say is true...it is very bad," Pharos said.

"Agreed," Arai added.

"I don't know why the Titan broadcast would be lying," Vincent said. "They don't have anything to gain by it."

"But Lunar City certainly does by reforming a dead government and trying to put everything back together," Fiona said.

"Whether it's a real government or not, what's important is what people *think* it is," Vincent said. "If they win the loyalty of what is left of the EDF then that is all they're going to need."

"This is true," Arai said.

"And most of them blame Solaris and the Clan for what happened to their planet," said Pharos.

Arai turned to look at Vincent, inquisitively.

"Yeah, that part's true. The Black Coats keep calling me the Great Traitor. I've been expecting to get shot any day now." He smiled but he was only half joking.

"Speaking of the Black Coats, when were you going to inform me of the conflict you had earlier?" Arai asked.

Vincent's eyes went wide with shock, how had she found out? A wry smile creased Pharos' lipless mouth. "It was a misunderstanding that went too far. I'm attempting to get in contact with their leader." He sighed and scratched his beard. "But that was before this whole *New Chairman* thing coming from Titan, though. I don't have a lot of hope for a peaceful ending now."

"Will this cause problems?" Arai asked.

"Oh, just a few." Fiona laughed sarcastically.

"We are handing it, but we need guns. Fast," Vincent said.

"The Armaments Cohort is already processing your request," Arai said.

"Intel," Fiona blurted out. Vincent raised an eyebrow in confusion. "If shit does go south with them, we don't have a fancy

Spy Master like you do. Can you tell us everything you know about the Black Coats?" Vincent had to admit, that was a good idea. They knew almost nothing about the Black Coats other than what they did in public and the local rumor mill. Neither of which happened to be useful when he was planning what might turn out to be a military operation. He had no doubt they had scouts, spies, and commandos at their disposal to go with their legions of Loyalists.

Pharos nodded. "I will forward you the files we have on them."

"Wait," Fiona said, her anger welling up in her voice. "You actually had information on them and didn't tell us?" Her words slowly seeped into Vincent's ears, and it took him a while to understand what she was saying. Arai was holding out information from him.

"Yeah, what the hell?" he exclaimed.

"Until yesterday you were not a Cohort Leader," Pharos said. "You were not privy to classified military information as a Consul."

"That's a bullshit excuse and you know it. You wanted him to face down these guys before you ever made him a Leader without any information or soldiers to back him up," Fiona spat. The fact she was making so much sense began to anger Vincent. Arai really had set him up for failure. A toothless figurehead in charge of no one and able to do nothing.

"It was a shortsighted and bad idea. This I admit." Arai crossed her thick arms. "We have righted the situation."

"Righted my ass," Vincent said. "You owe us."

"You are certainly forward towards the Warlord, human," Pharos said, disgust obvious in his voice.

"You have simply never met them before; they are always like this." Arai shook her head. "I admit, I owe you a debt for putting you in such danger, Vincent. It will not happen again."

Vincent was a little shocked she admitted to being wrong outright. He couldn't remember another time she ever admitted to any wrongdoing. He looked over at Fiona who was equally speechless.

"Uh, that's fucking right," she said, trying to save face.

Arai smiled in response. "Please, keep me updated on your progress with the Black Coat leader."

"Who I am assuming you two know by name?" Vincent asked.

"Former Colonel General Vasilli Brusilov," Pharos added.

"Why does that name sound so familiar?" Fiona asked no one in particular.

"Before being the Operational Commander on Grawluck, he was Military Governor of Mars," Pharos said. "His conduct during the Third Martian Uprising got him demoted and transferred elsewhere. I am told his behavior on Mars was quite terrible."

"*Brusilov The Butcher,*" Fiona seethed. "I only heard about him in scary stories when I was a kid. I had almost forgot his name. How the hell did he end up on Elysian? Shouldn't we have screened the people we were letting take refuge here?"

"You know as well as I do no one was screened. There is probably at least a few hundred war criminals, rapists, and murderers over in the Quarter," Vincent said. *And most of them are probably in my army now,* he thought to himself.

"Our good deed is certainly turning into a headache," Arai said.

"Well, I'll try to not let it get any worse."

"Be sure to do that." Arai's tone made Vincent sure their conversation was over. Vincent bowed slightly and turned to walk out. Smith and Huang were still standing at the door to the room, their faces one of shock.

"You two okay?" Vincent asked as he walked by them and through the doors.

"I'm sorry, sir, I've just never seen you speak...their language before," Huang said.

"Ma'am, are you not able to speak Mawr?" asked Smith.

"When I do, I sound like I have brain damage. Arai speaks Earth Standard; Vincent just thinks using their words is *respectful* or something," Fiona said.

"Well she is the Clan Warlord. Some respect is due," Vincent said, he was so engrossed in the conversation he ignored the Rhai soldiers bows and walked by without returning the honor.

"Why bother? She didn't think it was necessary to inform you of the war criminal living in our midst. She doesn't respect us." Fiona frowned.

"So, who is this Brusilov anyway?" Vincent asked.

"He must be pretty bad if he was actually demoted for his actions on Mars," Smith said.

"He was the Military Governor during the last uprising. Most Worms hate us, think of us as not as good as them, whatever. Brusilov thought Mars had to be cleansed of us Martians and the settlement restarted from the beginning. He was the one who started the *Earthian Resettlement Program* on Mars. It is what started the third war in the first place."

"Wait, they were still recruiting people for that when I enlisted," Huang said. Fiona laughed.

"Wait, you enlisted Huang?"

"Yeah. Turns out I was as much of a slacker as a soldier as I was a student." He shrugged. "Sentenced to four months additional service right before Grawluck. I was already starting my exit paperwork."

"Damn that is bad luck," Vincent said.

"Yep. They looked at my Ethics School marks and offered me a position on Mars studying medicine at Victoria Central University. I only made it for a few months there, partied too hard and started failing."

"So, you ran off to the EDF?" Vincent asked.

"Didn't have much of a choice. My Dad would have killed me if I went back home a failure. Guess I don't have to worry about that now." Huang faked a smile, but his eyes became watery at the thought.

"The program is more innocent these days," Fiona said. "When Brusilov started the program, they would send death squads out and wipe out all the men and boys in a town to make room for new Earthians they had recruited to move to Mars. They'd keep the women alive for breeding. Eventually all those small settler towns joined together and turned into Victoria. It's almost as big as Olympus now."

"What stopped Brusilov?" Vincent asked. He always assumed Military Governors were second to the Chairman himself on places like Mars, the Moon, or Titan. He had learned in school that only settlements, not Earth itself, would have Military Governors, as some kind of show of force from Earth itself.

"The Committee would never admit to it, but the uprising on Mars was more than just a thorn in their damn sides," Fiona said, digging in her pocket for a cigarette and lighting it. The tip glowed brightly in the darkness of the empty Government Quarter streets. "Thousands of soldiers dying, billions in lost revenue. We weren't going to win either mind you. By the end of the war people on Mars were starving to death and dying in droves from one terrible disease after another. The Committee agreed to terms of surrender by the main rebel group, on the grounds that Brusilov be tried for his crimes."

"Well, that obviously never happened," Vincent said.

"Nope. Just like the other groups warned them, as soon as they handed over their weapons, they were executed en masse. It didn't take long for the resistance to collapse entirely afterwards." Fiona blew out a stream of smoke. "Brusilov was fired by The Chairman himself, but not for slaughtering us like cattle."

"Then what was he fired for?"

"He made them look bad." Fiona forced a sad laugh. "He started his Resettlement Program with little Committee input, being a Military Governor he didn't really need it, but that also means he started a war without consulting them. A war he then went on to botch and kill half a million EDF soldiers in."

"So he got himself canned and put under the command of that Molke character on Grawluck?" Vincent asked.

"Seems that way," she said. Vincent remembered Molke vividly. He had been the one who had officially sentenced Fiona and him to death shortly before he ordered the EDF to turn on the Clan in the middle of the battle.

He also remembered murdering him in cold blood and Fiona stealing his ceremonial sword. The same sword she was wearing on her hip as they spoke.

"How the hell did we manage to kill Molke but miss this guy entirely?" Vincent asked. "We destroyed the entire command area."

"Sir, I think I know the answer to that," Huang piped up. "Brusilov was in charge was the eastern advance, meaning his camp was far away from where you must have run into the Field Marshal...I mean Molke. Molke's camp was Central Command, so you effectively wiped the overall commanders and their aides out. Their sub commanders were off near the fighting. From what I understand Brusilov's eastern advance got the worst of it."

"How did you hear that?" Fiona asked. "Weren't you busy being as far away from the battle as possible?" Vincent could sense ire rising up in Fiona's voice.

"I was ma'am, but do you talk to many people who fought on the eastern advance? I know I don't," Huang said. Vincent had to give the young soldier credit, most people shy away from Fiona's intensity, unwarranted or not. He didn't blink.

"I wonder why someone who is used to so much power is okay hiding away in secret," Vincent said. "He went from being a Military Governor to hiding in some basement somewhere in the Quarter. With all of the smugglers heading out he could have easily bribed his way back to human space by now. I don't get it."

"After being publicly shamed and fired no Committee will ever make him a Military Governor again. Here he has an army of assholes to do his bidding for him and no one to control him. He has got it made again." Anger welled up in Fiona's voice.

"And nobody ever becomes a Military Governor in the first place without being a shrewd, conniving, clever bastard," said Huang. "We shouldn't trust a thing he says."

Their conversation was cut short by a Black Coated man standing at the head of the Quarter's Tunnel. On either side of the angry looking sergeant was a grey uniformed member of Vincent's army. Above their head where it had once said 'The Chairman Lives' was now a badly painted phoenix. Vincent thought whoever had painted it had probably been drunk

"You came back," Vincent said, surprised. He never actually expected to see the sergeant again. If he had been given the same option, he would have left the other guy to die and never returned.

"Unlike your lot we real Soldiers have honor," the sergeant spat.

"Watch your mouth!" cursed Smith. Despite his having enough courage to yell at the Black Coats, the young soldier's oversized helmet drooping over his eyes and uniform that clear a size too big did not cut an intimidating figure. The sergeant scoffed derisively at him.

"And?" Vincent asked, trying to move the conversation along.

"The General will meet you."

"I want to meet him in a neutral area. The Consul's Office in the Government Quarter," Vincent said. The sergeant's expression was one of shock.

"Your office is hardly neutral," he said.

"The Clan doesn't care about your little Committee Loyalist bullshit and won't get in our way. I won't be surrounded by your people and he won't be surrounded by mine. It's our best option." Vincent shrugged. The sergeant scratched his chin where several days of stubble had grown. "We bring three people each and no more. Sidearms only."

"It will take me time to exchange messages again..."

"I don't want to wait for the back and forth." Vincent shook his head. "If he agrees to meet with me tomorrow at noon send up a flare at some point today. I don't care about the color. I'm sure you guys have some in your weapons stores."

"I will pass your message," the sergeant said. "And about—"

"Your comrade is the same place he was before. I'll have him brought out to you," Vincent interrupted.

The sergeant was obviously surprised.

"A lot of people here wanted to skin you two alive. Remember that I didn't let them."

The sergeant nodded and turned back down the tunnel out of view.

*   *   *

Vincent was unbuckling his armor when someone began to frantically knock on the door to their apartment. Fiona rolled out of bed, clad in only her underwear, and snatched her Riten out of its holster.

"Who's there?" Vincent called out. He regretted sending Zinvor out to find Nox. He had yet to return and the only protection he had were the two young soldiers who had most likely never fired their weapons before. Without his Mawr Guardian he felt naked.

"It's Private Huang, sir!" came the panicked voice behind the door. "A Reaper just landed outside!"

"A Reaper?" Vincent asked, puzzled. The Reaper, or officially the *Earth Standard Ship Frame #649,* was the EDF's main ship used for transport, resupply, and close air support, depending on its configuration. The bumblebee looking ship had earned its nickname through the years by being the ship that brought fire down on the EDF's enemies as well as being the ship that carted away their dead and wounded. He hadn't seen one since the evacuation off of Grawluck as the Clan had seized all of the surviving EDF spacecraft for use in the war effort.

He walked over to the window and peered out. Just like Huang had said, the fat grey shape of a Reaper sat parked in the middle of the marketplace.

"It's gotta be them!" Fiona cursed and moved to put her armor back on.

"If they had a Reaper, they would have bombed us to hell as soon as we shot at them. If this is the Black Coats, their plan doesn't make any sense," he said. "I'm going to see what the hell is going on." He re-holstered his Riten and opened the door. Huang saluted him, but his face turned bright red when he saw Fiona.

"What?" Fiona yelled at him. "This is the first time you ever saw a chick in her underwear before?"

"Uhh, actually yes ma'am," he stammered.

"Well, I was just fucking with you before, but now I just feel bad." She fought back laughter and pulled the covers over herself. Vincent pushed Huang away from the door and they walked down the stairs quickly.

The Reaper sat, its engines whirling quietly. Across the side of the cockpit the word *Shanna* was painted in baby blue letters. The troop compartment door of the ship slid open and Zinvor climbed out. He gave a nod to Vincent and motioned to the boxes stacked up inside of the cargo area.

"You ask for guns. I bring you guns." Zinvor grunted.

"Perfect timing." Vincent smiled and patted Zinvor on the shoulder. "Um, who's Reaper is this Zinvor?" As if on que, the engines slowly died away, leaving the night silent. The passenger side door swung open and Nox hopped out. "This is just getting more confusing." Vincent scratched his beard. "Did you steal a ship?"

"Sorry, sir," came a rough voice from Cockpit. Vincent looked up and saw a dark-skinned middle-aged man in a black flight suit. On his shoulders was the silver oak leaf of a lieutenant colonel. He heaved himself out of the cockpit in one fluid motion, stood up straight and saluted Vincent. Confused, Vincent slowly returned his salute. "I didn't mean to wake you."

"I'm sorry, who are you?" he asked.

"Lieutenant Colonel Vorbeck, formerly of the 56th Air Support Wing."

"Why the hell is a lieutenant colonel saluting me?" A lot of strange things had happened in the last year, hell even just the last few days. But a highly ranked officer throwing his lot in with him seemed just a bit too far.

"I'm a sentenced officer, sir," Vorbeck answered. "Reporting for duty." He gave a slight grin. "Unless you already have a pilot."

"We seem to be without one." Vincent smiled back.

"He was working for me until today," Nox joined in. "He heard about your conflict with the Black Coats and felt compelled to come join you."

"Welcome aboard then..." Vincent stopped himself, he just couldn't keep up the formality. "I'm sorry, what's your first name? There is no way I'm making a colonel call me sir."

"It's Ezra, sir," he said reflexively. "I mean, Consul." Vincent shook his head and Ezra ran a hand through his hair. "Vincent?" Vincent reached his hand out in greeting and Ezra took it.

"Welcome to the losing side." Vincent forced a laugh.

"Glad to be here."

"I have to ask, how the hell did you manage to keep a Reaper all this time?"

"I have my ways, sir." He winked

"Well, whatever you did I'm glad it worked out for us in the .end," Vincent said. "I'll have some people offload those crates. Help yourself to a drink, tell them it's on Blackwell."

"Will do, sir. Let me know when I can be of service." Ezra offered Vincent a salute and he waved it off. As if to cap off their conversation a green arcing light floated up into the sky. It bloomed into a neon star before dropping back down behind the housing projects of the Quarter.

A flare. He was actually going to meet Brusilov.

"Don't drink too much Ezra. I might need your help tomorrow."

CHAPTER SEVEN

"You are sure about this, sir?" Blackwell asked. Vincent was buckling down his armor to ensure it was loaded and trying to distract himself from the job at hand.

"Not even remotely," he said. "How would I know the first thing about negotiations with a former general and military governor?" Vincent knew he wasn't engendering a lot of confidence in the man who had become not only his recruiter, but also something of an aide. Blackwell handed Vincent his Riten, which he took and slid into its decorative holster on his hip.

"Tell him you're in charge and for him to fuck off back to the Moon," Fiona said from across the apartment. She was already ready, and Vincent noticed she made sure to wear the sword she had stolen off of the corpse of Field Marshal Molke. Brusilov would surely recognize it.

"Very diplomatic, Ma'am," snorted Blackwell. Blackwell handed Vincent the grey field cap that had come to round out his unofficial uniform. The Eagle and Star cap badge had been modified and the star snapped off. Vincent pulled his long brown hair back and tied it with a bit of string before placing the cap on his head.

"I'm sure he's only accepting this meeting because he already has a set of demands," Vincent said.

"Probably right," Fiona said. "Or the whole thing is a trap and we only have a few minutes to live."

"Or that." Vincent swallowed hard.

"The Quick Reaction Force is ready, sir," Blackwell said. "If anything happens, we will be out of the tunnel and into the Government Quarter as fast as possible." At the behest of Blackwell, Vincent let him assemble about twenty people to be ready in case anything happened. Vincent didn't really understand the point, because by the time the news traveled back to the Human Quarter that Brusilov started something Vincent was sure he would be long dead by the time they responded.

"Fiona, is the vanguard ready?" Vincent asked.

"Oh yeah. They couldn't wait." Fiona smirked.

"Good. Let's go."

Outside of the bar ten soldiers stood in the best uniforms they could find. None had any medals pinned to their chest. All of the volunteers to Vincent's new army had cast off all of their ribbons or awards rewarded to them for service to the Central Committee, and Vincent had done the same. Across their backs they all had black rifles slung, all of them EDF standard issue, smuggled in by Ezra. Under each field cap was a head of white-blonde hair on top of a pale skinned face. Blue, steely eyes stared straight ahead.

Admittedly, it had been Fiona's idea to make his vanguard an all Martian force. Once she brought the idea up Vincent couldn't agree fast enough. Once Fiona put the word out in the Quarter, they had dozens more volunteers than they had needed. Every Martian wanted a chance, no matter how small, to take a shot at Brusilov. Blackwell wasn't as excited as Vincent was, but he didn't give a good reason why. Blackwell was at least twenty or thirty years older than he was and stubborn in his ways. Vincent hadn't asked him if he had fought on Mars, but he was starting to suspect he had.

"Damn, I cannot wait to see the look on Brusilov's face." Fiona grinned.

"You are way too excited about this." Vincent sighed. "You know we aren't going there to kill him, right?"

"I know," she said, obviously disappointed. "A girl can dream you know?"

"Some people's girlfriends dream about vacations, others dream about kids, mine dreams about murdering old war criminals."

"You are one lucky guy."

"I am."

Fiona leaned in and kissed him on the cheek. "One for good luck."

Ezra's Reaper swooped in low before coming to a rest in the abandoned marketplace. Its side door was already open and Zinvor sat in its entrance. A mounted belt felt machine gun was in his hands. Through the passenger side window Vincent could see Nox still seated in the cockpit. Ezra climbed out of the cockpit and saluted Vincent.

"I see you got your vengeance vanguard ready." Ezra laughed.

"Caught onto that did you?" Vincent smiled.

"Was it supposed to be a secret?" Ezra asked.

"No," he said. "More like a giant middle finger."

"Well you certainly succeeded in that."

"And what's that?" Vincent asked pointing at Zinvor.

"I reinstalled Shanna's *defensive measures.*" Ezra seemed to make sure he put an emphasis on the last words. "Your bodyguard Zinvor seems to know his way around big guns."

"You have no idea." Vincent laughed. "Well, let's get this show on the road."

"Gladly, sir."

Vincent and Fiona climbed past Zinvor and into the two forward seats of the Reaper. Neither of them bothered to put on the four-point safety belt. The small legion of Martians squeezed in after them. Six of them managed to find seats while the remaining four sat down on the floor, their legs dangling off of the ship. They unslung their rifles and held them out, at the ready. Vincent really hoped they wouldn't have to be used.

"What are you still doing here?" Vincent asked Nox who was staring down at his co-pilot control panel.

"He does not have a gunner he can trust on this mission," Nox said.

"And you were the best option?" Fiona asked.

"Believe it or not," Ezra said, flipping multiple switches as computer screens began to glow in front of him. "Little Nox There is a damn good shot."

"I am normal sized for my race," Nox chimed in.

"Still as annoying as ever," Fiona groaned.

"That he is!" Ezra laughed, pulling a lever back. The engines to the Reaper began to wind up and they slowly started to lift off the ground.

"Shit. We are really doing this, aren't we?" Vincent said to no one in particular.

"Don't get cold feet now," Fiona said. "You have an entire population of rapists, murderers, deserters, and other various criminals that depend on."

"Damn, that has to be the least motivational thing I've ever heard," Vincent said.

"And it was only partially a joke." Fiona smirked at him. She leaned in and kissed him again. Her lips were cracked and chapped, but he didn't care. "If anyone can pull this off, it would be you."

"And if I don't?" he asked.

"Oh, that's too easy," she said, grabbing a rifle from the inside of the troop compartment. She pulled the rifle's bolt back and let it slam forward. "We kill every last one of those mother fuckers."

The Reaper slowly rose upwards and Ezra guided it expertly through the jungle of elevated Rhai-built skyscrapers and walkways. He brought the ship only inches away from the featureless sides of a metal skyscraper. Vincent watched as the distorted reflection of the ship flew alongside them.

Below them the Government Quarter was empty. Vincent had warned Arai ahead of time about the meeting with Brusilov. She had ordered the Quarter evacuated during the time it was to take place. That is evacuated except what Vincent had to assume was hundreds if not thousands of Gumi, hidden through the cavernous buildings of the Quarter waiting to strike if the meeting went sideways.

Vincent knew Arai wanted to swarm his office with the Gumi and snatch Brusilov, consequences be damned. He had somehow managed to talk her out of it. He convinced her that a bloodless and peaceful outcome was a possibility and it would look much better to the human population.

Explaining to a Mawr that a bloodless *anything* was a good option was one of the harder things he'd ever had to do. Thankfully, Pharos was there to help him. Though, admittedly now that he was looking down at the Quarter, with the Reaper swooping in for a landing, and he was going to actually have to go into his office and talk to Brusilov, Arai's wanton violence sounded much easier.

Just as Vincent had feared and planned for, Brusilov had completely ignored the manpower limit he had placed on the meeting. As the Reaper slowly floated down to the ground below Vincent spotted a platoon sized group of soldiers, armed with rifles. They stood ramrod straight in a parade perfect formation in front of the door to the Consul's Office.

"Good thing I talked you into ignoring your own rules," Fiona said.

"Sorry for trying to honor an agreement. It won't happen again." He forced a smile.

"Honor will get your dumb ass killed." She was right. Fiona and Arai had told him the meeting was nothing but a farce. There were two possible reasons why Brusilov was agreeing to the meeting. One: it was an ambush, or two: He was using it to measure what real strength Vincent's new piecemeal army had so he could kill them all at a different time. Or, as Fiona had put it "It's nothing but a dick measuring contest." He had only agreed to the expanded group of Martian soldiers after the so-called *Agents* of Pharos' Cohort had reported Black Coats trickling into the Government Quarter overnight.

Once again, everyone other than him had been proven right. Vincent was starting to think Fiona was right and he was leading them to their own deaths.

The Reaper landed so gently he hardly noticed. Before Vincent could get up the ten members of his newly formed bodyguard detail rushed out of the troop compartment and made a small formation of their own. They brought their rifles to their shoulder in a crisp *shoulder arms* position. A skinny blonde woman stepped out in front of the formation; a grey field cap sat on top of hair so short it was little more than a white fuzz. On her collars was the rank of a first sergeant.

"Detachment!" she ordered. "Present, Arms!" altogether the soldier's rifles were thrust out in front of them vertically. They turned their heads to face Vincent who had just barely stepped off of the ship. Vincent knew from his EDF training they were all saluting him in unison. He slowly raised his right hand to return their salute. "Presenting, Consul-Cohort Leader, Solaris!" the first sergeant barked.

On the other side of the now suddenly vast-feeling Government Square an older gentleman with the silver eagles of a solonel on his collar stepped out in front of the formation of Black Coats. A long silver sword hung from his belt, which he slowly unsheathed and brought up to eye level.

"Presenting, Field Marshal Brusilov!" At his booming command, the formation of Black Coats snapped to attention and saluted. Vincent had to admit their formation's movements were much sharper than his.

Slowly, a man who looked like he was easily in his seventies stepped to the front of the formation. He was short, almost an entire head shorter than Vincent, and had small circular glasses perched at the end of a crooked nose. Wrinkles were deep set into his weather-beaten face. His chest was heavy with medals and ribbons, though he wore no ceremonial side arm. On his collar were the four stars of a field marshal.

I see he decided to promote himself, Vincent thought. Why not just declare himself Military Governor of Elysian why he was at it?

"Fucking prick," Fiona spat from alongside him.

"Remember, we aren't here to kill him," Vincent said.

"Maybe you aren't," she said. "He even looks at you wrong I'm going to carve a trench through his skull."

"Good to see you're an optimist about the meeting." Vincent sighed. He saw Brusilov and the colonel leading his formation slowly make their way towards the Consul's office before disappearing behind its doors. Vincent began to walk that way when Fiona start to follow.

"No," Vincent said. Fiona raised an eyebrow at him.

"No?" she asked.

"I want you out here just in case something goes down," he said.

"Ugh, fine," she said. Though that was partially true he was mostly worried that once she got within close quarters with Brusilov she would snap and shoot him on the spot.

"Excuse me?" Vincent asked the first sergeant leading his entourage. "Could you come with me?"

"Me?" She looked around, confused.

"I don't want to go alone and if Fiona is in the same room, she will scalp him. You seem like my best bet."

"If I'm your best bet then we are in dark times, sir," she said, a slight smile on her face.

Vincent and the first sergeant marched towards the Consul doors. Though the Black Coats stood unmoving in their formation, Vincent could feel the soldiers' eyes burning into him as he walked past. He tried to ignore them but couldn't help but notice the first sergeant staring daggers right back at them. Vincent stopped before going into the doors.

"Sorry, what's your name?" he asked.

"First Sergeant Olympus, sir. Formally of the 20th Regiment of Light Scouts."

"Olympus, I guess I should have figured." He fought back a smile. Vincent remembered when Fiona explained to him that the EDF assigned a last name to Martian conscripts based on the city from where they came from. Almost every Martian soldier he had ever met had the same last name.

"Erin Olympus, sir," she clarified.

"Well, it's good to meet you—officially, anyway. I hope we both get out of this alive." He smiled.

"If we don't, I'll make sure I take as many of them with me as I can, sir," she said, her face stern.

"Good." He pushed open the door.

Brusilov had seated himself behind Vincent's desk and was scrolling through the dull light of his display screen. He knew he should have been perturbed or annoyed by this, but he also knew that Arai never sent anything important to him through the device. Instead it was just law enforcement updates and Gathering meeting dates. Both of which were public information.

The Mawr were not the most technologically advanced race in the universe, and if Vincent were to guess if they hadn't run into the Rhai and the Anarchs they would be little more than warring cave creatures on some rock somewhere. Because of this they were distrustful of using technology to send anything that could be considered secret, or even anything that pertained to Clan business. Arai sent runners to tell him information verbally or deliver notes which would then be destroyed by the runner once Vincent was done reading them.

"Solaris," Brusilov said. His voice deep and gravely. It sounded as if he had smoked for longer than Vincent had been alive. "So this is what the puppet of the toads does all day. Mindless paperwork." He set the display aside. "When he isn't shooting my men on the street."

"That was a misunderstanding," Vincent said, sitting down in the chair opposite of his desk.

"I can see that. If you wanted war you wouldn't be meeting with me."

"And if you wanted war you would have killed me already."

"That is correct," Brusilov said. He reached into a coat pocket, retrieving a small tin case and finding a hand rolled cigarette. "There is no need for war, as we both want different things."

"What do you want?" Vincent asked. He was honestly curious.

"To serve my Chairman, as all good humans should. I'm sure you heard the news."

"Yes."

"And I am going to assume you and your..." He trailed off a bit. "*Army.*" He used the words distastefully. "Have no intentions of heeding the Chairman's call to service."

"That is correct. We intend to stay here, as subjects of the Clan," Vincent said. He watched anger flash across Brusilov's face, but only for a second. Only a short time ago such traitorous statements would have seen Vincent shot on the spot. "I'm sure you know we would be executed if we returned anyway." A smile crept across the old man's face.

"Yes, I do." Smoke rolled out of Brusilov's nose. He probably relished in the thought of it. "This dirt ball of an uncivilized planet is the perfect place for your kind, if you are allowed to live anyway." At this, Erin balled her fists, clearly at her edge of putting up with the old man. Vincent turned back and gave her a look. "The Reds were never able to manage their tempers. Such primitive things." Brusilov smirked, obviously happy he finally got a reaction out of one of them. "And I hear you're fucking one of them." His voice was one of disgust. Brusilov knew he had tempers rising and he was going in for the kill. "I knew you were a traitor, but a race traitor as well?" Vincent pounded his fist on the desk, cutting him off. The colonel standing next to Brusilov jumped.

"You wanted to meet for talks. So talk, *Colonel General.*" Vincent growled, he knew addressing him by his real rank, rather than the one he had awarded himself, would irk him.

"Careful boy." Brusilov's eyes narrowed. "These talks only go on as long as I wish them too. You were a fool to only bring ten Reds to protect you."

"The Cohort of Mawr Warriors I have in waiting would be more than enough to handle most problems I would suspect," Vincent retorted. He was bluffing He wasn't sure how much Brusilov knew about the inner workings of the Clan and knew that in no way were any Mawr under Vincent's command and the only thing he had in waiting was a bunch of Rhai cops.

The bluff worked and Brusilov's face contorted into a frown.

"I underestimated you boy." He frowned. "That's good, because an idiot wouldn't be able to get me what I want."

"And why would I get anything for you?"

"Because if I get what I want, my soldiers and I will be off this planet." He tapped the end of his cigarette, the ash landed on Vincent's desk. He did so purposefully as there was an ashtray only a few inches away.

"Oh?" Vincent raised an eyebrow.

"As you know, the Toads took all military spacecraft when they allowed us to come here. I was incapacitated from my wounds at the time, or I would have never allowed such a shameful thing to occur, but here we are."

"The Clan needs them for the fight against the Anarchs," Vincent said. "Your backstabbing cost them a lot of their ships on Grawluck." The general ignored Vincent's jab.

"You can imagine how it would look if I showed up with my Soldiers to the Committee with all of my ships taken by the enemy." Brusilov crossed his arms. "I need at least an Air Wing's worth of ships back. If I squeeze them in tight and use the rest of the civilian fleet." The civilian fleet was what they called the non-military ships the Clan allowed them to keep for importing and exporting goods. In reality the civilian fleet was just converted to a Black Coat smuggling ring. "If you get me that, I can transport all of my men to Lunar City."

"You know you're asking a lot," Vincent said. "And I can't promise you anything."

"One hundred ships are hardly a large sacrifice for such a glorious fighting force as this *Clan*, is it?" His voice was dripping with sarcasm. "After all, they seem to have given you one." Vincent didn't want to make himself seem less influential by pointing out Ezra and his ship had just shown up the night before. "Without them I can't show my face to the Committee without being dishonored."

"It'll take me some time to bring this to the Warlord. Until then we need to come to some kind of ceasefire. I don't want the Quarter turning into a warzone," Vincent said.

"That seems agreeable." He tapped the end of his cigarette on the desk again. "As the current lines stand."

"Current lines?" Vincent asked, unsure of what he meant. Brusilov rolled his eyes.

"You'll have to excuse me; I was mistaken in thinking I was talking to an equal." He rolled his eyes. "By current lines I was speaking of the area your rabble controls." Vincent fought back laughter at Brusilov describing the marketplace and a rundown bar like they were strategic military positions.

"We also control the main tunnel out of the Quarter." Vincent smirked. "So, you're saying you won't try to leave?"

"You're dumber than I thought boy." Brusilov stubbed his cigarette out on the desk, leaving a small black burn mark. "You really think that is the only way out of the Quarter?" Brusilov stood up. "Also, no more weapons shipments."

"You're kidding," Vincent said. "You are armed to the teeth and have two times as many people than I do."

"Be that as it may I don't like the idea of you and your Toad masters gearing up to wipe us out." Brusilov stood up, pushing the chair back and nodded to his colonel, indicating that he was clearly done with the meeting. The colonel side stepped Erin and opened the office door for the general.

"My forces will keep rearming until they're done. I'm not going to debate that." Vincent rose to his feet. "However, I agree to the rest of your terms."

"Hmm." Brusilov turned to the colonel. "The boy thinks he has some balls, eh?" The colonel eyed Vincent with disgust.

"Nothing but a worthless race traitor, Field Marshal," he said.

"Go fuck yourself, you uptight prick," Erin snarled at the colonel.

"How dare you!" the colonel bellowed.

"Silence your mongrel boy," Brusilov said, by the tone of his voice Vincent was sure he meant it to be a command.

"I will when you tell your bootlicking colonel to shut the fuck up." Vincent shot to his feet. "If he disrespects the Warlord or my soldiers again and I'll put a bullet between his eyes."

Brusilov was obviously taken aback by being yelled at by someone who he considered so much lower than himself.

"The Warlord wanted to send her Warriors into the Quarter to slaughter your little army to a man. I told her to give you a chance. You are making me regret that, General."

"Colonel, please step outside." Brusilov nodded at him, the colonel quickly obeyed.

"Staff Sergeant Olympus, please join him," Vincent said over his shoulder. She squinted at him, clearly irritated, and walked out.

"Listen here you little shit," Brusilov spat, getting closer to Vincent as he did. He was a full head shorter than him and was forced to look up to scold him. His teeth were stained yellow and his breath stank of stale cigarettes and whiskey. "The only reason why I haven't killed you is I need those ships to get off of this damned rock. You can have your fake office with its fake title. It doesn't matter to me. The Chairman's glorious fleet will be here one day to wipe you traitors and your disgusting Toads from existence."

"I was there last time his *glorious fleet* tried to do that. It didn't go so well." Vincent poked the old man in the chest, ruffling his rows of campaign ribbons.

"When this is over, I swear I will hang you personally," he growled and made for the door.

"Someone told me that one before." Vincent shrugged. "I had a Martian shoot them in the head."

Brusilov's eyes flashed with pure hatred and he slammed the door behind him.

CHAPTER EIGHT

Vincent collapsed into his chair as soon as Brusilov left the room. His heart was slamming in his chest and watching the man leave without anyone getting shot was one of the biggest feelings of relief he had ever felt. He stood toe to toe with the Butcher of Mars and felt like he had won.

The door opened and in walked Fiona and Zinvor.

"Is everything okay? That old bastard looks pissed," Fiona asked.

"Yeah." Vincent smiled. "At least I think so. He threatened to kill me a few times but agreed to a ceasefire."

"I thought negotiations were supposed to be more cordial." Fiona smirked and sat on the desk next to him.

"Me too. He knows a lot about me somehow. It was off putting." Vincent had no doubt at least one of the people who had went to Blackwell to enlist in the Human Cohort was a mole. It was inevitable.

"Like what?" she asked.

"That we are dating. Which, by the way he *does not* approve of." He laughed.

She fake pouted. "Aw, darn I guess we have to break-up."

"Yeah. And I was really starting to like you too." He sighed and she leaned in and kissed him on the lips.

"I do not mean to interrupt, but Arai awaits your report," Zinvor said, snapping him out of his moment of relaxation.

"Yeah you're probably right. I guess I'll meet up with you and your squad of *subhuman Reds* when I'm done," Vincent joked. He knew he was probably the only one who could say something like that, even jokingly, around Fiona without getting attacked.

"Erin told me about what he said," she said. "He's glad I wasn't here. Good call on that."

"I know you better than you think." He smiled and walked out of the office.

Ezra was leaning against the side of *Shanna* and waved when he came close.

"Ready to go back, sir?" he asked.

"I have to go meet the Warlord, I'll meet up with you back at the Quarter," Vincent said and thought of something. "Ezra, how did you manage to keep you ship when every other military ship was confiscated by the Clan?" Ezra smiled a wry smile and stuffed his hands into the pockets of his flight suit.

"Forgive me sir, but I don't think the Mawr's knowledge of our weapons is very in depth. I took off Shanna's forward cannon and passenger's weapons and told them it was a supply ship. They didn't even question it." He looked a little guilty for admitting the lie. "Once I started working for Nox they didn't look into it too much more. He has a fair amount of pull with the Customs and Trade Cohort."

"Yeah, that sounds about right for Nox." Vincent sighed. "Well, I'm glad you managed to keep it."

"Me too, sir."

Vincent had to wave away Ezra's salute once again as he began to walk up the stairs to the Gathering auditorium. He assumed after decades of service in the EDF Ezra found it next to impossible to break his old professional habits. It also explained his flawlessly shined boots and sharp creases in his flight suit.

The Gathering auditorium was entirely empty with the exception of Arai and Pharos. They were busy, once again, pouring over piles of scrolls and displays.

"I see it went well," Arai said without looking up.

"Why do you say that?" he asked.

"You're still alive. I assumed if you failed, you would have been killed," she said. If that were her gauge of success, then Vincent could consider himself a downright optimist.

"It could have went better, but we could have a way out of this situation."

"He was willing to negotiate?" Pharos asked. "Interesting, I didn't see him as the type."

"Only as a means to an end," Vincent said. "He wants to heed the new Chairman's call and go back to Lunar City and take his group of assholes with him."

"Good riddance," Arai growled.

"That isn't all," Vincent said. "He says he can't face the Committee without at least some of the ships the Clan took from the EDF."

"He can't look like he aided the enemy," Pharos said.

"Right. They would probably shoot him on the spot," Vincent said. "He said he wants about an Air Wing's worth."

"We cannot sacrifice a single ship." Arai shook her head. "We have a shortage already! At this rate we will be forced to arm transport ships." Vincent knew the fight against the Anarchs was a tough one, but he had no idea of the kind of losses the Cohorts were taking. "I cannot abide by these demands."

"We barely have that many ships operational for planetary defense right now," Pharos said.

"What can we offer him instead?" Vincent asked.

"Nothing," Arai grunted. "I have trusted his people one time too many and it cost me tens of thousands of Warriors on Grawluck."

"Shit," Vincent said. "I understand why you'd feel that way Arai. But forcing him into a fight is going to cost even more Warriors."

"He speaks the truth, Warlord," Pharos said. "Brusilov's men would be more than able to force us to besiege our own city. This is an option we simply cannot risk." Arai gave Pharos a look annoyance.

"Then give me a better idea, Solaris," Arai snapped at him. It wasn't often that Arai showed emotion, but Vincent had seen it once or twice before. Something he had never seen was a Cohort Leader tell the Warlord *no*.

"We could offer to pack them into some transport ships and drop them off," Vincent said. "Let them keep the ones they came with. It can't be that many. Besides, maybe the Committee will see it as a good faith gesture and leave us alone."

"I do not like this idea," Arai grumbled.

"There is no good idea in this situation, Warlord," Pharos said. "But if it gets the Committee Loyalists off of our planet and does not turn into a civil war, we may have to consider it." It was becoming more and more obvious to Vincent that Pharos was more than just the Clan's spy master. He was something more like Arai's advisor and voice of reason. If any of the other Cohort Leaders had spoken to her so bluntly it would have ended at the barrel of a Riten.

"I agree with Pharos. All of our options here suck, but we have to pick the one that doesn't end in a bloodbath." The sound that came out of Arai's mouth was more like a guttural, feral roar. She slammed both of her fists down on the table in rage. A crack formed down the length of the table as it struggled to withstand her wrath.

"Fine!" she bellowed. "But this is it Solaris." She rose, her fists clenched. "If this fails, we do things *my way.*" Vincent knew what that meant. The Quarter would be flattened. Thousands of innocent humans would die. Any sort of bond that had managed to be made between the two races would be ruined. He had no doubt if Clan Warriors stormed into the Quarter nearly everyone would side with the Black Coats, if only for survival. Vincent would hardly blame them.

"Fine," he said.

"I will work on...alternative methods," Pharos said.

"Should I ask?" Vincent asked.

"Not yet." Pharos said. "If I find something that is of interest, I will be sure to inform you, Consul." Pharos picked up several displays and began walking towards the door.

"You are to deliver a message for me, Solaris. He has three days to inform us if he agrees to our terms. Past that time I will assume he means to wage war against us." Vincent bowed deeply and placed his hand over his heart, the Mawr version of a salute.

"Yes, Warlord."

"Do not fail me Solaris. You are dismissed."

CHAPTER NINE

Vincent set slammed his drink down on the table. Flakes of cheap pressed wood chipped and gave way underneath it.

"Why haven't we heard anything back yet?" He sighed. Fiona blew out a dark cloud of smoke from beside him.

"It hasn't even been a day," she reasoned. "The runner probably hasn't even made it to Brusilov yet."

Minutes after Vincent had made it back to the Quarter, he had Blackwell dispatch his best runner to hand deliver Arai's offer to Brusilov. The poor young runner would have to go through layers and layers of Black Coat security, deep into the Quarter. Deeper than Vincent had ever dared to go.

Blackwell had picked eighteen-year-old Private Miles, who had enthusiastically volunteered for the duty. The teen had been sentenced to two years of EDF service for shoplifting and trying and failing to run from the local Ethics Police.

"Why did Blackwell pick a guy who was arrested for getting *caught* for running from the cops to have to run for his life again?" Fiona asked.

"I don't know." Vincent took another drink. "I thought it was his version of a joke."

"He should have picked the medic with one leg," she joked. Vincent would have laughed, but Blackwell had indeed enlisted a young medic from Titan that had lost her right leg at the knee. Victim of a gunshot that had gone septic due to lack of medical care. Medical care that was withheld in the field due to her being a sentenced soldier. As it stood, she was the only medic that his new army had managed to sign up.

"They'd make a good couple," Vincent deadpanned.

"With their powers combined they create one entire person." Fiona smirked cruelly. Vincent laughed nervously. Fiona always had a mean sense of humor, though now it was directed at him since Nox had left the group...

"How's the drills coming with the new soldiers?" Vincent asked. Since he had been running around at Arai's orders and sitting through meetings with Pharos, Fiona had become his unofficial representative of the Consul's Office in the Quarter. Ever since Arai had greenlit his new army, the Consul's Office had turned into something like an accidental Mini-Cohort of Defense.

This had never been Vincent's intention. Neither of them had any experience commanding, let alone dealing with the logistics and organizational stress that came with outfitting a fledgling army. It had been what Fiona had best described as a "Cluster fuck." To make things easier, Blackwell had found a few former Quartermaster soldiers to tend to their fast-growing stockpile of weapons and ammo, both from black market means via Nox and legitimate supplies from the Clan.

A problem arose when it was discovered that none of the quartermasters that Blackwell found happened to be fit for the task. The young soldiers were used to having commanders and sergeants of their own to tell them what to do, of which Vincent's army had none. The situation quickly turned into a free for all. No one had any idea of how many weapons were now floating around the Quarter and how many had actually been put into the intended hands.

Vincent decided that wasn't something that Arai needed to know about. He had sent Blackwell on a mission to find some level of field grade officer. A major, a colonel; literally anyone who would willingly take command away from him. So far, he had turned up empty handed. He had momentarily thought of appointing Ezra, but when he broached the manner with him Ezra was quick to point out pilots don't know the first thing about field command.

"About as good as you would expect," Fiona said, nonplussed.

"So, bad?" he asked.

"Terrible." She laughed. "Half of them are drunk, the other half are hoping the Black Coats pop something off so they can kill them."

"Sounds like the EDF in a nutshell," Vincent said. "Bored and wanting to kill something."

"I guess you're right," she said. The bartender came over to refill Fiona's drink. Vincent noticed she was careful to avoid eye contact. She was about to refill Vincent's drink when he waved her off, suddenly noticing how tired he was from the events of the day.

"I'm going to go crash." He yawned. "All this *having to actually work* really took it out of me."

"Sweet dreams, wuss." She kissed him on the cheek before returning to her drink. "I'll be in my new office."

*   *   *

The rip of automatic gunfire jolted Vincent awake. He quickly scanned the dark room and saw Fiona snoring away, sprawled across the bedroll next to him. Tracers arced across the sky, lighting up the small square window of his apartment. Another long burst sounded, though this one was further away.

He quickly rummaged through a pile of laundry and pulled on a pair of dirty grey uniform pants. He nudged Fiona who was sleeping like the dead, deep in her booze aided sleep. He grabbed his Riten holster and tossed it around his shoulders before quickly heading out of the apartment door.

Zinvor greeted him on the other side, as always. At the foot of the stairs was two Martian soldiers that Vincent recognized from his meeting with Brusilov.

"What's going on?" he asked. The soldier turned and saluted.

"No idea, sir," the soldier said. Vincent remembered the young Martian's name was Tharsis, after the city he was from, but everyone called him Junior. "Sounds like it's coming from across The Pit."

The Pit as it was known was once a Rhai construction site, but since the humans moved in it had turned into a large open-air waste dump. Garbage, sewage, and all other refuse from the citizens of the Quarter was dragged there by hand and tossed. Since the split between the Consul's office and the Black Coats it had turned an unofficial border between the two sides.

"Damnit. Where's Blackwell?" he asked.

"He set up some kind of Operations Center in the Wine Cellar of the bar," Junior said. Of course he would have. He remembered when Blackwell had mentioned it was the only building they controlled in the Quarter that might be able to withstand a direct hit by one of the Black Coat's shoulder fired rockets. Of which they had many.

As the group walked towards the Bar several more gunshots shattered the silence of the night. The marketplace, normally busy even in the middle of the night, was completely abandoned. Even the most desperate street merchant was chased away by the possibility of catching a stray bullet.

Shadows flitted by in the darkness. Grey uniformed soldiers, half illuminated by the dancing light of the dull streetlamps, hustled by in small groups. The soldiers were lugging boxes and crates between them, laden heavy with weapons, ammo, or supplies. He couldn't be sure, but it looked like the soldiers were preparing for to defend the area. Then it hit him:

The machine gun fire. The sporadic rifle shots all around the Quarter. The Black Coats were probing their defenses in preparation for an attack.

Knowing Brusilov's history it would hardly surprise Vincent if he had strung him along long enough to get his personal army into position to overrun the Quarter. It had been over a day and he hadn't heard anything back from the runner. The chances that he would return alive were getting lower and lower as the hours ticked by and the shooting grew more intense.

The Eagle and Bar was a flurry of activity. The group pushed its way inside and by dozens of soldiers holding letters and paying close attention to Blackwell. The staff sergeant looked aged beyond his years. He was sitting behind the bar, a massive olive-green radio set was mounted on the wall next to him.

"You've got your orders! Now get out of here!" Blackwell screamed at them. The soldiers rushed past Vincent without noticing he was standing there. What he was watching was a product of his army's newest problem. An almost total lack of any communications systems.

According to a book titled *Standard Earth Defense Forces Manual of Ground Warfare,* they were missing one of the most important aspects of a fighting force. He had been reading the book, written by a field marshal whose name he could never remember, for the last few weeks. It turned out most of the book was a detailed explanation of things his new army just couldn't do or things they didn't have.

Instead, Blackwell had issued out the few precious radios they had to select units, the ones who could prove they actually knew how to use them and kept one for command and control. For the units left out in the cold without any link to anyone else, he had put together a small squad of runners that would physically hand carry paper orders to them. It was an imperfect system. Runners could get shot, lost, blown up, or refuse to run through gunfire. But it was at least a system.

"Sir, I'm sorry this business seems to have awakened you," he said upon seeing Vincent.

"Gunshots tend to do that. What's going on?" Vincent asked. Blackwell was making various marks on a hand drawn map of the Quarter.

"Black Coats are taking pot shots at the positions we've established near The Pit. I'm afraid they might be feeling us out for a full-on attack."

"And if they do?" he asked.

"Honestly, sir," Blackwell said, looking up from his map. "We'd get our heads kicked in pretty damned fast. Unless you can get your Warrior friends to come help us."

"I wouldn't count on that. They've got their hands full with other things." Like trying to stop the Anarchs from rolling over the entire universe without a second thought. "We handle this on our own. How many men do we have now?"

"About one hundred," Blackwell said, obviously full of pride of his small army.

"And them?"

"Err," Blackwell stumbled. "Somewhere north of two-thousand, sir."

"These are odds that I like," Zinvor grunted. Blackwell gave Zinvor an incredulous look. The group jumped as the bar doors slammed open and Ezra entered.

"Am I missing the fun?" he asked.

"Not quite," Vincent said. They're just feeling out our positions."

"I can let them know that's a bad idea," Ezra said.

"What are you—" Blackwell began, but Vincent cut him off.

"Do it," he said, crossing his arms. "Let us know how it goes."

"Yes, sir." He rendered a crisp salute and hurried out of the door.

"You didn't even ask what his plan was." Blackwell sighed.

"He's a colonel, I assume he knows what he is doing."

"Sir, if he sends a bunch of rockets across The Pit..."

"I hope he does," Vincent spat. "They're used to picking on people who don't defend themselves. They're still hoping we roll over and throw our weapons down. Throw ourselves at the benevolent mercy of their Chairman."

"I have no intention of doing that, sir," Blackwell said, determination in his voice.

"Good."

An explosion turned the dark of the night into a hazy dawn through the small windows of the bar. Glasses clinked together and dust shimmered down from the ceiling.

"Sounds like the Colonel is going to work, sir," Blackwell said, a smiling creeping up the side of his face.

"Great Traitor, this is *Shanna-one*," the radio crackled on the bar table.

"I assume you guys gave me that radio name?" Vincent raised an eyebrow. Blackwell fought back a laugh and motioned towards the radio. Vincent reached over and grabbed the handset.

"This is Great Traitor." He sighed.

"Roger. I confirm strikes on fourteen enemy positions. Unknown enemy casualties." Ezra's voice was garbled by static.

"Thank you. Feel free to do what you want *Shanna-one*," Vincent said.

"Your welcome, sir. I'll stay up here for a bit," he returned. Vincent heard the distinct *thump thump thump* of his Reaper's nose-mounted autocannon churning through rounds in the background.

The night past slowly. Vincent dozed uneasily, his head resting on a dirty bar table. He was jolted awake every few moments by another explosion. The shaking of the bar convinced him that eventually the whole structure was going to come down on his head.

The shooting faded away as the sun came up, basking the area in a sickly yellow hue. Vincent stood up from his table and stretched.

"So, we survived another night?" came the voice of Fiona, who he hadn't noticed came into the bar.

"Seems that way." He yawned. "How the hell did you sleep through all of that?"

"You'd be surprised what you can sleep through after half a jug of Titanian Vodka." She sat down at the table. "Hey Blackwell, can I get something to eat? I'm hungover as hell." Blackwell, who was still at his station behind the bar, listening intently to the radio perked up at the sound of his name.

"Uh, Ma'am I'm a little busy."

"You sent that little tart of a new Bartender away and turned this place into a commander center. Go get her or make me some damned food."

"Ma'am the area is still unsafe for civilians—"

"It's going to be unsafe for you unless you feed me," Fiona moaned.

Blackwell looked at Vincent, concern obvious in his eyes.

"Don't look at me for support, I live with her." He smiled. Vincent's stomach growled loudly at him and he sank back down into his seat. "And...as long as you're already making her something..."

"Of course, sir."

Slowly soldiers began to trickle into the bar. Many of the younger soldiers were wild with panic, their eyes red with exhaustion. To Vincent's surprise a young lieutenant marched up to his table and set down a hand-written note. Judging from it's hard to read scribble, it was written in haste.

"What is this?" Vincent asked.

"The butcher's bill sir," the lieutenant said. She was maybe a head shorter than Vincent with the olive skin of a Titanian. Her black hair was matted down with dirt and sweat.

"The what?" He raised an eyebrow.

"The night's casualties sir." She looked at him impatiently.

"Oh." He sat forward in his seat. *"Oh. "*How had that slipped his mind? There was hours of shooting, of course there would be casualties. How stupid could he be?

"In my opinion we got off light, sir. Only a dozen wounded, most of them lightly."

"None killed?" he asked, hopefully.

"No, sir," she said. He sighed, relieved. "Sir, if I may say. For a lot of these guys it was their first time in contact. Maybe you should say something to them?"

"Me?" he said. He noticed several dozen sets of eyes turning to look at him.

"You are their commander, remember?" Fiona said.

"What would you want to hear from your commander after something like that?" he asked. The lieutenant shrugged her shoulders, unsure. Fiona finished her drink and set her glass down.

"I have an idea," she said. "Drinks are on the Consul!" she shouted. The soldiers cheered, throwing their field caps into the air.

CHAPTER TEN

Vincent sat awake, sorting through various screens of his data display. He was exhausted and he could feel his eyes burning. He was going on his second night without sleep and no matter how much work he did, there seemed to be an endless amount remaining. To feed the growing number of people in the Eagle and Bar he had ordered Blackwell to distribute the Quarter's food stocks to the population at a daily ration. To deal with the growing number of wounded he ordered everyone to turn in their sheets and blankets to use as bandages.

He was happy for the work. The running of the Quarter, for how much longer it would last he was unsure, was a welcome distraction. The deadline of Arai's ultimatum to Brusilov was in the morning. If the fighting in the pit was any indication, the Black Coats did not intend on leaving Elysian peacefully.

Fiona was asleep next to him. She always had the ability to sleep through anything regardless of how stressed out everyone else around her was. Zinvor was seated across from them sitting on the floor. Even his eyes were closed. Vincent could count on one hand all the times he had seen the Tsarra sleep. It seemed the Mawr could operate for days at a time during times of strain without any sleep, food, or water. During the campaign on Grawluck they never even bothered setting up shelter, simply laying down in the mud instead.

He was proud his soldiers had taken the test given to them by the Black Coats and walked away alive. Blackwell was certain that the encounter would drive more people into their ranks. His theory was as the new army proved its mettle other soldiers, on the fence about standing up to Brusilov, would come forward. He wasn't sure how true Blackwell's theory was, but he was depending on it to make up for their manpower shortage.

The dull light of dusk began to show through the apartment's broken window. He sat his display down and stood up to stretch. Zinvor's eyes snapped open and he stood up. Vincent was momentarily taken aback.

"You're awake?" he asked.

"Excuse my indulgence, I rested far longer than I intended," Zinvor responded.

"You do know you're allowed to sleep right?" he asked. "I'm not going to tell Arai on you."

"A true Warrior only rests when his spirit exits the battlefield," Zinvor said.

"I'm not entirely sure what that means." Vincent sighed. The two walked through the apartment door and down the rickety metal stairs. The dusk air was brisk, and the wind carried with it enough dust to make Vincent's eyes water. At the bottom of the stairs was Huang, his rifle lazily slung over his shoulder and a cigarette glowing in his mouth.

"Good morning, sir," he said, still drunk with sleep.

"Where's Smith?" Vincent asked.

"Sleeping. It is my shift. Us and the Martian bodyguards you've acquired all take turns." He flicked an ash off the end of his cigarette. The Martian bodyguards, he was talking about the squad of Martians Fiona had assembled to meet Brusilov. She had said they were loyal to him because they all believed the rumor going around that he had purposely aided the Anarchs in destroying Earth.

"Were you involved in the fighting last night?" he asked.

"Yes, sir. Though, to be honest we couldn't see much of anything." Huang fiddled with his helmet nervously. "I was mostly just shooting at shapes in the dark."

"Well, either way I'm glad you're alright." Vincent smiled.

"Do you think they will attack again?" Huang asked nervously.

"I wouldn't doubt it," Vincent said. "For better or worse, we are going to find out today."

"Shit." Huang sighed.

"Let's hope Brusilov is smart enough to avoid a bloodbath," Vincent said. The area around the bar had been heavily reinforced. He wasn't sure how long the soldiers had been working but the entire building had been surrounded in sandbags, reaching up to the roof. Where they had run out of sandbags large broken off pieces of concrete were dragged into place. The marketplace, surprisingly, had several stalls being opened for business. In between the busy salespeople, soldiers sat behind low sandbag and debris bunkers.

On the far side of the marketplace was Ezra's *Shanna*. Its form shrouded in camouflage tarps in tones of brown and tan. A bored looking soldier stood watch over it, strolling around in a small circle.

Vincent pushed the Bar door open to find that along with being hastily converted into a command post, it has also been transformed into a barracks. Soldiers were fast asleep on the floor wherever they could fit.

"What the hell?" Vincent breathed to himself.

"Sorry sir, but it's the only solid structure we control. Blackwell thought it would be a good idea to sleep as many people in here as we could," Huang said.

"Makes sense I guess," he said. "Where's everyone else?"

"Mostly down through A Block," he said. The rows of human-built houses, most of them could be were hardly more than shacks, were known as A Block, B Block, and C Block. They were named after the tiers of a prison, only partially in jest. As the Black Coats had taken the majority of the rows of Mawr-constructed buildings, leaving the sentenced soldiers to fend for themselves in the *Tiers*, earning the area it's nickname.

"Those buildings won't take a hit at all," Vincent said, maybe a little too harshly. He noticed Huang flinched. Vincent cursed himself. Huang probably lived in the Tiers.

"We know sir, but it's closer to the Pit. They are the first to react if the Black Coats try anything," Huang explained. "The two groups rotate every few nights to make sure no one has to stay down there for long. We have done what we could to dig in and reinforce them." Vincent nodded. He was a little ashamed that a private had to explain to him how his army was running.

Blackwell was asleep in the back storeroom surrounded by kegs of beer and crates of liquor. Judging by the few empty bottles around him he had been pilfering the bars' stores. Vincent nudged him with a foot and the older man woke with a start.

"Morning, sir." He moaned, groggily. The old man rubbed his eyes, trying to focus.

"Any word from Brusilov yet?" he asked.

"No, sir. Not a thing," Blackwell said. He struggled to his feet, pulling himself up by a crate of bottles. It was the first time Vincent saw the tapestry of scars that wound their way from Blackwell's feet, which were missing several toes per foot, and up his thighs where the rest were covered by a pair of blue boxer shorts.

He obviously saw Vincent starring and cleared his throat, snapping him out of it. "An Anarch shell, sir," he said, motioning down to his legs. "More than one I suspect. I blacked out after the first one hit my tank. None of my boys made it out."

"Sorry...I didn't mean to stare," Vincent said, embarrassed.

"It's only natural when someone's legs looked up like ten pounds of ground beef." Blackwell coughed out a laugh. He fumbled with a pair of grey pants, his missing arm making the process a chore. "Anything else I can help you with sir?"

"I can't sleep." Vincent sighed. "I guess I should go see the guys out at the front, huh? That's something a commander would do, right?"

"Yes, sir it is." Blackwell cracked a smile. "I'll give you a tour."

"Thank you."

Once Blackwell was dressed, they slowly made their way through the maze of sleeping soldiers and out of the bar door. Vincent thought it was strange that he had ran into several officers working for the new army, but none had stepped forward to take command from Blackwell, who was still only a staff sergeant.

"So, none of the officers want to take over as the commander yet?" he asked.

"None of them have more than a few months service, sir. Most of them don't know what to do unless someone is yelling at them." Blackwell sighed.

"Sorry to hear that. I'm sure you're over it at this point," he said. "What about that Martian first sergeant?"

"Er, well sir, how can I put this politely..." He stuttered.

"You don't have to watch what you say around me Blackwell." Vincent brushed off his worries.

"Well, the Martians tend to keep to themselves..." Blackwell struggled to say. Vincent may have been young, but he wasn't dumb. He knew the pervasive hatred for Martians by segments of the human population from elsewhere was deeply entrenched. He knew that if he wanted to stop it from spreading in this new army he was trying to build, he had to stop it now.

"I'll let her know she's the non-commissioned officer in charge when we are done with our tour." Blackwell's eyes went wide. "And Martian soldiers are to be integrated at every level of every unit."

"Sir, if my job wasn't up to standard-"

"That isn't what I'm saying," Vincent said, cutting him off. "You were hired to be my recruiter, not to be in charge of an entire army. We need people. Badly. If you haven't noticed," Vincent said. "and you're the best recruiter we have."

"I understand, sir." Blackwell smiled. Vincent knew, deep down inside the old man wanted nothing to do with being in command. Hell, Vincent knew *he* didn't want to be in command. He assumed he was doing the man a favor.

The first position they came to was a repurposed grain store. The Black Coats had long since relocated most of the food stores to their side of the Pit, leaving the Sentenced areas little more than a food desert. It played right into the Black Coats hands of making everyone else dependent on them.

Several gun ports had been knocked out of the store's walls and he could see the large barrel of a belt fed machine gun sticking out. Vincent was very familiar with the weapon. His skill with it had led him to become a Squad Leader while still onboard the *ESS Victory*. He couldn't help but notice dozens of pock marks surrounding the port where the Black Coats had tried their hardest to take it out.

Out in front of the position was the wide-open area of The Pit. Mounds of garbage, burnt out ship hulks, and unneeded construction supplies from the rest of Elysian were piled up as far as he could see. He could just barely make out rows of brown brick buildings on the other side, where he had no doubt he was in someone's sights. Thankfully the Mawr couldn't build high enough to give the Black Coats a really advantageous position.

Vincent couldn't help but notice that several of the buildings in the distance were heavily damaged and smoke rose up from the skyline. It looked like Ezra's strafing runs had really taken their toll on the once much nicer area.

"Welcome to the fun, sir," smirked a soldier who was manning the machine gun. The soldier was wearing a helmet low over his dirty face and was surrounded by empty metal shell casings. There was a skinny Titanian soldier sitting in the store with him. He was staring straight ahead hardly even registering Vincent's approach.

"Looks like you guys had a lot of it," Vincent remarked. "*Fun* I mean."

"Something like that. Though, to tell you the truth I don't think they were trying that hard," the soldier said.

"I'd bet you're right. Keep your head up for when they come back," Vincent said as he and Blackwell began to move on.

"I wouldn't miss the chance to stack some Black Coats out there with the trash where they belong," the soldier laughed.

Before they could get to the next position a soldier called out from somewhere out in front of them.

"Stop!" The voice yelled, followed by the crack of a gunshot.

"Shit," Vincent cursed. "Let's go see what's going on." Blackwell led him to the sentry position that the shot had come from. The position was one of the few two-story buildings on their side of the Pit other than the Bar. Though, it seemed to be only standing through the strength of the men inside of it. It had caught the worst of the Black Coat attack with giant ragged hole punched out in various places and the roof collapsed in onto itself.

A soldier was standing up from where the second floor once was, a rifle held up on his shoulder. Vincent could see the helmeted heads of several other soldiers crouched behind the low broken wall. He and Blackwell walked into the first story of the building through a hole that was big enough to walk three men abreast.

Inside, ten soldiers were keeping watch over the Pit. Vincent pushed through them to get a view. It took a second to find what they were all staring at but when he found it, he was utterly confused.

A Black Coat with a hood over his head was stumbling his way through the piles of garbage. In his outstretched hands he held a black bag.

"Why the hell does he have a potato sack over his head?" Asked a soldier.

"That's a good question," Vincent muttered. "A very good question."

"That doesn't seem like a very *Black Coat* thing to do," Blackwell added. The rifle upstairs cracked again and sent a small spout of dirt up at the oncoming soldier's feet.

"Stop or I'll shoot your ass dead!" The soldier yelled out.

"This isn't right," Vincent said to himself. "Hold your fire!" he screamed. "Hold your damn fire!" Vincent turned to the group of soldiers huddled into the building with him. "Three of you go out and get that guy. Everyone, get ready to cover them if the Black Coats open up."

"Yes sir!" They chimed. Without hesitation three soldiers heaved themselves over the broken outer wall and bounded towards the Pit.

The three soldiers slowly approached the hooded man, rifles up and at the ready. One soldier snatched the bag from his hands, and another took the hood from his head. Blackwell's eyes went wide with shock.

"Who the hell is that?" Vincent asked him.

"It's Private Xi. He's been missing since last night," he said.

"He was captured?" Vincent asked.

"Sorry sir, we all just assumed he was buried under one of the collapsed buildings in A block. They got hit kind of hard with grenades," a soldier next to him said.

"Well, giving him back is a good sign," Vincent said.

"I don't like this" Blackwell trailed off.

The soldiers began to escort Xi back towards the blasted building. As they got closer Vincent could see the soldier's face was badly beaten and bruised. Blood, both fresh and dry was caked all over his face and head. Blood dripped from his lips.

One of the soldiers handed Blackwell the bag Xi had carried with him. The old man opened the sack, that now Vincent could see looked to be wet. A crimson drip fell from the bag and splattered on the ground. The bag was soaked through with blood.

Blackwell, his face frozen in horror, slowly withdrew a hairy, bloody, mass from the bag. The mass slowly rotated around, and Vincent could see the mutilated, pale face of a human. It dawned on him when he made contact with the head's cold, dead eyes. It was the head of Private Miles.

"Fuck," Vincent spat.

Blackwell slowly lowered the head back into the bag and handed it back to a staring soldier, who recoiled in disgust. His head swam with so many intertwined thoughts he couldn't make any sense of them. They had to know by sending this to them they were openly declaring war. But if they were declaring war, why weren't they getting shot at? They were well within range.

"Sir, if you'll excuse me, I need to get my reserves ready," Blackwell said.

"Get everything you can. We are going to need it. Get Ezra ready to be up in the air as soon as possible," Vincent said.

"Yes, sir."

"I have to go find the Warlord. She's going to want to know about this," Vincent said, before turning around and running off. He heard the crunch of footsteps behind him and saw the struggling, tired, form of Huang huffing and puffing to catch up. They sprinted past a group of soldiers who were sitting around half dressed outside of their quarters in C block.

Most of the buildings were whatever could be built with a tin roof slapped on top. A few others were nothing but large numbers of EDF tents stitched together. They eyed the running pair with confusion.

"Get to the line!" Vincent yelled at them. The soldiers pushed and shoved each other trying to get to their feet, grabbing their rifles and gear before running off. "Huang." Vincent addressed the private who was struggling to keep up with him. "I don't need your protection right now, find everyone you can who will fight and get them up there."

"But sir—"

"Just fucking go!" Vincent screamed. Huang didn't say another word. He pivoted on his heel and took off in a different direction. In front of him the Bar's doors were wide open, and soldiers were streaming out of it.

Fiona was waiting on the stairs. Her dull, rust colored armor and the silver saber dangling from her belt looked out of place in the sea of grey uniformed soldiers.

"Is it popping off?" she asked with a smile across her face.

"Not yet, but it is close. I have to go tell Arai." He coughed. The short run had so far winded him. He had let himself get out of shape since becoming Consul.

"Ugh," she complained running to catch up. "You're never any fun." Zinvor lagged far behind them. His short, stocky legs never having a chance to keep up with the humans. Mawrs may have been frightening Warriors on the field of battle, but there was a reason he had never seen a Mawr war formation move quickly.

The Government Quarter was crowded with its normal bustle of activity. The sheer mass of moving bodies prevented Vincent from running any further. They slowed to a shuffle as they tried to push through the sea of rushing government workers who pretended to not even notice them.

"Damnit, these bastards won't get out of our way," Vincent cursed.

"I will solve this," Zinvor grunted. He withdrew his Riten from its holster and fired a round into the air. The concussion made Vincent's ears ring, which caused the yelling and screaming of panicking government workers and the shouts from the Gumi to be dulled slightly.

Zinvor pushed to the head of the group and lowered his shoulder. Acting as a kind of bulldozer, they quickly advanced through the crowd. Squads of Gumi rushed out of the Gathering auditorium towards the commotion but stopped in their tracks and moved aside when they saw a Tsarra and a Consul pushing their way towards them.

Zinvor pushed open the double doors to the Gathering chambers. The group of Leaders sitting at the table stopped what they were doing and stared daggers at the group who had dared to interrupt their meeting.

"What is the meaning of this?" Cursed a Cohort Leader Vincent knew as Talous. A Rhai an old Rhai scout with blue skin.

"Silence!" Zinvor roared, slamming a fist down on the table. Several of the Cohort Leaders jumped. Zinvor's wide, black eyes cast heavy shade at the outraged gathering.

"Vincent?" Arai stood up at the head of the table.

"It was a ruse," Vincent managed to get out in between sucking breaths. "Brusilov killed our messenger. It's war," he panted. Arai rose to her feet, hands balled into fists, and turned towards Pharos. Before she could say anything, their meeting was interrupted by an explosion so powerful it shook the ground under their feet.

CHAPTER ELEVEN

Vincent struggled to keep his footing as the building shook. Dirt and debris trickled down from the ceiling.

"What the fuck was that?" Fiona cursed.

"Whatever it is, it has to do with Brusilov," Vincent said.

"Get me a situation report!" Arai yelled at the table of military leaders in front of her. "Now!" she commanded. At her order they scattered, the only one staying behind was the dark form of Pharos, who didn't seem to be worried about the situation. Pharos held a data display up to Arai, who took it.

"My Warlord."

"What?" she spat.

"I am getting reports that we have lost radio contact with the Port," Pharos said, one of their thin fingers scrolling through the glowing letters of the data display. Arai looked at the display again before casting it aside.

"He is going for the ships." Arai frowned.

"If that's true, he played us the whole time," Vincent said. "Hooked us in long enough to get as many people over there for the attack." Vincent cursed himself. This was, without a doubt, his fault. If they had listened to Arai in the first place none of this would have happened.

"Is our backup plan still ready?" Arai asked.

"Of course, My Warlord." Pharos nodded.

"Launch it," Arai ordered.

"Wait, what backup plan?" Vincent asked.

"We have been following Brusilov's movements since the sit-down you had with him. I have organized a strike force of Warriors to move in on his last known location and eliminate him," Pharos said.

"You can't be serious," Fiona interjected. "You really think you tracked this guy so easily?" She laughed. "He has had so many people try to kill him over the years at this point you can assume whatever location you think he is at, is one he wants you to think he is at."

"What do you mean by this?" Pharos asked.

"It's a trap," Vincent said before Fiona could say something disrespectful. "Whatever strike team you send out is flying right into an ambush."

Arai snorted and crossed her thick arms. "No human traitor could outwit my Warriors," she said.

"Arai, listen to me—"

"I listened to you once before. Now my port is under attack. You have no say in this matter Solaris, your judgement is clouded."

Vincent began to say something, but the heavy hand of Zinvor landing on his shoulder stopped him. He turned to look at his friend who gave him a stern look that told him to keep his mouth shut.

"They should be leaving momentarily, My Warlord," Pharos said.

Vincent had played every card he had to avoid fighting, and now he had nothing left. This was war. "I should be getting back to my Quarter," he said, gritting his teeth.

Arai nodded. "You should."

*   *   *

When they exited the Gathering chambers the Government Quarter was all but deserted. The masses fleeing the massive explosion that had shook them all.

"Stuck up mother fucker," Fiona cursed, her fists balled up.

"Don't blame her. She's right," Vincent said. "If I didn't stop her from killing Brusilov, none of this would be happening."

"You tried to do the right thing," Fiona said.

"*The right thing* is about to get a lot of people killed."

"Right and wrong," Zinvor began. "This is all relative. In this situation you attempted to save as many lives as you could. And by doing so will cause bloodshed."

"I know." Vincent sighed. "You don't have to make me feel any worse."

"I believe right and wrong depends on intentions," Zinvor said. "Your intentions were right for your people. Brusilov is the one who is wrong, not you."

"You're only making me want to kill this guy more." Vincent gritted his teeth.

"Good." Zinvor nodded. "Rage is a tool in many cases." Fiona drew her Riten from her holster and thumbed the hammer back.

"Then let's rage."

*   *   *

The ground rumbled with the impact of dozens of explosions. The whistles in the air told Vincent the Black Coats must have been hitting their forward positions with mortars or small field guns of some kind. In a normal battle, such guns wouldn't be so terrible, but in the Quarter with few hard structures to hide behind it was going to be a charnel house. The man-portable mortars might as well have been crew served artillery pieces. They would blast the thin barriers the soldiers had made like they weren't even there.

The bar had been turned into a casualty assembly point. His stomach lurched up into his throat when he saw several human-shaped forms covered by sheets. They were lined up neatly, like cords of wood. Several wounded soldiers were sitting on the ground outside, waiting for their turns to get seen by the few medics they had. When they saw Vincent approach a few of them tried to stand and salute.

"Sir!" One of them called out. "Did you come to fight?"

"You're goddamn right I did!" Vincent yelled. "Who has a rifle?" A wounded soldier, half of his face covered in a blood-soaked bandage, offered his up. Vincent grabbed it and slung it across his shoulder.

"Sir, they're shelling the hell out of us..." The soldier's voice trembled with fear and the terror in his eyes unsteadied Vincent. Could he really rally these soldiers to fight the Black Coats? In no way were the odds on their side. Vincent felt his throat thicken as he tried to think of the words.

"Good." Fiona smirked at the soldiers. "That means those pieces of shit are prepping to attack us over the Pit. This is what we have been waiting for boys." The wounded soldiers cheered at her words. "Did you want to live to a ripe old age or some shit?" she yelled at them.

"No!" A chorus of voices called back at her. Several wounded soldiers climbed to their feet, some better than others. They picked their rifles up off of the ground and began to walk back towards the sounds of battle coming from the Pit.

"Damn right!" she screamed. "Not a single one of you bastards is allowed to die until you kill at least five of those Black Coats!"

The soldiers, rejuvenated by Fiona's words, ran back out to the line. Some were slowed by their wounds, but as a whole they moved as if they were fresh.

"Holy shit," Vincent said. "You're good at this."

"Not really. You're just really bad at it." She laughed.

"We managed to make it so long without running into another war," Vincent said, pulling the bolt back on his newly acquired rifle. He saw a slug sitting on top of a full magazine. He had thirty shots. He had a feeling he was going to need every single one. He let the bolt slam forward.

"It's been a long, boring year babe." Fiona smirked.

*　　　*　　　*

The line at the Pit had been torn to pieces. Vincent could hardly see it as the constantly exploding mortar shells had obscured the area with dust and smoke. Shells shrieked overhead and impacted somewhere behind him, back towards B Block.

"Stay down damnit!" Screamed a woman's voice. Vincent had no idea who it was. It was hard to hear over the screams of the wounded and earth-shattering boom of incoming shells. "Stay behind cover! Keep low!" the voice commanded.

The group advanced at a crouch, though Zinvor was not too concerned of the incoming danger. He walked forward as if nothing was happening. A shell impacted only a dozen meters from him, showering the group with dirt and debris. Vincent reflexively forced himself to the ground as soon as he heard the wail of the incoming shell. Zinvor marched forward, as if the hail of shrapnel was water from a storm.

"Blackwell!" Vincent yelled into the swirling miasma. "Blackwell! Get over here!" From a shell hole in front of him rose the dirt covered face of Blackwell. Next to him was a dozen soldiers, curled up in balls, attempting to become as small as a target as possible.

"Sir!" he yelled. "You shouldn't be here!"

"I'm not going anywhere. Get on the radio, tell Ezra if he can't take out those guns we are going to get ripped to pieces."

"Yes sir, he said he's trying but he is running into heavy anti-air fire," Blackwell answered.

"Shit!" Fiona cursed. "They adapted quickly, didn't they?"

"Can your pilot pinpoint the gunner's positions?" asked Zinvor.

"Hold on!" Blackwell called out, jumping back into the crater and yelling into the ear of his radio operator. Blackwell took some notes on a data display before he climbed out of the crater and handed it to Zinvor. "Ezra sent us the position of their gun line," he said pointing at the display.

"I'm going to eliminate them," Zinvor said.

"Alone? Are you totally insane?" Vincent gasped.

"That's suicide." Fiona agreed. Zinvor frowned at the both of them.

Out of the smoke came the Martian first sergeant, Erin. Her once pale face was a mask of dirt and the cuffs of her uniform were stained crimson. She nodded at the assembled command group. It was then, Vincent remembered something.

"Erin," he addressed her informally. "You were a scout, right?"

"Yeah."

"Do you have any of your former unit with you?" he asked.

"Most of the guys I brought with me to the meeting you had with The Butcher were with me on Grawluck," she said.

"We have a mission for you," Vincent said. The corner of Erin's mouth curled into a smirk.

Erin starred down at the display, taking some notes on a display of her own.

"So, you want me to get across the Pit with this Alien and charge a damn mortar pit with only one squad?" she asked, her eyebrow raised. "Your bodyguard might have a death with, but I don't."

"It's the only way we can stop the shelling," Vincent said. "As long as those guns are on us, we don't stand a chance. The first sergeant rolled her eyes.

"I'll need some covering fire to get across that death trap," she said. "If we can get across no man's land without them noticing we might actually be able to pull this off."

"You'll get everything we got." Vincent nodded.

"Pretty ballsy idea there, sir." Erin nodded. "Didn't think you had it in you."

"He's not all bad." Fiona smirked. By looking at them, Vincent could have sworn they were related. With the twisting family trees of the Martian street kids anything was possible.

"Blackwell, find a radio for them," Vincent said. Blackwell hesitated and began to open his mouth to argue with the order. "I know we don't have a lot of them. Just find one." His protests ceased and he disappeared into the swirling smoke in search of one.

"If you'll excuse me Solaris, I have an enemy to fight." Erin nodded before turning and walking off.

"Good idea," Fiona said, patting him on the shoulder.

"Don't say that yet. Remember my last *good idea?*"

CHAPTER TWELVE

Vincent slowly peaked the barrel of his rifle over the lip of the shell crater he was laying in. He couldn't make out any of the structures on the other side of the Pit through the haze of the battlefield, but he knew they were out there somewhere. All around him soldiers were doing the same thing.

Blackwell waited at the bottom of the crater with a radio between his legs. Somewhere out in the Pit Erin and her team, Zinvor included, were crawling as slowly and quietly as possible. Erin had told them she would get them as close as they could to the enemy lines before requesting covering fire. They wouldn't be expecting a counterattack, certainly not one as bold as the one Erin was about to launch. It helped that the Black Coats underestimated them to the point of ridicule.

He hardly blamed them. Vincent didn't think much of the force he had managed to assemble either. Built from mostly discarded elements of Earth society, angry Martian conscripts, criminals, and the occasional decent person like Ezra, it didn't exactly inspire confidence.

But as they sat there in smoking shell holes while death rained down on them, his mind began to change. His thoughts went back to his unit on Ryklar. When Alliance plasma artillery slammed down on their heads, fusing hundreds of men to the rocks and maiming many more, not a single man turned and ran. They dug in their heels and faced their enemy. It dawned on him that he wasn't sitting around the ragtag outcasts that he thought he was. They with their heels dug in and facing a much more powerful enemy had become an army once again.

"Traitor Base, this is Red Eye," called Erin's voice on the radio. Her voice was little more than a harsh whisper. They must have gotten close.

"Go for Traitor Base," Blackwell answered.

"Requesting covering fire on all known targets," she said. "On my signal." As soon as her voice clicked off of the airwaves, the Pit erupted with gunfire. That must have been the signal.

"Covering Fire!" Vincent screamed and the line unleashed with a long burst of machine gun and rifle fire. The swirling smoke tail of a rocket twisted through the air at some unseen foe.

Vincent squeezed the trigger of his rifle at a steady pace, though he didn't switch it to automatic. He wanted some ammunition left when the Black Coats made their inevitable attack across the Pit. A Soldier next to him had no such qualms, letting rip with a long burst from his belt fed machine gun. The acrid fumes from powder smoke stung Vincent's nose.

"Cease fire!" Blackwell called, moving his hand up and down in front of his face, palm facing outward. The standard EDF hand-signal for the order. Slowly, the signal was passed down the line and the firing slackened and died off. A deathly silence fell across the line. He knew Erin would call for their cover fire to be lifted when they reached the Black Coat lines. All they had to do now was wait.

The tempo of the mortar rounds began to slow. Instead of a steady and accurate *thump, thump, thump* of shells exploding along the line, they at became erratic. Before, the gunners had the soldier's position dialed in, hitting almost every single building that remained on the line. Now, the shells were landing wildly and off target.

Then, as if a switch were flipped, the shelling stopped. The soldiers on the line slowly peaked their heads above the wreckage. Dust and smoke still obscured everything and stung Vincent's nose. He didn't know how long this lull was going to last for, but he knew they had to take advantage of it.

"Get the wounded out of here!" he yelled, snapping the soldiers around him out of their daze.

"Reinforce your positions!" Blackwell added. "Hurry up, you sorry sacks of shit!" All around them soldiers began to push and shove each other in every direction. Soldiers began to shore up their positions, stacking debris up where walls used to be. Others began to dig deeper into the shell craters around them.

Stretcher teams rushed out of the area and back towards the bar. Every step they took rattled the stretchers and caused the wounded they were carrying to cry out.

"Do we have an update on the scout team?" Vincent asked. "Or Ezra."

"I'll get on that sir," Blackwell said.

"They're going to come for us. That much I'm sure." Vincent frowned.

"We'll be ready for 'em," Fiona said.

"I fucking hope so."

* * *

138

Sweat poured from Vincent's face as he loaded armload after armload of broken cinderblocks and dumped them onto the defensive line they were building. It was rough and full of gaps, but it was better than being left out in the open. 'Better than nothing' had become the standard for their new army.

No word had come from Erin's scout team. The few hundred meters of the Pit might as well have been hundreds of miles. Every few minutes a burst of gunfire could be heard coming from the Black Coat position. Soldiers watched the tracers arc up into the air, powerless to help their comrades.

A sonic boom cut through the air. Vincent looked up to see the crescent moon-shaped forms of three Fidayi aircraft overhead. They were painted a dull yellow color and had the Clan standard marked on their wings.

"The hell is that?" Blackwell asked.

"I think that is Arai's back up plan," Vincent said. "She insists that they have pinpointed Brusilov's headquarters and they're going to kill him."

"You told her it was a trap, right?" Blackwell raised his eyebrow. "He has survived more assassination attempts than anyone I've ever heard of."

"We told her. Clearly we don't know what we are talking about," said Fiona. "I bet that bastard is already halfway to the Moon by now."

Rockets and tracers ripped through the air as the ships approached the Black Coat's position. The ships dived, cannon fire and missiles streaked downwards towards the enemy. Vincent could see the sides of the ships folding outwards, their highly trained and deadly cargo readying themselves to attack. The ships twisted and dove further, plunging through the cloud of incoming fire and behind the skyline. They were only gone from view a few seconds. The ships appeared once again, shooting straight up through the sky. Their cargo bays were empty. The strike team had already landed.

"They don't stand a chance." Blackwell grimaced. It didn't matter how dangerous one of Arai's teams was, the fact was they were going to be surrounded by thousands of Black Coats. It was a suicide mission. And worse, it was without a doubt Vincent's fault it was going to happen. Vincent frowned and hoped he would be wrong.

A fireball bloomed through the air as one of the Fidayi ships exploded, a missile finding purchase. Pieces fluttered towards the ground trailing smoke. Another ship was hit, fire erupted from its engines and it fell back towards the ground. The third ship was stitched with gunfire but managed to break free of the Black Coats kill zone.

"There goes their exfiltration route." Blackwell shook his head. Vincent's stomach dropped. Arai would blame him for this, just like she blamed him for Brusilov in the first place. His fuck up would hurt the view of humans in the eye of the Clan. They would be second-class citizens. *Again.* Damnit, he wouldn't let that happen.

"We have to save them," he blurted out.

"That plan might even dumber than going in there in the first place." Fiona laughed. She quickly stopped laughing when she saw he wasn't joking. "Shit, you aren't kidding."

"Blackwell, get Ezra over here," he said.

"Sir—"

"You heard the man," Fiona cut him off. "Looks like we are going on a suicide mission of our own." She stubbed out her cigarette and lit another one. Blackwell shook his head and went back to the radio. "So, what's your plan here huh?"

"We go in there and save as many Warriors as we can," Vincent said. "You were there. You know she blames me for all of this."

"So, what? Killing us in some stupid rescue attempt is the way to go?" she asked.

"I didn't say you had to go."

"You really are stupid," she spat. "You're not going into any suicide mission without me." She blew out a cloud of smoke. "But if we want a slim chance of this working, we are going to need more people."

"I can't ask anyone else to go with us. It wouldn't be right." He shook his head.

"Yeah you can you idiot. You're their commander," Fiona said harshly. "Commanders do that type of shit all of the time."

"We need as many people as we can to hold the line here," Vincent said.

"Ugh, I can't stand you when you're like this," Fiona fumed. She climbed on top of the barrier the soldiers were working on. She cupped her hands to her mouth and yelled out, "Hey listen up! Your commander wants to go on a dumb ass suicide mission into the heart of Black Coat country across the Pit. Who wants to go with him?"

All around them soldiers exchanged looks of confusion. Slowly they all started laughing nervously. Vincent saw in their eyes the sudden realization that they weren't kidding. Then, to his shock all around him, hands began reaching towards the sky. "Turns out you're not the only idiot in the crowd." Fiona laughed and slapped Vincent on the shoulder.

The *Shanna* appeared in the sky overhead and slowly floated down onto the blasted landscape, landing only a few feet away from Vincent. The door popped open with a hiss and the lanky pilot stepped out. His large black helmet, with its glowing overhead display, was turned off and set aside. He rendered a crisp salute to Vincent and shook Blackwell's hand.

"Sir, Sergeant Blackwell informed me of your plan. I have to advise against it," the colonel said sternly.

"I know, Ezra." Vincent nodded. "But can you do it?"

"You want me to fly into intersecting fields of anti-aircraft fire with a squad onboard to fight a couple thousand Black Coats all just to rescue some Aliens?" Ezra raised his eyebrow.

"Pretty much, yeah." Vincent shrugged. "The Clan pilots got torn to shreds. Are you telling me you're not better than them?"

"Sir, Sentenced or no, I'm the best pilot on this rock." Ezra smiled. "I'll fly up the Chairman's ass if you want me too."

"So, how do you get us in there without dying?" Fiona asked.

"Easy." Ezra shrugged. "I watched the Clan's approach. It's pretty clear to me their anti-aircraft weapons are in the streets. Like so..." Ezra quickly drew cross-hatched streets in the dirt with his foot with small squares on either side representing buildings. "Which is a good idea to protect them from you guys. It's hard for you to assault through buildings and take them."

"No shit." Fiona frowned.

"But it also gives them a restricted field of fire. You see..." He began to draw another line in the dirt. "If we come in low to the ground from across the Pit, they can't bring the weapons down on us. Not unless they want to shell their own buildings."

"How low?" Vincent asked.

"Oh, you'll see." Ezra grinned. "I can squeeze us into some small spaces, my gunner will give you cover fire while you pull the aliens out of the shit they got themselves into."

"Gunner?" Vincent asked. He looked over Ezra's shoulder and saw Nox sitting the passenger seat of the Reaper.

"That weirdo is going to be watching over us?" Fiona rolled her eyes.

"I haven't had a real gunner since Grawluck." Ezra frowned. "Nox is working fine."

"I guess they can't run away if their trapped in a ship," Vincent said. The diminutive alien had shown themselves to be a coward on more than one occasion during their previous adventures together. Nox insisted it was little more than a self-preservation tactic. "So, you're saying we can pull this off?" he asked.

"Oh, no." Ezra smiled. "But I can get you to the scene of our crash."

"I thought I was bad at optimism." Fiona laughed. Blackwell, his old, wrinkled face heavy with concern approached Vincent.

"Sir, this is a terrible idea. We need to hold—"

"Sometimes the only options we have are all terrible," Vincent interrupted. "Like it or not the Fidayi are our allies. Would you let one of our squads get surrounded and torn to pieces by the Black Coats?"

Blackwell recoiled at the thought. "Of course not, sir."

"Then let's fucking go."

CHAPTER THIRTEEN

The *Shanna* floated low and slow over the Pit. Ezra, the screen of his pilot's helmet glowing green as information about the ship's flight scrolled passed his eyes, pushed and pulled the throttle as the ship glided only a few feet above the mounds of trash.

The rattle of machine gun fire and the dull thump of explosions grew louder as they passed over the pit. The Fidayi squad, or whatever was left of it, was being hit hard. He hoped somewhere in the jungle of crumbling stone buildings Erin's scout squad was still lurking. Since the destruction of the Black Coat's mortar's they had fallen silent. Vincent had begun to fear the worst.

He tried to push the thoughts of the lost squad from his head as the *Shanna* approached the Black Coat positions. A massive Eagle and Star flag had been run up a towering flagpole that had been set up on the edge of the pit. The flag had been punched with multiple bullet holes and the edges were tattered as the harsh Elysian wind tore it slowly to pieces.

Ezra began to lift the ship into the air. Below them rows of sandbag reinforced bunkers lined the roofs of the buildings. Small black shapes were gathered behind each one. There was hundreds of them. The soldiers weren't scattering or running like Vincent assumed they would as a firefight roared in the streets somewhere behind them. Instead, they lazed around, like nothing was happening at all.

Slowly the ship's engines began to whirl, and it shuttered slightly. Ezra tipped the nose down and they started to pick up speed. The ten soldiers that had packed into Reaper exchanged nervous looks. Ezra leaned back between the pilot's seats, looking back at his human cargo. He held up one finger on his right hand and quickly point upwards. The hand signal for *Prepare to fire.*

He pressed a button in the cockpit and the two troop compartment doors slid out of the way. Soldiers swung the multi-barreled, chain driven, crew guns into position. Vincent's throat began to thicken. This was it. He grabbed his rifle in both hands, feeling for its charging handle. He pulled it back and let it slam forward. He swallowed hard and the relative calm of their flight came to an end.

Brrrrrt. The Reaper's nose mounted cannon spat out what had to be hundreds of rounds at once. A line of roof top bunkers exploded, sending black shrouded bodies cartwheeling into the air. *Brrrrrt.* Nox fired again. A building collapsed, flames erupted out of the collapsing structure, taking dozens of fleeing soldiers with it. The ship dropped into a stomach-churning dive. Ezra guided the ship towards the burning buildings below and in the direction of a main street.

Soldiers manning the crew guns began to fire as the ship roared past shocked Black Coats. Ezra leveled the ship out only a few feet above the cracked and broken road below them. It didn't take long for the Black Coats to snap out of their momentary confusion. Machine gun fire came at the *Shanna* like a thick winter storm. A soldier who was sitting near the open side door groaned as blood sprayed out of a wound in his neck. He collapsed forward and fell out of the ship.

Everyone in the crew compartment was firing whatever weapons they had at hand. The *Shanna* was flying far too fast for anyone to actually see what they were aiming at, but that didn't matter. Vincent raised his rifle, toggling the selector switch with his thumb to *automatic* and squeezed the trigger. He hosed half of his magazine in the general direction several of black shapes that ripped by the troop compartment in a blur. Another soldier pitched out of the ship, screaming. He left a slick of dark blood where he had once been sitting.

"I see their crash site up ahead!" Ezra yelled back. The ship swung wide as Ezra dodged an incoming rocket. "Shit!" Ezra yelled. "I can't get too close! I'll land as close as I can!" he said. Ezra jerked the ship hard, spinning it in a three-hundred- and sixty-degree circle. A long rip from the ship's cannon churned every enemy position around them to a pulp. A white streak from another rocket cut past the right side of the ship. It was so close Vincent could smell the burning rocket fuel.

"That was a close one, heh?" Ezra laughed as Nox unleashed another burst from the cannon. This one in the direction from where the rocket had come from, an alleyway exploded and collapsed. Below them Vincent could see the wreckage of a Fidayi ship, still smoldering.

"There they are!" Vincent yelled. "Bring us down!" Ezra shook his head.

"No goddamn way are we getting close to that!" he said. "Not unless you want to go down the same way they did!"

Ezra flew to the next street over and started to bring the ship down. Below them was a large intersection that cut in between the rows of buildings. Ezra guided the ship down expertly through the unending swarm of incoming fire. The sound of the Black Coats gunfire was almost overwhelming. The din of combat was so loud he couldn't hear himself think. Vincent wasn't sure of the thickness of a normal Reaper's armor, but he was sure Ezra's *Shanna* couldn't withstand this kind of punishment for long.

They had slowed down enough so Vincent could finally make out his surroundings. Below them he could see two dead Mawr Warriors lying face down on the street. All around them lay dozens of dead Black Coats. Nox's deadly cannon fire had laid waste to their attack on the ship and turned the surrounding area into a wasteland. A sea of flames licked up at the sky and thick black smoke choked the air. Wounded Black Coats struggled out of the flames, their coats melting to their backs. The ones who were able ran for their lives, leaving their stricken comrades behind.

The ship touched down in the middle of a wide opening. The remaining soldiers jumped off of the ship and spread out in a circle around it. Vincent was expecting to run into another storm of gunfire. Instead there was only a few random, badly aimed shots from the fleeing Black Coats.

He could hear the muffled screams of the wounded as they struggled to escape the burning buildings that had once been their positions. Had they actually swooped down and beaten them? Everywhere he looked was another dead, black coated corpse or a slick of blood leading down an alleyway. No. He shook the idea from his head. They would only need a few minutes to regroup before launching another attack.

"Where the hell are Arai's boys?" Fiona asked, he was glad he wasn't the only one worried.

"No idea!" he said.

"Should we just start calling for them like they're lost puppies or something?" Fiona asked harshly.

"Spread out!" Vincent ordered.

"Hey!" Ezra yelled. "We can't stay here long, sir; they'll be on us in no time once they get their shit together."

Vincent nodded. The circle of soldiers slowly began to fan out through the smoke, their weapons up and ready. As they walked further and further into the smoke, he could no longer see the soldiers next to him. He glanced in every direction. The line of buildings they had been dropped into had been turned into a killing field by Nox's cannon. Every step he took he found his foot landing in another pool of sticky blood. He walked past a Black Coat that must have been hit directly by one of Nox's shots. His legs had been completely blown away at the waist, leaving behind a scene that looked like a sausage factory dumpster.

A chill ran down his spine as his mind flashed back to the hilltop of Ryklar. Alliance ships had done multiple bombing runs on his Regiment's position, leaving a scene that looked a lot like the one he found himself in once again. Vincent struggled to bring his mind back to the task at hand when he came face to face with the enemy.

The wounded man was lying face down with blood pooling out onto the street. Around him was four other soldiers, attempting to load the wounded man onto a stretcher. Their rifles were slung across their backs. Vincent froze where he stood, his rifle pointing at them. He watched as they rolled the bleeding man onto the stretcher and began work to bandage a ragged looking stomach wound. The other four bent down to hoist him up when one of them looked over at Vincent. Their eyes locked and slowly, the Black Coat's eyes went wide with realization that they were being watched.

Vincent knew he had them dead to rights. With one burst from his rifle he could quickly dispatch all five of them. But he didn't. By the looks of it the man on the stretcher wasn't long for this world, and the other four were just trying to help their comrade. Just like any good soldier would. He couldn't bring himself to shoot a defenseless person, even if they were Black Coats.

The Black Coats held no such qualms. They dropped the stretcher, the wounded man bouncing painfully off of the ground. They fumbled for their rifles, their fingers refusing to work as adrenaline pumped through their veins. Vincent held his rifle at his waist, his finger tightening on the trigger.

"Get your wounded and get the hell out of here!" he yelled at them.

"Fuck you!" A Black Coat screamed back, his rifle finally coming up to his shoulder. He had waited too long and now the tables had turned. He should have known better than to think the Black Coats held any kind of battlefield etiquette. Or maybe he was just dumb for thinking such a thing existed anywhere outside of movies, books, or training.

Vincent flinched as a burst of gunfire erupted behind him, stitching across the group of Black Coats. They jerked and twitched awkwardly as their bodies were impacted by dozens of slugs before they fell to the ground, bonelessly.

"What the fuck are you doing? Trying to kill them through a staring contest?" Asked the voice behind him. Vincent turned around to see the dirt and smoke-stained faces of Erin's squad. Though, he noticed they were a fewer in number than when they had left. Zinvor stood next to her, his armor as dark as the billowing smoke.

"Something like that," Vincent managed to get out. "Have you seen the Fidayi team that went down about an hour ago?"

"Seen?" she asked. "No. But I know where their teams landed. It's been a shit show of a gunfight ever since. It's the only reason we were able to pull out from where we were."

"Do you think you can get to them?" Vincent asked.

"Shit sir, I don't know how many of them will be left by the time I did," she said. Seeing the expression on Vincent's face she paused, and then sighed. "You really are nuts, aren't you?"

"Absolutely. I need you to get whoever is still alive and get them back to our ship. You're the best scouts we've got, Erin."

"We're the only scout you've got," she corrected. "Fuck it, I'll round up my people and we will go save your precious aliens. If we aren't back in thirty minutes you best be getting on that ship of yours and getting the hell out of here."

"Deal."

CHAPTER FOURTEEN

The area around the ship was deathly silent. The screams of the wounded had fallen silent. Vincent wasn't sure how many of the pained voices that had called out had been a Black Coat or who had been one of his. In the hazy darkness of the burning city block around them, he couldn't be sure.

The group of soldiers that they had set out with had been violently cut down to just six. After Erin and her scouts had saved him Vincent had retreated back to the Reaper and met up with Fiona and the few other survivors. Unlike him no one else had given the wounded a chance. They bragged about how many Black Coats they had finished off. His stomach churned in disgust.

The Reaper sat in the middle of their small circle of soldiers, its engines whirling quietly as Ezra had insisted they keep the power going in case they had to make a quick escape. Vincent glanced down nervously at his watch every few seconds, keeping track of exactly how long Erin's team had been gone.

She had said thirty minutes. The red numbers of his watch danced above the display at *25:56.* The sounds of a distant gunfight coming from the direction where Erin and her soldiers had advanced through had not slowed. He began to feel the cold sweat dripping down his back under his armor.

"Vincent," Fiona said.

"Not yet," he said. "She said thirty minutes."

"Erin isn't a damn miracle worker," Fiona said. "We gotta get the hell out of here while we can. Maybe arrange for a defense or something."

"You can rub this in my face in—" He paused again to look at his watch. "Three and a half minutes."

"Noted." Fiona smirked. Before Vincent could give a retort, Ezra opened the cockpit door and waved him over.

"You gotta hear this!" he said. Ezra took his helmet off and handed it to Vincent. He slowly placed the pilot's helmet on, it smelled of stale sweat and the old man's musk. The ear cups of the radio were moist with Ezra's cold sweat.

"Red Ghost to *Shanna*," said a calm voice. "We've made contact with the Clan Assault team and we are heading back towards you." The voice was heavily distorted with static, but he knew it was Erin. "We've got enemy on our heels, estimated to be at least one Squadron in strength." The radio crackled and hissed. "Requesting immediately assistance!" Her voice wasn't rising in panic, but because a loud explosion nearby nearly drowned out her voice completely.

"This is Great Traitor!" Vincent called over the radio. "What's your location?"

"I'm sending it to *Shanna's* display now." Her voice came in warped and distorted. She could barely be heard over what had to be hundreds of rifles firing at once. "Make it fast or there won't be anything left of us."

"Sit tight, we are coming for you."

One of the many screens on Ezra's dashboard lit up with a new grid coordinate. A small green dot blinked on a topographical overlay of a city block Erin.

"I got it," he said. Ezra reached over and grabbed the helmet from Vincent's head and flipped down the facial display.

"Are we really flying in to fight an entire squadron?" Fiona asked. "I know I've been saying this a lot recently, but this is a really stupid idea." Vincent climbed into the troop compartment of the Reaper as its engines slowly began to wind up once again.

"The EDF might leave their people behind, but we don't."

"So, this is really going to happen then," sighed Fiona. The surviving soldiers rushed past her and climb aboard. Nox flipped a few switches on his control panel and the ship's cannon hummed with power. Fiona joined everyone else and sat down next to Vincent and he draped his arm around her.

"Sorry dear, I think some of your crazy is rubbing off on me." He smiled.

"It looks good on you," she said.

*   *   *

Unlike their low and slow approach across The Pit, this time Ezra brought the ship nearly straight up. The surrounding Rhai towers zipped by, turning into little more than an alloy blur. He twisted and spun the ship in between the multitude of walkways. The ship picked up speed and the occupants were forced back into their seats.

"This might get rough." Ezra's voice came through over the speaker in the crew compartment. "I'm going to try to come in right down on top of them."

"Get rough?" Fiona asked. Vincent shrugged. He couldn't see how it could have been any worse than the firestorm that they had just flown through.

"The human body is not prepared to handle this many G-Forces," said Nox. "Those without the proper equipment and training may suffer several side effects including death."

"Err," Ezra stuttered. "Thank you Nox. Don't worry guys you *probably* won't die. More likely you'll just black out for a few seconds." The ship's ascent slowed, almost like it was on an axel, it began to rotate. Vincent's seatbelt tightened as the nose of the ship tilted straight down.

The Reaper's engines rumbled with power and the ship rocketed towards the ground. Vincent's eyes were slammed shut and his head was forced back into his seat. He felt his heart throb in his temples as his chest tightened and his blood rushed to his head. He clenched his jaw so hard it felt as if his teeth would shatter from the force.

Vincent forced his eyes open and looked around him to see almost everyone limp in their seats. Fiona's eyes had rolled into the back of her head and she was gurgling spit. The ship shook as a number of missiles broke free from their mounts on the Reaper's wing platforms. They hurdled towards the ground, leaving trails of smoke in their wake.

As soon as the nosedive had started, it was over. It felt as if a ton of weight had been lifted from his chest. The blood drained from his head and his limbs tingled. Ezra had taken the ship out of the dive and leveled out. The soldiers around him began to slowly wake up, exchanging surprised glances with one another.

"So, let's not fucking do that again yeah?" Fiona cursed as she wiped drool away from the corner of her mouth.

"Ah good morning!" Ezra called out cheerfully. "Everyone alright back there?"

"Yeah. Can you see them?" Vincent asked.

"Yeah. Erin is trying to break contact and withdraw towards the Pit," he said.

"Is it working?" Vincent asked.

"No," Ezra said. "It looks like the Black Coats managed to get two companies in behind them. They're surrounded."

"Shit," he cursed.

"I'm bringing her down as soon as I can. But we can't stay on the ground for long," Ezra said. "Crew weapons ready?" The troop compartment doors slid open, but only barely. The doors creaked and screeched as the bent and battle-damaged metal grinded against each other. The doors became stuck halfway and were beaten open by soldiers swinging rifles like sledgehammers.

Ezra jerked the ship hard to the right as a rocket spiraled passed the cockpit. The chain guns on both side of the ship began to fire, showers of empty brass casings rained down as the soldiers manning the guns swept them back and forth. Vincent leaned out of the door and began squeezing off single rounds, at this height he couldn't make out any single target. Instead he aimed at where he thought he saw muzzle flashes.

The ship began a dive once again. As they got closer Vincent could make out the scene below much clearer. The crashed Fidayi ship, a repurposed EDF armed assault ship known as a Comanche, was surrounded on all sides by what seemed like thousands of Black Coats. About a dozen of Mawr and humans alike were dug in around the ship trying their best to hold them off.

"This is Red Ghost, please tell me that's you *Shanna*," Erin said, her voice coming through over the radio.

"Roger," Ezra answered. "Get low, we are coming in danger close." Vincent thought back to his training. He thought 'danger close' meant that supporting fire was landing so close to the people it was actually trying to help that the possibly of killing their own was very real. Ezra quickly reminded him that was exactly what it meant.

A cluster of missiles flew out from under the Reaper's wings, slamming down onto a row of buildings. Another cluster exploded amongst a group of Black Coats that were only a few dozen meters from the Fidayi ship. The explosion sent dirt, shrapnel, and debris crashing down on the huddle group of desperate soldiers and warriors.

Slowly, the Black Coats who had probably thought they were only minutes away from overrunning the tiny force gathered around the downed ship, began to waiver. The terrifying outpour of munitions from the Reaper into their ranks was too much for a body of normal soldiers to withstand.

"We're going in!" Ezra shouted. He brought the ship down fast. It was not a gentle landing. Instead the ship landed with a crash and a skid for a few feet across the street before coming to a halt. Vincent knew as well as Ezra as they were not going to keep the Black Coats at bay for long. Bullets smacked off of the Reaper's sides while the soldiers in the troop compartment tried their best to return fire.

"Get the fuck in the ship!" Fiona screamed, firing off a long burst from her rifle. Ezra had used the ship as a shield on one side of the encircled soldiers. While a good idea in theory, it had turned the *Shanna* into the main target of the attacking Black Coats. The soldier manning the crew weapon next to Vincent was hit and fell back into the ship. Vincent saw the other soldier's eyes wide with fear, obviously not wanting to replace him.

"Fuck it," Vincent said aloud. He pulled the wounded soldier, who trying in vain to staunch the bleeding from chest wound, back and sat down behind the large, multi-barreled chain gun.

The trigger of the gun was a flanged piece of metal at the rear of the receiver, flanked on either side by a vertical handle. Vincent grabbed both handles and pressed the trigger down with his thumbs.

The gun didn't make a bang like a normal one would. The barrels rotated so fast and the fire so quick it sounded more like a high-pitched whine. Vincent swept the gun to the left and right, never letting go of the trigger. Bullets snapped and cracked by his ears as every Black Coat rifle trained on him. He tried to make his body as small as possible behind the gun, but it was no use. Something stung his ear, forcing tears to well up in his eyes. He felt something warm running down his face and neck.

The ship rocked on its axis. Vincent steadied himself and without letting go of the trigger he glanced back over his shoulder. Erin and the remaining scouts piled into the troop compartment followed by four Mawr Warriors. Jumping in after them was three more Rhai soldiers.

"We're in!" Erin yelled. "Get us the fuck out of here!" Her calm radio voice finally melting away.

The ship lurched and quickly took off into the air. Vincent's firing finally stopped as the gun ran empty. It took him a few seconds to notice the barrels of his gun were still rotating but instead of a deadly cone of fire coming out, it was hundreds of empty *clicks*. The fire from the ground picked up and the ship rattled from the abuse.

Vincent leaned back and grabbed his rifle. He glanced down and saw his dark red blood staining his blue armor. He was still alive, so he assumed the wound couldn't be too bad. Vincent fired his rifle into the city below until the bolt locked to the rear, indicating it was empty.

"Incoming!" Screamed Fiona, pointing out of the door. Vincent could see a fireball cutting through the air to the right of the ship. The rocket was closing in fast.

"Hold on!" Ezra yelled and tried to pull the ship to the left. He was too late.

The ship was rocked violently by the explosion. Smoke engulfed the cabin as the ship's warning claxons assaulted blared. His eyes burned as he tried to blink through the smoke and his lungs begin to seize up.

Vincent could feel the ship dropping. The air rushed into the cabin from the forced descent and it pushed the smoke out. He felt something grab onto his arm and looked over to see Fiona holding onto him. Vincent wrapped an arm around her shoulder and pulled her in close. He wasn't entirely sure if it was because of their impending death, or to keep him from falling out of the stricken ship, but he held on tight either way.

Across from them Erin sat on the ground cross-legged, her face was the picture of calm. She reached into her breast pocket and withdrew a pack of cigarettes. She lit one and took a deep pull before handing it to Vincent. Vincent took it and drew the smoke in. He handed it back to Erin who smirked and nodded at him.

"Well, thanks anyways, sir," she said. "We almost pulled it off."

"I put us here in the first place," he said. "I got us all killed."

"Maybe," Erin said. "But you have balls." She tapped her cigarette. "If we didn't die, I'd follow you on another suicide mission anytime." She smiled.

"Thanks." He managed a laugh. "I'm going to hold you to that."

Ezra managed to level the ship out, though shaking and pouring smoke and fire from one of the engines. Vincent watched as the right engine broke off and tumbled towards the ruined city streets below. Ezra had one foot up on the control panel, bracing himself as he fought against the shaking controls. Vincent could see the entire windshield on the right side was shattered and blown away. Its jagged edges were covered in blood.

"Can you get us across the Pit?" Vincent asked.

"No idea!" Ezra said. "But I'm going to try!"

Despite his struggles the ship was falling fast. Though the ship was without any power Ezra had managed to bring it into a glide only a few feet above the Black Coat controlled city block. The ship jolted violently as it skipped across a roof top. Ezra pulled up hard on the controls, forcing the nose of the ship up. The rear of the ship dropped and bounced off of a pile of trash as they crossed into the Pit. The ship skipped and slid across the vast field of garbage before finally coming to a halt.

"Are-are we alive?" Fiona sputtered, coughing.

"I think so," Vincent gasped, his stomach finally dropping from his throat. "Barely."

"Just how I planned it." Ezra sighed and slumped back in his seat.

"I'm sure it was," Erin said. The solders in the troop compartment slowly climbed out of the stricken ship, their legs a little wobblier than before. Vincent stretched out, grateful to be back on solid ground. It was only when he stepped in front of the ship that he saw the true cost of the missile strike.

The entire right side of the cockpit was decimated and its cannon had been sheared away. The ship's windshield had been blown inwards. The explosion had sent thousands of pieces of shrapnel into the cockpit, right into the gunner's position. The small, frail body of Nox was pinned to his seat, impaled by shrapnel. They were slumped forward, hands still curled tightly around the useless controls of the cannon.

Vincent wasn't sure if he considered the two-faced alien a friend or not. But when he locked eye with the cold, dead eyes of Nox, something inside of him broke. He reached over and closed the Alien's eyes. Vincent's eyes began to burn as the tears ran freely down his face. He didn't try to hide them.

CHAPTER FIFTEEN

Vincent sat at the Gathering table, his head still swimming. His ears still rang with the concussion of battle. He could smell the copper tinge of his own blood. At the head of the table Arai was talking about something to do with the bombardment of the Black Coats, but her words were muffled by the endless ringing.

"Solaris," she said, her voice finally breaking through.

"Huh?" he answered.

"What were the loses of the Human Cohort during your rescue?" she asked.

"Uh..." Vincent struggled to gather his thoughts. "Twenty killed." *And Nox*, he thought. The skinny, backstabbing, little asshole Nox. Nox had saved him and Fiona from certain death on several occasions. Even if it were for their own gain at the time, the fact remained: if it weren't for Nox neither of them would still be here. They had died fighting for him.

Everything that had happened slowly began to wash over him. He had ordered the scouts to go looking for the Fidayi team, he had ordered Ezra to launch the attack against the Black Coats. His orders had killed twenty of them and countless Black Coats. He became overwhelmed with the need to vomit.

"You've shown us something here today, Solaris," Arai said. The rest of the Gathering's eyes were locked onto him. "That the humans of your army truly stand with the Clan against the darkness of the Alliance and the traitors of the Central Committee."

"The ships," Vincent said. "What happened at the port?"

"Unfortunately, the Black Coats succeeded in their goals," Arai growled. "I was premature in blaming this on you Solaris, their attack showed they had been planning this long before you ever got involved. Brusilov's meeting was clearly a ruse."

"So, they escaped." Vincent sighed.

"Yes," she said. "They managed to take at least two air wings worth of ships and evacuated the vast majority of their forces off of the planet."

"This brings...certain issues to the forefront," Pharos said.

"Indeed it does," Arai said. Vincent was having a hard time following the conversation.

"I'm not following you."

"The Committee is a real threat to us," Arai said. "They have proven that once again, they cannot be trusted."

"I want them dead as much as you do." Vincent frowned.

"I know," she said.

"So what issues are we talking about?" he asked.

"The issue is that we will now be fighting a two-front war," Pharos said.

"You mean, against the Committee?" Vincent raised an eyebrow. "You're going to war?"

"We clearly have no choice." Arai shook her head. "They wish us destroyed, so like always we must fight for our survival."

"But we are barely holding off the Alliance," Vincent said.

"I know." Arai frowned. "Our only hope in a fight against the Committee is to unify humanity against it." It suddenly dawned on Vincent what she was getting at.

"You mean *me?*" he asked.

"You are our Human Consul."

"We have arranged a meeting between you and Prime Minister Oscar Denta of the Union of Titan," Pharos said. "Certain members of their government recognize the danger that a renewed Committee could pose and are willing to speak with us."

"Seriously?" Vincent blurted out. The only thing most humans hated more than Martians were aliens. It was beaten into their heads in school that aliens, any aliens, were barbaric and violent that only wished for the destruction of Earth. The hatred ran so deep that no aliens were ever given permission to visit Earth. He knew attitudes tended to change from settlement to settlement, but the idea that the Titan government wanted to sit down and chat with an alien government was mind boggling to him.

"Some are not sure of our intentions, as is to be expected. Many within the Clan see all humans as bad as the ones who follow the Committee," Pharos said.

"Maybe if they see that we already work closely with humans, they will trust us," Arai said.

"They might just see me as a useless puppet," Vincent said.

"That is a possibility," Pharos nodded. "That will be on you to assure them otherwise." Vincent wasn't sure if could. He wasn't entirely sure if he had convinced himself if he wasn't a puppet yet.

"You managed to talk to Titan, what about Mars?" he asked.

"We were unable to make contact with any entity of a Mars government independent of the Committee," Pharos said.

"What does that mean?" Vincent asked.

"It means that the Committee is still mostly in control of Mars," Pharos said. "Though there currently a civil war ongoing on the planet's surface. My agents were unable to make heads or tails of the situation." To Vincent, that sounded exactly how Fiona had described what would happen to Mars after the destruction of Earth.

"Mars was the largest base for EDF troops, to destroy the Committee...we will have to go to Mars," Vincent said.

"You are observant Consul," Pharos said.

"We can hardly invade Mars with our Fidayi Cohorts alone. We have too many tied up on the Alliance front," Arai said. "An Alliance with the most powerful human settlement is the only way forward."

"Invade Mars?" Vincent sputtered. "You can't be serious!"

"We have no choice," Pharos said. "The Committee is a monster with many heads. We thought they would go away with their destruction of their home planet and we were wrong. It is clear that we must strike at all of its heads if we hope to succeed."

"Wait. There is more to this." Vincent thought for a moment. What could the Fidayi possibly offer the Titanians to get them to negotiate with an alien race? What did Arai say that got Titan's government to overlook generations of Xenophobia? That was when Vincent realized he was thinking about the situation from the wrong perspective. Arai didn't know anything about human space or settlements. But Pharos certainly did. What would Pharos do?

"You want Martian manufacturing," Vincent said. Mars, even before the endless civil strife, was known for their weapons manufacturing. Thousands of miles of manufacturing plants, as far as the eye could see, created almost everything used by the EDF from the smallest pistol to the terrifying Capital Ships like the *ESS Victory*. Almost every Martian who wasn't forcefully conscripted into the EDF was forced to work in one of countless plants.

"We have little use for human technology," Pharos said.

"But Titan does," Vincent pointed out. "And they would need the output of Mars to ever hope to fight the Alliance."

Pharos nodded. "Something like that."

"It will be your job to offer them that," Arai said. "Our full support in chasing the Committee off of Mars."

"What about the Martians?" Vincent asked. "I highly doubt they will willingly become slaves to a different overlord."

"That will be on Titan to negotiate, not us," Pharos said.

"Warlord, what about my soldiers?" Vincent stammered, changing the subject. "The dead haven't even been buried yet. I can hardly just leave—"

"With respect Consul, we do not have time for pleasantries," Arai interrupted. Pharos put his hand on Arai's shoulder, and she glanced sideways at him.

"You'll have to forgive the Warlord," Pharos interjected. "Your customs are still new to us. Is it normal for humans to honor their fallen?"

Vincent nodded.

"I was unaware of this before I scheduled the meeting with the Titanians. This can be fixed. And I assume the Warlord would send a delegation to give their respects?"

"Yes." Arai cleared her throat. "This would be acceptable after certain operations are complete."

"Certain operations?" Vincent asked.

"The Black Coat forces you were fighting in the Quarter was little more than a rearguard force." She thought for a moment.

"A distraction. While their main force attacked the port, they were left behind to stall us."

"It has worked, unfortunately." Pharos sighed. "We could not commit forces to chasing the stolen air wings while an enemy force held a portion of the Human Quarter. So three of our Rhai Cohorts have been finishing off what your *Shanna* left behind."

"Warlord." Vincent stood up and bowed deeply to Arai. "Please excuse my failures. They are mine alone and not my Cohort's." Arai held a hand up.

"Be seated, Consul." He did so. "I did not become Warlord without making a few mistakes. Neither did my Father, nor his before him. This failure is on the head of the Clan, not the Human Consul. Together, we failed in our mission. But what is more important than dwelling on this failure, is learning from it."

"I know what I learned," Vincent said. "I underestimated Brusilov. He played us for fools."

Arai nodded.

"Correct," she said. "It will never happen again."

CHAPTER SIXTEEN

Vincent stood at the crest of a large hole. Below him, laid side by side was twenty-one bodies shrouded in tattered bits of cloth. Military decorum mandated that they be in caskets covered by the flag of United Humanity. They had no flags or caskets, and humanity was far from unified. One of the bodies wasn't even human.

A loose formation of soldiers stood behind him. Their uniforms frayed and worn, many of them covered in blood stained bandages. The look on their faces wasn't one of despair, or sadness. Which, Vincent knew was plastered across his own. Instead, their hard eyes showed fierce determination.

On the other side of the hole stood a detachment of seven soldiers. They stood ramrod straight, their rifles held tightly in their hands. Blackwell stood in front of them, he slowly turned to face the soldiers.

"Present arms!" Blackwell commanded. The soldiers quickly pivoted, bringing their rifles to their shoulder. Everyone else in attendance slowly raised their hand to their eyebrow in a salute.

Standing far away from the formation of human soldiers was a small delegation of Fidayi Clan Mawr Warriors and Rhai Soldiers. At their head stood Arai, Zinvor and Pharos. The Fidayi did not have a similar sign of respect as the hand salute. So, at Arai's lead, the Mawr delegation slowly lowered themselves into a deep bow. The Rhai brought their balled fist to the center of their chest.

"Fire!" Ordered Blackwell. *Bang.* They fired in unison. *Bang.* They fired again. *Bang.* They fired their final shots. "Shoulder, Arms!" The soldiers smartly dropped their rifles back to their shoulder. "Burial detachment, post!" Blackwell's voice boomed. At that command, ten soldiers marched out of the formation behind Vincent, shovels held against their chest as if they were rifles.

As the soldiers began to dig, the rest of the soldiers broke from the formation and began to help throw dirt over the bodies of the fallen with their bare hands. Fiona, Erin, and Ezra stood next to Vincent at the lip of the hole, watching the soldiers work.

"We have to go to Titan," Vincent blurted out. He wasn't sure how to bring up the orders he had gotten from Arai. He assumed this was as good as time as any.

"Hmm," Ezra began. "We'll need a new ship."

"It's taken care of," Vincent said. "Erin, you're in charge while I'm gone."

"Wait, I'm not going with you?" she exclaimed.

"No, I need some kind of power structure here to help build this army. Who better than humanity's first Martian captain?" He smiled.

"Congratulations on your promotion, Captain." Ezra nodded.

"Wait, can you do that?" asked Erin.

"I'm the Cohort Leader, of course I can," he said. "I imagine you'll know how to handle anyone who opposes your command."

"Of course, sir," Erin said, Vincent could see a smile cracking across her lips. "May I promote Blackwell to be my first sergeant?"

Vincent smiled. "Good choice."

"Why in the hell are we going to Titan?" Fiona asked.

"Arai thinks they will join us in destroying the Committee," Vincent said.

"More war then," Ezra said, his eyes cast downward.

"I don't want it either. But if we don't bring it to them, they're going to bring it back to us," Vincent said.

"What about Mars?" Erin asked.

"Arai wants to invade with Titanian forces to kick out the Committee," Vincent said.

"Holy shit," Erin gasped.

"That is truly.... ambitious," Ezra said.

"It's hardly the worst idea any of us have ever had." Vincent frowned. It wasn't even the worst plan of the last twenty-four hours.

"Sir, if we are going to liberate Mars you can't leave me here," Erin said.

"You misunderstand," Vincent said. "I need you to stay here to build the army we will use to liberate Mars."

"It is a noble cause, Captain Olympus," Ezra said. "You should be honored."

"Fine." Erin crossed her arms in frustration. "But I'm not doing it because it's noble." She glared at Ezra.

"Good." Vincent smiled.

"You better not have any plans about me not going," Fiona said. Vincent smiled, putting his arm around her shoulder.

"I don't think I could do that if I wanted too," he said.

"Sir, I hate to interrupt but I should check out the ship we will be using," Ezra said.

"Good idea. And we should get packing, we won't be coming back for a long time," Vincent said.

"Just think of all of this that you're going to miss." Erin frowned, motioning out to the smoldering skyline of the Human Quarter. It was almost all that remained of the Black Coat controlled part of town, what had once been the nice part. After the Fidayi finished off the last pockets of Black Coat resistance, there wasn't much of it left.

"I am going to miss the free drinks." Fiona laughed.

"Those drinks weren't free, you just weren't paying for them," Vincent said. "Blackwell has been keeping your tab for a year."

"Sounds like we need to get off world before he notices then, eh?" Fiona smirked.

The Elysian Space Port was a ruined mess. The birthing dock, which was supposed to be a large, flat surface for landing thousands of ships at once, was a field of shell craters and corpses. Vincent's nose curled as he took in the smell of the battlefield. The three days of fighting that the Black Coats had sparked in order to take as many ships as they could was still very evident.

Rhai, Mawr, and human teams were making slow progress collecting remains and patching up the countless holes that had blasted the area apart. Giant Rhai-built towers, where the ships were parked when not in use, were still burning, one having collapsed entirely. There was still a bustle of activity in the sky above them. Ships of various different makes and models landed and took off all around them.

"The Black Coats certainly did a number on the place," Ezra said.

"Bastards," Fiona cursed.

To Vincent's surprise, five humans with their hands tied behind their backs were being marched towards the Port Control building by a squad of Rhai Soldiers. Their faces were stained with filth and their tattered pants were bloody.

"Holy shit, they took prisoners," Vincent gasped.

"Hey, buddy what to your people normally do with prisoners?" Fiona asked Zinvor.

"What is this word? *Prisoner?*" Zinvor asked, his brow ruffled.

"well, that certainly doesn't bode well for them," Ezra said.

"Couldn't happen to a nicer bunch of guys," Vincent said.

"Are you not going to stop them, sir?" Ezra asked, obviously concerned. It gave Vincent pause.

"Fuck 'em," Fiona said.

"I understand your emotions Fiona. But the Laws of Land Warfare clearly state how Prisoners of War are to be treated," Ezra said, his voice hard.

"Shit," Vincent said, scratching his beard. "Zinvor, go stop them from executing them."

"What else do you do with one who has dishonored themselves by being captured in battle?" Zinvor asked, clearly confused. "We could offer them the chance to kill themselves in penance."

"Please, just do it." Vincent sighed. Zinvor sighed and strode off after them.

"Why are you saving them?" Fiona asked.

"Because Ezra's right," he said.

"They wouldn't spare us," she snarled.

"I thought we were supposed to be better than them?" he said.

"*You* keep saying that." She folded her arms across her chest. "I'd scalp them alive if I thought you'd let me."

"Just because you fight monsters, doesn't mean you should let yourself become one," Ezra said.

"Says the criminal." Fiona laughed. "Besides, I never said I wasn't a damn monster."

"That is a good point." Ezra rolled his eyes.

"The story of how you ended up a sentenced soldier is still one I'd like to hear," Vincent said. The strait-laced Ezra was someone he still couldn't quite figure out. Though he was sentenced, he was a staff officer and pilot. While sentenced officers weren't unheard of, they were exceedingly rare. And generally the EDF allowed their prized pilots, who took years to train, to do whatever they wanted with little more than a slap on the wrist as punishment.

"A story for another time perhaps," Ezra said nervously. "How about that ship we will be using?"

"I don't know, Arai said we would be meeting with a Rhai pilot that would bring us to it," Vincent said, looking around.

"You must be Consul Solaris," came a high-pitched voice from behind them. Vincent turned and saw a red Rhai, clad in a skin-tight white flight suit.

"Yes," Vincent said.

"Good. I am Flight Cohort Leader Vols," it said. "And you must be Lieutenant Colonel Vorbeck, I have heard much about your skills." Ezra nodded. "Due to our current situation, we have only one human ship left that is undamaged."

"It will need offensive capabilities," Ezra said.

"Of course," Vols said.

The group followed Vols across the damaged birthing dock. More and More ships in varying degrees of ruin were landing amongst the wreckage. The Elysian air capabilities had been badly mauled in a frighteningly short amount of time. The pursuit of the escaping Black Coats had clearly not gone the Clan's way. Rhai ground crews were pulling dead and wounded pilots of out ships while others hosed blood from the inside of troop transports.

Vols stepped in front of a door and touched his hand to a display panel next to it and it silently slid open. It dawned on Vincent that this was the first time he had stepped into one of the Rhai sky towers. Though the outside was still smoking and stank of battle, the inside of the tower was eerily quiet and spotlessly clean.

In front of them was a Fidayi ship, its windshield blown out and the cockpit stained with dark blood. Its crescent shaped wings were stitched with bullet holes. Ground crews were hurriedly working on piecing the destroyed ship back together with mismatched parts. When it came to the Clan, nothing was truly destroyed or put out of service. Every piece would be reused or refitted for another purpose. Nothing ever went to waste.

Their footsteps *clanged* off of the metal floor as they followed Vols through the repair dock and into a small tube-shaped lift. The group was a tight fit in the cramped confines. Vols maneuvered around Zinvor's bulk and pressed a button on the lift's wall. The lift didn't make a noise before its door slid open and revealed they had been transported to the next floor.

In front of them was a ship Vincent had never seen. The cockpit area looked like a Reaper, including the deadly cannon that Nox had used to rain destruction on the Black Coats. Behind the cockpit was a different hull. This one was double the length of a normal Reaper.

"Hm." Ezra looked at the contraption. "Is that a Comanche hull?"

"Indeed," Vols answered. "We were going to use it to land Warriors, so the extra cargo space was going to be needed. We managed to find enough pieces from some of the wreckage you humans brought back with you from Grawluck."

"I trust that it is air worthy?" Ezra asked.

"It has been tested within the atmosphere," Vols said. "It has passed testing to show it should be acceptable for flight in open space."

"Acceptable?" Vincent raised an eyebrow.

"Is that Rhai-speak for it could still kill you?" Fiona frowned.

"Relax." Ezra smiled. "That's normal. The vast majority of EDF ships are tested for their rating in open space on the ground too."

"Comforting," Vincent said.

"Hey, I've made it flying for twenty years and never crashed once. That is until I met you." Ezra smiled. He got closer to the ship and inspected the thick welds that tracked the area where the Rhai had pieced the ship together. Ezra ran his fingers over the seams and whistled. "It's not pretty but it'll do the job."

"I have also stocked the ship's stores with everything you'll need for your travels," Vols said.

"Whoa!" Ezra exclaimed, looking through the windshield. "There's already a gunner in here?"

"Yes. Warlord Arai informed me of your loss. I have supplied you with a recent graduate of our Gunners Mate Academy," Vols said. Vincent peeked through the window and saw a small, blue skinned Rhai sitting behind the controls of the passenger seat. It flipped switches and turned dials while reading from a data display.

"Right..." Ezra said, his eyebrow raised.

"I assure you our graduates are adequate for your needs," Vols said. "Also... due to the requirements of the war effort Cadet Tyr is all we have to offer you. Our losses have been steep."

"Thank you." Ezra smiled. "I'm sure the quality of your Cadets is top notch. I'm sure we will be fine."

"Yes. If you have any more needs, please let us know," Vols said before quickly walking off.

"Hello!" Ezra said to the Cadet in the passenger seat.

"Greetings, Colonel," it said in the normal high-pitched, monotone Rhai voice.

"So is Tyr your first name or...." Fiona asked, trying to make conversation.

"I can be correctly addressed as Cadet Tyr, or Tyr. It does not matter which," Tyr clarified.

"Man, they really are all the same, aren't they?" Fiona said.

Vincent nodded. "It seems that way."

"I'm not even sure if it's a guy or a girl." She sighed.

"To be completely honest, I didn't know with Nox either," Ezra said.

"I have never understood the human race's strict gender definitions," Tyr said. "It all seems very counter-productive to me."

"Wait, the Rhai are genderless?" Fiona asked.

"The Rhai are Rhai," Tyr said.

"That doesn't answer anything!" Fiona objected.

"So, Ezra..." Vincent said, changing the subject. "How long will it take us to get to Titan?"

"Not long. A few days, assuming we don't run into any issues."

"Issues?" Fiona asked.

"Well, odds are that the Black Coats left a rear-guard picket or something to keep an eye on the Clan's movements. Not to mention the possibility of Alliance ships out for raiding," he said. "We'll be fine as long as we don't run into a destroyer of some kind." Vincent remembered the terrifying power of an Alliance destroyer vividly. He had no intention of ever seeing one up close again.

"Well, let's get to it." Fiona smirked. "Unless you're having some kind of second thoughts about becoming an intergalactic diplomat for the entire Clan."

"When you put it that way, I am full of optimism." Vincent sighed.

CHAPTER SEVENTEEN

Vincent had no idea where they were. Space gave no inclinations about their location and he had no idea how to read the ship's instruments. Though, he was glad to see the dead, black expanse in front of him was free from other travelers. Once they were out of Elysian space and the lines of thousands of merchant crafts faded away, they were left completely alone to float through the great beyond.

Ezra no longer had to sit at the controls. Instead he left his second, Cadet Tyr, in the cockpit. Tyr showed no want or need of their companionship in the preceding days, so the group had left them alone. Tyr would eat and sleep in the cockpit, with Ezra only checking in every few hours. Vincent was sure this independent command was exactly what Ezra wanted in a co-pilot, but as far as the group dynamic was concerned, it was strange. Even Nox had socialized with them.

The rest of the group sat in the troop compartment. Since the Clan had modified the ship, it was much roomier than Ezra's first

Shanna. This time, bed rolls were laid out with boxes of rations piled up in the middle. As they were human in origin, Vincent assumed they were looted from the Black Coats' stores after the fighting. He was happy to see them, as even EDF rations were better than the tasteless Mawr food.

Ezra slathered some kind of peanut spread from a brown pouch over the top of a piece of vacuum-sealed bread and took a bite. After a few seconds of tense chewing he cleared his throat.

"How did you two become sentenced?" he asked.

"Mines simple." Fiona shrugged.

"Ah, I figured you were first born, but didn't want to make any assumptions." Ezra took another bite.

"She's spent her years since making up for it on the crime front." Vincent laughed.

"He's not wrong," she said.

"And you, sir?" Ezra asked.

"I destroyed my Ethics Book." He smiled. "Damn, that feels like that it was a whole lifetime ago."

"It kind of was, wasn't it?" Ezra asked. Back when Earth still existed. Before he was a traitor to the Committee. Before he had started ordering people to kill each other. Before he had killed.

"Yeah, I guess so." Vincent sighed. "So, what did you do?" he asked Ezra.

"My commanding officer charged me with disobeying an order and insubordination," Ezra said. "I was quickly found guilty... by him." He laughed.

"Wait, he charged and judged you?" Fiona asked. "That seems a little screwed up, even for the EDF."

"Well, when your being charged by the Military Governor of a planet, they tend to disregard EDF regulation." Ezra sighed.

"You don't mean..." Vincent began.

"Yes, sir. I was charged and sentenced by Governor General Brusilov." Ezra said, adding more spread to his bread. "Former Governor General, anyway."

"You fought on Mars?" Fiona asked.

"I've been in the EDF for over twenty years, Ma'am. I fought against more than one Martian uprising," Ezra said. "Nothing personal. I hold no ill-will against your people."

"But you killed them?" Vincent asked. He didn't understand the idea of a Professional Soldier. Someone who could kill without hate or malice in their hearts, but out of duty or honor or out of some other concept he couldn't grasp. The only reason Vincent wanted to fight the Committee or the Alliance was because he hated them.

"Yes." Ezra nodded. "I did my job and they did theirs," Ezra said. "I was better at mine so I'm still alive."

"If you did your job how come Brusilov charged you with insubordination?" Fiona asked.

"Remember how I told you about the Laws of Land Warfare?" Ezra asked.

"Yes," Vincent said.

"Well, Brusilov thought such a thing was antiquated and didn't apply to the Martian Rebels. I disagreed," Ezra said.

"There has to be more to it than that." Fiona frowned, folding her arms over her chest. "Out with it." Ezra sighed and closed his eyes.

"I had been a Wing Commander and was ordered to do strafing runs on a Rebel unit outside of Olympus. Eventually they broke and ran, Brusilov wanted us to press the attack. Normally, this wouldn't have been much of an issue. But the Martians had a tendency to have a large group of civilians that followed their armies. Tailors, gunsmiths, families, stuff like that. Well, I could see clearly the only forces getting away were wounded fighters or panicked women and children." Ezra closed his eyes, clearly the memories bothered him. "So, I ordered my wing to return to base."

"That's it?" Vincent asked.

"I know you're too young to remember, but the last uprising did a hell of a lot of damage to the EDF. Morale was low, we all just wanted to go home. Some officers were openly talking about appealing to the Central Committee for Brusilov's removal from Command," Ezra said. "I was made an example. The trial lasted about ten minutes and I was sentenced to forty years of service."

"It sounds like you got about the same sentence as me," Fiona said.

"Effectively." Ezra nodded. "To further drive home their point to other officers who might think orders are flexible they sentenced my Wife and kids too."

"They can do that?" Vincent exclaimed.

"It's rare, but it happens," Ezra said. "A clause called Guilt by Blood. Normally they only use it against Martians so they can wipe out an entire generation of Rebels at once. Normally, families are given a reprieve if they sign a divorce decree and denounce their spouse. She refused."

"She really loves you." Vincent smiled.

"Shanna was always stubborn as hell." Ezra smiled. "I remember before I went to pilot's school her Dad tried to talk her into leaving me. She wasn't going to hear any of it!" he said. "Man, I really pissed him off when I proposed to her when I was home on leave."

"Does she know you name your ship after her?" Vincent asked.

"Oh of course," Ezra said. "She hated it. I told her it was my to always make sure she was close to me."

"Wait, she isn't a soldier, so what did they sentence her too?" Fiona asked. Vincent was surprised to hear a tone of compassion in her voice. It wasn't something he was used to hearing from Fiona.

"She was a Professor at the Central Engineering College on Titan. So, they shipped her to the Women's Reeducation Facility on Earth. She actually chose that one because it allowed her to bring our three daughters." Ezra's gazed dropped. Vincent saw tears well up in his eyes.

"No..." Vincent said. "They were still there..." Ezra reached into the pocket of his flight suit and produced out a photo that he handed it to Vincent. He took it and looked down. A much younger Ezra and his smiling in front of a rose garden.

"I'm so sorry Ezra," Fiona gasped.

"It's okay." He wiped tears away from his face. "At least they didn't feel anything. Just a flash and everything was gone, yeah?"

"That's what the Mawr told me," Vincent said.

"Vincent," Ezra said, his eyes locking onto Vincent's. "Can you promise me something?"

"Anything."

"This all of this works out somehow, and we get the chance. Brusilov is mine."

Vincent awoke as the ship began to rock. To his surprise, Tyr was asleep in their bed roll across from him on the floor. Like always, Zinvor lay on the bare metal floor, fast asleep in his armor.

Vincent was careful to not wake Fiona. She was curled up next to him, fast asleep. She lay amongst a small graveyard of cigarette butts. A small puddle of drool had formed around her mouth and she moaned as he pushed the covers off of himself.

Ezra sat at the controls of the ship. His feet were kicked up on the cockpit and he had a data display open in his hands.

"Sorry if the rocking woke you," Ezra said over his shoulder. "That'll pick up as we get closer." Vincent looked past Ezra and out of the windshield. In front of them, still a ways off, was a small green dot.

"Is that Titan?" he asked.

"Yes, sir." Ezra smiled. "I haven't seen that beautiful little rock since I graduated from flight school."

"It's my first time," Vincent said. "Actually, I've never been to any of our core worlds other than Earth." Vincent sat down in the passenger seat next to Ezra. "Unless we are counting Elysian now."

"I've seen them all," Ezra said, setting his display aside. "Titan is by far the best."

"What did you think of Earth?" Vincent asked.

"Ugly. Nothing but featureless grey buildings and featureless grey people," Ezra said. "I saw in old books that it used to look a lot like Titan. But after the unification the Committee just urbanized everything. Squeezed the life out of everything."

"Titan looks different?" he asked.

"Oh yes." Ezra nodded. "I remember taking the girls for walks through the giant Prime National Forest before I deployed to Mars. Trees as tall as buildings and lakes the size of city blocks."

"I don't think I've ever seen a real tree before," Vincent said. He had seen them in books and movies. And once onboard the *Victory* in a simulation. But never a real one.

"No wonder you Earthians are always so unhappy." Ezra laughed. "You exist in some Committee planned, concrete jungle. Did they still ban you from going off world?"

"Yeah. Though some people could leave their district if they had approval from the Central Office." Vincent forced a smiled.

"But that normally required you to get into some important school or something."

"They were afraid you would go to Lunar City and see how the members of the Committee really lived. Or come to Titan and see how they let us live."

"The Ethics Police would have probably just shot me if I tried to go off world," Vincent sneered. The Ethics Police. The jackbooted assholes who ruled every Earth District with an iron fist. They enforced the rules and directives of the Committee with extreme prejudice. It was the Ethics Police who had arrested Vincent and set him down the road that led him to sitting in the back of a ship with Ezra.

"We never had Ethics Police," Ezra said.

"You're kidding me," Vincent gasped. "How could there be a Central Committee without Ethics Police?

Ezra shook his head. "Tell me, was there any Titanians in your Regiment?"

Vincent thought for a moment. He couldn't remember ever seeing one. Lunar natives known as Loons, Martians, and Earthians all fought alongside him on Ryklar, but not a single Titanian. He thought it was strange at the time, but assumed it was just because waiting for Titan to send its conscripts to their sector of space would have taken too long.

"No," Vincent said. "Not that I saw."

"And why they sent Shanna to Earth as punishment," Ezra continued. "The Titan-Earth unification pact was a tense one. After the Wars, the Committee launched to put down the Martian settlements, they knew a war against us would be horrible. It could have even threatened the Committee's hold over Earth. We saw what they did to Mars and knew we couldn't let that happen to our beloved homeland."

"So you struck a deal?" Vincent asked.

"Precisely," Ezra said. "We would send a certain number of conscripts to the EDF, though they would serve in their own units. Travel between our worlds would be restricted, we would pay committee taxes, but in turn they would leave us alone."

"But why in the hell would someone as strong as the Committee bargain with Titan?" Vincent raised an eyebrow. "No offense."

"None taken." Ezra smiled. "Why do you think humans originally settled in the Titan cluster?"

"I don't remember." He scratched his chin. School had never been his strong point.

"Hydrocarbon Fuel," Ezra said matter-of-factly. "The lifeblood of humanity. It powers our lights, aerocars, ships, you name it. The Titan cluster is the only place we have ever discovered that it develops naturally."

"So, all the gas we used on Earth started on Titan?" Vincent asked.

"You got it." Ezra nodded. "It all forms on Rhea. We helpfully pointed out to the committee how easy it would be for us to move our settlements from Rhea to one of the other nearby moons and destroy their only source of fuel if we even heard a rumor of them trying to make a move on us. It didn't take long for them to see reason and come to an agreement."

"I know nothing they do should surprise me anymore but here I am, surprised. I would have figured the Committee would try to take over Titan with settlements, like they did Mars," Vincent said.

"Oh, they're there." Ezra nodded. "But the Committee was more scared of them turning to our side, rather than the other way around. So, their settlements turned into little more than walled off compounds that nobody ever leaves."

"So, when Earth fell, what do you think happened on Titan?"

"I would imagine every Titanian's taxes went down." Ezra laughed. "I'm sure over the years some loyalist sympathies formed, hell even the Martians have Committee loyalists, but I doubt the Prime Minister had a hard time crushing them."

"Wait, the Martian's have Committee Loyalists?" Vincent asked. He assumed every Martian was as full of hate towards the committee as Fiona was.

"Of course. It's been generations since the Martians had real independence. Just think, how many of your family members went to an Ethics School, ran by the Committee?" Ezra asked.

"Everyone. As far back as anyone can remember," Vincent said.

"Same with them," Ezra said. "How loyal were your classmates in comparison to you?"

"incredibly loyal for the most part," Vincent said. He had a vivid memory of his Father and brother waiting, silently, as his fate was decided. He got off lightly with just a few years of EDF service, but he had no doubt they would have waited with the same stoicism if the sentence would have been death.

He had volunteered his life in exchange for Fiona's on Grawluck when Molke's hangmen came calling. Meanwhile, his father sat there like a coward while some bastard from the Committee sentenced him. Their sentence could have killed him, instead it was they who were dead. All of them.

"Exactly," Ezra said, breaking Vincent's thought process. "Their hope is for every little rebel like you that pops up, the State eventually snuffs you out, or you shut up and go with the crowd to save your own ass. Same thing for Mars. It was working, abet slowly. They control the population by punishing entire families and elevating the loyal ones," Ezra said. "For instance, anyone you know with the last name Olympus was probably some element from the underworld, the family of a Rebel, or some other malcontent. If they were loyal to the Committee they would have been allowed to take a surname and move out to Tharsis or Victoria. Though, their first born still would have been property of the EDF."

"Fiona," Vincent said, he knew she was one of the Olympus' he spoke of.

"A street kid turned ganger I assume with those tattoos," Ezra said. "Not a lot of options out there for a first born with the conscription rules. She seems smart though, it's curious how the EDF recruiters were able to get their hands on her."

"What do you mean?" Vincent asked. Fiona was undeniably smart, though in an unconventional way. No one was ever going to confuse her for a scholar, but if you were going to find someone who could survive just about anything, it would be her.

"The EDF recruiters are notoriously easy to dodge in Olympus," Ezra said. "They have so many kids to track coming of age for conscription every year, it's impossible to keep up with them all. Most of them have no fixed address and going into any of the ganger areas would be a death sentence for a Recruiter. Any street kid with half a brain dodges them," he said. "Most who fall into the state's grasp are either dumb as a rock or running away from something."

"Fiona certainly isn't dumb." Vincent frowned. "And I don't think I've ever seen her run away from anything."

"There are outliers of course." Ezra held up his hands. "Just saying what I've seen." Before Vincent could cut in for her defense further, the ship's radio crackled.

"Approaching unmarked vessel," the voice came over the radio. "This is the Union of Titan Naval Vessel *Rebirth*. Identify yourself at once." Ezra leaned down and pressed a button before holding the microphone of his flight helmet up to his face.

"This is the Fidayi Clan Vessel *Shanna II.*" Vincent smiled when he heard the ship's new name. "Requesting Permission to land."

"Received *Shanna II,*" came the voice. "Request to land is accepted, we have been expecting you. You are clear to land on Grand Titan."

CHAPTER EIGHTEEN

The *Shanna II* slowed as it made the approached towards Titan. Fiona sat with her face pressed against the cabin window.

"It's so green," she said. Vincent sat down next to her and looked out. They hadn't yet broken through Titan's atmosphere, but Vincent could already see the world below them was a swirling marble of greens and blues, all coming together like a painting. Streaking through the sky next to them was the sleek, silver shape of another ship. Then, on the other side was another one. They were being escorted.

Zinvor sat on the ground behind them, cleaning his Riten, totally uninterested in the scene that unfolded around him. In front of him he had his armor taken apart and laid out. He spent hours cleaning every square inch of it during the flight. The black Tsarra armor shone under the white lights of the ship's interior. Vincent suddenly felt unclean.

He pulled himself away from the window and forced himself into the ship's cramped bathroom. A small piece of polished metal was bolted to the wall to act as a mirror. The reflection that looked back at Vincent was foggy and distorted.

He looked at his ear, or what was left of it. The bullet he had taken on Elysian had torn off everything below the middle of his ear. A well-meaning medic had tried to mend the wound, but it looked like her efforts had just mangled it further. Dried blood had crusted around the where the medic had sewn it shut and the skin around it was an angry red color.

He pressed down on a dull metal button above the sink's faucet and water gurgled out. He splashed the frigid water onto his face and watched the water bead off of his beard. He tried to wash away the crusted blood but winced in pain when the cold water met skin. He thought it best not to test the medic's handiwork too hard. Vincent sighed. He was going to meet the ruler of Titan while smelling like a battlefield and covered in his own blood.

He stepped out of the bathroom to see Fiona rummaging through the duffle bag they had brought with them. She had pulled out most of the clothes, throwing them onto the ground around her.

"What are you doing?" he asked.

"Blackwell got us some uniforms, I forgot where I put them," she said.

"Uniforms?" he asked. He had assumed this whole time their uniforms were their Mawr armor. Though, he had to admit that would look strange in a diplomatic meeting with his fellow humans. Worst still, he had never cleaned his armor and he was hardly presentable.

"Yeah. He says it's supposed to make us look all professional or some shit," she said, finally pulling two Khaki-colored uniforms out of the bag. She tossed one over to him and he caught the ball of cloth. When he unfolded it he saw it was a normal EDF uniform, though it had been dyed tan and the Eagle and Star flag on the right shoulder was replaced with a badly sewn Phoenix which had become the flag of the Elysian Humans. On the left shoulder was the Clan flag of a crossed Riten and sword.

"How did he dye these?" Vincent asked.

"Turns out this is the color they come out as when the cheap EDF uniforms are soaked with Blackwell's moonshine. Just bleeds the grey right out of them," Fiona said.

"Fitting," Vincent snorted. "But what does it do to our insides then?" Fiona shrugged, nonplussed.

On the hem of the uniforms pants was a black stripe, running from hip to ankle. That was normally reserved for commissioned officers of the EDF, not whatever Vincent was. Sure, Arai had appointed him Cohort Leader, but to be considered an equal of an officer he was pretty sure he would have attended at least one day of Officer's Academy.

Instead of the grey cloth field cap he had normally wore there was an officer's peaked cap, also khaki. The pin at its center was a mangled gold Eagle whose Star, normally held in its talons, had been snapped off. Vincent assume it was supposed to resemble a Phoenix, though now the bird was also missing its feet.

"Damn, look at you." Fiona whistled. "He just gave me this." She unfurled a plain khaki uniform with the new shoulder patches.

"Well, no one is really sure what rank or position you have. You didn't make it easy for them."

"I don't need a damn rank." She smirked. "They know who I am." Ezra cleared his throat from the cockpit.

"Maybe you two should get dressed. We'll be on the ground in about three minutes."

Vincent quickly fumbled his way into his new uniform. He had to give Blackwell credit, it fit well for what he assumed was little more than a guess at his size. The uniform was stiff with starch and sharp creases cut down the pants.

"How do I look?" Vincent asked.

"Like some asshole officer that neither of us wanted to listen to a year ago." Fiona laughed.

"You look better in armor," Zinvor grunted. "Warriors do not wear cloth into combat."

"We aren't going into combat, Zinvor," Ezra said in a slightly fatherly voice. Zinvor didn't respond. "I think you look presentable, sir." Ezra smiled. "You could use a haircut though."

"Yeah, you might be right." Vincent ran a hand through his hair, which was pulled lazily back into something resembling a ponytail. "They might think the Consul is some homeless dude."

"They wouldn't be far off," Fiona said, struggling to button the top button on her jacket, before finally giving up.

"Hey, we have an apartment," Vincent said defensively. "That...was turned into a field hospital last time I checked."

"Game face you two," Ezra said. "We are coming in for the final approach."

Vincent and Fiona stood watching the city of Grand Titan pass in front of them. Gone were the featureless grey skyscrapers that were the norm on Earth, when the Earth had a norm. Gran Titan was crowded with tall, glass sided towers of various shapes and colors. Neon lights and signs blinked advertising shops and entertainment. The sky was crowded with aero cars and ships. The endless rows of cookie-cutter Family Housing blocks were replaced with angled brick and mortar houses and blocks of apartment buildings.

The *Shanna II* circled and began to land. Below them was a featureless building that stretched up thousands of stories.

Hundreds of landings platforms branched off of it likes leaves on a tree, each crowded with ships and personnel.

"Where are we landing?" Vincent asked.

"At the Defense Directorate," Ezra said.

"And that is?" he asked again.

"Ugh." Ezra rolled his eyes. "The Military headquarters of Titan. I gave you a book to read up on this," Ezra scolded him. Vincent had meant to read it during the trip, but it had remained unopened in his bag.

"I...uh...was busy," Vincent said. He had actually been asleep.

The ship glided down to land in the middle of a circle of lights. Drummers and horn players began to play, muffled by the walls of the ship. When Ezra finally opened the doors, their music rose into a swell to greet them. Vincent froze in the doorway. There was at least a platoon of soldiers was on either side of a red carpeted walkway, their rifles held out in a stiff *present arms.* Camera drones floated along above them, their shutters snapping as fast as a machine gun burst.

This wasn't just a welcoming party. This was a welcoming party *for him.*

Fiona snapped him out of it by pushing past him and stepping out on to the walkway, followed by Zinvor. A few of the soldiers went wide-eyed at the sight of the Mawr Tsarra. Vincent forced himself to walk forward, his legs suddenly feeling like they were made of stone.

At the end of the walkway was an older man in a black suit and tie. His thinning silver hair was combed back over his head and he had a cane clasped in his hands. Next him was an even older man, stooped with age. He had glasses perched at the end of a crooked nose and a face framed with a white beard. The chest of his dark grey uniform was heavy with medals and he wore a sword on his hip. On his collar was the rank of field marshal.

"Consul Solaris," beamed the man in the suit, a smile splitting his features. The drones swooped in low to get more pictures, hovering only inches away from them. "Welcome to the Union of Titan."

"Th-thank you," Vincent struggled.

"Prime Minister Addler," Ezra whispered into Vincent's ear.

"Prime Minister," Vincent added.

"Shall we go inside?" Addler asked, his arms outstretched and motioned towards the massive double doors behind him.

"Of course." Vincent nodded.

The two old men turned and began to walk towards the doors and the welcoming party, now with their rifles shouldered, fell into ranks and followed behind them. The band's music died away as the doors closed behind them.

Vincent gasped in awe at the giant dining room they had walked into. High ceilings arced overhead, heavily decorated with scenes of Titanian Soldiers engaging in combat. Marble columns rose from the floor up to the scenes, each of them wrapped with intricate engravings. A long table, suitable for twenty people stretched out in front of them with as many seats.

"Are we eating dinner?" Fiona asked.

"Of course, Ma'am." Addler smiled. "It is Titanian custom to eat while we discuss important matters." He glanced at Zinvor. "Has your friend ever had human food before?"

"He's a fan of beer, that much I know," Fiona said.

"Er—we have been short of what you would consider regular human food on Elysian," Vincent said.

"I can only imagine," Addler said, his smile fading slightly. "Please have a seat."

Addler sat at the head of the table, with the field marshal sitting next to him. Vincent took the seat to Addler's right side. The table was set with fine glass plates and crystal glasses.

"I see you came armed," Addler said. "I can assure you that is not how we do business here." Vincent had hardly noticed that the three of them still carried Ritens. Ezra had, as always, been one step ahead and left his weapon in the ship.

"Oh!" Vincent exclaimed. "That isn't what these mean." He forced a smile. "You see, the Mawr consider these guns sacred. It would be considered a dishonor to be without them."

"Think of them as much of a weapon as an officer's saber," Ezra added, helpfully. Though, not entirely true, a look of understanding come over the Titanian's faces.

"Interesting. And both of you have one as well." Addler raised an eyebrow.

"Yes. The Warlord gifted them to use during our fight against the Alliance last year," Vincent said.

"Now that is something we would like to know about." Addler slapped the table, the glasses shaking. "Two humans running off and fighting with the...Mawr was it?"

"Well—" Vincent began, but was cut off by Fiona.

"The Committee left us to die on Ryklar and the Clan saved us. After the Committee got the Earth destroyed on Grawluck the Clan took in all of the survivors," she said. "We owe them our lives."

Vincent groaned. He was hoping to be more diplomatic.

"Right," Addler said. "They certainly seem much more pragmatic than the Committee ever was. Unfortunately, their good intentions were ruined by Brusilov I hear."

"You know about that?" Vincent asked.

"Of course," Addler said. "Warlord Arai filled us in."

"Well, we chased him off." Fiona folded her arms. "Piece of shit made off with a lot of the Clan's ships though."

"You chased off nothing," growled the field marshal. "You fell right into that old bastard's plan."

"Hey—" Fiona began. Vincent saw the anger welling up in her face.

"You misunderstand me, I don't mean to offend," the field marshal cut in. "Brusilov is a legendary tactical mind. By all accounts, your forces presented themselves on the field brilliantly, all things considered. You were even able to stop his secondary objective."

"Secondary objective?" Vincent asked. Arai hadn't told him about any secondary objective. He was under the impression that Brusilov's only goal was getting off of Elysian.

"To kill the Great Traitor of course." Addler smiled. Vincent frowned, his nickname had managed to travel through thousands of miles of space and to an entirely different planet.

"It certainly would have won him some points with the new Chairman," the field marshal laughed. "I must know, how exactly did you manage to survive?"

"Um..." Vincent thought for a moment. The Black Coats had been broken by their airborne assault against suicidal odds. "They were overconfident, I think. They assumed they had us pinned down and we launched a counterattack."

"You attacked them?" the field marshal exclaimed, a smile spreading across his face, clearly entertained by the story "From my understanding you were outnumbered ten to one."

"If I may," Ezra said. "We assaulted their stronghold with one Reaper gunship. On the ground a squad of Clan Warriors and a squad of our scouts attacked their air defense and artillery."

"If *I may*," Fiona cut in, her voice dripping with sarcasm. "We fucked them up," the field marshal broke into laughter.

"I don't believe I have introduced myself. I am Field Marshal Oscar Denta. Commander of the Union of Titan's military. And young lady I like you."

"I'm formerly Private Fiona Olympus of the Earth Defense Force." Fiona nodded. "Nice to meet you."

"Now that introductions are out of the way, how about we eat?" Addler grinned. With a clap of his hands two doors on either side of the room opened and a long train of people entered.

Each server was wearing a pearl white uniform. They had ribbons of awards on their chests and had various ranks pinned to the collars of their crisp jackets. Each of them had at least one platter of food held aloft in their hands, some carried bottles of wine or liquor.

"Now we're talking," Fiona said, her voice giddy. Vincent tried to keep his cool, but the aroma of the food was nearly intoxicating. One of the soldiers set a plate down in front of him, quickly flanking it with a tall glass of red wine.

His plate had a hearty slice of beef, red juices oozing out of the fresh cuts. A pile of mashed potatoes, with a small sprinkling of something green on them, and a dark gravy was poured over all of it. Vincent stared down at it, in wide-eyed shock. He hadn't had real food since he had left Earth. His dad was no chef by any means, but it was definitely better than Defense Force rations and Mawr food.

Next to him, Fiona attacked her food like it had offended her. She had the whole piece of beef held up to her mouth by a fork and was tearing at it with their teeth. Zinvor, clearly unsure of what to do in the situation, copied her. Ezra, giving sideways glances at the two, cut strips from his dinner and ate them carefully.

"So, Consul Solaris," Addler said. "Tell me, are the stories about the destruction of Earth true?"

"Which one?" Vincent asked. "The one where I did it, or the one that makes sense?" Addler laughed.

"As you can imagine we opposed the plan, but there wasn't anything we could do to stop the Committee's plans for Grawluck."

"Is that why only a few token units of the Titanian military were deployed to Grawluck?" Ezra asked.

"We convinced the Committee we would be useful as a blocking force against possible Alliance reinforcement. I am sorry you ended up being one of them, Colonel," Denta said in between bites. "We couldn't save all of Titan's children, but we saved as many as we could."

"We knew the operation was going to go badly. But as bad as it did? Not in our worst nightmares," Addler said. "You won't find many Committee loyalists in Titan, but we would never wish the Earth to be destroyed. I am sorry for your loss Consul Solaris."

"Yeah..." Vincent trailed off. "We were trying to destroy the weapons. To ensure they could never be used against anyone again...well, you see how that worked."

"A noble cause," Addler said, raising his wine glass. "To the fallen." Ezra raised his glass.

"To those who will fall," he added.

"And curse the bastards who need to fall." Denta raised his to join in. They reached across the table and clinked their glasses together before taking a drink. The wine tasted like bitter, rotten fruit to Vincent. He drank deep from his glass anyway.

"I think we all know who needs to fall," he said, finishing his glass.

"You speak of the new Committee I take it?" Addler asked.

"The Committee is a damned cancer. It'll keep spreading if we don't cut it out entirely," Vincent said as a soldier leaned in and refilled his glass.

"Add to it they are too stupid to work with the Clan to fight the Alliance," Fiona chimed in.

"And, if you were in charge," Addler said, leaning back in his chair. "What would you want to do?"

"It's not about what I want to do. I never *wanted* to go to war," Vincent said. "It is about what we need to do. About what we have to do in order to survive." He could see Addler looked uninterested while Denta was paying close attention. "I would do whatever we can do to ensure the Committee, and whoever calls themselves Chairman, is as thoroughly destroyed as Earth was. Until that happens, we can't pay full attention to the Alliance."

"You want Titan to go to war then?" Addler frowned.

"War is coming to Titan whether you like it or not," Vincent countered. "If the Committee secures Mars, say good-bye to your newfound independence." Vincent took another drink, feeling like he was on a roll. "If the Committee loses, they run back to their hide out in Lunar City and then the Alliance swoops in and kills or enslaves everyone anyway."

"Last I heard the Alliance was solidly defeated on Grawluck. Set to route even," Denta said.

"We gave them a bloody nose at best." Vincent shook his head. "They underestimated us, and we can bet they won't do that again. The Clan are holding them back for now, but the line is slipping. They can't do that for very long on their own."

"And what do you think of the capabilities of the Alliance, were they to direct their full attention to the Milky Way?" Denta asked.

"Demons," Zinvor growled. "You do not stand a chance against them." His ominous warning was slightly undercut by the fact he had gravy smeared all around his mouth. "No one can stand against them alone."

"I am forced to agree with him," Vincent said. "The Rhai tried to stand alone. Now they're enslaved. The Mawr tried to stand alone, they got their home destroyed too. We're next if we don't get our shit together."

"So what are you getting at here Solaris?" Addler said, dropping Vincent's title for the first time. It was clear his patience was running thin.

"Titan allies with the Clan, together we ensure that the Committee is kicked from Mars," Vincent said. "After that, we might be able to stop the Alliance."

"You pose a union with a gaggle of Aliens and Martians?" Addler stifled a laugh. "You must be mad." Vincent felt his face get hot. Even then, facing the greatest threat that humanity has ever faced, old human xenophobia reared its head.

"Says the man who has done *nothing* to fight the Committee or the Alliance," Vincent shot back, rising to his feet. "Instead you sit here and get fat and drunk while we do all of the fighting!"

"Boy, you forget yourself!" Addler yelled, getting to his feet to meet him.

"Go fuck yourself old man!" Fiona snarled at him. "You're the one too damn stupid to see that we need each other!"

"You would want me to send in my soldiers to fight *your* war on that red hellhole. Again," Addler spat. For all that Ezra had told him how much different Titan was than Earth, it had become clear to Vincent that the old feelings towards Martians still existed. "And the fact I even entertained having one of these *beasts* at my table," he said, staring daggers at Zinvor. At that, Zinvor rose to his feet and sent the chair he was sitting on slamming to the floor behind him.

"That is enough," seethed Denta, who had remained seated and drinking from his glass during the exchange. "I can see this is going nowhere. If you'll excuse us." Denta nodded to the doorman behind the table, who then opened a side door. Denta and the Prime Minster beat a hasty retreat. The doorman motioned for Vincent to follow him.

Vincent boiled with rage. He couldn't get out of the dining hall fast enough. He stormed off, following the doorman down a hallway. The hallway was decorated by military portraits of people Vincent had never seen before that hung in between each door. There seemed to be dozens of doors, each with ornately decorated silver handles. The doorman stopped at one door, rendering a crisp salute to Ezra.

"For Colonel Vorbeck and the...Mawr visitor," the doorman announced. Vincent could see that doorman, who he thought was little more than a servant of some kind, was wearing the rank of a staff sergeant on his collars.

"We have to share a room?" Ezra asked.

"Yes sir. We only have two rooms readied for diplomatic guests at the moment," the Doorman said.

"I am okay with this." Zinvor nodded and walked into the room. Ezra rolled his eyes and followed after him. The Doorman walked down to the next door and snapped to attention and gave another salute, this time to Vincent.

"Consul Solaris and Ms. Olympus this room his yours," he said.

"Thanks." Vincent nodded.

The room Vincent stepped into was without a doubt the nicest he had ever been in in his life. A wall to wall window gave them a flawless view of the Grand Titan skyline. The four-post bed had dozens of pillows piled at the head on top of a snow-white comforter. Fiona hurried over to a door and opened it, unveiling a full bathroom.

"I can take a hot shower," she gasped. She spun around and saw a towering liquor cabinet, an ornate wooden thing with gold trim. "And there's a full bar!"

"Look at that bed." Vincent gasped, his anger at Addler momentarily deflated. He hadn't slept on much more than a bed roll or a creaky bunk bed since he had left earth.

There wasn't much of a conversation after that. Fiona stripped off of her clothes and jumped in the shower. The hot water steamed up the entire bathroom and sent a dense cloud drifting into the rest of the room.

Vincent played with a clear screen that was mounted on the wall. After fiddling with it for a few moments it turned on, revealing itself to be a television. On it two people wearing entirely too much makeup talked about the goings on in Grand Titan that evening. A woman in a red jacket talked in excited tones about the Alien diplomats from what they called *The Clan of Elysian*. Soon the screen turned to photos and video of Vincent exchanging salutes with Addler and Denta. That bastard Addler smiled and welcomed them into the Directorate like he was actually willing to agree to something other than his own greatness.

Vincent sat down on the bed and cursed himself. He had let that old bastard get to him way to fast. They had to be playing some kind of political game, he just wasn't sure what it was. He was clearly working a few levels behind these damn professionals. What did he know about political intrigue? They wouldn't have invited him there if the idea of working with Aliens disgusted as much as Addler pretended it did.

And that Denta, relaxed and cool throughout the entire exchange. He sat back eating and drinking while they had screamed at each other like nothing what happening. And

Addler, the man who was supposed to be in charge, shut up when Denta told him. Was Denta really the one in charge?

"Hey," Fiona's voice came from the bathroom. Vincent's thought process was broken when he looked up and saw her standing in the doorway. She was naked and dripping wet from the shower. Her black tattoos stood out against her pale, white skin. "Get your ass up and get in here." She smirked. He got up, stripping off of his uniform and tossing it on the ground. He moved into her embrace and the steam enveloped them both.

*　　　*　　　*

Another night that Vincent couldn't sleep. Like always Fiona was long since passed out next to him. He stared at her, her slowly rising and falling chest, and the small bit of drool forming at the corner of her mouth. Her body was an illustration of a hard life. Her slender body was made of tough, sinewy muscle.

She was covered in various small, dimed sized black tattoos, all of which had obviously been done by an unskilled hand. Where there wasn't tattoos, there were the scars. Countless in number, and mysterious in origin. She had never elaborated on them and he didn't want to push the issue.

Vincent was pulled away by a soft knock at the door. He sat up, careful not to wake Fiona. Vincent walked slowly over to the door and opened it to reveal an empty hallway. A small white piece of paper was attached to the door with a strip of tape. He pulled it off and shut the door.

On the paper was a quickly scribbled note that said simple:

Tomorrow night be in the hallway at 1130. Consul comes alone.

-OD.

He had apparently not been that quiet. When he turned around Fiona was sitting up in bed rubbing the sleep from her eyes.

"Someone sent you a love letter?" she asked, still a little groggy.

"Yeah, someone named OD," he said.

"Oscar Denta," Fiona said. "I kind of figured he was really in charge," she said off handedly. He wondered if he was the last person to catch onto that fact.

"Then I wonder what that little charade was at dinner."

"A test," Fiona said.

"You think?" Vincent asked.

"I just assume everything with these old political fucks is a test. It's why I like the Fidayi more than humans these days. They might just want to shoot everything, but at least they're straight forward." She leaned across to a nightstand and retrieved a pack of cigarettes and lit one. "Who needs politics when you can just shoot the people that piss you off?"

"Why would they need to test me?" Vincent fumed. "It's pretty clear I'm not a damn committee loyalist."

"Maybe to see if you were still a loyal human?" she mused.

"But I'm not," Vincent spat. "The only beings I've ever met worse than humans are the Anarchs." He didn't have to point out he had a hand in killing hundreds, if not thousands, of his fellow humans only a few days before on Elysian. Or when he charged the trenches on Grawluck. Not to mention the small hand he had in destroying his own planet.

"Yeah, humans are pretty terrible." She grinned and blew out smoke.

"Ugh," Vincent moaned and sat down heavily on the bed. "I'm in over my head."

"You have been since day one," Fiona said. "But who wouldn't be?"

"A competent person." He sighed. "Someone that knows what they're doing."

"Believe it or not, you are competent." Fiona scooted across the bed to be closer to him. "That old bastard tried to show how much better he was than you and browbeat you into submission. You didn't take that shit. You stood up for everyone on Elysian. You stood up for what we stand for." That wasn't how Vincent remembered it. It was more like a whiney outburst because he wasn't getting his way. He was discovering more and more that was what politics were in the end.

"I'm just glad I'm getting another chance." Vincent scratched his beard.

"How about we celebrate then?" Fiona smirked. Vincent wasn't sure what there was to celebrate about.

"What are we celebrating exactly?" he asked.

"Being on Titan." She smiled. "If you don't remember..."

"It was our original plan." Vincent laughed. Before the destruction of Earth, before he had become Consul, before they found themselves in the middle of a three-way intergalactic war, they originally planned to run from the Committee and hide on Titan. She insisted it was the only place in the galaxy a Martian would be treated fairly. Their exchange with Addler at dinner had proved otherwise.

"Come on," She begged. "It'll be fun! When's the last time we actually had fun."

"Last night." Vincent smirked. Fiona pushed him and he laughed. "Fine, fine."

The streets of Grand Titan were unlike anything Vincent had ever seen. Narrow, neatly laid out walkways bustled with people going about their way. Above their heads aerocars jockeyed for position for miles. Skyscrapers with glass or brick facades held in place by ornately designed columns lined each side of the walkway. They stretched up into the cloudless sky, cutting through the sky traffic above.

At the base of each skyscraper were colorful store fronts ringed with flowers and plants. Crowds of people were lined up outside of them happily chatting away. Unlike the identical grey citizens uniforms of Earth which were mandatory when you traveled outside of the home, everyone's clothes were unique and vibrantly colored.

Groups passing by eyed them with curiosity. He wasn't sure if it was because they had seen the news from the night before or because it was the first time seeing a Mawr up close. Zinvor made himself more of a spectacle by plowing through groups of people as he walked, sending more than one of them sprawling to the ground. On Elysian, forcing your way through the streets was the custom. The alien races of the Clan had no real concept of personal space. Vincent had forgotten to tell Zinvor that doing the same thing in a human city just made you an asshole.

"This is the place!" Ezra called out. He had stopped in front of a small bar with a sign above the door that was decorate with a cartoonish version of a Reaper with arms and legs, drinking a beer. Under it said *Tipsy Wings.* "Haven't been here since before I got married." Ezra smiled.

"It looks like a dump." Vincent frowned. The bar had clearly seen better days. The large plate glass window near the door was cracked and smudged. Unlike every other store around it, there were no lights out front. Even the dingy bricks that had once been red, were stained with dirt, grime, and another substance Vincent thought looked like piss. Drunk young men and women in flight suits or dress uniforms were seated at several tables in a fenced off around in the open alleyway next door.

"The man who lived in an apartment above a bar that is full of corpses is calling this bar a dump?" Ezra raised an eyebrow.

"At least I have an apartment," Vincent shot back. "And besides, why would we leave that dump just to come to another dump on a different planet?"

"Because this is *my* dump." Ezra grinned.

They walked through the door of the bar and was unsurprised to see it packed with more uniformed soldiers. Large graphics of ships speeding through space in some unknown dogfight lined the walls. Bench tables stretched across the length of the building in neat rows, each with about ten soldiers apiece at it.

The bar, once loud and raucous, fell silent when they entered. Vincent, who had thought that the eyes were mostly trained on Zinvor, now felt the full force of their collective gaze. He couldn't read the room. He wasn't sure if their stares were of hatred, anger, or shock.

"So, are you going to fight us or buy us drinks you bunch of bitches?" Fiona barked, breaking the deathly silence. Slowly, a ripple of laughter went through the bar. Soldiers jumped up from their seats trying to offer Fiona or Vincent their drink. Several of them looked at Ezra, worried.

"Don't worry boys, I'm not a colonel in the EDF anymore." Ezra reassured them. "Do what you like." The bar erupted in cheers once again and someone handed him a tall glass of beer. The crowd had ignored Zinvor completely until he thrust one of his thick paws out and snatched a drink from an unsuspecting soldier's hand. The soldier recoiled in terror, giving up his beer without a fight.

"Cheers for the Great Traitor!" Called out a man with the shoulder insignia of a captain. The rest of the bar copied him.

"Great," Vincent moaned. "The name followed me here."

"I think you're just going to have to accept that you're not Vincent to anyone anymore." Ezra laughed.

"So why is this your bar?" Fiona asked.

"I nearly forgot," Ezra said. "Look." He led the group through the throngs of drunken, cheering soldiers to a table near the back of the bar. Next to the table was a picture of a Cadet, while decades younger, Vincent could tell that it was Ezra. A caption on a small metal plaque under it said simply: *The Vorbeck.*

"The Vorbeck?" Vincent asked. "I'm not sure if that's ominous or honoring."

"It's a drink," he said, obviously very proud. Ezra turned towards the bartender, an attractive young woman with dark hair. "Four Vorbecks!"

"How the hell did you get a drink named after you?" Fiona asked as the bartender rushed up to them with the drinks balanced precariously on a platter. The bartender passed the drinks out diligently to each person before hurrying off to the next yelling soldier. "Especially a strait-laced old fucker like you."

"It's a tradition from flight school," Ezra said, grabbing the small drink and downing it in one gulp. He winced in pain as the drink worked its way through his body. Everyone else followed suit.

Vincent put the shot back. The second the liquid touched his tongue it burned as if he had swallowed toxic chemicals. The shot was thick and coated his mouth with a consistency that reminded him of phlegm. It worked its way down his throat and hit his stomach with the force of a hand grenade.

"Holy shit that's terrible." Vincent coughed.

"Yeah. Like I was saying," Ezra continued. "It's tradition for every class valedictorian to have to drink whatever the underclassmen hand to him after graduation. The one that finally makes the valedictorian puke gets named after him."

"It tastes like we just drank that puke." Fiona frowned. "What's in this damn thing?"

"Hot sauce, cream liqueur, and grain liquor." Ezra smiled. "It's as bad as I remember."

"Why would you make someone drink this?" Zinvor said, confused. "I thought social drinking was supposed to be an enjoyable event for humans."

"Because Ezra hates you Zinvor," Fiona said. "He clearly hates us all."

"It tastes like there's a party in my mouth and everyone is dying from dysentery," Vincent spat. Before he could order another drink to wash the taste out of his mouth the bartender sped by and dropped off four more drinks.

"The Great Traitor doesn't pay for drinks here," the bartender said, smiling.

"Does that go for the Great Traitor's friends?" Fiona asked.

"Of course!" The bartender beamed.

"I knew dating you would finally pay off!" she smiled.

"Thanks," he said.

"Careful now, Vincent," Ezra said. "You are supposed to meet with Field Marshal Denta soon."

"Yeah I know," Vincent said. "I feel like it would be better if I was hammered for that."

"What are your thoughts on that guy?" Fiona asked.

"The Field Marshal?" Ezra asked, sipping his drink. "I have a feeling he holds the real power. He was Military Governor before Earth fell. He was considered something of a military genius when he was younger. Though, that was some time ago, he was still a household name here. He was the commander of Defense Force Staff Officer College for years."

"So, what's up with the Prime Minister then?" Vincent asked.

"Well once Earth fell Denta must have quickly set up something resembling a civilian government. Addler used to be the City Administrator for Grand Titan so hypothetically he should be good at his job. Putting a civilian face on a military government would be a good way to stave off any kind of dissent that could arise with the fall of the Committee."

"So, the Prime Minister is meaningless?" Vincent asked, drinking deep from his glass. The taste of The Vorbeck was sticking around like it had bonded to his tongue.

"Maybe, maybe not," Ezra mused. "I have a hard time thinking Denta would let Addler make a decision as important as this one. You don't become a Military Governor by giving power away. Maybe Addler is a figurehead."

"That explains all the cameras when we landed," Fiona said. "Addler was the only one to greet us when the cameras were around."

"Precisely." Ezra nodded. "Optics are important to a government, maybe you should take note." He laughed. "But Denta is a smart man, he knows what you and the Warlord say is true."

"Doesn't a war have to be voted on or something?" Vincent asked. "Does Denta really have that much power?"

"Technically, it should be voted on." Ezra swirled his glass around. "But it's more like a rubber stamp. Think of like how the Committee was to the Chairman." Vincent glanced down at his watch. It was nearly time to meet the field marshal. He suddenly regretted the several drinks he had downed during his and Ezra's conversation. Especially the first one.

"It's about that time," he said, his tone made it sound like he was going to his execution rather than a meeting.

"We await your good news." Ezra smiled and held a drink up in support. Zinvor slammed down his glass with such force a spiderweb of cracks crawled along the bottom of it and stood up.

"I will go with you," he said.

"Thanks." Vincent nodded. Fiona, surrounded by cheering soldiers, was well on her way to being outrageously drunk. She held up a glass so large it resembled a pitcher, its dark contents sloshed around as she gestured with it.

"You show that fucker we mean business Vinny!" she slurred. Vincent sighed, finished what was left of his drink in one swallow and made his way towards the door.

CHAPTER NINETEEN

The hallways of the Defense Directorate were empty other than a few roaming guards. Small glowing globe lights shined a bright white in between each door, casting sharp shadows out at various angles. Vincent could see in the hallway by the door of his room stood a woman in Titanian military uniform.

She looked to be the same age as Ezra with sharp, hazel eyes and olive skin. Her dark brown hair was pulled back into a tight bun, on her collar was the rank of a captain.

"The note said to come alone," she said, glancing back at Zinvor.

"Last time I did that I almost ended up hanging at the end of a utility chain. You'll have to forgive me," Vincent said.

"You smell like a bar." The woman twisted up her face.

"I imagine I would, as I just came from one." He smiled. "Shall we?"

"Ugh." She scowled and started walking quickly down the hallway. Vincent hurried to keep up.

They passed through the dining room and crossed into another hallway. She stopped in front of a set of double doors that were flanked with soldiers. The two guards quickly snapped to attention, rendering a sharp salute.

"Good evening, Captain Tirpitz!" Called out the soldier to the left.

"Let us in," the captain commanded without returning their salute. The two soldiers pushed the doors open and moved aside.

Denta's office was not what Vincent was expecting. A large, dark, cavernous room with almost nothing in it except the Field Marshal himself, seated behind a featureless desk. Hardly the office he expected the shadow head of state and Commander of Humanity's strongest army to have. Denta was busy scribbling notes on a data display while dozens of other small glowing screens went unattended on his desk. Behind him on the wall was the flag of the Union of Titan: A large Golden Eagle surrounded by eight black circles, symbolizing the Union's eight settled moons

He was still wearing his dress uniform, though the top button was undone, and his cuffs were rolled up. A pistol lay on the desk and his ceremonial sword sat, propped against the wall behind him.

"Good evening Consul," he said, looking up from his work. "I hear you were seeing the sights of Grand Titan."

"Just the bar, sir," the captain said harshly.

"Like any good soldier." Denta smiled. "Please, have a seat." Vincent sat down on the single chair facing Denta's desk. Zinvor stood at his shoulder. "Your bodyguard needed not come, I assure you I mean you no harm."

"I couldn't get rid of him if I tried sir. No offense is meant." Vincent smiled nervously. "He's a Tsarra so..."

"Your protection must be his mission then I assume?" Denta cut him off. Vincent was left speechless. Why would Denta know what a Tsarra is? "Know your enemy," Denta added after seeing Vincent's confusion. "Please forgive me, I spent years studying the Mawr when all we knew about them was their involvement with the Alliance. Clearly things aren't as cut as dry as I thought they were."

"Not quite," Vincent said.

"How lucky you must be to be fighting alongside Mawr Warriors. I have heard that each one is worth five men."

"Twenty," Zinvor grunted and Denta chuckled.

"Let me cut to the chase, as I think we both had enough bullshit for a lifetime during that farce with Addler. And as we both know, time is of the essence here," Denta said. "What are the Fidayi Clan's intentions with human space?"

"They don't have any other intention than making sure the Committee is eliminated as a threat to our safety. Obviously, a unified humanity helps them in the fight against the Alliance though," Vincent said.

"We have no intentions on unifying with anyone." Denta frowned. "We've made that mistake once; we will not do it again."

"Neither do we," Vincent said. It felt strange sitting in front of another human, using *we* to describe a clan of Aliens when only a year before the tables would have been turned. "In the end we both want the same thing."

"That is all well and good, but how do we go about pushing the Committee off of Mars? If the Clan is heavily engaged against the Alliance as you say, do they have many forces to commit to the fight?"

"Arai as promised to commit the Clan's strategic reserve. Along with the newly formed Elysian Human Cohort," Vincent said.

"You mean your army of EDF survivors?" Denta raised an eyebrow.

"Yes." Vincent nodded. He was more surprised that Denta knew anything about them. It shouldn't surprise him that Titan could have an informant as one of the thousands of smugglers that make the trip from Elysian to the outer Titan system.

"Sending in her reserves would mean if her forces dug in against the Alliance break, she would have nothing left to defend Elysian." Denta rubbed his chin.

"That should tell you how seriously she takes this threat," Vincent said.

"How many Warriors are we talking about?" Denta asked.

"I honestly have no idea." Vincent shook his head. "But it is sizeable. Minimum of at least two army groups if I had to compare it to a human military unit." Vincent had no way of knowing if the numbers he had just spouted off were true, but he assumed Arai would be able to scrape together a million Warriors and soldiers between the three races.

"Hmmm." Denta leaned back in his chair. "I don't believe the Martians will be so welcoming to yet another army of outsiders."

"We thought the same thing," Vincent said. "The Committee kept them in the dark, strangled off from fuel and power as punishment. We could give that back to them."

"So, we buy them off with our fuel?" Denta laughed. "That Colonel Vorbeck has taught you well. As good idea as that may be, I don't plan no give away our people's most important resource for free Solaris."

"Think of what their factories could do for Titan's military going forward if they owed you for fueling their newly independent planet?" Vincent asked. "We can't fight the Alliance with EDF hand-me-downs. My army has no navy and the Clan lacks the ability to manufacture much of anything on a large scale on Elysian. An alliance with Mars would help all of us." Denta laughed and slapped his hand on his desk.

"Damn kid, I have to give you credit. You're better at this game than I thought you would be." He leaned under his desk and pulled out a glass bottle and two glasses. "Tell me, is it true, you're a Sentenced Soldier?"

"Yes, sir." Vincent nodded. "Or I was, at any rate."

"As you can imagine, there are so many stories about you going around, I'm not sure which to believe," he said.

"I can assure you the least interesting one is probably the most true." Vincent laughed.

"I never thought I would be entering into a military alliance with a teenager and a bunch of Aliens. Strange times indeed." Denta poured two glasses and slid one to Vincent. Suddenly his words hit Vincent, he actually agreed.

"Wait, you mean—" Vincent stammered.

"Don't act so surprised. Your argument is a good one. Give yourself some credit." Denta sipped his glass.

"After that meeting with Addler though..." Vincent drank from his glass. The amber liquid inside was strong and smokey, but not bad.

"Addler is a tit." Denta laughed. "But the people like him. His talents don't stretch far beyond trade policy. Though, in his defense that has treated us well. But trying to explain military matters to him would be like explaining a good meal to a Martian."

"Sir, excuse my ignorance, but how are we going to plan a planetary invasion?"

"Well, we can't send our boys in blind, can we?" he said. "There are so many different factions on the ground during any good Martian rebellion, the key will be to find the largest that will work with us."

"How do we do that?" Vincent asked.

"It will require a small group of people to land on the planet before the main force," Denta said. He stared at Vincent for a moment, just long enough for Vincent to understand the implication.

"You mean us," Vincent moaned.

"I will send my personal aide as Titan's military attaché with you." Denta motioned for the captain to come over to his desk. "Tirpitz, pack your bags."

"But sir—"

"I'll hear none of that, now go."

The captain gave Vincent a look of pure hatred before storming off.

"You seem to have a large... intelligence network." Vincent tried not to use the word *Spies.* "What do you know about what's happening on Mars?"

"Next to nothing," Denta said. "Once it became clear that Titan had no intention of rejoining the Committee, they declared Titan to be in open rebellion and the few Titanian Regiments stationed on Mars were liquidated before we had a chance to evacuate them." Denta's fists tightened until the knuckles turned white. "From what we can gather is the Committee is in command of almost everything other than about half of Olympus. I can assume the Committee is still in control of the Mons Spaceport, keeping supply to Lunar City open."

"Any ideas of who is fighting who?" he asked.

"Not a clue." Denta shrugged. "That'll be on you to find out and report back to us so the Warlord and I can make a plan."

"Uh, sir..." Vincent mumbled. The idea that he wanted him to land in the middle of a war zone and stumble into Martian diplomacy between who knows how many different groups, was a few steps short of insane.

"I'm not going to lie to you and say this is going to be easy." Or even possible, Vincent thought to himself. Denta refilled his glass. "But unless we find whatever groups are in charge and get them on our side, we will just be jumping into a battle royale." Denta chuckled. "And besides, it seems like you're getting awfully talented at pulling off the impossible."

"I wish I wasn't," Vincent complained. "You have the most powerful military left standing in Human space. Why send me?"

"As you can imagine the Martians and the Titanians have a complicated history." Denta stared down into his drink. "The way they look at it, we and the committee were one and the same. After all we did help crush their rebellion, so I can hardly blame them for their feelings. They may reject any offer we have outright based on principle alone."

"Why would I have any better luck? I'm an Earthian." Vincent frowned.

"You're more than that. You're the—"

"I'm the Great Traitor," Vincent cut him off. "Damnit."

"To them you did something they could only dream of. You destroyed Earth and dethroned the Chairman."

"But I *didn't*," Vincent said.

"They don't know that. Haven't you ever heard the saying 'perception is reality'? Well, let them believe whatever they want to believe." Denta shrugged.

"You want me to lie to them?" Vincent asked. It would hardly be the first time he lied to get ahead in life. But lying to the Martians would mean embracing the idea that he was this *Great*

Traitor that Brusilov and his Black Coats vilified. It would mean accepting the story that he, not the Alliance had destroyed Earth.

"A means to an end," Denta said. "If we in power could move men based on truth alone, I have no doubt we would do it. Until that day..." he trailed off.

"Fine," Vincent said. As the words left his lips, he felt dirtier. "I'll do it."

"Good." Denta beamed. "That's my boy." He stood up and offered Vincent his hand. Vincent reached out and shook it, finding the old man's strength surprising. "On Titan we seal deals with a shot." Denta refilled both of their glasses. They raised their glasses together.

"Death to the Chairman," Denta cheered.

And long live the Warlord," Vincent added with a smirk. Denta laughed and they clinked their glasses together. The amber liquid splashed onto Vincent's hand and they drank deeply until their glasses were empty.

*   *   *

It was past midnight by the time Vincent made it back to the Tipsy Wings. Drunken soldiers milled about, melding into the bustling nightlife of the busy Grand Titan streets. He pushed through the doors into the bar. The air was clouded with smoke and the crowd inside had grown three times since he had left.

"Vinny!" Called out a familiar drunken voice. He turned to see Fiona, who had lost her uniform top and was now down to a white tank top, standing on top of the bar. "Get your sweet ass up here!"

Vincent laughed. "No, I think I'm good down here."

"Consul, sir!" called Ezra spinning around on a barstool, drink in hand. While he didn't slur his words, his face was red and his eyes hooded. "What's the good word?"

"You were right," Vincent said. "He agreed. We're going to Mars."

"Mars?" Fiona called out. She walked down the bar, kicking several people's glasses out of the way to stand in front of Ezra. "We're going to Mars?"

"We're going to war," Ezra said.

"You fuckers hear that?" Fiona screamed over the noise of dozens of people talking, slowly their chatter died down. "We're going to war!"

To Vincent's surprise the bar exploded into cheers. Glasses were thrust into the air, their contents sloshing and spilling out in small waves that cascaded down onto the bar patrons. "We're going Kill that Committee and burn Lunar City to the fucking ground!" Fiona cheered. Her crowd of drunken soldiers cheered with her.

"To the Great Traitor!" Ezra joined in, smirking at Vincent. The crowd joined in louder than ever and Vincent's ears began to pound as they stomped their feet in unison.

It was then, Vincent knew he could no longer fight it. He really was the *Great Traitor.*

CHAPTER TWENTY

Vincent watched as the *Shanna II* was loaded with supplies. Crews of Titanian soldiers struggled to with towering carts of boxes of food, ammunition, medical supplies, and water. Ezra guided the crates they were carrying, ensuring the loads were properly secured. Behind them crowds of Titanian soldiers had gathered to watch the strange crew ready their ship. The crowd grew as media crews arrived and began to set up cameras.

Captain Tirpitz arrived, but she was not alone. She was flanked by two soldiers who were heavily laden with bags.

"Good Morning, Captain," Vincent greeted her. She gave him a harsh sideways glance.

"Who pissed in your breakfast?" Fiona folded her arms. Vincent shot her a look. "What?"

"And who are you exactly?" Tirpitz asked harshly.

"Fiona. I'm an aide... or something to the Consul." Fiona sized her up. "Who are you?"

"Captain Anastasia Tirpitz. Official Titan military Attaché to the Fidayi Clan and Mars," Tirpitz said, maybe a little too proudly. Vincent knew that would set Fiona off.

"Well *Annie*," Fiona said, knowing how well the nickname would go over. "We tend to load our own bags in this crew." The two soldiers toting Tirpitz's bags exchanged glances with one another.

"That is ridiculous." Tirpitz laughed. "I am a captain in the Titanian Army, I am owed two porters. They were issued to me by the Field Marshal himself."

"Sorry, Captain," Ezra chimed in, not looking up from his data display. "She's right. We don't have the room to bring your porters. We are flying an assault ship, not a troop carrier."

"Unbelievable," Tirpitz gasped. At that, Ezra glanced up from his work and his eyes went wide.

"Wait, you're the military attaché?" He stumbled over his words. "*You're* Captain Tirpitz."

"Ezra?" Tirpitz gasped. "Ezra Vorbeck?"

"Err." Ezra straightened himself up and nodded. "Yes. The *Shanna II* is my ship."

"I take it you two have met before?" Vincent asked.

"Something like that. Yes, sir." Ezra nodded, his cheeks starting to flush.

"I feel like there is a lot to unpack here." Fiona grinned, eyeing the two.

"For a different time perhaps, Colonel." Tirpitz frowned.

"Definitely." Ezra sighed. "You two." Ezra nodded towards Tirpitz's porters. "You can go, leave the bags."

The two soldiers set down Tirpitz's bags and slowly backed away. Vincent couldn't help but laugh. He had been one of those young lower enlisted soldiers once and he couldn't think of a task he would have hated more than to be some uptight captain's personal slave. He watched with probably too much enjoyment as Tirpitz struggled with her two bags over into the ship.

Vincent settled back down onto his bed roll, which was now braced up against a stack of crates labeled *Rations* with a golden eagle stamp on it. Tirpitz sat down in a proper seat and buckled herself into its four-point restraint. Fiona sat down next to Vincent, her legs splayed out in front of her, her arms crossed. She eyed Tirpitz with distain. Vincent couldn't blame her for hating the captain, she looked and acted like the antithesis of Fiona's entire being.

Zinvor climbed in and sat down next to Tirpitz, leaning against her seat as a backrest. Tirpitz's eyes filled with horror as Zinvor settled in. She unbuckled her seatbelt, got up, and sat on the ground, as far away from Zinvor as she could get.

"Captain," Ezra said calmly. "Everyone on this ship are equals." He gave a reassuring smile. "Per orders of the Consul, isn't that right?"

"That's..." Vincent stumbled being put on the spot like that. "That's right."

"You not only expect me to work with the Martians, but these...beasts too?" she said, exasperated.

"Hey, I have to work with your annoying ass. We all have to make sacrifices," Fiona snarled.

"How dare you—" Tirpitz began.

Vincent had to interject. "You should probably stop." He held his hands up. "For your own safety."

Tirpitz huffed and crossed her arms in protest, though she kept further comments to herself. The *Shanna's* turbines began to whirl, and the ship hummed softly as they sped up. Out of the milling crowds of soldiers and media people, came Denta.

Somehow, he looked older than the night before. Maybe the hours of drinking had caught up with him. His uniform was still impeccable though, and the countless medals on his chest shone in the morning sunlight. The soldiers who were previously loading the ship stopped what they were doing and snapped to attention, salutes followed Denta as he got closer to them.

"I trust that these supplies will be enough for your travels?" he asked.

"Of course. Your generosity is appreciated." Ezra smiled. Vincent was a little surprised to see Ezra, the ever-dutiful soldier, not salute the Field Marshal. Denta nodded.

"The hopes of humanity's—and dare I say the entire galaxy's—freedom rests on this mission." Denta smiled. "Don't fuck it up."

The bright green shape of Titan slowly floated away from under them as they once again, drifted into the blackness of space. As Vincent watch, an overwhelming feeling of sadness washed over him. Surrounded by the luxury and ease of Grand Titan, he was loath to return to what had become his home since he had left Earth: the battlefield. From the purple hills of Ryklar where his Regiment was left to die to the muddy fields of death on Grawluck where his planet was destroyed, the slums of Elysian where Nox was killed. Now he was flying towards the chaos of a Martian rebellion.

Whenever a soldier stepped onto a field of battle it was like they were spinning the chambers of a Riten, putting it to their heads, and pulling the trigger. In each battle so far, the chamber at Vincent's head had been empty. Though for the thousands of soldiers who had fallen around him, that had not been the case. He wasn't sure how many more empty chambers any of them had left.

He had lost Nox on Elysian in the same battle he had nearly been shot in the head. He no longer feared his own pain or death. That all went away around the same time an EDF sergeant tried to strangle him to death with an old utility chain. What kept him up at night was how many more people were going to die following him into the messes he kept getting himself into.

"Hey," Fiona said, breaking him away from his own thoughts. "Everything alright? You look hungover or something." Fiona was never particularly great in handling emotions, but she wasn't entirely wrong. His head was pounding.

"I...just wasn't ready to leave yet," he said.

"Yeah it was pretty nice." She smiled. "Waking up in that nice warm bed, taking that hot shower," she remembered. "But we had to leave. Those things weren't ours to enjoy."

"Huh?" Vincent turned to her. "Why not?"

"I'm gutter trash and you barely passed school." She shrugged. "He got shunned from his own race." She pointed to Zinvor. "And he's just a plain old criminal." She nodded to Ezra. "People like us exist to scrape together a living that is just barely considered humane while fighting and killing each other so people like that fucker"—she pointed to Tirpitz—"can live on Grand Titan and their only worry is if the corner store runs out of ice cream or their favorite pair of shoes or some shit."

"Excuse me?" Tirpitz cursed.

"Oh!" Fiona faked shock. "Excuse me ma'am! Which wars did you fight in? What street did you beg for change in?" Her questions were met with an angry, offended glare. "Whose dick did you suck so you could eat?"

Tirpitz's eyes went wide.

"Yeah. I didn't think so." Fiona scowled. "That's her world. Ours is whichever one is currently at each other's throats."

"I guess I'm coming to accept that," Vincent said. "I just don't want to drag anyone else with me."

"It's a noble cause, sir," Ezra said. "I can't speak for anyone else, but I'm with you because I want to be," he said. "I could have left you on Titan or stayed on Elysian. Any one of those soldiers back on Elysian could have never picked up a weapon for your cause. But you know what?"

"What?" Vincent asked.

"They're smart enough to know that the war isn't over," Ezra said. "And instead of debating it in council chambers or the parliament floor like Denta and Addler do they simply picked up their rifle and went to work. So, what if Fiona said is depressingly true? We might be criminals, and street kids, and dropouts, but we are smart enough to know when it's time to go to work." A smile began to creep across Vincent's face. "This is who we are. This is what we do."

"Damn, that might have been the most motivation thing I've ever heard." Fiona burst out into laughter.

"Yeah, maybe you should be the Consul." Vincent scratched his beard, fighting back his own laughter. "You seem like you would be a lot better at it than me."

"You lead in a different way." Ezra smiled. "Hundreds of thousands of people once thought they were the lowest of the low. EDF grunts, Martian conscripts, Sentenced soldiers. Every single one of them probably thought they were nothing but a pawn to the Committee or the Black Coats. I know I did."

"And now what?" Vincent stifled a laugh. "I showed them if they keep failing eventually someone will take pity on them and give them a job?"

"You showed them a pawn can turn around and kick King's ass every once and a while."

"I thought, in human chess, the pawns did not have legs." Zinvor scratched his chin. "Kicking would be an impossibility."

"No, Zinvor." Ezra rubbed his eyes. "It's a metaphor. Like saying that the lowest Warrior of yours could way day rise up to become Warlord."

"This would be treason," Zinvor growled.

"Ugh, never mind," Ezra conceded.

*   *   *

Warning claxons ripped Vincent out of his sleep. Several alarms were going off at the same time, all at different pitches and locations. He sat up in his bed roll, throwing the covers back. Ezra was awake and sitting in the cockpit. He scrolled through a multitude of different screens on the ship's main control panel. Slowly, the sirens went silent.

"What's going on?" Tirpitz asked. Vincent heard an edge of fear in her voice.

"Nothing yet," Ezra said. "I'm picking up several signatures up ahead though.

"Shit, the EDF is onto us," Fiona cursed.

"Not yet," Ezra replied. "I can spoof their signals, if anything they will just think I'm another one of them."

"Will that work?" Vincent asked.

"Yeah." He rubbed his eyes. "At least until we get close enough for them to notice we are two ships bolted into one. Not many EDF ships look like ours does." Ezra laughed. "I think we will be able to get to the surface of Mars. But if we don't strike a deal with them and have to leave without the Titanian Navy, we'll be out of luck. I won't be able to trick them twice."

"How far away are they?" Vincent asked.

"Nearest signature is almost one thousand miles off," Tyr responded. Tirpitz jumped at the sound their shrill voice. Almost like he hadn't noticed them until then. "I recommend a deviation from our current flight path."

"Negative," Ezra said. "We plotted this path with the hope the EDF wouldn't notice us amongst their supply ships."

"This will lead to confrontation with EDF forces," Tyr said.

"Understood." Ezra frowned.

"Are they right?" Fiona asked.

"It is a possibility," Ezra said.

"I am right," Tyr butted in, this time with urgency.

"That's enough Gunner's Mate," Ezra barked at Tyr. They showed no outward signs of emotion but said nothing else.

"What kind of confrontation?" Vincent asked.

"Well, this hunk isn't built for dogfighting," Ezra said. "Our best bet is the spoof works and we can slip past them."

"And if it doesn't?" Tirpitz asked, her voice thick with dread.

"Our mission ends at the scene of the crash." Ezra shrugged.

"Comforting." Tirpitz sighed. "Do the Martians have any anti-air capabilities?"

"If the current rebellion is anything like their last one, they're going to have enough to carpet the sky with missiles," said Ezra, fearful. "It was the only way they could slow the EDF supply routes and try to strangle off the garrison on the surface."

"Have you seen Olympus? Doesn't look like anyone stopped anything." Fiona snorted.

"That's because the EDF eventually resorted to orbital strikes," Ezra said. "Indiscriminate ones at that. Before the strikes we were targeting Rebels and places where they would hideout, but the loss of so many pilots to ground fire changed higher command's mind," he said in a pained voice. "The strikes eventually caused the rebels to surrender."

"It's hard to keep fighting when the water extractors are destroyed, and you start watching your family die of thirst," Fiona said, folding her arms. "Or destroying the surface of the planet so thoroughly that you undo a thousand years of terra forming."

"Well, their plan for the future of Mars didn't exactly involve Martians," Ezra said. "Hence the waves of new settlers after the war."

"I cannot wait to get my hands on those pieces of shit." Fiona clenched her fists.

"We aren't going there to fight settlers Fiona," Vincent said, putting his arm around her shoulder. She quickly shrugged it off.

"We are going there to free Mars," she seethed. "Mars will never be free without kicking out those leeches."

"Careful, Fiona." Ezra held up a finger. "That's how the Committee sold the settlement program to the Earthians. The rebellious blood would have to be bred out of you and all that."

"Did you just compare me to them?" Fiona raged.

"Hey, if the shoe fits." Tirpitz shrugged.

"You shut your damn mouth!" Fiona screamed at her. To Vincent's surprise, Tirpitz stood up from her seat.

"I've had about enough of you." She stood, fists clenched. Even in her decorated military uniform, Vincent had to admit Tirpitz did not cut an intimidating figure. Fiona, with her ragged tank top, battle scared Mawr-armor pants and skin pock-marked with scars should have probably scared Tirpitz at least a little bit.

Instead, Tirpitz squared off with her. She unbuttoned her jacket and set it aside. Beneath her uniform she was tightly wound bundles of muscle. Vincent wasn't sure which one he was more afraid of anymore. The two women locked eyes. Finally, it happened: Fiona lunged at her, swinging a wild punch at Tirpitz. Tirpitz grabbed Fiona's wrist, and deftly twisted at her hips. She sent Fiona crashing into a stack of ration crates. Fiona popped back to her feet and rushed at her once again. Tirpitz ducked under Fiona's punch so fast it made Fiona look as if she was moving in slow motion.

Tirpitz wrapped one arm around Fiona's hips and one leg in front of her feet. With a heave she sent her attacker to the floor. Fiona landed flat on her back and her head bounced off of the metal floor with a sickening thud.

"That's enough!" Ezra yelled from the cockpit. Vincent, made speechless by Tirpitz's obvious skill, didn't think Ezra's warning was needed. Fiona was limp on the ground. The impact having rendered her unconscious.

"Where the hell did you learn to do that?" Vincent gasped. He had watched the uncontrolled fury of Fiona level an entire bar of drunken soldiers on multiple occasions. He had seen her take beatings from men and aliens three times her size and walk them off. He never thought he would watch her get picked apart so easily.

"You may have been right earlier," Tirpitz said. "I've never fought in battle, nor struggled to make ends meet," she conceded. "But what I did do was bust my ass and trained for years. Eventually I became the Field Marshal's personal aide." She crossed her arms over her chest. "And the Union of Titan's Grand Judo Champion," she added. "So, I'm just about over your little girlfriend questioning my dedication."

"I don't think she will do that again." Vincent laughed. Fiona awoke from her impact-induced slumber. Blood trickled from a small on the back of her head.

"Ugh," she groaned. "Did I just get my ass kicked?"

"Yup," Vincent said, wiping away the blood. "Convincingly, may I add."

"Damnit." She sat up. "She only won because she didn't stand and fight me," she spat. "What kind of shit was that?"

"I won because I know how to fight. You ran straight at me like some kind of bar room drunk." Tirpitz laughed. "I hope that the cut isn't too deep."

"It's nothing!" Fiona contested. Though Vincent could see the side of Fiona's lip curling into a smile. Fiona was a complicated woman, but if it was one thing she respected, it was strength.

Zinvor chortled, clapping his huge, gnarled paws together.

"Again!" he cheered. "Again!" To Vincent's surprise he watched as Tirpitz's hard face cracked into a smile and then began laughing.

"So, I guess to get you to lighten up all we had to do was get assaulted?" Vincent chuckled.

"Excuse me?" Tirpitz feigned outrage. "I was defending myself." She fought with her hair, fixing the few strands that became out of place during the struggle. "Also, Solaris you didn't seem too upset that I smashed your girlfriend's head into the ground."

"I used to be concerned when she got herself into stupid situations." He shrugged. "Something like this doesn't even register to me anymore."

"Doesn't sound like you make it easy on him." She laughed.

"Hey, he knows what he got himself into," Fiona said.

"True, I do this to myself." Vincent sighed. "What about you? Who are you leaving behind?"

"No one." Tirpitz shook her head. "In between my duties to the Field Marshal and training I never had time for much of a personal life. Just as well, I always found dating to be tiring."

"I wouldn't know," Vincent said. "We didn't really date. It just kind of happened." He thought about it and they had still never really had a single real date the whole time they were together.

The one night they had in the luxurious state room on Grand Titan was about as close as they ever came.

"Oh?" Tirpitz raised an eyebrow. "So, you're not really together?"

"Oh no," Fiona said. "He's mine." She slapped him on the shoulder.

"Lucky guy," Tirpitz said.

"Damn right he is."

Another warning siren broke up their conversation. Ezra turned his attention back to his control panel, and quickly exchanged panic words with Tyr.

"Is everything okay?" Fiona asked.

"We're about to find out," Ezra said nervously.

"What does that mean?" Vincent asked.

"We're being tracked," Ezra said.

"I thought you said you could spoof their signal?" Tirpitz yelled at him.

"The Clan captured this ship over a year ago!" Ezra yelled back. "The EDF must have changed their signals or something since then!"

"You didn't think the EDF would change their security encryption a whole damn year after having thousands of ships get captured at Grawluck?" Tirpitz screamed, rising from her seat.

"It was our only option!" Ezra shot back. "Besides, the signal package we have might be close enough for them to leave us alone. The outer picket ships routinely track ships as they get closer. Even friendly ones."

"That's a pretty big fucking gamble." Tirpitz frowned.

"It is the only gamble we had," Ezra said, his irritation growing. He reached down and pushed a lever forward. The ship lurched forward. For the first time during the flight Vincent could hear the ship's engines winding up. The ship vibrated slightly, and a few cans rattled across the floor.

"Attention unflagged ship," came a voice over the speakers. "This is EDF patrol ship *ES 19*. Identify yourself or be fired upon."

"Fuck," Ezra spat. "We are going to have to run for it."

"Wait," Tirpitz said, putting a hand on his shoulder. "Use your old call sign and credentials. There's no way they know you're involved with the Clan, right?"

"Maybe," Ezra said. "I'll give it a shot." Ezra reached over and fiddled with some buttons before pulling his helmet mic close to his mouth. "This is the *Shanna I*, current registration number 9826." Vincent knew he had painted *Shanna II* on the side of his new craft, but the *Shanna I* was the ship he had made his way to Elysian with and the one that the EDF would most likely have on record.

The speakers hissed with empty static. Everyone in the ship stared at them, holding their breath. Ezra didn't wait for an answer. He hammered down on the lever again and the ship's engines whined with strain. The once dull vibrating rose into a rattling shake that made it feel as if the ship was going to tear apart. Vincent quickly sat down in a seat and strapped himself in. Everyone else followed suit.

"Hold on boys and girls," Ezra said. "And Tyr," he added. Ezra ripped back on the lever and jerked the yolk back. The ship slammed to a dead stop, violently jamming everyone into their seatbelts. Pain seared through Vincent's shoulders as the seatbelt pulled taut. Suddenly, the occupants of the ship were pushed back into their seats as Ezra accelerated once again, this time bringing the ship into a steep climb.

"The fuck are you doing?" Fiona screamed.

"Brusilov saw me during the meeting!" Ezra yelled. "He would make sure to note me as one of the Elysian traitors. That silence means they are running my credentials through the database. No way I pass that check." Through the cockpit windshield Vincent could see the dull grey line of several Reapers facing them. "Guns free Tyr!"

"Guns free," Tyr repeated. The ship's cannon let out a long burst of fire. It stitched across the line of ships, and they erupted into orange blooms of fire.

"Holy shit!" Tirpitz yelled. "Nice flying!" she added.

"That'll buy us some time," Ezra said. "But it's only a matter of time before we run into the rest of the picket, that was only the advanced guard. Time to see what this baby can do."

"Multiple targets approaching," Tyr informed them.

"Engage. Closet targets first," Ezra commanded.

"Roger," Tyr responded. "Firing." Rockets screeched away from under the ship's weapons mounts. Trailing smoke and fire as they raced off into space. A few seconds of silence passed before Tyr said. "Target down." Only then did it dawn on Vincent that Tyr was now firing on other ships that were so far away they couldn't be seen with the naked eye. Instead they must have been tracking them using the targeting system in their flight helmets. He was curious how many people were doing the same thing to them at that very second.

Vincent's question was answered when Ezra quickly brought the ship into a dive and a bright light streaked by, only feet from the ship. He looked over and saw Fiona's eyes clamped shut, her knuckles white as she gripped into her seats arm rests. He wanted to reach over and reassure her, but the steep dive had pinned Vincent to his seat.

A fire ball erupted in front of them and the ship rocked violently. Ration boxes broke free and tumbled across the crew compartment.

"Damn air burst missiles!" Ezra cursed. "Bastards!"

"Are we dead yet?" Fiona moaned.

"Not yet. Getting there it seems though," Vincent said.

"Damage report?" Ezra asked.

"minimal   damage   to   the   rear   stabilizers. Recommendations?" Tyr asked.

"Sure," Ezra responded.

"Disengagement," Tyr said.

"Not a fucking option anymore," Ezra seethed.

Vincent wasn't sure how he hadn't noticed, maybe from being busy frozen with fear, but up ahead was the small, red shape of Mars. Still far away enough to be as small as a distant star. A siren wailed, snapping Vincent back to the confines of the ship.

"Someone has locked onto us," Tyr said.

"Deploy chaff!" Ezra ordered, the panic rising in his voice.

"Deploying," Tyr said. A *poof* barely audible over the ship's engines sent thousands of small pieces of metal flying into space. A rocket that was heading straight for the ship twisted off course and exploded, rocking the ship with distant shock waves.

"What's our ETA?" Ezra asked. Tyr momentarily looked down and then locked their wide unblinking eyes back into her helmet targeting system.

"Five minutes until we are in the Martian atmosphere," Tyr said.

"Good." Ezra breathed a sigh of relief. "Going good so far." As soon as the words were out of his mouth the ship shook as if it had been slapped by a meteor and the interior lights flickered.

"Shit!" Ezra screamed. Smoke began to fill the crew compartment and burned Vincent's eyes. Fans kicked on and began to vent the smoke out of the troop compartment but struggled to keep up.

"What hit us?" He coughed.

"A small caliber missile from a scout ship I think." Ezra coughed. "If it were a Reaper, we'd be dead. Tyr where is that bastard?"

"Six O' clock high," Tyr said. "Reader says a Mantis pattern scout ship."

"Little bastard," Ezra growled. The ship rose into a steep climb and banked hard to the left. The few straps that remained holding supplies back gave way. A wave of ration packets and ammunition boxes cascaded over the occupants of the troop compartment.

"We will not catch the Mantis, Commander," Tyr said.

"No shit," Ezra said. "Watch this." Ezra jerked the ship hard back to the right and in front of them was the small tear drop shaped scout ship. A missile streaked out from under the *Shanna* and reduced the fast-moving ship into a cloud of debris and flames. "My first assignment was a Mantis. They're fast as hell but can't maneuver worth a damn." He grinned.

"Fuel leak detected from the number four fuel cell," Tyr said, bringing the mood down.

"Damnit." Ezra sighed. "No more dogfighting. We won't have the fuel for it. We have to make a break for the surface."

Bright lights, trailing fire behind them burned across the blackness of space. Ezra deftly made the ship dance around them. Countless explosions lit up the darkness all around them. Vincent noticed every time Ezra accelerated thick black smoke would fill the cabin, only to be cleared by the fans.

"Why aren't we shooting back anymore?" Tirpitz asked.

"We are currently out of indirect fire weapons," Tyr answered.

"Only thing we have left is our cannon," Ezra said. "And I don't really feel like getting close enough to use that again."

A dark fluid began to pool around Vincent's feet and a pungent smell rose up from the floor.

"What the hell is this?" Vincent asked, watching as the liquid beaded up on his boots. Ezra glanced back.

"Looks like fuel," he said, seemingly without concern. "It's incredibly toxic, so don't let it touch your ...anything really."

"Damnit." He sighed. Fiona, who had snapped out of her frozen state of fear was fumbling with a cigarette, trying to light it. Vincent reached over and slapped it out of her hand. "There's enough people trying to kill us right now, we don't need you helping them!" Before Fiona could respond the ship rocked again.

"That was a close one," Ezra said, laughing nervously.

"Entering Martian space," Tyr said.

"About damn time!" Fiona cheered. Out of the cockpit windshield the only thing Vincent could see was the rust colored surface of Mars.

Long chains of ships were queued up in a neat row next to a massive supply barge. The barge was an immense structure, large enough to be crewed by hundreds of Naval personnel. In comparison the Reapers around looked like remoras to a shark. Once the smaller ships were loaded up, they would dive and race towards the surface of the planet, no doubt heavily laden with supplies and reinforcements for the fighting going on below.

"This is too good to pass by," Ezra said. "Do it Tyr." The gunner let loose with a barrage of cannon fire. The Reapers were sitting ducks. Five of them exploded into flames as the others attempted to escape the gunfire, crashing into the barge in the confusion. Tyr then directed cannon fire tore into the supply barge as the *Shanna* raced by. Impacts traced their way along the length of the barge, spurting flames into space.

"Main cannon is having a malfunction," Tyr said. "Switching to close range impact rockets."

"Get that barge!" Ezra screamed. Even though he said he wouldn't Ezra banked the ship back for another run on the barge. The line of Reapers had been reduced to floating wreckage with the few surviving ships fleeing towards the planet's surface with their cargo. Smoke poured out of the barge from where the cannon had landed several direct hits. The large ship was listing heavily as its stabilizers failed, and small escape pods began to trickle down towards Mars.

White streaks erupted out from underneath the *Shanna*. Arcing forward, looking like angelic wings.

"Guns dry," Tyr said. Vincent knew what that meant. The *Shanna* had nothing left. The few rifles and pistols held within the crew compartment meant nothing in the vacuum of space. Fire bloomed across the top of the barge. The tall conical tower that must have been their command deck, exploded. Fire rippled down the spine of the giant ship until it reached the rear where it's two huge engines sputtered and died.

"Powerplant failure detected Commander," Tyr said. "Recommendation?"

"Sure." Ezra sighed.

"Fuel levels low and guns are dry. I recommend immediate course for the surface."

"Agreed." Ezra nodded. "Let's bring her down."

CHAPTER TWENTY-ONE

The *Shanna* struggled through the Martian atmosphere. Vincent wasn't sure if it was from the fuel leak or Mars itself. The Martian air was thick with red dust, making it look like they were flying through an impenetrable wall of red. Fiona insisted it was just "the windy season." Though she couldn't rightly explain the Martian season to them in any real sense.

"So, it's like this for six months?" Tirpitz asked.

"Yeah," Fiona said.

"Six months isn't a season. That's just half of the year," Vincent said.

"Well, it rains every once and a while too during the windy season."

"With all the dust in the air...." Ezra started.

"It's more like a toxic mud storm." Fiona scratched her chin. "It'll burn your skin."

"Lovely," Tirpitz said.

"Is there a season that is, you know, conducive to human life?" Vincent asked.

"Not anymore." Fiona shrugged. "Once the wind dies down it's just hot as hell."

"Why did we settle this place?" Tirpitz asked, frowning.

"Before the terraforming was ruined, it was pretty nice," Ezra said. "Olympus was always kind of rough, but the rolling fields outside of it were about as green as anything on Titan."

"Unbelievable." Tirpitz sighed.

"Where are we landing?" Fiona asked.

"The only intelligence Denta could give us was that the last he heard that the Central District was held by rebel groups. So, I planned for there," Ezra said.

"That's where I'm from." Fiona smiled, though Vincent could tell it looked forced.

"Know anyone who might be involved in the war?" Vincent asked.

"Oh, probably," Fiona said. "Draft dodgers, gangers, criminals," she said. "You know, real winners."

"Sounds like we'll fit in for the most part." Ezra laughed.

"All of us except" Fiona looked at Tirpitz.

"So, what, I need a cover story or something?" Tirpitz sighed.

"It would probably be helpful," Ezra said. "Just in case."

"Umm," Tirpitz thought. "Maybe insubordinate to some asshole commander?"

"Huh." Ezra looked a Vincent. "Haven't heard that one before."

The Martian skyline approached. Gone was the seamless construction of Grand Titan. The Olympus skyline looked like shattered, jagged glass. The city had been utterly broken by who knows how many explosions over countless years. The dust began to clear up as they got closer to the planet's surface. A rust-red haze remained, clouding everything to a nearly unrecognizable static screen.

"Any ground forces, this is Elysian Defense Force ship *Shanna II*, requesting permission to land," Ezra said. The radio hissed with empty static in return.

"Any luck?" Vincent asked.

"Not unless they're answering me in some unknown static based language," Ezra groaned. Warning sirens blared and Vincent was sure the EDF had found them again.

"We are being locked on by multiple ground-based weapons systems," Tyr said.

"Well, they aren't firing so that's a good sign," Vincent said.

"Who the hell are you?" Hissed a man's voice over the speakers.

"This is the *Shanna II*—" Ezra began to repeat.

The voice on the other side cut him off. "Yeah we heard that part. But I ain't never heard of no fuckin' *Elysian Defense Force*."

"I assure you we are here to help you fight the Committee," Ezra said. "We have the Great Traitor on board." Vincent sighed at his name.

"We'll see about that," the man said. "I'm forwarding you the coordinates for a place to land. If you so much as go ten feet in a different direction, I'll blow your ass out of the sky."

"Your people are so nice." Tirpitz frowned at Fiona.

"Hey, they didn't kill us outright." Fiona shrugged. "Already going better than I thought it would."

"That makes two of us," Tirpitz said.

The ship dipped lower into the dust. Unlike other cities he had been to, there was no traffic. No aero cars or other ships were in the air around them. There was no foot or vehicle traffic in the streets below either. Martian weapons probably made sure of that. Through the hazy air he couldn't see one bit of light coming from the city. The few windows that remained intact were dark. There were no streetlights or headlights. It was if the entire city was dead.

"Man, the Committee really did a number here," Vincent gasped.

"It's been like this as long as I can remember," Fiona said.

"They never rebuilt?" Tirpitz asked, shocked.

"Not Olympus." She shook her head. "I hear the settler cities are nice though," she said, her voice thick with hatred.

"Did it always have no power?" Vincent asked.

"They don't transport fuel to Olympus," she said. "A few of the rich gangers got their hands on a few generators though. They make good money robbing the transports that go to the settler cities, it's really the only way fuel makes it Olympus at all."

"Sounds like you know something about that?" Tirpitz laughed.

"A girl has to make a living." Fiona smirked.

"You think your old gang is fighting?" Vincent asked.

"Probably. There is a lot of money in stolen EDF gear," she said.

"So. they wouldn't be fighting for freedom or anything?" he asked. Fiona laughed.

"I'm sure a few gangers are fighting the committee, but it ain't about freedom," she said.

"What about the glorious Martian Revolution we hear so much about?" Tirpitz asked. Fiona shrugged

"That was kind of a thing once. Now it's just a bunch of gangers fighting each other over turf trying to carve out their own little fiefdoms. I don't think anyone actually wants to govern this mess. They just want to make as much money as possible before the orbital strikes come down on us again."

They hovered low over what looked like what used to be some kind of sports stadium. The structure had long ago been reduced to a few broken walls and a few sections of seating. A field, that was probably supposed to have grass, was an expanse of shelled cratered dirt.

"This is it," Ezra said. "You guys ready?"

"Not even remotely." Vincent sighed. "Not like we have a choice though."

The ship began to make its final approach as the crew compartment door slowly slid open. The opened doors unsealed their quasi-sterile environment of recycled air. Martian wind blew into the compartment, assaulting Vincent's senses. The smell of burning rubber, shit, and rotting corpses burned his nose.

As the ship's engines blew away the shroud of dust it revealed a crowd of heavily armed people waiting for them. They wore a combination of torn street clothes and pilfered EDF body armor. Their faces were covered with bandanas and goggles that made them look like insects. They were armed with a combination of EDF rifles and what looked like homemade shotguns.

As the door opened the armed group rushed them, weapons raised.

"Show me your fuckin' hands!" Screamed one of them. "Make one stupid move and I'll top ya!"

"Whoa!" Vincent yelled. "We're here as friends!"

"You don't look like any fuckin' friend of mine, Worm," the man spat. Rebels approached them and snatched their Ritens from their hips. This was something he was worried about. He looked back at Zinvor who stood, hand on the butt of his Riten, staring down a rebel. The rebel had a sawed-off shotgun in his hand, pointing directly at Zinvor's chest.

242

"Give it to him Zinvor," Vincent said.

"I will not," he grunted.

"Tell your boy there if he doesn't give up his gun your all fuckin' dead," growled the rebel standing in front of Vincent.

"It's just temporary damnit!" Vincent yelled at him. Zinvor wouldn't budge. The rebel standing in front of him pumped his shotgun threateningly. Ezra, who had finally exited the ship, snuck around behind Zinvor, and quickly pulled the weapon from its holster. He tossed it at the rebel before Zinvor could grab it.

Zinvor wheeled around and punched Ezra square in the nose. Ezra stumbled back, his nose erupting with blood, before having his fall broken by the ship.

"You are a dead man!" Zinvor roared, he began to stomp towards Ezra who was sitting in the dirt, braced against the side of the ship.

"Zinvor!" Vincent screamed. "Focus damnit!" Zinvor stopped in his tracks and turned around. He glanced down at the rebel's shotgun which was still trained on him, seemingly noticing it for the first time.

"Alright, that's enough of this bullshit, let's go," ordered the rebel in front of Vincent, who was obviously in charge.

"Where are you taking us?" Fiona asked.

"To where we're gonna shoot your asses if we find out you're lying to us," the rebel leader spat.

"Why the hell would we fly right to you if we were lying?" Tirpitz asked.

"Because you're a Committee spy," growled one of the rebels.

"I am a captain in the Titanian Army!" she yelled at him. "Why would I spy for the Committee?"

"You served those bastards once," the rebel leader said. "Why wouldn't you again?" Tirpitz frowned, her face turning red with anger.

The leader walked off and the rest of them fell in a loose circle around the group ensuring none of them would try to run off. Tirpitz helped Ezra to his feet, his nose noticeably more crooked than it was before Zinvor punched him. Drops of blood had stained Ezra's flight suit, leaving a trail from his collar down to his waist.

The rebels led them further into the dead city. The streets rumbled under their feet from far off explosions and Vincent could hear the distinct sound of long bursts of machine gun fire in the distance.

"So, who are you guys with?" Fiona asked.

"Pfft," said the leader. "The Head Hunters, who else is there?" He held out his arm where he had an armband with a cartoonish severed head was displayed. The other rebels laughed at his answer.

"Are the Cutters still around?" she asked.

"That asshole Marcus's crew? Yeah they're still around," he said. "They control most of the east side. Why?"

"I used to run with them before the EDF picked me up," Fiona said.

"You were dumb enough to get drafted?" The leader laughed. "The legendary Great Traitor sure surrounds himself with the best." The rebels broke into laughter again.

"Oh, go fuck yourself," Fiona shot back. "Your war seems to be going great. You control what? Ten, fifteen feet of a shit hole? Big fucking man you are!" Tirpitz stifled a laugh and glanced around nervously. The rebel leader stopped in his tracks, turning on his heel and punched Fiona in the stomach. Her armor protected her from any real damage, but she reeled back, trying to catch her breath.

Vincent rushed forward, reeling back and delivered a punch to the man's jaw. The leader stumbled back before catching himself. Before he could attack again Vincent was brought to his knees by a powerful blow to the back of his head. He felt a warm liquid dripping down through his hair. Vincent turned to see the rebel with the shotgun standing over him.

Tirpitz rushed to his aide. She grabbed the man at the wrist, thrusting her hips into his waist, and tossed the rebel onto the ground. She didn't stop there. Instead she twisted his wrist hard and snapping it in half so loudly it sounded like a gun shot and he dropped the shotgun. His stomach turned when the rebel's arm flopped at an unnatural angle when she released it. Tirpitz grabbed the shotgun and pointed it directly the leader.

"I dare you, bitch," the leader laughed, rubbing his jaw. "You'll be dead on the spot."

"Sure. Probably." Tirpitz grinned. "But at this range you'll be just as dead as I am." The leader's eyes widened, and he looked around at the other rebels.

"Alright, alright," the leader said. "That's enough fucking around." He held a hand up, trying to calm the situation.

"Pussy," Fiona spat at the leader. Vincent dabbed at the back of his head and sighed when he felt the jagged edges of split skin. "Are you alright?" she asked.

"Yeah." He sighed. His head throbbed, but it was hardly the worst thing that had happened as of late. Bleeding from one wound or another had become a normal part of his life.

"Your *Great Traitor* hits like a bitch," the Leader laughed. Vincent clenched his fists and started walking towards the Leader again but was pulled back. He looked down and saw Fiona's hand on his arm. She shook her head at him. "That's right," the leader said, turning around. "You should listen." He snickered and began walking off once again.

"I don't know who that bastard is," Vincent seethed. "But I'm going to beat his ass."

"Of course you are, dear." Fiona patted him on the shoulder.

The rebels led them further into the city. Every few steps Vincent could hear the whimpering of the rebel with the broken arm. Large tarps and frayed blankets were tied up at various intervals, seemingly at random. Bricks and other debris had been shored up into defensive lines with bored looking rebels leaning against them.

"Hey!" The leader called out to them. "Let the Boss know I got them." A few of the rebels got up from the wall and shuffled away. Out of the wreckage of the heavily damaged cityscape came a mostly intact city block. The area looked like it used to act as a municipal complex in a previous, far gone era. The roof had been blown off of one of them and was replaced with a tapestry of tarps and scrap wood.

The windows were boarded up and the doors had been replaced with blankets that were in various stages of falling apart. A large, badly made flag that showed the same cartoonish severed head as the rebel's armbands hung from a pole over the main door of the complex. The hum of what sounded like a generator could be heard over the blowing wind.

"Alrighty girl, you can hand over the shotgun now," the leader said, his hand outstretched. Tirpitz exchanged glances with Vincent.

"Go ahead. If they were going to kill us, they probably would have done it by now," Vincent said. Tirpitz sighed, looking defeated and handed the shotgun to the leader. The leader grinned, upended the shotgun, and delivered a crushing blow to the side of Tirpitz's head. A gash was torn over her eyebrow and she collapsed bonelessly into the dirt.

"I'm not gonna kill you. But we did owe you that one for my man's arm," the leader said.

"You piece of shit!" Vincent screamed.

"We should have just left you to rot!" Ezra seethed.

"Now you want some old man?" The leader laughed. Zinvor stepped forward, his dark eyes burning into the leader. Vincent stepped up to be shoulder to shoulder with his Mawr bodyguard.

"If you touch another member of my group, I promise you I'll leave your piece of shit rebellion to die on this backwater hellhole," Vincent said through gritted teeth. "But not before I let Zinvor here tear you apart with his bare hands."

"Oh, so the *Great Traitor* has some balls now?" The leader chuckled.

"I will when I rip yours off," Vincent said. The two were now so close together he could make out the leader's pale blue eyes and the small black tear-shaped tattoos that ringed his eyes. Rebellion or no rebellion, he wanted to kill this man. No. He was going to kill this man.

"You wanna do this Worm?" The leader growled.

"You're fucking right I do," he said, their chests were now touching. The leader was a full head shorter than Vincent and at least twenty pounds lighter. But after fighting side by side with Fiona he knew to never underestimate a Martian because of their slight size.

"Hey!" Screamed a voice over the blowing wind. The leader, suddenly snapped out of their confrontation, looked over at the direction of the voice. "Xan! Do you have them?"

"Yeah!" the Leader responded.

"Well the Boss is waiting!" The man yelled back. "Hurry the hell up!" the Leader, Xan, turned to Vincent, his eyes narrowing.

"The Boss saved your ass Worm. This ain't over," he hissed before stomping off.

"Is she okay?" Vincent asked Ezra, who had his arm around Tirpitz. She had woken slightly, but it didn't look like her feet were working yet.

"I'm fine," Tirpitz moaned. "I just need a minute."

"A doctor would be a good idea," Ezra said. "But I don't think that's an option around here."

"And your nose?" Vincent asked.

"Definitely broken," Ezra said. "Is it bad?"

"Well, it ain't good." Fiona slapped him on the shoulder.

"I should have killed you," Zinvor grunted at him.

"No killing Ezra," Vincent said, a command he never thought he would have to give. The group was pushed forward by the rest of the rebels, towards the complex.

The rebels standing around in the complex's courtyard stared daggers at the group of newcomers as they walked through the area. Xan swept the entry curtain aside and they stepped inside. For what felt like the first time in hours Vincent's face wasn't being assaulted by the rough sand and the Martian wind.

What he saw inside did not look anything like the headquarters of a planetary rebellion. Loud music played, heavily polluted with static from frayed speakers. Men and women drank and danced in various stages of undress. The air hung heavy with cigarette smoke and was tinged with the smell of unwashed bodies. Most of the people drunkenly dancing around still had rifles slung over their backs or pistols shoved into their waist bands.

In the corner a crowd of people were gathered cheering on as two men, bleeding heavily from various cuts on their faces, fought each other. Flickering lightbulbs hung from the ceiling by their bare wires. Their poor power supply ensured the lights were only working at half strength, basking the whole area in an eerie yellow-green glow.

"Bring 'em here!" Called out a voice over the ruckus. Xan pushed through the crowd, making a small gap for everyone else. The drinking crowd of rebels and civilians turned to gawk at the new people in their midst. He noticed more than a few sets of eyes remained locked on Tyr and Zinvor.

On the opposite side of the dance floor was a long table. It was chipped and damaged, unlike the pristine banquet table on Grand Titan. A small feast of EDF rations were scattered about, the packages ripped open. A ring of drunk rebels sat around it, most of them sporting the same type of facial tattoos as Xan. At the head of the table sat a man that looked about as old as Ezra. His pale head was shaved bald and instead of hair was covered in small black tattoos.

Half of his face was covered with a rough white-blonde beard. The other half was disfigured by a burn scar. The scar started at his eyebrow and went down the right side of his face and neck. His right eye was milky, white, and dead. He wore the tattered grey top of an EDF colonel general, undoubtedly looted off a corpse.

"So, you're the ship that destroyed a Worm supply barge," he said. His voice sounded like it was the product of a life-long smoking habit. It was a statement, not a question. "You." He pointed a finger at Vincent. "I hear you say you're the Great Traitor." The table burst out in laughter. The man at the head of the table did not join in.

"That's what the EDF says," Vincent said.

"Hm." He grunted. "And what do you say?"

"I say I'm Vincent Solaris. Human Consul to the Fidayi Clan. Cohort Leader of the Elysian Defense Force." Ezra coughed loudly from the back of the group. Vincent sighed and added

"Destroyer of Earth." The crowd of rebels talked to each other in hushed tones. They turned back to Vincent, eyeing him with suspicion.

"That is a hell of a claim to make kid," the man said. "My boys." He nodded around the table. "They don't believe the shit that's coming out of your mouth."

"I have a hard time believing your shit either," Vincent said, scratching his beard. "If you thought we were some random assholes landing in the middle of this war zone with no worth to you or your cause you would have killed us and took our ship without going through all of this trouble."

"That's still a possibility." The man grinned.

"No, it isn't." Vincent shook his head. "I know you want our help. And I promise you if my group and I come to any harm the Clan will turn your planet into glass." He wasn't sure how much of a bluff the last part was, and he didn't want to find out.

"And you want my help. Why else would you have come to this damned rock?" The man stood. "I'm Murat, and *this* is my army."

Vincent had to say, he was not impressed with the people Denta had sent him to help.

"The Head Hunters?" Vincent asked.

"That's right. Strongest gang on the east end." Murat gave a toothy grin, obviously proud of the boast. He was missing most of his teeth and the ones that remained were the shade of butter. "And you're going to have to prove you're worthy of working with us."

"What?" Vincent said, exasperated. They had traveled from a different solar system to aid them in their fight for independence, been beaten on arrival, and now wanted them to prove themselves? He couldn't believe it.

"If you want to fight the worms you're going to need the rest of the gangs. And they sure as shit ain't gonna to trust you unless you have someone to vouch for you," Murat said.

"Let me guess," Fiona cut in. "*You* want to take something before the other gangs do, but you need our help to do it."

"My boys could do it without you!" Murat waved her off unconvincingly.

"Maybe without them," Ezra said. "But not without my ship." Vincent saw Murat's eyes dart around his table to his comrades. Ezra had him dead to rights.

"If you want our ship, you're going to have to arm it," Vincent said. He didn't want them to know they were out of ammo, he wanted it to sound more like a deal than anything else. "Arming an attack ship isn't cheap you know." He saw Ezra start to cut in before slowly seeing what Vincent was doing.

"We've raided enough of the Worms bases that we have some of their bombs laying around," Murat said. "We've just been using them to ambush their patrols." The table broke into laughter once again. "We can spare a few."

"So, what is it you want to do?" Vincent asked.

"We got some spooks in with the Worm work crews on the west end," Murat said. He rummaged around in his pockets before pullout of a data display. He clicked it a few times before it finally turned on. Its screen was cracked and barely readable. "They told me they're moving a huge shipment of missiles towards their positions here." A map that flickered with static was shown to Vincent. If he was reading the map correctly it showed the Headhunters, whose area was colored green, were almost entirely surrounded by EDF controlled areas. A small corridor remained opened connecting them to another area that was colored green.

"They're going to threaten the corridor you have with your allies?" Ezra asked.

"It's how they snapped up the North End," Murat said. "Cut off the gangers and snuffed 'em out one by one."

"I don't understand," Ezra said. "The EDF I was a part of would have just sat back and strafed your forces until there was nothing left. Why would they want to engage you on the ground on your own turf?"

"That was the old EDF." Murat waved him off. "Once Earth was gone, they lost their endless supply train. No more Capitol ships. All they got is a few destroyers. Even the smallest Reaper is worth its weight in gold these days. They won't risk 'em. Conscripts on the other hand..." He trailed off. Vincent gasped in disbelief. The massive Capitol ships, like the *ESS Victory* he had lived on, were all gone. The once mighty EDF naval fleet was in tatters after being mangled by the destruction of Earth and lost fighting the Clan and Alliance above Grawluck.

"How do you have such a huge supply of anti-air weapons?" Ezra quizzed him. "If you don't even have a supply of anti-armor missiles that is."

"This wreck we're sitting in now?" Murat began, Vincent could see him swelling with pride. "Was the command center for the 100th Air Defense Regiment. Their fat ass commander didn't expect us to hit 'em while they were asleep." Murat laughed. Now he knew where he got the stolen colonel general's uniform from. "Got most of their wares in the ambush."

"You're forcing them to move their supplies on the ground?" Vincent asked.

"For the most part," Murat said. "Large shipments have to go to Victoria and Tharsis before being trucked into Olympus. The Mons Spaceport is still open, but they only risk shipments there once or twice a week and it is more of a fortification than a spaceport at this point." Vincent was impressed. The rebels surrounding were not much to look at, but they had managed to stand against the EDF.

"I imagine the shipments are under heavy guard?" Ezra asked.

"Tanks, APCs, you name it." Murat said. "Enough that we can't mess with 'em without some support."

"So, we fly in blow up their armor and you take their supplies?" Vincent said. "Seems easy enough."

"That's where you're wrong boy." Murat pointed a finger at Vincent. "You will be with me on the ground. If I'm gonna to vouch for you I need to see if you got a sack between your legs."

"Ridiculous," Tirpitz gasped. "You can't expect the Consul to charge into battle like a common soldier!"

"That seems like a pointless risk," Ezra agreed. Vincent sighed.

"Fine," he said. "I'll do it."

"What?" asked an exasperated Ezra. "Why?"

"I need him to vouch for me if any of this is going to work," Vincent said. "Obviously, none of you have to come with me."

"Fuck that." Fiona laughed. "You know I'm going."

"Your battlefield is mine as well," Zinvor said.

"Err," Tirpitz thought aloud. "I suppose my choice is made for me."

Vincent fought back a smile.

CHAPTER TWENTY-TWO

Vincent sat, propped against the dirt wall behind him. Murat had put the group up in a dank, filthy room at the far end of what had become the Head Hunter's command post. Though they had come up with a battle plan together, they were still being treated like prisoners.

They had not been given their weapons back and Vincent had heard the distinct sound of a lock slamming shut on the door behind them when they were shown their rooms. The bed rolls they had been given smelled like they had belonged to soldiers who were two months deep into a campaign.

While he and Tirpitz had decided that it was for the best to sleep on top of the bed rolls, Ezra and Fiona didn't seem to mind the stench they emitted and were curled up inside, soundly asleep. Zinvor lay on his back, his arms folded over his thick chest and snoring so loudly that Tyr had used their bed roll to cover their head to try to drown him out.

Vincent, as always, was wide awake. He wasn't stressed about the upcoming operation. Instead he was incredibly suspicious of their new so-called allies. Murat was little more than a ganger or a warlord and his men didn't even qualify as rebels. They were little more than thugs wearing the drapery of rebels. He knew they couldn't trust them. He cursed Denta. He had put them in the unenviable position where they had no choice *but* to trust them.

Throughout the night, or day, Vincent was unsure of which, the floor rumbled with the impact of far off shelling. Every few hours he would hear the shriek of low flying rockets or artillery. He was sure if it was incoming EDF artillery or some other gang that Murat had pissed off. At some point a wide crack split the floor of their room in half as the ruined foundation of the building finally crumbled under the abuse. Smaller spider cracks had begun to branch off of it. He was certain one direct hit would bring the entire building down on their heads.

His head throbbed from where his skin had been split open. Vincent worried that with his current surroundings it was going to get infected. There was no water to speak to clean it out and he had to instead use the booze the Martians were drinking. He wasn't sure of its origins, but it smelled only a few proof shy of the fuel he watched Titanian ground crews pump into the *Shanna II.*

The door to the room clicked and was flung open. Standing in the doorway was Xan. Now, with his face uncovered Vincent could see he was no older than he was. He wore stolen EDF body armor with an ammo harness thrown over it, tattered grey cargo pants, and a black tank top. The dented and worn rifle he had slung over his shoulder had its butt stock sawn off.

"You pussies ready?" he said, glaring at them. Fiona pushed the bed roll off of her.

"Hard to be ready when you assholes still haven't given us our guns back," she said.

"You'll get 'em back when the Boss says you can get 'em back," Xan spat. "Not a second sooner." Vincent knew he would have to fight the urge to shoot Xan as soon as Murat returned his Riten. He knew he would be able to restrain himself, but he wasn't so sure about Zinvor. "You have a few minutes to get your shit together. We gotta move before the dust dies down."

The group slowly started rising once Xan had left. With each other's help Fiona and Vincent strapped on their Armor. Zinvor had never taken his off. Tirpitz slipped on body armor she had brought with her. Though it looked much the same as the EDF's, it had pouches for ammunition and grenades attached to it, rather than requiring an additional webbed harness. Her armor also had additional flaps that buttoned around her neck and down over her groin.

The room that was packed full of drunken party goers the night before was full of passed out gangers. They lay unconscious, mostly likely wherever they fell, from a hard night of drinking. Shame didn't seem to be a common trait amongst them. Several were naked and wrapped around one another. What they had been doing before finally blacking out was plainly obvious.

"Do they have any decency?" Tirpitz gasped, wrinkling her nose.

"I think they answered that question very clearly," Vincent said. The overwhelming combination of smells was causing his eyes to water.

"Man." Fiona coughed. "It smells like a bunch of armpits fucked each other all night."

"Wouldn't you want to spend the night before going out to fight getting drunk and banging your brains out?" Xan asked. He was seated at the table in the corner that the gang's leaders had been seated around the night before. He had a jar of clear liquid in his hand and was smoking a hand rolled cigarette.

"Wait, these guys are going to be fighting with us today?" Vincent asked, incredulous.

"You don't see any other army around, do you?" Xan asked sarcastically. Vincent didn't see any army whatsoever. Just a bunch of drunk gangers and what he assumed were prostitutes.

"What are they going to do?" Ezra asked, his nose curled. "Puke on the EDF?"

"They'll rally here soon enough don't you worry." Xan nodded, smoke curling out of his nose. The cooks made some food out back. By the time you get a bowl they will be up." Xan put a thumb over his shoulder towards open doorway behind the bar area.

The group went through the door and found what the Head Hunters considered a Kitchen. Also, Vincent found the source of the thick blanket of smoke that clung to the ceiling of the entire complex since they had arrived. Two cook fires roared in the middle of the floor with two large pots sat down right on top of them. A thick, dark substance boiled within.

The smell coming off of the pots was not what Vincent would describe as welcoming. The concoction smelled like a mixture of sour meat and rotten potatoes. An older man, or at least old in comparison to the Martians Vincent had yet seen, stood between the two pots. He was stirring his concoction with what looked like a piece of rebar.

"Did ya what some?" he asked, his voice deep and guttural.

"Umm," Vincent said, exchanging concerned glances with Tirpitz and Ezra.

"Oh, calm down guys it's just black broth," Fiona said. The man dipped a tin bowl into the mixture and handed it to Fiona.

"It's not going to kill us?" Tirpitz asked.

"I'm not dead and I ate it all the time." Fiona shrugged. She handed bowls to them one at a time. Vincent took his and looked down at it. It looked more like oil than food. He watched Fiona drink straight from the bowl, slopping some of the black mess around her mouth. Ezra and Tirpitz watched Vincent and waited.

He dipped the bowl up to his mouth and drank deep. The soup hit his tongue with the force of an artillery shell. The *black broth* tasted like a pure decay. His body fought against what he was trying to force into it. It took every inch of Vincent's will to not projectile vomit all over the kitchen area.

Cold sweat beaded at his hairline and his heart raced. Finally, the mouthful of soup went down, and he tossed the rest aside. His tin bowl clanging off of a nearby table before clattering to the floor.

"What the fuck did you just make me eat?" He coughed. Ezra and Tirpitz set their bowls aside, uneaten.

"I told you, black broth," Fiona said slurping down the rest of her bowl.

"But what is it?" Vincent asked. He grabbed a tin of liquor off of a counter and chugged it back trying to chase away the rotten taste that lingered on his tongue.

"A pig," the man stirring the pot said.

"Like, a whole pig?"

"Entrails, feet, tongue. The soup's base is pig's blood. It's whatever is left over at the end of the month."

"I don't think you are supposed to keep pork that long." Tirpitz grimaced.

"Aww what the fuck Fiona?" Vincent cried. "Why would you feed this to me?"

"I thought you were sick of rations," she said.

"I am. Next time I'll just eat from the ship's latrine," he cursed. "It'll taste the damn same."

*   *   *

True to his word, when the group left the kitchen and reentered the main room the vaunted Head Hunter "army" was awake. Xan was addressing them as they finished getting dressed. Nobody seemed to be paying any attention to him.

Murat entered the room. He wore a pistol on each hip and a had a short carbine on a three-point sling hanging off of his chest. To his surprise he was wearing the same Titanian type body armor as Tirpitz. Though his looked much worse for wear and had several dark stains around the neck area.

"I assume you still have our weapons?" Vincent asked.

"I do not go to war without my Riten," Zinvor growled.

"Relax, I still got 'em." He motioned to a ganger standing nearby who dropped a duffle bag in front of the group. Zinvor bent down and opened it. He picked through the pile of weapons until he found his Riten. He cradled the pistol in his hands and smelled its barrel. His dark eyes shot open in shock.

"You fired it," he growled. Vincent sighed and put his hand on the Warrior's shoulder.

"Calm down," Vincent told him, hoping his duty as a Tsarra still held some weight. It was the only thing keeping Zinvor from putting a fist sized hole in Murat's chest.

"This is unforgivable," Zinvor said, while holstering his Riten. He glanced angerly at Vincent for forcing him to restrain himself.

"Save it for later," Tirpitz said, glaring at Xan. "I know I am." Zinvor nodded, understanding. Vincent holstered his Riten and slung his rifle over his shoulder.

He walked over to the metal crates that Murat had pointed to. Inside were thousands of pilfered EDF magazines still loaded with slugs. Several of the magazines were dented and had dark red stains on them. After loading up his pouches he searched for grenades but found none. Instead he found glass jars with a clear liquor sloshing around inside. A wick was poked through the top of the jar's metal lid.

"What the hell is this?" he asked, holding it up.

"A Chairman Cocktail." A nearby ganger grinned. "You light the wick and toss the bastard at whatever you want to burn." A regular hand grenade would have been much more useful, but that was clearly not an option. He stuck several of the cocktails in his harness before rejoining the group.

"Good luck down there." Ezra patted Vincent on the shoulder. He put something in his hand. Vincent looked down and saw it was a small radio and microphone that could clip onto his shoulder. "If anything goes sideways, you let me know," Ezra said. "We'll drop down and grab you and get the hell out of here."

"Let's hope that isn't necessary." Vincent smiled. "You just bring the fire down on those tanks."

"I always do." Ezra nodded. He straightened to attention and gave Vincent a sharp salute before pivoting on his heel and marching out of the room. Tyr straightened and saluted Vincent by holding a closed fist to their thin chest and chased after Ezra.

"Ready?" Fiona asked him, a cigarette poking out from her teeth. He took it from her and inhaled it deeply. He blew out a cloud of smoke into the already smoky air.

"Not even a little."

*　　*　　*

The Martian wind and dust abused them as they stalked through the ruined city. Vincent had tied a strip of cloth over his face in a vain attempt to protect himself, much like everyone else. The dust had turned what he now knew was day into a red tinged dusk.

The few civilians that still survived in the district of the city were hunkered down indoors until the dust settled. Vincent had learned that this was one of the few times of the year where the gangers turned revolutionaries had an upper hand. The EDF, being mostly from Earth and the Moon, simply couldn't operate in such a harsh climate. Instead they would sit in their well defended and supplied bases until the weather cleared up. The windy season was what was known to the Martians as The Fighting Season.

The Gangers of Olympus were born into the dust storms. First born Martians were forced into the elements almost as soon as they were born. They had little choice other than to adapt to their world or die. All of those curious times when Vincent watched Fiona thrive in situations where others would fail started to make sense.

The remains of the city made the going slow. It would have been easy to simply march down the road, but the EDF would have seen that coming a while away. Instead, Murat and his gang picked their way through dozens of miles of bombed out alleyways and the tunnels of what had once been an underground transit system.

After hours of walking Murat called for the group to stop. The gangers dispersed into the broken subway tunnels and the surrounding buildings, which Vincent could tell were little more than a shell, their innards having been burned out long ago.

"This is the spot." Murat nodded.

"So, what's the plan?" Vincent asked.

"One of my boys is going to put a mine out that way." He pointed up the road in front of them. We hit the lead vehicle and hit the rear vehicle. Trap 'em in." He wasn't sure what they planned on attacking any of the EDF vehicles with. The heaviest weapon any of them had brought was a machine gun. That was when he saw a ganger pull a long tube out of a duffle bag he had been carrying with him.

The tube looked badly welded together with the trigger mechanism of a light machine gun bolted onto the bottom of it. The ganger produced a homemade rocket, which looked as if it would explode at the slightest touch and slid it into the tube.

"I don't know what that is, but it looks like it's going to end badly," Tirpitz said, a worried expression on her face.

"Anti-tank weapons are kind of hard to come by, so we make these little babies in house," Murat said. "We use 'em all the time."

"What's their success rate?" she asked.

"A lot to a little," he said, not bothering to point out which meant success or failure. Vincent made a mental note to stay far away from the ganger and his homemade rocket launcher when the ambush started.

Vincent and the rest of the group got comfortable in the remains of the subway tunnels. Murat sent another group of gangers to the head of the road, so they could fire on the convoy from two sides. He watched as gangers unloaded medium and heavy machine guns from their packs and set them up on the parapet of the tunnel. Fiona crouched down next to him.

"So, what happened down here?" he asked.

"The transit system? An EDF earthquake bomb. One of those bastards that they fire from orbit."

"A what?" he asked.

"One of those bastards that they send down from orbit. It penetrates a couple hundred feet below the surface and then explodes."

"But why target a train station?"

"It was easy for rebels to use the transit tunnels to move freely throughout Olympus. They could hit the EDF and vanish back down into the tunnels."

"Smart."

"For a while it was." She sighed. "Civilians got sick of worms kicking in their doors looking for rebels or getting their houses strafed by Reapers. Soon they took their families and moved into the tunnels too. It kind of became something of a second Olympus, just below the surface."

"What happened to them when the EDF blew up the tunnels?"

"Dead. All of them." She balled her hands into fists. "The explosion was so big that the ones who survived the fireball had their lungs blown out of their chest by the overpressure. Drowning on dry land like a fish out of water. A half a million people gone in seconds."

The attack had done a number on the tunnel, but he could still see shades of what it would have looked like without years of warfare. Marble brick walls, which would have shone brightly under white lights. Large, faded murals were painted across the bricks showing a triumphant Martian soldier standing atop Olympus Mons, his rifle held over his head.

On another wall—it's marble deeply cracked and crumbling— was a red backdrop with a single blue star in its center. The proposed flag of an independent Mars. The heroic tapestry of a war for independence that he thought must have looked different than the one he was currently living through.

"What happened to that version of Mars?" Tirpitz asked, motioning towards the walls. She sat down on the rocks next to him, taking in the surroundings.

"Looks like the same EDF propaganda shit they showed us before stuffing us into a ship and sending us after the Alliance," Vincent said. He remembered the rows of posters that wall papered the bastard Rostov's office. Rostov, the EDF officer that forcefully conscripted him under a court order. The man who had more to do with the destruction of earth than he did. "How do they trick people into enlisting on Titan?"

"There's no tricks," Tirpitz said. "Everyone has to serve two years before going off to college. It's just a part of the community."

"But not you." Vincent prodded. The captain still hadn't shared much about herself, but he felt that the enigma was about to give.

"No." She shook her head. "I did well enough on my tests that I was accept into Officer's Academy when I was sixteen. I couldn't turn that down."

"What did you parents think of that?" he asked. "If my dad had a choice, I never would have even looked at a uniform." He laughed.

"Wanted you to follow in his footsteps?" she asked.

"Something like that. Wanted me to go to school and learn a trade like him," he said. "I kind of derailed that by passing school by the skin of my teeth and getting rejected from every college on Earth." While he was exaggerating slightly, he really had been rejected from every school in his home District. Tirpitz stifled a laugh.

"Mine were much the same. My dad wanted me to be a pilot like him." She frowned. "I wanted to be on the ground."

"I guess I never asked," Vincent said. "What is it you do in the army?"

"Why do you think I was sent with you?" She gave a wry smile. "I'm in the Pathfinder Corps." She pointed to the badges that she wore on either collar. Two small, crossed torches. "We go ahead of the army and set up landing zones, call in orbital strikes, and lay the groundwork for the main offensive. We can act as light scouts in a pinch."

"Now things are starting to make sense."

"keep it down!" A ganger hissed at them in a harsh whisper. "They're coming!" Vincent saw dust cascading down from the subway ceiling and the ground began to shake. He remembered that feeling when he saw an EDF armored column roll by for the first time on Ryklar. Tirpitz held a finger to her ear where she had a small earpiece. In hushed tones she whispered.

"*Shanna II*, this is *Pathfinder*. Be advised, contact with the enemy incoming. What's your location?" Vincent couldn't hear her radio, but the receiver he had clipped to his armor hissed static before he heard the familiar sound of Ezra's voice.

"Read you loud and clear *Pathfinder*. *Shanna II* is on station."

"Received," she said. "Standby." She turned to Vincent. "He's above us. Probably low enough that EDF pickets can't get him but high enough to hide up in the dust." Murat slid down the side of the broken tunnel, moving quickly from street level to the underground. He landed next to the group. A twisted smile was spread across his burnt face.

"You ready?" he asked.

"Always." Fiona smirked.

"I mean you, *Great Traitor*. Don't let us down," he said.

"I was going to say the same thing to you," Vincent shot back.

"Your gang better be worth our time," Tirpitz joined in. Clearly affected by his gang being challenged, Murat puffed his chest out and began to climb back to street level.

"Oh, you'll see!"

*   *   *

Vincent peeked his head over the broken tunnel's edge. The ground's shaking intensified as the EDF column inched closer. The column's lead vehicle slowly came into view. A Lunar pattern tank, it's once black paintjob had been stained rust-red by the planet's unceasing wind and dust. Its tracks chewed up the ground and it drove slowly on. Its cannon swung back and forth, searching for targets.

Behind it was a transport vehicle. It was little more than a truck cab with a flatbed, cruising along on a pair of tracks less than half of the size of the tank's. A large metal shipping container was strapped on its flatbed, nearly two times the size of the truck itself. That had to be Murat's target.

Behind the transport vehicle was a troop carrier, which looked like an armored box on tracks. An EDF trooper poked out of the carrier's gunner's hatch, a heavy belt-fed machine gun in his hand. He had never ridden in one, but Vincent knew a normal transport could carry at least thirty soldiers. Not only were they outnumbered, they had to fight a tank. He cursed himself for allowing Murat to lead him out to the ambush.

The rebels had stacked a small pile of rocks on the side of the road. According to Murat, it acted as a flag for the triggerman whose job it was to detonate the mine they had planted. Vincent assumed at the beginning that Murat was talking about an actual landmine, but he wasn't. The mine had actually been a homemade bomb. It was little more than a few anti-air missiles bound together with utility tape. They had wired a radio to the bomb so when that radio was contacted on a specific channel, the bomb would explode.

A rebel sat near them, his legs crossed under him like a school kid. In his hands he had a small black radio. He was fiddling with the dials on top of the radio, looking increasingly frustrated.

"Any time now!" Murat called down to him.

"I'm trying boss!" The rebel whined. "It ain't working!"

"What?" Murat screamed. "Xan put that together himself!" It did not take long for their voices to draw attention.

Machine gun fire stitched across the lip of the tunnel. The rebel holding the radio had is head torn in half by the incoming burst. Vincent dove for cover into the debris.

"*Shanna II,* this is *Pathfinder.* We are compromised!" Tirpitz screamed into her earpiece. Vincent had forgotten, through all of her education and years of military service, this was the first time anyone had ever shot at her. "Requesting immediate air support!" Ezra's response came back so broken and garbled with static Vincent couldn't understand it.

Rebels, grouped together in small clusters, began to fire wildly over their cover. Dozens of them were reduced to red mist by a single well aimed tank shell.

"Spread out!" Vincent screamed. He took off running down the length of the tunnel. Rifle fire joined the chorus of machine guns already pouring down onto them. The air around Vincent's head became filled with so many bullets it sounded as if he had stuck his head into a hornet's nest.

The troop carrier's back ramp dropped, and a platoon of soldiers charged out. The soldiers took up positions and began pounding the rebels with well-aimed fire. Vincent fell to his stomach to take cover as the debris around him exploded with gunfire. A rebel dropped next to him, clutching a ragged throat wound. Blood pulsated from between his fingers.

Vincent rolled onto his back and pulled one of the Chairman Cocktails from his vest pouch. He stared down at the wick, cursing himself for not carrying anything to light it with.

"Fiona!" he yelled. She was only a few feet away, ducking behind the remains of a subway directory sign.

"What?" she screamed back. The sign was getting smaller and smaller as incoming fire chipped away it's edges.

"I need your lighter!" he said. She gave him a confused look before rummaging around in her pockets. She found one and tossed it to him. He flicked the flint a few times before a flame popped up. Vincent lit the Cocktail and panicked as fire surged dangerously down the wick.

He pushed himself to a knee and flung the cocktail out into the street. He heard the sound of shattering glass and watched as group of six soldiers were engulfed in flames. They ran, their screams being drown out by gunfire, as their uniforms burnt and melted to their skin. One by one they dropped to the ground.

Another tank shell screamed overhead and exploded amongst a group of rebels. Dirt, debris, and body parts rained down on the surviving occupants of the tunnel. Then, Vincent saw something he never wanted to use: the homemade rocket launcher, still being held onto by its late gunner, his chest blown open by machine gun fire.

"Shit," he cursed. Crawling across the ground, arm over arm he got to it. He couldn't tell if it was too damaged to fire or not, as it had always looked unsafe to be anywhere near. He sighed, picking the thing up in his hands. He was as good as dead in the moment anyway, so he might as well give it a shot.

"Hey!" he yelled back to the gathered rebels, which included Fiona, Tirpitz, and Zinvor who were all trying in vain to fire back at the EDF soldiers. "I need covering fire!"

"You don't plan on actually using that thing, do you?" Tirpitz asked.

"Are you going to give me covering fire or not?" he yelled back. Zinvor, seeing the plan unfold in his head, walked over to where a wounded rebel lay, a belt fed machine gun next to him. He dropped his rifle next to the man and picked up the machine gun.

"Ready!" Zinvor called out.

"Now!" Vincent ordered. Zinvor stepped up onto the parapet of the tunnel, fully exposing himself to enemy fire. He let out a long, unbroken burst of machine gun fire, sweeping it left and right. His border-line suicidal move emboldened the rebels around him, and they joined in. Vincent saw his chance and ran for it.

He leapt over the parapet and onto the road. He knew he was going to have to get close if he had any chance for the slapdash launcher to work. The road was littered with the dead and dying. Their blood had soaked into the red soil and congealed into dark pools on the street. The air was thick with the copper smell of human blood and the burning cordite of machine gun fire. As he got closer to the rear troop carrier, the EDF soldiers hiding from the rebel's suppressing fire saw Vincent and began to fire at him.

Vincent dove to the ground. Finding himself behind a wounded soldier, he grabbed the man and pulled him onto his side. The man's body twitched as bullet impacted and his blood oozed through holes in his body armor. It seeped towards Vincent, coating his hands and arms. Vincent rolled on his side, unholstered his Riten and waited. The soldier's fire slackened and died off. In their panic, their fire had become undisciplined. They had all begun reloading at once. A rookie mistake.

Vincent sprang to his feet and rushed the soldiers, launcher cradled in one arm and his Riten up and at the ready. He quickly emptied the six chambers of his Riten, striking one soldier in the neck and another in the chest. The other five turned tail and ran. He fumbled with his holster, the adrenaline pumping through his body making his fingers unable to line the gun up with the leather. He dropped to one knee and brought the launcher up to his shoulder. He clenched his teeth and slowly squeezed the trigger.

Nothing happened.

The piece of shit wasn't going to work. With almost perfect timing the gunner on top of the troop carrier noticed him in the middle of the road, launcher aimed directly at his vehicle. The gunner disengaged from the rebels in the tunnel and quickly began rotating towards him. Vincent frantically slapped and punched the launcher. He pressed the trigger over and over again. Finally, out of frustration he spiked the launcher to the ground and prepared to run for his life.

With a *pop* a rocket erupted out of the launcher. Fire and smoke streaked through the air in a wild spiral. The rocket skipped across the ground as its motor died out after only a few feet. It began to tumble, bouncing end over end down the street. To Vincent's utter amazement, the rocket exploded under the lowered ramp of the carrier. A fireball sent the carrier into the air, the smoking hulk completed a front flip before finally crashing back to the surface upside down. Flaming wreckage rained down on the battlefield, scattering the soldiers around it.

A cheer went up from the rebel positions before a tank shell silenced them. The tank had turned and began moving back down the road. It had pulled to the side of the transport vehicle, trying to protect its cargo from the rebels incoming fire. The EDF soldiers had also retreated from where they had dismounted from their carrier. Running back to the area around the transport vehicle, joining in with the tank in hammering the rebel positions.

Their return fire kicked sparks up from the road. Bullets snapped and popped only inches from his head. Vincent, unable to stand the incoming fire, retreated back to the tunnel with everyone else.

"Why isn't Ezra bombing the shit out of them?" he screamed at Tirpitz.

"I don't know!" she yelled. "I think the dust is messing with my signal!"

Ezra, it turned out, wasn't going to wait for his pathfinder to find him targets. Out of the dust came the gunmetal grey shape of the *Shanna II*. It hovered over the battlefield like a predator scoping out prey. Vincent could imagine Tyr picking through targets on the ground and hopefully being able tell which ones were friendly. A cheer came up from the EDF soldiers. They had seen a Reaper enter the battlefield and assumed their friends had come to help them. They had no idea what was about to happen to them.

The *Shanna II*'s cannon belched a cone of fire down the road. The cheers quickly turned into screams. The burst cut right through the huddle of soldiers taking cover behind the tank. Two rockets hissed out from under the ship's stubby, wing-like weapons mounts. They both impacted the tank right below the turret.

An explosion rippled through the street and severed the tank's turret and sent it cartwheeling into the air, trailing smoke behind it. The *Shanna II* turned and lifted back into the dusty air, it's job, Vincent hoped, done. Fire from the EDF soldiers all but ceased as they broke and fled into the city. Rebels ran out into the street and fired at them as they ran. Vincent saw several soldiers crumple and drop from gunshots to the back.

Now, with the EDF in full retreat, the Head Hunters strode out into the street like conquering heroes. The doors to the transport vehicle creaked open and three EDF soldiers slowly crawled out, their hands raised above their heads. Their faces were white with terror.

One, a soldier wearing the two collar stripes of a corporal shouted.

"We surrender!" His voice was shaking with fear. "Please you can have the truck just let us go!" A shotgun blast from Xan blew open the young corporal's chest and he fell to the street bonelessly.

"Hey!" Vincent screamed, he quickly advanced on Xan and pushed the shotgun away from the other two soldiers. "They surrendered!" Xan let out a harsh laugh.

"No such thing as a prisoner here kid." He smirked. He pumped his shotgun and a single empty red shell fell to the ground. "Get outta my way." Xan aimed is shotgun at one of the other soldiers and Vincent shoved him, sending the Martian stumbling back. Vincent went to draw his Riten, only to remember it was empty.

"Hurry up and get that damn transport out of here!" Murat ordered. "They're goin' to have artillery painting this whole damn area any second." He looked over at the two surrendered soldiers. A dark stain had begun to slowly work its way down one of their legs. The other, a slightly older looking Private First-Class was sobbing uncontrollably. "And someone clean up that mess."

Three gangers stepped forward and squeezed off bursts of automatic gunfire into the two soldiers. Their blood splattered into the crew compartment of the transport vehicle. Laughing gangers stepped forward and began to pick through the pockets of the dead men as their bodies twitched and groaned.

Rifle and pistol reports could be heard all over as members of the Head Hunters executed the wounded that the EDF had left behind. Vincent stood, frozen in the middle of the road in shock. He had not seen such brutality since the Alliance massacred the wounded after the doomed last stand of the EDF on Ryklar.

He felt a hand on his shoulder and looked over to see Fiona.

"That's just how it is here," she said. "They would have done the same to us." He looked over and saw Tirpitz's face turning several shades of pale green. "We need to go," she reassured him, her voice softening.

The gangers piled up their wounded on the remaining space on the back of the transport vehicle. Everyone else climbed onto the sides, hanging off. Vincent sat down with Fiona next to a man who had his arm amputated above the elbow. A tourniquet had been tied on, but his skin was getting pale even for a Martian.

After a bit of struggling the ganger who had been ordered to drive the transport vehicle got it in motion. Just as Murat said, EDF artillery began to rain down on the area, but thankfully they were long clear of it. Overhead he saw the *Shanna II* flying low, a single hand stuck out of the cockpit window giving them a thumbs up.

CHAPTER TWENTY-THREE

The Head Hunter's headquarters had turned back into the booze-fueled party that it had been the night before. Vincent couldn't tell the difference between the regular drinking from before and the celebratory drinking they were doing now. Thankfully, they were no longer being treated as prisoners. Unfortunately, this meant they were having shot after shot of gut-wrenching liquor pushed their way.

Someone had stolen a large Committee flag from one of the EDF vehicles and had set it on fire. People kept walking by, using it to light their cigarettes. Another person had been mixing drinks together in a dented EDF helmet and dolling it out to anyone who walked by. It was one drink Vincent made sure he turned down.

Murat had left, leaving his sadistic underboss Xan in charge. Murat explained he had to go talk to the other Bosses to set up a time for a meeting and let them know Vincent was the real deal.

The idea that someone as reprehensible as Murat or Xan was vouching for him made Vincent's stomach turn.

After fighting with the Head Hunters, he hoped the other gangs knew what they were doing. The rabble he had just fought with had no idea of spacing, disciplined fire, or tactics. They could hardly use cover effectively. Vincent watched more than a dozen of them get wiped out at once because they were hiding behind something wouldn't stop common rifle fire, let alone the heavy machines or tanks. The Clan and the Titanians couldn't get here fast enough.

Vincent sighed, putting back another drink. His tongue had grown numb to the Martian rotgut. Fiona, as always had been the life of the party. Slamming back drink after drink and hitting the dance floor. She found herself with a group of Martian women. They were feeding each other drinks and chain smoking.

Zinvor stood behind Vincent, one hand on the butt of his Riten, on guard as always. Tirpitz sat next to him, looking down into her drink, mentally checked out from the party around her. He knew that look. He had felt that way once before. When the massive adrenaline dump of combat wears off for the first time and you suddenly feel how incredibly close you just came to a violent death.

"Everything alright?" he asked.

"Hm?" She picked her head up. "Oh. Yeah."

"It'll pass."

"Unbelievable." She sighed. "I've been an officer in the Titanian Army longer than you've been alive and you're reassuring *me.*"

"If it makes you feel any better there's probably a couple Martian preschoolers who've seen more combat than me." He forced a laugh and relaxed a bit when he saw her smile.

"I didn't even fire my weapon," she said, deflated. "How do you go through all of that and not even fire your weapon?"

"Really?" he asked, shocked.

"I had one job and I fucked it up," she cursed herself. "I almost got us all killed."

"No, that idiot Xan's half assed bomb making job almost got us all killed," Vincent retorted. "You can't help it if the radio sucks."

"Well, I didn't help matters," She pouted. "I should have known the dust storm would have caused problems with the radio."

"And what if you did?" Vincent asked. "What could have you done differently?" She began to tear up, before quickly drying them with her sleeve.

"Nothing," she sniffed. "I could have done nothing."

"We survived, Anastasia," he said. "Sometimes, that is all that matters." She didn't say anything. Her eyes were locked onto her drink, the tears flowing freely now she made no further attempt to hide them. Ezra came up behind them, putting a hand on either of their shoulders.

"Looks like you need some fresh air," he said to Tirpitz and she nodded wordlessly. She left her half full drink on the table and followed after him.

"Talkin' shit about my bomb, are you?" came the drunken voice of Xan from behind him. He spun on his seat and met him. He wasn't sure if he had enough liquor in him not to care, or he was finally sick of the ganger's attitude.

"You mean the one that didn't work? Yeah," Vincent said.

"I'm about sick of your shit, Worm," he slurred. He poked Vincent in the chest with a single outstretched finger. Vincent grit his teeth. He was trying to control his emotions but was failing. *This pompous, drunken asshole had almost got them all killed.* His blood began to boil. He tried to force it down and kept remembering he had to work with these people. Vincent noticed the music died away and people stopped their conversations to look over and see what was going on.

"Step back," Zinvor growled. Zinvor stiff armed Xan square in the chest, his immense strength nearly knocked the small man over without trying. "Last warning." Xan spit at Zinvor's feet.

"Worm bitch," he cursed. "Nothin' without your toad slave watchin' your ass." Xan reached for a small pistol he had on his waist and Vincent's heart jumped into his throat.

Zinvor quickly unholster and cocked his Riten in one fluid motion. Xan was staring down the barrel of a Riten before his weapon had even budged. Vincent braced himself for the exchange of gunfire that was sure to be coming, but instead of shooting at him, Xan tossed his pistol on the floor.

"On your manhood, worm." The room exploded in a mixture of excited talking and cheers.

It was obvious Vincent was supposed to know what that phrase meant, but he had no idea. Fiona, barely able to walk, stumbled over to where Vincent sat at the bar.

"He wants to fight you," she managed to get out.

"What?" Vincent exchanged glances between the two of them. "That's stupid. I'm not going to fight him." Even though every inch of him screamed to punch Xan in the mouth he knew the best way to build allies for the coming the war was not to get into bar fights.

"Babe." She wrapped her arm around his shoulder. "You have to fight him. He's challenging your manhood."

"What kind of backward shit is that?" Vincent exclaimed.

"Martian shit," Fiona said. "Your manhood is your life."

"Wait, is he challenging me to a *fight to the fucking death?*" Vincent exchanged looks with Fiona and Xan. "Are you insane?"

Xan, by this point, had stripped off his tattered grey uniform jacket revealing his pale, tattoo covered chest.

"If you don't, he'll probably order his boys to kill us all," Fiona said. "He's trying to act like the big boss since Murat is away."

"Your whore is right," Xan spat. "You outsiders have no place here. Murat can't see that, but I can. I'll do what I do best: clean up the Boss's mess."

Vincent didn't wait any longer. He unholstered his Riten and set it on the bar. He kissed Fiona on her forehead and stepped towards Xan, then quickly launched himself forward, throwing a hard, right punch. Xan ducked out of the way and sent Vincent sprawling onto the floor face first. Xan was on him immediately, jumping on his back and began trying to wrap his arm around Vincent's neck. He tucked his chin down against his armor, saving him.

Vincent through his head back, slamming it hard into Xan's nose. Xan let go of his hold and fell off of his back. He felt a warm liquid dripping down the back of his head. Zinvor stepped forward, ready to aid him.

"Stay out of it," Vincent growled. "I fucking got this." Zinvor stopped in his tracks. Vincent jumped up to his feet quickly and blasted a kick into Xan's face as he began to stand up, sending him falling onto his back.

Now, he saw his chance and pounced on him. He mounted him and began to rain punches down on his stricken opponent. Xan, though caught in a bad position, brought his arms up to protect his head and face. Vincent's punches were deflected harmlessly away. Xan bucked his hips upward and sent Vincent flying up and over Xan's head.

Vincent quickly rolled over and found their positions reversed. Xan straddled him and connected hard with a quick left to his jaw. Stars bloomed in Vincent's eyes and he felt his teeth rattle as a copper taste filled his mouth. A second hard punch landed on the bridge of Vincent's nose and he felt it give way with a *crunch.* His eyes welled up with tears and he fought to see straight.

Through his blurry eyes he saw Xan reach behind his back and produce a small knife. Vincent reached out, putting his hands on Xan's hips and pushed hard. He wiggled his way out from underneath him and wildly kicked out, trying desperately to keep him back.

"I'll wear your damned skin when I'm done with you!" Xan cursed and pressed the attack. He slashed wildly with his knife and Vincent ducked and spun around as the sharp edge passed only inches from his face.

He was beginning to think telling Zinvor to stay back was a bad idea. His head swam and blood was dripping down his face and the back of his head. His eyes were starting to swell up and his vision blurred. He shook his head, trying to get his bearings as Xan attacked once again.

His knife glanced off of Vincent's shoulder, his armor thankfully holding strong. He shot his arm under Xan's armpit and pivoted into him, attempting a hip toss. Xan lowered his weight, stopping his attack. He only had a moment to curse himself for giving his opponent his back as Xan grabbed the back of his head and slammed it hard into the edge of the bar.

He felt his legs give out from under him and he flopped to the ground. He pushed himself over and rolled onto his back. Xan was moving in for the kill. He was pumping up the crowd, holding his knife up as his gangers cheered around them. Xan had his back turned, flexing his thin arms and laughing.

Vincent saw something fly in front of his face and stick into the ground next to him. His eyes focused and he saw the silver glint of Fiona's sword swaying back and forth next to him.

"Get up and kill that piece of shit!" she screamed at him. Vincent forced himself to his knees and wrenched the sword from the wooden floor. Slowly, he managed to command his legs to function and stand up. His vision narrowed to a tunnel and he wobbled, using the sword as a crutch.

Xan began to turn around, the crowd noise swelling to a fever pitch. The smile on his tattooed face faded to one of terror as he saw his prey standing and armed. Mustering up all the strength he had left, Vincent attacked. He swung the sword wildly, hacking and slashing at the blurry form of Xan as he tried in vain to escape.

Xan howled in pain as the blade found purchase. The tip of his nose was sent flying in the air with a squirt of blood. Vincent stepped back, did his best to line his target up, and slashed again. Xan brought up his small knife in an attempt to defend himself.

His sword cut straight through the hilt of Xan's knife. It kept going, slashing straight through Xan's wrist. A pulse of hot blood sprayed up into Vincent's face as he heard the wet slap of the severed hand hitting the floor. Xan screamed, using his other hand to cover his bleeding stump and dropped to his knees. The crowd with deathly silent.

"Kill him!" Fiona screamed. "Gut the bastard!"

Vincent brought the sword up high over his head. He lined it up with the whimpering face of Xan, a mixture of blood and tears running down his face. Vincent scanned the faces in the crowd. Though, they had grown silent from watching their hometown favorite get his hand chopped off, their faces were still excited. Some of them were snapping photos on small data displays.

Disgusted, Vincent stepped back and lowered the sword. As much as he hated the man, he wouldn't kill a man for a crowd's entertainment. He slumped back on his chair, the sword clattering to the ground. His head swam from the fight and he fought to keep his bearings.

"Why didn't you end it?" Fiona asked.

"No." Vincent struggled to get out. He was starting to get tired. "I'm not going to stoop to their level."

"If you could see what you look like right now you may have." Fiona frowned.

The crowd began to get restless. They gathered around Xan, who at this point had managed to staunch his stump's bleeding with his discarded shirt. Vincent looked on, assuming he was going to watch the gangers turn against them for maiming their Underboss. He couldn't have been more wrong.

The gangers started to hurl insults at Xan. Xan held his hand up in apparent surrender, but the crowd of angry gangers began to kick and punch him. Xan got to his feet and ran towards the door, the crowd on his heels. Xan managed to escape, leaving a small trail of blood behind him. The crowd stopped chasing him once he made it outside. Almost like nothing happened, the music queued back up and they began partying once again.

"What the hell did we just watch?" Tirpitz asked, a look of shock frozen on her face.

"He challenged Vincent's manhood and lost," Fiona said. "He *should* be dead but since Vincent decided he was above that the gang excommunicated him. He's not a man anymore."

"Shit," Vincent said. "Murat's going to be pissed." He couldn't imagine any situation that the gang leader would be happy he chopped up his Underboss and got him kicked out of his own gang.

"Doubt it." Fiona shrugged. "It's the life."

"So, what happens to Xan now?" Tirpitz asked.

"Probably goes out in the street and bleeds to death." Fiona laughed. "If he doesn't maybe some other gang might take him in. Or he turns snitch for the Worms."

"Your planet concerns me." Tirpitz frowned. Fiona smiled.

*　　　*　　　*

Vincent winced as a man who called himself a Doctor stabbed a needle into the back of his head. He watched as the thread unspooled as the Doctor pulled the needle up, sewing the ragged gash on the back of his head together.

"Sit still," the Doctor said.

"I'm trying," Vincent whined. This was the second time in as many weeks he had been forced to get stitches without any pain medication. The Doctor had offered him a shot of spirits to prepare for the procedure, but he had rejected it. His head was pounding, and he wasn't sure more booze would help with that.

The Doctor's Office was unlike any other he had ever sat in. Back on Earth when he went to see the Doctor at the District's Healthcare Complex the exam room was a near flawless, pearl white. This Doctor had set up shop in a mostly intact house, one of the bland square brick ones the Central Committee liked to build by the thousand. The walls were cracked and crumbling and its roof, which had been blown away, had been replaced by bits of tin and scrap wood. What had once been the living room has full of the wounded gangers from the botched ambush on the convoy.

The air was tinged with the smell of sweet almonds and booze. It turned out the same thing they had been drinking down the street at the bar doubled as a medical antiseptic. Unfortunately, for the stricken gangers laying out in the living room the gangrenous stench of the almonds told him it wasn't

282

working very well. On the table in front of him lay a blood-soaked power saw, indicative of the Doctor's treatment methods.

The blanket that served as the room's door was pulled open and the ugly, burnt face of Murat entered. Despite what Fiona had said, he still expected the worst.

"I see you're no worse for wear eh?" Murat said, sitting down on a rickety stool next to the bloody saw.

"Listen..." Vincent started.

"No worries," Murat said. "Xan was dumb enough to challenge you and lost. Whatever happens to him is his problem to deal with. I came to talk about the meeting."

"Oh." Vincent perked up. "How did it go?"

"After how I told them how you single handedly routed a Worm platoon, everyone was in agreement." Murat lit a hand rolled cigarette, discarding a spent match on the ground. Smoking in a Doctor's Office would be unheard of anywhere else. "We are going to hold a Great Crawl to discuss the war plans moving forward." Murat stood back up. "It is in the morning. We will go together." He turned and left the room.

"What the hell is a Great Crawl?" Vincent asked out loud to no one in particular.

"A meeting of all the gangs of the city's four boroughs," the Doctor said. "It started as a bar crawl where they'd all compete to see which gang could drink the most."

"Of course it did." Vincent sighed. He suddenly didn't feel so bad for founding an army at the Eagle and Bar.

"Since the rebellions it's kind of morphed into a political meeting." The Doctor tugged hard on the last stitch and set the needle down.

"Are all the rebels gangers?" Vincent asked.

"Mostly," the Doctor said. "Though one group calling itself the Mars Liberation Brigade has been operating in the north end."

"And you work for the gangs?" Vincent asked.

"I work for whoever has wounded," the Doctor said.

"But not the EDF?"

"I'd treat them," the Doctor said. "But none of them seem to make it to my hospital alive." Vincent stood up and offered a hand to the Doctor.

"Thank you, sir." The Doctor took the offered hand and shook it.

"Please, call me Doctor Sombart." He smiled, his deep-set wrinkles creasing his pale face.

"No offence Doctor, but I hope I don't need your help again," Vincent said.

"That makes two of us," Sombart said. "You should probably get some rest. It'll help with the headache."

"You wouldn't happen to have any medication for it would you?" Vincent asked, climbing to his feet.

"Not unless you want to get trepanned," Sombart said, cleaning his hands off in a small basin. The water in the basin was dark red.

"I'm sorry?" he asked confused.

"It means I drill a hole in your head to relieve pressure off of your brain." Sombart gave a slight laugh. "Without anesthetic."

"You don't really do that." Vincent frowned. Sombart motioned over to a small hand powered drill that sat soaking in a plastic bucket. Small chunks of meat floated in the bucket's red water. "You do that," Vincent gasped. "I guess I'll be going."

CHAPTER TWENTY-FOUR

Vincent stood in front of a broken mirror attempting to clean the dirt and blood off of his once dark blue armor. The collective filth had formed a crust that had worked its way into every scale of leather. He wondered to himself how the Mawr's armor always looked nearly spotless at all of their meetings.

Since they had proven themselves in battle and badly mangled his Underboss, Murat had gifted them their own room. Zinvor, as always, stood guard outside of it while Ezra and Tirpitz and their own rooms down the hallway. Tyr's stayed with the ship.

Fiona did not have the same qualms when it came to the cleanliness of her armor. Hers was still covered in the dirt, grime, and blood. Vincent was sure the brown specks around the neck of her armor was vomit. She sat, her back against the wall on their bed roll having her morning smoke and cleaning her Riten.

"I keep telling you they're not going to care about how clean your armor is," she said.

"And I keep telling you I don't care about them; I just feel disgusting," he said.

"We don't have time for that crap. We have to get the other two and get going," she said, pushing herself to her feet. She holstered her Riten and made for the door.

"Fine," Vincent said. "You were in a gang, have you ever been to one of these Crawls before?"

"Nope." Fiona shook her head. "You could say I didn't have the status to be invited. I heard they're fun as hell though."

"I don't think *fun* is what we're going for here," he said.

"Maybe you're not." Fiona tapped the ash off the end of her cigarette.

Vincent sighed and pushed the door open. It creaked angerly as the hinges struggled to hold on. While the room was still falling apart, it was the most intact room they had been in since they had landed on Mars. He was amazed to see the roof was the original and it even had a door rather than a sheet. Cracks spread out across the ceiling like the legs of a spider and the black orbs that used to be alight with power hung dead.

Vincent pushed the torn green blanket that was Ezra's door aside and found his room empty. A tattered bed roll lay in the middle of the room. An empty ration packet sat torn open and half eaten next to it.

"He must be with the ship," Fiona said. "What other hobbies does the old bastard have?"

"You're probably right." Vincent shrugged. The sound of rustling bodies from further down the hallway made them both turn around. Ezra and Tirpitz appeared from another doorway. Ezra was bare chested, wearing only his dress uniform slacks. He had his jacket folded up in one arm, and his knee-high officer's boots in the other. Tirpitz was clad only in her underwear, her normally tightly pulled back bun a mess of dark curls.

"Oh shit," Tirpitz gasped. She ducked back into the doorway in an attempt to cover herself. Vincent's eyes lingered on her tightly muscled body a little too long before he pulled his gaze away.

"Good morning, sir," Ezra sputtered. "I was just waking up Captain Tirpitz for the Crawl and I—"

"Waking her up is right!" Fiona gasped in between bouts of laughter. Vincent elbowed her in the ribs, and she winced away. "I didn't know you had it in you!" she giggled.

"Get it together," he said, though he himself was fighting back laughter after watching the normally unflappable Ezra blush so brightly he could see his dark skin turn red.

"Sorry," she said, still laughing. "I didn't know people that old still banged."

Tirpitz, who had in the meantime managed to get on her grey uniform pants and a white undershirt, stuck her head back out of the door. "How old do you think I am, you little shit?" Tirpitz screamed at her, her hand busily pulling her hair back into her bun.

"So, this is what you meant by getting fresh air eh?" Vincent laughed. He hated to join in, but it wasn't often the implacable Ezra lost his cool.

"Not so fresh anymore," Fiona cackled.

"Can we just handle this like adults?" Ezra tried to mediate.

"Clearly not." Vincent sighed. "Can we just go to the meeting?"

"It's a Crawl," Zinvor corrected.

"Whatever!" Vincent exclaimed, throwing his hands up.

The group stepped out into the wind-blown streets and Vincent was relieved to see the dust storm had largely died down. The sky was still a swirling red haze, but for the first time since they had landed on the planet, he could clearly see out into the devastated city that surrounded them.

The first signs of civilian life he had seen since he had been in Olympus sprang from the ashes. Hunched old women pushed carts with wares for sale. Vincent couldn't help but notice nearly none of them were selling food. If they were it was looted EDF rations or strange looking meat that had been hastily wrapped in newspaper. Insects buzzed around the carts in thick clouds.

The sides of the roads had large trenches dug into them. Not for defensive positions as he would have assumed, but for garbage and waste. Years of war had destroyed anything resembling a municipal plumbing network and made garbage collection impossible. Vincent watched an old man dump a bucket that was full of piss and shit into the frothing trench below. It sloshed back and forth with bags of discarded garbage and empty liquor bottles.

Ragged, wild strands of wire looped from one ruined building to another, all planning having long ago been discarded. What had to be power transformers sat at the top of wooden poles sending out bursts of sparks every few minutes. What little power this end of the city had looked to be as big of a safety risk as the incoming artillery. Of which, there was plenty.

The ground shook under his feet as he walked. The explosions were a steady drumbeat, never ceasing or slowing down. Though from the lack of the telltale sound of overhead shrieking or any of the civilian populace making any attempt to get to escape, told Vincent the combat was far away.

Gangers milled around the entrance of the Head Hunter's command complex. Wearing little more than pants and ammunition harnesses, their faces uncovered for the first time since Vincent had landed, showed they were as relieved as he was the dust storms had ceased. To his surprise, parked outside of the complex was the captured transport vehicle.

The vehicle had undergone a transformation since the last time he had seen it. The shipping container that once sat on the vehicle's flatbed was gone. In its place was sheets of metal and sandbags built up to act as armored walls, creating their own version of a troop carrier. Two heavy machine guns were mounted on either side of the armor, giving it offensive abilities. Though he questioned the protectiveness of the scrap sheet metal they had bolted onto the side, he assumed it was better than nothing.

Murat stood outside of the vehicle looking it over. He was surrounded by other gangers who looked on as their leader inspected it.

"Good Morning, Solaris," Murat boomed. He stood, hands on his hips, as he marveled at the ramshackle assault vehicle in front of him. "Hell of a war machine, isn't she?"

"Umm, sure," Vincent said.

"Those damned Cutters won't think they're so great now with all of their war wagons. We're catching up."

"War wagons?" Vincent raised an eyebrow.

"Well, they certainly ain't fuckin' mare they?" Murat frowned. "Let's get going. Don't want to be late to your own party, do you?"

"My party?" Vincent asked. Murat motioned for them to climb into the back of the vehicle where two gangers were manning the flanking machine guns. They did so, finding the space in the back surprisingly roomy.

"Well, yeah," Murat said. "We don't hold these Crawls very often. Too easy a target for the Worms. So, you better make it worth our while." Murat's burned features twisted into a grin. Murat hefted himself into the back with them and the vehicle rumbled to life. Choking black smoke erupted from the twin exhaust pipes that jutted straight into the air over the cab.

The tracks clanked and the exhaust blanketed down into the newly constructed troop compartment. Vincent coughed and fanned his hand uselessly trying to clear it away.

"Talk about a design flaw," Fiona hacked.

"We're still working out the kinks," Murat coughed.

As the vehicle picked up speed the flowing air mercifully cleared away most of the exhaust. After being forced to breathe in the fumes the polluted air of Olympus felt wonderful in comparison.

Vincent stood up and looked over the shoddy armor siding. He was hoping they would eventually leave the thoroughly destroyed East End and he would get to see what Olympus really looked like.

"Are we leaving the East End?" Vincent asked the ganger who stood, leaning against the machine gun on the right flank of the vehicle.

"Yep." The girl nodded. "Goin' over to the Cutters turf on the West End. They're the only ones with a place big enough to hold the Crawl."

"Cool," Vincent said. "I want to see what normal Olympus looks like." He saw the girl raise an eyebrow. "I mean, you know, without all the...damage." The girl laughed.

"You're gonna be disappointed then. Only place that's still standin' is the North End. And we're going to have to kick the Worms out of it before you get to see it."

To Vincent's shock, the girl was right. The vehicle passed through the thin corridor that connected the Head Hunter's territory to the Cutter's, he could tell where they were from the intense fortifications they drove past.

The gangers had dug in. Deep, intricate trenches had been carved into the streets themselves with sandbag and bunkers layered into the surrounding buildings. He quickly lost count of the number of gangers he saw manning the line, but the number was easily equal to that of an EDF regiment. Vincent had to admit he was impressed. He couldn't imagine the Gangers he had ambushed the EDF with manning a functional defensive line.

Vincent finally saw the Martian's way around their critical fuel shortage. Small horses pulled carts filled with stolen military supplies. The animals were mostly skin and bones, their stumbling, fatigued steps made it seem like they were on their last legs. Once the carts were at their destination they were unloaded by groups of boys and girls who looked like they should have been in elementary school.

"You're using kids?" Vincent asked Murat. Murat waved off and laughed.

"A gun can't tell if your 50 or 15," he said. "The bullet kills all the same. Ask your girlfriend how old she was when she started doing jobs for the Cutters." He nodded at Fiona.

"Shut up," Fiona spat at him. Murat smirked. "You think those kids have a choice?"

"No." Murat shook his head. "Ain't nobody around here eatin' for free."

The vehicle jerked to a stop next to a long line of other War Wagons. Each one was a little different than the one next to it. Farm tractors, gasoline powered trucks, flat beds, and every other kind of vehicle had been transformed into a slap dash armored behemoth. One, which looked like it used to be a dump truck, had an entire artillery piece bolted to where its trash compartment had once been.

Behind them were the remains of a large auditorium. It stretched up into the air for several stories and was capped with a long arcing roof. It was not built in the plain, grey, block style indicative of the Committee-era colonization of the planet. There were tall, decorated columns flanking a large arched doorway, over which there looked like there had once been an inscription. The words of the inscription had been lost to the decades of conflict and erosion from dust storms. The building was scarred with thousands of bullet marks and its roof mostly collapsed inwards.

The stairs that led up to the grand doorway were collapsed and blown away. The Martians had replaced them with a pile of debris that acted as a ramp instead of fixing them. A monument in concrete showing a relief of a valiant looking Martian Soldier holding the flag of an Independent Mars lay toppled over and shattered, it's feet still attached to the base.

"What is this place?" Vincent asked.

"The Cutters' base," Murat said. He climbed out of the back of the war wagon and the rest of the group followed him.

"I mean, before that."

"Shit kid, I don't know," Murat said. "The Cutters set up shop here years ago. Been runnin' tricks and powder out of here as long as I can remember."

"I'm sorry, tricks and powder?" Vincent asked, distracted.

"Hookers and drugs," Fiona chimed in.

"It was the People's Congress," Ezra said from the back of the group. He had placed his peaked officer's cap on his head. Other than his Elysian shoulder patches, he was wearing what looked like a full EDF officer's uniform. Gangers who were milling about looking at the parked war wagons gave him hateful glances.

"The what?" Fiona asked.

"Before the rebellion," Ezra said. "Before the Committee's unification. It was what the Martian settlers set up as an independent government. It lasted for a few years before...well, you know the rest."

"Before the unification ya say?" Murat asked scratching his chin. "You don't look that old. How do you know that?" Ezra looked at Murat in disbelief.

"What?" he asked, confused. "No, I didn't see it. That was hundreds of years ago. History classes are a thing you know. They have entire degrees in that field even."

"Not around here," Fiona said.

The group made their way up the debris ramp and through the archway. The inside of the Congress was filthy and the air thick with dust. The similar Martian scents stung Vincent's nose, now punctuated by the smell of burning wood.

In the middle of the floor was a large bonfire. As there was no roof, the smoke went straight up and into the air above. Vincent knew he was naïve to assume he was going to walk into some council room like the one on Elysian or Grand Titan. Though, he never assumed he would be sitting around a bonfire in the middle of a destroyed Congress building.

Dozens of men and women sat around the bonfire in excited conversations. Boys and Girls dressed in mostly homespun rags brought them food and drinks on platters so large they had to be supported by several of the children at once. Vincent looked on in disgust as one of the older gangers smack a younger girl on the backside as she walked away.

"Gentleman!" Murat called out. "Now we can get started!" The conversation around the bonfire died away and they rose to their feet. Vincent wasn't surprised when he saw several of them stumble as they tried to stand up straight. He was starting to think no official business could be done on Mars sober.

"Is that boy the Traitor we've heard so much about?" Mocked a voice at the head of the group.

"That is Marcus, Boss of the Cutters," Murat said.

"Damn right I am." Marcus grinned. His pale face was decorated with the normal ganger tattoos around his eyes and an ugly scar going from the corner of his mouth up to his left ear. His blonde hair was pulled back into a rough ponytail much like Vincent's. He was wearing stolen officer's pants, evident from the red stripe going down the side of the pantleg, and a ratty tan tank top. Unlike most of the Martian's Vincent had met, Marcus wasn't thin. Instead his arms were bundles of muscle and his thick chest stretched out his tank top to the point it barely fit.

"Vincent Solaris, Consul to the Fidayi Clan and Cohort Leader of the Elysian Defense Force," Vincent said, trying to remain somewhat formal. He held his hand out and Marcus took it in his.

"And is that Fiona Olympus?" Marcus raised an eyebrow, looking over Vincent's shoulder.

"Yeah," Fiona said quietly.

"Oh," Vincent said. "Do you two know each other?"

"Of course we do!" Marcus said, a smirk pulled his scarred face back. "She used to work for me. Before she ran off and joined the damn EDF."

Vincent looked over his shoulder at Fiona, who was staring down at her feet. Her eyes looked up and met his. In her eyes he saw something he almost never saw in Fiona: panic. They told him she wanted to be anywhere but where she was currently standing.

"Man, Solaris you look like shit." Marcus recoiled after taking a good look at him. While the swelling in his eyes had gone down, dark rings still surrounded them.

"I feel like it too." He sighed. His head was still throbbing, the rough trip in the back of the war wagon didn't help matters.

"Xan worked 'em over pretty good before Solaris cut off his damn hand." Murat laughed.

"Impressive," Marcus said. "Xan was a scraper." He grabbed Fiona by the shoulder and gave it a squeeze. "Must have learned somethin' from this one. She was always a feisty one." Fiona pulled her shoulder away from his grasp but said nothing.

"We should get started. We have a lot to go over," Tirpitz said, stepping in between Fiona and Marcus, sensing the discomfort.

"Yeah." Marcus eyed Tirpitz. "Good idea."

"Let's cut to the chase," came a voice from near the bonfire. He was someone Vincent hadn't noticed before. Unlike the rest of the gang leaders, this man was older. His grey hair was a neat crew cut and he was cleanly shaven. "Why do you want to help us?"

"That's Erik Olympus. *Brigade Commander.*" Marcus spoke the man's title dripping with sarcasm. "Of the Mars Liberation Brigade."

"Well, Commander Olympus," Tirpitz addressed him. "Prime Minister Addler and Field Marshal Denta understand the plight of the Martian people, and—"

"Oh, cut the shit," Marcus interrupted.

"Fine." Tirpitz sighed. Vincent fought back laughter as she dropped her façade of formality. "We need your help to keep the EDF away from Titan and you need our help to kick them off Mars."

"And the Aliens?" Erik asked.

"The Clan wants revenge for the EDF stabbing them in the back on Grawluck," Vincent said. "And your help to fight the Alliance when the time comes."

"Why the hell should we get involved in some alien turf war?" Marcus crossed his arms.

"Because once the Alliance is done with us, they'll come for you. And you stand even less of a chance alone than we do," Vincent said. Erik laughed harshly.

"You want us to jump into a war ten thousand miles away when we don't have enough rifles or goddamn boots for the war we are fighting now. We can hardly feed the fighters we have, let alone the rest of the city. We haven't even had clean water in months."

"It's all in the aid agreement." Tirpitz produced a data display and clicked it on. "Unlimited military and civilian aid as soon as possible and unlimited aid for rebuilding an independent Mars as soon as the planet is secured." The gathered gang leaders exchanged glances, clearly looking for a counter argument.

"And how exactly are you going to land a full Titanian invasion force?" Erik asked.

"The plan is for a combined force of Clan and Titanian ships to gain air superiority over Olympus while we on the ground secure the Mons Spaceport. It's the only place in the city large enough to land an invasion force." The Martians burst out into laughter.

"You want us to march straight up the Mons and attack the most reinforced Worm position on the fucking planet?" Marcus gasped in between bouts of laughter. "That's about the dumbest shit I've heard in my entire life."

"If we could do that, we wouldn't need your damn help in the first place," Erik said. "We would have taken it a year ago!"

"You would have the full support of the combined Clan and Titanian fleets." Tirpitz folded her arms across her chest. "As many airstrikes and orbital bombardments as you could want."

"It would require every bit of manpower we have," Erik said. "And even then...." He trailed off, pinching his chin. "If we lost, we wouldn't have anything left to resist the EDF."

"You can't be seriously considering this," Marcus snapped at Erik. "It's insane."

"It certainly has its flaws." Erik pinched his chin. "But what we have been doing sure as hell hasn't been working. They've been pushing us back for weeks now. Another month and Murat's boys will be surrounded."

"He's right," Murat said. "We are holding that corridor by the skins of our sacks. As soon as the dust dies down for good, we're expecting them to launch an offensive. Even with those new launchers we just looted I don't think we will last through the season."

"Sure, it won't happen as fast as if this attack fails," Tirpitz began. "But the reality is you'll all be surrounded and destroyed. Once they beat the Head Hunters and get rid of the threat of their anti-air weapons they'll have control of the sky again. How long will you last once you're getting bombed and strafed?"

"We've survived that way for years!" Marcus cursed. "We've survived without these fuckin' Head Hunters and his fake Brigade coming onto my damned turf."

"This is bigger than your stupid gang turf war shit!" Vincent snapped.

"You don't know what you're calling stupid boy!" Marcus seethed through his teeth. Marcus jabbed Vincent's chest with his finger. "There are generations of history here."

"History of what?" Vincent shot back. "Being forced to live surrounded by your own shit? No running water, food, or electricity?" Vincent watched as Marcus' pale face turned red with anger. "A proud history of being crushed under the Committee's boot? A history of not being in control of your own fucking history?"

"You little—" Marcus bellowed, but was cut off by Erik.

"He's right Marcus and we both know it!"

"You think I'm going to join hands with these two assholes and forget about everything that's happened in these streets?" Marcus seethed, turning his rage towards Erik and Murat.

"The feeling is mutual." Murat frowned.

"Wait, I thought this meeting was about working with us, not for you guys to debate *working with each other*?" Vincent asked, confused.

"Have you not been fighting alongside each other this whole time?" Tirpitz asked.

"Fight with them?" Marcus asked, incredulous. He gestured at Erik. "With that boy fucker?" And then Murat. "And that mouth-breathing idiot." Erik, who had seemed like the voice of reason so far during the meeting, had heard enough. He landed a punch square on the chin of Marcus, who barely stumbled back. Marcus only smiled. "Like I thought, you hit like a bitch. Maybe you should sic your boyfriend on me next."

"What the hell have you been doing this whole time? Why protect the corridor if you hate each other?" Tirpitz asked.

"To keep open a path to trade our loot obviously," Murat said.

"And these pieces of shit haven't been paying their debts!" Marcus yelled.

"because *you* won't accept Committee Units as currency!" Erik yelled back.

"Why would I accept the damned Worm's worthless scratch?" Marcus contested. "You bring me fuel or flesh, you know the deal."

"Flesh?" Vincent asked quietly over his shoulder to Fiona. Fiona nodded wordlessly to the child who were waiting near the bonfire. Their small arms were tiring under the weight of the platters they were carrying. "Slaves?" Vincent gasped.

"*Child slaves?*" Tirpitz mouthed and Fiona nodded. "Why in the hell are we working with these people?"

"A means to an end," Ezra said. "We need them."

"The Affirmations of Paterazm have a passage," Zinvor said, his voice a low croak. "It says *be wary of when you craft with substances that are toxic, for you too will be poisoned in time.*"

"We need them." Vincent repeated Ezra's words. He wasn't sure if he was talking to the group or reassuring himself. In the meantime the three Martian leaders had been engrossed in a lively argument, each screaming over the other. "Excuse me," Vincent said, trying to get their attention, but they ignored him. His temper rose and he balled his fists.

"Shut the fuck up!" he screamed, his voice cracking embarrassingly. Their argument stalled and the three turned to look at him. "What if you can, temporarily, work together." Vincent held his hands up to stem the flow of their complaints. "And in return and I can promise each side gets equal military assistance and when it's all over you can settle this any way you want, and we will stay out of it."

The three exchanged glances and turned back to Vincent.

"You ain't going to try to dictate how we live our lives?" Marcus asked.

"I plan on staying out of your lives entirely," Vincent said. After seeing how the Martians lived, he wanted absolutely nothing to do with them. "Trust me."

"What is considered over?" Murat asked.

"When the Alliance is defeated," Vincent said. "Or at least no longer a threat to our existence."

"And our forces stay under our commands?" Erik asked.

"Yes," Tirpitz said. "While Field Marshal Denta and Warlord Arai will be in overall command of the effort, no Martian forces will be led into combat by our officers."

The three gang leaders turned and huddled in a small circle. They talked in hushed tones in a much friendlier way than Vincent had expected to see three people who were just talking about how much they wanted to kill one another.

"You got a deal," Marcus said. "But if I see so much as one more bullet go to either of these two than my boys and we are gonna have an issue."

"And I ain't sharing my missiles." Murat crossed his arms.

"And what aren't you sharing?" Vincent asked Erik. Erik laughed off the comment and walked towards Vincent.

"How would you like to join my Brigade for the attack, Solaris?" he asked. Vincent raised his eyebrows and was unsure of what to say. He wasn't sure if this was considered some kind of honor in their society or not. What he did know however was that he didn't want to be anywhere near the Head Hunters during the next battle.

"Um, sure." He forced a smile. Erik placed a hand on Vincent's shoulder and smiled warmly.

"Good. I would like to show you firsthand what I don't want to share with them." He nodded. "If we are all set here, I would like to go. I need time to go over this plan with my Troop Commanders, I'm sure these two would like to do the same."

Erik exited the Congress with the group quickly following in tow. His Brigade's War Wagons were parked away from the rest. The three wagons were parked in a neat row and a dozen gangers were standing in a loose formation in front of them. Their uniforms were almost matching. They were wearing what looked like EDF uniforms that had been dyed red and a shoulder patch that depicted a blue star on a red background. The same flag he had seen in the transit tunnels.

The formation snapped to attention, their boots cracking off of the concrete in unison so loud it sounded like a rifle shot. A ganger standing at the head of the formation gave Erik a salute, though his palm was facing outward, a difference compared to the EDF norm. Erik returned the salute and climbed into the first Wagon. Vincent followed after him, once inside he realized the wagon looked like a converted farm tractor.

The vehicle's engine rumbled to life and the Brigade's wagons arranged themselves into a convoy. Two gangers jumped into the vehicle behind the group and grabbing ahold of two small handles by the rear door slid a metal sheet over the rear door and over the exposed top of the crew compartment.

"Let's go home boys," Erik said.

"Yes Comrade-Commander!" answered a voice from the front of the wagon. The wagon's tracks lurched forward and soon the convoy was racing down the street into an unknown direction.

Vincent exchanged looks with Tirpitz and Ezra. They were coming to the same conclusion as he was: Erik wasn't leading a gang. He had created a small, functioning, independent army.

"So, you used to work for Marcus?" Erik asked. Fiona, who had fallen into something resembling a catatonic state since the Crawl, suddenly snapped back to reality. The misery that had been painted across her face vanished.

"Once, yeah," she said.

"Should I ask what you did?" Erik raised an eyebrow. Anger flashed across Fiona's face.

"You know what I did," she spat.

"Well, I don't," Vincent said. "You've never talked about it. And he said you *joined* the EDF? I thought you were drafted."

Vincent meant to hold onto the questions for later, knowing the sudden barrage would infuriate her, but Erik had opened the flood gates.

"Of course I joined!" she yelled. "You have any idea how easy it is to dodge the draft when you don't even have a last name?"

"But you said—" Vincent began, but she cut him off.

"I know what I said!" she exclaimed. "I fucking lied to you, Vincent!"

"Vincent!" Tirpitz cut in. "Maybe now isn't the time for this." Her voice ceased sounding like a stern military officer and instead sounded like a scolding parent. Vincent gathered his senses and looked around. The awkward glances from the other occupants of the wagon told him she was right. A crowded armored vehicle was no place for a couple's argument.

"Right...," he said. "I'm sorry." After a moment of strange silence Erik spoke up.

"I volunteered too," Erik said. "I showed up the EDF Conscription Office on my seventeenth birthday just like they told me to."

"I thought everyone here hated the Committee?" Tirpitz asked, confused. "Why would anyone volunteer to work for the people who destroyed their planet?"

"There wasn't much else out there for a first born. You see how Marcus and Murat's gangers are. I didn't want that for me," he said. "A life of soldiering is a lot better than a short, violent life running guns or drugs for one of those madmen."

"Wait, if you were serving, how the hell did you get away?" Vincent asked.

"When you get to a high enough rank, they eventually forget where you're from. I was the Command Sergeant Major of the 615th Infantry Regiment stationed in Victoria. Until you destroyed Earth that is." He grinned, sarcastically. "When I saw that I knew what it meant. I and most of the other Martians deserted as soon as we saw an opening. Together we started the Mars Liberation Brigade."

Vincent couldn't help but smile and feel an affinity for the man. Though he was decades older than him, they had much of the same path that led them both to be sitting in that wagon.

"You know I didn't destroy Earth," Vincent said flatly.

"Of course I do," Erik said. "The idea that a teenager destroyed Earth is insane. Good idea using it as an in with those two idiots though. Otherwise they probably would have just shot you and took your ship."

"You don't seem to like them very much," Tirpitz said. "Why are you working with them?"

"Same reason you are," Erik said. "I can't hope to liberate my planet without them."

"And when it ends?" Ezra asked.

"I think we all know what needs to happen for the betterment of Mars and her people," Erik said ominously. Vincent glanced nervously at Tirpitz and Ezra. The group of Martian leaders had promised only moments before to put their bloody histories behind them and here Erik was talking about how killing them was the only route towards peace. "Don't worry," Erik said, sensing the awkwardness. "I have no intentions of violating our deal."

"Good," Tirpitz said. "Can I ask you an honest question?"

Erik nodded.

"Can we trust Murat and Marcus to hold to the deal?" Tirpitz asked.

"Of course not." Erik said, his voice grim. "It's not a matter of *if* they will break the agreement. It's when."

CHAPTER TWENTY-FIVE

The convoy came to a halt. The ride had lasted the rest of the afternoon and late into the evening. The time felt like it slowed to a crawl inside in small in closed space of the wagon's crew compartment.

The rest of the group had fallen into a restful sleep. Tirpitz had dozed off, her head on Ezra's shoulder and Fiona on Vincent's. Erik had stayed awake, silently scanning through maps and plans for the upcoming offensive. Vincent attempted on more than one occasion to engage him in conversation. Each time Erik would lose Vincent in a long-winded explanation of military concepts he didn't understand.

The two soldiers seated in the back stood up and slid the metal curtain back down, forming a ramp. The cold Martian air blew into the compartment and reminded Vincent he wasn't wearing anything under his armor.

"Welcome to civilized Mars." Erik smiled, standing up and stretching deeply.

While the sun had set long ago, the area was brightly lit by glowing lamp posts. A small, but busy marketplace moved with life. Throngs of men and women in uniform with small children running around at knee level crowded the streets. The shops were hardly bursting with supplies, but people loudly bartered over the price of rations or the rare piece of meat.

Instead of rows of slapped together buildings like back at the Head Hunters camp, a small suburb had been maintained. The buildings, while still damaged, had been repaired with real skill and care. Waste trenches still lined the streets, but they had been covered with paving stones, creating something like a normal sewer.

"Wow," Tirpitz gasped.

"Now you know what I am protecting." Erik smiled. Outside of Grand Titan, Erik's little slice of Olympus was the nicest place he had been since he had left Earth.

"But how?" Vincent asked. "In the middle of all this shit, how did you build this?"

"Say what you will about the EDF, but it does give you an education." Erik laughed. "I didn't just bring tens of thousands of grunts with me. I brought carpenters, engineers, Medics, and logisticians." As they walked down the street, kids rushed up to them. Dozens of pale-faced Martian kids tugged at the hems of Vincent's armor and cheered Erik's name. Erik smiled and them and patted them on their heads.

They passed a small guard post, little more than a shack in the middle of the road, manned by two bored looking soldiers. One of the soldiers manning the post was of a fair complexion and under his red garrison cap was a head full of brown hair.

"Is that a—" Vincent began.

"A settler?" Erik smiled. "Yeah, we have a few hundred of them."

"You allow settlers to fight with you?" Ezra asked, his eyes wide.

"They're as Martian as I am," Erik said. "They just came to the planet a couple hundred years late is all."

"Unbelievable," Ezra gasped. "Forgive me, but after years of fighting on this planet that is never something I'd expect to hear."

"What do the others think about it?" Tirpitz asked.

"About what you would imagine. Called me a traitor, a spy, threatened to flatten the areas under my control. You know, the normal stuff." Erik shrugged. They walked past a row of houses and into what Vincent assumed was the main army's encampment. Houses gave way to tents in neat, uniform columns stretching out as far as Vincent could see. "As you know, in the EDF, in the lower ranks at least, everyone is treated the same, everyone is equal. It is the same here. And will be the same on all of Mars one day."

"So, you thought you could bring the two sides together through the military?" Tirpitz said. "Good idea. Much of Titanian society is organized the same way."

"I know it's hard to believe, but after Earth was destroyed a lot of the settlers began to see through the Committee's lies. Staying with the EDF or the Committee wasn't an option for them, and everyone knows the gangers have a standing bounty on the head of any settler. We gave them a home."

"How do you hold back the gangers?" Vincent asked. "I'm sure they're itching to get their hands on all of this."

"Have you ever heard of the idea of mutually assured destruction?" Erik asked.

"It was how we stopped the Committee from turning Titan into another Mars during Unification," Ezra said. "Create a war that would cost both sides so much it would be pointless."

"Exactly," Erik said. "Well, the gangers outnumber us, there is no getting around that," Erik explained. He led the group through the rows of tents where soldiers lay sleeping, playing cards, or reading. "They even have more war wagons than us." Erik pointed up ahead where dozens of rows of artillery were sitting. Their long, black barrels pointed up into the air at an angle. The guns' crews sat around smoking and lazing in the cool night air. Nearby another row of tents held other crews, fast asleep. "But what they don't have is three entire batteries of trained artillery crewmen and officers."

"Impressive," Tirpitz said.

"I see them make one move towards me, their territory is well within the guns' range," Erik said. "I keep crews rotating through around the clock just to be safe."

"And the EDF?" Ezra asked. "With all these lights and a large laid out camp area...they leave you alone?"

"Not entirely," Erik said. "But this isn't like the last rebellion. The endless legions of reinforcements coming from Earth and Titan don't exist anymore. The uppity rich people in Lunar City are hardly going to waste their high-born sons and daughters by marching them through intersecting fields of fire and artillery bombardments."

"So, they attack the gangers?" Vincent asked.

"They are a much easier target. Though we make sure to support them with our guns. Just like Murat covers the skies over us. It's in all of our best interests that the other survives. For now anyway," Erik said.

"So the EDF avoids you for the most part?" Vincent asked.

"Attacking the gangers gets their officers some glory for their reports to send to their senior leadership without the risk for major casualties. Senior leadership can report to the Committee and show them their victories and save themselves from the firing squads for the time being. A time will come when we will be the last ones standing and they will have no choice though."

"Not if we succeed," Vincent said.

"If we fail Mars is as good as pacified," Erik said. "And I don't intend on letting that happen." Erik sighed and rubbed his eyes. Vincent hadn't noticed before, but the man's eyes were beat red and tired. Vincent felt about as bad as Erik looked. He hadn't had a good night's sleep since before the war against the Black Coats had started. "I'm sure you all must be exhausted," Erik said and waved to a nearby soldier. The soldier stopped what he was doing and ran over to Erik, presenting him with a salute.

The soldier had dark red stripes going down either side of his pants, showing him to be an artillery officer. Though his collar didn't show any officer's rank he had ever seen. Instead, two pins of crossed cannons were pinned to his uniform. "Comrade-Ensign," Erik addressed him. "Show the Consul and his party to their quarters please."

"Yes, Comrade-Commander." The Ensign saluted again.

"We don't have much, but it's probably better than whatever Murat put you up in." Erik nodded before walking in an opposite direction through the Artillery line.

"Follow me, please," the Ensign said warmly and began to walk back through the army's camp, towards the lines of block houses.

"Sorry to pry, but what's an Ensign?" Tirpitz asked. "It's not a rank I am familiar with."

"Oh you're not prying." The Ensign smiled. "Comrade-Commander Victoria reformed the Brigade's Officer Corps. As I'm sure you know Martians were not allowed to be officers in the EDF so we kind of had to start from scratch. So, Comrade-Commander Victoria created the Olympus Officer's Academy, over that way." The Ensign pointed over to a small cluster of buildings near the market. "The first Martian Officer Academy called for a new rank structure. Or at least he thought so. I was a member of the first graduating class earlier this year."

"Well congratulations, Ensign." Ezra smiled. "I remember when I first graduated the academy."

"Yeah," Tirpitz added. "Then the hard work started." She laughed and Ezra joined in. The Ensign led them to a small house on the corner that had been repaired with concrete blocks of various colors. The windows were boarded up and the roof had been replaced with a handmade metal one. Bullet marks still stitched across the original structure and it looked like a bomb had blown away what would have been a small front yard.

"This is where the Comrade-Commander has said you will be billeted, I hope it is acceptable." The Ensign saluted. Vincent, Ezra, and Tirpitz all returned the young officer's salute and he walked away quickly.

Vincent jumped as the sky above them flashed. At first, he thought he was seeing lightning, but the light did not arc across the night sky like he expected it too. The one light soon blossomed into countless other flashes. The lights streaked across the sky like shooting stars before they would stop and quickly change direction. In only a few moments blinking, flashing, and shooting lights of red, orange, and yellow stretched from one side of the sky to the other.

Civilians walked out of their houses in awe, pointing at staring up at the mysterious light show. Soldiers from the encampment let out a loud cheer and several of them fired their guns into the air in celebration.

"What the hell is going on?" Vincent asked.

"I know those lights anywhere. It looks like the Field Marshal is making his move," Ezra said.

"I hope our pilots fight as good as they look." Tirpitz smiled warmly at Ezra. He blushed slightly, barely visible on his dark cheeks.

"They do," he said, grinning sheepishly.

"Ugh." Vincent sighed.

"Not as good as Fidayi pilots!" Zinvor grinned broadly, obviously not understanding the nuances of the exchange.

Fiona pushed the door open to the house, ignoring their conversation. She let the door slam behind her. Ezra whistled and put a hand on his shoulder.

"I wonder what's going on with her," Vincent said. "I should probably go see what's wrong."

"I wouldn't do that," Ezra said, holding him back.

"Huh?" Vincent said. "Why not?"

"When you piss off a girl like that, they tend to need space for a little while," Ezra said. "And for a girl as Fiona as her I'd give it a long while."

"I pissed her off?" Vincent raised an eyebrow. "how?"

"You missed that?" Tirpitz laughed. "You guys don't fight a lot, do you?"

"Actually, I don't think we've ever had a fight before." Vincent thought aloud. Fiona was at her best, a boiling cauldron of undirected rage, but he had never been the target of it before.

"Welcome to adulthood, sir." Ezra laughed and patted him on the shoulder.

"Are you telling me relationships are full of arguments?" he asked. Ezra and Tirpitz doubled over in laughter and Vincent scowled at them. "Hey!"

"Sorry, Consul." Tirpitz gasped between bouts of laughter. "Now you know why I spend most of my time with books, not men."

310

"That isn't what I saw earlier." Vincent folded his arms. Just because they were twenty years older than him didn't mean they knew everything.

"Grand Titan's book selection was lacking," she shot back. "And it seems Olympus' does as well." A smirk curled the corner of her lip. "I think I'm going to go find my room. Goodnight Consul." She brushed past him, and the blushing Ezra was left in her wake.

"Going to bed too, I assume?" Vincent said.

"I am kind of tired..." he said, searching for an excuse. "Goodnight, sir."

Vincent sighed, resigning his fate to the anger of Fiona, and walked into the house. The house, though damaged from the war, was still in good shape. Everything smelled like disinfectant and lemon-scented cleaner. It was obvious Erik had called ahead and had the house turned into the closest thing Mars had to a dignitary's suite.

The layout of the house brought Vincent back to his destroyed home he had grown up in. Or was it was officially called, the Central Committee's Ministry of Family's Standard Medium Family Domicile. Looking around, he saw the living room was to the right of the stairs, meaning this was a Type Two. He knew up the twelve stairs in front of him there would be three bedrooms, if it had been Vincent's house his would have been the first one on the right.

Vincent was so lost in his moment that he jumped when he heard the sound of muffled sobbing coming from the couch. There Fiona sat, her knees drawn up to her chest, sobbing into her legs. She didn't look up or acknowledge him, leaving Vincent to be the one to try to find something to say. He sat stood speechless, having never seen Fiona in such a state before.

"I'm sorry," she sobbed. He wasn't sure what he had expected, but he knew an apology wasn't one of the possibilities. He cautiously walked over to the couch and sat down.

"What are you sorry for?" he asked, putting a hand on her knee. "You didn't do anything."

"I lied to you," she cried. She picked her head up from her knees and looked at him. Her eyes were red from crying and tears were streaming down her face. "I should have told you the truth."

"Fiona, I don't care that you showed up to the conscription office. None of that matters now," he said, brushing her hair behind her ear.

"It's more than that. I told you I was some hardcore ganger. I wasn't."

"You do know that's a good thing, right?"

"I did work for Marcus, that part was true." She sniffed.

"But I thought you weren't a ganger?"

"I wasn't. You saw the girls serving them drinks at the Crawl."

"So, you were a waitress? Who cares?" he said, trying to reassure her. His thoughts wandered back to the meeting. They wandered back to Marcus slapping the young girl on her behind and the look of abject terror on Fiona's face when she saw him. "No!" he blurted out.

"I didn't have a choice!" she bawled. "He found me on the streets and took me in. Fed me, clothed me." She fought to speak through her crying.

"Oh Fiona..." Vincent gasped. He felt his skin begin to burn and his throat thicken. His hands clenched into fists until his knuckles turned white.

"I was one of his personal girls," she sobbed. "At first, I tried to fight him—we all did. If we fought, we were beaten. Our food was taken away. The one's that didn't break were given over to the rest of the gangers. I tried to escape once...they caught me a couple days later. You've seen the scars of how he paid me back for that. So, I escaped the only way I knew he would never find me. When I turned seventeen, I ran to the conscription office."

"And I brought you right fucking back here," Vincent cursed. Tears began to well up in the corners of his eyes. His fingernails began to dig into the palms of his hands.

"I would have told you, but I assumed he would have been dead by now."

"I'll fucking kill him," He seethed. "I'll cut out his goddammed heart." Vincent shot to his feet.

"You can't!" she cried. "We need him for the war, otherwise I would have shot him on the spot."

"I don't give a damn," He spat. She grabbed him by the hands and pulled him back down to the couch.

"I love you," she said, a small smile finally perking up the corner of her mouth. Vincent got up and began to walk for the door.

"I love you too," he said.

The cold Martian night breeze cooled his burning face. He wiped away his tears and started walking for the Brigade encampment. He knew he had a new deal to make.

CHAPTER TWENTY-SIX

The Brigade's encampment was bustling with activity. The sight of the allied Fidayi-Titanian fleet engaging with the EDF picket forces sent the soldiers into a wild party. Music was playing from sound systems, a bonfire had been started, and soldiers, mostly half dressed, danced around drinking from unlabeled bottles of spirits.

Countless soldiers offered Vincent drinks from their tin cups or clear bottles, but he ignored them. His mind was racing. He had begun to plan on how he would kill the most powerful ganger on Mars. He knew the one man on the planet who had the same plan and he did.

Erik, ever the sergeant major, hadn't moved into one of the houses in his district. He had set himself up in a tent just like his men. Abet, a tent that was four times larger than that of a normal soldier. Two young soldiers, dressed in full battle gear, stood guard outside of its entrance and rendered stiff salutes to Vincent as he approached.

"Good evening Comrade-Consul Solaris," called the guard to the left who had the stripes of a corporal sewn onto his sleeves.

"I need to see Commander Victoria," he said shortly.

"I'm sorry Comrade-Consul, but he has ordered that no one bother him for the night," the corporal said.

"I don't give a shit." Vincent frowned. "It's important."

"Like I said, I'm sorry, sir," the corporal said, this time more forcefully. The professional tone of voice turning into one of mild annoyance.

"Like *I said*," Vincent seethed, stepping forward. He had no idea what he was going to do, but he was sure the two guards were more than capable of beating his ass.

"What the hell is going on out here?" came a voice from inside the tent. The tent flap folded back, revealing Erik. He was wearing his red uniform pants, held up by a pair of suspenders and nothing else. "Vincent?" he asked, puzzled.

"We need to talk," Vincent said. He hoped the urgency in his voice was enough for Erik to pick up on.

"Um." Erik thought for a moment. "Sure. Come on in." Erik held the flap aside and Vincent entered the tent.

The inside of the tent was barebones. A few trunks of clothes lined one side with a small portable desk against the other. Maps, data displays, and artillery charts were strewn across it. At the center of the tent was a standard issue soldier's bedroll. Vincent was immediately taken aback when he saw a man about the same age as Erik laying in it. Vincent felt his face begin to burn as it turned red.

"I'm sorry I—" he stammered.

"My guards were turning you away for a reason. Solaris, that is my Husband, Nat," Erik said, a tone of annoyance in his voice. Nat was sitting up in the bedroll, awkwardly trying to slip pants on underneath the covers without exposing himself. "And you can imagine we do not get to see each other often."

His Husband. Vincent didn't mean to stare, but he couldn't help himself. He remembered back to the Crawl, when Marcus insulted Erik bad enough to where Erik would punch him. Now he understood.

"Sexual Incontinence doesn't bother you does it?" Erik asked, his words dripping with aggravation. *Sexual Incontinence* has been the term the Central Committee had used to condemn anyone who's sexual orientation did not apply to strictly black and white standards laid out by the Ethics Police. Anyone who had been accused of such acts would be disappeared for reeducation.

"No." Vincent shook his head. "Of course not."

"I assume you didn't come here for a lesson on traditional Martian sexual practices." He sighed. "So to what do I owe the pleasure?"

"I want to help you kill Marcus," Vincent blurted out.

"Excuse me?" Erik raised an eyebrow. "What happened to the truce?"

"I mean afterwards." Vincent steadied himself. "He needs to die."

"If we kill him that means war with Murat too."

"I don't care. I can't speak for Titan or the Clan, but I can promise you my forces in reclaiming Mars," Vincent said. He tried his best to sound as firm and commanding as possible, but he heard his voice shaking.

"Why?" Erik asked. "Why would you get involved in a Martian civil war?"

"To be honest I don't care about Mars." Vincent frowned. "But I can't leave this planet until Marcus is dead." What little professionalism he had managed to keep melted away, replaced by uncontrolled rage.

"Well, I appreciate the honesty." Erik laughed. "What did he do to you?"

"Not me. My girlfriend, Fiona...." Vincent fought to find the words. His brain swirled with images of the tapestry of scars that covered her pale body. His thoughts went back to Marcus fondling the poor girl at the Crawl.

"She was one of his girls," Erik said knowingly.

"You knew?" Vincent gasped.

"No." Erik shook his head. "But after hearing that she used to work for him and that she surrendered herself to the EDF I could put the rest together. If you noticed, he doesn't tend to have any women in his actual ranks. He has other...uses for them."

"You don't...." Vincent began to say but was immediately cut off by Erik.

"I know you're not about to ask me if my Brigade has the same practice." He frowned. "I think you can tell by my present company that I don't have any use for women on that front. And if any of my men are caught frequenting the ganger's brothels my sergeants have ways to correct that behavior."

"I'm sorry, I didn't mean any offense," Vincent said.

"I don't blame you for asking. After working with those two, I would think all of us Martians are disgusting creatures too." He laughed. "You went to the People's Congress; do you know the history behind it?"

Vincent shook his head.

"Generations ago, before unification, all of the Martian settlements got together to form a central government. They knew what was happening on Earth and knew they couldn't ever accept a government with a single man at the center of it."

"But isn't all government based on one single asshole telling people what to do?" Vincent asked.

"That was why they people all got together to elect the People's Congress, the same body that met in that building. Five hundred delegates met to vote on matters that were brought to their attention by the people they represented."

"But who led them?"

"Nobody." Erik shrugged. "In times of crisis the Congress would appoint a Commander. That Commander would control defense policy and the armed forces until whatever the emergency they were facing would be handled."

"And you're the Commander," Vincent said, starting to put things together.

"I am." He nodded.

"So, what is with all the Comrade stuff?" Erik laughed.

"The Congress isn't stupid," he said. "They knew giving certain people absolute power or command of military units ran the risk of someone attempting to take power themselves. Addressing everyone no matter their rank or station in life as Comrade reminds us that we only have these positions because of the People of Mars."

"And when all of this is over you are just going to give up power and what? Retire?" Erik smiled.

"I don't think I'll ever retire. But yes, I will give power back to the Congress, which will be elected as soon as Mars is finally unified." Vincent walked over to Erik, his hand outstretched.

"I don't know what I can do. But you have my full support in making that happen," he said. Erik stood up and gripped Vincent's hand hard. His strength was crushing.

"And you have mine." Over Erik's shoulder Vincent noticed a large map. It wasn't like a military map he had ever seen before. It was painted with vibrant colors and had the name "Mons

Spaceport" in large cartoonish letters over the top of it. Erik noticed.

"Oh that." He sighed. "It was the only map of the Spaceport I could find. It's a tourist map I found on a settler."

"Mars has tourists?" Vincent wasn't sure which part was more surprising to him. The fact that people actually wanted to visit this place or that a major military operation was being planned on a tourism map.

"Not really. Not in the traditional sense anyway. It was part of a package they would give to prospective settlers to try to get them to move here," he said.

"So, what's the plan anyway?" Vincent asked, trying to move past what he saw as pretty major flaw in the plan already.

"You haven't been briefed?" Erik asked incredulously.

"I might be Consul and Cohort Leader but that doesn't mean I know what I am doing. Denta is taking the Command so I assume Tirpitz would have told you," Vincent explained. "If she would have explained it to me, I probably would have only understood half of it." He laughed nervously. He had done many things since he was made Cohort Leader but attaining a military education was not one of them.

"She has." Erik nodded. "So, assuming the fleet gains superiority, they will bombard the EDF defensive positions on the Mons plateau." He pointed to jagged lines that had been drawn all around the Spaceport. "Scouting the area is hard, but from what we can see we should expect concrete reinforced trenches and pillboxes. We can assume they are hardened against airstrikes. So, we will most likely be assaulting those on foot. The roads leading to the Spaceport will in all likelihood be covered with landmines. Our only available route of attack his up the sides of the Mons itself. They wouldn't expect it."

"A frontal assault?" Vincent gasped. "Up a mountain? The losses...."

"Will be terrible," Erik finished his thought. "We wouldn't stand a chance if it wasn't for the planned bombardment."

"When will the Titanians and Clan land?" Vincent asked.

"Not until the Spaceport is secure. All the fighting on the ground will be on us," Erik said.

"So, what exactly will we be fighting?" Vincent breathed, trying to calm himself.

"They have at least twelve regiments of field artillery, another dozen of armor, and a full army group of infantry." Erik pointed to small colored squares on the map. Vincent thought back, trying to remember army logistics. An army group alone was nearly half a million men. Vincent felt his jaw go slack and lose the ability to form words. Erik did not seem troubled by the information in the slightest.

"I am hoping—" Erik began, snapping Vincent back to the conversation, "That a defeat here will break the EDF's will to hold Olympus."

"And if they win?" Vincent asked.

"Well, you don't have to worry about the Anarchs if you're dead." Erik laughed. He leaned over to a small flask that sat on his desk and poured a small measure into a tin cup. He offered it to Vincent. Vincent held his hand up in refusal. He had just about enough of Martian booze for a lifetime. Erik glanced down at his watch and smiled. "For the nerves."

"The nerves?" Vincent asked confused. The tent rumbled and a thunder boom cut through the air. Then another. Then it felt like an earthquake had struck the city. The bombardment of the Mons had begun.

"Just on time," Erik said, offering Vincent the drink again. He took it. "For Mars."

CHAPTER TWENTY-SEVEN

The next morning Erik's army went on the march. Vincent watched from on high, secure onboard the *Shanna II*. What looked like a giant red snake uncoiled from its encampment as hundreds of thousands of soldiers set out. Hundreds of War Wagons rumbled across the pavement alongside of the Brigade's column. Their engines vomited black exhaust into the air as they went. Piles of soldiers were crammed onto and into the wagon's anywhere they could fit in a vain attempt to save themselves from the rigors of marching.

Far behind the column were Erik's vaunted Artillery batteries. Unfortunately for its gun crews there wasn't enough vehicles to go around. They instead had their guns strapped to pack animals. Horses and donkeys that looked one meal away from dropping dead kicked up clouds of dust as they struggled to pull their loads.

"I do not miss that," Fiona snickered, tapping a cigarette out of the door, the ash raining down on the columns below. Vincent smiled. He was happy to see Fiona slowly returning back to her normal self. Though he still couldn't get the vision of her breaking down out of his mind.

"Me either," Vincent agreed.

"I don't know," Tirpitz said, her legs dangling off the side of the ship. "I feel like I'm missing out."

"Shit." Fiona laughed. "I keep forgetting you've never been on a real march before." Tirpitz frowned.

"We marched clear across Ryklar," Vincent said. "Until my boots nearly fell off my feet and people started dropping dead."

"And that was before we got our asses kicked by the Alliance." Fiona blew out a cloud of smoke. "All that marching and the only thing it got them was dying tired."

"And I'm sure every single guy down there wishes he was us right about now," Vincent said. Tirpitz didn't respond, she returned to staring down at a map overlay on her data display. Vincent noticed it was a digital version of the same tourist map.

The horizon was aglow with explosions. Since the orbital bombardment began the night before, it had been a steady drumbeat ever since. Orange and red streaks broke through the red dust clouded sky above and slammed into the Spaceport.

"How long can the fleet do this?" Fiona asked. "Eventually they will run out of ammunition or something right?"

"Back in the day of the Capitol Ships they could shell a planet until it was uninhabitable for human life," Tirpitz said. "Like the Victory you two were on. It had enough orbital shells for years."

"How is that possible?" Vincent gasped. The ship had been the size of a small city, so it shouldn't have surprised him it carried enough ammunition for a prolonged campaign.

"Well, the orbital guns aren't like a piece of artillery firing powder charges. They're more like your rifle and fire a giant rail slug. It doesn't even explode." Tirpitz smiled, her expression turning from a scowl to slightly smug. "It's a tungsten rod the size of a tank that strikes the planet's surface with enough force to cause everything below it to atomize."

"Can I get that in *not officer* talk?" Fiona said.

"It's like it's punching the planet really hard," Ezra joked. Fiona expressed her feelings about his ribbing by tossing her cigarette butt at the back of his seat.

"Regardless," Tirpitz continued. "Since they're magnetic munitions they don't take up as much space. Kind of like our rifles can carry way more rounds than the older versions you see some of the Martians carrying."

"You've never been in a big battle before, right?" Vincent asked her.

"No." Tirpitz frowned.

"But you read a bunch of history and stuff."

"Of course," she said.

"Historically, what are the odds of an irregular army winning with a frontal assault against a superior foe that has had years to fortify their position?"

"As far as I know it's never happened before," Tirpitz said. "I'm going to go out on a limb here and say the odds aren't in our favor though."

"This isn't the first time the Martians have tried to take the Mons," Ezra said.

"I can imagine how it turned out last time." Vincent sighed.

"You might sleep better if you don't," Ezra said. "Though last time they definitely didn't have air superiority and a long barrage beforehand."

"Is that you being optimistic or pessimistic? I honestly can't tell," he said. Ezra didn't answer, he looked back into the crew compartment and winked.

*　　　*　　　*

The army came to a rest after six hours of marching. They picked what used to be a large apartment complex to act as encampment for the night. The complex had long before been leveled by shell fire, leaving the rare piece of wide-open land in the city. They could not have found the area soon enough. The Martian Liberation Brigade may have been the best rebel group that Vincent had seen on the planet, but it had wholly fallen apart during the march.

It turned out that the backyard engineering that went into building the war wagons didn't have the highest reliability rate. Nearly half of the machines had broken down along the way. One had caught fire and had to be abandoned before it exploded. Vincent had to look away when one of the Artillery Battery's pack animals fell into a shell crater and broke its legs. The only recourse for the soldiers was to put the poor beast of its misery.

The soldiers had once again set up orderly rows of tents. The loud partying and drinking of the night before was gone. Most of the soldiers had collapsed into their bedrolls, fast asleep as soon as they had been set up. The few awake were patrolling outside of the camp area, their feet dragging with fatigue.

Vincent found Erik supervising the exhausted mechanics who were struggling to get the war wagons running once again. One of the wagons, a repurposed farm combine outfitted with duel heavy machine guns, was torn apart and its components strewn about on the ground.

"Everything okay?" Vincent asked.

"Far from it." Erik sighed. "Looks like we are going to have to take the parts of this one to fix the others. We need every wagon we can get."

"You don't have any spare parts for any of these?"

"Hardly." Erik laughed. "Most of these damn things are older than me. We only have whatever our mechanics can piece together. How's the ship?"

"Ezra says it's running fine. He said the Rhai outfitted it with some kind of dust filter," Vincent said.

"What do you think of them?" Erik asked.

"Who?" Vincent said. "The Rhai?" He laughed. "The first time I met one they tried to sell Fiona and I to the Alliance."

"Hmm." Erik frowned. "That isn't promising."

"You can trust the Mawr," Vincent said. "They're a bit much to get used to, but they would never betray anyone they trust."

"And the Titanians?" Erik asked. "Their soldiers once supported the Committee, right here on this soil," he grumbled.

"I can't say that I trust them, they're only in all of this for their own sakes," Vincent admitted. "But I do know they hate the Committee as much as us and know for any of us to live in peace they have to go."

"Then why would they back the Committee before?" Erik asked.

"Because they saw what happened to Mars and knew they didn't want to put Titan through the same carnage," Vincent explained. "Looking around, it kind of makes sense."

"So, they only support the side that they think is going to win." Erik frowned.

"This time that side is us," Vincent said, and Erik grinned.

"Damn right it is."

*   *   *

Vincent lay next to Fiona, his arm around her as she slept. The ground's ceaseless trembling and the thundering explosions from the Mons ensured Vincent was going to stay awake throughout the night. He was careful not to wake Fiona as he clambered out from underneath the covers.

He climbed out of the crew compartment of the *Shanna II*, where their group had bedded down for the night, and made his way through the camp. A few soldiers were obviously having the same issues as he was. They were gathered in small circles playing cards by dimmed, red lensed flashlights.

The Martian breeze was cool, and enough time had passed so that Vincent hardly noticed the smell of the decaying city around him. The blowing dust had calmed a bit and no longer stung his face or eyes. His armor had not been so lucky, as its dark blue hue was now almost entirely rust red.

The sharp report of a nearby rifle shot made Vincent dive to the ground. He slid to the ground, coming to a stop alongside several soldiers, their playing cards scattered around them.

"Are we under attack?" Cried one of them.

"They're supposed to be pinned down on the Mons!" Screamed another. Another single rifle shot barked out of the darkness.

"Get to your positions damnit!" roared a sergeant who had come running out of the darkness. "Move!" At the sergeant's command the prone soldiers leapt to their feet and began running in various directions. Vincent unholstered his Riten and took off after one of them.

Vincent crouched behind a low wall with dozens of other soldiers. The wall, only half a foot tall, forced everyone behind it to try to get as low as possible. Vincent carefully peaked his head over the top. He had expected to come under withering fire at any moment.

"Hold your fire!" Came a voice out of the darkness. "Don't shoot!" Vincent exchanged confused looks with the soldiers around him.

"Flash?" Called out a soldier next to him. On closer inspection Vincent could see it was an Ensign.

"Thunder!" Yelled the voice.

"Alright. Approach slowly!" The Ensign ordered.

"What the hell is going on?" Vincent asked the Ensign.

"Flash is the challenge word we gave our night watchmen. I say that when they're coming close to our lines and they answer with 'thunder'. If they don't answer correctly, we open fire."

"Oh," Vincent said, making a mental note of the password just in case.

Out of the night came two dozen shapes, walking slowly. As they got closer Vincent saw they were wearing the grey uniforms of the EDF. The soldiers shambled forward, some of them half dressed. Others had white shirts tied to the end of their rifles, held up over their heads. Behind the surrendering EDF soldiers were two of Erik's soldiers, their rifles pointed at their backs.

"They're surrendering?" The Ensign gasped. The soldiers along the wall slowly climbed to their feet. As the EDF soldiers approached the soldiers fell into a hushed silence and stared at them. Vincent found himself doing the same thing. It was the first time he had seen a normal EDF soldier up close and not a Black Coat since Grawluck.

Their faces were covered in dirt and dust. Blood matted their hair and their eyes were wide with frozen shock. Many of them were limping from various wounds, others had stained bandages wrapped around them. At their head was woman, a blood-soaked bandage covered half of her face, the pins of a staff sergeant on her frayed collars.

Erik met the column of EDF soldiers, two armed soldiers at his side. Vincent noticed he was wearing a clean and pressed uniform. Sharp creases went down the center of his pants and sleeves. He stifled a laugh. The Brigade Commander had been just as filthy as the rest of his soldiers from the march but had to have gone and changed into a clean uniform when he got word there were prisoners.

"Good evening," Erik said. "I am Commander Erik Victoria. Who might you be?"

"Staff Sergeant Scarn, Army Group Olympus, 245th Scout Regiment, 1st Squadron, Charlie Troop, 3rd Platoon," she answered. "Do what you will with me, but please do not harm my soldiers any further."

"I respect the dedication you have to your men, Sergeant, but that won't be needed." Erik nodded. "Consider yourself lucky you fled the bombardment in this direction. A few miles in any other direction and the gangers would have had you." Scarn's eyes went wide. "I accept your surrender, Sergeant. My men will disarm you and lead you back to the holding area."

"Th-thank you, sir," Scarn stuttered. The surrendering soldiers' faces of abject terror began to relax. They tossed their rifles down onto the dirt and were led away a few of Erik's men. As one of the EDF soldiers walked by Vincent, a young private, he heard him mutter.

"Anything is better than those damned Black Coats." Vincent reached out and grabbed the soldier by the collar of his uniform.

"What did you say?" he asked. The young private's eyes turned to saucers and he fumbled for words.

"I didn't say anything, sir!" he yelled, clearly terrified.

"Did you say something about Black Coats?" Vincent shook the private, trying to bring him back to his senses.

"Yes, sir!" The private said. "I didn't mean to speak out of turn!"

"I'm not going to hurt you," Vincent reassured him. "Are you saying there are Black Coats up at the Mons?"

"Yes. The assholes think they are better than everyone else," the private said, tears beginning to cloud his eyes. "They're shooting anyone who even talks about trying to break out towards Victoria."

"Who are these, Black Coats?" Erik asked.

"They were sent by the Committee to root out disloyalty in the EDF," Sergeant Scarn said. "Their definition of disloyalty turned out to be very broad. They shoot anyone they think is hurting the war effort."

"I had a run in with them on Elysian," Vincent told Erik. "We chased them and their Zealot of a leader off of the planet. Guess we know where they ended up."

"Who is leading this death squad?" Erik asked.

"Field Marshal Brusilov," Vincent said grimly.

"The Butcher," Erik growled. Erik nodded to the prisoner's escorts. The escorting soldiers nudged the EDF soldiers with their rifles and the procession marched away down the camp.

"You look like you've seen a ghost Solaris," Erik said.

"The last time I saw Brusilov a lot of people died." Vincent sighed. "I was hoping I would never see him again."

"There hasn't been anywhere he has gone that he didn't leave a trail of corpses in his wake. You should count yourself lucky you were able to walk away from it." Erik smiled.

"By all means I shouldn't have," Vincent said. "I'm no officer." He laughed.

"If your soldiers followed you into combat against Brusilov they certainly see you as one," Erik said. "Don't sell yourself short, you made it this far."

"I was a corporal. And a bad one at that." Vincent sighed.

"I was a corporal once," Erik said, patting him on the shoulder and yawning. "I'm going to try to get a few minutes of shut eye before we step out in the morning. I suggest you do the same." Vincent nodded at Erik as he walked away.

He made his way back through the camp, which had already fallen back silent. Vincent sat back on the edge of the *Shanna II*'s crew compartment and watched the geysers of fire and smoke erupt on the Mons as it continued to be pounded with shells. He had no idea how anyone could survive such a thing, but he knew at least one would. The idea that Brusilov was staring back at him all but assured he wouldn't be sleeping that night.

In the morning, the soldiers of the column began to march once again. They left their tents behind to be packed up by support soldiers and placed on one of the carts being dragged along by the surviving pack animals. Erik was trying to make up for lost time, not even giving the soldiers time to eat before setting out. Instead, they marched with their rifles slung and clumsily tried to eat while they walked.

The *Shanna II* floated overhead. As they got closer to the Mons Reapers, Comanches, and the crescent shape of the Clan ships dove low over the column. The column erupted into cheers each time. The ships welcomed the cheers by rocking their wings back and forth in greeting. In moments they were racing back up into the sky and diving onto the Mons.

Vincent's throat went thick as he saw several of the attacking ships reduced to fireballs by return fire. Tracers and missiles streaked through the air from the Mons towards the incoming ships. Dozens of them vanished with a poof of smoke and debris.

"They still got some fight in 'em," Fiona said.

"Seems that way," Tirpitz said.

"How can anything be alive up there?" Vincent gasped. "The fleet has been hitting them for two days."

"Erik said about two more days of marching at most," Tirpitz said.

"Almost a week under that kind of fire?" Ezra scoffed. "No way anything survives that."

"Even roaches survive when everything else dies," Zinvor growled.

"They should have been crushed under the weight of the shells." Tirpitz grimaced.

"Why the pause?" Vincent asked. "Why send in close air support when you have guns big enough to level a planet I mean."

"After a certain amount of shelling the guns need to be checked for any damages and cleaned. The magnets that power the rail cannons are so powerful they tend to mess themselves up if they fire for too long. It only takes a few hours at most. The close air support keeps the attack up and doesn't give the targets time to reinforce their positions," Ezra said, adding with confidence "Two more days of the orbital strikes will snuff out what fight they have left in them."

"Over confidence kills more Warriors on that battlefield than any weapon," Zinvor said. Tirpitz frowned.

"Man, he really is grim, isn't he?" Fiona sighed.

"Not just him. It's his whole race. They make the Martians look downright upbeat."

"That is terrifying," Tirpitz said.

"Wait until you see them fight," Vincent said. "I've been on both sides of them on the battlefield. I think I would rather sit through that bombardment then fight a Mawr Cohort again."

"What is the human saying?" Zinvor said. "Like hot knife through butter?" He grinned and began to laugh, his hoarse laugh sounded like a human coughing up something. Fiona began to laugh with him while Tirpitz looked on in confusion. Vincent scratched his beard.

"They bond over violence. It's best you don't try to figure out their dynamic."

"Noted," Tirpitz said.

*　　*　　*

The march had begun to claim soldiers as well as machines. Medics carried away numerous soldiers on litters. Their uniforms were smoking and their features a sickening charred black.

"What the hell happened?" Vincent asked.

"One of the new soldiers decided smoking in his war wagon was a good idea." Erik shook his head. "Damn thing went up like a lighter."

"Oh," Ezra gasped.

"Last thing we can deal with his losing another damn wagon," Fiona said, crossing her arms.

"Fiona!" Vincent gasped and nudged her shoulder. Even for Fiona that was terribly callous.

"No, she's right." Erik sighed. "But the damage to the wagon itself wasn't too bad. It can probably be fixed."

"And the soldiers?" Vincent asked.

"Well, I hope the Titanians bring some burn specialists with them or they're as good as dead," Erik said, rubbing his temples. "That isn't even the worst of it."

"Something is worse than a bunch of soldiers catching on fire?" Tirpitz asked, horrified.

"One of artillery carriages," he began, but seeing the confusion on everyone's face, elaborated. "They are the trailers that carry all of the artillery's ammo. An axel snapped off of one of the damn things and rolled over on six soldiers. Including a battery captain."

"I imagine you don't have a lot of extra trained officers to replace them with," Ezra said.

"No," Erik said. "I barely had the last class graduated to make up for the losses we suffered over the last couple of months. I even cut their education short to fill the holes."

"I believe they told us in academy that a march was a dangerous to an army as the enemy was. I never understood what they meant until now," Tirpitz said. "We have a saying in the Cohorts when you are a *krtser*—" Zinvor said, his switch to the Mawr language producing looks of confusion from everyone else.

"*Krtser* means a Warrior that hasn't earned their armor or Riten yet," Vincent said.

"You understand their language?" Erik asked.

"He barely passed Ethics School, yet took up a completely alien language in a couple weeks. It was nuts." Fiona laughed. Zinvor cleared his throat in annoyance.

"Sorry Zinvor, go ahead." Erik nodded.

"Cohort Leaders tell the Krtser *March or die*," Zinvor finished. "If a *Krtser* falls during the march they are left."

"Man, you weren't kidding about these guys." Erik laughed. He rubbed his face. "But goddamned if he isn't right."

Erik's army plodded on. The billowing, swirling dust that had kicked up in the morning had finally died back down. Before anyone could breathe a sigh of relief it began to rain.

It wasn't a type of rain that Vincent had ever seen before. Red-tinged mud slapped against *Shanna II* so loudly it sounded like incoming fire. Ezra fumbled with a couple of switches before small wipers turned on, smearing red mud across the windshield.

"What in the hell—" Tirpitz gasped as the mud splashed into the crew compartment. Ezra acted quickly and with the press of a button the compartment doors slid shut, protecting them from the onslaught of mud rain.

"The rainy season," Fiona said without any kind of reaction. Vincent twisted his face up.

"Doesn't look like any damn rain I've ever seen before."

"All the dust from the windy season gathers up in the clouds and mixes with the rainwater. Now our rainy season is like something out of your nightmares," she said. "You can thank the Committee."

"We have to fight in this?" Tirpitz cursed.

"If it makes you feel any better it's a thin mud," Ezra added. "Not like the shit on Grawluck."

Vincent shuddered at the thought of the flooded trenches and the sticking mud of the dead world. He could have gone the rest of his life, however long that was going to be, without ever seeing mud again.

"You still feel like you're missing out on the march?" Fiona asked smugly.

Tirpitz's nose turned upright, and she frowned. "Not quite."

*　　*　　*

The army finally came to a rest about one mile from the Spaceport. The Mons had once been the tallest mountain in all of human space, maybe even the galaxy. The committee, besieged on all sides for decades by Martian Rebellion and in need of an easily securable lifeline, blew the top off of the mountain and turned it into a Spaceport. They went even further by turning the approaches into a fortress.

In the rebellions of the past, their plan had worked flawlessly. No matter how bad the situation got in the streets of Olympus, the EDF could retreat to their mountain fortress as endless supplies and reinforcements streamed down to them from the Committee fleet who sat uncontested in the skies above. It didn't matter what the rebels tried; they could never dislodge the EDF from the Mons.

What Vincent was watching unfold in front of him was a much different story than the one the history books told. The Mons was exploding with the force of thousands of orbital shell impacts. What had once been the strongest point of Committee power on Mars looked like an erupting volcano. Fire and smoke billowed out from its top and the scent wafted down through the army camp. For the first time since Denta had come up with this insane plan, Vincent was feeling confident.

Erik's soldiers had begun to dig in. Dropping their packs they retrieved small folding shovels and began to dig hasty fighting positions. The odds of the EDF counter attacking through the hail of orbital artillery was incredibly low, but no one wanted to be caught unprepared.

The Brigade had stopped in a clearing. What had once been a suburban area during the time of unification had been flattened. It had been cleared by the EDF to create wide open fields of fire to better service their entrenched positions on the Mons that looked down on them. The Committee had spent years creating the perfect killing fields, ensuring there was nothing for any attackers to hide behind.

Vincent, Fiona, Zinvor, and Tirpitz began to hack away at the ground while Ezra watched from the cockpit of the *Shanna II.*

"What?" Fiona laughed. "Are colonels too good to dig their own foxhole?"

"He's not staying with us," Tirpitz said, an undeniable tinge of sadness in her voice. "He's going to join the fleet soon."

"Well it makes sense," Vincent said. "He's too valuable to fight down here with us."

"Yeah. You're right." Tirpitz sighed. Sweat began to bead around her brow as she looked back at Ezra who was typing something into the onboard computers, not paying any attention to the digging soldiers.

"You really like him huh?" Fiona asked. Tirpitz's dark skin turned as red as fire.

"What?" she asked, incredulously. "How could you—"

"You guys are terrible at hiding it," Fiona cackled, obviously enjoying getting under her skin.

"Is...that wrong?" Tirpitz asked. "He outranks me and—"

"You're not in the EDF anymore," Vincent pointed out. "I'm not sure what Titan rules say, but there's no regulations about that sort of thing in the Elysian Defense Forces." He smiled. Tirpitz grinned broadly.

"Two Warriors are perfect mates. Will make strong offspring," Zinvor grunted, tossing a shovelful of dirt over his shoulder. Tirpitz's face went even redder at his remark.

"Offspring?" she screamed. "No one is saying anything about any offspring!"

Zinvor shrugged and chopped his shovel back into the dirt. "Is waste," he grumbled.

The dirt crunched behind them and Vincent turned around to see Ezra approaching. The somber look on his face told Vincent he was having the same worries as Tirpitz.

"So, fleet Command just radioed me. They want me to—"

"I know," Tirpitz cut him off, her eyes downcast. They stood, awkwardly separated by a few feet, neither wanting to make the first move towards the other.

"You guys are killing me." Fiona sighed. "Stop hiding it will you?"

"Sir, I—" Ezra looked at Vincent.

"Just cut the shit, will you? Do you really think I am going to stand in between you two?" Vincent smiled.

Ezra, ever the stickler for the regulations, was holding his emotions back for the old EDF regulation that forbid any sort of relationships between superior officers and anybody below them.

"Right." Ezra smiled nervously. Tirpitz finally broke the stalemate, jumping out of the small entrenchment she had been working on, and embraced him. Ezra held his arms out in shock for a moment before wrapping them around her tightly.

"You know, if we weren't about to charge up a mountain to fight half a million damn people this might remind me of those stupid romance books my Mom used to read." Vincent laughed.

"Still a better love story than ours." Fiona shrugged.

"No way," Vincent said, throwing an arm around her shoulder and pulling her in close. "Star crossed lovers brought together from across the warring galaxy into each other's arms."

"More like a one-night stand on a shitty bunkbed surrounded by hundreds of other soldiers while we awaited our deaths." Fiona smirked.

He rolled his eyes. "Well, when you put it that way."

The two finally let each other go. Tears cut lines through the dust covered face of Tirpitz. Ezra's eyes were growing mistier by the second. He reached into the collar of his flight suit and produced a necklace—his standard issue identification tags—and gave them to Tirpitz. She put them around her neck and tucked them into her top.

Ezra wiped his eyes with his sleeve and turned towards Vincent.

"Well, sir, I'll see you at the top." He began to bring his hand up into his normal parade-perfect salute when Vincent stuck his hand out.

"Take care of yourself, Ezra." He smiled. Ezra's hand came down and wrapped his hand around Vincent's, squeezing it hard.

"You too, Vincent." He smiled. Ezra turned back to Tirpitz and kissed her passionately. "I'll see you soon, okay?" he said. She couldn't find any words, instead she just nodded. Ezra turned and walked away, back towards his ship.

Tirpitz frantically began to wipe the tears away from her face before turning to look and them.

"I'm sorry." She sniffed. "That wasn't appropriate for an officer to do in front of others."

"Damn, you guys are so much alike it's creepy." Fiona laughed. Vincent couldn't help but join in the laughter. At the sight of the two of them laughing Tirpitz's tears turn to anger.

"And why exactly are you two laughing?" She pouted.

"I think you two might be perfect for one another," Vincent said. The red began to fade from Tirpitz's face, and she smiled

"Yeah," Fiona agreed. "I think you share the same stick up your asses." She laughed again. Tirpitz huffed and kicked dirt at Fiona who playfully returned a kick full of her own. Their small argument was ended when the sound of the *Shanna II*'s engines whirled to life and the ship rose into the air over them.

Tirpitz's expression sank as the ship sped off into the red clouds overhead and out of sight.

"he's going to be fine," Vincent reassured her. "he's been through more than we could ever know."

"I know," Tirpitz said. "But what if someone can only go through so much before their luck finally runs out?" The tears reappeared in her eyes.

"There is no luck on the field of battle," Zinvor said. "Only skill. And Warrior Ezra has many skills."

"And have you seen where you're standing?" Fiona asked. "You should be worried about you right now."

"Yeah, I like his odds a whole lot more than I like ours," Vincent said.

"Oh please," Tirpitz scoffed. "Nothing is going to be alive on that plateau. It just isn't possible."

And that was when, as if on cue, the ground stopped shaking for the first time in a week.

CHAPTER TWENTY-EIGHT

"Battalions!" Boomed out Erik's voice. "Commanders!" he yelled "Form up your Battalions." Soldiers dropped what they were doing, grabbing their weapons, and ran to take their places in their formations.

Small, tight squares of about one hundred soldiers apiece materialized along the lines of foxholes they had just been building. Vincent ran over to where Erik was standing, joining in on the meeting with his Commanders. A dozen officers wearing the ranks of captain and major on their collars eyed Vincent suspiciously.

"That's the signal," Erik said, pointing up. "We are officially too close for them to keep up the fire without the risk of accidently hitting us." Vincent's stomach began to churn. Erik's voice sounded artificially loud now without the deafening eruptions of fire from on the Mons.

"When do we move Comrade-Commander?" asked a young looking major. An Earthian with a tightly groomed mustache.

"We are going to wait for the close support ships to take positions above us and—" Erik was interrupted by the far-off sound of rifle and machine gun fire. "What in the—"

"That sounds like it's coming from the west side line of advance, Comrade-Commander," said a captain.

"Fucking Marcus!" Erik screamed. "We were supposed to advance at the same time! Get me my radioman!"

A smaller soldier broke from a rank from one of the Battalions behind the command meeting. He had a large, incredibly old looking radio strapped onto his back. A long antenna swung back and forth over the soldier's shoulder as he ran. The soldier stopped in front of Erik, gave him a quick salute, and then handed him the radio's receiver at the end of a curling black cord.

"Cutter Actual, this is Red Command. What's going on over there?" Erik asked. The receiver hissed for a few moments before the acid voice of Marcus broke through the static.

"Did you actually think I was going to sit by and let some traitor get all the glory for taking the Mons?" Marcus said.

"You stupid fuck!" Erik spat back at him. "We need to work together for this to work!"

"Eat shit, boy fucker," Marcus cursed, and the static stopped as the line went dead. Erik handed the receiver back to the radioman and took a moment to compose himself.

"I want artillery cover before we advance. He might be okay with a suicide mission, but I'm not," Erik said slowly, his eyes closed in thought. "How long until we can have a smoke cover thick enough for us to advance?"

"twenty minutes, Comrade-Commander." Answered a major with a red stripe on his pants.

"You have ten," Erik commanded. The artillery major saluted and ran off screaming commands. "We advance behind the wagons. I'm going to need you all to control your men and stay in formation. Those wagons are going to be the only cover we have during the advance."

"Yes Comrade-Commander!" they barked in unison.

"I'll see you at the top." Erik nodded. "Mars Eternal."

"Mars Eternal!" they roared.

In comparison to the prior week's orbital bombardment, the report from the battery's artillery was pathetic. The guns boomed and the slopes and ridges of the Mons became cloaked in a thick white smoke. Vincent stood next to Erik who had a pair of binoculars up to his face and was scanning the horizon.

"Wagons forward!" Erik called out. Wagon's tracks tore at the ground, flinging dirt through the air and onto the assembled soldiers. The phalanx of mismatched tanks gathered in front of them. Soldiers hung out of hatches with multiple different weapons mounted along the top of the Wagons. Somehow, this unconventional display made Vincent feel better about their chances.

Fiona nudged his shoulder and held out a pack of cigarettes. He took one and lit it.

"For Mars?" He grinned at her. The tip of her cigarette sparked as she inhaled.

"Fuck Mars," she said. "For Elysian."

"And Titan," Tirpitz said.

"And the Warlord!" Zinvor roared.

"Forward, March!" Erik commanded. The brigade erupted into a cheer.

"Mars Eternal!" They called. "Death to the Chairman!" and finally "Long live the Great Traitor!"

The army stepped off.

Vincent followed close behind Erik as they inched up the slope of the Mons. The War Wagon in front of them churned the blasted landscape under its tracks as it spewed black exhaust over their head. Artillery shells crashed down on the slope above them. Smoke screens were mixed with the power of high explosive shells.

The soldiers advanced behind them, bayonets bolted onto the ends of their rifles, their eyes darting all over as their nerves overtook their earlier cheering. Vincent had cursed himself for not grabbing a bayonet before they had set out. Though he had a sinking feeling that there would be plenty of them on the ground soon.

The advance was deathly silent with the exception of the grunting, overworked engines of the wagons and bursting artillery. He could hear his feet crunching across the dirt with each step he took and his heart beating in his temples. The sound of a nearby soldier's gear jingling as he walked was clear as day. The flick of a lighter as someone lit a cigarette sounded like it was right next to him. Vincent could have never imagined two hundred thousand soldiers could ever be so quiet.

The quiet was short lived. The buzz saw of machine gun fire tore into the advancing formation of soldiers. The sharp crack of rifle fire soon joined in and all the air erupted with angry snap and pop of bullets cutting through the air around their heads. Soldiers began to be ripped away from the advance, but no one stopped.

Vincent, close to the rear of a war wagon was as safe as anyone could have been. Thousands of rounds sparked off of the wagon and soldiers behind him forced themselves as close to him as they could. The slope behind them was already thick with the dead and dying.

Reapers dove low through the clouds and sent a cluster of rockets towards the ridge ahead of them. The rockets twisted through the air and burst into flames when they impacted. The war wagons began to pepper the ridge with whatever weapons they had. Machine guns, rockets, and grenades arched out from the wagons and exploded around the enemy's trench line.

Vincent peaked out around the wagon and fired blindly at the enemy positions. Tirpitz and Fiona did the same. The heavy machine gun mounted on top of the wagon had fallen silent, so Zinvor clambered up the back of the vehicle. He shoved the gun's previous operator's corpse off of the side of the wagon and it flopped into the dirt. Afterwards, long burst of gunfire began to sweep across the top of the ridge line.

An explosion cut through the advance off to Vincent's left. A wagon had been hit by a rocket and fire blew out of its sides. The crewmen inside leapt from the burning vehicle, screaming. Their uniforms melted to their backs as they burned up like human candles. The soldiers who had taken cover behind the stricken Wagon ran for their lives as burning fuel splashed over them. Their screaming pierced Vincent's soul. He could hear their unspeakable misery over the sound of thousands of rifles.

"Hold the fucking line!" Erik screamed. "Not one step back roared. The soldiers around him cheered and fired at the EDF positions. Vincent watched as one of the cheering soldiers had his stomach blown out through his back by a rifle round, his insides cascaded onto the soldiers behind him.

The grade of the slope was beginning to even out. Mercifully, their climb turned into a regular walk. He knew they had to be getting close. Though, Vincent hadn't dared to stick his head out to see how close they were.

Another nearby war wagon exploded. It was sent cartwheeling backwards end over end before landing like a fiery meteor on the surrounding soldiers. The burning wreck cut a devastating swath through what had once been an entire Troop.

"Reform damnit!" Screamed out an officer. "Reform on me!" The surviving soldiers began to advance once again. What was left of the Troop gathered together behind a different wagon.

Above the explosions and gunfire, Vincent heard something he was sure he wasn't going to hear: the horrible shrieking of incoming artillery shells.

The ground behind the advance exploded, silencing the wounded who had been left out in the open. The whistling and screeching of various different sized artillery and mortars rose to a crescendo.

"They still have artillery!" Fiona screamed. "How the fuck do they still have artillery?"

"I'm on it!" Tirpitz yelled back. She dropped to a knee and produced a data display from a pouch on her vest. A few seconds passed and another volley of artillery filled the air with the sounds of impending death. The gunners had adjusted their aim considerably as the shells impacted amongst the advance.

Vincent watched as a platoon disappeared in a cloud of smoke and fire. Another shell crashed down onto the roof of a War Wagon and it detonated. The explosion sent burning hunks of metal and boiling hot fuel in all directions, cutting through the surrounding soldiers like a scythe through wheat.

"I got it!" Tirpitz yelled. She activated the small radio she kept on the shoulder of her vest.

"*Shanna II, Shanna II*" she shouted over the cacophony of the destruction around her. "Fire mission!" A few seconds passed and she spoke again. "Counter Battery!" She glanced down at her data display. "I say again, Counter Battery! Grid AB 34726351. Fire for effect!" As she finished a shell landed a short way away from them. It exploded amongst the midst of the soldiers advancing behind them and covered them with a mixture of dirt and blood.

Vincent sat up slowly, his ears were ringing so loudly that he couldn't hear the guns going off around him any longer. The slope behind him that had once been full of soldiers, packed shoulder to shoulder, was completely desolate. It had been pounded into a killing ground by machine gun fire and punishing artillery.

"Get those fucking guns off of us!" Erik screamed.

"I'm trying!" Tirpitz yelled. "There's too many of them!" as if to underline her point another group of Reapers dive bombed the Mons, sending up columns of flames. The artillery fire continued unabated. Another wagon was turned into a fireball, sending soldiers for their lives.

"We must close the gap!" Zinvor bellowed. "So close they cannot use their cannons!"

Erik climbed to his feet, his once pale complexion had been darkened with dirt and filth.

"He's right," Erik said.

"I don't see how it could make this shit any worse!" Vincent said.

"Just get me close enough to kill these bastards!" Fiona growled.

"Soldiers of Mars!" Erik screamed. Thousands of pairs of terrified eyes looked towards their Commander. "This is our damn hill!" he roared. "This is our goddamn planet!" Erik pointed up the hill as the ground around him ruptured with gunfire. "Every single second they are allowed to stay on it disgraces the memories of all of those who came before us! Sacred Martian land is right in front of you! So go take it!" The wavering soldiers pumped their fists into the air and cheered. "Charge!" Erik bellowed, his voice hoarse.

Vincent had never been a part of a large infantry charge before. He had thankfully missed out on most of the slaughter on Grawluck. It was something he had never felt before. The soldiers around him, having only seconds before being torn to shreds and on the verge of breaking, let out a determined shout. Their battle cry was part uncontrolled rage, part desperation, and part determination. They rushed forward into the hail of bullets and artillery fire, heedless to it all. Whether he wanted to or not, Vincent found himself carried along like he was being pushed to the shore by a wave.

They sprinted past the War Wagon and like he had thought, they were nearly at the ridge line of the Mons. They were so close he could see the black helmets of the EDF soldiers sheltering in their trenches. The charging soldiers fired wildly at the trench and Vincent joined in. Sweeping his rifle to the left and right, he burned through his magazine in just a few seconds.

The soldiers in the EDF didn't fire at first, having been momentarily spooked by the sudden charge of someone they had thought defeated only a few moments before. They were only a few meters away when their shock wore off and the defender's fire picked back up in earnest. Machine guns and rifles at such a close range were devastating. The men around him were blown apart and jerked back, falling into the wave of soldiers behind them.

Vincent grimaced, waiting for the impact of a bullet. He knew it was coming any second. As close as they were his armor offered virtually no protection. Then, it happened. His rifle exploded into pieces as it absorbed an incoming bullet. His hands burned with pain and his fingers went numb. He didn't stop, he couldn't have if he had wanted too. He kept being shoved forward by the human wave at his back.

Vincent didn't want to look down and see what remained of his hands. Instead, he charged forward, empty handed. The dozen meters that remained between the two sides felt like the distance of a marathon. A grenade exploded in front of him and he felt the countless impacts of shrapnel, dulled by his armor. Something cut through his right boot, and he felt it begin to fill with hot liquid.

Finally, at the lip of the trench he kicked out wildly. He connected with the head of an EDF soldier and they reeled back. The advancing soldiers poured into the trench, their screaming human wave breaking across the concrete reinforced line. Vincent pounced on the soldier he had kicked. Straddling him, he began to rain punches from his damaged hands into the man's face until his eyes rolled into the back of his eye. He stood, drawing his Riten from its holster and fired a single round between the man's eyes.

Fiona lashed out next to him with her Riten in one hand and her sword in the other. Erik speared a man in the neck with his bayonet while Tirpitz dropped two more with a burst from her rifle. It quickly became clear that the soldiers that had been left to defend the trench did not want to fight the screaming horde that had descended upon them. They were wavering and were about to break entirely. First it started as a trickle, the odd grey uniform would see an opening and flee over the trench towards the spaceport. After a few minutes it turned into a flood.

Every soldier that still could heaved themselves over the opposite side's wall and fled trying to get away from the Brigade. Unfortunately for them, now in the open, they were sitting ducks for the circling close air support of the fleet. The Reapers and Clan craft turned the wide-open area of the spaceport into a shooting gallery. With each pass a dozen or more fleeing EDF soldiers would vanish in a cloud of gore.

The few EDF soldiers in the trench quickly through down their weapons in an attempt to surrender. Despite Erik's standing orders, the soldiers of the Brigade had just watched hundreds, if not thousands of their comrades get shot down and they were in no mood to give quarter. The surrendering soldiers were hacked and shot to death where they stood, their cries went unheard over the surrounding battle.

It had only lasted a few moments, but the grey, concrete trench had been turned into a charnel house. Vincent couldn't take a step without standing on a dead or dying soldiers from either side. His nose wrinkled with the smell of bloody copper and burning cordite. Slowly, the soldiers around him began to notice, despite the hideous slaughter, they had taken the trench.

The fighting had not ended though. Gunfire could still be heard coming from all directions.

"What's going on?" Vincent panted, trying to catch his breath.

"I don't know," Tirpitz gasped, her eyes wide. That was when Vincent saw the tip of a broken off bayonet was lodged in Tirpitz's body armor. "Did we win?"

"I think so," Fiona said, flicking the blood off of the end of her sword.

Erik strode down the length of the trench, his once perfect uniform in tatters. He smiled when he saw Vincent's group.

"Good to see you in one piece," he said.

"You too." Vincent smiled. Erik looked at Tirpitz, who's face had terror plastered across it.

"Thank you, Captain. If it weren't for those strikes who knows how many more men would have died." He smiled warmly. "You saved my army."

"I..." She stumbled.

"Have a seat. Catch your breath," he soothed. Tirpitz sat down unsteadily on the firing step of the trench. She sat her rifle across her lap, the white of her knuckles began to fade.

"So, what now?" Vincent asked.

"It seems like we are the first to secure our objective." Erik grinned. "I've sent the medics down the slope to help who they can. We aren't advancing any further today." He sighed. "I'm bringing the Battery up the hill so they can support Marcus and Murat. Enough of our blood has been shed today. It's time they pay their fair share."

"I can help," Tirpitz said, her voice steadying.

"Are you sure?" Vincent asked. "You don't have to."

"Yes, I do," she said. "It's my damn job."

"Well, you might find this useful then," Erik said, handing her a damaged data display. "I pulled it off of a dead colonel over there. It has all of their positions on it. Turns out they aren't so good on information security." He smiled again. "Bring the rain, Captain." She stood a little taller and her eyes took on a determined gaze as she slung her rifle over her shoulder.

"I will," she said. She took the display and marched off down the trench line, ignoring the salutes that followed her.

"Solaris," Erik said, looking at Vincent. "You need to go to the medics."

"I am fine," he said. His combat high had begun to fade, leading his various wounds to begin burning with pain. He slumped against the trench wall as he watched the blood from his boot ooze out and intermingle with the thin swamp of offal that had filled the trench floor. "Alright maybe not." He sighed. He felt Fiona's arm loop under his shoulder and lift him up.

"I got him," she said. The tone of her voice made it sound like it was just another day. Though, he had to admit this was far from the first time she had dragged him, wounded, from a battlefield. "This isn't as bad as last time." She smirked.

"Yeah." He whimpered as she shoved him over the lip of the trench. "At least I can walk this time."

"Your face is still busted though." She chuckled.

"That'll heal," he said, cringing as he put weight on his feet on the other side of the trench. "But you'll still be a bitch." They both burst out into laughter. Vincent quickly stifled his laughter when he saw litter teams picking amongst the countless bodies on the slope, looking for those who could be saved.

A solder, a white arm band on his arm indicating that he was a medic, walked along with the litter teams. Every few feet he would kneel down next to a wounded soldier and look them over. After a few seconds he would mark an "X" with a black marker on their forehead before walking off to the next one.

Vincent knew that meant no matter what that medic did, that soldier was going to die. The soldier was termed *expectant*. Or they expected them to die within minutes. The medic's time was better used on the soldiers who had a fighting chance. It was cold and the first time Vincent had seen it he thought it was heartless, but it was the way it had to be. In a field hospital time was everything and could never be wasted.

The slope had been carpeted with the dead and dying. No more than a foot of space anywhere was free of a red-jacketed body. The walking wounded slowly shuffled to the ad hoc field hospital like zombies. He watched as a few of them, only a short way from the medics, drop bonelessly to the ground, their wounds having claimed them or their shock finally wearing off.

The field hospital was what had once been a hardened concrete pillbox. It's two-foot-thick walls had been obliterated by a bomb, turning its former defenders into little more than a thin coat of paint on the interior walls. Now, dozens of wounded men lined its shattered floor with medics and men in stained white coats tending to their ugly wounds.

A medic walked up and looked at Vincent.

"Consul, sir?" The young medic asked, a Martian girl with a buzz cut. Her red uniform was stained up to its elbows in blood. "Are you hurt?"

"Yeah." He moaned as Fiona sat him down on an ammunition box. The medic knelt down and looked at his feet.

"Well the good news is your toes are still intact," she said.

"The bad news?" he asked.

"You're gonna need a new boot," she said. She produced a pair of scissors and cut away what was left of his boot. She wrapped a previously used bandage around his foot. He tried not to think about what had happened to the bandage's previous owner. His hands, thankfully, weren't as bad as he originally feared.

His rifle had taken the brunt of the damage, leaving his palms slightly burnt. There was no question, however, that he would have been dead if it weren't for the armor Arai had gifted him. Small scratches in its scales were scattered across his chest and legs. The marks of deadly shrapnel that would have killed anyone else.

"I would say try to take it easy but by the looks of your face you don't take a hint," the medic joked. "Just try to keep the wound clean."

"I'll try." He winced, pushing himself back to his feet. Vincent and Fiona were politely hustled out of the field hospital as several more litter teams had returned, bringing with them their grisly cargo, and space was at a premium.

He stepped gingerly back into the trench line where soldiers were going about the business of reinforcing their new positions. They were rifling through the pockets of the dead and then tossing their bodies out of the trench. A soldier approached Vincent, a pair of boots held in his hands.

"You look to be about a size twelve, sir." He smiled.

"Thanks," Vincent said. He knew, no matter how terrible it felt to be taking the boots of a dead man, the soldier was trying to be helpful. Vincent took them. The boots were tied together by the laces and he couldn't help but notice they looked almost brand new. An identification tag was looped through the laces on the left boot. It was a common practice amongst soldiers on the frontline, as sometimes your boots were the only thing left of you.

Private Soule, Silias
4-14-2129
ABPOS

The soldier had only been seventeen years old. The Mons had undoubtedly been his first battle. It had also been his last. Vincent untied the tag and put it in his pocket.

"Hey look!" Fiona said. Vincent pulled himself away from the dead man's boots and looked over the trench. Long lines of grey uniformed soldiers were streaming from the uncaptured positions around the perimeter of the Mons. Vincent's heart leapt. At first, he thought they must have beaten back Murat and Marcus' attack and they were launching a counterattack to drive the Brigade from the hill.

Then he saw that their raised hands. A white shirt was tied to the end of a rifle. It had to have been at least two battalions, running towards them. Fear, panic, and desperation painted across their faces. At the sight of such a large surrendering force the fleet above stopped their strikes and Erik's artillery went silent.

Reapers and Clan ships circled them overhead like vultures. The surrendering soldiers jumped up and down waving their flags at the ships. Brigade soldiers leaned over the trenches, waving the surrendering soldiers on, their rifles close at hand. Fiona and Vincent limped to where Erik, Tirpitz, and Zinvor were standing.

"Is it over?" Vincent asked.

"Certainly seems like it," Erik said. "The fight's gone out of 'em."

"Can you blame them?" he asked.

"No." Erik shook his head. "I don't think I could have kept my Brigade together under that kind of fire for so long." He sighed. "But." A grin began to creep across his face. "We stood toe to toe with them and beat them in the field." His grin broke into a broad smile. "I never thought I'd see the day."

Brigade soldiers climbed out of the trenches to meet the surrendering EDF. After a quick pat down each soldier was pushed into the trench where they were gathered. Medics began picking through their belongings for any first aid kits, as they were always in short supply.

The firing from the other sides of the Mons had slackened and then died away. Jubilant gangers appeared on the other side of the spaceport, firing their weapons into the air in celebration. While the two sides still hated each other, the soldiers of the Brigade erupted into cheers with them. Soldiers climbed to the top of the trench and fired into the sky.

"We fucking did it!" Fiona screamed. "I can't believe we actually did it!" She wrapped her arms around Vincent and Tirpitz, jumping up and down. Tirpitz's frozen features began to break, and a smile slowly appeared on her face. Vincent winced in pain but couldn't help but get caught up in the mood.

He unholstered his Riten, joined by Fiona and Zinvor. Tirpitz unholstered her sidearm with them. Together, smiles across their face, they pointed them up into the air and fired.

CHAPTER TWENTY-NINE

"You want to do what?" Vincent exclaimed. He wasn't the only one that was packed into the small bunker that was confused. Erik had called for a staff meeting in one of the few intact bunkers that remained. Vincent was invited along with a few colonels and a dozen or so captains.

"I've ordered the EDF dead to be buried with our own," Erik repeated himself.

"Sacrilege!" shouted a colonel. He was an older man with a well-maintained beard. A chorus of agreeing voices piped up afterwards.

"Listen, I know it's hard to understand," Erik said. "How many soldiers did we lose taking the Mons?"

"We are still counting, Comrade-Commander," a different colonel said. This one was younger and bald. "Right now we are looking at least twenty thousand casualties." The colonel swallowed hard. "We expect the number to rise."

357

"And how do you expect to replace those numbers?" Erik asked, it was a rhetorical question. The officers in the room exchanged angry glances. "We have several Academy classes months away from graduation and the next crop of new recruits will take at least a month to finish their basic training. And if you haven't noticed the Committee still controls Victoria and Tharsis."

"So, you're hoping that the surrendering EDF soldiers join you?" Vincent raised an eyebrow.

"A few won't. That much is to be expected," Erik said. "The loyal ones will be interned until the campaign is complete."

"We expect them to be loyal to us after they change sides?" Laughed a captain.

"If they turn against the Committee, we would be their only option. Going back would be a death sentence," Erik said.

"what do you hope to gain by burying our dead together?" Scoffed the bald colonel.

"To show them that we aren't enemies. We are one in the same, the enemy is the Committee," Erik said. Vincent understood where he was coming from. Only a short while ago he managed to convince thousands of disenfranchised soldiers that the Black Coats were worth going to war over in the service of an alien race.

If he had broached that subject with the same soldiers that would eventually form the Elysian Defense Force within their first few months on the planet, he was pretty sure they would have shot him dead. After over a year of mistreatment, hunger, and oppression by the Black Coats had changed them.

The soldiers that stood against them on the Mons were probably the same. Moderately loyal until they watched their home planet get destroyed. Until they were forced to fight a tenacious enemy in the streets of Olympus. Until they watched their commanders stay far away from battle, comfortably in their billets in some high-class area of Victoria, while they were abandoned to get relentlessly bombarded from space. Then they watched their fellow soldier get gunned down by Black Coats sent by their commanders to scare them into holding the line.

It seemed the gathering of officers had come to the same conclusion that Vincent had, as their facial expressions softened. A few of the Martian officers were still clearly unhappy, but they had stopped voicing their displeasure.

"I need everyone to begin reforming their units, I want a hard count on our fighting numbers before the fleet lands." The officers all nodded. "Dismissed," Erik ordered. The gathering saluted and exited the bunker.

"Do you think it'll work?" Vincent asked.

"No idea." Erik shrugged. "It's worth a shot."

"But you seemed to confident a few seconds ago," Vincent said.

"Consider it a teachable moment." Erik smiled. "Subordinates want their Commanders to believe in the orders they're giving are fool proof and are always going to work. If you don't believe in them, why would they?"

"So, when you ordered the charge on the hill?" Vincent asked.

"I certainly didn't think we would be sitting here talking about it." Erik laughed. "Your Titanian pathfinder pulled our asses out of the fire." Vincent laughed nervously. "We owe her."

"She thinks she failed," he said.

"She's still raw," Erik said. "Young officers always think they could do better. They beat themselves up with the 'what-if' game." Vincent swallowed hard. He was guilty of running the events of Grawluck through his head every night when he closed his eyes. "You do it too?" Erik asked.

"Just a little." Vincent scratched his beard.

"It doesn't do you any good," Erik said. "I once led an attack on the EDF garrison in the west end. It went from being a genius plan to being a slaughter in a couple of hours. I lost an entire Troop and gained nothing." He sighed. "It's something I have to live with, but not something I can dwell on right now." He pointed in the direction of the slope where thousands of his soldiers had been cut down. "If I worried about every single life it took to make it up that hill, I could have never ordered the attack." Erik stood and made for the door of the bunker. "We have a war to win right now. We'll have the rest of our lives to morn."

Soldiers in dirty, threadbare grey uniforms stood in a loose formation. Many of them were holding shovels and pickaxes, their hands filthy from hours of digging. The looks of shock and terror from being captured had begun to fade. They had been replaced by eyes tired from a week's worth of bombardment and the last few hours of grave digging.

Erik, flanked by Vincent and Tirpitz, approached the gathering. The soldiers eyed them with fascination. They exchanged words in hushed whispers.

"Good evening Soldiers," Erik began. "I am Commander Erik Victoria of the Mars Liberation Brigade." The crowds whispering died away. "With me here is Consul Vincent Solaris of the Fidayi Clan, and Captain Tirpitz of the Union of Titan." When Vincent's name was spoken a mix of emotions spread through the gathered formation.

Anger, hate, and curiosity, sometimes all at once played across the faces in front of him.

"The Great Traitor!" called out one of the soldiers. Vincent couldn't help but roll his eyes.

"You can believe that if you want too," Erik said. The crowd busily began to talk amongst themselves. "But that would require you to accept that an eighteen-year-old sentenced soldier outsmarted The Chairman, the Committee, and the entire EDF." Vincent struggled to fight back laughter.

The idea, which he hated to admit a large amount of his Elysian Defense Force believed, was so insane when spoken aloud he couldn't help but laugh. The formation took Erik's words in and stopped talking.

"Or, you can accept that the Committee lied to you, just like they always lied to us," Erik said. "How many of you are from Earth?" he asked. Most of the soldier's hands went up. "How many from Mars?" a few more hands went up. Vincent noticed they weren't Martians, but settlers. "Now many from Lunar City?" Not a single hand went up. The soldiers looked around and then back to Erik.

Erik strode closer to the formation, his hands clasped behind his back. "Not a single one. And why do you think that is?" he asked, not expecting anyone to answer. "Trust me when I say I have been fighting the Committee for a very long time. I have never seen any committee member's children putting on a uniform and shipping out. They are perfectly fine sending you off to freeze, sweat, starve, and die while they stay at home in their warm beds, never wanting for anything." The whispering amongst the soldier began to get louder. They were still angry, but their anger wasn't directed at Erik anymore. "They don't get draft notices. They don't send anyone they care about to be shelled to pieces for a week or to fight to the death in some trench."

"Shit, the Red is right," spat a sergeant. Vincent saw nods of agreement amongst the formation.

"I can't give you your home back. The Alliance took that away from you. But if you fight for me, I can promise you a new place to rebuild your lives, like we will be doing."

"What if we don't want to fight anymore?" Came an unsteady voice. Vincent saw it came from an undersized private, her hair a mess of brown curls.

"We have plenty of non-combat roles that need to be filled as well." Erik smiled.

"What's the difference between fighting and dying for you and fighting and dying for the Committee?" Asked a corporal.

"You'll get the chance to die a free man," Tirpitz said.

"If we fight for you, will we get a chance to torch Lunar City?" Asked a tired looking first sergeant.

"Together, we will make the whole goddamn Moon howl." Erik smiled broadly. The formation broke into a cheer. Several soldiers shed their uniform jackets and tore off the Eagle and Star shoulder patch. Erik turned to a Brigade soldier who was following at his heels. The Martian girl looked no older than sixteen and was carrying a large data display. "Can you begin processing them please?"

"Yes, Comrade-Commander," she said.

Erik turned and began to walk away, seemingly unaware how easy he had just made turning thousands of EDF against their own government look.

"That was amazing," Vincent said.

"Soldiers are simple, Solaris. The officers on the other hand..." Erik sighed.

"How many of them turned?" Tirpitz asked.

"Only a few," Erik said.

"Brainwashed rich kids from high up families," Vincent said. "Not too surprising."

"Speaking of rich kids." Erik said, turning to Tirpitz. "When can we expect your field marshal to make his grand appearance?" Tirpitz wrinkled her nose at the slight. As if on cue, the sky darkened, a long shadow was cast down on the Mons. An immense shape, black, and almost entirely featureless descended through the clouds. Smaller ships buzzed around its vast bulk in tight formations. The Titanian Navy had blotted out the entire Martian sky.

The ship at the head of the formation was nowhere near as enormous as the ESS Victory, but the Titanian landing barge was huge in its own right. The Mons Spaceport, the largest port on the entire planet, only barely had enough room to handle one of the ships at a time.

"I suppose I should get my welcoming party together," Erik said. "Maybe you should clean yourselves up."

*　　*　　*

The landing strip of the Mons Spaceport had been ravaged by the week of shelling. Crews of Brigade engineers and gangers had labored for hours in an attempt to fill the countless shell craters. They had only succeeded in making the Spaceport barely serviceable.

Now, a parade field of sorts had been formed. On one side of the strip stood two battalions of the Mars Liberations Brigade in a tight formation. Their rifles resting on their shoulders, they stood rigidly and staring off somewhere in front of them. Erik stood out in front of his gathering with Vincent and the rest of his group.

Vincent had tried his best to clean himself up, but it was mostly a failed endeavor. Using only a canteen of water and a rag, he felt like he had only managed to scrub away the top layer of filth out of many. Fiona had tried no such thing. She elected to nap on the flight instead and looked like she had just stepped out off of the battlefield. She looked much more like their counterparts on the other side of the strip.

The Head Hunters and Cutter gangs were gathered together in the closest thing they could manage to a military formation. Murat and Marcus stood together as their gangers lazed about behind them. Many of them were smoking or drinking from flasks. More than a few were sitting in the dirt and eating from stolen ration packs or playing dice. The tattered rags that acted as their flags were stuck in the ground, their frayed edges flapping in the wind.

"An impressive sight." Tirpitz sniffed, looking at the gangers. Zinvor grunted in approval. Though the stoic alien wouldn't say it, Vincent thought he had to hate the gangers as much as everyone else.

"You fight with army you have, not the one you want, Captain," Erik said. Tirpitz groaned.

"That's no army," she said. "Criminals and thugs at best."

"Sounds like ours huh?" Fiona laughed.

"That isn't entirely fair," he said. Fiona raised an eyebrow at him. "I think," he added reluctantly. He had made it a point to not look into the charges his soldiers had been charged with before allowing them to enlist into the reformed Defense Forces. Beggars couldn't be choosers.

The barge began to descend. Its matte black paint had been scarred by the battle in Martian space. Small gun turrets poked out from its armored walls every few feet, spinning around on the lookout for targets. A massive Titan Eagle was painted across the length of the barge in gold. A towering command bridge poked out from its head with several antennae crowning it.

Tirpitz had explained the barges they were using were originally for running massive amounts of supplies from Capitol Ships to the surface of a warzone creating a 'skybridge'. Since the Capitol Ships were all gone, the Titanian supply of Barges were retrofitted to act as troop transports and assault ships or any other roll the Titanian Navy needed them to fill.

Just in front of the barge was the unique shape of the *Shanna II*, holding formation with four other ships. Vincent watched as a small smile broke turned to toothy grin across Tirpitz's face. Though his reasons were much different, Vincent couldn't help himself but smile along with her at seeing him emerge unscathed from the battle.

Small, stubby, legs popped out from the belly of the barge. With a hiss of air pressure the barge came to a rest, the ground under Vincent's feet rumbled slightly as its bulk came to a stop. Erik turned on his heel towards his soldiers.

"Brigade!" he called out. The two colonels standing in front of their formations parroted his command. "Attention!" the thousands of heels snapped together in unison, giving the sharp report of a thunderclap.

Under the barge's cockpit a rush of steam vented into the air and the front of the massive ship began to open. A ramp began to creak towards the ground, opening a door large enough to drive two tanks abreast. A hush fell over the soldiers on the Mons. The sudden silence allowed Vincent to hear something that sounded like music coming from the ship.

Not just music. He heard drums. The rapid tapping of snare drums got louder and louder as the ramp descended. The ramp touched the ground and the drumming was so loud that the Brigade soldiers, formerly rigid at the position of attention, began to give each other confused looks.

People began to emerge. Two soldiers marching side by side were the first ones down the ramp. Both of them carried flags. Vincent's eyes went wide when he began to recognize what he was looking at. The soldier on the left, wearing a crisp Titanian combat uniform, was carrying a large Titanian Union flag in gold trim.

Next to him was a uniform Vincent had never seen before. A khaki colored uniform with a garrison cap slouching over one side of the soldier's head. The flag in the soldier's hands was a was a golden phoenix emblazoned across a blue background. The adopted symbol of the Elysian Humans.

Behind the two humans was the squat, muscular form of a Mawr Warrior. Its armor was the deep, dark yellow of Arai's personal Cohort. The Mawr marched a few steps faster than its human counter parts to make up its shorter stride. The Warrior carried the Clan flag lazily over its shoulder, the pomp and circumstance of human military traditions escaping them.

Then came the drummers. Dressed in Titanian dress, at least a Troop's worth, filed out of the ship rank by rank, their drumming never missing a beat. Once they were off the ship they stopped, marching in place, and pivoted on their heels so they were facing towards the center, lining either side of the ramp.

Field Marshal Denta emerged. He was as always, resplendent in his dress uniform. His peaked cap making him nearly half a foot taller than normal and chest full of medals taking up the entire left side of his uniform. Next to him was Arai, clad in her dark yellow armor, a small rainbow of ribbons streaming from her pauldrons. A third man marched behind him; one Vincent had never seen before. He was at least as old as Denta and he wore the same Khaki dress as the man who carried the Elysian Human flag. He had one silver star each on the collars of his uniform.

"Who the hell is that?" Fiona asked.

"No idea," Vincent said. "That's our uniform though."

Erik began to walk towards the disembarking command staff. He stopped after a few steps, turning towards Vincent and

Tirpitz and motioned for them to follow him. They quickly caught up to him. Across the expanse of the Spaceport, Vincent saw Murat and Marcus slowly strolling in the same direction. Vincent thought they were purposely going as slow as possible in an attempt to try to show the Titanian and Mawr that they were not impressed by them. A lit cigarette dangled from Marcus' lips.

Vincent felt thousands of eyes upon him as they began to walk through the line of drummers and flag bearers. The drumming was so loud that now that he was so close it felt like gunfire assaulting his ears, but he tried to play it off. Both sides exchanged salutes, though Murat and Marcus ignored the gesture. The drums stopped, as if the saluting were their signal to do so.

"A pleasure to meet you, Comrade Field Marshal," Erik said.

"And I you, Commander Victoria. Your forces are certainly impressive," Denta said.

"As is your fleet." Erik smiled.

"Where's the rest of your army, eh?" Marcus asked. "Or do you plan on smacking the Worms upside the head with a snare drum?" Erik shot him a venomous look.

"Our Armies will not land on the field until terms are agreed upon," Denta growled.

"We already made a deal," Murat said, his burned features contorting in shock.

"Those were terms for our support," Denta said. "Now that Olympus is all but secure, we have a bit more to talk about."

"Agreed," Erik said.

"Shall we?" Denta motioned to the barge behind him. "I have a room set aside for us to talk while the Engineers offload the ship."

Murat and Marcus went along without further complaint, but the annoyance was clear on both of their faces. The group made their way up the ship's ramp and into its cavernous interior. The cargo area was packed with row after row of modified storage containers secured to the floor by thick chains. All of them were the same drab grey color, a large golden eagle was stenciled on each of them.

Engineers were rushing around, unhooking chains and struggling to coax a forklift into operation to begin unloading their tons of cargo. They stopped what they were doing to salute the group as they approached them. Denta waved them off and they quickly got back to work.

The inside of the barge reminded Vincent of the *Victory*. It stank like burning oil and dust. Every inch of space was taken up by cargo, people, or the countless miles of wires and pipes that facilitated the operation of the ship. Very little space was left for simply moving through the ship. The hallway Denta led them down required all of them except the Mawr to duck to make it past the bulkheads.

Finally, they arrived in Denta's office. While it was a small room in comparison to his stately office on Grand Titan, it was still large for any ship. His desk was a single piece of metal bolted to the floor. His chair was little more than a metal stool, with a small grey cushion on top of it.

Vincent wasn't surprised when Denta reached behind his desk and produced a small amber bottle and several tin cups. He poured out a measure of dark liquid in each one and passed it around. He was starting to accept no military matters could be handled without a drink. He was also beginning to be thankful for that.

"So, what are your terms?" Marcus asked, getting to the point.

"I'd say it's pretty clear you have no intention of working with us," Denta said, looking at Marcus and Murat. "Your little show at the Spaceport told me as much."

"Smarter than ya look old man." Marcus grinned.

"Watch your damned mouth," spat the man in the khaki uniform. "You'd be dead without the fleet."

"And you would be dead if we didn't want you here," Marcus sneered.

"Marcus," Erik said curtly. "This isn't going to get us anywhere."

"Either is his kneeling down and licking this bastard's boots." Marcus folded his arms. "This is our damn planet."

"And if the EDF wasn't here I would want nothing to do with this backwater." Denta scowled. "We aren't here to take your pile of rubble from you. We are here to give it back to you."

"So," Erik began. "What Solaris said is true?"

"Yes," Denta said. "I'm not here to make any claims on Mars and neither is the Warlord."

"We have the same enemy," Arai added. "All other arguments are unimportant to me."

"And you expect my boys to just fall in line and follow your commands?" Marcus asked.

"No," Denta said. "I don't want your filth polluting my ranks. I think it is best that the gangers operate independently."

"In all due respect—" Erik began.

"What does that mean?" Murat asked.

"The organized formations press the advance into Tharsis and Victoria while the gangers stay in Olympus to root out possible EDF stragglers and loyalists," Denta said. "Besides, no one knows these streets better than you, right?"

"Hmm." Marcus thought it over. "But you'll still arm us, right?"

"I can't expect you to clear this place armed with that crap you have right now." Denta nodded. Murat and Marcus exchanged looks. "I'm surprised those damn rifles didn't explode in your hands."

"I'm pretty sure some of them did," Vincent interjected.

"Deal," Marcus said.

"Good," Denta said. "Then I assume we are done here?"

"I have a city to run, don't I?" Marcus smirked before turning and walking out of the office. Murat hurried to keep up.

"Comrade Field Marshal, this is a terrible idea," Erik said once they were out of the room. "You just gave them control of the Capital of our planet!"

"Give the *Comrade* shit a rest and in all due respect Commander, the capital of your planet hardly exists anymore." Erik's face twisted at the barb. "I can't depend on them during a military advance. Leaving them in charge of Olympus' ashes is our best immediate option," Denta said. "And all of our reports say there are minimal EDF forces in the city's outskirts. Either way, they will be out of our hair."

"And... Erik and I were talking..." Vincent began to say.

"Captain Tirpitz briefed me on your deal. I couldn't agree more, Consul. As does the Warlord." Arai nodded. "Surprisingly pragmatic on your part. I am impressed." He wasn't sure if he should have been offended by that or not.

"Just like that?" Vincent asked, shocked. Denta just greenlit what amounted to two political assassinations in the blink of an eye.

"You say we cannot trust them," Arai said. "That is all I need to know."

"To be completely honest I don't have time to get involved in Martian political intrigue. Just don't let it come back on us. We have a beast of a fight ahead of us, Commander Victoria. Are you with us?" Denta asked.

"The people of Mars cannot rebuild their lives until the Committee and the Alliance is taken care of. That much is clear to me," Erik said. "The only way to do that is together." Denta smiled and Arai nodded.

"Can I ask a question?" Vincent asked.

"Of course." Denta nodded.

"Who is he?" Vincent nodded to the man in the khaki uniform.

"Excuse my manners, Consul," the man answered. "I am Brigadier Vadim Presan. I was appointed to be your Deputy Cohort Leader by Warlord Arai."

"My what?" Vincent asked confused.

"Both Field Marshal Denta and Warlord Arai thought it would be appropriate if a staff officer helped you run the Elysian Defense Forces." Vincent knew he was beating around the bush, but he understood. While Vincent had lucked his way to victory on a few battlefields it was clear to everyone that he wasn't going to be able to command an actual army.

"You have no idea how glad I am to hear that." Vincent laughed. Presan laughed with him. "You were on Elysian this whole time and never joined before I left. Why is that?"

"Permission to speak freely, Consul?" Presan asked.

"You always do." Vincent nodded.

"Until your raid on the Black Coats I didn't exactly have a lot of faith in the Clan," he said. He cleared his throat. "Or you."

"Understandable." Vincent sighed. He hardly believed in himself, asking others to do so always felt like a stretch. "Are you Sentenced?"

"Of course not, sir."

"Then why not join the Black Coats?" Vincent asked.

"Brusilov is a goddamn monster. I couldn't serve him anymore." Presan shook his head.

"But you did before," Vincent said.

"As did you, Consul." Presan said, an obvious tinge of offense in his voice. "Before, there was no other choice."

"I understand where he is coming from," Denta said. "Like him, we saw an opening and took it." Denta poured another measure of liquor in their cups. "From what I understand he has turned your rabble into something of an actual army."

"Your Captain Olympus and First Sergeant Blackwell did a fine job. I really just had to put on the finishing touches," Presan said.

"I would imagine having a Brigadier in charge made it seem a little more legitimate," Vincent said.

"Your words sir, not mine." Presan laughed. "Though after the battle recruitment certainly increased."

"Oh?" Vincent asked, surprised. He had been rushed away from the Quarter to meet with Denta and then rushed once again to Mars. He had been so busy dodging EDF gunfire he had completely forgotten about the goings on back on Elysian. "So, a couple people actually wanted to join?"

"You could say that," Presan said, a small smile creasing his face. "We are working on our second full Regiment right now, sir." Vincent opened his mouth to speak, but nothing came out. "And with the full assistance of our Titanian allies, we have enough uniforms, guns, and foficers to go around."

"Officers?" he asked. "How?"

"Well, our Cohort is severely short on officers," Presan said. "Most of the officers turned loyalist with the Black Coats. As talented as our NCOs are, we can't ask them to fill in all of the gaps."

"I simply supplied you with our newest graduating Academy class," Denta said. "They are as fresh as the driven snow, mind you." He scratched his chin. "But they need the experience and you need their leadership. We have also begun to accept applications from the Elysians to our Officer's Academy."

"That is incredibly generous of you," Vincent said. "Thank you."

"It'll also make our battle plans easier," Presan said.

"Yes. I fully intend on using your Elysian soldiers with my own," Denta said. "It will be easy for them to work together."

"And mine?" Erik asked.

"As you can imagine I think some of your men would object to fighting side by side with Titanians," Denta said. After a moment of hesitation, Erik nodded his head in agreement.

"There's bound to be a few," said Erik.

"So," Denta began, turning towards a small display and clicking it on. Green light flickered and a digital map appeared in the air above the display. Laid out in detail was a large city.

"Victoria," Erik said.

"Precisely," Denta said. "The seat of their power on Mars. Consider it a political and moral victory for your new forces."

"I am grateful for the opportunity, but in all honesty, I don't think the Brigade has the forces at its disposal that I would need to take the Committee capital," Erik said, frowning.

"You will be supported by ten Regiments of Titanian Infantry, Armor, and close air support." Denta added more unit symbols to the map with the tap of a finger.

"Oh." Erik raised his eyebrows. "That should probably be sufficient."

"Unfortunately, because the city is backed up to a mountain a full envelopment would be impossible. This leaves only with only one front of attack. They knew what they were doing when they made this the only damn city on the planet that was remotely defensible."

"A frontal assault?" Erik gasped.

"Our advance will be covered by limited airstrikes and nerve agents. Once they dissipate our infantry will advance behind a combined force of Titan armor. Our goal is to breach their defensive lines and launch a decapitation strike on the Military District, where Brusilov will be. Once he is gone, resistance will surely crumble."

"Let's back up a little there," Vincent interrupted. "Did you say *nerve agents*?" he asked, disgusted. "Even Brusilov hasn't used that!"

"That's because they haven't felt threatened yet," Denta said. "We can expect them to be used against us soon."

"Still!" he said. "How can we drop nerve agents on these people? It'll wipe out the entire civilian population!"

"You're refusing something you don't understand, Consul." Denta grimaced, a small mask of respect still lingering. "We only need these weapons to clear their frontal defensive position so we can break through. They are heavier than air and will sink to the ground of their trenches and foxholes. It becomes inert in only a few minutes. The city's populace will be spared."

"I agree with the Field Marshal," Erik said. "After everything they have done on Mars having them drown in their own lung fluid is acceptable to me. Though I must admit I would rather your fleet flatten the entire city without further delay. It would save us the battle."

"The amount of military and human intelligence in Victoria is simply too valuable to turn to dust so easily, Commander. And besides, think of it as a new capital. You'll be able to rule Mars from the former seat of Committee power." Denta grinned, clearly thinking Erik would love the idea. The stern gaze Erik was giving him said otherwise.

"I also agree." Arai nodded. "What is the difference between shooting them or blowing them to pieces and stealing the air from their lungs. I long for the day we have a weapon like this for the Anarchs."

"Make no mistake Consul, this Command structure is not a democracy, but it seems you've lost," Denta said. Vincent folded his arms.

"Fine. But Elysian soldiers won't be taking part in any fucking gassings," he said. Denta rolled his eyes and the meeting continued like he hadn't objected at all.

"Sir, the forces in Victoria are sure to be Black Coats and Brusilov's best units. They're not going to surrender," Tirpitz said. "It'll turn into a siege."

"Understood, Captain," Denta said. "I did not expect them to surrender. Though, once we drive through and kill Brusilov, they will waiver."

"Forgive me, Field Marshal," Vincent began, studying the map. "If you simply break through and force your way into the Military District, won't you leave your flanks exposed?" Presan nodded in agreement.

"That does seem risky," he said. Denta waved them off.

"It is about the violence of action, Consul. I do not expect you to understand it. It is like a jab in a boxing match. You hit them so hard they cannot gather themselves before the final blow." Vincent wasn't convinced. Presan's look of concern told him he wasn't either.

"What about Tharsis?" Erik said, changing the subject. "They have another entire army group stationed there."

"Not just any army group. All of the EDF vehicle repair facilities happen to be in Tharsis, meaning it is where the majority of their heavy armor is as well." Denta swiped his hand over the map and it quickly changed to the map of a much smaller city. "Tharsis wasn't constructed with defense in mind, most human settlements weren't. It's surrounded with mountains and ridges. If we simply surround the city with the Clan forces, we can pin them in and make them fight within the city streets."

"Paterazm willing," Arai said.

"Right." Erik raised an eyebrow at Arai invoking the Mawr god of war.

"I will lead my personal Cohort in this effort," she said. "My *aspet* will churn them to dirt."

"Your what?" Denta asked, looking at her sideways.

"Tanks," Vincent translated.

"Thank you, Consul." Denta nodded. "And I'm glad you're so against our Victoria plan Consul, because you and your forces will be taking Tharsis with the Warlord."

"Good," Vincent said.

"Well gentlemen," he said, before glancing at Arai. "And ladies," he added. "We have a lot of gear to offload and not a lot of time to do it. I think your forces need to rest and ours need to get to work." Erik and Vincent nodded in agreement. "And Solaris, if I may say, get some sleep. You look like shit."

"Yes," Arai agreed. "I will send one of my Armor Melds to repair the damage to your coverings."

"Thanks," Vincent said.

"It looks like you went a few rounds with a Mawr," Presan added, stifling a laugh.

"Can't argue with you there." Vincent sighed. His foot was throbbing, and his broken nose made any sudden movement of his face or head painful. "I feel like I just charged a trench line or something."

Denta and Presan both laughed.

"We will meet again before we step off." Denta nodded, dismissing the group. "Tirpitz, if you don't mind, I'll have you stay with the Consul for a while longer as a liaison."

"Yes, sir." She saluted smartly. Vincent saw the corner of her mouth curl into a smile.

"We're lucky to have her." Vincent smiled at her, knowingly.

CHAPTER THIRTY

Over the next several days an endless stream of grey barges descended on the Mons. Each one unloaded supplies or tens of thousands of soldiers, Warriors, and vehicles. The grey storage containers on Denta's ships, it turns out, were not storage containers at all.

The containers had been converted to act as officer's billets, field hospitals, and planning rooms. Thousands of them were unloaded and placed into neat rows on all sides of the birthing strip, creating a small village seemingly overnight.

Hundreds of thousands of soldiers had pitched a city's worth of tents around the ruins of the Spaceport. The Mawr, as always, simply kicked the larges rocks out of the way before laying down on the ground. Mawr and humans intermingled for the first time, gathering around cooking fires and looking over each other's weapons. He watched human soldiers get sent tumbling into the dirt during friendly wrestling matches.

By Fiona and Presan's insistence Vincent hadn't been helping with the planning or logistics of the sprawling camp. Instead, he had laid in bed in the billet Denta had issued him and had his multiple wounds tended to by a Titanian Army doctor. The doctor was a man who had to be pushing seventy years old. The old man grimaced as he rewrapped Vincent's foot in fresh bandages.

"You're lucky you didn't lose these to rot," the doctor said, looking at his toes.

"Sorry." Vincent winced as the doctor put the finishing touches on the wrap. "Not a lot of medical care around here."

"And whoever stitched up that ear of yours needs to have their eyes checked," the doctor scoffed.

"I'll let them know." Vincent frowned. The doctor packed up his small black bag and stood up.

"Don't get smart with me, Consul," the doctor said, his finger outstretched. Vincent couldn't help but feel like he was being scolded by a professor back at Ethics School. The door to the billet opened and Presan stepped inside, flanked by another man Vincent hadn't met.

"Sorry to interrupt, sir," Presan said.

"I was just leaving," the doctor said curtly and exited the small billet. The man standing next to Presan straightened to the position of attention and saluted.

"Cohort Command Sergeant Major Aron Victoria reporting, sir." Vincent, without standing, returned his salute. The sergeant major was easily in his late fifties with pale skin and deep-set wrinkles. He had the piercing blue eyes of a Martian but the thick, dark hair of an Earthian.

"Um, hi," Vincent answered nervously. He wasn't sure what decorum said he had to show in a situation like this. He wasn't even sure if his army had decorum yet.

"I'm sorry I wasn't there with Brigadier Presan during the landing," Victoria said.

"A sergeant major's duty is to be with the soldiers, Consul," Presan added helpfully. "And with our ranks growing so fast the sergeant major has had his hands full."

"And those Titanian kids they sent us aren't making my job any easier." Victoria growled. "Most of 'em don't look old enough to drink, let alone to lead a fucking Troop into battle."

"How are the soldiers?" Vincent asked.

"They're ready, sir." Victoria nodded.

"Good." Vincent nodded. "I wish I could say the same." Vincent looked down at his foot.

"From what I hear you're lucky to be alive," Presan said.

"People keep telling me that," Vincent said. "Are we moving soon?"

"Not quite yet," Presan said. "Scouts are just reporting back in, so we should be making final plans soon."

"You should know sir, our scouts got closer to enemy lines than any others," Victoria said with a grin. He was talking about Erin. "One of Captain Olympus' privates stole a radio right out of those bastards' fighting positions. Turned it over to one of those skinny bastards to be evaluated for intelligence value." He must have been talking about Pharos.

"May I suggest putting them in for commendations?" Presan said.

"Do we have those?" Vincent asked. Presan let out a laugh.

"We have adopted the award structure of the Titanian Army, sir," Presan said. "To streamline things."

"Oh, okay," Vincent said, scratching his beard. "Go ahead and do that then."

"Of course, sir." Presan nodded. "We should get going. Denta loves his staff meetings"

"He is getting pissed with the supply lines getting raided," Victoria said. "Probably a bunch of Black Coats held up in a hole somewhere."

"Raids?" Vincent asked. "EDF stragglers? I thought the gangers were supposed to be rooting them out."

"Part of the plan for the advance is to set up forward camps on the outskirts of Olympus. The supply trains that link the Mons and the camps keep getting attacked," Presan explained. "The gangers were supposed to protect the lines."

"And it turns out those gangers are terrible at their jobs. Who would have thought?" Victoria frowned.

"And as you can imagine advancing on Victoria and Tharsis is a bad idea while there is a sizable enemy raiding force at our rear," Presan said. "I'm sure Denta has a lot to say. I'll update you as soon as I can, sir."

"Thank you, Vadim." Vincent smiled. Presan gave a quick salute before ducking through the small door. Victoria turned to follow him but stopped and turned around.

"Don't be so nervous Consul, you're doing fine." He said with a smile before following after Presan.

*   *   *

Victoria, it turned out was correct in his assumption that the Gangers were bad at their jobs. Throughout the night the distant sound of gunfire could be heard. Every few minutes the high-pitched whine of Reaper engines would pierce the night. The ships were most likely racing off to try to catch the EDF raiding parties before they melted away back into the city. From the ongoing sound of gunfire and explosions, it seemed like they were failing.

Laying on a soft bed in his billet Vincent felt a million miles away from the rest of the war effort around him. He decided he had rested enough; doctor's advice be damned. When he sat up in his bed and began to put weight on his foot he winced. He slipped his boots on over his bandages and left them untied.

He had yet to receive his armor back from the Mawr Armor Melds, their name for an armor repairman, so he decided to put on his khaki army uniform instead. He limped out of his billet, it's flimsy door smacking closed behind him. He walked out into a small town of billets just like his own. Each one housed at least two staff officers. Their aides created a human traffic jam of people all trying to push past one another. Upon seeing Vincent slowly making his way through the recently created alleyways they hurriedly moved aside. One aide in the khaki uniform of the Elysian Cohort snapped to attention and saluted Vincent.

"Good evening Consul, sir!" The young woman barked.

"Don't let me slow you guys down." He winced as he stepped. The bustling traffic picked back up around him as he inched his way along. It didn't take him long to find Denta's billet.

Two of the containers were pushed together to create a much larger building. Two flags were stuck into the ground outside of its door: A golden Titanian eagle, and the five stars of a field marshal. Two soldiers stood on either side of the door in field uniforms, rifles in hand.

"Good evening, Consul!" They called in unison as they saw him approaching.

"Evening," he said. "Is the Field Marshal busy?"

"They are in the middle of a meeting, sir," the soldier to the left of the door said. "I assumed you knew." Vincent sighed, not feeling like explaining that the Doctor's insisted he rest. He walked past them in silence.

Denta stood at the head of the table with Arai off to his left and Erik to his right. Presan stood amongst a large crowd of Titanian, Rhai, and Mawr leaders. The gathering sounded more like an argument than a meeting.

Denta was struggling to be heard over the bickering Titanian and Mawr leadership who were screaming at each other in languages the other didn't understand. Presan was engaged in a yelling match with a Rhai half his size while Arai was berating one of her own Cohort leaders.

"Sorry I interrupted," Vincent said, and the five different arguments ceased as the attendees turned to see who had just entered the room. Multiple maps were strewn about the table, both paper and digital. There were countless drawings, showing possible plans, only for them to be scribbled out on another map and replaced with a different plan. It seemed each member of the meeting had their own plan they wanted to put into action.

"Good to see you on your feet Consul," Denta said, his voice tired.

"So, should I just pick someone from the meeting and start yelling at them?" Vincent asked. Presan muffled his laughter with the sleeve of his jacket.

"The Field Marshal seems to think that his forces would be best to take out these raiders. My men know Olympus like the back of their hand!" Erik said.

"I helpfully pointed out to the Commander here that if the Gangers see his Brigade's troops stomping through their turf, he'll start another damned civil war!" Denta snarled at Erik.

"What about the Clan?" Vincent asked.

"My forces do not excel at irregular warfare," Arai said. "I say we advance on our primary targets nonetheless."

"The raiders will sally out of Olympus and strike at our rear!" Denta yelled. "Our supply train will be cut off before the battle even starts!"

"Then we will fight them in open ground!" Arai shot back.

"You're mad!" Denta retorted and at that all sides of the room began yelling once again. Arai flipped the table over, scattering maps and displays all over the floor and a Mawr Cohort leader shoved a frail looking Titanian colonel. Erik managed to separate the two before Denta gained control of the meeting once again. "That's enough!" Denta held his hands up in mock surrender. "I have a compromise."

"Go on," Erik said.

"I'll send a company of my pathfinders out with a Troop of Erik's soldiers and I'll put someone you know and trust in command," Denta said. *Pathfinder*, Vincent thought for a moment. He was going to send Tirpitz. "They will ride in the supply train and as soon as they get hit my pathfinders can bring in the rain and finally snuff these bastards out."

"This is a good plan." Arai nodded. "not as good as mine, but still good."

"You're going to send them out to get ambushed?" Vincent asked. "Why not just launch an offensive through the areas the supply trains keep getting ambushed in?"

"We tried that already." Denta shook his head and rubbed with temples with his fingers. "Cohort Leader Lyrs there." Denta nodded at the Rhai Leader. "Sent in over five thousand of his soldiers and found miles of nothing. Didn't even fire a shot. It's clear they have no intention on standing up and fighting with us toe to toe if they can help it."

"What about the Gangers?" Vincent asked.

"When they do work it's because we bribe them with fuel and weapons. If we increase the damn bribes it will cost us more than the raids currently are!" Denta sighed. "I expected nothing from them, and they still managed to disappoint me. I thought they hated the EDF enough that they could at least be trusted to do this much." Denta pulled a flask out of his jacket pocket and took a pull from it. "Instead the only thing they did is take the weapons we gave them and sell them off to someone else."

"That is impressively corrupt," Vincent said. He knew Marcus and Murat were allies of convenience, but like Denta, even he was shocked at their level of incompetence.

"That's only the damned beginning," Denta fumed. "I asked for rosters so my logisticians could figure out how much supplies we needed to send them. The rosters they gave me were inflated three or four times of the numbers they actually had so they could sell even more of my damned supplies!" Denta drank again. Erik rolled his eyes.

"I could have told you this was going to happen if you would have just listened to me."

"I'll admit you were right." Denta waved him off. "You can gloat later."

"Noted." Erik smiled.

"Pick your best Troop and get them ready. They'll be on the next supply convoy out to the north," Denta said. Erik nodded.

"They'll be ready in thirty minutes," Erik said before turning and marching out of the meeting room.

"You're sending Tirpitz out?" Vincent asked.

"She's the most experienced pathfinder I have. It certainly helps she is the only one that the Martians trust," Denta said. Vincent couldn't help but wonder if experience that was barely two weeks old actually counted as experience at all. "I can give you another Liaison if you want."

"No, that won't be needed," Vincent said. "She'll be an asset for the operation, I'm sure. I should go wish her luck before she leaves."

"I'm sure she would like that," Denta said.

"I will brief you on the rest of the meeting, sir," Presan said. "When you're done."

"Thank you."

*   *   *

Vincent left the meeting behind and began to walk towards where the supply convoy was being put together. A group of fifteen trucks was parked in the middle of the Spaceport's landing area. Dozens of soldiers formed a line from a pile of crates and boxes back to the trucks. They were passing one box at a time down the line until it reached the trucks and was then tossed into the cargo area. Each truck was stacked high with boxes, their contents having been secured to the bed of the trucks using large fabric straps.

Alongside of the cargo trucks sat a dozen small, tracked vehicles. The vehicles were little more than grey rectangles with machine guns mounted on top of them. The Titanian Golden Eagle was painted on the side of them. On a few of them he saw small, badly painted stencils of crossed torches. The sign of the Titanian Pathfinder Corps. Outside one of them was Tirpitz, addressing roughly a platoon of soldiers. Fiona watched, sitting in the dirt, smoking a cigarette.

"Dismissed!" she ordered, and the platoon fell out, running back to the tracked vehicles. She turned to see Vincent approaching and a look of concern formed on her face. "Consul?" she said. "You should be resting."

"I can't have you leave on a mission without me seeing you off," he said.

"Thanks," she said. "I wish I could take our crew out with me."

"Trust me, I'll be asking for my liaison back for the advance on Tharsis," Vincent said. While he hadn't known Tirpitz for very long, they had already been through a lot together. Charging an enemy trench line and nearly getting murdered in space tends to bring people together. It was the same bond he once held with Ikari and Richardson. One forged in blood and fire.

One thing was for sure, despite her high-class upbringing, she had become part of the strange collection of people that had turned in Vincent's staff. He wasn't sure if they could have survived without her. "I could always use a Pathfinder Corps in the Elysian Cohort you know. Its Commander could stay real close to a certain pilot." He smiled.

She laughed. "You're kidding."

"I'm not," he said. "If you haven't noticed, I have no clue what I'm doing. The more of you competent people I have around me, the more things will fall into place."

"You're serious," she said, her eyes wide.

"I can't promise you pay, decent lodging, or anything resembling a pension. I actually can't even promise that you'll survive to see Titan again. But I'm serious." Vincent heard the ground crunch behind him. He turned and saw Ezra approaching. He was legitimately shocked to see two days of beard growth on the man's dark cheeks and his flight suit dirty from days of constant work.

"I think you should take it." Ezra smiled. He didn't wait for an answer. Instead he walked quickly towards her and kissed her deeply.

"You're nuts," she said breathlessly.

"I never said I wasn't," Ezra said. "If you don't, it's only a matter of time before the war takes us to different places. It might not be pretty, but Vincent will keep us together."

"Is that true?" she asked. "We haven't even been dating that long..." Her voice trailed off.

"I didn't even know you were dating," Fiona said. "I thought you guys were just banging."

"Same," Vincent added.

"Do you always have to be so crass?" Tirpitz spat at her before turning back to Ezra. "I don't know if we are or not. But I want to give it a chance. Can Vincent really do that?"

"I managed to keep Fiona and I together from one near death experience to the other." Vincent shrugged. "Shouldn't be too hard to do it for another couple."

"The Field Marshal would never allow it," Tirpitz said, her voice dropping.

"Then I'll ask for you to be my permanent liaison. Or on some kind of training mission," Vincent said. "I'll think of something."

"Thank you, Consul Solaris," she beamed, her eyes shimmering with tears.

"You guys need to stop thanking me." Vincent laughed. "I should be thanking you. You all make it look like I know what I'm doing. And stop calling me Consul."

"Eh, you're alright." Fiona smirked, leaning back onto her hands. "We make a good team." Ezra and Tirpitz kissed again before Tirpitz pulled away.

"I'm sorry. I should get my bearing before my soldiers notice." She dabbed at her eyes with her shirt sleeve.

"Sorry dear." Ezra smiled. "I didn't mean to make you look bad." He gently brushed a piece of stray hair back behind her ear. "Just come back, okay?" he said, grabbing her by both shoulders.

"I just have to root out some stragglers," she said. "Compared to charging up the Mons this will be nothing."

"I know, but still..." Vincent noticed squads of soldiers piling into the tracked vehicles and the dull rumble of the cargo truck's engines. Tirpitz glanced over at them and turned her attention back towards Ezra. It was clear she had to leave, but it didn't seem like she could make herself say the words.

An older man with the chevrons of a staff sergeant on his collars approached from the convoy. He looked unsure about interrupting the moment the two were having. The staff sergeant cleared his throat.

"Ma'am," he said. "We are ready to go."

"Of course," she said, reluctantly breaking contact with Ezra. "I'll be there in a moment."

"Yes, Ma'am," he said and hurried back to the convoy.

"I'll see you in a few hours," Tirpitz said.

"I will." Ezra smiled. Ezra eyes lingered, watching as she walked away. When she finally climbed into one of the tracked vehicles, he managed to pull himself away. "Well sir, do you want a tour of the Cohort's camp?"

"I guess," Vincent said. "That is something a commander does isn't it?" he asked, unsure.

"Yes, sir," Ezra said. "Also, I need a distraction. This will work nicely."

"Then lead the way."

CHAPTER THIRTY-ONE

If the camp the Titanian Army had built reminded Vincent of a small city, the one his Cohort built reminded him of a slum. The Elysians, still attempting to run an army on scavenged goods and hand-me-downs, had cobbled together a wide array of tents, tarps, and other bits of scrap to erect their housing. Though, Vincent noticed they did manage to arrange them in neat lines in an attempt to mimic their Titanian neighbors.

Cook fires burned, sending spirals of smoke into the air at regular intervals. The soldiers milled about half dressed and they appeared drunk. Try as they may to have all of the trappings of a functioning army, little things like these kept reminding Vincent that he had slapped together an irregular force made out of criminals and malcontents.

Groups of soldiers were gathered around. Their chests bare, cigarettes dangling from their mouths, their rifles in their hands. Another soldier standing off to the side would throw a rock into the air and the line of soldiers would fire at it. After each volley, the soldiers would erupt into wild cheering and exchange cigarettes, rations, or Bits.

Other groups were gathered together and fighting in the dirt. He was relieved to see they weren't bare knuckle boxing like the Martians had been back at the Head Hunter's camp. He wasn't sure if they had enough medical supplies to clean up the mess. Instead, they were wrestling, twisting each other's arms at odd angles until one of them tapped out in submission. Again, an exchange of goods went with each conclusion.

"What kind of fighting is that?" Vincent asked.

"It looks like the gutter trash version of what Tirpitz used on Fiona," Ezra said.

"Why a gutter trash version?" he asked.

"I don't think the refined fighting of the Titanian upper class allows for eye gouging or fish hooking." He nodded over to a soldier who had a piece of bloody cloth covering one of his eyes.

"Fair point." He sighed. A piece of broken wood had been repurposed into a bracket outlining some kind of tournament. He noticed a sergeant named Ibram had cleared half of the board with little effort. It made him want to watch the next fight that paired Ibram against a mechanic named Baskerville. Ezra ushered him on towards the next part of the camp instead. When Vincent opened his mouth to protest, Ezra stuck a finger out like a disappointed Father.

"Betting on these human cock fights is no place for a Commander," he shamed.

"I wasn't going to place a bet." He frowned. "I didn't bring any money." Ezra furrowed his brow at Vincent and folded his arms across his chest. "Sorry, *Dad.*" Vincent rolled his eyes.

As the two walked on Vincent was taken aback by a number of civilians that seemed to be wandering through the camp. It was hard to tell who was who because almost no one was wearing a full uniform. But old men, stooped women, and young kids pushed carts through the line of tents. Soldiers crowded around the carts and loud, aggressive haggling would begin.

"What are those people doing?" Vincent asked.

"Locals," Ezra said. "Selling whatever they can get their hands on. Goods or services. They probably did the same thing for the EDF before we chased them off."

"Really?" he asked.

"Oh yeah," Ezra said. "When I was stationed here during the rebellion they would do or get whatever you needed. Find you booze or smokes, fix a pair of boots, tailor your uniform, you name it. Not like there is much of an economy out there anymore. A campaigning army is kind of their meal ticket."

"That sounds... depressing," Vincent said.

"You want to be depressed, you should see what the Gangers or Martian extremists do to them if they catch them working with the EDF." Ezra grimaced. "Luckily for them, we killed most of the extremists last war."

"Extremists?" Vincent raised an eyebrow.

"Supremacists. Racists. Nationalist. Whatever you want to call them." Ezra waived his hand. "They think are the master race, totally different from Earthians. Unlike the independence fighters, they didn't believe in surrendering when they saw the war was lost. Once most of the rebels turned their weapons over the extremists sank into the underworld and turned into little more than murderous Gangers. Anyone who took part in normal society was considered a collaborator, so they would explain away their behavior and crimes as just another way to resist Committee dominance." Ezra sighed. "If they caught people working with the Committee or doing commerce with the EDF they would shoot them. After a couple of years the violence turned from resistance struggle to economic competition."

"What ever happened to them? I haven't seen any of them running around here."

"And you wouldn't either." Ezra shook his head. "The EDF never cared so much about the local gangers. Sure, there was some low-level violence, but it was normally directed at other Martians, not them. But the second you start calling yourself a Resistance your neighborhood would get bombed off of the map. So being little more than Gangers was bad for business," Ezra continued. "But I will say I have never seen lowly Gangers be able to field entire battalions of fighters before."

"Wait, you mean the Head Hunters and Cutters?" Vincent asked. "But then why would they work with us if they were extremists?"

"No idea, sir. I'm just spit balling here." He shrugged. "Nothing on Mars is black and white though. Everything blends together into shades of grey after a while. It is hard to get a bead on Murat. I am not sure if he is a stooge or just an idiot. But I don't think it is outside the realm of possibility to assume that Marcus' hatred towards us goes further than just being suspicious." Vincent rubbed his temples and sighed. Not only did they find themselves teamed up with a complex web of blood thirsty street gangs, but some of them might have also been violent racists.

Before he could grill Ezra more on the matter, a bout of screaming from a nearby tent attracted his attention.

"Get your fucking asses out of here!" Vincent heard a muffled voice yell from the inside of a tent. It was a familiar voice, but he couldn't place it. The tent rustled for a few seconds before it was tore up from its stakes altogether. The rippling canvas shell was flung into the air like it was caught in a gust of wind and there stood Sergeant Major Victoria, his grizzled face as red as a tomato.

A young Martian girl quickly covered herself with a tattered homespun dress before fleeing in terror of the rampaging sergeant major. Two soldiers, neither looking over the age of twenty, struggled to dress themselves as Victoria hurled insults at them. Vincent winced in sympathy when Victoria delivered a slap to the face of one of them, a dark skinned Titanian. When the other soldier, an Earthian with a buzz cut, smirked at his friend getting slapped Victoria delivered another to the side of his head. He was nearly knocked off of his feet.

"Um, did I interrupt something?" Vincent asked. The two soldiers stood to attention, still stark naked, and saluted him.

"It's nothing for the Consul to bother himself with, sir," Victoria said, his temper barely contained. It wasn't in disrespect, his tone of voice told Vincent whatever was going on was supposed to be below him.

"Entertain me," Vincent said.

"If you insist, sir." Victoria straightened his uniform which had become rumpled by his outburst. The two soldiers hurriedly began to put their clothes back on. "These damned skin merchants are selling their whores to the boys," he spat. "Brigadier Presan gave explicit orders against it, but he won't let me kick the lot of the merchants out of the camp for the sake of morale."

"Skin merchants?" Vincent asked, embarrassed by his cluelessness.

"Pimps." Victoria frowned. Vincent felt his face begin to go red.

"Oh," he said. "Where did they come from?"

"Those damned Head Hunters and Cutters. It's easy enough to tell, they got their women branded like cattle. Once we secured the area, they turned it into one giant marketplace for their wares. Drugs, booze, and girls. In between this and skimming supplies from the Titanians they've got to be making a killing." Vincent thought back to the conversation with Fiona. About what Marcus made her do to earn her keep. His throat thickened and his skin began to burn.

"They aren't *whores*." His voice became hard. "They're *slaves.*"

"I had no idea," Victoria stammered.

"Slaves," he gasped.

"What is the punishment in the regulation for disobeying an order from a general?" Vincent asked, his eyes burning into the two soldiers who now stood, swaying back and forth from obvious drunkenness. One of them had managed to put his pants on backwards.

"Violation of Defense Force Code of Uniform Justice, Regulation A, section two stipulates the firing squad, sir," Victoria said. Vincent flashed his eyes back to Victoria.

"What's below that?" he asked. As angry as he was, he didn't think he could ever order his own men shot down like animals.

"The cane, sir," Victoria said. "Ten lashes." Vincent thought for a moment about actually ordering a man caned. As horrible as it sounded, the pain those women had gone through was immeasurably worse.

"Do my orders supersede a generals?" he asked, legitimately curious.

"Yes, sir." Victoria nodded.

"Twenty lashes. And make sure it is done so everyone can see. Consider it an example to the others," Vincent said. "and no more trading with the Gangers. Kick their peddlers out of our camp immediately." He thought for a moment. "And shoot any Ganger you see with one of those girls," he added. It turns out, he felt fine with ordering Marcus or Murat's men shot.

"I'll alert the Sentries, sir." Victoria nodded, a smile spreading across his face.

"What?" Vincent asked, seeing the smile.

"Nothing, sir," he said, his smile growing.

*   *   *

Vincent sat as his desk unable to sleep. Presan had been passing on piles of notes from countless meetings that he had missed. So much had been going on behind closed doors he could hardly keep track of it all. The Brigadier's notes were a mess of acronyms, abbreviations, and other military jargon that he had been communicating in for what Vincent assumed was decades longer than he had been alive.

He was reading a display that had notes going on at length about the exact number of boots that had been requested from Titanian High Command. The green glowing text began to blur together, and Vincent sat it down on the desk. He rubbed his eyes when the ground shuddered slightly.

He stood up and looked around. The ground shook, this time harder. His desk rattled across the floor and the piles of data displays crashed to the ground. He could hear voices shouting outside of his billet's paper-thin walls. A few seconds later the roar of Reaper engines could be heard as they tore through the sky seemingly only feet above their roof. Fiona awoke in a start, flinging the covers off of her.

"What the hell is going on?"

"Another supply raid?" Vincent said. Then dozens of explosions cracked. These were closer and much sharper. It was the report of an artillery battery sending shells miles away, flying somewhere into the city.

"Sounds like Annie found those stragglers," Fiona said. Vincent was suddenly overcome with an intense feeling of guilt. Over the previous hours of ordering his soldiers caned as punishment and ordering others to shoot human traffickers he had forgotten Tirpitz had rode out with the supply convoy.

"Oh, right," he said.

"Must be a big group." Fiona sighed. "Can I tell you something?"

"Of course," he said.

"You have to promise not to tell either of those two."

"Ezra isn't one for the latest gossip, so sure."

"I think they make a good couple." She sighed. "I hope she can stay with us."

"Aww." Vincent grinned and nudged her with his shoulder. "Did you make a friend?" He knew she would never admit respecting someone, let alone actually liking them. They had hardly even spoken about their relationship, it just kind of formed without either of them acknowledging it. Emotions made her so uncomfortable it made her skin crawl. He had to admit, he did enjoy watching her squirm sometimes.

"Ugh," she moaned. "Being around you people is making me soft." Vincent wrapped his arms around her, and she playfully tried to fight him off.

"It's okay you can admit it."

"Never!" she giggled. She punched him in the side before leaning over for a kiss. A sharp rapping at the door ended their moment.

"Sir!" called the voice of Presan. Vincent climbed out of bed and fumbled as he rushed to put on his khaki pants.

"Come in," Vincent said. The door sprung open and an exhausted looking Presan entered. The strange absence of Victoria didn't go unnoticed.

"The convoy was hit," Presan said. "Hard."

"Shit," Vincent cursed.

"The artillery and air strikes are keeping the EDF back but it's only a matter of time until they're overrun," Presan said. "I told Field Marshal Denta that Captain Olympus' scouts could handle it."

"Good," Vincent said. It was a good choice by Presan, they had been by far the best unit in the Cohort. "I'll get my kit; can you call Ezra?" Vincent asked.

"Sir, in all due respect you're not in the shape to go," Presan said, his voice hard.

"But—"

"Sir," Presan interrupted. "Captain Olympus is more than qualified to lead this mission. I must insist you stay here until you're healed."

"I'm going," Fiona said, still in bed. She tossed the covers off. Presan's face reddened slightly at seeing her wearing only her underwear. Fiona began to hurriedly put her armor on.

"That would be fine." Presan nodded. "I'll tell Captain Olympus."

"Why can she go?" Vincent whined.

"Because she isn't healing from the last batch of wounds she received," he said. He quickly added a "Sir." Presan furrowed his brows at him. It was then, seeing the little sign of respect that Presan offered, that Vincent remembered he was the one in charge. Somehow, between him and the grizzled soldier that was standing in front of him, he was the one who was technically in control of the situation.

"Fuck that." Vincent frowned. "Tirpitz is our friend; we don't leave our friends behind, Presan."

"You can hardly walk," Presan said matter-of-factly. "Your foot looks like ground meat."

"Good thing we will be flying then," he shot back. Presan rolled his eyes, reaching down to where Vincent's uniform top was. He picked it up and tossed it to him. He still hadn't had his armor returned to him. He might as well be going into combat naked.

"I should have known better." His wrinkled features frowned. He turned towards Fiona. "Don't let him die."

"I'll do my best." She grinned, strapping on a load bearing vest over her armor. "You're not going?"

"Me?" Presan gave a dry laugh. "I have a war to plan, remember? One of us has to do it." The old man's eyes bored into Vincent. He knew the man didn't like the idea of taking orders from a punk like him, but he wasn't going to let that bother him while Tirpitz was in danger. Presan gave a salute before turning and marching out of the quarters.

"I think he hates me." Vincent sighed, buttoning up his top and throwing on his Riten belt.

"Imagine going to the Defense College for eight years and serving in the military for decades only to end up being second in command to, well, *you*." Fiona fought back a laugh. "I would hate you too."

"Thanks." He frowned, throwing his ammo vest over his unarmored chest. "I don't think I'll ever forgive Arai for having faith in me."

"You can hate yourself later, let's go pull Annie's ass out of the fire." Fiona grinned and stepped through the door. He followed her, trying to make his walking motion as normal looking as possible. Every step he took sent a jolt of pain through his foot, but he tried to play it off.

The Spaceport was a hornet's nest of activity. Soldiers and groundcrew hurried in every direction. Reapers, loaded heavily with weapons, rushed off into the air as others landed. As soon as the ship's landing skids hit the ground soldiers sprinted to the Reapers, pulling carts full of chain gun shells and rockets and quickly went back to work reloading the empty ships. The dull thump of artillery could be heard from their gun pits on the other side of the Port.

Ezra's *Shanna II* was off to the side. It's pilot and Co-pilot were hurrying around the ship, going through their pre-flight checks. Another ship was parked alongside it, with its crew going through the same motions as Ezra. Erin's scouts were standing in a formation, her soldiers standing in rigid ranks as their captain yelled instructions at them. Erin saw Vincent and Fiona approaching, stopped what she was doing, saluted them.

"Are you coming with us, sir?" she asked.

"Wouldn't miss it," he answered. The Scouts broke from their discipline and began to smile and exchange looks with each other. A harsh look from Erin snapped them back to their senses. She walked close to Vincent and leaned in so the other soldiers wouldn't hear.

"Is this a good idea with your injuries, sir?"

"We don't leave people behind Erin, remember?" he said. It was not that long ago where he had been told to leave her behind. She smiled.

"Oh, I remember." Erin nodded before turning back to her gathered soldiers.

"Mount up!" she ordered. With a cheer they broke from their formation and ran towards the two waiting Reapers. The *Shanna II*'s engines were already roaring with Ezra and Tyr seated in the cockpit. At the tail end of Erin's scouts came Zinvor. The Mawr awkwardly sprinted as fast as his short legs would take him. He bounded side to side as he ran, making it look more like a high-speed waddle.

"You were going to leave me!" He managed to get out in-between gasping breaths. Zinvor had left Vincent's side for all of an hour to train with his fellow Mawr for the first time in months and he had run off. The Tsarra's devotion, if you could call it that, to him was something Vincent still hadn't learned how to handle. Not to mention it had been so long since Zinvor had been attached at his hip that he had assumed he would just show up when the time came.

"I didn't want to ruin your training." Vincent scrambled for an excuse. Zinvor didn't answer. Instead, he jumped aboard the Reaper and sat down on the edge of the troop compartment, his legs dangling off of the side.

"You are unarmored," Zinvor said, his voice showing the most amount of concern a Mawr was capable of.

"I'll be fine," he said.

"Tsarra." Zinvor slapped his chest. "Will be your armor."

"Let's hope that isn't necessary," he said.

"Ready?" Ezra yelled back. Erin gave him a thumbs up. At her signal, the two Reapers jumped into the air, leaving a dust cloud in their wake. Vincent fought his way through the seated soldiers and poked his head into the cockpit.

"Hey," he said, getting Ezra's attention.

"I'm a little busy, sir," he answered flatly.

"We'll get her, okay?" Vincent reassured.

"I'm sure Captain Tirpitz will be fine, sir. She is a pathfinder." Vincent couldn't see his friend's eyes, the flight helmet hiding them away behind a glowing display. He could hear the pain in his voice, though he was doing his best to cover it up with a professional screen. Vincent patted Ezra on his shoulder.

"Are you sure—"

"Sir, we are going to be entering Anti-Ship Artillery range shortly. I advise you to return to your seat." It was then Vincent saw a new picture. It was posted up above the windscreen, next to the picture of Ezra's late wife and children. It was a picture of Ezra and Tirpitz. They were making kissy faces and half covered by crisp white bed sheets. Tirpitz, her normally tightly bound hair was a curly mess. Her dark cheeks were red, and they didn't have a care in the world. They had been hiding their relationship longer than they had let on.

He turned back to his seat and sat down next to Fiona.

"How's he handling it?" she asked.

"Not well," he said. "But I don't think I would be doing any better."

"Eh." Fiona shrugged, checking the action on her rifle. It snapped closed. "I'd be alright."

"You would be fine with me being trapped, surrounded on all sides, and about to die?" Vincent asked, slightly offended.

"You'd be fine," she said. "You're always fine."

"That is only true if your definition of 'fine' just means I haven't died yet," he said.

"Pretty much, yeah," she said, nonplussed. He rolled his eyes. Before he had time to respond the ship jerked roughly to the left, sending its occupants desperately reaching for a handhold.

"Incoming enemy fire," Tyr droned.

"Make sure you're ready to hit the ground fighting!" Erin called out. Her scouts quickly began to go over their weapons and gear one more time. "Colonel Vorbeck, do you have any word from the elements on the ground?"

"Negative," Ezra said. "Their comms have been dark for the last twenty minutes. No response or situation reports."

"Twenty minutes?" Vincent cried. "Why in the hell did we wait so long to send out help?"

"A lot can happen in twenty minutes," Fiona said, quietly.

"They're still fucking holding!" Erin spat. Fiona held up her hands in mock surrender. "You hear that?" she yelled. The scouts around her called out in unison:

"Yes Ma'am!"

The ship dropped in altitude and the broken city below emerged from the clouds. Tracers, lasers, and fireballs lit up the terrain below them. As soon as they saw the city, the city must have seen them. The ship was rocked with the hailstorm-like *tak tak tak* of incoming small arms fire.

"Door gunners!" Ezra yelled. "Hold your fire! We don't know who is who down there!" The two young Elysian soldiers frowned as their guns remained silent.

"Where we are landing?" Erin asked.

"Rear of the supply train's last known location. You'll have to work your way up from there!" he said.

"How far out?" Vincent asked.

"Two minutes till touch down," Ezra said as the ship's nose tipped downward, and its speed increased. "We will not be touching the ground. I'll slow down just enough for you to jump off." Vincent cursed to himself. Maybe he should have stayed behind. He was jumping into a swirling blind firefight wounded, unarmored, and unprepared. He unholstered his Riten and checked it make sure it was loaded and re-holstered it. He nervously worked the action on his rifle and the bolt snapped forward smoothly.

Vincent was jolted back to the present when a rocket streaked by in front of the ship's nose. It was so close he could smell the acrid cordite fuel burning off its motor.

"Thirty seconds!" Ezra yelled. The scouts shifted so that their legs were dangling off the edge of the ship. A wide highway was below them. Several of the same cargo trucks that Vincent had watched soldiers load only a few hours before were now looted and ablaze. One of the pathfinder troop carriers had a fist-sized hole blown in its side and there were several dead bodies around it. A few figures could be seen picking through the bodies.

"Go!" Ezra yelled. The scouts jumped out expertly, tucking and rolling as they impacted the street. Vincent, Fiona, and Zinvor hit the ground like a sandbag being tossed to the ground. He attempted to roll when he hit the ground but instead landed straight on his ass.

"Shit!" Fiona screamed.

"Status!" Erin yelled.

"I'm alive!" Vincent moaned, slowly climbing to his feet.

"I think I am," Fiona said, dusting herself off. The next ship swooped down, and another thirty soldiers leapt out and crashed to the ground.

Bullets snapped and cracked past Vincent's head as the air around them became thick with incoming rounds. The soldiers in the street dropped to the ground and the road sparked with impacts.

"Spread out!" Erin screamed. She turned towards the soldiers, standing and exposing herself to the fire. "First squad, get a base of damn fire over there!" She pointed to a half-ruined building. Second squad, clear those buildings!" She pointed to the opposite side of the road where a warren of small, dilapidated structures stood. Vincent could see a gallery of muzzle flashes coming from within its walls. "Third squad, on me!" she ordered. Erin advanced up straight up the road as her other two squads broke off to their flanks.

Vincent wasn't sure what squad he belonged too, so he chased after her. A scout to his left dropped to the ground, blood spurting from a neck wound. Another burst of automatic weapons fire cut through the middle of the squad and he could have sworn he felt a bullet pass through his hair. As they advanced up the road, the true toll of the ambush became known.

A cargo truck had been turned over on its side, a massive crater was blown into the street under it. Everywhere he looked there was another grey or red uniformed body lying motionless in the street. The air was thick with the smell of burning gunpowder and flesh.

They took cover behind a destroyed troop carrier.

"First squad!" Erin yelled into her headset. "Report!"

"In position!" Came a static clouded voice.

"Suppress those fucking guns, we are getting chewed up out here!"

"Roger!" Said the voice. As if a light switch was flipped a torrent of machine gun fire roared out from the right side of the street. It raked through the enemy positions and momentarily silenced them.

"Move!" Erin ordered. She ran and Vincent did his best to keep up. Each step sent a jolt of pain through his foot and up his leg. He could feel his sock squish in his boots and knew he was bleeding through his bandages again. Now that the nearby enemy weapons weren't trying to take them out Vincent could see muzzle flashes and tracers arcing up into the sky form further up the stricken supply train.

"Someone is still fighting up there!" he yelled.

"I see 'em," Erin said. "But we have to wait until the flank is secure or we will end up trapped out here like they are."

"Fuck!" he cursed. "Tell those bastards to hurry the hell up!"

"Second squad!" she shouted into her headset. "Great Traitor says hurry the fuck up or he will kill you himself!"

Rifle fire began to smack into the ground near them once again and they dove for cover behind the wheel well of a supply truck.

"I did not say that!" Vincent whined.

"Consider it motivation." Erin smiled. She leveled her rifle on the truck and began to fire well aimed shots into the distance. Her scouts followed suit. Vincent, Fiona, and Zinvor lined up with them. He rested his rifle on the truck and scanned for targets. A group of grey clad soldiers rushed in an unorderly mass from the left side of the road, chased from their positions by the flanking scouts.

"Targets in the open!" Yelled one of the scouts. Vincent lined his sights up and placed the meaty portion of his finger on the trigger of his rifle. He pulled the trigger once and three slugs zipped out of the barrel in quick succession. Everyone else on the line with him did the same thing. The soldiers were mowed down as methodically as if they had been standing in front of a firing squad. The soldiers dropped, twitched, and crawled as they died. A few rounds were fired into them after they stopped moving for good measure.

"Right flank secure!" came the voice of the second squad's leader over Erin's headset.

"Let's go!" Erin yelled. Using the truck for assistance, Vincent climbed to his feet and slowly plodded off after everyone else. He didn't feel like he was slowing everyone down until he looked over and saw he was in the back of the ground and running alongside Zinvor.

The burning trucks and troop carriers coated the area in a dense, harsh smoke that obscured everything ahead of them. Every step he took he ran past another dead soldier. Though he was relieved to see at least some of them were wearing grey. He was surprised to find several of them with long hair and unkempt beards.

The gunfire sounded much closer now. He could hear distant shouting and even what he thought could have been people laughing. Clearly the EDF had no idea they were coming up from the south. They were still relishing their victory over the supply convoy. He turned to Erin to tell her, but she had dropped to a knee, halting the advance. She had heard the same thing.

"Any pathfinder unit, this is Red Ghost Command. Status?" she said into her headset. First there was some static. Then the sound of gunfire coming though the mic. "Any pathfinder unit, this is Red Ghost Command. If you're still out there give us a sign." Vincent's eyes darted around, looking for anything. The tempo of gunfire didn't slacken, and no one answered Erin's radio traffic. Then it happened: a single flare arced into the sky. It bloomed a brilliant red in the night and slowly floated down back towards the city's blasted skyline.

"They're alive!" Erin roared. "All Red Ghost units, close the distance!" she called into her headset. Vincent knew what that meant. He reached back onto his belt and felt for the scabbard of his bayonet. The knife fit snuggly over the barrel of his rifle and locked in place. "Any surviving pathfinder units, do not fire to the south. I repeat. Do not fire to the south we are coming for you. Red Ghost Command out."

"Are we doing this?" Fiona asked.

"Oh yeah," Erin said. Zinvor let out an inhuman, guttural roar that was so loud it drown out the drumbeat of the nearby battle and rushed forward. The rest of the occupants of the middle of the street followed after him.

The first EDF soldiers they came upon were taken completely by surprise. A group of about ten of them wearing bits of civilian clothes. A strange combination of cut off shorts and EDF standard issue body armor. The odd collection was standing behind a barricade made out of a ruined troop carrier when they were slaughtered. They were shot dead so quickly one of their lighters was still lit, flicked for a cigarette it's owner would never get to smoke.

The element of surprise from there on was mostly gone. Vincent brought his rifle up to his shoulder and fired two rounds into the chest of a pale, young looking woman who hadn't had the chance to grab her weapon yet. Fiona dropped another one next to her, an old man who fumbled trying to bring his carbine up to his shoulder. The scouts on their right flank poured withering machine gun and rocket fire into the EDF soldiers who attempted to rally to the defense of their southern flank.

The incoming fire to the south began to slacken and then broke entirely. Before long Vincent could see the fleeing shapes of grey jacketed soldiers attempting to run back into the city. It didn't stop him or the rest of the advancing unit from shooting them down as they ran.

"Who's out there?" Came a panicked voice over Erin's headset.

"It's Red Ghost. Let's get you the fuck out of here," Erin responded. Out of the dusty, smoke filled darkness came a soldier. Everyone reflexively brought their weapons up only to see the uniform of a Titanian pathfinder, a sergeant, who was holding his hands up.

"How many of you are there?" Erin asked

"About ten left, fifteen counting the Brigade soldiers," the sergeant said, now that he was closer Vincent could see a bandage wrapped around his upper leg. "But they're still hitting us from the northern approach." He sighed. "I've never seen the EDF fight this way before."

"Only the north?" she asked. The sergeant nodded.

"Call for air support all along the northern approaches. In the meantime we will deploy with your guys until they show up."

"Ma'am, I'd rather get the fuck out of here," the sergeant said, defeated.

"I can't call a ship into this mess if it is just going to get shot down and we can't carry all of your wounded. Man the damn line, Sergeant," Erin snapped. The sergeant saluted and led them back through the smoke and to where the pathfinders had hunkered down.

They had managed to pull a dozen of the trucks and troop carriers into a small circle, a few dozen meters wide, in the middle of the street. While clearly assembled in haste, the position might as well have been a fortress in the middle of the open highway. The EDF had been throwing themselves at the fortification for what had to have been hours. Grey coated bodies littered the ground all around them. Every step Vincent took required him to step on the remains of someone's blasted corpse.

In the middle of the circle was their one still functioning orbital radio along with their wounded. One tired looking medic made her rounds, checking bandages and pulses. Another dozen next to them were draped with ponchos, hiding them from few. The Medic ignored those ones.

"Get on the radio and get the Reapers to hit our Northern reference points!" The sergeant yelled at the young soldier who was sitting next to the radio. The soldier nodded and went to work. "And hold on boys, they might try to run us over one last time!"

"With losses like these..." Fiona looked around. "...Why didn't they pull back?"

"No idea," the sergeant said. "Their ambush was well laid. Front truck hit a mine of some kind; rear truck got hit with a rocket." He shook his head. "Trapped us on the road and we started taking so many damn casualties we couldn't move. The captain ordered us to circle our wagons and wait for help."

"And now?" Erin asked.

"It was like the ambush was the only thing they had planned," he said. "Once we managed to get something together that looked like a defensive line, they just started attacking us in waves. But not all at once, if they had we might have been rightly fucked. But Piece meal like their commanders couldn't agree on what to do."

"Well, you did a good job, Sergeant..." Erin began, searching for a name.

"Flynn," he said, helpfully.

"Sergeant Flynn."

"Where's Captain Tirpitz?" Vincent asked, interrupting. The sergeant's face turned grim and he looked away.

"Come with me," he said. Flynn led him passed the moaning and crying wounded. Vincent looked around amongst their blood-stained faces, unable to recognize a single one of them. Even through their contorted, grimacing faces made their features hard to make out he knew none of them were Tirpitz.

His heart jumped into his throat when Flynn kept walking, towards the human shapes under the grey ponchos. Flynn knelt down next to one of the shapes and pulled back the poncho.

Her once perfectly done dark hair was matted with blood and stuck to her face. Her dark complexion was mottled and pale from blood loss. Vincent knew who he was looking at. There, under a ripped standard issue army poncho, in the middle of some godforsaken highway, lay Captain Anastasia Tirpitz. He gasped and fell to his knees.

"No!" he cried. His eyes began to burn as he felt tears coming. A hand grabbed onto his shoulder he turned and saw Fiona standing next to him. Her pale eyes shimmering with sadness. On the other side of him was Zinvor. His dark eyes were emotionless, but he bowed his head and placed a single giant fist over his chest.

"We will avenger her ten times." Zinvor growled. Vincent couldn't speak. Instead he just nodded.

"Come on." Fiona tugged at him. "We have to go," she said. He pulled himself back to his feet. The scream of jet engines overhead pulled his attention away as Reapers flew in low overhead. Their cannons cut swaths through the streets and orange fireballs of outgoing rockets streaked through the air.

The ground shook with hundreds of impacts, finally breaking the EDF's assault. The smattering of rifle and machine gun fire turned into random pop shots, before dying away completely. Unlike most victories, there was no cheering this time.

CHAPTER THIRTY-TWO

The *Shanna II* floated down weightlessly onto the battlefield. The cockpit door swung open and out stepped Ezra, with Tyr at his side. Ezra's face was ashen with dark circles under his eyes. He walked slowly towards Vincent, willing each step forward.

"I..." He stammered. "I want to see her," Ezra said.

"I don't think that's a good idea," Vincent said quietly.

"I need too, Vincent." His eyes welled up. "Please." His dark eyes, normally so full of wit and intelligence were replaced by a depth of sorrow Vincent couldn't possibly comprehend.

"Okay," he said. Vincent led him behind the troop carrier where Tirpitz still laid. Six pathfinders stood guard around her, never letting her out of their sight. Ezra sank to his knees and pulled the poncho back.

"Oh no," he gasped. "Oh baby." Ezra leaned down and kissed her forehead and brushed her hair away from her face. A small smile tugged at the corner of his lip. "If you could see your hair," he moaned. Tears fell from his face and landed on her blood-stained uniform. He looked back at Sergeant Flynn "Was it fast?"

"She didn't feel a thing, sir," the sergeant said, no longer fighting back tears. Vincent stopped trying to hold his emotions in check. He felt the tears flowing freely down his face.

"I'm so sorry, Ezra," he managed.

"May she rest with Paterazm for time eternal." He wasn't sure if Mawrs could cry, but the Tsarra's voice broke as he spoke.

"We have to get her back," Ezra said, rising back to his feet. "So, she can be laid to rest proper."

"Yeah," Vincent nodded.

"Sergeant, can you form an honor guard?" Ezra asked.

"Of course, sir. It would be my honor," Flynn answered. Ezra turned and began walking back towards the ship. "Tyr," he said. "Can you bring the *Shanna* home?"

"Yes, sir," Tyr said.

"Thank you," he said. Vincent watched Flynn and the pathfinders load Tirpitz's body onto a stretcher. A young Private knelt down and took the front two handgrips, walking it towards the ship. Pathfinders, Scouts, and Brigade soldiers formed a line on either side of them as they slowly walked her body towards the *Shanna.*

"Present, Arms!" Barked Flynn. At his command everyone snapped to attention and brought their hands up in a salute. As the stretcher passed by Vincent, he could see not a single pathfinder was holding their emotions in check. They were outwardly sobbing for their fallen commander. Many of them cried out audibly as the stretcher passed them. Ezra stood like a statue next to the troop compartment of his ship, his hand held rigidly next to his eye.

"Consul, sir," came the voice of Erin. Snapping Vincent away from the scene.

"Yeah?" he asked, he dabbed his cuffs at his eyes.

"I know it isn't the best time. But can I have a moment?"

"Yes." He pulled himself away from the grey colored poncho laying on the floor. "Of course."

"I..." She fought with the words she was trying to say for a minute. "I don't think this was the EDF."

"What?" he gasped. "Well it certainly wasn't the Alliance."

"We were both EDF once," she started. "How many soldiers did you ever see with beards?" She pointed at a nearby dead body. Its blonde beard was thick and untamed. Fiona frowned, marching up to the body. "What EDF commander would order frontal assaults against a fortified position?" she asked, not waiting for Vincent to answer. "Have you ever seen thousands of EDF troops run into combat without body armor or helmets?" She kicked one of the nearby bodies. "And look at these weapons." She knelt down and picked one up. It was a badly modified Standard Mag Rifle. The buttstock had been sawn off and a scope, originally meant for a hunting rifle was grafted on top of its receiver. "You ever see a soldier's rifle that look like this?" Fiona walked up to a nearby body a knelt down close to it.

"Wait, what are you doing?" Vincent asked.

"I have a theory," Fiona said. She unclipped the bayonet from her rifle and slung the rifle across her shoulders. "How many Martians do you think are still enlisted?" She pointed her bayonet at the body's pale face. Fiona knelt down and slipped the edge of her bayonet under the corpse's uniform top. She slid the blade upwards, cutting its shirt down the middle.

The corpse's stomach was blown open by a slug, oozing thick chunks of gore onto its surface. But, past that Vincent saw something else: small, badly inked, black tattoos dotted the man's chest. At the center of the man's chest was two crossed knives under a severed, cartoonish looking head. The symbol of the Head Hunters Gang.

As the *Shanna II* lifted into the air, Ezra sat down in the troop compartment with them. He seated himself at the head of the stretcher, looking down at the poncho shroud. He reached back into the cockpit, grabbing the radio.

"Titan Command, Titan Command, this is Shanna II," he said.

"Go ahead Shanna II," crackled the radio.

"Pathfinder Command is down," he said.

"Repeat last," said the voice. Vincent now recognized the voice as Denta's.

"I repeat. Pathfinder Command is down." His voice cracked.

"Confirmed," Denta responded. Ezra handed the mic back up to Tyr.

"Why would they do this?" asked Erin. "We gave them everything."

"Marcus has always been a two-faced little shit," spat Fiona. "I'll fucking gut him."

"Wait." Vincent put a hand up. "We have to tell Denta and Arai. We need to come up with a plan."

"Fuck a plan. We have an army!" Fiona shouted.

"So do they!" Vincent yelled back. "And we armed it to the teeth!"

"Who are you?" She pounded her fist on the wall of the ship. "The old Vincent would have rushed in there and starting shooting people!"

"And the old Vincent would have gotten his people killed," he said. Fiona balled her fists up, and he was sure she was about to take a swing at him until Ezra opened his mouth.

"He's right," he said, disarming Fiona. "We have to do this right or everything that we've fought for will be lost. What she died for will have been for nothing."

"You too?" she snarled.

"Rushing into things is how she died in the first place. Use your head," Ezra said, his eyes boring into hers. For the first time since Vincent had known her, she backed down from his stare and instead looked down at Tirpitz's body in silence.

*　　*　　*

The *Shanna II* touched back down at the Mons. Since the skilled hands of Ezra were not at the controls, the landing was a little rougher than normal. Zinvor pushed open the troop compartment doors and they laid eyes on their solemn welcoming party.

The Mons was packed, shoulder to shoulder, with somber looking Titanian soldiers. Many were supporting their comrades with arms around the shoulders. Others were openly weeping into their hands. Some were letting the tears flow freely down their face.

There was no organization among them. There was no neat formations of soldiers or tightly regulated firing salute to welcome Titan's fallen daughter. On the fringes of the gathering was a few curious Rhai and Mawr, who were still trying to understand their new human allies.

Vincent stayed in his seat as the surviving members of the pathfinders hoisted Tirpitz's stretcher onto their shoulders. The poncho that covered her body fluttered and flapped in the Martian breeze. At the sight of her body the few Titanians who remained stoic broke down.

Through the crowd of sobbing soldiers came Denta. He was dressed down and not wearing his heavily decorated dress uniform for the first time that Vincent could remember. Denta was wearing a wrinkled, grey field uniform and dirty boots. His eyes were bloodshot red and his sunken. The man, aged with grief, suddenly looked the seventy or so years old he undoubtedly was.

He stopped, straightened himself as best and his bent back would allow and brought his left hand up in a rigid salute. All around Denta, the soldiers followed their leader, though unlike him they made no attempt to stop their outward expressions of grief.

A utility truck slowly drove through the crowd as it parted to make way. A red eagle was on its door, showing that it belonged to the Medical Corps. Flynn's small detachment met the truck and placed the stretcher on its flatbed. Then, the wounded pathfinders climbed in with their fallen leader.

Denta turned to begin following the truck as it drove off when Vincent stopped him. Denta jumped slightly when he placed a hand on the old man's shoulder. When he turned to look at him, Vincent could see he was no longer trying to control his tears.

"We need to talk," he said. Denta raised an eyebrow.

"You'll have to forgive me, I don't feel up for a chat right now," Denta said as he swallowed hard. "I need a damned drink. And to get off of this rock. Unfortunately, I can only settle for one of those things."

"Denta," he said, his voice hard.

"Fine." Denta waved him off. "Never thought it would be you who would be hard at a time like this."

"We've cried enough," Vincent said. "I'm ready for blood."

The Command room was empty except for a few aides. They were running around doing their best to clean up the mess that

Denta seemed perfectly fine with simply living in. Trash littered the ground, crumpled up paper was everywhere, and food and liquor were spilled over all of the tables.

"Out," Denta spat. The aides dropped what they were doing and scurried out of the room. He slowly walked over to his table, Vincent noticed a noticeable limp, and sat down heavily on a small metal stool. "So...talk," he said. Pouring a large amount of brown liquor into a dirty tin cup. He poured one more for Vincent. He motioned over to Zinvor with the bottle who shook his head.

Vincent sat down on another stool and it creaked as he settled on it. He sipped his drink and the burning liquid comforted him.

"We weren't attacked by the EDF," he said. Denta sat his drinks down, a small amount of its contents splashed out.

"Then by who?"

"Gangers," he said. "I don't know about Murat, but they were definitely Marcus's fighters."

"All of our intelligence said they were EDF. Maybe they're just pressing Martians into service now. They're getting desperate."

"No," he said. "I fought with the Gangers, remember? These guys used the same ambush tactics then closed in so we couldn't use air support or artillery." He sighed. "They were disguised as EDF regulars, though badly." He took another sip from his glass. "They were throwing themselves desperately at the pathfinder's last position trying to overrun it. They knew any survivors would see right through their ruse." Denta drained his glass and refilled it. Vincent could see his knuckles turn white as he gripped the bottle.

"Can I tell you something?" he asked.

"Of course." Vincent nodded.

"I never had any children of my own," the old man said. "With the constant traveling and then the duties of the Governorship, I simply never had time. My soldiers ended up becoming something like adopted children of mine." He put his glass back in one swallow and refilled it again. "At least that was what I told myself. Though, Annie..." His voice trailed off. Vincent couldn't help but wonder if she would have been as mad at Denta for calling her that as she was at Fiona. "...She was like a daughter to me. A real daughter." A smile creeped across his face as he remembered. "She had been at my side for nearly twenty years. I watched her graduate the Academy and earn her first Command." A single tear trailed down his face. "I thought one day she would take over for me." At that, he was balling. Tears were pouring down his wrinkled face and he made no attempt to stop them.

"She was dating Colonel Vorbeck," Vincent chimed in, though he wasn't sure why he told him.

"I know." Denta smiled. "They had been high school sweethearts."

"Really?" He coughed as his drink went down the wrong pipe.

"Until they both went into the Academy and Vorbeck began to date Shanna." Vincent eyed with curiosity. "Oh relax. She told me everything." Denta laughed. "She had a lot to say about him. You as well."

"A lot to say?" Vincent asked. "You're making her sound like a spy or something."

"She was." Denta sipped. "At first, anyways." He shrugged. "But you can hardly blame me. Some teenager showing up in an Alien suit of armor claiming he wants to destroy the Committee." Denta chuckled. "You can imagine my disbelief."

Vincent broke out in laughter. It all still sounded ridiculous. "So, what did she say?"

"That you were honest," Denta said, becoming somber. "That you were a man of character. Someone who really believed in their mission." He smirked. "If a little clueless and totally in over your head."

"Ain't that the damn truth," Vincent said, finishing his drink. "I'm not so sure about that other stuff, but I am still in over my head."

"You're doing alright," Denta said. "All things considered."

"So, what do we do with the Gangers?" He brought the conversation back to the topic.

"We take out their leadership." Denta frowned. "Not a single of them lives through this. Personal vendetta aside. They lied to our faces, stole from us, and killed my damn soldiers. They hamstrung our entire operation to the point that who knows how much more the EDF managed to dig into Victoria and Tharsis."

"I couldn't agree more." Vincent nodded. "But how?"

"We give them what they want," Denta said.

"More guns?"

"No." Denta shook his head. "Importance. You saw their little chest thumping theatrics when we landed." He drained his glass yet again. "We pulled their asses out of the fire and they act like we did nothing. They don't want to be seen as equals. Not like Erik or you or the Warlord. Everything they do is to show us how little they think of us. How much better they are." He filled his glass again. "They crave importance."

"So, you want to use their arrogance against them?"

"Precisely. We tell them that, damn no matter how hard we try we just can figure out this pesky assault on Victoria and really need their input."

"Then what? We take these two assholes out and two more just take their place."

"These Gangers aren't soldiers, even if they like to play dress up. I learned that during the Rebellion. They're a bunch of individuals occasionally held together by someone they're afraid of. Without that little King Shit, they break. They fall apart. They run back to the holes they came from."

"Sure, I get it," Vincent said. "But if it was that easy why didn't you do that during the rebellion rather than just flattening Olympus?"

"Because we never gave them another choice then," he said. "It was either they fight for their independence or join the people who probably killed someone they were related too." Denta shrugged. "Most of them would have rather died than swear allegiance to The Chairman. And they did. By the tens of thousands." He drank deep from his cup. "Well, we aren't the Committee, anymore are we?"

"Once they show up to the meeting we have planned, your scouts, my pathfinders, and the Mawr's...ugh I can never remember these damned words. Their scouts."

"The *Urvakan*," Vincent helped.

"How did a kid who barely graduated school manage to learn a damned alien language?"

"I'm a natural." Vincent smiled, sarcastically.

"Fine, whatever," Denta spat. "Our combined forces surround their known bases and kill anyone who won't surrender."

"Then what?" He laughed. "Ask them to promise to never be street trash ever again?"

"Not quite." Denta smirked. Vincent wasn't sure he liked the look in the old man's dark eyes. "Join the Martian Liberation Brigade or the Elysian Cohort or die."

"You've got to be kidding me!" Vincent cried. "Erik would never approve!"

"And you?"

"Of fucking course I don't approve!" he cursed.

"Your army is already made of criminals and Reds, what's a few more? You could certainly use the numbers." Vincent's temper began to rise hearing Denta casually insult the Martians.

"You would be forcing them into service. What is the difference between that and sentencing soldiers? That is the exact opposite of what we stand for!" Vincent slammed his tin cup down as a way of underlining his displeasure. Denta smirked. "This is just a continuation of the Chairman's disgusting racist policies of oppression against the Martian people and I will have no part in it."

"Ugh," Denta groaned. "You idealist are so hard to reason with. Fine. I will give them positions in Titanian labor battalions. I could use the extra manpower so I can free up some real soldiers who are stuck toiling away here."

"I doubt they are going to willingly sign up for a future of manual labor." He frowned.

"Who said anything about willingly," Denta said.

"That sounds an awful lot like outright slavery, Denta," Vincent said.

"I never said I wasn't going to pay them," he said.

"That is a shit excuse," Vincent said, his temper rising as Denta once again filled up his cup. "I got a paycheck when I was a sentenced soldier and we both know what that arrangement was."

"Your morals won't fill your ranks, Solaris," he said, clearly tired of the conversation.

"Maybe not," he said. "But my Cohort will not take part in anything that strips someone else of their freedom."

"Yes they will," Denta said, a slight smirk spreading across his face.

"The fuck they will." Vincent rose to his feet.

"Need I remind you that your forces are under my command for this Campaign?" Vincent balled his fist. He could see the conversation was going nowhere and stormed out of the command center.

*   *   *

The meeting had left Vincent with a bad taste in his mouth. And it wasn't just because Denta insisted that he drank something that tasted like it was dug out of a peat bog. It was because Denta had turned out to be a two-faced asshole. Since he had first met Denta he had always seemed like a fatherly figure. If not to him, then at least to Tirpitz. It had all clearly been a façade to hide what he was really capable of. What his true intentions were.

When they first touched down on Titan, he was the only one who welcomed them with open arms. When Addler tried to treat them like he was above them, rightly so, Denta stepped him and defended them. He even sent Titan's vast army to Mars at Vincent's mere suggestion. Had that even been a play? Had Denta told Addler to dismiss them just so he could slide in and come to their support?

Since he had landed on Mars it was almost as if he was a different person. Despite the small bits of humanity he showed at the death of Tirpitz each idea he has had as been more terrible than the last. He casually planned out the chemical bombing of their fellow humans and only a day later suggested bringing the impressment of Martians into military service. Somehow, his backup plan to that was even more vile.

Vincent was so distracted by his own thoughts that he didn't notice the crowds of soldiers around him until they began bumping into him. They were busy back and forth through the tight corridors of the Command area. All around him were busy Titanian soldiers going back and forth, data slates and papers tucked under their arms. Barely one in ten that he could see was one of his own. Then, it dawned on him: Denta didn't see him or his soldiers as a partner. He saw them as underlings. They were tools to be used.

Denta had clouded his vision with shiny things like new uniforms and a damn parade when they landed on the planet. Those stupid drummers might as well have been Denta pissing all over the battlefield. He wanted to show how powerful he was. It was a statement to Vincent, to Erik, to everyone. Arai probably hadn't understood human shows of strength and didn't know better. A Fidayi show of strength would have probably just involved fighting the enemy commander one on one while the rest of them watched.

He cursed himself for being so damned trusting. Why else would a superpower like Titan help him for any other reason than to get ahead? Denta wanted to spread Titan's sphere of influence through human space, that much was to be sure. But he had to know a legendary field marshal who had led the Chairman's armies would have been looked at suspiciously by just about everyone. He needed someone to hide behind. Someone like Vincent.

He could use Vincent as a figurehead, the Great Traitor, to do something the Chairman never could: control Mars. Of course, he could never control it directly. That would lead to the never-ending cycle of rebellions that the Committee had to deal with. They would let a Martian run it. A Martian that was indebted to him for liberating his planet from the Committee. A Martian like Erik.

Before he could curse himself again his line of thought was broken by the sight of his quarters. Outside of his quarters a small, ragged looking Phoenix flag was stuck in the dirt. Next to it was two soldiers he had never seen before in full battle uniform. Upon seeing him they brought their rifles up to their shoulders in salute.

"Good evening, sir!" Barked the soldier to the left.

"Who are you two?" he asked.

"We were posted here by Consul's Aide Fiona Olympus to watch over your quarters, sir."

"You take orders from Fiona?" he asked. The soldier leaned forward, his voice falling to a whisper.

"Wouldn't you?"

"Fair enough." Vincent laughed. "It may be a good idea if you stay here though," he said, with a new paranoid feeling coming over him since the meeting with Denta. He walked inside his quarters and found Fiona seated behind his desk. His desk was little more than a fold out field table, but since Blackwell decided it was a good place to stack the paperwork he had to do, it had turned into a working desk.

Fiona was flipping through the glowing screen of a data display. She didn't seem to be taking in what she was reading, instead squinting hard and flipping to the next page.

"You've been slacking," she said.

"Slacking?" he asked.

"Have you even been looking at what Blackwell has been leaving you?"

"No," he admitted. He had attempted to read through them on a few occasions but always felt like there was too much to do around the camp and would get distracted. "Is it important?"

"Important?" She laughed. "It's literally orders for running the Quarter back on Elysian. Laws, regulations," she said, flipping to another one. "This one is about establishing a Police Force." She flipped to another slate. "This one is about elections? Seriously, how did you manage to space out on this?"

"Is this really what you want to do right now?" He frowned, trying not to think about that he had an entire population back on Elysian depending on his governance. "I got a fucking D in Government back in Ethics School," he moaned. "How did I end up in charge of one?"

"Look at this one," Fiona said, tossed a data display to him. He caught it and turned the screen towards him. It read "*Elysian Public Hospital reports the birth of forty-six children during the month of August.*"

"Is it August?" he asked.

"Depends on what calendar we are going off of." She shrugged. "Which is..." She pulled out another display. "...what this order is trying to clear up."

"Shit." He sighed and sat down heavily on the bed.

"Did you read what I read?" she asked. "Kids are being born Vincent. Kids are being born into this clan, or whatever we are, that *you* are in charge of. People are being born into the world that we are creating." She sat the display back down on the pile on the desk. "I want to sit down and cry about Annie too, but we just aren't allowed to do that anymore."

Vincent cradled his face in his hands. The last thing he needed right now was the affairs of a planet he was pretty sure he was never going to see again clouding his mind.

"Who is handling these issues now?" he asked.

"According to Blackwell they're being forwarded and handled by the Fidayi Clan...and then it's a string of letters I can't pronounce." She screwed her face up staring down at the screen. He held his hand out and she gave it to him. Vincent looked down at the twisted runes of the Fidayi language and read "The Fidayi Cohort of Outer Races"

"They're going to have to handle it for now," he said, running his hands through his greasy hair. "I'll try to play Consul back on Elysian if we escape this planet with anything resembling an army alright?" Fiona frowned, but didn't press the issue. Instead she dug into her pants pocket and tossed him a pack of cigarettes. Vincent took one and lit it.

"Can you do me a favor?" he asked.

"Sure." She smiled.

"I want a command meeting." He blew out a cloud of smoke. "Only our people."

CHAPTER THIRTY-THREE

The last person to enter Vincent's quarters was Presan. Dark circles were around the man's bloodshot eyes. He had the look of someone who had just been woken up and was not happy about it. Victoria was seated on two duffle bags he had piled together and was sipping from a canteen. Erin was sitting on the bed next to Fiona, sharing a cigarette. Zinvor was standing outside, joining Vincent's two other guards, looking for anyone who might be listening in. And anyone in a Titanian Army uniform.

"Sir," Presan yawned. "I hope everything is okay."

"I have to ask you something...I never thought I would have to ask you," Vincent said. "And I need your complete honesty. And in turn I will promise you mine."

"Of course, sir," answered Erin.

"Do you think I am the best person for this job?" Vincent asked. The room went silent. Presan furrowed his brows and exchanged glances with Victoria.

"We are permission to speak freely, sir?" Presan asked.

"I already told you, you always do," he said.

"Well, then...no," the old Brigadier answered. "You're not." Vincent felt his heart sink. "I mean no disrespect, sir," Presan added.

"No." Vincent countered. "I need your honesty right now. Don't try to sugarcoat it."

"No," Fiona said. "Of course you're not the best person for this job."

"Agreed," Erin said.

Vincent leaned heavily against the wall and folded his arms across his chest.

"Then why are you following me?"

"Because," Presan said. "Being a good military leader doesn't make the man. Brusilov is a magnificent military leader and he's a bastard. The people believe in you. I saw that on Elysian. I see it here in the camp. People weren't enlisting to fight for you because they thought you were some battlefield genius. They chose to serve you because you were just like them, and you not only stood up to The Chairman, but *you won.*"

"You did something no one ever thought they would be able to do in a million years," Victoria said. "You went from being some pissy little kid to being the Great Traitor." Victoria smiled when he saw Vincent's face drop at the mention of his hated nickname.

"No one would ever confuse you with strategist." Presan laughed. "But that's why you have us, sir."

"Do you really believe I can lead the Elysians?" Vincent asked.

"No one stands alone, sir," Erin said. "Not the Warlord, not Denta. And we would never let you stand alone either."

"Is everything okay, sir?" Presan asked, taking a step closer.

"So, you've been honest about me...tell me what you think of Denta." He wanted to be sure he wasn't being paranoid. These grizzled army officers would have felt the same thing as him if it were real right?

"He certainly likes the sound of his own voice," Presan said, his face sour.

"And his insistence on that musical display when we landed. Looked like a mutt pissing on his territory to me," Victoria said.

"And since then?" Vincent asked. He didn't know a lot about staff officers, but he did know they cared entirely too much about their honor and prestige. They wouldn't stand silently by as someone made them look bad.

"He's a cock." Erin laughed.

To Vincent's surprise he saw Presan break out into laughter with her. "A fucking racist too," she sneered. "I've seen how he looks at me and my boys. Just like how they looked at us when we were doing a life sentence. Bastard didn't even accept my salute as an officer."

"I cannot disagree," Presan added. "He's a snake and I wouldn't trust his intentions past the battlefield, sir."

"I agree." Vincent nodded. "I'm assuming you've heard about our plans for the Gangers?"

"My aide informed me of the plan, yes," Presan said.

"They probably didn't tell you about Denta's plan to turn them into Sentenced soldiers once Murat and Marcus are dead." At that the room froze.

"You can't be serious," Fiona spat. "He wants to conscript Martians into service?"

"This plan is repulsive," Presan said.

"I'll beat that old bastard's head in," Victoria growled. Vincent held up his hands.

"I already told him we wouldn't do it," he said.

"He'll just impress them into the Titanian Army!" Erin screamed.

"I know!" Vincent said. "Just like you said, we shouldn't trust him. And I don't anymore." He sighed. He knew he had to tell them the next part. "Captain Tirpitz was sent to us as a spy for him."

No one said a thing, but Fiona took a pull from her cigarette so hard sparks flew off of its tip.

"Make no mistake, Denta is using us."

"Honestly, when I first accepted this command sir, I thought you knew," Presan said.

"I spent enough of my life being used by uppity old bastards. I don't know about you guys, but I'm over it," he spat.

Victoria nodded. "Damn right."

"Denta thinks the Elysian Cohort are an after-thought. That they're his play-things." Vincent tapped the end of his cigarette, dropping ashes onto the ground. "So, let's turn the tables on that fucker."

"How so?" Presan raised an eyebrow.

"His plan is to capture Marcus and Murat as they come to the Mons for a meeting. Well, we are going to capture them first."

Erin grinned. "I like it!"

"Presan you sit in on all of his meetings, right?"

"Of course."

"So, you'll know Denta's exact timetables when it comes to the operation."

"Yes, sir. The man never deviates from his precious timetables." Presan frowned. Vincent remembered sitting in on numerous meetings where Denta would go on for hours about the importance of his set times. If this one company did not make it to this particular street by this particular hour, the entire operation would certainly go to hell. He cared more about sets of data than he did about people.

"We simply send out Erin's scouts along the route the day before. In the middle of the night so not even the Titanians know about it. Can you do that Erin?"

"They don't call us the Red Ghosts for nothing, sir." She smiled.

"Then what?" Fiona asked. "We shoot them, right?"

"Eventually," Vincent said. "But Denta wants to frame this as a revenge mission against the Gangers who stole his shit and killed his adopted daughter."

"But they did do that," Erin said.

"They did," he agreed. "But if you were going to shoot them *for* the Martians rather than for us, what would you do?" he asked.

"Put them on trial for their crimes against the Martian population," Presan said.

"But who would try them?" Vincent smiled knowingly.

"Erik." Victoria grinned broadly. "Martians prosecuting Martians for the betterment of Mars." He slapped his knee. "Damn sir, I did not give you enough credit."

"I have to admit Consul, you are learning this game quickly." Presan smiled.

"I can't take all the credit." He sighed. "Denta has forced me to turn into a backstabbing bastard."

"It suits you." Presan nodded. "Not all great men are good men. And great men are needed to lead."

"And the good men?" Vincent asked.

"Not sure," he said. "But there is probably a lot of good men in those grave sites down the hill back there."

That one stung him. He didn't want to think how many so-called good men his plan would end up killing.

"So, when do we start?" Erin asked, snapping Vincent's mind back to reality.

"Immediately," he said. "Presan start digging around for the timetables. Erin, prep your scouts for the mission...." He thought for a moment. His mind was running a million miles a minute and he couldn't think of what else they should do.

"We should inform the Fidayi," Victoria said. "As strange as they are, they are true allies."

"Their input would be helpful," Erin agreed. "More Mawr Warriors never hurt a battle plan."

"Right." Vincent nodded. "I'll do that." He stubbed out his cigarette on his desk.

"Sir, in all due respect, what do you hope to achieve by doing this?" Presan asked.

"Respect," he said. "Not just respect for myself." He swallowed. He had to admit, the idea of being treated like little more than a joke by some high class Titanian field marshal irked him more than he ever thought possible. But it was more than that now. Soldiers volunteered to fight and die for him against the Black Coats on Elysian. They followed him across the galaxy to fight the Committee on Mars, ready to fight for him again. He could not allow their lives to be thrown away in the service of someone who didn't care about them. If he did, he wouldn't be any different than The Chairman.

Vincent breathed deep and tried to gather himself. "If I let him treat me like a joke. Or like a pushover. That means I accept the sacrifice our boys and girls made, and are yet to make, and the world we are trying to build is nothing but a joke as well. And I just can't do that, Presan."

Presan stood, straightening his uniform and saluted. "I understand now, sir."

Vincent waived off his salute. "I know you don't think I am the best person for this job," he began. "And I respect that. But I'm asking for your help."

"Sir, you may not be the best man for the job right now, but—" Victoria began.

"Either was I when I first enlisted," Presan said. "That doesn't happen overnight. You're just swimming upstream from the start. But I have a feeling you'll get there, kid."

Vincent stood up and joined Presan near the door. "Thanks. Now let's go piss off Denta, yeah?"

Presan nodded. "For Elysian."

"Always."

CHAPTER THIRTY-FOUR

Vincent walked up a small walkway that had been packed into the Martian dust. The towering form of Arai's Command Ship stuck out of the dirt like a sharp, black, obelisk. The ship was obviously a captured Anarch design, though Vincent wasn't familiar enough with their vehicles to know which class it was. It was half of the size of the Destroyer that they had fought in the skies above Elysian, but impressive, nonetheless. The craft was a seamless spike, unlike most Fidayi ships which were slapped together from anything remotely flight worthy.

Rhai and Mawr rushed around one another down the path back towards the Human Command quarters on the other side of the Mons. Much like the streets of Elysian, they paid no attention to personal space. Bumping and shoving their way past one another and occasionally into Vincent. While he had gotten used to the pushy aliens, the other humans who were delivering data displays to the Fidayi Command area had not. They waited on the side of the path for someone to make room for them, like they were trying to merge into traffic. They stood looking flustered and straightening their uniform as the races of the Fidayi paid them no mind.

As he got to the base of the ship, he saw a small village of tents erected in neat rows. Different colored banners fluttered from each one. Warriors in different colored armor milled about the area. It finally dawned on him that these were the command tents of the Fidayi Cohort Leaders. Vincent wanted to laugh because despite most of the Cohort Leaders distaste for humans and the humans distaste for the Clan, both of their camps ended up looking exactly alike.

The only difference between the two was the stoic aliens were not playing card games or gambling. Instead they were gathered in small reading circles, studying their Affirmations. Other groups were engaging in hand to hand combat at the direction of an older Warrior. It wasn't drunken brawls like Vincent's soldiers, but rather methodical training. He noticed that unlike the humans, they were using real blades. He glanced over at Zinvor and it looked like he would much rather be training with them than acting as his bodyguard.

"You can join them if you want." He smiled. Zinvor grumbled to himself but did not answer.

The ship's entrance was a good twenty feet off of the ground and required walking up black metal ramp. Though the ramp itself looked as thin as a piece of paper it didn't shake or wobble as he walked up it.

At the top of the ramp, on a small landing, stood two of Arai's Personal Guards. Their ornate armor a deep yellow and their pauldrons thick with fluttering ribbons. By this point they knew Vincent as well as any of the Cohort Leaders. He wasn't met with any challenge, instead they snapped over at the waist in a deep bow. The door they were standing in front of soundlessly slid open and they stepped aside.

The inside of the Command ship was identical to that of the Anarch Destroyer they had stormed in the skies above Elysian. The hallways were an almost sterile white color. Unlike a human ship, there wasn't a single rivet or bulkhead to be tripped over. It was like the whole ship had been formed out of a mold somewhere and peeled out all at once.

He knew the Mawr would never be able to keep such a ship in working order. Outside of their armor and guns they were hardly engineers. His thoughts were proven correct when a few seconds later a team of the ship's crew—all of them Rhai—walked by checking the ship's systems on a data display.

"Warlord's office?" Vincent asked. The Rhai stopped in their tracks and exchanged glances. A Rhai with light purple skin stepped forward.

"Down. Hallway." It pointed down the path to the right as it struggled with human speech, the Rhai's high pitched voice stung his ears. He nodded and the two of them began to walk that way. Like most Alliance buildings or Ships there was no signs telling them where they were supposed to go. Vincent remembered aboard the *ESS Victory* there were hastily made signs stuck everywhere so the ground soldiers wouldn't get lost.

"Your sister certainly got an upgrade," Vincent said.

"I don't like it," Zinvor growled. "Demons made this ship." He eyed the walls like he loathed them. Vincent was never sure if Zinvor gave the Anarchs that nickname because of how much he hated them, or because he actually thought they were some demon from an unknown part of space. After fighting them himself, he was so sure what he believed either.

They had to have been going in the right direction as the foot traffic in the hallway turned from studious Rhai engineers to stern faced Mawr Warriors, who could not have looked more out of place if they were standing in the middle of an operating room or science lab.

He pushed his way through the Warriors and found himself at Arai's door. More of her Warriors were blocking the way, seemingly in the middle of an argument about something. They were pushed aside, their conversation coming to an end. In their midst was Pharos. His dark grey skin almost blended into his black shimmering cloak. A smile crept across his face when he saw him.

"Consul Solaris," he rasped. Every other Rhai he had ever spoken to had a high-pitched voice. Not Pharos. Their voice was a dull rasp, hardly ever growing louder than a loud whisper.

"Pharos," Vincent said. "I would say long time no see but that is kind of your thing."

"Clever," Pharos said. "I imagine you are here to see the Warlord?"

"Yes."

"She has been waiting for you." Pharos turned and when they did the door behind them silently slide open. Inside was the Warlord's Office, or at least a room that she had attempted to turn into an office. The featureless white room was draped in flags and banners. The gleaming white floor was covered with a fur rug, from some animal Vincent had ever seen before. No matter how hard she had tried it didn't look like any office Vincent could picture her in.

A low rectangular metal desk was bolted to the floor and was surrounded by small cushions. At the head of the desk was Arai. The Warlord was without her Armor and instead wore her Riten in a simple over the shoulder holster.

"Warlord," Pharos announced. "Consul Solaris is here to see you."

"Oh," she said. "They allow you out of the Titanian Command Center now?" He wasn't sure if this was an attempt at humor or not.

"I've been dealing with some... things." He stumbled, looking an excuse. He hadn't made it to a single meeting of the Cohort Leaders since they had landed on Mars.

"Do I need to remind you that you're a member of the Fidayi Clan and not the Titanian Army Solaris?" she growled. "The Cohort Leaders have been talking. And I cannot say they are wrong to do so."

"Let them talk," Zinvor growled. "While they have been chatting away like broodlings the Consul has been fighting." He glanced over at Zinvor. While the Tsarra had charged into combat to save him more than once, he had never stood up to his sister in his defense.

"Hm," Arai grunted. "So why are you here now?" Vincent had never thought of how to sell his little operation to the Clan. Explaining it to a group of human soldiers who had a history of being taken advantage of by strongarm military leaders was easy enough. But telling her that they wanted to go behind the back of one of their allies just to make the Martians feel better about them being on the planet wouldn't work. The Mawr were not exactly a compassionate race.

"The Titanians are planning an operation that by all means should be mine to lead," he began. Arai didn't look up from a map she was looking down at, taking notes. Well, that didn't work. "They are trying to steal our glory and it is an affront to Clan's honor."

"How so?" she asked, her brow furrowed. He knew a challenge to his perceived honor or that of the Clan would immediately get her attention.

"The Gangers betrayed us," he said. "They lied to Denta, sure. But Marcus and Murat looked me in the eye and lied to me. They dishonored a Cohort Leader of the Fidayi Clan and by doing so dishonored the Clan itself."

"A serious charge," Pharos said. A knowing smile spread across Pharos' lipless face.

"Indeed," Arai said.

"But." Pharos held up a slender finger. "There is more to this, is there not?"

"I wouldn't lie to the Warlord." Vincent frowned.

"Withholding information is not lying, Consul." Pharos grinned. "Maybe something personal perhaps?" Vincent should have known Pharos would have known everything before he had even opened his mouth.

"Yes." He nodded. "Something very personal."

"Like?" Arai said. Vincent thought for a moment. He had no idea how he could explain that Marcus had abused and tortured Fiona for years. He wasn't sure if the Mawr even had intimate relationships outside of breeding.

"The one they call Marcus committed outrages against Vincent's Broodmate," Pharos said. Vincent's jaw dropped. Pharos turned back to him. "That correct is it not?" He couldn't form words, instead he just nodded his head. Arai rose to her feet, her fists balled.

"What do you need of me?" she asked.

"I want to capture their leaders and have Commander Erik put them on trial for their crimes. But to make sure this doesn't blow up into a city-wide civil war we need to deploy our Warriors to surround their encampments and capture them before they can rally to their defense," he said.

"Trial?" Arai roared. Pharos held up a hand.

"This is actually a good plan, Warlord," he rasped. "The Consul means to cut the head off of the Gangs while delivering justice to the Martians, the Titanians, and the Elysians all at once. While at the same time making Commander Erik look like the true hero of Mars."

"You scare me sometimes Pharos," Vincent said.

"You mean to bring the entire Martian population under this Erik character." Arai scratched her chin. She glanced at Pharos who nodded at her. "You are getting better at this."

"People keep telling me that," he said.

"A good idea." She smiled. "It is time that Denta recognize the glory of our Clan. I have been waiting for the opportunity since we landed."

"I will dispatch our Cohorts, Warlord." Pharos nodded.

"Good. I hope you know what you're doing, Consul."

"I would never lie to you, Warlord." Vincent shrugged. "I have absolutely no idea what the hell I'm doing."

CHAPTER THIRTY-FIVE

Vincent was in Arai's Command Office listening intently to Blackwell's radio set. The One Armed newly promoted first sergeant sat next to the set, fiddling with the knobs until its signal came in clear. Arai and Pharos sat on the floor on cushions while he paced back and forth across the room. Presan joined them, looking somewhat uncomfortable sitting on the ground with the Clan leadership.

"I can't believe you made me stay here," he grumbled.

"Many things can go wrong in an operation such as this, Consul," Pharos said.

"You let Fiona go!" he whined.

"Your Broodmate is not Consul," he said.

"But I'm the damned Cohort Leader! I should be allowed to go in with my soldiers."

"My Cohort Leaders are not allowed to risk themselves like idiots," Arai grunted. Vincent sat down on the edge of the table and folded his arms. He hated this feeling. Ordering people off on missions that could kill them while he sat around and did nothing. He hated it more because Fiona had run off without him. Zinvor only stayed behind with him because he was bound by a sacred oath.

*   *   *

At a few minutes after midnight Ezra led a flight of a dozen ships of a combined Clan air wing packed full of Erin's scouts, Erik's Soldiers, Clan Scouts, and several of Pharos' Agents. Vincent had never seen Pharos' Agents before. Soldiers of the Special Activities Cohort. They were Rhai clad in jet black armor and equipment. They carried small carbines that were linked the face screens of their helmets, ensuring pinpoint accuracy wherever they looked.

Arai assured him that they were the best soldiers available to capture Marcus and Murat alive. Though he had no reason to distrust Pharos, he couldn't help but be made uneasy around him.

To make matters worse Presan was worried about the Titanians listening in to their radio communications. And rightfully so. They used the same radios, vehicles, and as far as Vincent knew, they had probably trained some of his soldiers too.

It would be incredibly easy for them to listen in on their transmissions during the mission. They decided to work around this threat by simply not saying anything over the radio unless they absolutely had too.

"Three minutes out from target zone A," crackled a voice over the radio. It was hard to tell but it sounded like Erin. Vincent rushed over to Arai's desk. He rummaged through the haphazard pile of maps until he found one that said "Target Zone A" scribbled across the top of it. Murat's main encampment at the eastern edges of the Olympus city limits.

According to Erin's scouts it had once been an EDF command post, which made it a solid structure to defend. Though, years of ganger neglect and conflict had left the complex in ruins. Photos from Pharos' Agents showed a rotted and collapsing roof and a perimeter wall that was little more than rubble at this point.

"On Target B" came another voice. It was the voice of Rhai agent. "Awaiting package delivery."

By package, they meant Murat and Marcus. Before the operation could be launched, and before Denta could catch onto their little game, they had to somehow manage to trick Murat and Marcus into thinking that something was an even better deal than the fake one that Denta had laid out for them. That was where Pharos' vast intelligence network came into play.

Using Pharos' Agents, the same ones now stalking the road, they had met with the two Gang leaders. Posing as dissident Rhai Soldiers looking to make extra money, the Agents offered them Rhai weapons in exchange for human women. The two leaders were quick to agree.

Pharos set a meeting spot in one of Olympus' old, ruined factories, far away from the eye of the Titanian military garrisoned on the Mons. As intricate and detailed as Pharos' plans were, they all hinged on the combined force of Mawr, Elysian, and Brigade Soldiers being able to simultaneously capture their objectives.

Vincent had little doubt that the combined forces of Erin's Scouts reinforced with two Troops of Elysian soldiers would be able to force Murat's surrender. And if worse came to worse they would have little issues bleeding it out of them. He didn't worry about Pharos' agents, backed by a small war band of Mawr Warriors led by Zinvor either. Though Target B was the stronger of the two, defended by the stronger of the two gang's, he had little doubt Zinvor Warrior's would make short work of them if they decided they wanted to fight.

It was the capture of the so-called package that worried Vincent. In order for this plan to work, and to legitimize Erik as the rightful leader of Mars, him and his soldiers had to capture Marcus and Murat's convoy as it pulled into the ruined factory. Their forces, once ramshackle and pieced together with bits of stolen EDF gear was now several times stronger than they had once been. Their shoddy War Wagons, repurposed cargo trucks loaded down with weapons, were now actual Tanks and Troop Carriers, both gifted and stolen.

"Package located" Came the voice of Erik. "Heading due east towards the rally point." He paused. "Estimated strength, approximately one Battalion of mixed light and heavy armor."

"A battalion?" Vincent spat. Nearly eight hundred heavily armed gangers were heading towards Erik's three hundred or so Soldiers.

"It seems they did not trust your Agents very much," Presan said to Pharos.

"It was wise of them." Pharos nodded.

"Presan!" Vincent yelled.

"Yes, sir?"

"How many ships can we get in the sky?"

"The Elysian Wing is about a dozen strong now, but if we scramble them, we will alert the Titanians."

"Worry not, Consul," Pharos said.

"Worry not?" Vincent mocked. "Erik is going to get steamrolled!"

"Do you really believe I would leave this entire operation up to something I could not control?" Pharos asked.

"And just what the hell does that mean?" Presan folded his arms.

"Targets are exiting their vehicle," the radio speaker hissed.

"Moving on target A," Erin said immediately.

"Inbound on target B," screeched the Rhai voice.

"I asked you a question!" Presan demanded. Pharos, nonplussed, tossed Presan a Data display. Vincent rushed over to see what it was. The display was playing video feed of some kind. A skyline whipped by in a blur. Shapes came into view, the crescent shaped ships of the Clan.

"You had ships there the entire time?" Vincent asked.

"I knew using the Mons would alert the Titanians. Like you said." Pharos nodded at Presan. "I deployed a squad of light scout ships directly from the fleet. They have been stationed miles above Commander Erik's position for hours." Pharos turned towards the display. "Always control every element of an operation, Consol. Leave nothing to chance."

The display camera feed continued. The ships were diving onto the factory area. It looked to be badly damaged and surrounded by a wasteland of a ruined district. Outside of the largest factory stretched a long column of vehicles in various shades of black, grey, and rust red. Hundreds of tanks, armored personnel carriers, and trucks sat parked with still more people milling about outside of them.

"Is that—" he began.

"Erik's position," Presan gasped. "He doesn't stand a chance."

"Watch" Pharos said. The scout ships spread out. As they got closer, the bright plumes of rocket fire streaked from their wings. Explosions tore through the ranks of Ganger vehicles, throwing them through the air like toys being thrown by a child.

The ships quickly pivoted around and made another pass on the column. Tracers began to arc up into the air as the Gangers tried in vain to fight off their assailants. The pilots nimbly dodged around the incoming fire.

The ships strafed the vehicles once again and dozens of tanks erupted into flames, their turrets blowing away from their hulls. By the time the ships made a third pass on the column there was not much left to attack. Survivors fled into the surrounding city while still others jumped on the few vehicles left operational. It did not take long for the ships to seek them out too.

The room fell into an eerie silence.

"Like I was saying." Pharos cleared their throat. "Leave nothing to chance."

"You could have told us you had air support waiting this entire time." Presan frowned.

"And ruin that wonderful look of surprise on all of your faces?" Pharos grinned. "I think not."

"We have the package!" Erik's voice crackled over the radio, breaking the silence.

"Target A captured!" Erin answered.

"B, secure," came the gruff voice of a Mawr.

"What is the meaning of this?" screamed Denta. "You dare betray me Solaris?" Try as Pharos may, even the Clan Master of Spies could not conceal a large air strike in the middle of a deathly quiet city. Denta, flanked by Titanian officers of just about every rank had met them on the berthing area of the Mons as soon as he had returned from Arai's command ship.

"I don't work for you," Vincent answered flatly. "This was a Clan operation, sanctioned by Warlord Arai herself."

"With Martian assistance," Pharos added helpfully.

"Don't work for me," Denta grumbled. "Your forces are under Titanian Command!"

"As you will see," Pharos withdrew a Data display from a pocket and handed it to Denta. "Our Glorious Warlord Arai has rescinded those orders as of last night."

"This is horse shit Solaris and you know it!" Denta spat.

"It might be horseshit Denta, but it's official horseshit." Vincent smiled. Denta his dark face turning even darker broke from his flanking officers and closed in on Vincent. His breath smelled of smoke and liquor and his tired eyes were bloodshot.

"Where the fuck do you get off, kid?" he seethed.

"I warned you," Vincent said, not backing down and getting even closer to Denta. "I wouldn't stand for slavery. I wouldn't stand for racism. I wouldn't stand for you trying to turn Mars into what The Chairman always wanted it to be."

"After everything I've done for you!" Denta growled.

"You used me," He shot back. "You used me, and you used my soldiers. And it will not happen again."

Denta backed up, folding his arms across his chest. He turned his nose up and readjusted his glasses. "I underestimated you, Solaris."

"If you'll excuse me, I have prisoners to handle," Vincent spat.

Denta and his entourage turned on their heels and stormed off.

Vincent felt the grip of a hand on his shoulder, and when he glanced around to see who it was, he saw the grinning face of Victoria.

"You showed that old bastard," he said.

"Are the men coming?" Vincent asked.

"Yessir," Victoria nodded.

"Good." He smiled. Presan had suggested, and Vincent had agreed, to the idea of a large welcoming ceremony for the soldiers who had gone out on the mission. Part as a way to show that they were all in this together, Earthian, Fidayi, and Martian alike—but also partly to rub it in Denta's face. Vincent liked the second part the most.

The fare was distinctly different than the Titanian parade when they landed. There were no drums or flags or tight formations of ornately dressed soldiers. Word had quickly gotten out that the operation had been a success and the soldiers who rushed to the field were what Vincent assumed an Elysian greeting party would look like. Shabby looking soldiers in mismatched uniforms. Some of them were drinking, others were already drunk. Many had their rifles slung across their backs, others did not.

Music played from speakers that someone had brought with them. Not the pomp and circumstance of Denta's absurd army band. Instead it was grinding guitar riffs and the shouting of a band that Vincent had never heard of before. The Mawr and Rhai contingent who had showed up looked on at their human comrades with equal parts confusion and amusement. Large bottles were passed from the humans onto their Mawr counterparts and they drank deeply from them. He fought back laughter when he watched a Mawr Warrior eat a cigarette that was offered.

As the crowd began to swell, dark shapes appeared in the sky. First a few and then a dozen. The box like shapes of the Reapers appeared out of the dark red Martian clouds. At the head of the arrow shaped formation of ships was the *Shanna II*. Her odd, cobbled together body shape always easy to point out.

They circled the landing area to whoops and cheers from the crowds of soldiers. Several fired their weapons into the air in celebration causing a few others to dive to the ground, thinking they were suddenly under attack. Presan did not look entertained.

The *Shanna II* led the procession of ships onto the landing zone that had been growing smaller and smaller as the crowds pushed in. Ezra landed his ship so gently he hardly disturbed the dust that covered the ground.

The crew doors were thrown open and out stepped Erik. The crowd erupted into cheers once again and Vincent could see the normal stoic, grounded, Martian's face crack into a broad smile. The rest of Erik's men piled out of the ship behind him. They tried even less than he did to remain calm and professional. Instead they pumped their fists into the air, riling up the crowd further.

Only after all of Erik's soldiers emerged from the transport ships did they fetch their prize. The last Reaper in the flight had its doors opened by Erik and inside two of Pharos' Agents sat. In between them were two hooded, shackled, prisoners in the stolen, tattered uniforms of EDF generals.

The Agents climbed out and the Martians grabbed their prisoners, pushing them forward. The crowd began to get restless. As Martians, Elysians, and Titanian fury began to build at the sight of the men who had betrayed them. In some cases they had probably had several of their friends killed by them. The crowd began to vent their rage by throwing anything they could find at the captured gangers. A rain of empty bottles, ration tins, and rocks cascaded down onto the shackled prisoners. Murat was knocked off of his feet by a rock the size of a fist. officers and sergeants left to control their soldiers flailed their arms around and shouted orders in vain.

A pistol was fired into the air and angry shouting died away. Vincent looked over and saw Erik, pistol held out over his head, smoke curling from its barrel.

"Enough!" Erik shouted. The crowd, still obviously riled up and rearing to tear apart the two gangers with their bare hands, withdrew just a little. "These men are in my custody and will be tried by law as laid out by the People's Congress of Mars. Not unruly mob justice in the street!" Erik's procession of soldiers created a path through the still growing crowd. Now, instead of shouts of anger directed at the captured Gangers, there was cheers of support for Erik.

"What do you think of him?" Vincent asked Presan. He raised an eyebrow, apparently surprised that he would want his opinion. "I keep telling you, you can always speak freely."

"I'm still getting used to it." He laughed. "I think he is a good leader. He can obviously bring people together. I heard he even created his own Officer's Academy."

"It's true. I've seen it," Vincent said. "And I fought with them on the Mons, what he built works."

"Then we should seize the initiative here," Presan said. Vincent felt his face get warm with embarrassment as he had absolutely no idea what Presan was talking about. He must have picked up on his cluelessness. "We already stole the Gangers from Denta, now we have to cozy up to the Martians before he does. He has the money, guns, and supplies. We have to give the Martians something they've always wanted."

"Recognition," Vincent said.

"Now you're getting it." Presan smiled. "Recognize the People's Congress of Mars and Erik as its duly elected Commander."

"I don't think he was actually elected though," Vincent said.

"Hardly important." Presan waived him off. "Right now, Titan is the senior member of this alliance that we have. It is possible that they even rival the Clan in power. If we are the first ones to win over the Martians, have them on our side, Denta is no longer the loudest voice at the table when it comes to planning. We still have an entire other war to plan. It could come in handy."

"You want an alliance inside of the alliance that we already have?" Vincent asked.

"It's politics, Consul. You will have to trust me on this," he said.

"Were you a politician, Vadim?"

"I was a general officer in the EDF, it is virtually the same thing." He smirked.

"Okay, but do I have the power to do that? I'm hardly the damn Warlord," he asked.

"Arai won't care." Presan waved him off. "She already said she wants nothing to do with Mars and she barely understands humanity. That's why she has you. You are the Human Consul after all."

"Uh." Vincent thought for a moment. "How do I go about officially recognizing a new independent planet?"

"I will have my aide draft the official letter, sir. I will have it sent to Commander Erik by the end of the day." Presan laughed and slapped him on the shoulder. "You should really get an aide." Vincent's eyes widened and he fought for words. "You know what, I'll make sure you get one of those too."

"Thank you, Presan." He smiled.

The crowd pushed on, following the prisoners as they marched across the Mons and into the Martian encampment. Out of the crowd came Blackwell. His wrinkled face was normal defaulted to a mild irritation. Now, it was beat red with anger. Vincent's first sergeant was a man of strict rules and regulations, even in a slapped together army such as Elysian's. It was obvious he was one of the sergeants who had tried in vain to keep the crowd away from the prisoners.

"Are you ready Blackwell?" Vincent asked him.

"Ready?" Blackwell seethed. "For beating the discipline back into these dogs?" Presan let out a cough of laughter.

"No." He laughed. "We have a trial to attend."

CHAPTER THIRTY-SIX

Vincent awoke with a start as the door to his quarters slammed open. Standing in the doorway was a Mawr he had never seen before. He rubbed sleep from his eyes and noticed the Mawr had a clothes stand in tow. Draped across it was his armor.

"Good Morning..." Vincent yawned. The Mawr bowed low and it was then that he noticed it was not a Warrior. It was not clad in the scaled armor of the Mawr Warrior class and did not carry a Riten. He remembered Arai telling him about a class of Mawr known as *Ashtogh*, or the ones who were incredibly skilled tradesman. They were the builders, engineers, and what Arai called Melds. The ones who crafted their armor and built their Ritens.

"Greetings, Consul," the Meld said. "Our Warlord insisted your Armor be ready by today and it has been done." At the Meld's deep grumbling voice Fiona stirred in bed, finally waking up.

"What the hell is all this about?" she moaned.

"Apologies Consul Broodmate," the Meld grunted.

"What did he call me?" she asked, still drunk with sleep.

"Oh, go back to sleep." Vincent hushed her. He turned back towards the Meld. "Thank you, the armor looks amazing." The Meld bowed low again.

"May Paterazm guide you."

"Uh, sure. You too." The Meld turned and left. "Hey Zinvor." His face popped in through the door. "Could you do me a favor and stop letting people just barge in here while I am sleeping in my underwear?" Zinvor didn't answer, he just frowned and went back to his position outside.

"Your bodyguard sucks," Fiona whined.

"Just as well." Vincent reluctantly climbed out of bed. "We have to get ready for the trial." Fiona sighed. "Are you going to be okay?"

"Better than okay," she said. "I've been waiting for this for years." She put on a strong front, but her eyes betrayed her true emotions. Her blue eyes were watery, and she fought back tears.

"You don't have to go," he said, reaching back and brushing her hair behind her ear. She bristled.

"If you think I would miss this you don't know me."

"You can't just shoot him you know," he said, and she smirked.

"I know. If I could he would have been dead yesterday." She rolled over to her armor that laid in a pile on the floor. Fumbling around with a pocket she found her cigarettes and lit one. "But I'll be damned if I'm not on that firing squad."

"I'm sure Erik wouldn't mind."

Vincent walked over to where his newly refurbished armor sat on its stand. It's dark blue scales that had been pitted and damaged by countless fights had been replaced. Across the chest a crimson phoenix was emblazed, the bird's wing tips reaching each pauldron. Gone were the sarcastically placed corporal's chevrons. He wasn't sure if it was because the Melds had no idea what they were or because they thought they were tacky. In their place were several scrolls. He noticed a new one, a dark red scroll that read in Human Standard, *"Liberator of Mars."*

The Mawr were certainly being liberal in their award names.

He stepped into the pants and noticed they felt heavier than normal. He flexed his legs and felt the once light and almost cloth like armor restrict his movements for the first time. It was tight and stiff like an unbroken in boot. He slipped on his top and found it just as tight. He suddenly got the feeling he had done so much damage to his last set of armor they just built him a new one altogether.

"Ready?" he asked. Fiona had quickly gotten dressed and was sliding her Riten into its holster at her left hip. Smoke curled out of her nose and she tamped her cigarette out on the table.

"Let's fucking do this."

* * *

The Brigade camp's atmosphere was thick with tension and anger. The small village of tents that had popped up at the foot of the Mons was crowded with soldiers of every race and faction. All of them were mummering to themselves, their facial expressions fierce. The gangers had managed to piss of every section of the alliance that had formed to liberate Mars, and every corner of it was here to see justice served.

As Vincent entered the camp, flanked by Zinvor and Fiona, the crowd parted to make way for them. He small amount of the soldiers rendered salutes to him as the group walked past, the Mawr dropping to one knee to honor Zinvor. The trials had been going on for hours already. Erik had scheduled the trial to take places in phases, which would take hours if not days to get through. The gangers had such a wide array of crimes to answer for, there was no way Erik was going to settle for only prosecuting Marcus and Murat. He had a long list of names to get through before he got to the main event.

At the center of the camp they came upon an area that had been turned into the gallows. A crude wooden frame had been propped up. Each of the four uprights had a post branching off of it laterally. From each branch a half dozen bodies swung lifelessly from ropes. Their bulging, dead eyes, stared lifelessly back at them as they walked by. A few red-uniformed brigade soldiers stood guard over the area to ensure the crowd didn't attempt to exact more vengeance on the already dead bodies.

They walked past row after row of tents only big enough to fit four soldiers at a time, which was EDF standard to keep fire teams sleeping together. Finally, they got to what had to be Erik's Command area. A tent four times as large as any of the other ones was popped up in a clearing and surrounded by a small wall of sandbags. Soldiers in full combat gear stood guard outside of it, roving back and forth.

At the tent's entrance stood Presan, his arms crossed and looking upset. He quickly straightened to the position of attention and saluted Vincent. He returned his salute and shook his hand.

"Damn mob justice, sir," Presan said. "These courts Erik set up are just hanging everyone they see."

"They deserve it," Fiona seethed. "Fuck them." She pushed Presan aside and went into the tent.

"You'll have to forgive her—" Vincent began.

"I understand, sir," Presan interrupted. "Emotions and justice do not mix."

"We agreed to let Erik do this," he said. "Now we have to let him do this."

"I don't like it." Presan frowned. "This is something the Committee would have done."

"I know," he said. "I sat through that once remember?" "Twice actually," he corrected himself.

"Err..." Presan stumbled. "That isn't what I meant."

"I know." Vincent waived him off. "Any word on the rest of the gangers?"

"Many of them are enlisting in the Cohort, sir. As you can imagine they are wary of joining Erik's Brigade." Presan sighed. "I can get the full roster to you later, but I believe the main trials are starting soon. We should go inside." He pulled back the flap of the tent and stepped inside.

Crowds of soldiers were packed into the tent leaving standing room limited. They were each carrying on individual conversations that when joined together created an almost deafening level of noise. Smoke from countless cigarettes combined with the smell of hundreds of unwashed bodies to create a miasma of sorts. Vincent winkled his nose at the stench.

"Order!" Screamed out the voice of Erik, who Vincent could still not see. They pushed through the crowd, finally getting to the front. What had been the Brigade's operational planning area had been converted into a something resembling a court room. The table that had once been used to for planning now reminded Vincent of the Committee Court he had sat in front of back on Earth. Erik and four other officers sat behind the table, each with numerous data displays in front of them.

Murat, in shackles, sat on a lone folding camp chair in front of them. He had been changed out of his stolen military uniform and instead was now wearing little more than homespun rags.

His feet were bare, and face stolen and distorted with the signs of abuse.

The defiant, commanding gang leader that Vincent had met when he had first landed on Mars was gone. Murat's eyes were red, puffy, and bloodshot. It showed that he had spent the night sobbing in his jail cell. He was shaking and his gaze was set down towards the ground. The Martian officers sitting behind the desk with Erik were staring hatful gazes at the shackled ganger.

"Murat Olympus," Erik began. "You stand accused of charges of murder, extortion, kidnapping, rape, looting, theft, human trafficking, slavery, and high treason. What do you have to say in your defense?" Murat raised his head, his shaking intensifying. Murat wasn't a bright man, but even he knew he was only minutes away from his death.

"Marcus told me to do it," he stammered. "All of it!"

"You fucking lie!" screamed a voice from the crowd.

"Coward!" yelled another.

"I don't lie!" Murat countered.

"Enough!" Erik roared. "You have dishonored the Martian people and this court finds you guilty on all counts. Due to your crimes this court finds as long as you live you will remain a threat to the security of the people and the state. We hereby sentence you to death. The sentence is to be carried out immediately." Erik waived his hand at two of the soldiers who were standing guard. They rushed over and dragged Murat away. Murat had devolved into a sobbing messing, his legs no longer working. They dragged uselessly behind him as the soldiers took him towards the gallows.

"Next!" Erik said.

The tent flap at the rear of the tent was thrown open and two more soldiers entered. In between them was Marcus. His cold, blue eyes looked out at the cheering crowd emotionlessly. Unlike

Murat, he showed no fear. His chest was puffed out, standing defiant in his ragged, torn shirt and pants. Someone had attempted to break him physically. His left eye was swollen, and his lips were cracked and bleeding. But he was not broken. His lip curled into a smirk.

"Piece of shit!" Fiona spat, her voice joining the chorus of boos and hisses as he shuffled towards the chair. "I'll gut you myself!" she screamed. Vincent put his hand on her shoulder. Erik looked over at her and nodded. Marcus didn't want to sit down as he was instructed by his two escorts, so they had to force him down.

"Marcus Olympus," Erik began.

"Go fuck yourself you boot licking piece of shit." Marcus laughed. "Your court has no authority."

"You stand accused of Crimes against humanity. Including murder, rape, slavery, looting, human trafficking, forced enlistment of child soldiers, theft, and high treason. What do you have to say in your defense?" Erik brushed off Marcus' insults like he had said nothing at all.

"My defense." Marcus laughed. "What do you have to say in yours?" he shouted. "You're turning this planet right back over to those damned Worms!" Erik rose from his chair.

"Your actions caused the death of sixty-eight of our planet's allies in direct action. By standing against our alliance you have emboldened the Chairman's war effort against us. In doing so you have betrayed the people of Mars!"

"Fuck you!" Marcus spat.

"This court finds you guilty on all counts. As Commander of the People's Congress of Mars I also accept the request of the Consul of Elysian of the evocation of the Martian law of Blood Vengeance."

"What?" Fiona gasped.

"You're welcome," Presan growled.

"What the hell is blood vengeance?" Vincent whispered.

"It means the court can decide that the victim or the family of the victim of a crime can dispense the justice of the court up to and including execution," Presan explained. "I may have put in the request." He nodded towards Fiona. "I hope you don't mind I forged your signature, sir."

"I'll allow it." Vincent nodded.

"You are an unredeemable criminal against your own people, and you will be punished as such. This court sentences you to death. The sentence is to be carried out immediately," Erik said and with the wave of a hand, two soldiers came forward to grasp Marcus, but it was not needed. Marcus rose to his feet on his own.

"I can fucking walk on my own," he hissed. "You're the traitor to your people!" he yelled, walking towards the exit. "You serve the Worms and the Titanians and the fucking Toads!" Fiona broke free from the crowd and delivered a wild haymaker straight into Marcus's face. Her punch stopped him mid-insult and he stumbled back, only to be caught by his two escorts. Vincent rushed forward and grabbed her, but not before she hauled a kick straight up into Marcus' groin. He buckled at the knees as he gasped for breath. The escorts, once again, dragged him towards the door.

*   *   *

If the gallows were out of control before, they were now a mad house. Erik's soldiers had given up keeping any peace outside of a small ten-foot circle around the wooden structure. Murat's body was already hanging dead from its far-left branch. Erik's soldiers shoved Marcus to the base of the structure, but no one made any move to string him up by one of the gallows many ropes.

Erik, with the rest of his ad hoc court in tow, marched out to the small circle. The crowd that had just been pulsing with hate and vitriol fell to a hush.

"Fiona Olympus," Erik said. "I have accepted the Consul's request for Blood Vengeance on your behalf." He took a few steps forward and place and hand on her shoulder. She did not flinch. "I know you are one of countless victims. But through your hand, you will bring justice in all of their names. Now, Sister of Mars, do what you will."

"You?" Marcus laughed harshly. "You want one last fuck before I go eh?" he cackled. Vincent felt his face get hot and before he could stop himself his hand was at his hip, his fingers curling around the handle of his Riten. Presan took a step in front of him.

"This one isn't yours, sir," he said. "This is all her." Vincent gritted his teeth. He could only imagine how long she had been dreaming of this moment. Vincent had felt intense hatred for Molke, Rostov, and now Brusilov. For the Court who had sentenced him to the EDF. But those were new feelings compared to hers. She had been plotting this man's death, he had no doubt, since before she was even ten years old. Ever since he had picked her up from the street her family had banished her to.

Fiona stepped out, taking her place at the center of the small circle. Marcus, back against the gallows, smirked.

"You don't want to kill me," he said. "After everything I did for you, you fucking owe me! I took you in. Gave you food, I clothed you when your own family tossed you out like trash!" he yelled. "If it wasn't for me you would be dead!" Fiona shook. For the first time since he had known her, she hesitated. Her hand was on the handle of her Riten, but she didn't draw it. She didn't speak and her eyes welled up with tears. Her hands trembled.

"Death would have been better than what you did to me," she said quietly, her voice barely audible. "You're the fucking devil." Tears began to stream down her face. Marcus broke out into laughter.

"You're damn right I am," he said. Her hand let go of her Riten. She stepped forward. Vincent could see Marcus meant to step back, but with his back against the base of the gallows there was nowhere for him to go. Fiona's hands reached out, her pale fingers closing around his throat and gripping tight. He stumbled, trying to get away and fell over. Fiona was on top of him, straddling him as he tried to struggle and fight her off. The shackles made his fighting futile. Her grip got tighter and tighter while his eyes bulged from their sockets and turned a bloodshot red and his lips turned blue. His mouth moved wordlessly as she stared straight down into his dying, panicking eyes. She said nothing has the life drained from them.

Marcus bucked and kicked wildly, trying to free himself. As the oxygen escaped his body his kicks turned to spastic twitches. His legs curled up underneath of him reflexively and his balled fists loosened as his muscles lost control. His tongue lolled out of his mouth, a sickening purple color. Fiona did not let go. Instead, she started screaming. A heart wrenching, blood curdling scream. A scream that let out over a decade of pain, torture, and heartbreak.

The once wild crowd was now so quiet Vincent could hear his pulse racing in his temples. The soldiers around him slowly took off of their hats and held them to their chests. He could see several of them openly sobbing sympathetically. Presan dabbed a shirt sleeve at the corner of his eye.

Fiona screamed and she screamed. Marcus's body finally went limp. But her outburst of pent up emotions went on. Her tears flowed straight down onto the body she had just been strangling as her voice grew hoarse and began to crack.

It was only then she let go. Fiona covered her face with her hand and sobbed uncontrollably. Her wails of pain pierced Vincent worse than any wound ever had. As much as he wanted to help her, he knew there was nothing he could do.

"You should take her back to your quarters," Presan whispered. He nodded and went to her. She had been ignoring everything else around her, trapped in this moment a decade in the making. When he touched her shoulder she jumped. Her bloodshot eyes turned towards him and after a second of pause, she wrapped her arms around him.

She buried her face into his chest and continued crying.

CHAPTER THIRTY-SEVEN

Since the trials, the planning for the final push on the last EDF held cities had gone into overdrive. Denta had insisted the Martian's trial had set the planning back days, if not weeks. But Vincent was sure he was still pissed that they had managed to capture the Gangers from under his nose.

The fact that the Clan, or more precisely Vincent's Consulate, was the first to recognize Erik's People's Congress probably only fueled his anger. Erik declaring himself the ruler of Mars changed nothing as far as Vincent was concerned, but he knew beating Denta to the punch was just another way to score a win against the old man.

Denta's anger was evident. Once he had been charitable and friendly to him and his army, but that was over. After the trials Denta had ordered all of the Titanian junior officers he had loaned to the Elysians withdrawn, leaving Vincent's forces severely lacking leadership at almost every level. Though he was shocked when Presan said several of the Titanians had ignored

Denta's orders and resigned their commissions, only to be quickly reinstated as captains within the Elysian Cohort.

Pharos, Presan, Vincent, and Arai had been locked away in the Clan's Command ship for so long Vincent had lost track of time. He tipped another cup of Kaff back and rubbed his eyes.

"Denta is not taking this well," Arai said, he noted a hint of pleasure in her voice.

"Not at all," Presan said. "Even with a few dozen Titanian officers staying with us, we are short hundreds of Platoon and Troop Commanders. It is going to make command and control a nightmare."

"When one of my Cohort Leaders is outdone by a Warrior. I simply pick that Warrior to be a Cohort Leader. I do not understand why further schooling would be necessary," Arai said.

"Well—" Presan began, but Vincent cut him off.

"She has a point," he said. He knew Presan, though seemingly a lifetime away from the days where he attended Officer's Academy, was stuck in his insistence that they could not simply *make* an officer.

"What if we make *brevet* lieutenants?" Presan offered.

"What's that?" he asked.

"A system that they used back in the day. Hundreds of years ago. During times of strife they could temporarily promote people and if they lived up to the expectations of their new positions, the rank became permanent. We could have the Sergeant Major make a list of the most capable sergeants and see what they can do with a command."

"Hm," Vincent said. "That should work. *Brevet* Field Marshal Presan." He smirked. Presan gasped.

"You can't be serious. I am only a Brigadier, sir I—"

Vincent interrupted him again. "Show the men you deserve it, and you can keep it."

A smile creeped across Presan's face. "I will not let you down, sir."

"I know you won't," Vincent said. "Can you go inform Victoria to start making that list? We have a lot of slots to fill and not a lot of time to do it."

"Of course sir." Presan saluted and marched out of Arai's office. As soon as the door closed behind Presan, it opened once again. Ezra stepped into the office and took a seat next to Vincent on Arai's ring of floor cushions.

"I'm sorry I'm late, sir," he said. "Final preparations for our air wing are going badly."

"Badly?" Pharos asked.

"Yes," he said. "Since our little stunt, the Titanians are no longer supplying us with replacement parts for our ships. They're framing it as they are running low and have no more to give."

"And you do not believe them?" Arai asked.

"Their ships certainly seem to be in perfect working order." He sighed.

"Petty assholes." Vincent frowned. "How bad are the ships?"

"Well, they're working as well as you can hope for an air wing scraped together from captured and damaged EDF hulks. But we will need those parts if we have any hope to transport our entire force, artillery included, to Tharsis." Ezra leaned over and grabbed Vincent's cup and took a drink. "I'm going to need something harder than this." Pharos reached into his pocket and produced a flask, pouring a measure of clear liquid into the cup. "Thanks," Ezra said.

"In time we can rectify the ship issue," Arai said. "But not on such short notice."

"What do you propose?" Ezra asked.

"An overland march?" Vincent said.

"That would take far too long," Pharos said.

"Agreed," Ezra said.

"What if our soldiers just rode with the rest of the Clan? What is left of your air wing join in with the Clan's close attack craft," he said. "Can your transport ships hold us?"

"I'm sure I could *find* an extra supply barge." Pharos said.

"I'm not going to ask." Vincent sighed. "But if you can just miraculously find an entire supply barge I would be in your debt."

"It will be no problem," said Pharos.

"Any other issues?" Arai grumbled, clearly going tired of the constant stream of problems.

"No, Warlord." Ezra said, scratching his face.

"How are you doing Colonel Vorbeck?" Arai grunted. "I understand your Broodmate fell in battle."

"Yes...my...Broodmate." He swallowed hard. "She did."

"I know this can be difficult," she said. "I also lost my Broodmate in battle years ago." Ezra sniffed and a tear ran down his cheek. Arai reached across the table and placed a large, paw on his shoulder.

"How did you get over it?" he asked.

"I did not. I have not" She said in as soft of a voice as Vincent had ever heard her speak. "But I owed it to my Clan to work through the pain. We can mourn our fallen when the enemy is finally defeated."

"Right." He sniffed again and wiped away a tear.

"But we must win this battle before we can get there," Arai said.

"Of course Warlord," Pharos said. "We have much to do and not much time to do it in. We will meet in the morning for final preparations."

Ezra and Vincent were joined by Zinvor as they exited Arai's office. It was then Vincent finally got a good look at his air wing commander. Ezra, normally spotless and always in tight military regulation looked like he hadn't showered or shaved since the day Tirpitz had been killed. His flight suit was ragged, dirty, and torn. His once flawlessly shined black boots were scuffed and caked with Martian dust.

"Are you okay, really?" Vincent asked. Ezra sighed and rubbed his stubble covered face.

"How could I be?" he moaned. "How would you be handling it if Fiona got killed?" Vincent shuddered at the thought. They had been through so many situations together that neither had any business surviving he didn't even think about it anymore. The idea of losing her was almost inconceivable to him.

"When you put it that way, you're handling it pretty well," he said. "You look like shit though." Ezra choked back a laugh and dabbed at the corner of his eye.

"Thanks." He chuckled. "I guess I have been letting myself go huh?"

"You look worse than me," Vincent said. "And I look a few shades above homeless these days."

"Yeah." Ezra grinned. "You really have to cut that beard off." Vincent didn't mind the ribbing; he was just happy his friend was smiling again.

"I would, but Fiona likes it," he said. "And it makes me look older, I try not to look my age during all of these meetings with field marshals and alien warlords, you know."

"Good point," he said. "So, tomorrow is the big day."

"Yeah." Vincent sighed. "One way or another, it'll be the beginning of the end."

"I'm looking forward to seeing the look on Brusilov's face as we tear his little empire apart," Ezra said.

"I'd prefer to never see him again if I could help it."

"So, you've never said what you're going to be doing during the offensive," Ezra said.

"On the ground with everyone else," Vincent said.

"I would try to talk you out of it, but I know it's pointless."

"You're learning."

"One of these days you're going to get killed." Ezra warned.

"And one of these days this war will be over. Let's see which one happens first."

"I guess we will find tomorrow. Till the morning, sir." Ezra turned and rendered a salute which Vincent returned.

"I guess we will."

*　　*　　*

The Mons was as busy as ever. Soldiers rushed around in full combat gear, leaders screamed and yelled directions at them. He saw a Troop of his Elysian soldiers in formation being inspected by a major he had never seen before. Titanians were spray painting letters and numbers onto the side of armored vehicles with stencils. It didn't seem like a single person on the Mons was asleep that night.

He made his way through the normal tide of officer's aides back to his quarters. To his surprise a young lieutenant he had never seen wearing Elysian khaki was standing by his door. A short girl with a tight raven-haired bun and dark skin with a stack of data display under her arm quickly brought herself to attention and saluted.

"Evening, sir!" she said.

"Evening...Sorry, who are you?" he asked.

"I was assigned by Field Marshal Presan to be your aide, sir," she said.

"I mean, you name. What is your name?"

"Junior Lieutenant Felicity Haagen, sir."

"It's been a long night, what do you have for me Felicity?" The young officer was obviously surprised he was addressing her by her first name.

"The Field Marshal requires your signature on the Brevet promotions, sir," she said.

"Every single one?" He sighed. "Isn't there hundreds of them?"

"Yes, sir. Four Hundred and sixty-three to be exact, sir."

"I'm sorry Felicity there is no damn way I am doing that tonight." He frowned.

"But...err," she stumbled.

"You're my aide, right?"

"Yes, sir."

"So that means you'll be going into combat tomorrow, right?"

"I go where you go, sir."

"Have you ever been in combat before?"

"No sir. I graduated the Grand Titan Military Academy last month." Vincent rubbed his temples.

"Okay." He breathed out. "Just tell Presan I signed them all and if we survive tomorrow, I'll get around to it."

"I can't lie to a field marshal, sir," she stammered.

"You can if I'm telling you to lie to a field marshal." He winked. She thought for a moment.

"I suppose you're right."

"Can I ask you a question?"

"Yes, sir."

"Why did you leave the Titanian Army for...us?"

"Permission to speak freely, sir?"

"Yes, and you always do."

"Well, because you brought down the Chairman when Field Marshal Denta was sitting on his ass on Grand Titan." Vincent gritted his teeth for a moment, but relaxed. He let a smirk crease his face. Denta had pushed the idea that he really was the Great Traitor so hard his own people had fallen for it.

"Thanks." He smiled. "And Felicity, make sure when you show up in the morning you have a radio with you so I can talk to Presan."

"Of course, sir!"

"Have a good night." He turned, ready to walk into his quarters when Felicity clapped her boots together and rendered a salute.

"For Elysian sir!"

"Always," he responded. "And stop with the sir shit, it is getting old."

"What, what should I call you then?" she asked, puzzled.

"Vincent works pretty well." He smiled. She nodded before hurrying off to do what it was that aides did.

Inside of his quarters Fiona sat on the bed, still fully dressed as if she had just left the trial grounds. The quarters were clouded with thick smoke and Fiona was surrounded by a small graveyard of cigarette butts.

"Run into your new government issued girlfriend?" she asked, her voice still hoarse.

"Presan thinks I need an aide apparently," he said.

"I think you need about a dozen of them." She laughed, smoke curling out of her nose.

"Probably," he said, sitting down next to her. Her head sank onto his shoulder.

"He's dead. But he doesn't feel dead to me," she breathed. "It still feels like he is going to burst through that door any minute and drag me away again."

"He can't do that anymore," he said, brushing her hair back. "You made sure he can never hurt anyone again."

"You know what the bad part is?" Her eyes welled up once again. "He's dead. But I still feel him," she spat. "I have his ink. I have his scars. He is literally under my skin. He marked me like territory." She took a deep pull from her cigarette. "No matter what I did to him, he was always going to win."

"But—" he started, but she didn't give him a chance.

"He knew that though." She gave a sarcastic laugh. "The piece of shit died with a smile on his face."

"Maybe, you should stay here tomorrow," he said. The look she gave him could have killed him on the spot.

"You think I'd let you take Tharsis without me?"

"Not in a million years, but I thought I would at least suggest it to sound like a good guy."

"You sound like a jackass." She smiled, her eyes shimmering.

"I normally do." He scratched his beard.

"You know I love you right?" she asked.

"I know. I love you too," he said.

"Are you nervous about tomorrow?" she asked.

"No," he said.

"You're lying."

"No," he said. "I'm really not. Denta expects me to fuck up, Arai hopes for the bare minimum, and the Soldiers think I am some kind of Chairman deposing demigod." He laughed. "No matter what I do I'm fucked. I'm bound to let someone down, so why worry?"

"That is the most depressing kind of optimism I've ever heard," she said.

473

"Presan will be in control once the fighting starts." He shrugged. "As much as anyone is in control out there."

"Is that why you promoted him?" she asked.

"He has the job of a field marshal," he said. "Why not? Not to mention if we fail tomorrow none of this will matter anyway."

"If he can pull us through this, he deserves to be a field marshal." She laughed, and Vincent joined in. He stood up and walked over to his desk. It was still cluttered with Data displays and paperwork he had continued to ignore. He told himself if he survived the rest of the Mars campaign, he would take a crack at actually governing the Quarter.

He pushed it all aside and pulled out a small metal flask. Stamped across it was the Titanian Eagle. He tossed the flask to Fiona and she grinned.

"Where did you get this?"

"Stole it from Denta's Office during our last meeting," he said. "It's that gross smokey whiskey that you like so much."

"You really do love me." She giggled and tipped a mouthful of the flask into her mouth. She winced as brown liquid hit her tongue and smacked her lips. Vincent peeled off his armored jacket to allow himself to breathe. Fiona smirked. "Not going to get some sleep before tomorrow?"

"I couldn't if I wanted to." He sighed. "I wish I could sleep through anything like you."

"If you're staying awake, I'm going to need you to drop the pants too." She grinned devilishly.

"Now?" He laughed.

"One more for the road." She smiled, taking another swig from the flask. She pounced on him, her lips pressing against his. She tasted like smokey Titanian Whiskey, but he didn't care. His frenzied hands stripped off her armored jacket and he buried his face into her neck.

CHAPTER THIRTY-EIGHT

Vincent and his command staff were seated on a gathering of ammo boxes staring down a Data display. The sun hadn't even cracked the horizon yet, so its screen was even brighter than normal. The screen was cluttered with small circles, triangles, and squares all of them green in color. Denta had given the slate to Vincent's new aide, Felicity. Clearly, he was still not ready to sit down and talk to him since he had betrayed him.

"The hell is this thing?" Erin looked down at the screen.

"You've never seen one of these before, Captain?" Presan asked.

"You have?" Vincent asked.

"Of course," Presan said. "It is a Combined Arms Tracker," he added, like that title should have been all they needed to know.

"You'll have to forgive me, sir." Erin frowned. "I ain't exactly been a captain for very long." Presan swallowed hard when he realized his mistake.

"Right," he said. "Forgive me." He reached down and fiddled with the screen. The map zoomed in and out. When he zoomed in far enough, he saw each shape had a title. One triangle was labeled *Elysian 1st Squadron* a square was labeled *Clan Armor No. 1.* "It allows Operational Commanders to keep track of everything on the ground no matter where they are. Hypothetically, the Man Above could feed you orders through this thing," he said. The Man Above was a somewhat derogatory nickname for an EDF Task Force Commander who would stay onboard a Capitol Ship and command his troops on the ground from thousands of miles away. "But as we don't have those anymore, it's pretty much an interactive map."

"But it will let you keep track of everything, right?" Vincent said.

"Yes, sir," Presan said. "I was hoping I could—"

"Talk me out of going with them?" He cut him off. "Not going to happen."

Presan sighed in defeat.

"I already tried," Fiona said.

"I thought if he could follow the operation on the Tracker, he would change his mind," Presan said.

"Nice try." Vincent laughed. The deadly silent of the morning air was broken by the roaring of engines. Their backwash blew gale force winds down on the Mons and Erin's garrison cap went flying through the air. Soldiers laying around the landing strip grabbed their gear in vain attempts to stop it from being snatched away.

It was the Fidayi's second transport barge. Its hulking form floated for a moment and landed next to the first, with only inches to spare.

"He pulled it off," Presan said.

"At this point I just assume Pharos has some kind of magical powers that we aren't aware of," Erin said.

Gravel crunched under approaching footsteps, when Vincent turned to see who was approaching, he saw Ezra. He was wearing a crisp, new flight suit. While it was still EDF grey, it had the Elysian Phoenix patch sown over his heart. His black boots shined even more than his bright silver colonel's oak leave rank on his shoulder boards. In his hands he was holding a small brown bottle.

"You look just about fuckin' reborn." Erin laughed. "Er...Colonel," she stammered, still not very good recognizing her new lot in army life. Ezra chuckled.

"Cut that out," he said. "It doesn't suit you. Besides, I can't go into battle looking as homeless as the Consul here." He laughed. Vincent smoothed his beard, suddenly self-conscious. Ezra held the bottle out in front of him. "A pre-battle tradition." He smiled. "I raided it from Denta's stores."

He passed the bottle to Vincent, who took a swig. The smoky burn of Titanian whiskey stung his throat and he passed it to Presan. The old field marshal sniffed the bottle and his nose wrinkled.

"I'd kill for a regular beer," he said, before tipping back a mouthful. He handed it to Erin who took a pull longer than Vincent's and Presan's combined. She smacked her lips

"You and Zinvor have the same taste." Vincent laughed at Presan.

"Speaking of Zinvor, where is he? I thought he was supposed to be glued to your hip?"

"Not before battle," he said. "He is with the other Tsarra doing their affirmations."

"Hm," Ezra said. "Does he have the same mission as the rest of them?" he asked.

"No. He is doomed to be my bodyguard forever it seems," he said. "What are the others doing?"

"You didn't hear?" Erin said, taking another swig from the flask. "They're going to charge Tharsis' defenses to break a hole for the rest of us."

"That's suicidal!" Vincent exclaimed.

"That's the point I suppose," Ezra said. His pointless objection was cut off by the sharp report of a whistle. Ezra looked up. "I think that's our signal." Vincent's heart sank. In the middle of that setting, despite the fact they were sitting around on a bunch of ammo crates, it felt like a gathering of old friends. He didn't want to remember that he and about one million other people were about to board barges and run into gunfire again. He wanted their little gathering to continue for just a minute longer.

The whistle was blown again. Slowly the group began to get up.

"Are you ready?" Presan asked, the question seemingly aimed at the whole group.

"I'm ready for this to be over." Ezra frowned.

"Agreed," Vincent said.

"Like you said," Fiona said. "For better or worse, this ends today."

"I should get going," Ezra said. "Have to make sure the flight crews are getting ready."

"Good luck," Vincent said.

"Same to you, sir." Ezra saluted. He returned the salute. "You can keep that." He nodded at the bottle in Erin's hands.

"I planned on it." She smiled.

*   *   *

The landing strip was packed. Soldiers, Mawr, and Rhai were stuffed shoulder to shoulder in neat lines. In front of them were the gaping maws of the transport barges. In the distance Vincent could see legions of Titanian soldiers in neat ranks marching in lock step onto their transports.

In comparison his army was a mismatched quilt of khaki, black, and grey. The soldiers that had come with the Clan from Elysian were still mostly uniform in their khaki dress and matching body armor and helmets. Since the Gangs had been forcefully disbanded and found joining the newly declared People's Congress of Mars distasteful, they had swelled the Elysian ranks in by the thousands.

Victoria ensured they were broken up and dispersed amongst the units as best he could. The last thing he wanted was small gangs reforming within the ranks. Unfortunately, no one thought to bring several thousand spare uniforms, so the gangers were wearing whatever they had laying around. Most of it was stolen EDF gear in various states of wear and tear. Many of the gangers had managed to buy, find, or steal armor from the thousands of EDF dead left on the Mons after the battle. Many did not.

While he may not have thought much of his own army the jet-black Cohort of Tsarras who were lined up at the front of the line gave him the creeps. While all the other soldiers and Warriors exchanged words or doubled checked their gear as they waited to board. The Tsarras did not. They stood, unmoving, like a giant shadow had descended upon the formation.

Two barge crewmen walked out onto the loading ramp and motioned for the soldiers to begin loading. Shouts from sergeants and officers goaded the soldiers forward.

"I suppose we should get in line," Fiona said.

"Yeah." He breathed. The rumble of engines caught his attention. He looked over at the second barge, parked to the right of the one the soldiers were crowded around. A small parking lot of tanks waited their turns to drive up the ramp. Some of the vehicles had giant Phoenix's painted on the side and sat on huge metal tracks. Some of the others jet black seamless Rhai creations that hovered inches off of the ground silently.

Rhai crewman peeked their heads out of hatches, only to retreat from the cloud of exhaust fumes pouring out of the human tank's engines. He was surprised to see Arai seated on top of a massive tank of her own. It was clear a creation of the Mawr Melds. Plates of metal were bolted together haphazardly to form a hull that was the size of two human tanks.

It had two turrets, each armed with the short, sharp barrels of Rhai plasma cannons. Their sleek appears standing in stark contrast to the rest of the vehicle. The tank was so enormous it sat on four sets of tracks, each in pairs on either side of the hull.

"She's riding with the armor?" Vincent asked.

"Yes," Zinvor grunted. "As she normally does." He couldn't help but become incredibly jealous of her. He longed for meter thick steel walls to protect him from whatever the hell they were about to run into.

Slowly, the soldiers trudged forward into the barge. Suddenly, he felt a nudge at his elbow. He turned and saw Felicity. Her helmet was oversized, and her body armor was swallowing her whole. On her back she was wearing a large radio complete with a four-pronged orbital antenna. The effort required to simply find him caused her to sweat profusely. He could hardly blame her, as her collected gear probably weighed about half as much as she did.

"You made it." He smiled.

"Yeah," she panted. "I think I got the last orbital radio from the stores."

"Good." He nodded. "That way we can talk to the fleet in case we need to pull ourselves out of the fire."

"Let's hope we won't be needing that," Fiona said.

Presan stood off to the side of the slow-moving body of men. He was surrounded by his staff; colonels, majors, and other generals Vincent never bothered to learn the name of. All of their arms were raised in salute, their piercing eyes looking down on the soldiers.

"For the Consul!" Presan boomed.

"For the Consul!" Cheered the soldiers. Vincent's face burned with embarrassment.

"For Elysian!" Vincent countered.

"For Elysian!" The army copied. Presan's face broke into a smirk.

The sound of thousands of boots clanking off of the barge's ramp was nearly deafening. He wasn't sure what he was expecting once inside the craft. Seats perhaps. What he saw instead was row after row of cargo netting. It was strung low from the walls of the barge at about chair height. It was only once soldiers began sitting down on top of the contraption, he realized that they were the seats. Flown into combat like a bunch of cargo. Like material. He thought it was kind of fitting.

The barge's door creaked and moaned as it rolled back up. It closed with a crash and the air locks began to hiss. As its engine started to wind up the barge vibrated and shook like it was under fire. An unknown black substance began to leak from the overhead pipes and tubing. The air stank of burning oil, dust, and unwashed bodies. Soldiers frantically began looking over their weapons as if they had changed in the last few hours.

He watched a few of the older soldiers write their blood type on their boots. He saw others looking longingly down at photographs of some long dead loved one from back on Earth.

The lively chatting of a few minutes ago was over as the reality of their situation was about to set in: they were going to war for the first time.

Most of the frontline soldiers who had fought on Grawluck had died there or been so badly wounded they could no longer fight. This meant that the majority of the soldiers who had enlisted in the Cohort were the support soldiers handling supplies or paperwork. Others were the reserves from miles behind the line. Some of the soldiers had been with him since he fought the Black Coats in the Quarter, but not many. For hundreds of thousands of them, this would be their first taste of real combat.

As the barge lifted into the air, Squadron, Troop, and Platoon leaders leapt into action. They began barking orders. First it was "check your gear!" and then "check your buddy's gear!" Vincent fell in line with the rest of them. He grabbed his short Titanian pathfinder carbine and pulled the charging handle back. It slammed forward with a *clack.* He went through the pouches hanging from his armor. One pouch held six magazines, around two-hundred and ten rounds. Another held five grenades. He unholstered his Riten and spun its chambers. It clicked through each one smoothly.

He felt a cold hand slide over his own. It was Fiona. She wasn't fumbling through her gear like a rookie as he was. Instead she was getting in one last cigarette, the smoke curling up above her head and mingling with the fetid barge air.

"We have to stop going on dates like this." She forced a laugh.

"When this is all over, we can go out to dinner and a movie." She grinned. "In Lunar City."

"It's a date."

The barge rocked and swayed, and soldiers fought to stay on their cargo net seats.

"Five minutes!" came a crackling voice through the barge's intercom. "five minutes until touch down!"

CHAPTER THIRTY-NINE

Vincent's body tensed and his heart began to race. Five minutes out. This was when the EDF would hammer their ships with anti-ship fire. He remembered back in the Quarter when he was zipping over their lines aboard the *Shanna* and got smacked out of the air like an annoying insect. He thought back to Grawluck and watching the ships all around him erupt into flames in the middle of the planet's perpetual darkness.

He knew their time was coming. He felt the barge jerk around, pulling a tight left turn to bring the rear of the ship forward. The cargo nets they were sitting on swayed back and forth and several soldiers fell to the oil slicked ground. The Tsarra marched through the lines of cargo nets and took their place next to the ramp.

"This is weird," Erin said. "I thought we would be getting torn apart by now."

"Maybe Ezra's wing took out their anti-ship batteries?" he mused.

"Doubt it," she said. "They would have a hard time mapping them without scouts or pathfinders on the ground. Orbital scans only do so much. They were going almost blind. And anyone with half a brain would have held their fire to target the troop transports."

"What the hell is Brusilov planning."

"Maybe they're saving it for when we are an easy target on the ground." Fiona frowned.

"Make sure Presan is updated on this." Vincent turned to Felicity.

"On it," she said and began fiddling with her radios.

"I don't fuckin' like this," Erin said.

"Me either." He sighed. "Ideas?"

"Once the Tsarra hit the ground, we hold back. I can call in strikes on the positions that target them," Erin said. She saw Vincent's facial expression drop. "They're out here to get killed anyway. You really think any of them are going to survive the breakthrough? We might as well use their suicides to our advantage." He sighed again. As much as he hated it, she was right. He couldn't tell them to hold back if he wanted too.

"Fine." He nodded. "Spread the word to the Squadrons. No one is to advance until ordered."

"Yes, sir," Felicity said, and began talking into the radio.

"How many squadrons do we even have now?" Fiona asked.

"Uhh..." Vincent didn't want to admit he had no idea how many soldiers he just issued orders too.

"We have five Squadrons, sir," Felicity said, before going back to her radio set.

"See?" he said. "This is why I needed an aide."

Fiona laughed. "This is why you need a damn clue."

A warning siren blared, an ear-piercing shriek and made everyone wince and cover their ears. "Prepare for landing!" Boomed the intercom.

"Get on your feet you lazy bastards!" Screamed a commander.

"Weapons check!" bellowed another.

The landing ramp whined and hissed as it slowly made its way back down. The punishing Martian wind cut into the troop compartment and Vincent covered his eyes with his arm. Through the blasting dirt and dust he could see they were only a few hundred feet above the ground and quickly making their decent. The Tharsis skyline jutted out of the barren Martian landscape like a well-maintained garden. The low, uniform block houses and cookie-cutter high rises that made up any Committee controlled city loomed before them.

Unlike most committee-controlled cities however, thick black smoke poured from the tops of many of the buildings. The smoke rose in pillars before coming back down, blanketing the city in a thick blanket. He could see the shapes of dozens of Reapers buzzing around the city, their weapons silent.

"What the hell is going on?" Fiona yelled over the wind.

"I have no idea!" Vincent spat, gritty sand finding its way to his mouth. "Get Ezra on the radio!"

"Here sir!" Felicity handed Vincent her headset. He placed the headphones over his head, the ear cups slick with her sweat.

"Sir?" Came the voice of Ezra.

"Yeah. What is going on?"

"We aren't sure," he said. "It looks like the EDF set a bunch of fires so we couldn't see their defenses. We aren't taking any fire either, though."

"What are your suggestions?"

"I'd move up real slow. They're planning a trap of some kind. With Brusilov nothing is as it seems."

"Right. Thanks," he said, handing the head set back to Felicity.

"And?" Erin asked. "What did he say?"

"He has no idea." He sighed.

"Just the way I like it." Fiona grinned and racked the bolt on her rifle.

The barge jolted as it touched down on the ground. The landing was so rough that many of the over encumbered soldiers were dragged back to the ground by the weight of their gear. True to their mission the Tsarra charged down the ramp, letting out a roar as they did so. Zinvor stood next to Vincent, eyeing them with a bit of jealousy.

"You can join them if you'd like," he said, only half-joking.

"That is not the plan Paterazm has for me," he grunted.

"Sorry buddy. Guess you're stuck with me forever," he said.

Soldiers cautiously made their way out of the barge. Two long lines snaked their way out and formed into something resembling a military formation on either side of the barge. Some soldiers laid down in the dirt, their rifles up at the ready while others took a knee. Vincent awaited a barrage of machine gun and artillery fire from the city that never came.

The Tsarras were so fast in their dash towards the city that they had nearly covered half the distance in the time it took for the Cohort to get off of the barge. Arai's barge landed a few hundred feet away, its tanks rolling down the ramp. They organized themselves into a line, like a broad armored wall, for the infantry to get behind.

Erin's scouts had deployed a large digital scope, though it looked more like a fat, green, box the size of a suitcase rather than a scope. One of the scouts fumbled with the controls on the side, causing the scope to whirl and click as it zoomed in on the burning city.

"Anything?" he asked.

"Not a damn thing," she cursed. "The smoke is throwing off the thermal sights."

"Shit," he said. "We really are going in blind."

"Seems that way," she said. "I'm sorry, sir."

"It's not your fault Brusilov is torching a city to slow us down," he said. "Give the order to move out," he said.

Arai jumped down off of her tank and met with Vincent on the ground.

"Curious timing for a fire," she said.

"It's blocking our air wing and our scout's sights. He knew what he was doing."

"Hm," she said. "The Tsarra are already within city limits. We must join them."

"Agreed." He nodded. She clambered up the back of her tank and settled into its commander's hatch. Before long, the armored wall began creeping towards the city.

Vincent could hear is heart pounding in his temples as the prickling feeling of nervousness creeped up his back. He held his carbine close to his chest and his eyes darted around, looking for anything through the smoke. He couldn't see anything. He hoped the EDF soldiers on the other side of the smoke were just as handicapped as he was. At least on Grawluck he could see the Alliance positions from miles away.

The soldiers around him were just as on edge. They had their rifles up and pointing at an enemy that they couldn't see. Commanders busily talking over their radio headsets. Hundreds of different Commanders all talking over each other trying to figure out what was happening. Sergeant Major Victoria appeared among the throng of soldiers, screaming and yelling.

"Spread the fuck out!" he yelled. "If one goddamn burst of machine gun fire gets through the gaps in that armor your whole Troop will get wiped out!" A young lieutenant stammered and sputtered his words in response before frantically waving his arms to order his soldiers to spread out.

"And you!" he screamed at young Trooper. "Where in the fuck is your helmet?"

"I...I" The Trooper fought to find words.

"I don't want your excuses. If you survive this shit heap you come find me and I will straighten you out!" Vincent tried not to laugh. In the middle of all of this he was stomping around and still managing to scare the younger soldiers.

"Yes, Sergeant Major!" The Trooper squeaked. Victoria marched up to where Vincent was and rendered a sharp salute.

"Everything okay?" he asked.

"Oh." Victoria laughed. "You saw that?"

"It was hard to miss."

"Just lighting a fire under their ass. It keeps their head in the game." He smiled.

"If you say so." Vincent shrugged. The wind had changed directions, pushing the acrid, black smoke into the face of the marching army. Combined with the exhaust from the tanks, it was like they were in the middle of a gas attack. Everyone frantically covered their faces with their sleeves or hats. No matter what they did everyone was breathing in a thick cloud of toxic fumes and dust.

Sensing their desperation for air the tanks picked up the pace and the soldiers ran at a slow jog to keep up. Eventually they came through the worst of the smoke, now it formed some eerie barrier. It draped down at their heels closing off the sky above and the ground behind them.

The Tharsis skyline once again came into view. In the center of the city, the largest building stuck out of the city like a grey spike. Hundreds of stories tall, it must have been, like back in his home district, the city's Committee Center. Fire lapped out of thousands of the building's windows, spreading ash and embers down onto the surrounding city and spreading the fire. Rows of grey block houses were already gutted from the growing fire with geysers of flame bursting through their roofs.

The Tanks broke the wall formation and paired off into their platoons. They quickly began to make their way towards their assigned positions in the city. The Tsarras stood around at the City's entrance, milling about in confusion. They had charged headlong into a fight that simply wasn't there. It was then that the horror of the city began to be seen.

A large metal, arching, sign across the central road heading into the city. It read simply "Tharsis". Hanging from the sign was dozens of bodies, their hands tied behind their backs. Men, women, and children swung in the wind. Their lifeless, bulging eyes gazed down on the advancing soldiers as their purple, swollen tongues lolled out of their mouths. Around each one of their necks read a hand-written sign that read *TRAITOR.*

"What in the fuck?" Fiona gasped. Soldiers stop to gawk at the sight. Many of them taking off their helmets and covering their hearts with them.

"What are you looking at?" Victoria screamed at them. "Get fucking moving! Sergeants, get ahold of your soldiers!" The soldiers pulled themselves away from the scene and quickly began advancing into the city.

"look," Erin said. She pointed over to a pile of baggage stacked under the corner of the sign. "They were trying to run."

"And they strung them up." Victoria scowled. "Animals."

"Regular EDF wouldn't have done this," Felicity said.

"I seem to remember almost getting strung up just like them by regular EDF soldiers once," Fiona said.

"It's true," Vincent added. "Make sure the soldiers know anyone who executes a prisoner will be shot."

"Yes, sir," Victoria said. Vincent could see the grizzled sergeant major did not look too pleased at the order.

"Just because they did shit like this doesn't mean we can act like them in return, Aron." Victoria did not seem convinced, but he did not voice his objection.

"Of course, sir." Victoria nodded before turning and walking down the street towards the soldiers. Vincent heard his booming voice assaulting every soldier he came across until it faded off into the distance.

"Someone cut those poor bastards down," Vincent said. A group of passing soldiers heard them. They dropped their packs and began to climb the sign, knives in hand. As soldiers streamed into the city, he kept expecting to hear the sound of gunfire any minute. But it never came.

"Word from Field Marshal Presan is to have the soldiers begin clearing the buildings that aren't on fire," Felicity said looking up from her radio. "He thinks they could be hiding inside, trying get us into a position where they can pop out and surround us."

"Go ahead and spread the word," he said. Presan's fears were not unfounded. Being trapped in the middle of a city and besieged by all sides from tens of thousands of different windows and alleyways sounded terrifying. He checked his watch. They had been in the city for almost an hour, wouldn't they have sprung their trap by now?

Reapers flew in low, their troop compartments open. They touched down on the roofs of skyscrapers and dislodged squads of soldiers to clear them. Rhai soldiers, clad in shimmering black armor emerged from houses, empty handed. Soldiers, their rifles slung over their shoulders, exited what looked like what had been the District Food Distribution Center. Its shelves were bare. It had clearly been picked clean, leaving nothing behind.

"Sir," Felicity said.

"Let me guess? They found more nothing?" he said, probably a bit too harshly.

"No," she said. "A group of soldiers from Dog Troop found something they said we should see."

*   *   *

Vincent and his command staff made their way through the cluttered, clogged streets of the city until they found their way to a large grey building. The single-story structure lacked windows. Cameras lined its roof near guard towers that now sat empty. By the front door, a sign read *Tharsis Central Detention Center*. A few soldiers lazed around outside of it, nominally on guard.

When he approached, they both came to attention and saluted. One, an older looking Martian with a blond beard sighed.

"It's a fucking slaughterhouse in there," he said. "Here, sir." He handed Vincent a hanker chief. When he held it to his nose, he discovered it had been soaked in booze. He walked up the flight of stairs that led to large double door. Emblazoned across them was the Eagle and Star flag. When he pushed the doors open the smell hit him.

It was a smell so strong he could physically feel it wash over his face as he stepped inside. The stench burned his face and his

493

eyes began to water. He quickly put the hanker chief to his face to stop himself from retching. It was a smell of rot, shit, and blood.

The rest of his staff wasn't so lucky as Felicity began to dry heave. Fiona gasped, doubled back, and ran out of the room. Zinvor watched her with a look of confusion, not seeming to notice the smell.

The layout of the detention center brought Vincent back to his short incarceration prior to his sentencing. From the sterile white floors, to the Committee propaganda posters mounted on the walls, the center was a carbon copy of the one back on Earth.

Walking down the entry hallway, he passed the front desk where he knew under normal conditions there would be an ethics officer to read off the condemned person's charges before throwing them into the holding area. The large sliding door next to the desk, normally locked, was jammed open.

Once he walked through the door the smell overpowered the liquor-soaked rag. He fought back the urge to vomit and attempted to breath only through his mouth. But he could taste the toxic air. Now that he was further into the building there was no mistaking the overwhelming stench of death.

The uniform lines of slate grey benches faced a wall sized flat screen display. The screen was still on. The rules of the center crawled slowly across the screen. No speaking unless spoken to by an officer from the Ethics Committee. No questioning your charges until brought to the Committee. No personal effects allowed in the holding area. You will proceed without pause to the door at the rear of the holding area when your name is called. Any violation of these rules is an affront to the Chairman and will be dealt with accordingly.

The rules looped back around and restarted.

Elysian soldiers milled around, their faces covered in

whatever kind of cloth they could get their hands on to shield themselves. It was in the central holding room Vincent discovered the source of the smell.

Hundreds of grey uniformed soldiers lay face down in neat rows on the ground. A thick pool of sticky blood had mixed together and covered the once white floor. Each one had been shot a single time at the base of the neck. A soldier wearing captain's bars on his collars approached Vincent.

"Welcome to the party, sir," he said, his voice muffled by a tan shirt he had wrapped around his entire face.

"What the hell is this?" Vincent asked.

"Damned if I know, sir," the captain shrugged. "Word is they've been finding sites like these all over the city though."

"Any idea why they were shot?"

"We have someone going through the records right now." The captain shook his head. "Evil bastards, but they kept meticulous records. Looks like each one had their rank ripped off their uniforms before they got shot."

"Poor bastards probably just wanted to surrender." Vincent shook his heads.

"This has the Black Coats written all over it," the captain said.

"Why would they not also burn this building?" Zinvor asked.

"They wanted me to find it," Vincent spat. "Send a message to show what happens when you throw your lot in with the *Great Traitor.*"

"Trying to intimidate us?" The captain laughed. "I thought this Brusilov was supposed to be smart."

"Sir!" Felicity moaned, her sleeve trying in vain to block the smell from assaulting her senses. Her eyes cried out that she wanted to be anywhere else than where she was at that very second. "Units have captured the City's Committee building. We should probably get going."

"I guess that is my signal to leave," Vincent said. "Thank you, Captain. let me know if you find anything here."

"Yes, sir."

Vincent tried not to make it too obvious he was happy to get out the reeking house of horrors and back out into the street. The air outside was thick with the scent of burning smoke, but anything was better than where he had just come from. Soldiers in the street were picking buildings seemingly at random and kicking the doors in.

"Welcome back," Fiona said. "Learn anything?"

"Brusilov is still an asshole. What is going on out here?"

"Presan ordered the city be cleared room by room, nothing is to be spared." She took a pull from a cigarette. The smell of her cigarette was somehow a welcome relief. "So far they've just found some civilians who managed to hide from whatever the hell the Black Coats were up to. Not a single man above the age of ten though."

"Think Brusilov drafted them all?" he asked.

"Either that or just shot them." A chill ran down his spine as his mind flashed back to the execution grounds he had just left.

They walked through the streets watching sergeants and officers direct soldiers towards buildings that had not yet been cleared. Other soldiers ran buckets of water towards the burning buildings, trying to put them out. Mawr Warriors gathered in groups to watch the humans in confusion, not entirely sure what they were doing.

"Any word on Denta and Erik?" he asked.

"The EDF's front broke pretty easily by the sounds of it," Fiona said. "By the time we were in the city, so were they."

"Sounds like Denta's plan is working then." He sighed.

"Don't act so excited." Fiona laughed. Vincent rolled his eyes.

"Forgive me if I feel like this all going just a bit too well so far."

They walked by a group of soldiers who were tearing down a Committee billboard that read "Strength in the Chairman". A fire had been started in the middle of the street and it was being fed by the collection of posters that the Committee had hung around the city. A red banner that read "Death to the Great Traitor!" curled up and wilted as the flames ingulfed it.

The crowded streets gave way to a wide-open city center. In the middle of the center a large ornate white marble fountain jutted from the ground. The once flowing fountain ran dry. Emerging from the center was a giant statute of an EDF officer, a sword held triumphantly over his head. A group of soldiers were busily tying a rope around the statue's neck and tying it to the tow hitch of a waiting Troop Carrier.

As he got closer, he saw a name plate was stamped to the base of the statue. It read *Governor General Brusilov.* Vincent sighed, suddenly wishing the soldiers would tear the damn thing down faster. He jumped at the sudden sound of gunfire. He turned and saw Fiona laughing, her smoking Riten in her hand. A large chunk had been taken out of the statue's head and had fell into the fountain's dry reservoir.

At the head of the city center was city's Committee Headquarters. A wide set of stairs led up to the grey, one hundred floor, obelisk that had once acted as the command center of the entire city. Smoke poured from the top floors, but soldiers milled about casually at its doors. Scraps of burning paper and debris fell like a blizzard, piling up in banks at the building's base.

The soldiers saw them approaching and quickly stubbed out cigarettes, straightened their uniforms, and unslung their rifles.

"Good evening, sir!" One of them called out, an older corporal with a thick, drooping mustache.

"Hey, guys," he said. "Is the building secure?"

"Yes, sir!" he said. "We have several squads of soldiers doing their best to put the fire out on the upper floors. Sergeant Major Victoria thinks it was Brusilov's personal quarters."

"Sounds about right," Vincent said. "No EDF at all then?"

"None, sir." The corporal frowned. "Bastards gone and ran." The doors to the building swung open and there stood Victoria.

"Shouldn't you rabble be patrolling?" he cursed. The soldiers exchanged worried looks and ran off. "Our scouts have reached the northern edge of the city, sir." He beamed, his wrinkled face creasing with a smile.

"And?"

"Nothing. Not a damn thing," Victoria said. "It seems like the Earth Defense Forces have abandoned the city entirely."

"So...we won?" he asked.

"We won."

CHAPTER FORTY

Vincent stood in front of a window that spanned length of the entire room. In front of him, ninety stories down, lay the entirety of Tharsis. The fires had long since gone out, replaced by the cook fires of thousands of soldiers. Brusilov had made sure to destroy anything of use to the invading army before he withdrew. Food stores, ammo, and fuel had all been taken with them when they ran. The retreating EDF even made sure to blow up the power plant, plunging the city into darkness.

While everyone knew there would be irony in staying the night in Brusilov's private quarters, he had made sure to torch it before he withdrew making sure not to give them the satisfaction. They would instead have to settle for the Committee of City Ethics as a billet, ten floors down. The dropping night temperatures had chilled the building. It had the effect of turning the unheated concrete walls into something akin to a refrigerator.

The double doors swung open with a groan. Blackwell and

Felicity entered the room. Felicity was carrying a tray with several mess kits on it. Fiona rolled over from her bedroll moaning in annoyance.

"Can't a girl get some damn sleep around here," she whined.

"She can if she doesn't want to eat." Blackwell frowned. Fiona groaned and covered her face with her blanket. "It's fresh meat," Blackwell added enticingly. Fiona tossed off her blanket and sat up.

Felicity sat the tray of tins down on a large metal desk. A nameplate read *Chief of Ethical Law Enforcement Edwin J Wheeler*. Fiona slapped the nameplate onto the ground and sat on top of the desk. She grabbed the first tin and opened it. A thick stew with meat, vegetables, and a piece of warm bread topped the entire thing. The smell curled into Vincent's nose and he suddenly remembered how hungry he was. He grabbed a tin and sat next to Fiona on the desk.

"Where did you get this?" he asked.

"Search parties found it amongst the personal stores of our friend Brusilov. One of the few stores we've found so far." Blackwell snickered. "So, Dinner is on him."

"Any word on Denta and Erik?" Vincent asked between mouthfuls. He didn't dare ask what kind of meat he was eating. He hadn't seen anything alive on Mars outside of half dead pack animals and as far as he knew all of the farms had long since been destroyed.

"Their last update has them at the gates of the Planetary Governor's Headquarters," Felicity said, hardly holding back a smile.

"It seems that bastard Brusilov wasn't as smart as we all gave him credit for." Blackwell laughed.

"I don't know," Fiona said, pointing a plastic field spoon at him. "He outsmarted all of us and Arai back on Elysian and jacked half of the damned reserve air wing."

"Even Pharos didn't see that one coming," Vincent added. "And he sees everything."

"Right." Blackwell cleared his throat. "Anyway, Field Marshal Presan wanted me to let you know he will be moving his headquarters into the city tomorrow now that we have secured it."

"Secured it," laughed Fiona, brown flakes of stew flying from her mouth. "That old bastard abandoned it and now we have a city with no power and a bunch of starving, scared civilians."

"Are you always this negative?" Felicity scowled at her.

"Oh, I'm sorry were you talking?" Fiona sarcastically cupped an ear. "I'm afraid my ears can't hear an officer who hasn't fought in an actual battle." Vincent stifled a laugh and forced himself to be composed.

"Thank you," Vincent said, bringing the subject back to the task at hand. "I'm glad Presan can come enjoy the jewel of our campaign." He feigned righteousness and Blackwell laughed.

"Don't be too upset that you're missing out on the fighting," Blackwell said. "By the sounds of it, Denta's boys are getting it pretty bad out there, and honestly I want no part of it if we can help it."

"Agreed."

Blackwell smiled. "Well, we will leave you be to get some rest."

"Thank you." Vincent smiled, he was doing his best to contain himself, but as soon as the two walked out of the room and closed the door behind him he upended the tin into his mouth, drinking the stew back. He felt the warm sauce drip into his beard, but he didn't care. He was so sick of Titanian Army rations that anything resembling a home cooked meal was otherworldly.

"Your aide has a mouth on her." Fiona frowned.

He laughed. "She's learning from you, you know."

"She's got a long way to go then." She grinned and wiped the stew from his chin.

A Reaper circled above the city center. The statue of Brusilov that had once stood proudly in the middle of the square had been ripped down and dragged away. The last anyone had seen it several soldiers had set in on fire and dumped it into a nearby ravine.

A small gathering of soldiers and civilians crowded the city center. The civilians were still unsure of the new occupiers. They weren't sure if they were supposed to treat them like oppressors or liberators. They gave the Elysian soldiers and especially their alien allies a wide birth.

The Reaper touched down gently in the middle of the gathering. The troop compartment door slid open and Presan stepped out. The soldiers in attendance rendered him countless salutes and the old field marshal was grinning ear to ear. Vincent shook his hand and Presan pulled him in for a hug.

"We did it huh?" grinned the old man.

"Looks that way." Vincent smiled. "Word from Denta?"

"No." Presan shook his head. "But I've been following him on the tracker. I didn't believe his plan would work either, but he punched right through the EDF defenses like he said he would. His forces will be at the gates of the Military District of the city soon enough."

"So, now what?" Vincent raised an eyebrow. Presan smiled again and nodded to his aide. An overweight captain with a goatee and a bowl cut. The man was struggling to pull a trunk off of the Reaper, with the help of the Reaper's crew.

"Our army is young, and the influx of these new gangers complicates things. We have quite a bit of reorganization to work on."

"That sounds terribly boring." Vincent sighed.

"Don't worry, sir. You put me in charge to work on these things. From what Blackwell and Haagen have told me you have quite a few other things to work on."

"Other things?" Vincent asked. Felicity cleared her throat behind him.

"Civilian administration of Elysian's Human Quarter, sir." She whispered.

"Ugh." He sighed. "Can I put that off for a little longer?"

Presan cleared his throat. "I do not recommend it, sir."

"Fine," Vincent said, throwing up his hands in defeat. He turned, getting ready to lead Presan to their quarters when the crowd began to grow restless around them. Soldiers began to yell, and civilians ran even further away from them. Mawr and Rhai soldiers looked around, unsure of what was happening.

The scowling face of Victoria burst through the throng of soldiers. He was dragging an EDF soldier by his uniform collar, a major by the look of it. His hands were tied behind his back with repurposed wire.

"Unhand me! This is no way to treat an officer of the Chairman's Army!" The major screamed. His nose was bleeding and his lip was cracked.

"What is going on, Sergeant Major?" Presan asked. Victoria dropped the major like a sack of flour on the ground, straightened himself up and saluted.

"Sir!" Victoria said. "Captain Olympus' scouts found this Black Coat sheltering in the basement of a civilian's home in the Northern District." Vincent exchanged glances with Presan.

"How do we know he is a Black Coat?" Vincent asked.

"I saw him on Elysian!" Screamed a voice from the crowd.

"Me too!" Yelled another. Vincent scratched his beard and turned back towards Presan.

"What should we do?" he asked.

"Shoot him," Presan answered flatly. "We cannot allow these animals to live after what they have done."

Vincent took a deep breath. The major sat on the ground like a petulant child, his hate filled eyes staring directly at him. Every part of Vincent wanted to draw his Riten and drop the man where he sat. But he knew he couldn't.

"I gave an order to not shoot prisoners." Vincent frowned. "I can hardly go about giving orders to the soldiers and then ignore them myself, can I?"

Vincent reached down and tore the major's rank from his collar and tossed it onto the street. "Fuck you!" The major screamed, spit flew from his mouth and he fought to get his feet under him, the strong hand of Victoria on his shoulder made his flailing futile.

"The people are watching, sir," Presan said into his ear. "We must show them we aren't weak."

"No, Presan," Vincent began. "We must show them we are different." He nodded to a group of nearby soldiers. "Take this man away. He will be imprisoned until we can bring him back to Elysian to stand trial for what he and his people did in this city." The soldiers nodded, grabbing the major and dragging him away. Vincent began to notice the crowd was exchanging hushed whispers, the Elysian soldiers and the Tharsis civilians talking amongst each other for the first time. They were all looking at him.

"I...uhh," he started. He fumbled, trying to come with something to say. He suddenly regretted skipping out on his public speaking class back in Ethics School. Or most of his classes for that matter. "The Chairman is gone. He's never coming back. We will make sure of it." He sighed. "I don't know where the future is going to lead us, but I can tell you as long as we are here those goddamn Black Coats aren't going to hurt anyone anymore."

"I would rather die tomorrow fighting a free man than live one more day under the boot of that despot!" Presan bellowed. The crowd cheered at his words and Presan patted him on the shoulder. "Your public speaking needs some work." He grinned.

Vincent laughed. "What part of me doesn't need work?"

"You letting that Black Coat walk really seems to have brought everyone together," Fiona said, frowning.

Vincent shifted uncomfortably.

"What?" she asked, seeing him.

"I've never executed anyone for a cheering crowd before." He sighed. "I don't intend on starting here."

"We normally use a firing squad for things like that," Presan said.

"I couldn't order them to execute someone just because I wanted them too. Didn't feel right," he said.

"I would have done it." Fiona shrugged. He shot her a sideway glance. "Wouldn't even have to give the order. I'd do it for fun."

"I'll keep that in mind for next time." The crowd, intermingling for the first time, began to peter out back into town. "Shall we?" Vincent turned towards Presan who nodded.

Before they could go anywhere Fiona froze, her eyes locked onto the skies. "What in the hell?"

Vincent followed her gaze. In the deep red Martian sky he could make out the small form of a Reaper. It was coming towards the city quickly and was trailing fire and smoke. It looped wildly through the sky. The pilot was fighting a losing battle to keep it in the air.

"Is that one of ours?" Vincent asked, panic rising in his voice. "Or one of theirs?"

"Look at the tail!" Fiona responded. The Reaper swung around. Through the stream of black smoke Vincent could see the worn stencil of a Titanian Eagle showing through. "Why the hell is he crash landing all the way out here?"

"Everyone get the hell out of the square!" Presan bellowed. The once cheerful crowd made a run for it, with the rest of the Command staff trying to keep up.

Ship was rapidly losing altitude. It was becoming clear that the pilot was no longer trying to land and instead was just trying to control how badly they crashed. The pilot fought hard, bringing the stricken ship's nose up just in time. The ship slammed into the ground with a thunderous jolt. Sparks erupted from underneath the Reaper and showered onto the fleeing crowd as the stricken ship screeched across the ground. It finally came to a stop when it slammed into the fountain, breaking it into dozens of pieces.

"Get a medic!" Someone screamed from the crowd. Vincent took off running to the ship. He grabbed ahold of the troop compartment door and pulled, but it wouldn't budge. A soldier jammed his bayonet into the crack of the door and pried on it like a crowbar. The door gave way. Inside was several limp soldiers, their limbs and torsos twisted at odd angles from the crash. The ship's floor was covered in thick pool of blood.

Medics pushed through way through the crowd and began to pull the men from the ship. They flopped bonelessly onto waiting stretchers.

"Consul Solaris? Is that you?" the pilot asked. He pulled off his helmet, blood had dripped down his dark Titanian skin and was going into his eyes. His co-pilot sitting next to him was slumped over the controls, unmoving. The controls had collapsed downward, pinning them in. Blood oozed from where their legs should have been.

"Yeah, I'm here. Are you okay?"

"I think my legs are broken," he moaned, wiping the blood from his eyes. "Sir, I have a message from Field Marshal Denta. It's urgent."

"From Denta?" he asked, confused. "Why doesn't he just use the radio?"

"It was a trap!" the pilot yelled. "Brusilov allowed his center to collapse and let them drive right in." The pilot coughed and specks of blood flew out. "He had tens of thousands of soldiers in hiding, once Denta got to the Military District they pounced on his exposed flanks and encircled them!" Je paused to catch his breath. "The bastard must have done something to the radio arrays in the city because all of our transmissions have been jammed ever since they launched their trap." The pilot dug into the pocket of his flight suit and handed Vincent a small scrap of paper. The medics had finally worked around to the pilot's door and began to force back the control panel in an attempt to free the man's legs. The pilot howled with pain as they worked.

Vincent unfolded the paper. Denta's neat, looping handwriting looked out of place on the crinkled paper. The note said: "*Encircled as of 0230 hours. Comms jammed. Unable to contact fleet support. Send reinforcements immediately. Will fight until last. FM Denta.*"

The doors slammed behind them as Arai and Pharos joined the Command Staff. Presan's aide had brought out several maps charting routes over the vast wastelands between Tharsis and Victoria. Maps of Victoria were laid out with the last known locations of Denta's soldiers. Another data display with the units of the Clan sat next to it.

"So, what are our options?" Arai grumbled.

"We attack and we do it now," Vincent said immediately. "What other option is there?"

"Why wouldn't it be another trap?" Presan asked. "He walked right into his last one. We should dig in around Tharsis and see what happens."

"You mean, do nothing." Arai frowned.

"I— " Presan stuttered. "That isn't what I said."

"But it is what you meant," Arai said.

"Don't put words in my mouth!" he yelled. "If Denta is lost, that is one entire army group gone!" he clapped his hands together to underline his point. "We cannot risk our second!"

"We can't risk losing one at all!" Vincent countered. "We have to save them."

"If I may," Pharos cut in. "Where do you think we obtained intelligence regarding the hidden bases of the Gangers after we discovered them raiding our supply lines?"

"I thought you used scouts?" Vincent asked. The way Pharos always had a tendency to speak like he was the smartest person in whatever room was standing in always irked Vincent. The spy master reminded him of a teacher's pet who would gloat about their grades.

"Not quite," he said. "My agents gleaned the information from captured EDF documents."

"This is hardly the time for rhetorical questioning," Presan said. "Can we get to the point?"

"The EDF knew about the gangers. I suspect Murat and Marcus were double agents of some kind, but they were executed before I was allowed to interrogate them." He shot a glance in Vincent's direction. "Brusilov was almost certainly using them to drive a wedge into our alliance. He would know how tenuous it would be, and as we found out recently, he was very right in that."

"So, they did that knowing we would eventually find them out and want to double cross Denta by capturing them first?"

Vincent gasped. "And he knew we would most likely support the Martians over the Titanians when that time came."

"Yes." Pharos nodded. "Meaning, he hoped the situation between us at the time of the offensive he already knew was coming had become so bad that when he launched his encirclement plan we wouldn't want to commit to relieving Denta in order to save our own position."

"Why are you only telling us this now?" Presan pounded a fist on the desk.

"I was unaware of the nature of the trap," Pharos said, clearly disappointed. "It was truly a masterful move." They shrugged. "We did warn Denta that his plan was foolhardy. He did not listen."

"We must relieve Denta at once," Arai said, her voice let it be known that no other arguments would be considered.

"We can't just pick up and go," Presan said. "It will take hours to get everything packed up and ready to move again."

"This is time we do not have," she said flatly. "We must be ready to depart within an hour. Leave everything that is not needed for an immediate attack."

"That is insane!" Presan yelled.

"Was there something in my order that made it seem like it was up for debate, *Field Marshal*?" Shouted Arai, using his rank as a curse. She slammed a fist into the metal desk. When her hand moved away a large crater was left in its surface. Presan gathered himself, going to the position of attention and bowing.

"Yes, Warlord, of course," he said. Vincent notice his knuckles were turning white at his sides. "Forgive my outburst."

"You humans," she said, pinching her chin. "You let emotion take control of you too often. Why do you not simply act?"

"It is our emotions that make us human," Vincent countered. "Acting without compassion or without concern for others. That would make us as bad as the Anarchs."

"Human compassion sounds like Mawr cowardice." Arai folded her thick arms across her armored chest.

"You know I am not a coward," Vincent shot back. She knew the Mawr thought process was much different than his own but calling him and his people cowards was not something he was going to stand for. He was sure he was out of bounds challenging the Warlord, but he really didn't care. "And you know damn well my people aren't cowards!"

"Consul, you forget yourself," Pharos said, trying to be helpful. It was the closest the spy master had ever come to telling him to shut up.

"No, she forgets herself!" he yelled. He felt his face get hot and his fist ball up. "She forgets everything we have been through together." Vincent took a step closer. Every second Arai didn't flatten him with a punch was another surprise. "You Mawr always talk about honor and respect, well it is about time you show us the respect we deserve damnit!"

Arai took a step towards him. Though she was a full head shorter than him, her bulk was nearly three times his own. Her piercing eyes bore directly into his. This was it. He knew it. She was going to deck him and pulverize his jaw into bone dust. Instead a grin spread across her wide face.

"Earn it," she said in a low growl. "The Clan will *give* you nothing." She turned her back to Vincent, dismissively. "We leave in one hour."

The outskirts of Tharsis had been transformed into a field of chaos. The barges had landed only a few hundred feet where they had landed two days before. Hundreds of thousands of men, women, and aliens bumped shoulders. Hundreds of small, uneven lines formed as they pushed and shoved their way back onto the ships.

The soldiers were traveling much lighter this time around. Due to Arai's forced march orders, Presan had directed them to ditch anything and everything they wouldn't need to fight as soon as they hit the ground. Sergeants and officers were screaming for the soldiers to line up by units, but it was lost in the ruckus of their panicked mobilization.

"This is a goddamn mess." Presan rubbed his temples.

"I am slightly impressed they could pull this mess off at all," Vincent said.

"We don't even know how many people we are missing. Not a single unit leader had enough time to count their personnel. Only Paterazm knows how many of them are sleeping off a night of drinking in a local's bedroom." He sighed. Vincent laughed at the old Earthian invoking the name of the Mawr god of war to curse his own soldiers.

"I'll let you know how this all goes when we land," Vincent said. "I'm sure it is bound to be interesting to say the least."

"You won't have to," Presan said. "I'm going with you this time."

"But—" Vincent began.

"They're jamming our transmissions, keeping our air support at arm's length..." Presan seemingly thought out loud. He reached into his pocket and pulled out a cigarette, lit it, and took a deep pull. "I'm going to have to run this the old-fashioned way." He blew out a thick cloud of smoke. "Damn it has been too long."

"I didn't know you smoked," Vincent said.

"I don't. Or at least I didn't. Promised the old lady I would quit after I got home from Mars." He laughed. "If she can see me now, she would slap me." Vincent looked at him, confused. He had never spoken of a family before, though he never really talked about himself at all. "She was on Earth," he said. "Gone. Like everyone else."

"I'm sorry," Vincent said, unsure of how to respond. "I didn't know."

"I would have retired last year," he said, smoke coming out of his nose. "If it wasn't for one last action on Grawluck, I would have been back at home when it all ended."

"Do you wish you were?" he asked. "With her, I mean."

"I did," he said. "At first." He tapped ashes onto the ground. "But now? Look at what we've made. Look at what we are about to do. She would understand she will have to wait just a little longer for us to meet in the great beyond. My soldiers, my people. They still need me."

A throat was cleared behind them, and Vincent turned around. Fiona, Felicity, and Zinvor were standing together. Felicity, unlike every other soldier, still had a large backpack, along with her radio. Knowing her, she hadn't even unpacked during their one night of calm.

"I don't mean to interrupt but we should board," Felicity said.

"If we miss our flight, I'm pretty sure Arai will shoot us," Fiona said. "Well, she will definitely shoot you." She grinned at Vincent.

"Only if I'm lucky," he said. He bent down and picked up his carbine from the ground and slung it over his shoulder. He checked to make sure all of his gear was still in place and joined the line of unruly soldiers.

A tank's engines roared as they backed into their barge one more time. Vincent managed to catch one last glimpse of Arai's massive command tank, this time it had multiple flags and banners fluttering in the wind. Though something was missing from the armor barge this time, the artillery. Taking it apart and hooking it back to their towing vehicles would have taken too much time. Now, the Elysian artillery soldiers joined the queue with the regular infantry.

Once again, they all sat back down on the sea of cargo nets and settled in for the flight. The ramp slammed behind them. Almost immediately the pitter patter of the thick, muddy Martian rain began to assault the barge, and everyone let out a collective moan.

"Ugh. Now we have to fight in this shit?" Fiona whined.

"We are landing in a contested landing zone, relieving a totally cut off army who is being attacked by one of the best officers in EDF history and you're worried about the rain?" Felicity asked, incredulous.

"Never had to slog your way through a Martian rainstorm, have you? I'd rather assault a damn machine gun nest," she said.

"By the sounds of it we will get to do both," Vincent groaned. The ship rocked and several soldiers were thrown off of their seats. A warning siren blared, and a red light flashed in the troop compartment.

"Attention!" Came the voice of someone from inside the cockpit. "We have been locked onto by multiple anti-air weapons and are attempting to jam them. The Clan Airwing is on their way to try to take the heat off of us. Hold on tight back there!" The ship began to shake and dive wildly.

Vincent's stomach jumped up into this throat and he felt the Kaff he drank for breakfast began to churn and bubble. As soon as the ship's dive was over, it leapt back into the air at a steep climb. Several soldiers doubled over and began to vomit onto the floorboards, others rushed to avoid the puke, only succeeding in falling from their seats and into the mess.

The ship rocked violently, and smoke began to fill the compartment. The ship's internal venting system kicked on and whirled loudly as it pushed the smoke out. They didn't work fast enough and soon the smell of burning plastic assaulted Vincent's senses. Soon, soldiers were pulling their shirts over their faces in an attempt to protect themselves.

Vincent got up from his seat and pushed his way through the masses of nervous, yelling, and vomiting soldiers. He eventually found his way to a staircase so small he had to turn sideways to fit while wearing all of his gear. The door at the top of the stairs read *Authorized Personnel Only.* He pushed the door open anyway.

The barges cockpit was a tornado of activity. Two pilots sat in front of a panoramic windshield while their various assistant pilots were running back and forth to the banks of computers that lined the walls. Each beeping light and siren undoubtedly telling them more than Vincent ever wanted to know about the health of the ship he was riding in.

"Consul?" A pilot asked looking back. He was sweating heavily, and the collar of his flight suit was soaked through. Through the windshield in front of them Vincent could see the sprawling city of Victoria in the distance.

"What hell is going on?" Vincent asked. The pilot was about to answer, but quickly turned back to his control panel and jerked the stick sharply to the left. A red light burned through the sky just as he did so, and the barge managed to dodge it by what had to be only meters.

"Taking a ton of flak, sir. Thankfully, Colonel Vorbeck and his boys are keeping the worst off of us," the pilot said. "We lost our left rear stabilizer, but we'll be okay as long as we don't have to go into orbit any time soon." He watched as a small swarm of Reapers, he assumed Ezra's, dove down onto the city and an entire city block went up in a plume of fire.

"What about the orbital guns?" Vincent asked.

"We would use them if we could," the pilot said. "But with the jammers in place we can't be sure where the field marshal is exactly. A full broadside onto the city could wipe him out." The

514

pilot jammed the control panel's sticks downward and brought the ship into a nosedive. A cluster of missiles screamed past, so close Vincent felt like he could reach out and touch them. One of them found purchase, and the ship rumbled as more sirens began to screech.

"Report!" The pilot screamed.

"We lost our oxygen supply!" Called out one of the assistants.

"Son of a bitch!" The pilot cursed. He brought the ship lower and lower until it felt like they were only a dozen or so feet from the ground.

"Fire on the starboard wing," the co-pilot said calmly.

"Fix it!" Yelled the pilot. Another cluster of missiles arced out of the city. Their glowing trails looked like a hand of light reaching out of the city, trying to smack them out of the air. Vincent could see Arai's barge flying alongside them, right in the path of the oncoming missiles.

"Dodge it!" Vincent found himself screaming aloud. The missiles got closer and the ship began to climb slowly.

"They're too heavy!" The pilot screamed. "They're not going to make it!"

The missiles slammed into the underbelly of the ship, exploding into a massive fireball. It pitched sharply downwards. As it did so its left wing broke off and plummeted to the ground. The rest of the barge fell in an uncontrolled dive towards the ground trailing a stream of fire and debris. After a few minutes it vanished from view, falling behind a nearby ridgeline. A bright orange light flashed, and the cockpit fell silent.

"They could have crash landed," the Pilot said, seemingly trying to reassure himself. "These old barges are sturdier than they look." He turned back his headset. "Clan Flight Two-Bravo, this is One-Bravo, come in!" The pilot called over his headset. After a moment of silence, the cockpit filled with empty dead static. The pilot bent over the control panel and fiddled with some of the countless buttons and dials that surrounded him. "Clan Flight Two- Bravo, this is One-Bravo. Status?" Again, his call was greeted only by static.

"How far out are we?" Vincent asked.

"Sir, we can't possibly put you out there without armor. That's insane," the pilot said. "We should turn around."

"We don't have a choice," he said. "They need us."

"But—" The pilot began to say but stopped himself. "Of course, sir. We are three minutes out. We are getting you as close as we can without getting shot out of the sky." The Pilot turned back to trying to raise Arai's ship on the radio.

Slowly, what he had witnessed began to settle in. Vincent's heart slammed so hard he could feel it in his temples. He leaned heavily against one of the computer banks, his legs going weak. All of their armor was gone. Arai was gone. The whole goddamn Clan's Warlord was gone, and he had tens of thousands of her Warriors in the barge behind him, all rearing to go into battle, who had no idea what had just happened. He wanted to faint. He wanted to puke. But he couldn't. He knew he couldn't let himself give in to the panic that was suddenly flooding him.

He turned around and walked back towards the troop compartment.

Zinvor was waiting for him at the top of the stairs. Vincent put a hand on the Tsarra's shoulder.

"I think your sister is dead," Vincent said.

"The Warlord has fallen?" he asked, emotionlessly.

"I watched her ship go down," Vincent said. Zinvor frowned and placed a hand over his chest.

"Thank you, Vincent," he said.

"What about the Warriors? Are you going to tell them?"

"Yes," he said. "They must know the enemy have cut down

their Warlord." He turned to the crowd sitting on the cargo nets below, using the staircase like a balcony, he yelled, his Mawr deep and guttural. "Warriors of the Fidayi Clan!" The Warriors stopped what they were doing and looked up at him. Most of the humans followed their gaze, curious what the alien was shouting about. "Our Warlord, Arai the Great, has fallen.

Then something happened that Vincent was sure he never thought he would see. The Mawr prostrated themselves onto the ground, others covered their faces with their hands. Then, they began to cry. Not quiet sobbing like a human normally would, but loud, painful, mournful screams of grief. He felt his eyes begin to burn with tears. He tried to sniff them back, but he failed.

Arai was a heartlessly cold creature; of that he was sure. He wasn't sure why she had taken him, and nearly one million of his suddenly homeless brethren under her wing. He had no idea why she came to trust him and give him a purpose after everything he knew was destroyed. He, and the entire human race, would always been in her debt.

"Zinvor, we are three minutes out from landing," he said, hoping he could control the outpouring of unrestrained emotion.

"Warriors of the Fidayi Clan!" he called again. "We land on the field of battle against the foe who has struck down our beloved Warlord in a short time. We will lay our wrath onto them without mercy! Long live the Warlord!"

"Long live the Warlord!" The crowd screamed. The Mawr, done with their outburst were now ramping up into their more common emotion: anger. Tears were still pouring down their faces as they began to slap their chests with their huge hands.

"Before she died..." Vincent said, hardly audible over the noise. He repeated himself louder so the occupants of the barge could hear him. "Before she died, the Warlord talked to me about honor and respect. She told me neither of those things are given freely," he said. "She told me we had to earn it."

"Thirty seconds!" The pilot yelled. Vincent swallowed hard and unslung his carbine from his shoulder. He felt the barge swing around, bringing the rear of the ship forward.

"So, let's go fucking earn it!"

CHAPTER FORTY-ONE

A furious storm slammed into the landing ramp. It sounded like a relentless hailstorm was battering the ship and the ramp began to dent and give way under the assault. The jet black Tsarra once again moved their way to the front of the ship. They carried a wide array of weapons Vincent had never seen before. Large, belt fed machine guns, rocket launchers, automatic grenade launchers, and various Rhai crafted laser weapons. The rest of the Mawr Warriors joined them at the front.

"What is going on?" Vincent asked.

"On this day," Zinvor grunted. "We are all Tsarra." He pounded his broad chest and held his rifle over his head. "For the Warlord!" A battle cry ran through the ranks. It wasn't restrained by race. Humans, Rhai, and Mawr alike slammed their fists against their armor and screamed. Unleashing all of their pent-up anxiousness, releasing it into the air in one ear shattering cry.

The ramp slammed to the ground and a shower of small arms fire greeted them. It crashed into the body of soldiers and cut dozens of them down all around Vincent. He winced and waited for his turn to get hit.

"Get off the ship!" Screamed Presan, attempting to make himself heard over the earsplitting din of combat. "Go!" Other leaders took up the chorus of shouting. But people didn't move. They couldn't move. They had been packed in so tightly it required organized formations marching onto the ship to fit just right. Now that the front ranks were dead or wounded from the incoming fire, it had created a human traffic jam. Now, panicking, all order was gone. People fought and clawed their way through, trying to get out of the death trap.

Soon Vincent was joining in and pushing the people in front of him. They were trapped in the barge like fish in a barrel. He felt something warm and wet splash into his face as a young soldier next to him was reduced to a mist of gore from the neck up. The Tsarra began to charge off of the ship, vaulting over growing pile of the dying.

Soldiers tripped and fell over the growing pile of bodies that was being churned up by the torrent of gunfire. Vincent felt his legs go out from under him as he slipped. He watched his feet fly up in front of his face before slamming back down. His head bounced off of the metal floor. Several soldiers around when crumpled on top of him as their bodies were torn apart by machine gun fire.

His vision bloomed with stars. His limbs burned, and his fingertips tingled with pins and needles. A strange copper taste he knew to be blood filled the back of his mouth and he blinked rapidly to try to get his bearings. He coughed and sputtered, trying to make sense of where he was but before he could, someone fell on top of his face. Vincent fought back nausea as he felt the dying soldier twitch and gurgle as the life drained from him.

Suddenly, his vision was cleared as the smothering bodies were thrown off of him. Standing over him was Zinvor and Fiona. Fiona's eyes were wide with terror as she looked down at him.

"Are you hit?" she screamed and frantically began patting him down, looking for injuries. Her hands came up, soaked in blood no matter where she felt. His head was still foggy, and it took him a minute to think of the words to say. "Are you hit?" she screamed again. There was so much blood everywhere Vincent wasn't sure if any of it was his. He wasn't even sure how long he had been lying there.

"No," he said. "I don't think so." When he looked around, he saw they seemed to be the only living thing still in the troop compartment of the barge. What remained was a horror show of torn and mangled bodies. The wounded moaned and crawled around looking for medics. Several terribly maimed men shuffled about the deck in shock, their faces snow white and holding their own severed limbs, their gaze was otherworldly and dead.

"Come on!" she yelled. "We have to get the fuck off of this ship!" Zinvor wasn't taking any chances this time. He grabbed Vincent by the collar and began to sprint, Fiona ran along beside them. Zinvor was forced to climb over some of the piles of the dead, his short legs making the effort a struggle.

Zinvor ran down the ramp and tossed Vincent like a ragdoll behind a ridge. Behind the same ridge the survivors of the barge were taking cover. Many of them were peaking over the top, trying to fire back at the unknown number of guns that were firing in their direction. Though their fire was sporadic and undisciplined.

Medics had created small triage points where only a few of the wounded were able to be brought to. The rest of the wounded had been left on the line, waiting their turn. But most of the soldiers stayed, their backs against the ridge, cradling their rifles and frozen in terror.

The ridge wasn't large, only about four feet high in some places, but it may as well have been a fortress wall compared to the hell that had just unfolded inside of the barge. Vincent peaked his head up over the ridge to get his bearings. In front of him was a few hundred meters of open ground, without so much as a ditch, rock, or single obstacle in between them and the city.

He could see the EDF positions brimming with activity. Black helmets could be seen over the parapet of their fortifications running back and forth. Muzzle flashes lit up across the line, keeping the panicking Elysian troops pinned down. The turrets of tanks scanned across the ridgeline. The tank's standard issue black paint had become shrouded in a thick layer of red Martian dust. Their cannons boomed and whole sections of the ridgeline vanished in an orange plume of fire.

In the charts and maps Denta had given them the area around Victoria was supposed to be heavily forested from years of forced cultivation and covered in craggy boulders and ditches like the rest of the planet. He wasn't sure how old the maps were, but they may as well have been for an entirely different planet.

Vincent had lingered with his head over cover for too long. A burst of gunfire stitched across the top of the ridge right in front of his face, missing his head by only inches. He dove to the ground trying to catch his breath.

"Where is Ezra?" he yelled, spitting out a mouthful of dirt. "Can he take some of this heat off of us?"

"His Wing had to pull back to the Mons to rearm," Felicity said. "He had them dump all of their fire on the city's edge just so we could make it this far." Vincent cursed Arai in his head for forcing him to leave all of their artillery back at Tharsis. He was even madder that he would never get the chance to say it to her face.

"Shit," he cursed. "Presan?"

"He is setting up a command post on the east end of the ridge, sir," Felicity said. "I'll bring you to him." They ran at a crouch down the ridgeline, the back of Vincent's head throbbed with each step. Suddenly remembering he had lost his carbine back on the barge, he bent down and grabbed one that lay discarded on the ground. Its forward grip was sticky with blood.

Presan had set up a command post with the help of the rest of the surviving commanders. He had piled up supply crates into something resembling a series of desks, on them were tattered maps and cracked data displays. The small circle of commanders was gathered around a map and having an animated argument when Vincent and Felicity approached.

"What did I miss?" Vincent asked. Victoria pulled himself away from the argument long enough to render a salute, none of which the rest of the commanders noticed.

"A shit show, sir," the sergeant major said.

"I can tell," he groaned. "How can we get off of this ridge?"

"Ask them." Victoria shook his head. The commanders were yelling at one another, all semblance of command and control was gone. At one point a major sent a broken data display flying at the head of a colonel, hitting the old man right between the eyes. A young Martian captain tossed a pile of ammo crates, causing Presan to jump out of the way.

"Sir?" Presan asked, shocked.

"I thought you guys were supposed to be more professional than the rest of the army?" Vincent forced a laugh. He saw Presan's surprised look did not fade. "What's wrong?"

"Someone told me you were killed on the barge," he said. "Word got around." It was then that Vincent turned back towards the soldiers who were hiding alongside them. Their wide eyes were locked onto him. They weren't the stares of horror like he thought. They thought they were staring at a dead man.

"If it makes you feel any better, I didn't believe the rumors," Victoria said.

"Thanks," he said. "So, I go and die for a few minutes and now everyone is at each other's throats?"

"Well, sir..." Presan began. "The Warlord is the one that left us out here with no artillery or armor and now she's dead."

"We're stranded!" screamed a major, whose name Vincent never bothered to learn. He was a rail thin Earthian with a bald pate.

"And we can't get the damned Mawr leaders to even talk with us about strategy," Presan said. "They're just over there plotting revenge!" the old man rubbed his temples. "and their revenge sounds an awful lot like a suicide charge."

"Without the rest of the Clan we can't hope to get to the city," Vincent said. "We need to work together."

"Well, they aren't going to listen to me." Presan folded his arms. "And that barge isn't going to fly anywhere with all that damage."

"Wait..." Vincent said. "You can't mean retreating on foot back to Tharsis."

"It's our only option!" yelled a colonel with a blond beard.

"Zinvor," Vincent said. "Get a handle on your Cohort Leaders, will you?"

"My leaders?" Zinvor asked. "They are not my leaders."

"Your sister is dead, that makes you the Warlord doesn't it?" he asked. He had no idea how the Mawr line of succession ran, but that sounded right in his head. Zinvor glanced around with the sudden realization he probably had never thought about it.

"At least until a Clan wide Gathering can be held to select the new one, yes. But my Tsarra mission—" Zinvor began.

"Is to protect me," Vincent finished. "And I am about to charge across open ground into a city full of EDF soldiers. The best way to protect me is to control the damn Clan."

Zinvor bowed slightly before turning and walking off back down the ridgeline.

"Sir, you still mean to attack the city?" Presan asked. Vincent looked around at the crowd of frowning officers. Many of which had just been screaming for them to retreat so loudly that several of the soldiers had heard them. A broad grin spread across his face.

"I'm still here, aren't I?" As if to underline how bad of an idea that was to make, the air filled with deafening shrieks. His smile vanished as he glanced upwards at the red sky.

"Is that—" a captain began to ask before his question was cut off as the ridgeline exploded in fire and dust.

"Incoming!" someone screamed. Vincent dove to the ground, pulling himself as close to the ridge as he could. It was only a matter of time before the EDF got their artillery dialed in on them. He cursed Presan and the rest of the bickering officers for taking so long to get their shit together. A shell screamed through the air and slammed into the stricken barge and detonated.

It erupted into a fireball that sent massive pieces of flaming ship parts cartwheeling into the sheltering soldiers. Burning oil and gas splashed through the air raining down on the sheltering soldiers. They screamed inhuman screams as their uniforms melted to their skin. The ones that ran away from the wall of oncoming fire and shrapnel were cut down by machine gun fire as they broke from the cover the ridgeline.

Vincent's brain rattled in his head and he felt his bones shake with every impact. He had never felt anything like it before in his life. Every few seconds the ground would shake as if the entire planet were seized by a giant set of celestial hands and throttled.

It felt as though the planet itself was going to crack in half. The artillery was coming down as fast as the rain.

The soldiers around him began to scratch and dig their way into the base of the ridge. They used bayonets, shovels, and their bare hands to try to get away from the bombardment. As fast as they dug the mud would wash back into their hole. He watched as an entire platoon vanish in a geyser of mud, fire and smoke as they ran for cover. Another squad of Rhai soldiers were blown apart as a shell exploded amongst them.

Felicity, who had hunkered down next to him, was frantically trying to get her radio to work. She turned to him and began to mouth something. The ringing in his ears blocked out whatever she was trying to say. She motioned frantically off into the distance behind them. She rolled her eyes, got to her knees, and tossed her radio over her shoulders. With one last look at Vincent, she took off running. Bullets slammed into the lip of the ridge as she sprinted away.

"Where are you going?" he screamed, unable to hear his own voice. Thick, black smoke curled down from the burning wreckage of the barge, concealing most of the line from what he could see. Out of the smoke, crawled Fiona. She had a cut across her forehead that leaked blood and her pale face was smeared with mud. She crawled up to him until her face was right next to his ear.

"Did she lose her mind?" Even while screaming, he could hardly hear her.

"I don't know!" he yelled back. She winced as another shell impacted what felt like only a few feet away. A spout of mud sent up by the impact splashed down onto them. The gritty sludge dripped down through his hair and into his armor. "I don't blame her though!"

Suddenly, it felt like he was hit by a car. His feet were no longer on the ground, and before he understood fully what was happening, he was flying end over end through the air. He came crashing back down awkwardly amongst a dozen other soldiers. The soldiers pushed him to a seated position, many of them patting him on the shoulders.

"Fiona?" he called out.

"I'm here!" She crawled out from behind what looked like a large piece of the ship's engine. Vincent looked around and got his bearings. He found the small command post had been reduce to little more than a smoking crater. A direct hit. He looked over himself to see if he had left any parts of his body behind in the crater and was relieved to find everything still attached.

"Shit!" he yelled. "The command center!" He struggled to his feet and ran towards the wreckage, Fiona at his heels. Bullets traced along the ridgeline only inches from his head, each impact sending small spurts of mud into his face. The steady drumbeat of impacting artillery never slowed. The command center had been reduced to rubble. Shards of supply crates were intermixed with the shattered bodies of the Command staff. A miasma of cordite mixed with burning scraps of maps and charts fluttered down in the hazy air.

"Presan!" He picked up a supply crate and tossed it. Under it he found the broken corpse of a captain. Under another was a mangled heap of flesh that wore the black oak leaves of a colonel. Vincent rolled the colonel out of the way, discovering another body. This one began to move. Its face pulled away from the sucking mud, revealing the blood face of Victoria. He gasped for air and spat out mouthfuls of a mixture of mud and blood.

He was badly rattled by the trauma of the artillery strike. His eyes were wild. He began to reach for Vincent's arms and kick out with his feet. The old sergeant major wasn't even sure what planet he was on anymore. For all he knew the person looming over him was an EDF soldier coming to finish the job. Vincent pulled an arm away and slapped him hard across the face.

"Aron!" he called. "It's me, Vincent!" He stopped fighting and shot panicked looks in every direction.

"What the fuck happened?" Aron shouted. His eyes were bugged out of his head. He brushed off his face and rubbed his eyes. Slowly the look of familiarity returned, and he surveyed the damage around him.

"Are you hit?" Vincent asked.

"No." He coughed. "I think I'm good."

"We need your help, Aron. Can you move?" The sergeant major gave him a hard look and nodded. He got to his knees and joined Vincent in searching through the wreckage. Finally, they found him.

Presan was lying on his stomach, near a destroyed radio set. Both of his legs were torn to shreds below the knee. Everything from the shins down was gone, what remained having been churned into something that resembled ground meat. The back of his uniform was stitched with small, ragged holes that oozed blood and stained his once tan uniform a dark red.

"No!" Vincent screamed, dropping to his knees, and rolled the old man over. His face was obscured by a mask of filth. His eyelids fluttered and Vincent saw his chest rise ever so slightly. "He's alive!" he yelled. "Get me a Medic over here!" His body went into auto pilot and his brain began to work through the steps that he had gone through a hundred times before in first aid class.

He drove his knee into the old man's groin to try to slow the blood loss from his broken lower extremities. He rummaged through the wreckage around him until he found the body of a young sergeant. Vincent quickly undid the dead man's belt and tied it tight around Presan's shattered legs. He wretched down on the strip of leather until the spurting blood was finally shunted off.

Just then a stretcher team arrived, dropping their stretcher next to Presan and unloading their packs. They quickly checked his pulse and one of them, a slightly pudgy medic with black hair and the dark skin of a Titanian, jammed an IV into his arm. In only a few seconds they had him rolled onto their stretcher, strapped down, and were off running again all while shells crashed down all around them.

Vincent leaned back against the rocks and sunk his face into his hands. He felt Victoria and Fiona join him, their shoulders brushing against his. It finally happened, something he probably should have done days or weeks before. Or maybe even when he was back on Grawluck.

His eyes began to burn and before he could stop himself tears ran down his face and into his hands. What the hell was he doing out here? His stupid ass had gotten him, the woman he loved, and thousands of people who trusted him stuck in a death trap. He had no idea how many people he had already gotten killed. It was only a matter of time before a shell with his name on it was fired from one of Brusilov's guns and ended it all.

As if on cue another shell detonated along the ridgeline. The chorus of screams that met Vincent's ears after the smoke cleared was deafening. Another group of people he had led towards their deaths. He wondered what they were thinking in the seconds before the shell landed on them.

Why did they ever trust him? Arai put him out there and she at least had the good sense to go and die before she could watch him fail. As he sobbed Fiona wrapped her arm around his shoulder and pulled him into her chest.

That was when the sky opened, and hellfire begun to rain down.

CHAPTER FORTY-TWO

The thick red clouds over their head flickered and flashed. The air rumbled like a storm and rolled in within seconds. Bright orange streaks cut through the sky, crashing down onto the EDF positions in front of them. It was as if someone had flipped a switch and the constant drumbeat of shelling stopped. Vincent looked up from his hands in awe and the incoming fire.

"What..." He gasped.

"The fleet!" Fiona screamed. "The fucking fleet decided to finally show up!"

"But how?" Vincent asked.

"Haagen." Victoria frowned. "She told Presan she would get to somewhere where she could transmit." He pointed a finger to a hill, nearly a half mile to their rear. The same direction she had pointed out to Vincent, but he had not understood. "We told her it was suicide. Running that far in the open up an exposed hillside. She would have had worse chances than staying here under the bombardment."

"That's where she ran off to," he said. The ground shook once more, though this time it was from the ferocity of the fleet bombardment of the city's defenses.

"She could only bring the fire down on their frontline positions, anything past that risked Denta's forces." Victoria reached in the pocket of his jacket and pulled out a flask and took a pull. "She just saved our damned lives."

"We have to go get her!" Fiona said.

"We don't have time," Victoria said. "If we are going to take that damned city, we have to get our forces together and get to work."

"We don't even have a Commander anymore!" Vincent countered.

"Yes, we do," Fiona said. "We have the Great Traitor."

"Me?" he said, incredulous. "You want me actually command want is left of us? It was my stupid idea that got us in this situation in the first place!"

"Do you have any idea how important that city is to Mars?" Fiona asked. "Do you have any idea how hard my family fought in the past to even dream of having them cornered like rats in their little fortress?" Her fist balled. "I'm not walking away from this one."

"She's right." Victoria nodded. "And if you think of it, how much fight do you think the Committee has left in it?"

"What do you mean?" he asked.

"If the so-called Great Traitor was on your doorstep with an army of aliens and Gangers at his back you would probably send our best commander and every soldier you could muster to stop him, wouldn't you?"

"Wait, so you're saying Brusilov's army is the last EDF army they could field?"

"The units stationed around Lunar City have always been rich kids whose daddies had paid off the committee to make sure they got a comfortable posting led by officers who were connected to important people. The Lunar natives were all long deployed here or died on Grawluck. Whatever reserve force they have left on the Moon is probably made up of pompous rich kids led by incompetent politicians." He took another drink. "Brusilov's got an army of veterans with him. He's the backbone of the entire government right now." Vincent sighed, standing all the way upright for the first time since he had stepped off the barge. "We take him down. We take down the Chairman."

"I guess I have an army to get together then."

*   *   *

The army that survived the landing and bombardment was not the same army they had taken Tharsis with. The enthusiasm and cheering had dried up. In its place was the screams of thousands of wounded and the mourning sobs of the survivors. The soldiers who still manned the line had been so thoroughly coated in red mud, they looked as if they had risen up from the surface of Mars itself. Their eyes were locked onto something in the distance that only the trauma of sustained combat could make visible.

The blasted landscape of the ridgeline had been reduced to little more than a crater filled graveyard. The mud and debris churned up by the bombardment had buried many of the dead in unmarked graves. There didn't seem to be any kind of cohesion remaining amongst the units. Plain clothed Martian gangers sheltered in the same holes as Rhai soldiers and Mawr Warriors carried human wounded to Earthian medics.

"Commanders!" Victoria's voice boomed over the shrieking of the fleet's incoming rounds. "Assemble your units! We attack within the hour!" Soldiers exchanged looks that ran the gamut from shock to absolute horror. "If your unit no longer has a commander, consider the ranking sergeant officially breveted to a lieutenant!"

Zinvor grumbled orders to what remained of the Mawr Cohorts and they fell into a tightly packed formation along the ridge. The Rhai soldiers instead fell in with the Human Cohorts. Zinvor strode past the hurrying soldiers to where Vincent and Victoria were trying to get a handle on the situation.

"I guess you managed to control them after all," Vincent said.

Zinvor nodded. "Though I had to shoot two Cohort Leaders to assert my authority. They were no loss."

"Err." Vincent scratched his beard. He knew the Mawr leadership style shouldn't surprise him anymore, but there he was, speechless.

"I promised them revenge once the attack begins. I intend on following through with that."

"They can be the first ones over the top if you would like."

"It would be our honor." Zinvor nodded.

"Hope I'm not late," came a voice from behind Vincent. He turned to see Erin standing with a wide grin spreading across her dirty face. Her head and left eye had a bandage covering them. One of her pantlegs was torn off around the upper thigh revealing a series of small black tattoos spread across pale skin. "I heard you died."

"Yeah." Vincent laughed. "I heard that too."

"You look like shit," Fiona added.

"Feel like it." Erin smiled. "I heard about Presan, does that mean you're in charge Consul?"

"Seems that way. You feel like being a Squadron Commander? I just lost most of them."

"Uh," Erin started. "You want me to do what?"

"Here." Victoria tossed her the black oak leaf pin of a colonel. "Found those on someone who doesn't need them anymore."

"They're yours if you want them," Vincent added. "I need someone I can trust and isn't going to start screaming about retreating."

"Sir, it would be my honor," she said.

"Great." Vincent smiled. "Your first mission is to assemble this mess for a counter-attack. The sooner the better. And for fuck's sake, call me Vincent."

Erin held the colonel pins her in hand and stared at them for a moment. She quickly pinned them on her collar and straightened her uniform top.

"Thank you, Vincent." She nodded before turning on her heels and marching towards the hurrying soldiers, screaming orders so loudly Victoria winced.

*   *   *

As Erin brought the shattered remains of the Clan army together Vincent cast a glance towards the sky. The constant flashing from behind the clouds had not ceased. The incoming bombardment resembled a concentrated rain of fire. A rising cloud of smoke grew around the city. Geysers of flame erupted as ammo dumps or artillery positions caught fire and exploded. The twisted, bent shape of artillery barrels tumbled through the air like matchsticks in the wind.

It's terrifying isn't it?" Fiona said. "We know exactly what they feel like right now. Trapped like rats in a box with a giant boot overhead trying to stop their life out while they scurry around in circles with nowhere to run. But here we are sitting here like it's some kind of Sunday at the movies." He knew every time his bones rattled with the impact of the fleet's bombardment countless EDF soldiers were being vaporized.

He quickly chased away any feelings of remorse.

"Remember what those animals did in Tharsis," he said. "They had this coming."

"Damn right," she said.

"Uh, sir," Victoria said. "If we go charging across no man's land here, who is going to tell the fleet to stop shooting?" He stopped for a moment. He hadn't thought of that. They can't talk to the fleet, but could they see them?

"I have no idea," Vincent said. "I guess we are going to depend on Felicity still being alive out there and call it off when we start moving."

"That is a hell of a gamble." Victoria folded his arms.

"Unless you have a cup and a string that will go into space, it's the only gamble we have." He shrugged. He hoped wherever Felicity was, she was alive. Or at least alive enough to call off the fleet.

"We have another problem," Victoria said.

"Of course we do." Vincent sighed. "What could be worse than having no tanks, artillery, or a fucking commander at this point?"

"We have no supplies either," he said. "They were still on the barge when it got hit. All we have is what we have on our backs."

"I'll pass orders to take what we can from the dead in the meantime."

"Thanks," he said. Victoria nodded and walked off.

"Keeps getting better and better," Fiona said. Her stomach let out a loud growl and she frowned. "I hope someone has food or water in their bag, because I watched all of mine explode."

"No water either?" he asked. She turned around to show him her standard issue EDF canteen that dangled from her load bearing vest. It had a hole punched through one side. He assumed from one of the millions of pieces of flying shrapnel they had dodged in the last few hours. "Talk about some bad luck."

"It was full of booze anyway." She frowned. "But it was the good Titanian stuff. I won't be able to replace that any time soon."

"I'm sorry for your loss." He grinned. "Here." Vincent handed her his own and she drank from it greedily. She smiled and handed it back. She handed him a cigarette in exchange, and he took it.

She leaned over and grabbed his hand. Together, they watched as the bombardment seared through the sky and slammed into the EDF positions. He thought he saw something that looked like a tank get thrown into the air like a child's plaything.

"We are a long way from the *Victory,* eh?" she said.

"A long way from just about everything at this point," he said. "I feel like I'm living in a bad movie I can't turn off. Or a nightmare. I'm not sure which."

"I don't know," she said. "It could have been a lot worse." He chuckled, smoke curling out of his nose.

"How in the hell could it be worse?"

"You might not have me." She smiled. He leaned into her and kissed her on the top of her head. Her white-blond hair was gritty and smelled like cordite, but he didn't care. He stopped for a moment, taking in everything around them. He had been thinking about asking her something for a long time but thought that he should wait until they were out of a warzone. Then he remembered, war was who they were. This was how they met, how they fell in love, and how they survived. Besides, if he didn't ask her soon, he may never get the chance. They could only dodge death so many times. He took a deep breath and looked her into her piercing blue eyes.

"Marry me," he said. The cheaply made Martian cigarette that had been dangling from their lips dropped to the ground. The side of her face was covered in dried blood and smeared with various kinds of filth. None of that mattered. She was still beautiful. "I mean..." He stumbled. "Will you marry me?" Her face broke into a wide grin and her eyes grew misty.

"Of course I will, stupid." She pushed herself up onto her toes and kissed him. He wrapped his arms around her and hugged her tight. Suddenly, she began to laugh so hard the tears that she was holding back, broke free.

"What's so funny?" he asked.

"Proposing in the middle of all of this shit." She barely managed to get out in between bursts of laughter. "I couldn't think of anything that was more fitting." After a moment, he joined in with her laughter.

"Our first date was nearly ruined by getting shot out of space by Anarch artillery." He laughed.

"And our second was almost ended by getting overran and bombed on a hilltop." She chuckled. Vincent's smile faded somewhat remembering the faces of Richardson and Ikari and all the others who didn't survive Ryklar. She put a hand on his cheek and smirked. "You owe me a ring now, eh?"

"I guess I do." He smiled. The edges of their little world blurred as her eyes swallowed him whole. She leaned up and kissed him on his lips again. Her lips were as dry and cracked as his were, but he didn't care. His hands slid up to the back of her messy hair and pulled her in tighter.

They let go of each other when Vincent felt the ground under his feet begin to shake. They exchanged confused glances. It was not the constant *thump, thump, thump* of the crashing orbital strikes. It was a steady rumble. Like a drum roll amidst a bass line. He broke away from Fiona to look around. The rest of the soldiers had the same confused look on their faces as he did.

"What the hell is that?" she asked.

"I don't know," he said. The Victoria skyline flashed for an instant. The light was so bright Vincent's eyes seared and he had to shield his eyes with his arm. After a moment he was able to look back at the city. He saw a thin, arcing yellow light streaking into the sky, leaving a puffy white contrail of smoke behind it.

Vincent and Fiona broke from their embrace. He strode quickly over to where Erin and Victoria were standing with crowds of exhausted looking soldiers. No one was trying to organize the troops anymore. They were all staring straight up into the sky like he was. The ground rumbled again, and another streaking light came from the city, following after the first.

"What the fuck is going on?" Vincent asked.

"Orbital counter fire," Victoria said, rubbing his temples. "They should have known they would have batteries around the city. Of course he would have those hidden away until the Fleet showed up to fight."

"Are you really suggesting Brusilov lured in the fleet so he could attack it?" Erin frowned.

"I don't know!" Victoria spat. "I wouldn't put anything past him!" The two missiles vanished from view into the thick red clouds. Three more launched, following the smoke trail of the other two.

"Now," Erin said. "We have to attack now."

"Right." Victoria composed himself. "Before their line has enough time to reform. It may be our only chance."

Vincent looked at the soldiers. Many of their eyes looked like they were on another planet. After escaping the barge and sitting through a barrage, any confidence they had gained from taking

Tharsis was long gone. He noticed there were significantly fewer former gangers in the ranks. He wasn't sure if they were dead or did a runner when no one was looking. He thought the latter was more likely and he hardly blamed them.

"Are they ready?" Vincent asked.

"No," Victoria said.

Zinvor appeared, pushing the crowds of soldiers aside. His black armor was now heavily laden with weaponry. Along with his Riten with hung low at his hip, he had a belt fed machine gun in his hands, one that would normally take a crew of humans to use correctly. Across his back he had a rifle slung, a bayonet already mounted under its barrel.

"Warriors are always ready to do battle," he grunted. His eyes darted back and forth as he searched for words. "Sometimes, you just have to give them a reason."

"A reason..." Vincent thought aloud. What could he tell these soldiers that would ever make them want to leap over this ridge and charge into a city? They had just sat by and watched their friends and comrades get ground to a pulp from an artillery barrage. The fact that they were still here at all felt surprising enough.

"I know why I want to go fight," Fiona said.

"As do I," Victoria added.

"I'm not going anywhere, sir," Erin said, her arms crossed. Vincent saw the new colonel's rank on her collar. "I'm here to either take that city or die trying."

"Why do they want to fight?" he asked them, pointing over to the soldiers. The soldiers sat around in small groups. Their rifles on the ground and he witnessed more than one flask being passed in between them.

"They're here for you," Victoria said. "Remind them why." She smiled and shoved him forward.

"Soldiers!" the old sergeant major's voice boomed over the dull roar of thousands of side conversations. "Your Consul wishes to address you!" Unlike before, the soldiers didn't get up from where they were sitting. Instead, they simply offered a glance towards the direction of their sergeant major.

It was clear to him that the original aura he had as the Great Traitor character that had been created for him had begun to fade in the face of the ordeal they found themselves in. Part of him was happy. It was a lie used for the benefit of both the committee and Denta to rope as many people as they could to their causes, no matter how different they were.

At the same time it was that lie that helped build the army that brought them to this point. It was the same lie that motivated them to climb on that barge in the first place and held them there while the EDF dropped hundreds of rounds of artillery on their heads. They all could have broken and ran for their lives, but they didn't. They were still here.

"I can't lie to them anymore."

"What?" Victoria raised an eyebrow. "What do you mean?"

"I can't do this anymore." He owed it to them, he thought. They deserved the truth.

"I'm not this *Great Traitor* Denta or whoever told you about," he began. The soldiers exchanged confused looks with one another. "I didn't slay the Chairman or destroy Earth. I was trying to *save* Earth. I am an Earthian and I wanted nothing more than to protect my home, my family, and my friends." Their eyes were locked onto him now. "The Clan and I did our best, but it was the EDF. They double-crossed us and got everyone killed anyway."

Vincent sat down on the ridgeline and breathed deeply. "Like most of you I was a sentenced soldier who just wanted to go back home. I missed my stupid little house, my asshole dad, my little brother that outdid me in everything. They were what I missed. I didn't miss Ethics School or being locked up for drawing in a damned book. But I still missed being home." He saw a few soldier's eyes begin to get watery and a few Martian soldiers frown.

"And when they stuck me aboard the *Victory,* nearly got me shot out of the stars, and left us all stranded on Ryklar, I still just wanted to go home." Fiona stepped up beside him and put a reassuring hand on his shoulder. "Then, when I watched Earth and everything along with it blink out of existence... I felt like I died with it. I know a lot of you felt the same way." He saw a few nods amongst the soldiers.

"And then Arai welcomed us all to Elysian. It's a dirty, gross, cramped place. But we moved in anyway. We didn't have any Committee or Chairman to tell us what to do. We created our own place in the universe. Then when the Black Coats came around, we sent them packing." A few cheers went up from the gathering of soldiers. He knew, amongst the soldiers, if one could prove they had been with Vincent since the fight in the Quarter, it had become a badge of honor.

"That little dirty, cramped Quarter gave us something to fight for again," he said. "It brought us all together to fight for something we all needed: a home. A place to rebuild. A place to raise a family." Vincent pushed himself to his feet. "We fought for a home that is now building schools and hospitals. A home where people are having children..." He looked over at Fiona and took her by the hand. "...A home where people are getting married and planning their futures." A few soldiers began hooting and clapping. "And if The Chairman and that asshole Brusilov have their way, all of this will be gone as fast as we created it. I don't know about you guys, but as long as I am alive, and as long as I have all of you standing with me, that ain't going to fucking happen."

The soldiers went wild. Standing up and pumping their rifles into the air in celebration. Screams and cheers went through the ranks, with the few officers they had left joining in.

"They stand high in their little castle, looking down on us. They underestimate us. They think us Criminals, Reds, Toads, or race traitors. But they're wrong. They aren't fighting an army of Earthians, Martians, and Titanians," he added. "They're fighting a whole goddamned Clan of Elysians!"

"And that means they're fucked!" Fiona added. The celebration and outpouring of emotions spread to the Mawr and Rhai who began yelling and pounding their chests with their human comrades, though Vincent was unsure if many of them even understood what was going on. The feelings were infectious.

Vincent climbed down off the ridgeline and walked back to where Zinvor, Erin, and Victoria stood. Victoria's wrinkled features creased with a broad smile and Erin nodded in approval.

"So?" she said.

"Colonel." Vincent looked at her. "Prepare to advance." She grinned ear to ear and saluted before marching off. "Zinvor?" the Tsarra turned Warlord grunted in response.

"Let's go get some fucking revenge."

CHAPTER FORTY-THREE

The half mile expanse of land between them and the EDF defenses around Victoria was dead silent. The rain slowed and died away, leaving a muddy morass. Thick plumes of smoke rose from the city and Vincent could see flames licking up into the air from the EDF line. Their once reinforced line flanked with tanks and artillery had been reduced to a field of ruin in only a few minutes.

As Zinvor climbed on top of the ridgeline, Vincent expected him to come under immediate fire, but the enemy line remained deathly silent. Slowly the black shroud of the Tsarra Cohort moved forward. They fanned out over the open ground, their weapons up and scanning around the wreckage of the EDF positions. Once they had pushed out a few hundred feet, the rest of the Mawr Warriors pulled themselves over the rocks and followed after them. Still, there was no firing.

The momentary relief of the rain drying up ceased as the Martian winds began to kick back up. Clouds of dust blew through and slightly obscured the advancing Mawr behind a curtain of rust red. Vincent looked down at the rifle he had found on the ground. It was filthy after being dragged with him through the mud. He pulled its bolt back. The metal ground loudly against the filthy receiver. At this point, the only thing he could do was hope the damn thing still worked. He reached down to his belt and withdrew his bayonet, fitting it snuggly over the barrel.

The sharp crack of a whistle – Erin's whistle – broke the silence. The signal to advance. Slowly, the soldiers pulled themselves over the ridge and entered no man's land. A soldier near Vincent was too short to heave himself over the rocks himself, so he placed his shoulder under the soldier's rear and shoved him over the top. Vincent quickly followed after him.

Once clear of the ridge, he could feel the cold Martian wind on his skin. The dust scored his face like sandpaper. He looked over at Fiona who had an extra shirt wrapped around her face for protection. Most of the other Martians had done the same thing.

That was when a soldier only a dozen feet away from him vanished in a geyser of mud. The explosion was so close Vincent could feel the heat on his face. Then another. *Boom.* The torn remains of a soldier was sent cartwheeling into the sky. Their body parts and gear rained down on those below. *Boom.* The legs of a sergeant were shorn clear off and her torso vaporized into mist. *Boom.* A black clad Tsarra vanished and its Riten sent flying.

"Landmines!" Screamed a voice.

"Stop fucking moving!" Yelled another. Vincent froze, not daring to take another step. All around him soldiers were doing the same thing. A Rhai, apparently not understanding the command in Earth Standard inched forward, the resulting explosion left nothing behind that Vincent could identify. He nervously looked around. Every single dip and rock in the Martian soil could be hiding another landmine.

"Single file lines!" Erin ordered. Right. Vincent told himself. Standard EDF tactics dictated that if you were in a minefield you had to fall into single file lines, with whichever low ranking private you liked the least taking the point. Each man was supposed to follow in the exact footsteps of the man in front of him. Unfortunately, the Soldiers would have to actually get in those lines first.

More explosions cut through the air. When the dust cleared the howling wounded could be clearly heard over the orders being shouted by officers and sergeants. One of the shouts was silenced by another fireball that covered one unfortunately squad in the gore of their former leader.

Vincent looked around at the dirty, scared faces of the soldiers around him. Their eyes were so wide with fright their pupils looked like pin pricks.

"Stay in line!" he yelled at them. He saw a young soldier, he didn't look a day over seventeen, maybe younger, at the head of the line. "You need to move or we're all going to die. All of us are depending on you right now." The soldier was belly down in the red mud. It was clear by the look of absolute horror on his face the soldier had no intention of going anywhere. Whatever Vincent said to the young soldier wasn't going to penetrate his human survival instinct telling him to stay glued to the ground.

Vincent cursed and began to walk up the line of soldiers. They all stared at him as if he were insane. He tried to stay close to each one as he passed, careful not to step on any untrodden mud. Somewhere to the left of him someone wasn't so lucky. The sharp crack of an explosion tore a grey uniform apart, raining its former wearer's remains down on a horrified squad.

Once at the head of the line Vincent forced himself to walk. Each time his boots touched the mud he winced, waiting for the ground to explode under his feet.

"Don't stop!" Came a voice to his right. He looked over and saw Fiona leading another group of soldiers through the minefield. He wasn't sure if she was talking to him or the soldiers behind her. She marched on, upright, without any fear. He did his best to mirror her.

The EDF positions were only a few dozen meters away. After each step he told himself to take another. His legs got heavy and resisted his orders. His brain was doing the smart thing and telling his limbs to stay where they were. The only safe patch of ground was the one he was standing on.

Snap

An incoming round streaked past his ear. Angry red tracers cut through the air all around him and stitched through the line of soldiers. The remains of the ravaged trench lines and pill boxes sprang back to life with dozens of machine guns. He dropped to the ground, landing with a splash. The air around his head sounded as if it was thick with angry buzzing insects.

Bullets impacted all around him and spat mud at his face. He heard the flat meat packing sound of a lead slug smacking into flesh somewhere behind him. Vincent cursed his own commands. He should have ordered an attack as soon as the orbital strikes began. Instead he sat on his ass and let the EDF get back into position.

He chased the thoughts from his mind. Beating himself up wouldn't change anything now. He got them stuck out in a goddamn minefield he had to get them out of it. Vincent rolled over on his back so he could look back at the soldiers behind him. None of them were still moving. Their twisted corpses had been chewed apart. He was alone.

"Fiona!" he yelled. "Erin!"

"Yeah!" He heard Fiona's voice over the gunfire.

"I'm still here!" called out Erin. "Is that you, sir?"

"Yeah! I'm still alive!" A slug smacked into the mud next to his head. "For now, anyway." He shivered as cold mud worked its way into his ear. "We need to take this damn trench! We can't stay out here!" he screamed. "Pass the word down to Zinvor to get a base of fire on the—" He lost his train of thought as he saw something he never thought he would see: his soldiers turning and running for their lives.

Khaki-clad soldiers jumped to their feet and tried to run back towards the staging area. Most of them were immediately cut down by machine guns or were blown to pieces by mines as they ran. At first it was a few. A few soldiers turned into entire squads. Then he saw entire platoons break and run for it.

His army was falling apart.

"Get back here or I'll shoot you my damn self!" spat Fiona.

"Hold the line!" ordered Erin. She grabbed a soldier who was running by her and shoved him back towards the advance. Sergeants repeated her order to the soldiers around them. Sergeants physically held soldiers in place, refusing to let them budge. "Hold the line in the name of the Consul!" Screamed Erin, her voice changing from a stern order to a shrill cry of rage.

He got them there. He had to get them out. Vincent grabbed some grenades from his vest, primed them, and tossed them as hard as he could while staying low to the ground. Vincent took a deep breath and pushed himself to his knees.

"Soldiers of Elysian!" he yelled as loud as he could. He heard the dull thump of his grenades detonate in the trench line in front of him. "You came here to kill Black Coats! Well, they're right over there! Let's go say hi!"

He stepped off, feeling for the selector switch on the side of his rifle and flipped it straight up to 'auto'. Without aiming he squeezed the trigger and swept the gun back and forth as he ran. Mud kicked up all around the lip of the trench, an EDF trooper who peaked over had a hole punched through their skull.

Vincent heard the battle cry of the Mawr Warriors and the excited shouts of humans. The soldiers in the trench were recovering from the grenade blasts and returning to their firing positions. Vincent dropped one with a burst, three rounds smacking into her chest, their vest was useless at such a close range. The soldier next to the one he shot got the drop on him. That was when he felt it.

A sledgehammer blow to his midsection. He felt his ribs shatter and the air be forced from his lungs. He wheezed and fell face first into the mud, only a few dozen meters from person who shot him. His lungs spasmed as he gasped for air.

He worked his hand up to the spot, a few inches below his sternum. He felt broken scales of armor under his fingers. The second layer, a kind of soft leather, was still intact. He coughed and tasted the copper tinge of blood in the back of his throat. His rifle was gone. It must have sunk into a mud puddle when he dropped it.

He pushed himself up with one arm and reached down to grab his Riten with the other. In one swift motion he leveled on the shape of a black helmet and pulled the trigger. The shot punched straight through the helmet, spraying pink mist into the air. He got back to his feet, stumbling for a few steps before collapsing over the top of the trench.

The trench was a scene of total mayhem. Swirling masses of Khaki, black, and yellow spun around one another. Each was trying to kill the other with whatever they had in hand. Fiona had her saber stuck in the ribcage of a soldier wearing sergeant's stripes and shot another dead with her Riten. Zinvor twisted a human's head at a sickening angle with his bare hands. An EDF trooper stabbed a young Martian in the neck with a bayonet.

Vincent got to his feet and immediately felt a blow to the back of the head. Knocked off balance, he turned and saw the pale, terrified face of an EDF trooper, his features obscured by mud. He had rifle held aloft from just clubbing Vincent with it. Two shots from his Riten sent the trooper to the ground, bonelessly.

Now that they were in the trench, the tides were turning. Khaki uniforms poured into the position to meet the EDF soldiers who did not look like they had any intention on running. When rifles were broken in half soldiers began throwing rocks at once another. A Rhai soldier's head was sunken in by a shovel by a screaming soldier wearing a Black Coat. Vincent dropped him.

"Reinforcements!" Shouted a soldier. Vincent peaked over the opposite side of the trench to see what looked like an entire Squadron running towards them. They were firing blindly at the trench with little regard of the fact that their own people were still inside.

"Shit!" Erin cursed, shooting two more EDF soldiers down. "We can't hold another damned squadron off!"

"I know!" he yelled. "We can't retreat! We'll die out there in that fucking minefield!"

"We'll hold as long as we can!" Erin said. "Bring it in!" she yelled. "Stay with your units!" Soldiers shuffled closer together, trying to bring their dwindling firepower together against the growing number of enemies. The few EDF holdouts still fighting from the trench were emboldened by the arrival of their reinforcements and were now refusing to budge.

The Clan soldiers, now behind solid cover, were holding on by their guts. Vincent grabbed a rifle from a fallen soldier and began pumping slugs into the coming EDF reinforcements.

Zinvor had grabbed a squad light machine gun and was firing it from his shoulder. Swaths of the incoming soldiers were cut down in front of him.

To their left, the original surviving EDF soldiers were beginning to advance on their flank. Fighting on two fronts, the Clan didn't have a chance. The soldiers on the left side begun trying to fall back, finding nowhere to go. The soldiers who were fighting the reinforcements blocked their way. They were being herded together like cattle with no way out.

A blue light cut through the air in front of the trench. The world around them burned with plasma fire, turning the mud to glass in an instant. The ground shook with the thundering of cannons and shorter bursts of blue plasma seared through the air.

"Shit!" Vincent screamed. "What now?"

"Someone give me a goddamn report!" Erin bellowed.

"Incoming tanks!" yelled somebody, their voice filled with fear. "On the right flank!" Vincent heard the metal on metal scraping of tracks. More cannon fire and spouts of mud and fire erupted on the other side of the trench. Plasma fire burned through the left flank. Soldiers, human and alien alike, screamed in pain as they were melted. The low, deep throated chug of heavy caliber machine guns tore the on rushing EDF Squadron to shreds.

"Those are ours!" Erin shouted. "That's our armor!"

Vincent peered over the lip of the trench and saw something he never thought he would see again. Arai's massive tank leading a column of armor that stretched across the horizon.

"It's Arai!" Vincent cheered. "She's alive!"

The Mawr Warriors led out a triumphant roar as the EDF broke and ran while others tossed down their rifles and surrendered.

The Warlord lived.

CHAPTER FORTY-FOUR

The trench had been converted into a field hospital. Hundreds of soldiers of varying races laid around with medics checking over bandages or dispensing medication. It was a cramped space, hardly big enough to lay side by side and the orbital strikes had collapsed large stretches of it.

The few soldiers who had managed to make it through the ordeal unharmed were already back at work. They had only managed to take a foothold into the city, and they would need to make sure to be ready to hold it. They were hacking away at the collapsed sections of the line and doing their best to turn the ruined pill boxes into something serviceable. Unfortunately, a full broadside from the Titanian fleet did not leave them much to work with.

Vincent sat, leaning against the trench wall. He winced in pain as a medic poked at his chest. The skin had bruised to a sickening deep purple where the slug had slammed into his armor. It if wasn't for his armor, he would have been dead before he had hit the ground.

"Yep," the Medic said. She was a young, dark-skinned sergeant with dark circles around her eyes. She had a bulge in her lip and spat a dark liquid over the edge of the trench. "You definitely have some broken ribs." She pressed his chest one last time. "Not a lot we can do for that. I don't even have any basic pain killers left."

"Don't worry about it," Vincent said. "I'm sure there is someone else who needs your help more than I do." He forced a smile. "Now I have something to distract me from the pain in my foot." She nodded before moving down the line.

He pushed himself to his feet and slid his armored jacket back on. He climbed over the trench wall and made his way towards Arai's tank. The armored behemoth's dull yellow paint job was scarred and beaten by scorch marks and divots. On the tank's front slope a screen had been set up, on it was a map of the battlefield.

Arai was standing with a group of Mawr, Rhai, and human leaders. When Vincent approached a broad grin spread across Arai's face.

"I am happy to see you are alive," she said.

"Same goes for you," he replied. "I thought you were dead."

"We all did," Erin said.

"It was not my time to join Paterazm. Not yet," she said. "It seems I showed up at a good time."

"We wouldn't be alive if you were any later," Vincent said.

"Well." Fiona frowned. "Those pieces of shit who ran would still be alive."

"Hm?" Arai snorted.

"During the battle," Vincent began. "When were trapped out in the minefield, a few of my soldiers retreated."

"Disgraceful," she growled.

"That was one of the things I was going to ask you, sir," Erin said. "The garrison we left behind in Tharsis arrested the deserters who managed to survive the hike back. What should I tell them to do?"

"Shoot them." Arai frowned.

"And then throw their asses in a ditch," Fiona added.

"No." Vincent held up his hands. Fiona and Arai looked at him, their eyes wide in shock. "They're human soldiers so they fall under me, right? It was my orders that got them stuck out in a minefield and getting shot to shit. Anyone in their right mind would have run." He sighed. "If anyone should be punished it's me for throwing them into such a hopeless situation. Release them. Tell them to return to their units."

"Yes sir," Erin said, nodding.

"Are you kidding me?" Fiona yelled.

Arai scratched her chin. "I must admit," she began, "just when I think I have you humans figured out, you do this."

"Gotta keep you guessing." Vincent shrugged. "So, what is the plan now?"

"We have sent scout teams on ahead into the city to find Denta's forces," Erin said. "What's left of them anyway."

"And we have more prisoner's than we know what to do with," Victoria said.

"Any of them talking?" Fiona asked.

"Singing like birds." Victoria laughed. "Turns out the Black Coats in the city are pretty much in control of everything. Brusilov lets them rule over the regular soldiers like Kings over peasants. Forcing them to do all the shit work, taking their pay, their food. They even had machine gun positions set up behind the regular soldier's positions, forcing them to stay in place."

"Just like on the Mons." Vincent pinched his chin.

"That Explains why they sat under that bombardment without running," Erin said. "They would have been shot by their own men if they had retreated. That is certainly one way to motivate your army."

"Do you think if the Black Coats didn't have them at gunpoint, they would have fought so hard?" Vincent asked.

"Hard to say," Victoria mused.

"I remember back at the Mons soldiers saying they wanted to surrender, but the Blacks Coats wouldn't let them. A couple of them even ran through the fleet's bombardment to surrender to Erik," Vincent said.

"And that was back when most of them probably still thought they could win." Erin ran a hand through their peach fuzz hair. "Now? Will Olympus take the enemy at the gates? I bet they couldn't wait to run."

"Can we put something together to try to get the soldiers who are still fighting to surrender?" Vincent asked. "If things are that bad it shouldn't be too hard to win them over, right?"

"Like what?" Victoria asked.

"I don't know." Vincent scratched his beard. "Radio broadcasts, drop them leaflets or something? Show them that if they surrender to us the Mawr won't eat them."

"Eat humans?" Arai grunted. "Who says these things?"

"The Chairman and his cronies have been spreading this crap about us ever since we joined you guys," Fiona said. "Last I heard I was whoring myself out to the Rhai for drugs."

"Lovely," Vincent said.

Victoria smiled. "One of the Prisoners said that the Great Traitor was having a bunch of bastard kids with the Mawr."

"Truly an abomination," Erin mocked.

"How would that even work..." Vincent rubbed his temples. "Okay." He held his hands up trying to get the conversation back on track. "How can we broadcast anything to them if they are still jamming all of our signals?"

"Pharos' agents are working on that as we speak," Arai said.

"Good." Vincent nodded. "Anything you need me to do?"

"Yes," Arai said. "Go rest with your soldiers. You look terrible." A deep growl that passed for Mawr laughter came from her mouth and she gave him a hard slap on the shoulder. It nearly floored him. "Once you're rested you can go meet with Denta. Once we find him anyway."

He grinned. "Right."

"Sir!" someone called out. Vincent awoke with a start. "Sir are you awake?" the voice asked again. He felt like he had only been asleep for a few minutes, but the sun was down, cloaking the entire city in front of him in darkness. The skyline occasionally lit up with a streak of orange tracers or a flash of brilliant orange from some far-off explosion. He rubbed his eyes and saw Victoria peering down into the trench over him.

"Yeah." He moaned. His entire body ached, and he felt a sharp pain in the center of his chest when he spoke. Fiona was asleep on the ground next to him. Her armored jacket was bundled up under her head as a pillow and drool gathered at the corner of her mouth.

"We found Denta. He wants to talk with you."

"I'm coming," he said. Vincent pulled himself up by the trench wall. He reached down and grabbed a rifle, slinging it over his shoulder. "Hey, out of curiosity have you heard anything about Haagen?" Victoria shook his head.

"No, sir." He frowned. "We are still trying to gather all the names of the people we lost today. We should know by morning..." He thought for a moment. "...where she is." He was clearly not wanting to say what they both were thinking: that Felicity had died on that hill calling in the fleet.

"We owe her our lives," he said.

"I know, sir." Victoria held his hand out for Vincent to grab and he took it. He pulled him up and over the top of the trench. "We will do right by her."

"How far out is Denta's Command Center?"

"Not far," Victoria said. "But the city is hardly secure. The EDF is still hunkered down in a couple buildings and Erik's army are trying to force their way through to link back up with Denta. Everyone seems to be fighting over a few city blocks. I can't seem to wrap my head around the situation maps, they change every twenty minutes."

"Sounds like Olympus," Vincent said. The two of them were joined by several khaki uniformed soldiers and Zinvor, who had been waiting for them. Many of the buildings around them had been leveled by the orbital bombardment. Collateral damage from shelling the line. Military trucks and a few tanks had been melted to the road, reduced to little more than scorched black husks.

"Except worse," Victoria said. "See those?" He pointed ahead and saw the faint outline of engineer's tape. The tape was actually a kind of white cloth used by combat engineers to mark out minefields and other dangers on the battlefield. The white strip was wrapped around a light pole that had long gone dark. "That means we've cleared this route. Any other road without those could mean you're walking into an ambush."

"We cleared these?"

"Well, kind of," Victoria said. As they walked the soldiers moved out in front of them in a loose formation. They lowered themselves into a crouch and their eyes darted through the darkness at the surrounding buildings. "The Titanians did."

"But the Titanians got pushed out of here and the EDF retook it."

"Correct."

"So, it isn't clear at all."

"Also, correct." The air snapped next to Vincent's head and he instinctively dropped to the ground.

"Sniper!" screamed one of the soldiers.

"Told you!" Victoria yelled. "Hey!" He screamed at the four soldiers at the head of the line. "Put down some suppressing fire so we can get Consul Solaris out of here!"

"Yes, Sergeant Major!" answered one of them. They began to squeeze off shots into the darkness. Their tracers arced wildly into the night in every direction. Because they could not tell where the sniper was hidden, Vincent assumed they were simply trying to suppress everything.

"Ready?" he asked.

"I guess, you ready back there Zinvor?"

"I am always ready," he grunted. Victoria pushed himself to his feet and took off running. Vincent chased after him, each step sent a jolt of pain up his unhealed foot and through his chest. The soldier's suppressing fire slowed down as one by one they stood up and ran after them.

Victoria stopped at an intersection that was lined with what looked like it had once been a market. Glass store fronts had been blown out during the fighting and several aero cars laid grounded, shot to pieces. Posters on the walls of apartment blocks espoused EDF soldiers to hold back the traitors and beasts from beyond human space.

One of the posters had a photo of Vincent. He recognized it as one that had been taken when he had been arrested. There were crosshairs over his face with large bold red letters at the base that read "Death to Traitors".

Victoria's eyes found a fluttering piece of engineer's tape and took off running to the right. Another sharp crack of a sniper's bullet dropped one of the soldiers that were running with them. The sprinting khaki uniform in front of him dropped wordlessly. Victoria and Vincent dove into an alleyway. Vincent looked over at the old sergeant major. Despite him being old enough to easily be Vincent's Dad, maybe even a younger Grandfather, he showed no sign of having just been sprinting through the streets. Vincent gasped for air; each breath felt like he had rebroken his ribs.

"That bastard has a bead on us," Victoria growled. The three surviving soldiers heaved themselves into the alley. Zinvor leaned out from the wall, firing blindly into the night.

"They're watching the route between us. Fuckers," spat one of the soldiers. She was a pale skinned Martian woman with the tattoo of a meat cleaver under her right eye and a buzzcut. She was wearing civilian cargo pants paired with a tattered Khaki jacket. She must have been one of the gangers who had just joined them. Vincent noticed she was carrying a worn wooden hunting rifle with a scope on it. "Let me take a crack at that fucker Boss," she said to Victoria.

"Sergeant Major," he corrected her.

Yeah, whatever."

"You think you can hit them? We don't even know where they are," Vincent said.

She smiled. "I need one of you to run across the street, the Worm will take a shot at you and I'll plug one right between his fuckin' eyes."

"You're not going to get much more than one chance."

"Shit, one chance is all I need." She was overflowing with confidence. The problem was Vincent couldn't tell if it was confidence or bullshit.

"You there." Victoria pointed to one of the other soldiers. "You're the runner." The Soldier's eyes went wide with fear.

"That ganger bitch will just let me die!" The soldier protested.

"What the fuck did you just say?" The Martian seethed. Vincent was sure she was about to shoot him but the crack of another bullet on the corner of the alley tempered her fury.

"Did I fucking stutter, Soldier?" Victoria yelled. "I gave you an order." Vincent could feel the tension rising and knew he had to act.

"I'll do it," he said. "If you wanted a chance to get back at the guy who killed your old Boss, now is your chance." The Martian smiled fiendishly.

"We'll see," she said.

"Sir, in all due respect, I have to object," Victoria said.

"You're not the first sergeant major whose orders I ignored." Vincent smiled. Victoria rubbed his temples in resignation. "Ready?" he asked. The Martian nodded.

Vincent took a deep breath and thumbed the selector switch on his rifle from safe to auto. He locked eyes on the burning wreckage of an EDF cargo truck. It had been blown onto its side and surrounded by discarded supply boxes. It was only maybe fifty feet away. At that moment it might as well have been a mile.

Vincent peaked around the corner, brought his rifle up to his shoulder and fired a burst into the night sky. He had no idea where the sniper or snipers were, he just had to get their attention. He fired off another burst and was answered immediately by the smack of a slug impacting the wall directly above his head. His heart leapt into his throat and he took off running.

He made sure he ran in a zig-zag pattern to try to throw off the sniper. It seemed every few seconds another slug slammed into the ground near his feet or cracked by his head.

"Any fucking time now!" Vincent screamed over his shoulder.

"Can't rush perfection!" The Martian answered. He got closer to the truck and a slug sparked off of it. He fired another burst in the general direction of the sniper's perch only to be greeted by another slug, this one hitting the magazine of his rifle. Vincent dove behind the truck only to realize he was now holding one half of his rifle in each hand. He rolled on his back and saw the Martian peering out, her rifle scope pressed tightly to her eye.

Bang. The rifle bucked hard against her shoulder with tremendous recoil.

She lowered the rifle, a grin slowly spreading across her face. Vincent exhaled in relief, his bruised ribs burning with pain.

"Perfection." She smiled.

"Perfection." Vincent laughed.

"The name is Skylar by the way. Skylar Olympus."

"Right." Vincent nodded. "Skylar. Good job."

Victoria led them to the beginnings of a forward camp. They had passed several small observation posts manned by Martian or Titanian soldiers before reaching Denta's main camp. The city around them became more and more effected by the fighting the further they went in.

Whole buildings had been gutted or leveled by explosions and fire. This led to the soldiers to just turn the wreckage into more fortifications. Sandbags and large chucks of twisted rebar enforced masonry were stacked up ever few feet creating makeshift barracks, hospital, and command post. Not a single building was without some kind of damage.

Vincent could see the barrels of machine guns peeking out of the windows of the buildings that still stood. The distance the constant staccato of gunfire could be heard. He wasn't sure which side of the line it was coming from. Every few seconds the ground rumbled with the report of an explosion.

Tarps and blankets were strung up between fighting positions and the doorways of buildings, shielding the movements of soldiers from the watchful eye of snipers.

Wherever soldiers walked they moved quickly and at a crouch, hoping beyond hope that the next slug that went hurdling through the air didn't find them. Every one of the sniper screens had been pock marked with countless bullet holes.

"Man, these guys look ragged as hell," Skylar said.

"They've spent the entire time we've been gone under siege from all sides." Victoria frowned. "We would look a bit ragged too."

"Lucky for them, we saved their asses." She laughed. A helmeted head popped out from behind a half wall of sandbags and concrete.

"Consul, sir?" the soldier said.

"Yes?" Vincent answered.

"Field Marshal Denta wanted me to bring you to him as soon as you showed up. Follow me please." The soldier jumped out from behind the wall and began to run towards a building. Vincent sighed and jogged after him, without doubling over. The distant crack of a sniper rifle convinced him to change his mind and crouch like everyone else.

Once they made it inside the building Vincent could hear the telltale whistle of incoming artillery. The ground shook and dust cascaded down from small cracks that had formed in the ceiling.

"Solaris!" Boomed a voice he recognized as Denta's. The old man limped towards them. His left leg was heavily bandaged, and he was leaning hard on a cane. "Good to see you're alive."

"Certainly not from a lack of trying," Vincent said. "Could say the same for you it looks like."

"Oh this?" Denta looked down at his leg. "Just the price of playing the game. Where is Presan? I would like him to be here before we begin the meeting." Vincent shuddered at Denta calling all of the brutality he had seen in the last few hours a game.

"Last time I saw him he was getting the stumps of his legs tied off with belts," Vincent said.

"My god," Denta gasped.

"He's alive," Victoria added. "Last I heard, anyway."

"The Warlord is handling things at our position, until then she has given me permission to stand in for her in our meeting."

"What about that spy of hers, Pharos?" he asked.

"Pharos is working on something important," Vincent said. "I can fill you in." Denta frowned, clearly not comfortable being treated as equals with him. Vincent knew the old man thought he was little more than a dumb teenager. At one point, Vincent confessed, he probably would have been right. But after surviving so much and rescuing this puffed up stuffed jacket, he wasn't going to accept being treated as anything other than exactly what he was.

"So, you're in command then?" Denta smiled, seemingly amused.

"He has always been in command." Victoria frowned. "You just wouldn't accept it." Denta glared at him.

"Presan's gone and Arai doesn't want to deal with you after you ignored all of her warnings. I'm all you have left." Vincent folded his arms across his chest. Denta's façade of friendliness faded completely. His features turned into a snarl.

"Listen here—" he began.

"We told you not to underestimate Brusilov, but you charged right into a trap just like we told you would happen!" Vincent said.

"How dare you!" Denta began, but he wasn't given a chance to finish.

"Then, after capturing my objective, I had to lead my soldiers through a damned minefield to rescue you!" The soldiers watching the exchange began to exchange looks with one another. Their looks of anger went from targeting Vincent, to glaring at Denta. He could only imagine how much suffering these soldiers had to sit through because Denta's decisions.

"Enough!" Denta roared. "Not in front of my men." He turned and hobbled to a backroom, which he had turned into an office. "Clear the room!" he ordered. Several aides dropped what they were doing and hurried out of the building. Denta turned awkwardly on his one good leg and sat heavily on a fold out chair and sighed.

The old man's features were already heavily wrinkled and creased with time. Since Vincent had last seen him, it looked like he had aged another ten years. His eyes were sunken in their sockets and they were ringed with dark circles. He no longer wore the heavily decorated uniform Vincent was used to seeing him wear. Instead, he was wearing a tattered grey field uniform, his field marshal rank was missing off of his shoulder boards.

"I know," he said, his voice defeated. "I know I fucked up. I should have known better but the thought of ending this thing fast was just too good to pass up. Now?" He sighed. "Now I am missing an entire Regiment." He reached into a pocket and produced a flask. He took a long pull and breathed deeply. "I have been fighting on this planet longer than you have been alive kid, but I lost more men in the last few days than I have in my entire career."

Vincent could swear he could see the old man's eyes begin to get watery. And right about then he started to hate himself. The whole way to Denta's office, after watching Arai's ship get shot down, after sitting through an artillery barrage, and then forcing his soldiers to run through a mine field he couldn't wait to rub in the fact that he was saving Denta's skin. But now, he felt sorry for him. He knew exactly how he felt. They really had become equals.

He reached across the table and grabbed the flask from Denta and took a drink.

"So have I," he said. The smoky Titanian whiskey washed away the scorn he had for the old man. He exhaled. "You done with this shit?"

"With what?" He quickly dried his eyes with a sleeve.

"Trying to get one over on us to put Titan in a better position when all of this is over." Vincent took another drink. Denta's eyes went wide. "Because this is what it gets us." He sighed and rubbed his eyes. He was exhausted. Only about three hours of sleep curled up in a ball on the dirt did not do wonders for the function of his brain. "We get thousands of dead. I lose the commander of my army. The Clan almost loses its Warlord. Our plan is almost dead before it fucking starts." Denta's glance was cast down at the desk. "Your position...the power of Titan... none of that means shit if the Anarchs sweep through here and enslave humanity."

"Okay!" Denta finally said. "Okay..." He repeated. "I get it, damnit." He reached over and took the flask and tipped it back. The sudden silence alerted Vincent to the distant crackle of gunfire. The rumble of an explosion shook the building. A small spout of dust twirled down from the ceiling and sprinkled across Denta's snow white hair. "Fine." He straightened himself once again. The defiant sharpness once again returning to his eye. "So, Consul. Tell me your plan."

The screeching metal tracks of Arai's armored column arrived in Denta's camp as the Martian sky burned red with daylight. Rhai, Mawr, and human soldiers were crowded into every conceivable space on top of the tanks and armored personal carriers. Behind them marched row after row of soldiers, forming a multicolored snake that crawled its way through the broken city.

Above the city, formations of Reapers were joined by the crescent shaped jets of the Mawr, and a few sleek black Rhai ships. Due to the ongoing communications jamming they flew so low they could search for threats with their naked eyes. None of the EDF snipers thought it was a good idea to take a shot at the column with air support so close by. They made it to Denta's camp without an issue.

Fiona was riding alongside Arai on top the turret of her armored beast. A cigarette dangled from her lips and she held a battered Mawr rifle across her lap. She climbed down from the tank and kissed his forehead.

"Did you tell that old bastard he owes us?" She blew out a cloud of smoke.

"No," he said. "Maybe I'll rub his face in it when we win this thing."

"Yeah," she said. "These guys look damn miserable. Got it worse than us."

"Way worse," he agreed, though picking out the biggest loser in the situation seemed pointless to him. Arai finally climbed down from her mount and fussed with her armor, fixing her scrolls.

"Hm," she grunted. "Looks like we missed a good fight."

"You were a little late to our fight. Maybe we should have saved you some?" Fiona folded her arms. Arai did not acknowledge the slight. Either because she didn't understand it was an insult or because she just ignored it. "I am sure you told him of our plan?" she asked.

"Yes." Vincent nodded. "It turns out he was pretty agreeable."

"How did you get through to him?"

"It turns out losing thousands of soldiers through negligence changes a man's mind," he said.

"If this is the case why do his soldier not shoot him?" Arai mused.

"Good fucking question," said Fiona.

"Whatever the reason, we should be thankful for it or I would get shot too." He frowned.

"But you were victorious," Arai said, clearly confused.

"Right. That is what winning looks like." He sighed. He certainly didn't feel like a winner and he wasn't sure how Arai could either.

The door to Denta's headquarters opened and his aide appeared. He was a smug looking captain. His nose resembled a downturned beak that gave him the appearance an uptight butler that Vincent had seen in a movie. He had a permanent upturned scowl that made him look like he was constantly smelling something sour. In the middle of everything he had somehow managed to keep his knee-high boots spotlessly clean.

"The Field Marshal will see you now," he said. The aide had not been there the night before. Vincent assumed that now Arai was with him Denta had to put on the façade of being a strong-willed military commander rather than a broken-down old man. If he had known that all of these human gestures were lost on Arai, maybe they could save some time and actually been honest for once.

They were escorted through the lobby of the building. It was crowded with officers and soldiers of every rank going about their daily duties. As the various units of the Titanian and Martian armies could no longer rely on radios, they had gone back to using hand carried messages written on scrap paper. Commanders would issue orders, from the smallest mundane thing to ordering a unit into combat, and then give them to the fastest soldiers in the unit to sprint off through the city. More than a few messages were never received. EDF snipers or ambush groups claimed a fair share of them.

Once they were back in Denta's office, Vincent saw he was once again the man he knew from before. He was dressed in his parade perfect uniform, cleanly shaven, and even seemed well rested. He was charting out known EDF positions on a large display on the wall. Clan positions to his south and a thin secure corridor connecting them had been added to the map with a yellow highlight.

The EDF positions were marked with small red squares and were dotted across the city. They formed thick red lines at various points, indicating where they had dug in and fortified entire city blocks. The positions grew larger and larger until an entire District of the city was colored red. It was labeled as the *Military District.*

"Good morning, Warlord." Denta smiled. She nodded in response.

"Is this up to date intelligence?" she asked, gesturing to the map.

"The best we can do," he said. "Cobbling together reports from my unit's runners has been a bit of a chore. The EDF has laid out traps and ambushes for them all over the city."

"You haven't rooted them out yet?" Vincent asked.

"A lack of resources." Denta frowned. "Erik and his forces are trying to push west." He pointed to a group of small circles to the west of Denta's position on the map. "We are just struggling to hold here. If your forces push east, it will take pressure off of us and allow us to move again. Regardless, these small ambush teams will be nipping at our heels the whole way."

"Shit." Fiona laughed. "Why not send in the Gangers?"

"What do you mean?" Denta asked.

"Can you think of anyone else we have in our ranks that would be better at sneaking through a city in the middle of a battle and ambushing people?" Fiona asked.

"That is an outstanding idea," said Erin in agreeance.

"Can we trust them?" Denta asked. "They stabbed us in the back before."

"We don't have Gangers anymore," Vincent corrected. "We just have some Martian soldiers with interesting tattoos and histories." He nodded at Skylar and nodded. "I trust all of my soldiers. They've earned it."

"We don't have any Ganger officers, sir," Erin said. "Who would lead them?" He turned and looked at Skylar.

"You want the job?" he asked. She looked around before realizing that he was talking to her.

"You want me to be the Boss?" she asked. "Seriously?"

"I want you to be the *lieutenant*." He rolled his eyes.

"I'm your girl, Boss." She smiled.

"*Consul,*" Erin corrected her.

"Whatever." Skylar shrugged.

"Take the next couple of hours and put together a team. I'll bring you orders before nightfall," Erin said.

"Got it, Boss." Skylar nodded, giving an ugly salute, and walked out of the office.

"You sure know how to pick them, sir." Erin rolled her eyes.

"I picked you, remember?" He smirked. Denta cleared his throat.

"Solaris said something about Pharos clearing the radio jammers. How is that coming?" he asked.

"It is done," Arai said.

"What?" Denta asked shocked. "Then why aren't we bombing them into dust? Why are we not linked back to the fleet so we can be fucking resupplied?" he sputtered, spit flying out of his mouth. "My soldiers are low on food, water, you—"

His complaints were cut off by the door to the office opening once again. In the doorway stood Pharos, cloaked in black shimmering armor and a small, compact pistol on their narrow hip.

"Because, Field Marshal," the smooth, almost whisper like voice said. "We do not want to let them know yet."

"What do you mean?" he asked in shocked, disbelief.

"The fleet is not in position," Pharos said.

"Why do we need the fleet to broadcast the Consul's little message?"

"Because, Field Marshal." Pharos' voice dripped venom when he addressed Denta by his rank. "The EDF is demoralized, but they are not broken. A simple message asking them to lay down their weapons would have an effect, but not at the scope we would like."

"Get to the point, would you?" Denta frowned.

"During my time with you humans I have learned that you are a race driven by fear." Denta's mount opened to object, but Pharos continued. "I do not mean that as an insult. It is self-preservation technique that I am sure led to the survival of your people. I simply mean to harness that fear response."

"How so?" Denta folded his arms across his chest. He was clearly over the Rhai's long winded explanation.

"As the message demanding their surrender is broadcast across every channel on the EDF network they will look up and see the entire Fidayi Clan and Titanian Fleet."

"I will end my message with a threat that if they don't surrender, we will lay waste to the entire Military District," Vincent said.

"You're going to bluff them?" Fiona raised an eyebrow.

"Consider it a push in the right direction." Pharos smiled.

"I thought we were not leveling the city," Arai said.

"We are not," Pharos said. "But they do not know our intentions. If the stories the Consuls tell are true, the EDF command have been spreading horrible rumors about our brutality through their ranks. It is time we use those to our advantage and scare them into giving up the fight."

"Driven by fear," grunted Denta. The old man's hard expression broke with laughter and he slapped his desk. "I'm happy you're on my side." Pharos said nothing. It was clear to Vincent the only side Pharos was on was Arai's. Pharos' black eyes showed no emotion. Vincent wasn't sure why, but no matter what the Spy Master said, he was sure he was holding something back.

"About the radio message," Vincent said. "I thought that the EDF soldiers who surrendered could say something, it shows that they are still alive and well. That the Mawr didn't eat them or whatever."

"Good idea." Denta nodded.

"You should say something," Erin said. Vincent's eyes went wide.

"Me?" He laughed nervously. "Have you ever heard me give a speech?"

"There is a reason that people cling to the Committee, other than loyalty," she said.

"Fear?" he asked.

"Normalcy," she corrected. "They just want a normal life, and their entire life that normal has been the Committee. We have to show them we have a different option. A new normal." Vincent thought back to the Human Quarter. Cramped, hot, and stinking. And that was before it had erupted into a warzone and few decent buildings had been blown up.

"Do we have normalcy to offer them?" He laughed.

"No," Fiona said. "But we can offer them freedom from the Committee that exploits them. Freedom to control their own lives. A blank slate where we can create a better future, together."

"Humanity without masters." Erin grinned. "Martian, Worm, or otherwise."

"I must admit," Denta said, rubbing his chin. "I like this idea. Even if the kid sucks at public speaking."

"Really?" Vincent raised an eyebrow. "You like one of our ideas?"

"I think it's a bunch of horse shit." He laughed. "But, if it takes even one soldier away from Brusilov, I'm willing to listen."

"I'll consider that progress."

CHAPTER FORTY-FIVE

Vincent sat with the rest of his command staff inside what remained of a small store. Its shelves were barren, and the original walls were missing. Soldiers had replaced the bombed-out sections with sandbags and bits of plywood.

In front of the store there was what had been a main thoroughfare in better times. A pedestrian walkway that cut through the heart of the commercial district. During the time of war it had been turned into a main deployment route for soldiers of the EDF until Erik and Denta's forces had seized it. Aero cars had been grounded and stacked up against one another to create a roadblock. Tired looking Titanian soldiers manning the roadblock were reinforced with three of Arai's tanks and several disheveled looking squads from the Elysian cohort.

Everyone was on edge. Vincent among them. He wasn't sure if this grand plan had any hope of working. It hated that he found himself agreeing with Denta. He wasn't sure of why surrendering soldiers would tell them misleading information. Why try to fool them? It was common knowledge that surrendering meant certain death at the hands of the Black Coats.

Unless the deployment of surrendering soldiers with fake information was just another one of Brusilov's plans. He was starting to feel like Victoria. He expected another Brusilov plot around every corner.

"Hey." Fiona snapped him out of it. "Are you ready?"

"No." He sighed. Her hand found its way onto his shoulder and she pulled him closer. "You're going to do great." She smiled.

"You really think so?" he asked. She reached into one of the pouches on her vest and pulled out a pack of cigarettes. They were a Lunar brand, pilfered from the corpse of an EDF soldier he assumed. She put one in between her cracked lips and lit it.

"If you don't, we go in there and skin the Worms alive. I'm fine with either one, Sweetheart." Her smile did not fade or change in the slightest whether she was encouraging him or threatening terrible violence.

"Lovely." He planted his face into his hands. Erin handed him a portable radio. It was a small thing, covered in dings and scratches.

"Pharos said they would transmit a signal to let us know when we were good to go," she said. He took the mic in his hand, hoping words would come to him. Denta had insisted that he write a speech down. Vincent had spent the last several hours looking down on a blank piece of paper, unable to think of a single word to say. He did however burn through an entire pack of Martian cigarettes, leaving his voice rough and his throat sore.

"I assume he is the EDF guy who wants to talk?" Vincent asked motioning towards a soldier who stood behind her. He was dressed in a grey field uniform with several days of beard growth covering his face. Erin nodded.

"Major?" she said. The man walked over to them and saluted.

"Major Ikagi, 2nd Squadron, 10th Infantry Regiment." He stopped for a second. "Or, at least I used to be." Vincent nodded and Ikagi dropped his salute. Ikagi looked to be in his mid-30s, with pale features and a pair of wire frame glassed perched on the end of his nose. He looked like he hadn't slept in days.

"Your unit didn't surrender with you?" he asked.

"Not entirely, no. I took as many as I could."

Erin smiled. "Well, hopefully today you can take away more."

"I just want this to be over," Ikagi sighed.

"Me too, Major," Vincent said.

The radio emitted a high-pitched squeal. He assumed that was the signal. "Shit." He frowned. "I guess this is it." He brought the mic up to his mouth and pressed the button down. "Uh..." Vincent began, his voice shaky. "Soldiers of the Earth Defense Forces. My name is Vincent Solaris, Consul of Humans for the Fidayi Clan. Formerly, of Earth. I know you have heard a lot about me, probably all of it bad, but hear me out. There was a time before all of this, when Earth was still alive, when I was just like you. I was cold, hungry, and scared on a planet far from home being left to die by an uncaring, lying government."

He paused and looked over at Fiona. She smiled, encouraging him to keep talking. "I watched my entire unit, people just like you, get massacred by the Alliance. They fought bravely for the government they trusted to care from them only to be abandoned. The Fidayi took me in and together we tried to save Earth from the Alliance, but the two-faced Chairman stabbed us in the back. Their greed, lust for power, and racism led to the death of everyone we love and hold dear to us when the Earth was burned out of existence. The very ideals we were taught to memorize and worship in Ethics school were the same ones the Chairman was following when he killed our home and left us to pick up the pieces. I know this is hard for you to accept, but we built a new home alongside our allies in the Fidayi Clan. It isn't much, but Earthians, Martians, Titanians, Mawr, and Rhai all live side-by-side and serve alongside each other to protect what is left of this universe from the Alliance." His confidence began to grow as the soldiers around him began to pay close attention to his words.

"I can't promise you a comfortable life. I can't promise a warm bed or food on your plate. Not yet anyway. What I can promise you is a fighting chance to build something that we haven't had since before we were unified by the Committee: Freedom. So, soldiers of the Earth Defense Force, I beg you to join us. The only thing you have to lose is your shackles." He stopped and had the mic over to Ikagi.

"My name is Major Shinichiro Ikagi formerly of the 10th Infantry Regiment. I am standing alongside Consul Solaris today because I have seen the true enemy of Mankind. That enemy is the Chairman of the Central Committee. It is clear to me now that the Committee has done nothing but lie about our so-called enemies in the Fidayi Clan and the Consul. While Brusilov's vile Black Coats steal your paychecks, food, and equipment. While they force you into slavery, the Consul and his army have provided my men with the first hot meal they have had since they landed on this planet and a bed to sleep in. We have not been treated as prisoners, but as comrades. I invite anyone who is listening to cross the lines today and join us and be welcomed with open arms." Ikagi handed the mic back to Vincent.

"The city is surrounded. The sky above you is controlled by our fleet which will soon reduce Brusilov and his Black Coated dogs to ash. Our fight is not with you, it is with the people who ordered you here. Do not stand between us." Vincent set the mic down and sighed heavily. He stared down the empty road in front of him. "Do you think that worked?"

"I think so," Erin said. "Think of how many people are trapped in their ranks and the only thing keeping them there is the fear of being shot by a Black Coat. You just gave them a way out."

"While still also possibly being shot by a black coat." Fiona smirked.

"What do you think, Major?" Vincent asked and Ikagi's posture immediately went rigid, snapping to the position of attention as all good EDF soldiers are trained to do.

"I believe what Lady Erin said is true, sir," he said.

"Lady Erin?" Fiona cackled with laughter. Erin's pale skin began to turn red.

"*Lady*?" Erin seethed. "I am a fucking colonel!" she roared. Fiona's laughter was infectious and soon Vincent fell victim to it.

But the laughter quickly died away, and the street returned to its state of eerie silence. Wind howled down the deserted street and soldiers talked in hushed whispers. Vincent's wasn't sure what he was expecting but standing there in the middle of the empty street made him feel a little bit like being stood up on a date.

He slumped against the side of a tank and waited.

The sun began to dip behind the broken skyline of Victoria. Vincent fought to stay awake as the days of sleep deprivation began to catch up with him. The rest of the Soldiers were not doing any better. Their heads bobbed up and down as they periodically fell asleep before jolting back awake a second later.

Suddenly, one of the tank commanders perked up in their hatch. The Commander leaned forward and squinted at something off in the distance. He started frantically waving his hands as if he were trying to get someone's attention. He began mouthing words, but what he was saying was drowned out by the rumbling engine of his tank.

That was when Vincent saw them.

Where before the road was completely devoid of life it was now teeming with people. They were too far away to make out quite yet. But it looked like a group of soldiers walking shoulder to shoulder. The tank commander fumbled around inside of his turret for a few seconds before bringing out a microphone.

"Who goes there?" His voice boomed, thick with static from being amplified. Vincent's heart began to race. Where people really trying to surrender, or was this some kind of trap?

"Should we shoot?" Fiona asked.

"No!" Vincent yelled. "They could be surrendering."

"It could be one of Brusilov's tricks!" She scowled.

"No, goddamnit!" he shot back. "We just invited people out to join us you can't shoot them!"

"Walking towards a line of dug in infantry and tanks is one hell of a trick." Victoria raised his eyebrow. "This is probably legit."

"We should be ready just in case," Erin said. "Major, come with me," she said and began marching down the line. Ikagi rushed to stay at her heels. She began shouting orders to soldiers who quickly ran to where they were directed.

"Don't shoot!" Screamed out a voice in the darkness. "Please, don't shoot!" As the voices got closer the true composition of the crowd could be made out. Soldiers clad in grey field uniforms that were little more than torn to rags walked alongside old men and women, many of whom were carrying children. Military utility vehicles flanked the mob, their cargo beds stacked high with people, equipment, and suitcases.

"Holy shit," Vincent gasped. Fiona's eyes went wide.

"They brought their entire families."

"Wouldn't you?" he asked. "Imagine what the Black Coats would do to someone's family if they found out they surrendered."

"Look at those poor bastards," she said. The soldier's uniforms were falling off of their backs and many of them were limping from various untreated wounds. Others were being carried on litters. Their faces were gaunt, and their eyes were sunken into their sockets. Many of them were not even wearing boots, instead they had bits of rags wrapped around their feet. Most of them were still armed, with their rifles slung across their backs.

The soldiers began to trickle past the roadblock. Their eyes grew as wide as saucers when they saw a Mawr or Rhai up close for the first time. Once they had made it past the aliens, they saw Vincent. Their eyes locked onto him, thunderstruck. He wasn't sure if it was because they had previously only seen his face on a propaganda poster or because they believed the lies about the destruction of Earth, but they made sure to keep their distance.

"I guess it's time to say hi, huh?" Vincent shrugged and began to walk towards the surrendering soldiers.

"What are you doing?" Fiona hissed. Vincent walked over to the first soldier he saw, a raven-haired girl who looked no older than he was and extended out his hand. She looked down at his hand looking like she expected it to be holding a gun.

"I'm Vincent," he said with a smile. "Thank you for joining us."

"You're Vincent Solaris?" she asked, her voice shaking.

"I am."

Her hand slowly extended out and grabbed his, giving it a tentative shake. She let go and rejoined the group. He shook the next soldier's hand. A tired looking sergeant who met him with a broad grin. An older captain with several days of stubble and a deep scar cutting across his face greeted him with a salute. Soon, the rest of the soldiers on the roadblock broke from their line and joined him. The Mawr and Rhai, still not entirely sure about the situation, stayed back.

Han shakes and hugs quickly spread through the ranks and soldiers began to help the fleeing civilians carry their belongings. The roadblock quickly turned into something of a strange party atmosphere when one of Vincent's soldiers started handing out boxes of rations and former ganger with a face covered in black tattoos began to pass out canteens. Judging from people's facial expressions after they took a drink from them, the canteens were not full of water.

Erin appeared from out of the crowd looking frustrated.

"Why does everything with our soldiers always turn into a damned drinking party?" she fumed.

"Because they're soldiers." Vincent laughed. "Don't act like you forget what it was like being an enlisted person."

She frowned and folded her arms.

"Besides, let them enjoy this."

"Have you ever seen humanity so united?" Fiona laughed. "You have people who were in the EDF ten minutes ago saluting a Martian colonel and drinking alongside the same aliens they had been taught their entire lives would destroy everything they loved." She paused for a second and lit a cigarette. "Oh sorry, I mean *Lady* Erin."

"I hate you so much." Erin rolled her eyes. Fiona and Vincent broke out into uncontrollable laughter. The impromptu get together moved onto the side of the roads as the tanks backed out of the way to let the cargo trucks through. "I never thought I would ever see anything like this." She smiled. "Unbelievable."

"This," Vincent said. "This is what we are fighting for."

Vincent approached a soldier who was passing out the spike canteens. A swaying Martian who was greeting everyone with a too friendly kiss on the cheek. He had clearly been celebrating longer than anyone else. Before he could take a canteen, a voice cut above the din of hundreds of conversations.

"Long live the Chairman!" It screamed. Soldiers stopped what they were doing and glanced around, confused. Vincent looked up to see a cargo truck pulling passed a tank. He saw the driver. A rough looking man with long brown hair. His knuckles were white and glued to the steering wheel. The truck got closer and he saw he was wearing a black coat. "Death to the Great Traitor!" The driver shouted.

Before he could do anything, the truck erupted into a bright flash.

CHAPTER FORTY-SIX

"Vincent?" A voice called out from the darkness. The voice sounded so far away it was almost a whisper. "Vincent!" It called again, now it was louder and sounded urgent. The edges of the darkness began to melt away. He recognized the voice as Fiona's, but why was she yelling at him? He was so comfortable and warm. They must have been in bed. But she always slept in longer than he did. "Vincent! Wake up damnit!" Her voice cut in once again. This time the darkness vanished completely.

When he woke, he saw a dull gunmetal grey ceiling above him. Various pipes and wires strung across it with thick cobwebs weaving between them. He tried to look around and get his bearings when he locked eyes with an overhead light. Its bright white glow seared his eyes and they clamped shut independent of his control. Tears flowed freely from his eyes. The burning in his left eye traced a line through his head and caused an explosion of pain that caused him to scream. The wave of pain washed through his brain and felt like someone was flash frying his head.

"Hey!" Fiona screamed out. "He's awake! Somebody get over here!" as fast as the pain began it ended, as if someone had flipped a switch. Vincent blinked. The vision in his right eye was worse than normal. It was blurry as if was trying to look over a fire. Out of his left eye he couldn't see anything. He knew he had his eye open, but the only thing he could see was impenetrable darkness. A dull throb replaced the vision in his left eye. "You said it would fucking work!" Fiona cursed at somebody Vincent couldn't see.

"I'm sorry Ma'am," a voice said. It was an old voice tinged with bitterness. "These things don't always take right away. Adjustments are sometimes needed." Vincent coughed. His throat was raw from screaming.

"What—" he croaked; his mouth was so dry it was hard to speak. "Where am I?" The vision in his right eye began to clear. The shape of Fiona and Zinvor began to form alongside him along with a dark skinned Titanian man in a white coat. The air smelled like burning oil and dust.

"You are aboard the *TSS Mercy*, Consul," the man in the white coat said. His was the older voice Fiona had been yelling at.

"A hospital ship," Fiona added. Vincent felt his heart drop.

"A hospital ship?"

"Do you not remember what happened?" The man asked, taking notes on a data display.

"I remember meeting with the EDF soldiers..." He thought hard, his mind was jumbled and confused. "And then a bright flash."

"They drove a bomb into our roadblock," Fiona said. "A fucking insane person drove a bomb right into us." She frowned.

"They drove a bomb into us?" he asked. The idea was absurd.

"A Black Coat suicide bomber," she said. "He killed hundreds." She shook her head. "hundreds of people were wounded too. Most of them were civilians."

"Many of ours as well," Zinvor grunted.

"...including you," Fiona said, apprehensively. He picked his head up and glanced down at his body. His armor was gone and instead he was wearing a white hospital gown. Various tubes branched down from a bank of computers leading to IV sites in his arms. A machine was plugged into a hole in his stomach and electrodes were taped to his chest. Every time he breathed a computer next to him would let out a *beep.*

Everything was still attached that he could see. Though his foot was now gnarled with scars from the Battle on the Mons and his chest was still badly discolored from where he had been shot. "You were blown through a window," Fiona continued. "I thought you were dead." Her voice trailed off as she choked up.

As he picked up his head a little higher, grabbed the back of his head and tugged him down. A sharp pain stabbed at him from behind his left ear. He traced his hand back over his head he was surprised to him his head had been shaved, leaving behind only a prickly stubble. His fingers also found a small wire. The thin wire went from a computer at the side of his bed up and into the back of his head.

"What in the—"

"Do not pull on the wire," the man in the white coat ordered. "We are still adjusting the augmentation."

"The what?" Vincent asked. Fiona placed a comforting hand on top of his. The look on her face only made him more concerned.

"The left eye was far too damaged to save," the man said. "We were able to salvage the nerves however, which allowed us to implant an augmentation."

"I lost my fucking eye?" Vincent gasped, sitting up quickly. The spot behind his ear stabbed at him again. The thick, paw like hand of Zinvor forced him back down.

"The pain you felt upon waking was the augmentation absorbing light for the first time. We will have to dial it back so it works correctly. But, rest assured, the pain is a good thing!" The man smiled. "It means the implant took."

"It felt like my brain was on fire!" Vincent snapped. "How is that a good thing?"

"It takes time for your body to get used to the new processors, sir." The man nodded. "This is good progress for only two weeks."

"Two weeks?" Vincent exclaimed. "I've been here for two weeks?"

"Yes. Placing the augmentation and allowing it to set correctly meant we had to place you in a medical coma."

"I can't be gone for two weeks!" he yelled. "Who is running the army?" His mind raced. "What is going on in Victoria?"

Fiona squeezed his hand again. "Everything is fine," she said. "Erin is running things on the ground." She smiled and leaned in closer, kissing him on the cheek. "So, you should be happy somebody who knows what they're doing is in charge again."

"You're right." He sighed. Erin had earned the right to command soldiers through years of clawing her way through battles while he had been put in charge by default. "That doesn't mean I'm happy about it though," he added. "How much longer to I have to be chained to this computer?"

"Just the rest of this night cycle, assuming the tests come back favorable," the man said. "It will still take the augmentation time to bind correctly to your neural pathways, but the direct connection will not be necessary."

"Can I at least sit up?" Vincent asked.

"Of course." The man reached behind the bed and tugged on the wire, moving it around the side of the bed and coiling it onto Vincent's chest. He was still tethered to the computer, but at least he had more slack now. He tried to push himself into a sitting position, but his arms trembled and he fell back down.

Fiona stifled a laugh. "Feeling a bit weak, I imagine." She pointed to the machine plugged into the side of his stomach. "They've been feeding you with liquid for a week and you haven't moved."

"Ugh," he groaned. "How embarrassing."

"*That* isn't embarrassing," she said. "Just wait until you find out how you've been going to the bathroom." Vincent felt his cheeks begin to burn. "Now that," she stroked his hand. "That is embarrassing."

*   *   *

When Vincent woke up again, the overhead lights, once so bright he thought they would scorch his brain to ash, were off. He knew this meant that the ship was officially in its night cycle. The light cycle was an artificial cycle of lights that would brighten or dim every twelve hours. It was put in place after numerous studies showed that without a normal day/night cycle, human bodies and minds quickly began to break down. People would become fatigued, make mistakes.

The cycle would simulate day or night, allowing normal shifts to go to work as if they were planet side. Back when Vincent was aboard the *ESS Victory* the cycle had never worked on him. He was only able to sleep a few hours at a time and his body was always confused and tired. A crewman had told him that it took months to years for a normal navy recruit to become accustomed to their way of living. In the meantime, Vincent was still unable to sleep.

He forced himself to a sitting position, his midsection cramping from the exertion. He finally got to look around the room that he had just learned he had been in for over a week. It was small, hardly bigger than his bedroom back in his father's house. Even with the musty stench of oil and dust, it was still cleaner than his room had been.

Unlike his old bedroom, it was devoid of furniture or warmth. Across from his hospital bed was a small cot where Fiona was curled up in a ball and fast asleep. Her armor lay splayed out on the ground next to her. The only other thing in the room was a series of computers and a spider's web of black wires and tubes that led from them and were plugged into his body in one way or another.

He knew Fiona and the Doctor who was watching over him would disapprove, but he wanted to get up and walk around. After having such a hard time simply sitting up, he wasn't sure if his neglected muscles had the strength left in them to support his weight. Vincent flexed his legs and brought them to his chest. After a few minutes of struggle he managed to rotate his legs over the side of the bed.

Vincent sighed as he realized he wasn't going to be able to force his legs to work again while balancing the computer that was plugged into his own skull. He wasn't sure what would happen if that wire came unconnected, but he was certain he didn't want to find out. The door to the room swung open and a figure, backlit by harsh white light stepped in.

"I kind of figured they wouldn't be able to keep you trapped on that bed once you woke up," the figure said. It was a woman's voice. She closed the door behind her. Standing in front of the door was Felicity Haagen. Her right arm was in a sling and she was balanced on a crutch. Her thick black hair, once pulled into a painfully tight bun, had been buzzed short like his own.

"Felicity?" he gasped. She straightened herself up the best she could and saluted. "Cut that shit out!" He waved her off. "I thought you were dead!" She hobbled closer to him.

"I was," she said. "Twice."

"What happened?" he asked. "I mean, when you ran off."

"When I climbed that hill, I made myself a really easy target for them. It also turns out that orbital radio transmissions are really easy to triangulate for artillery strikes." She shrugged.

"You seem to have gotten off okay," he said. Felicity bent down and lifted up her left pant leg revealing a metal augmented leg, going into a black boot.

"I lost it at the thigh." She sighed. "I'm still learning how to use it, but it could be worse." She shifted uncomfortably. "I'm sorry I ran off like that without telling anybody."

"Don't be ridiculous, Felicity," he said. "You saved our lives. More than that, you saved the entire mission. I don't know what I can do to ever repay you."

"I already got her a promotion." Fiona waved her hand and him.

"A promotion?" Felicity gasped. "It is customary for a junior lieutenant to stay at that rank for two years."

"Customary where?" Fiona frowned. "Titan? You're Elysian now. Remember?"

"Wait, how did you do that? I was in a coma," Vincent interjected.

"I forged your signature and Erin accepted it," Fiona said. "So congratulations, First Lieutenant." Felicity's eyes began to tear up. She opened up her mouth to speak when Fiona interrupted.

"Now if you could, *Lieutenant Haagen*, I'm trying to sleep, and he is supposed to be resting. Get out." She pulled her blanket over her head and rolled over.

"Okay," the man in the white coat said. "I'm going to turn on the augmentation again."

"Is this going to set my brain on fire again?" Vincent asked.

"All of our tests say the augment is perfectly synched to your neurons." Vincent turned and looked at him, raising an eyebrow. "Okay." The doctor held up his hands. "As perfectly as it is going to be."

"Why can't you be sure?" Fiona frowned.

"A lot of reasons." The doctor pinched his chin. "The augments are perfectly engineered pieces of technology. Truly flawless. The human body, however, is not. Everyone's body does not take the augments like they should. Some outright reject them. Sometimes the shock to the system can kill people if they are too weak." He read the look of concern that was painted across Vincent's face, because he continued. "But the Consul's body accepted the augment as good as can be expected. There is no reason why it won't work. Are you ready?"

Vincent sighed, wincing as he remembered the pain of the last time they switched on his new eye.

Fiona put a hand on his shoulder. "It's got to work better than it looks right?" she said. Vincent turned and looked at her, his cheeks growing flush. He hadn't had the opportunity to look at himself in the mirror since he had woken up and it had suddenly dawned on him that he had no idea what his new eye looked like.

"Wait, what?" he said. "What does it look like?" Fiona burst out into laughter and was joined by Felicity who quickly stifled her laughter when he looked at her. "Ugh," he groaned. "Just turn the damn thing on." The Doctor leaned over and began to type on the computer that was attached to his head. After a few moments, a crackle of pain surged through the back of his head and seared through his left eye.

The pitch blackness faded away and a picture began to form. First it was hazy and full of static, as if he were trying to read a damaged data display. The world slowly began to come into focus and after a few minutes the picture in his new eye was significantly sharper than the one in his right.

"Whoa," Vincent gasped. "It's working." He put his hand up in front of his face. "I think it is working better than the real one." A grin spread across the doctor's face.

"Maybe you'll actually be able to shoot now." Fiona laughed.

"I'm a righty." Vincent frowned. Fiona patted him on the shoulder. "Can I see it now?" the doctor handed him a small mirror and Vincent held it up in front of his face.

What he saw shocked him. A twisted series of stitches wound their way across the left side of his face, leading up to his new eye. A slate grey globe replaced the natural white one. In the center, where the iris used to be, a small black dot replaced the brown eye he expected to see.

"Creepy, right?" Fiona asked.

"A little. Yeah." Vincent reached up and poked the augment, getting even more creeped out by the fact that he felt nothing. "You already said you would marry me. You can't back out now."

"Yeah, yeah." Fiona waved him off. "It's kind of growing on me. It's a little badass too."

"Yeah?" He smiled.

"Not as cool as Felicity's robot leg over there though." She folded her arms.

"You think?" Felicity beamed.

"You kidding me?" Fiona grinned. "Think of how much street cred you're going to have with your soldiers when you put a metal foot up their ass." She nudged Felicity's shoulder and the young girl's smile spread further across her face. And that was when Vincent understood what Fiona was doing. His augmented eye didn't look cool and he was sure Felicity wanted nothing more than to have her leg back. She was trying to make them feel better in the only way she knew how. He couldn't stop himself from grinning like an idiot and joining in.

"You remember Rostov?" Vincent asked.

"How could I forget that bastard?" Fiona asked.

"He had an augmented leg and he scared every soldier who ever looked at him." That was until he killed him on Grawluck. She didn't have to know that part. Felicity began to laugh, looking genuinely relieved. Fiona winked at Vincent and sat down on the bed next to him.

The Doctor reached behind Vincent's ear.

"This might pinch a bit," he said, and unplugged the wire. It sent a strange jolt of electricity through Vincent's eye and down his jaw.

"So, I'm good to go now?" Vincent asked.

"Not quite." The doctor held up his hand. "After the augments are installed, we like to make sure they are working correctly for at least a week before you are cleared for field operations. Not to mention getting those stitches out. You go back to the front with all those open cuts you'll get an infection in no time. It is a miracle you didn't already have one. There are another thousand or so soldiers on this boat who would wish for luck as good as yours."

"But—" Vincent began.

The doctor quickly cut him off, holding up a finger. "I don't care if you're the Consul or Field Marshal Denta himself. You aren't running off with my augments until I know they aren't going to rot and fall off of you. It's a waste of material that could have been spent on someone who might actually listen to their Doctor."

"Fine," Vincent groaned. "So, do I have to change batteries in this thing or something?" He tapped his eye.

"Don't be ridiculous," the Doctor frowned. "All augments are powered by the electricity that naturally occurs in the human brain."

"Right..." Vincent forced a smile. "I was totally kidding. The electricity in the human brain..." He sighed. He copied off his friend Chester throughout Biology and Human Anatomy classes and he still managed to get a D. He had no idea what he was talking about.

"He wasn't kidding," Fiona stated.

"I know." The doctor rubbed his temples and yawned. "Now if you'll excuse me, I have other patients I need to check on."

"Of course." Vincent stood up, his legs unsteady under him. "I never got your name." He extended his hand and the doctor shook it.

"My name is Doctor Colonel General Lars Trotha, Chief of Augmetic Engineering for the Titanian Armed Forces. Field Marshal Denta wanted me to ensure that you received the best treatment available." He nodded at Felicity. "And your Aide, of course." Trotha turned and exited the room.

Vincent sighed. "So, I can't leave this damn ship for another week. What now?"

"Well, the Doctor wanted me to walk as much as I could," Felicity said. "Something about the more I use it the more it syncs with my nervous system. I didn't understand half of what he said. I assume he would want you to do the same thing."

"At least you didn't think your leg ran on batteries," Fiona giggled, and Vincent rolled his eyes.

"How about you show me around the ship?" he asked.

"I thought you hated ships, sir."

"I do. But I don't have much of a choice, do I?"

The *TSS Mercy* reminded Vincent of every other human ship he had ever been on. It was a maze of small, cramped hallways with bulkheads acting as tripping hazards every dozen feet or so. Wires hung down from the low ceilings, interweaving themselves between pipes and ductwork. Vincent was by no means a large man, but the effect was claustrophobic. Crowds of Titanian soldiers in white uniforms shoved by them, fighting over the little free space they had.

Even though he was on a hospital ship, it felt as though he was in the middle of an industrial factory. The stench of Burning oil, dust, and stale sweat mixed with the tinge of anti-septic and the coppery smell of blood. The dull humming of the ship's engine made everything vibrate just enough where you could not ignore it. How anyone lived aboard one of these ships for years at a time, Vincent had no idea.

"The chow hall is down this way," Felicity said as she maneuvered her crutches over a bulkhead. "Are you hungry?" Vincent's stomach began to growl, and it suddenly felt like he hadn't eaten in a week. His memories of shipboard dining were haunted by the taste of the food aboard the *ESS Victory* and he frowned at the thought.

"Don't worry, it's better than that crap they gave us before," Fiona said, reading his facial expression. "Apparently, you have to almost die in order to get real food."

"I enjoy the human space food," Zinvor said. "It is nourishing."

"Bland, tasteless, mush?" Fiona frowned. "It would probably be a Mawr staple."

"This is an insult, is it not?" he grunted. Fiona laughed.

"He's catching on." Felicity led them through a door and into a large bay. Rows of metal tables were filled by soldiers sitting shoulder to shoulder. There were multiple different uniforms between them. Tan, grey, red, and even people in civilian clothes and a few Rhai sat side by side one another eating.

"Civilians and EDF soldiers?" Vincent raised his eyebrow. "I didn't think Denta would ever sign off on that."

"He didn't," Fiona said. "You did."

"You forged my signature on this too?" Vincent asked. Fiona was a lot of things, but compassionate towards the plight of Earthian settlers and EDF refugees was absolutely not one of them.

"No," Fiona spat. "She did." She pointed at Felicity.

"I thought you would want these people cared for, sir." Her face began to turn shades of red. "I'm sorry for breaking protocol."

"Why would you be sorry for helping people?" He smiled. "I'm just shocked Denta went along with it." Vincent supposed the talk he had with the old man had done more good than he originally thought. Fiona shrugged.

"The Clan pulled his ass out of the fire. He owed us."

As they stepped into the room, Felicity stepped to the side of the door, straightened herself to the position of attention the best she could and bellowed.

"Consul Solaris!" At her command, the rows of soldiers stopped eating and shot straight to their feet if they were still able to do so. The ones who couldn't stopped what they were doing and sat rigidly, staring straight ahead. Vincent froze in place, unsure of what to do. He looked over at Felicity accusingly, it was his turn for his cheeks to flush. "As you were!" she yelled out after a couple of seconds. The soldiers went back to eating as if nothing had happened.

"What was that?" Vincent asked, feeling his face burn.

"It's standard aboard a ship for the presence of a superior officer to be announced when they enter a room, sir," Felicity said.

"Consul isn't a military rank," he said, then thought for a moment. "As far as I know."

"But you are Cohort Leader, sir," she reminded him. He rubbed his temples. She was right, but he failed to see the purpose of introducing rank into the act of eating lunch. Felicity led the group through lines of tables and Vincent couldn't help but notice that while soldiers from Mars, Titan, or Elysian paid him no mind. The novelty of his existence having worn off, the surrendered EDF soldiers and their civilian counterparts stopped what they were doing at gawked at him.

By the time they sat down at a table near the back the crowd was no longer entertained by Vincent's presence. The sounds of countless conversations and the clanging of forks and spoons against metal bowls grew to a dull roar as people turned back to their food. As soon as they had settled into their seats ship crew in white cook's jackets and hairnets were standing behind them holding trays of food.

Vincent was handed a small, dinged up metal bowl full of a green-brown mush. He poked it with his spoon, and it swayed a bit. He spooned a mouthful of the stuff in and swallowed it without chewing.

"How is it?" Fiona asked, chewing a mouthful of the stuff down.

"Terrible," he said, swallowing. "What is it?"

"Space stable yeast product." Felicity frowned. "Meat doesn't tend to hold up well during long space travel and there isn't exactly a lot of room onboard for storage. So, everything is reconstituted yeast or algae mixtures."

"Well." Vincent sighed and took another bite. "This is still better than that soup that Fiona tried to feed me."

"Humans complain too much," Zinvor said, dropping his empty bowl on the table. Vincent pushed his bowl across the table to the hungry Tsarra and he took it, shoveling the food into his mouth with his hand. "You did not even have to hunt for this meal. A blessing from Paterazm," he said, spitting brown flecks of something across the table.

"Gross." Fiona giggled. A siren began to wail throughout the chow hall. A screaming claxon was followed with three loud chimes. After a few moments of the siren blaring, the chimes repeated themselves.

"Alert!" boomed a woman's voice over the ship's intercom system. "Alert!" she said again. "Mass Casualty event! All available personnel report to the landing dock!" without delay, the chow hall erupted into a tornado of chaos.

Soldiers, ship crew, and civilians dropped their dishes and began pushing against one another for the exit.

"What's going on?" Vincent asked.

"Mass casualty event," Felicity said, repeating the intercom voice. "It means they're bringing in the wounded from the surface. A lot of wounded." Vincent stood up and fought into the crowd trying to exit the chow hall.

"Sir!" Felicity called out. "Where are you going?"

"We're available, aren't we?" he said.

When Vincent got to the docking bay the entire area was a chaotic blur of activity. A Reaper had already landed, and its landing ramp deployed. The ship was badly damaged. Smoke trailed from one of its engines. Lines of white jacketed medical crew were working in a chain to pass stretchers from inside the ship, down the ramp, and onto the landing area. After every few stretchers one was set aside, the soldiers laying on them were no longer moving.

He watched another ship pull in. Its normally flat, grey metal was scored with bullet marks, as if it had flown through an asteroid field. Its windshield was cracked, and it looked like a minor miracle had held it together to as it exited Mars' orbit. Its ramp dropped, slamming against the docking bay with a sharp clang. The first ones out of the ship were the wounded who were still able to walk.

A soldier stumbled out from the ship. His face covered with blood-stained bandages, and his left arm reduced to a ragged stump. He was being led down the ramp by the next wounded man. After them came a group of shirtless soldiers. They had been seared by some kind of thermal weapon. Their once pale Martian skin had been scorched black and red. It flaked off in flecks of ash as they shuffled. It was then that Vincent noticed they were not shirtless. Their uniform jackets had seared to their skin.

Screams of pain and misery melded with the shouting of orders. Medical personal ran down to the ship and bellowed over to the gawking crowd for assistance. Vincent took off running at their orders, Fiona at his heels. Ship crew were passing off stretchers when a Titanian sergeant in a stained white uniform and handed one to Vincent. The soldier laying on the stretcher seemed a thousand miles away. Her blue eyes were staring up, unblinking, as her hands held a large brown bandage over her stomach.

"This one needs to go to surgery now!" the sergeant said. He pointed to a collection of tables that had been set up in the middle of the bay. Doctors in long white jackets were working on a long line of charges. The high-pitched whine of their bone saws didn't muffle the screams of the wounded. The grey metal deck around their feet was thick with sticky blood and littered in discarded bandages.

Fiona grabbed the other side of the stretcher and they made their way into the crowd. At first, he tried set off lightly, worried he would cause the soldier even more pain, but it soon became apparent that it didn't matter. Medical personnel, orderlies, and civilian helpers were bumping into each other, running at a dead sprint, and dropping stretchers all in an effort to get the wounded person to one of the dozen operating tables.

The surgeons who were not actively operating would look over a stretcher and either order the soldier placed on their table or to be set aside. Vincent knew being set aside was a death sentence, he had watched this grim practice before. Either their wounds were too grievous, or they were so far gone they were not even worth the surgeon's time. In battlefield medicine time was everything and it was better spent on someone they knew they could save.

Vincent waited in line behind a stretcher being held by two soldiers who wore tattered grey uniforms. The wounded man on it had been stripped down to his underwear. His chest had been blasted open and his innards were clearly visible. The mess had been pieced back together with bits of plastic and adhesive in what looked like a vain attempt to stop his organs from spilling out. The soldier didn't seem to be breathing.

He glanced over his shoulder and saw the woman he was carrying had quickly begun to circle the drain. Her arms had contorted at strange angles and her fingers froze into fists. Her breathing had changed from slow but normal to a gasping snore. Each time she breathed in her chest would heave and blood would bubble from her stomach wound.

The Surgeon looked down at the soldier in front of them and nodded to an Orderly that stood nearby. Two Orderlies took the stretcher from its original bearers and dumped the wounded soldier onto the ground next to them, where a growing pile of the dead and dying was forming. The Orderlies then handed the stretcher back and the two soldiers who had brought it. The soldiers hustled back to the landing ships to find more wounded.

The Surgeon looked down at the wounded soldier Vincent and Fiona were carrying and again, turned towards his Orderlies and nodded. Before the Orderlies could take the stretcher from them Fiona kicked at one of them.

"Fuck off!" she hissed.

"This one is already going into shock!" An Orderly yelled back. The Orderly was a young man, younger even than the woman who was dying on the stretcher.

"If you were dying would you want something to throw you in a pile like a piece of garbage?"

"It's a waste of damn time!" The Surgeon yelled. "Now get out of my line before I order you arrested!"

"Touch me and I'll fucking gut you," she growled. Vincent pulled the stretcher away from the line and towards the pile of human suffering that had been created next to the Surgeon's tables. Other white uniformed Orderlies were going through the pockets of the dead and dying. They were at work taking off their Identification tags and adding them to a bag they were carrying. The bag was growing so large the Orderly carrying it was visibly beginning to strain under its weight.

Fiona and Vincent set the stretcher down next to them. He reached over and pulled her tags from around her neck. Stamped in on the thin metal tag it said:

Anahit Brunet
First Infantry Regiment, Elysian Cohort. Fidayi Clan.
AB NEG

He sighed and handed the tag over to one of the Orderlies who tossed it unceremoniously into the bag with the others. The soldier's snoring finally went silent as her body finally gave in. How many people had Vincent led to such an undignified death? Cast aside like trash to have their body picked over so it could be tallied in a command room somewhere. There was a good chance the poor woman didn't even have loved ones to miss her anymore.

The siren began to wail once again. The last flight of transport ships had hardly departed, and more were already coming in. Even soldiers who had been deemed worth the Surgeon's time were piling up around the operating tables, waiting their turn. Others were being brought into the hospital bays, their wounds packed with gauze for the Surgeons to get to later.

Fiona lit a cigarette and handed one to Vincent, which he took.

"It's going to be a long night," she said. The sirens screamed out again, followed by the calm woman's voice.

"Alert!" she said. "Mass Casualty Event! All available personnel to the landing dock!"

An endless stream of medical transport ships began landing on the *Mercy*. Soldiers and civilians came out in waves. They had been shot, blown apart, and burned alive. The lines to the Surgeon's tables were quickly disregarded when children were brought out of the ships, cradled in the arms of desperate medics.

The worst was the gas victims. A some point the EDF holed up in the Military District and their backs against the wall began to launch gas rockets and shells. There was even rumors of Reapers, loaded heavily with explosives and poison, crashing into crowded marketplaces and command posts in horrific suicide runs like the one that had wounded him.

After Vincent took the radio and spoke to the entire city something about the defenders had changed. The Black Coats knew they were losing not only the city, but the people too. In return they were doing their best to turn the city into a giant graveyard. One big enough to bury them all.

The gas victims came off the ships with their eyes bulging out of their heads and their lips and skin badly discolored. Blisters formed across their skin, they bled from every orifice, and their skin sloughed off the bone in thick slabs at the slightest touch. Most of them were discarded as lost causes as soon as they came off the ships. Others were led screaming into the hospital bays, their ruined eyes covered with wet cloth.

Vincent and Fiona worked alongside everyone else for hours in an almost automated series of movements. After their initial argument with the Surgeons, they didn't bother speaking up in defiance of their emotionless methods. Vincent knew they were right, but he didn't want to give them the satisfaction.

Mercifully, the transports stopped coming. He wasn't sure if that was the last of the wounded or the *Mercy* had simply run out of beds and there was another Hospital Ship they were being sent to instead. Fiona and Vincent were sitting on the ground, watching as dozens of Orderlies mopped up the pools of blood that had filled the dock area over the last few hours. Their cleaning was making slow progress. Every motion of their mops smeared the blood across the grey floor in a crimson arc.

The night cycle lights flickered off and bright overhead arc sodium lights kicked on, giving off an audible hum and bathed the butchery of the landing dock in an orange light.

"Before I was blown up, we were winning. What is going on down there?" Vincent sighed. "Are we losing?"

"I don't think so. This might just be what winning looks like," Fiona said, smoke curling out of her nose.

"Fuck," he said. He watched an Orderly wring out a mop into a bucket, filling it with red water. "I don't think I can do this anymore."

"You don't have that choice anymore Vinny. None of us do." She put an arm around him, pulling him in close. "We either win this or we die."

"How many more people are going to die," he began, his eyes beginning to burn with tears, "gasping for air on the floor of some ship while everyone steps over them like they are just some obstacle." He motioned over to the door to the Hospital Bay. "Or have their eyes burned out of their skulls and drown in their own blood from gas?"

"We did that too," she said.

"That wasn't me!" he cried. "I said not to use it!"

"But," Fiona held up a hand, "it worked against them. And now it's working against us."

"So, what are you saying?" he asked. "That Denta was right and I'm an idiot?"

"You're not an idiot." She smiled. He knew she was trying to look reassuring, but she only looked like she was humoring him. "You're an optimist. You think that just by doing the right thing all of the time things will work out. That we will win by virtue of being the good guys."

"That makes me sound like an idiot."

"It's one of the reasons I love you. If everyone thought like you the universe would be a better place." She stubbed her cigarette out and tossed it into a pile of discarded medical bandages. "Until then, you're going to have to start thinking about how to beat Brusilov. Not about what a good person would do."

"You want me to be a monster," he said. She lifted his chin up so his eyes would meet hers. Her blue eyes locked onto his and swallowed him whole. "I want you to fucking win."

CHAPTER FORTY-SEVEN

The inside of the hospital bay was one of the foulest places Vincent had ever laid his eyes on. Bay D, according to the fading painted stencil on the door, had been set aside for Elysian and Civilian casualties ever since the Titan fleet touched down at the Mons. It had since been filed up with thousands of the dead, dying, and miserable.

The bay was wide enough for a transport ship to dock within its walls. The space was short and dark, with a spiderweb of wires and tubes coming off of the walls from medical computers and machinery. Each bundle of the web went to a soldier who lay on a bed recovering. If they were lucky, they would have a cot to lay on, many did not. The *Mercy* had run out of beds during the initial attack on Victoria and had since soldiers who were considered less likely to survive were forced to lay on the floor. They were given only a thin wool blanket in between them and the cold metal deck plates.

The smell was so overpowering that it burned his eyes and nose. The swirling stench of blood, burned flesh, bile, and infection combined together to create something truly overwhelming. The warm, stale air of the hospital bay only made things worse.

"Presan is in here?" He coughed, trying to force his lunch to stay down.

"Yes, sir," Felicity said. "When they brought the Field Marshal in, they couldn't tell who he was due to his uniform being burned off." She swallowed hard, trying to keep her composure as they walked down the aisles of human misery. "Once they found out who he was he refused to be moved away from the soldiers." Vincent felt his throat thicken.

He had been sleeping in his own private room and being tended to by the head Titanian Military Augmetic Engineering while the people who fought for him sat and rotted in a place that resembled a repurposed meat locker.

"Sir, you were in a coma," Felicity said, sensing his shift in mood. "You couldn't object."

"And you're only going to be here a few more days," Fiona pointed out. "Ol' Presan can't say the same thing."

"Wait. Why not?" he asked. "You lost your leg and you hardly even need that crutch anymore."

"This is my last day with it actually." Felicity smiled slightly. "But, remember when the Doctor told you about how some body's reject the augments?"

"Yeah."

"Field Marshal Presan is one of those." She sighed. "They tried twice, but each time his body rejected the augments. The last time he ended up with an infection of some kind." In a place like this of course his wounds got infected, Vincent thought to himself.

Felicity led them further into the bay. Orderlies bumped shoulders with Elysian Medics in their stained khaki jackets, and Martian ones in their red coats. When they reached the rear of the bay, they found an area that was surrounded by army-issued green wool blankets suspended from the ceiling by bits of string. A soldier's attempt to salvage some bit of privacy.

A young Titanian corporal in a khaki uniform sat outside the blanket wall on a field chair. When he saw Felicity approaching, he got to his feet and saluted.

"The Field Marshal is expecting you."

"Thank you, Corporal," she said. He turned, pulling a blanket out of the way.

Field Marshal Denta lay in his bed propped up to a sitting position by several pillows. He had several data displays in front of him and he was making notes. Vincent notice his skin held a deathlike pallor. His eyes were bloodshot and his lips bluish. A heart monitor beeped in a stead rhythm next to him and several IV bags hung on hooks around his bed, their lines going into both of his arms. He looked up from what he was doing and smiled weakly.

"Consul Solaris!" he croaked. His voice sounded hollow. "You look well."

"So do you, Vadim." Vincent faked a smile. The man looked like he should have died days before.

"Don't lie to me son." Presan coughed. "I know I look like shit. That's why I asked you to meet with me. Denta is holding a meeting aboard his flagship and invited me." Presan looked down at the stumps where his legs used to be. "Clearly, I am not in the shape to attend. I know Erin was put in charge temporarily, but it would probably be good if one of us went as well."

"Of course." Vincent nodded. "What happened? Did Denta get scared off the surface?" He smirked.

"Sort of." Presan handed him a data display. "Have you not been reading the reports?"

"What reports?" he asked. He looked over at Felicity who shrugged.

"Don't look at me, they haven't been sending me anything," she replied.

"Hmm." Presan rubbed his chin. "They were probably not aware you were awake."

Vincent took the display and looked it over. It was casualty lists by unit for each of the human armies. The Titanians had several units being withdrawn back to the fleets for rest and reinforcing. The Elysians had several units that had been stricken from the list altogether. "Once their encirclement was broken the main EDF forces pulled back to the Military District." Vincent knew that part. Brusilov had turned an entire city district into a citadel of layered defenses. "But they left several thousand soldiers all around the city in small groups. These are the diehard Black Coats. They are held up in every building, every nook and cranny, refusing to surrender. They're forcing our forces to have to fight for every single room of every single house on every single street. And when we get too close, they blow themselves up or crash a Reaper full of nerve gas into a command post. I've never seen anything like it."

"Madness," grunted Zinvor.

"They're too stupid to understand that they lost," Fiona said.

"Regardless, it isn't the best situation for an old man to try to command an army from the front," Presan rasped. "Wish I would have taken the same damn hint."

"How can we end this damn thing?" Vincent asked. Presan sighed, looking defeated.

"Fighting like we are now?" He shook his head. "It'll take years to root them all out. And that is just to move a secure line forward to start the assault the District. And by then High Command in Lunar City would have probably got their shit together enough for a counterattack."

"You think they can still scrape one together?" Vincent asked.

"If we gave them enough time. Same could be said for the Anarchs. Every second we waste kicking down doors in Victoria is a second that is needed to get ready for our real fight." Vincent wasn't sure how long it took to assemble an Anarch fleet, but he was sure he never wanted to find out. "But," Presan held up his hands in mock surrender, "I could complain about Denta's battle plan all day. You're the one who has to go deal with him. I don't even think getting my legs back is worth putting up with that."

"Lucky me," Vincent sighed. "I suppose I should go get ready."

"Yeah," Presan said. "You smell like you have been hanging out in a hospital bay."

Vincent slipped back into his Armor. The jacket still had dried blood around the neck. He assumed it was from when his eye was blown out of his skull by a flying piece of debris. Numerous other new cuts, scrapes, and gouges decorated the dull blue armored scales from his boots up to his chest. A large divot in the center of his chest remained from where he was shot while storming the city limits. Zinvor was the only Mawr on the ship and without Arai's Armor Melds there was no way to get his Armor cleaned or repaired.

Fiona wiggled into her armored pants and slid her boots on without lacing them up. She carried her Riten in a shoulder holster and the weight of it made it droop down on one side. Her armor was surprisingly unblemished. She always did find a way to escape every situation where he found himself wounded, totally unharmed.

They stepped out of the room and were met by Zinvor and Felicity. Felicity led them back to the landing docks which were now busy loading and unloading cargo. No hint of the previous night's scenes of unfiltered suffering remained. Vincent noticed one of the barges that was docked was taking on several pallets of freight. Each one was full of multiple stacks of six-foot-long metal boxes. From their grey color, Vincent thought they must have been made out of Zinc.

Docked next to the barges was a heavily modified Reaper. A large red Phoenix was painted across its side and the name *Shanna II* was stenciled under the cockpit window. Ezra stood outside of his ship while Tyr busily checked over its exterior.

"What are you doing here?" Vincent asked.

"I'm your ride to the meeting." Ezra smiled. "And besides, the old girl has taken a beating and needs some repairs." Felicity snapped to attention and saluted Ezra who waved her off. "And who is this?"

"Felicity," Vincent said. "She's my aide."

"Wait, she's the junior lieutenant who scaled a cliff to put out that radio call?" Ezra stared at her wide eyed. "Felicity Haagen, right?"

"*First Lieutenant* Felicity Haagen," Vincent corrected with a smile. Ezra nodded.

"My apologies, First Lieutenant."

"How did you know who I am?" she asked, her cheeks growing red. Ezra read the looks on their faces and laughed.

"You haven't been off the ship yet, so I guess you don't know. Everyone has heard of Lieutenant Haagen. You're the hero of Victoria."

"The Hero of Victoria?" she repeated, her face growing deeper shades of crimson by the second.

"Congrats on being a celebrity." Fiona slapped her on the shoulder. Felicity lowered her head.

"Everyone knows who I am?" she asked, her voice hardly above a whisper.

"*Everyone.*" Ezra confirmed.

"Permission to launch myself into the Sun, sir?" Felicity moaned. Vincent grinned.

"If I have to deal with it so do you."

"Can we go now?" she asked weakly.

"Nice change of topic," Ezra said. "She is right though; we should get going."

"Is it a long flight?" Vincent asked.

"Not normally. Denta's ship is in a holding pattern not far from here." Ezra shook his head. "I tend to get slowed down when the EDF tries to shoot me down though."

"Does that happen a lot?" Felicity asked.

"Well, *I* certainly didn't decorate my ship that way."

The deep blackness of space above Mars had been turned into a gridlock. Ships from three different races and countless different makes, models, and sizes crowded each other. They jockeyed for position amongst the wrecks of hundreds of ships, long since destroyed by orbital counter fire and left to float in orbit around the planet forever. It was as if a busy highway passed directly through a cemetery.

A continuous stream of barges and Reapers crisscrossed from one ship to another before turning back towards the planet's surface. A similar stream made the return trip an endless supply chain for the endless war still going on below them.

"How many people does it take to run a fleet like this?" Vincent gasped.

"Millions," Ezra said. "Most of them aren't technically people though." He nodded at a huge black destroyer. The ship was identical to the one Vincent had boarded and destroyed with the Clan in the skies over Elysian. A seamless obsidian blade that nearly blended into the darkness of the void. This one must have been captured during unknown battle and pressed into Clan service.

"Do we have ships?" he asked. "I mean, other than yours." Ezra nodded.

"A few. Mostly what we have captured from the EDF in varying states of repair, most of it bad. The Clan have given us some too. Nothing like that though." He pointed to a Titanian ship. It was the second biggest ship Vincent had ever seen.

It was a large rectangular ship. It looked as if an Earthian skyscraper, slate grey in color, had been ripped off of a settlement and floated into space. Every few feet weapons platforms jutted from the flanks of the ship, bristling with short cannons and rocket pods.

"What the hell is that?" he asked.

"A Dauntless-Class Carrier," Ezra answered. "It's the flagship of the Titanian Navy after their only Capitol ship was destroyed above Grawluck. It is about half of the size." Vincent felt his mouth drop. He had never actually seen a Capitol ship in person like this, though he had lived inside one for months. The only passing glances he had of the *Victory* were of its shadow as it plummeted to its death.

"Oh, so that's Denta's flagship?" Fiona asked. "How much do you want to bet he named it after himself?" Vincent and Felicity laughed.

"I do not understand the humor," Tyr piped up from the co-pilot's seat. "The *TNS Denta* is a fine ship."

"He really named it that?" Vincent asked. "There is no way."

"Technically," Ezra sighed, rubbing his temples. "He named it after his Father, Field Marshal Petr Denta, He was a legendary commander of the Titanian Army." Fiona doubled over with laughter and began snorting. "He did conspicuously leave out his father's first name though."

*　　*　　*

The orbit around the *Denta* was chaotic. Dozens of landing bays alongside the side of the ship had grinded into traffic jams. Long lines of ships trying were trying to get in and out at the same time. Many of them were Mawr craft, undoubtedly bringing Arai and the Clan leadership to the meeting. One of the bays was left open and Ezra guided the ship towards it. Soon, the ship swallowed them whole.

Denta, always one for pomp and circumstance, had stationed soldiers in full dress uniform in lines along the landing bay. They snapped to attention as the doors of the *Shanna II* opened and saluted them as they stepped out.

The soldiers stood, their chests full of golden metals and boots so polished Vincent was sure he could see himself in them. The smell of recycled atmosphere, polluted from countless trips through the ship's air scrubbers, stung Vincent's nose. The familiar smells of burning oil, dust, and machinery greeted them. Part of him was happy to discover no matter how much self-importance Denta afforded himself his namesake ship was the same as everyone else's.

The head of the honor guard stepped out of the rank of soldiers and turned towards Vincent.

"Welcome to the *TNS Denta* Consul Solaris," he said. The soldier was a man pushing forty. He wore first sergeant rank on his collar and his dark skin was creased with the hard life of a soldier. His gaze was not one of respect, but professionalism in his job. "The Field Marshal instructed me to bring you to the War Room as soon as you boarded the ship. Follow me please." The Soldier didn't wait for a response. Instead, he turned and began marching further into the ship.

They followed him until he brought them to a room guarded by two more soldiers. These ones were not in dress uniform. Instead they were fully equipped for combat. An officer wearing a Martian uniform in front of them had been stopped by combat soldiers and they seemed to be in some kind of argument.

"I need some identification," one of the soldiers said in a clipped tone.

"I am a colonel in the Martian People's Army." Vincent guessed that while he was out Erik had continued his consolidation of power on Mars. Gone was the Martian Liberation Brigade. They weren't a rebel completing for power amongst others for supremacy. Now they were the *Martian People's Army*. "Do you think some ganger crawled their way through the goddamn void to come and sabotage your pretty ship?" The Martian barked at them.

"Identification, *Colonel,*" the soldier shot back. He added sarcastic venom to the colonel's rank. The fight out of him, the Martian officer grumbled and searched around in his pockets until he produced a small piece of paper. The soldier glanced at it suspiciously before waiving the Martian through. It was clear that though the two sides were allies, generations of discrimination and racist was not going to go away overnight.

The soldiers on guard didn't ask Vincent or anyone with him for any credentials. The same soldier who had just given the

Martian colonel a hard time waived them through with a nod and a salute. The War Room was huge. A large circular table took up the bulk of the room. Officers from the various races had gathered into groups and were carrying on with side conversations. Vincent wasn't sure who many of them were. He found Arai, Pharos, and Erin standing to one side.

Erin looked like she had aged five years since he had last seen her. The dark circles around her eyes were magnified by her pale skin. Her khaki uniform was rumpled and dirty, unadorned with any rank or awards. She looked like she had slept or showered in days.

"Good to see you well, Solaris." Pharos nodded.

"Yeah," Erin added. "I heard you got your face blown clean off. Looks about that way too."

"They stitched it back together." Vincent smiled. "How are things going?" Erin gave him a hollow look that told him everything that he needed to know. "Yeah," he said. "That's what I heard."

"The last flailings of a dying beast," Arai grunted. "We have them cornered."

"An animal cornered is an animal at its most dangerous." Pharos countered. The banging of a Denta's palm on the table pulled Vincent's attention away from the debate.

"Commanders!" Denta called out. "Please, have a seat and we can get started." The grumbling group of officers took their seats, but Arai and a few Mawr remained standing.

At first Vincent thought it was a sign of disrespect. Then he noticed one of the Cohort Leaders, a short Warrior wearing dark yellow armor, spinning a chair around in circles in obvious confusion. They were not being disrespectful; they were simply uneasy about human chairs. The Rhai did not have the same problem, quickly taking their seats. Vincent sat down next to

Pharos. The Mawr pushed the chairs aside and stood in their place.

Officer's Aides began to pour drinks and serve plates of food to the officers sitting at the table. The plates were piled high with mashed potatoes and a thick cut of meat, they certainly weren't going to eat reconstituted mush. Even the aliens at the table tucked into the meal. Seated across from him, sat Erik in a dirty red uniform with no food or drink in front of him. His aide was the colonel Vincent had seen get harassed at the door to the meeting. He stood behind Erik, unmoving. Felicity bent down and whispered in Vincent's ear.

"Do you want me to get you something to eat?"

"You're my aide, not my butler," he said.

"It is tradition to serve dinner before a planning meeting," Felicity said. Denta was never one to shy away from tradition, no matter how ridiculous. A dull roar of multiple different conversations filled the room. It was as if they were at a mess hall back like he had just found himself in on the *Mercy* rather than on a ship above a battlefield where millions of people were fighting for their lives.

"Gentleman!" Erik barked, pounding his fists on the table. Metal dinnerware clattered and a few drinks sloshed out their contents. "I thought we were here to plan an offensive, not to have a goddamned dinner party." The other human officers stopped eating, glancing towards Erik with looks of disgust. The aliens looked on in confusion. Arai continued to eat her dinner, not bothering herself with the human intrigue.

He wasn't sure if it was for his lack of tact, or that this was the first time that any human at the table had ever been spoken to by a Martian of equal or greater rank than they were. Up until a few weeks before, such a thing had never existed. A general who sat to the left to Denta, brown sauce from his dinner was at each corner of his mouth, clenched his fists and pouted.

"It is custom—" he began, but Erik wouldn't let him finish.

"If we were following customs, General, I wouldn't be allowed to sit at the same table as you. And either would any of them." Erik gestured to the Clan leadership, Vincent included. Vincent heard Fiona fight back laughter next to him. "But as we are building a new world here, I'd like to get to the fucking point."

"Seconded," Arai said. Vincent noticed her plate was already empty. Pharos had left theirs untouched.

"I agree," Vincent said. Erik nodded to his aide who produced several data displays and handed them to him. Denta angerly put his fork and knife down and dabbed at his lip with a napkin.

"I assume this means you think you have something worth sharing with the group?" He grinned, clearly feeling superior.

"I do, Field Marshal," Erik said. "Some of us stayed on the ground rather than running off of the planet when your last plan failed." The table erupted into a chorus of haughty displeasure and forced outrage. The Clan representatives laughed between themselves.

"I like this Martian." Arai nodded between bouts of laughing.

"Me too," Vincent said, trying to keep a straight face. After a few seconds of uproar, Denta managed to quiet down the hooting chorus of officers around him.

"So, what is your master plan then *Commander*?" Denta asked, the scorn dripping from his voice.

"It is very clear to anyone who has been paying attention that Brusilov hasn't been trying to actually *win* this battle since Consul Solaris and Warlord Arai broke the encirclement of Field Marshal Denta's forces."

"That is because we have them beaten!" bragged a colonel with a handlebar mustache and a double chin.

"We do. That much is certain," Erik agreed. "But they aren't fighting like a cornered animal trying to get some breathing room." Vincent exchanged looks with Pharos.

"Their suicide attacks?" Denta asked. "Clearly the acts of desperate men."

"You would think," Erik said, turning one of his data displays to the rest of the table. "But each one has been ruthlessly effective." He pointed to blue dot on the map. "The first was an attempted assassination on the Consul. Not only did they almost succeed, but their assumed secondary goal of dissuading other mass surrenders like what was happening definitely succeeded. We haven't had more than a few dozen surrenders ever since." He pointed at another blue dot near a square labeled *Titan Command.* "The second was the attempted assassination of Field Marshal Denta with nerve gas. That did not succeed either, but they did successfully force the Titanian Army to abandon the position." Denta frowned and folded his arms high across his chest. "And of course, the suicide reaper attack here, on our rear camp which was meant for me and our main supply base. I was unharmed, but many of my high command were not so lucky."

"We know of all of these attacks, why are you pointing them out?" grumbled a general.

"Brusilov was trying to decapitate our forces," Erin cut in. "Strikes on leadership and our supply network."

"Precisely." Erik nodded. "While their forces fought a stalling action around the Military District, which is what we thought they were doing. Their other forces launched an unconventional counterattack. But what good would such an attack do if you thought your back was really against the wall?"

"They're waiting for reinforcements," Vincent said. "Field Marshal Presan thought the same thing." Erik smiled and nodded at Vincent. "They're trying to buy as much time as possible."

"Brusilov can't win this battle on his own regardless, even if he managed to kill every officer in this room," Erin said. "But if he succeeded in killing Denta or Erik that would put an incoming army group or two with a fleet at their back from the Moon in a very good position to push us back."

"Exactly," he said. "How long do you think it'll take EDF high command to slap together an army to relieve Brusilov?"

"Two months at the latest," Pharos said. "Assuming they still think it is worth the risk. And if I may, it is in their best interest to keep us away from Lunar City for as long as they can. They will reinforce Brusilov. It is only a matter of time."

"Let them come!" Roared a general who sat to the right of Denta. He had so many medals on his chest Vincent wasn't sure he couldn't fit another. "We will crush them too!"

"We won't." Denta sighed. "Commander Erik is right."

Vincent noticed there was no hate in his voice when he addressed the Martian Leader anymore.

"We cannot hope to fight a prolonged siege on this planet." The generals around him fell into a shocked silence, their jaws slacked. "The emergency mobilization of our forces for this operation has left our capabilities..." He thought for a moment to find the right words. "...strained." Denta reached over to his cup and drank from it. "So, I assume you have plan to end this quickly?"

"Yes," Erik said. "We end it now." Erik's display switched to show a planetary map of Mars. The Fleet was shown above it in small blue boxes. "We bring the full force of your fleet's orbital guns onto Victoria."

"You mean to destroy the city." Denta frowned.

"Yes." Erik nodded. "You and your staff spoke at length before we began our offensive about preserving Victoria as a gem of the new Mars. But Victoria is a relic of the old Mars. Built by the Committee and lived in by settlers whose entire purpose was to snuff out our way of life and our people. To turn us into mindless servants like them."

"You'll rule over a pile of ashes," said Denta, folding his arms. His aide refilled his glass.

"We built this planet from the dust. We will do it again."

"I support this." Arai nodded. "We have the ability to end the battle immediately and face the true enemy. Not using it is negligence."

"I do not," Pharos said. Arai seemed as shocked as Vincent that the Spy Master would disagree with the Warlord on something. "It is a waste of valuable military intelligence that we may need when we assault Lunar City."

"In all due respect," Denta began. "I do not believe Aliens should be the deciding vote on whether my fleet levels a human city or not," Arai grumbled in annoyance. Vincent wanted to point out that Arai would most likely be willing to level any city regardless of the race that lived in it, but he didn't.

"I am forced to agree." Erik nodded. "This should be between us. If the time comes, I assume we will give them the same respect." Denta nodded.

"What about the people?" Vincent asked. "There has to be hundreds of thousands of people trapped in the Military District."

"We have taken nearly half a million people into displacement camps in the time between your announcement and the bombing," Erik said. "We can assume anyone still with them does not intend to, or cannot, surrender." Denta turned and spoke with a few generals around him. None of them seemed too pleased with the plan. After a few moments Denta turned back towards the table.

"I cannot support this Operation," he said. "Cohort Leader Pharos is right. The sheer amount of military intelligence we would lose by leveling the city is too much. You do know we will have to contend with what remains of the Committee on the Moon even if we carry out this plan?"

"It is a risk I am willing to take," Erik said, turning towards Vincent. Suddenly, Vincent's throat thickened. He realized that with one vote for, one against, and Arai's was not counting, it all came down to his vote.

Vincent turned towards Erin and Fiona. "What should I say?"

"Support it," Fiona said. "Erik is right about Victoria."

"I can see where Denta is coming from," Erin added. "We cannot fight this battle and think our next is going to be some kind of cake walk. The information we could get from the District could give us the upper hand." Fiona stared daggers at her, but Erin's face remained stoic.

"Can we win the battle without destroying the city?" he asked. Erin sighed, exhausted. She rubbed her temples.

"Not without losing a lot more soldiers. Soldiers I don't really think we are in the position to replace at the moment." Vincent remembered back to their marathon night of helping the wounded and dead off of the medical ships. How many more nights just like that one would occur if they allowed Brusilov to fight over every nook and cranny of Victoria? How many more people would die because he didn't think something sounded *right* to him? What even was the right thing at this point?

Vincent slowly got to his feet, reaching over to a Titanian major's glass that was half full of an amber liquid and tossed it back. The smoky booze burned the whole way down. "If we would have had this conversation two weeks ago, I would have still been on Denta's side. But when I was aboard the *Mercy,* I saw the aftermath of what Brusilov is doing. In Tharsis I saw what he has planned for the people who are left alive when all this is over..." He took and deep breath, still not entirely sure of what he was about to say. "When I saw people who swore to fight for me, people who swore to free the universe from the Committee and the Alliance, stumble around blind, missing limbs, their bodies discarded like trash on the floor...I knew what I had to do, what we have to do." He trailed off, staring down into his now empty glass.

"Well?" Denta raised an eyebrow, spreading his arms out in front of him.

"We await the Consul's vote." Vincent raised his glass towards Erik.

"I vote we fucking win."

CHAPTER FORTY-EIGHT

Vincent sat at a table in the Chow Hall alone. The chow hall was busy with crewmembers of the *Denta* coming off of their work shifts and grabbing a bite to eat. The clattering of their spoons was interspersed with tired conversations about whatever it was naval staff talk about after a long day at work.

He stared out of a viewing port trying to lose himself in the endless void of space. It wasn't working. His mind raced and he felt sick to his stomach.

He had been the deciding vote that will undoubtedly kill tens or hundreds of thousands of people. His mind flashed back to the obliterated Martian transit tunnel that he had stalked through with the Gangers. Only a few weeks ago he had been disgusted by the wonton destruction and murder. A few minutes ago he had voted to do the exact same thing. Vincent tried to chase the images of a burning city from his mind with a cup liquor he had bought from the ship's crew, but it only made him feel worse.

He felt a hand on his shoulder and jumped slightly. He turned and saw Fiona, balancing two bowls of food in her other hand. She slid him one and he poked at it with a fork. It was the usual reconstituted byproduct that they had eaten aboard the *Mercy*. He pushed it aside.

"How has everything gone so crazy that I just decided the fate of a city?" He buried his face into his hands.

"I don't know," she said. "But here we are."

"The universe has gone insane."

"But fuck it, why not you? Why not us?" Fiona shrugged. "Look at the universe people like Denta built. People like the Chairman built. Like the Anarchs and the Alliance built. They carved sprawling Empires built on murder, oppression, and genocide." She finished her drink and turned her back to the viewing port. "Why shouldn't we get a shot at running things? How could we do any worse?"

"Because we are a bunch of fuck ups, criminals, and gangers. I'm in command of an army and I never even made sergeant. Shit, I hardly passed Ethics School."

"And Denta graduated from the best military academy in human space and you just rescued him. You commanded an army that forced Brusilov from Victoria's outskirts. Your pedigree, schooling, or where you were born doesn't matter anymore. Only your ability."

"None of that matters!" he cried.

"What the hell do you mean?"

"How can I be proud of beating him if I am becoming just like him, Fiona?" He shot to his feet and slapped the table. "I just ordered the destruction of an entire city!" She moved to speak but he cut her off. "I am a fucking monster!" He slumped back down into his seat. "Why would anyone believe in a world I am building?"

"We don't have a choice," came a voice behind them. When Vincent turned, he saw Erik standing in an open doorway. "We did a pretty good job of destroying the old one and besides, you already sold those EDF deserters on a new world. It's about time you started believing in it."

Vincent laughed. Not in happiness or humor, but in nervousness.

"Do I?" he asked. "Do you?"

"I believe in a new world. A free world in one way or another. But you can't lead a revolution with white gloves, Vincent," said Erik.

"I'll drink to that." Fiona grinned.

"As will I," Erik said. "Another thing we can drink to is the end."

"The end?" Vincent asked. Erik nodded.

"The soldiers have all been pulled out of Victoria and the gunships are getting ready," Erik said. "And this happens to be the perfect place to watch the bombardment."

"Victoria is..." Vincent said, trailing off, searching the featureless Red orb for anything resembling a city. He could find nothing. Erik laughed.

"You can't see the city from here." Vincent felt his face go red. You couldn't see Elysian from orbit even though the city sprawls across the entire planet. Of course he wouldn't be able to see Victoria. "I have just never been on this side of a full orbital broadside."

"I'm a little surprised. I figured Denta would have done something to try to stop it," Vincent said. He was hoping the old man's pride would get the best of him and he would cancel the bombardment. It turned out even Denta had come to realize the battle in Victoria couldn't be won while their soldiers were fighting over each street and house.

"No. the intelligence loss is a small worry for him," Erik said. "Otherwise he would have never put it to a vote." Vincent shook his head. "I thought as much during our previous meetings, he just couldn't be seen as being the one who launched the strike."

"But why?" Vincent asked.

"Optics, mostly." Erik shrugged. "He can't be seen to use the vaunted Titanian military to wipe out a city full of settlers, many of whom probably had family ties on Grand Titan. Now, he can say he rejected it, but the Clan and Martian vote overrode his in an Alliance that Prime Minister Addler forced onto the Titan Military."

"So, we destroy Victoria and we still manage to lose he pulls Titan out, blames Addler, and gets to keep his job?" Fiona gasped.

"Precisely," Erik said.

"The more you tell me about him the more I hate him." She frowned.

"And what about the loss of life?" Vincent asked. "That doesn't bother him?"

"This wouldn't even be the first time he leveled a Martian city," Fiona scoffed. "If anything, this is just old hat for him." Erik nodded in agreement. "But that was Olympus, Titanians don't care about shelling a bunch of Martians."

"If he wasn't our ally, I would string him up in the middle of Olympus myself."

"Here, here." Fiona raised her glass and took a drink.

"Look," Felicity said. "The Battleships are lining up." She pointed out the window and the gunships that Erik had been talking about previously, he was sure Felicity couldn't wait to correct him on their proper name, were lining up in neat rows. They were not even a quarter of the size of the *Denta* but looked like a fearsome crossbreed of a spaceship and a tank. Every bit of space on the outside of the ships was covered by squat turrets with large rail cannons. Each ship must have had hundreds of guns.

The ranks of the Titanian Navy fell in line and soon there were dozens of Battleships in multiple stacked formations over the planet. Dozens turned to hundreds. Soon, a solid wall of ships formed that obscured Mars with an impenetrable screen of slate grey. Their turrets all turning to be trained on a target so far below them nobody pulling the triggers could have possibly seen it.

"Out of curiosity when you called in that strike when we were trapped in the mine field, how many of these things responded?" Vincent asked. He remembered what felt like. The sky itself falling down in front of him, churning an entire city block to dust and destroying a squadron's worth of tanks in only a few minutes.

"Just one," Felicity said. "The *TNS Dagger.* The bombardment of the Mons was only ten ships."

"Holy shit," he gasped.

"That's right." Erik grinned. "I have been looking forward to this."

There was no sound in space, Vincent knew that. But deep down inside he still expected to hear something when the thousands of rail guns laid out in front of him began to rain down fire on Victoria. Instead, there was nothing. Small puffs of grey dust plumed out from the barrel of the guns. The casings of the high velocity rods sheared off and disintegrated into dust in the vacuum of space. Every few seconds each ship would take its turn firing again. Soon the entire formation was obscured with grey particles floating around the ships like a cloud. Vincent's throat went thick.

"So, this is how a city dies," he gasped.

Fiona grinned. "It's a thing of beauty."

"Makes me wish I could have joined the Navy." Erik laughed. "Doing more damage in ten seconds than an entire Regiment could do in a week." Erik tipped the rest of his drink back and swallowed. "We should get ready to head back down. We have a pile of rubble to claim."

*   *   *

The *Shanna II* rumbled and shook as it reentered Mars' atmosphere. A dust storm swirled around the ship as it descended. The dust mixed with the thick, black smoke of the burning city scape of Victoria creating an impenetrable blanket that seemed to cloak the entire planet. The once impressive skyline of Victoria, the of the gem of Committee rule on Mars, had been reduced a mass grave. Its skyscrapers had been shattered and the symbols of Committee power had been churned to ruin by the bombardment.

The ship circled what remained of the city. A few stubborn buildings remained standing, their facades crumbling away, twisted rebar poking out from their ruined slate grey walls. Fires burned within their husks, gutting what the bombardment had managed to leave behind. The curtain of anti-aircraft fire that had previously defended the city was gone. Flames licked through the burned-out defense towers where the gunners had once been.

Felicity gasped. "The city is...dead."

"Good riddance," Fiona spat.

"Hm." Zinvor frowned. "Smiting your enemy without seeing them somehow cheapens the victory."

"Brusilov would have done the same thing if he had the chance," Vincent said. He wasn't sure if he was trying to convince Felicity or himself.

"He did," Fiona said. "When he targeted the transit tunnels under Olympus. And to be honest I'm happy to return the favor. The only thing I regret is we didn't get to see the look on his face as we tore down his little empire around his ears." The radio inside the ship crackled, interrupting Fiona's revenge fantasy. The dust storm had clearly been playing hell with transmissions. What came through was garbled and heavily polluted with static.

"*Shanna II, this is Cohort Leader Pharos.*" Vincent raised an eyebrow and made his way through the troops compartment towards the cockpit. There he saw Tyr trying to dial in the radio signal.

"Go ahead, Pharos," Ezra answered.

"*Do you have the Consul on board?*"

"Affirmative."

"*A planetary scan revealed a bunker complex under the Military Governor's Palace. We can assume that Brusilov and his inner circle survived the bombardment. Advise him that we are sending in a team to root them out.*"

"Of course he fucking did," Fiona seethed. Vincent felt his face begin to burn. They leveled an entire city to beat him and he still survived. "The only thing that could survive a full bombardment like that is cock roaches and Vasilli fucking Brusilov." She kicked the wall of the ship in pitiful anger.

"Fuck that," Vincent spat. "Tell him we want to go into that bunker with them. If anyone is going to kill that old bastard it is going to be us." A smile spread across Ezra's face.

"Pharos," Ezra began. "Be advised. The Consul says if anyone is going to take the bunker it will be him." The radio waves crackled and hissed. Vincent was sure the painfully logical Pharos would retort that his request didn't make any sense.

"*The glory will be his.*" Came Pharos' voice. "*Please land at the beacon I have sent to your navigation display.*"

"He actually agreed," Vincent said.

"Are you surprised?" Felicity asked.

"Yeah." He laughed nervously, scratching his beard. "I was kind of banking on him telling me to go away."

"Being Consul has its privileges," said Felicity.

"Right." He sighed. "Privileges."

The ship swooped down low into a clearing, of which there was now plenty. Buildings that had been hit directly by kinetic shells had been atomized, but it did not take the impact of a shell to cause destruction. Just the energy of a shell passing through the air was enough to set surrounding buildings on fire and reduce others to ash. The streets had been churned to rubble while aero cars, tanks, and military transports were scorched to little more than husks.

The area they had landed looked like it could have once been a parade ground. The foundations of a fountain lay in the middle of a concrete square. It looked as if one of the burning buildings around them acted as a reviewing platform for the Military Governor. Now they were pulverized by countless shells. The reviewing balcony had been blown away and the building it was attached to had collapsed inwards, fire vomited outwards from the windows that remained.

The door to the *Shanna II* slid open and Martian dust assaulted them. Vincent pulled a scarf that Fiona had given him over his face and stepped off the ship. Soldiers were hunkered down around what remained of the square, taking cover from the weather amongst the ruins of a nearby fountain. The smoke from the burning city settled down on them like a curtain and made breathing even more difficult. Vincent ran at a crouch towards the fountain.

The soldiers sat, their backs against the broken walls of the fountain, shielding their faces from the dust storm. Around them, embedded into the slate grey concrete was crazed black outlines of something. As he got closer, he could make out the distinctive parts of rifles. The trigger guard, buttstock, even a magazine.

He kneeled next to the soldiers. Leaning against fountain and the melted rifles. But the rifles weren't alone. A faint outline, hardly visible to Vincent's real eye began to take shape through the dust. He closed his real eye and let his augment focus. It was the faint, ghost like shape of a human, their dead arms reaching out for the melted rifles they would never fire again.

"They call those the *Shadows of War," Erik said.* Vincent pulled himself away from the human shapes.

"What?"

"The shells come down so fast that they atomize anyone and anything around them. It burns flesh into the concrete. Freezing them for eternity doing whatever it was they were doing when it all ended." A shiver ran down Vincent's spine. He wondered if those soldiers even knew what was happening when their bodies were blasted into dust. He thought it might be better if they didn't.

Pharos appeared out of the dust. They were wearing their shimmering black armor, their face obscured by a Rhai battle helmet shielding them from the elements. Behind them was a dozen of what they called *Agents*. With them, however, were several humans.

"Consul," rasped Pharos, their voice sounding somewhat computerized through the helmet's voice box. "The bunker is ahead."

"Thank you," Vincent said, squinting his unprotected eyes against the dust storm. His augmented eye felt no effects from the blistering wind. He soon found it easier to simply close his remaining real eye and let the augment take over.

"It is of no substance to me," Pharos said. "Ideas of battlefield glory are not something my people care about. I only care that Brusilov is dead."

"Humans are emotional creatures," Vincent said, smiling under his scarf. "I think you taught me that."

"Yes," Pharos said. "Though the Warlord instructed me to keep you safe. No disrespect to your Tsarra, of course." He nodded towards Zinvor, who grunted at the slight. "I also sent for your *Irregulars.*" He paused for a moment, clearly choosing his words wisely. "They have had many successes hunting EDF units before the bombardment."

"Irregulars?" Vincent asked. That was when he noticed a Martian woman wearing a grey jacket and a checkered scarf around her face. Her blue eyes protected from the dust by a set of goggles that bulged like the eyes of an insect.

"Hey Boss!" she said, giving a lazy salute.

"Skylar?" Vincent asked.

"*Captain* Skylar now, Boss."

"Glad to see you're okay, Captain."

"Same to you, Boss. Though that eye is a bit freaky."

"Thanks." Vincent sighed. "So, you're going in the bunker with us? What do we know about it?"

"Well," Pharos interrupted. "Scans show the complex goes a few floors down. Hypothetically, they could keep as many as one hundred soldiers within comfortably."

"I bet it's crawling with Black Coats," Skylar said.

"So, what is the plan?" Vincent asked.

Skylar shrugged. "We go in the tunnel, we kill them, we win the war."

"Truly a military scientist that one," Felicity said.

Vincent shook his head and sighed. "I'm ready when you guys are."

"I will let my agents know," Pharos said, before turning and walking off. Vincent walked back to the *Shanna II* to grab a rifle when he spotted Ezra. He had slipped a regular soldier's body armor over his flight suit and covered his face with a scarf. He strapped a load bearing vest over his chest and was loading it down with shotgun shells and hand grenades.

"Ezra?" he asked. "You're coming with us?"

"Remember what you promised me back before we landed on Mars?" Ezra asked.

"That you would get to be the one who killed Brusilov," Vincent said.

"I plan on holding you to that, sir."

"Ezra, you're our Wing Commander now. Soon, when we have a real Navy, I plan on putting you in charge of all of it. You're worth way more to the war effort out here, with your ship." Ezra grabbed a shotgun from the weapons rack of the *Shanna II* and racked its pump action.

"Honestly, sir." He slid a pistol into a leg holster. "I don't care about any of that right now. I hope that means you won't stop me."

"Nope. I thought it might be worth a shot though," Vincent said. Reaching passed Ezra and grabbing a carbine from the weapon rack. "I don't think you would listen to me if I tried." Ezra winked at him.

"Good," he said. "Let's end this thing."

The entrance to the bunker had been buried under layers of rubble. Several of Skylar's soldiers were working to uncover it.

The going was slow, so Vincent and the rest of the crew joined them. Vincent and Ezra teamed up and still strained to throw what looked like a piece of marble out of the way but succeeded in only moving it a few feet. He watched Zinvor pick up a piece of concrete larger than he was and throw it ten feet away. Eventually, several Mawr Warriors found their way into the work gang and things began to speed up.

Vincent froze in horror when he uncovered the twisted, blackened form of a human. Soon, they uncovered several more. Some were smaller than others. Two of them had their hands intertwined, their fingers fused together forever as their lives were flashed out of existence. Their corpses flaked away to black dust when soldiers grabbed them. What remained were stacked off to the side like chords of wood. He was snapped away from the scene when he heard a soldier.

"I think I see an opening!" they called out. Vincent huffed and wiped the sweat from his forehead. It had mixed with the dust to create a red mud that smeared across his face. A Mawr in red armor joined with the soldier who had alerted them to lift a large piece of debris when the ground erupted with a violent explosion. Vincent was forced to the ground as the shockwave shook him to his bones.

A fireball tore through the debris pile, vaporizing the two people nearest to it. Dust and debris cascaded down on the survivors.

"Did they fucking booby trap it?" Fiona cursed. Zinvor pulled himself to his feet and looked down at where they were clearing debris.

"Yes. But it looks clear now."

"We can assume it will be this way throughout," Pharos said, trying in vain to clean the dust from their once flawlessly black armor.

"Leave it to us," Skylar said. "We have been taking apart their traps for weeks."

"Your man did not see the trap he just triggered," Pharos said.

"In this game there is no such thing as an expert, just people whose luck hasn't run out yet. That guy?" she said. "His luck was up when he woke up this morning.

Vincent sighed. First the minefield and now a tunnel full of booby traps. He was starting to miss just getting shot at. Skylar's soldiers slowly crawled through a hole in the debris. They began to slowly pick around the area, one hand on a flashlight, the other on a pistol. They eventually kneeled and waved everyone else forward.

They climbed through the debris and came to a short staircase. The reinforced walls of the staircase had given way under the force of the barrage. The walls had cracked, and the red sand-like dust was trickling in. In front of them a large set of grey metal double doors stuck out from the ground. A red colored display panel was on the left side of the door.

"I assume nobody brought a password?" Vincent joked nervously. Pharos walked forward, a small data display in their hand. They placed it over the panel on the door and tapped it. The panel turned from red to green and Vincent could hear the whirling and clicking of the door unlocking. "How in the hell?" He sighed, looking at Pharos. Pharos shrugged and placed the display in a pocket.

"Human systems are very easy to crack when you have spent years monitoring the Anarchs."

"Comforting," said Ezra. A soldier stepped forward and pushed the left door open. Vincent was expecting some dank, uncomfortable tunnel. Maybe he was just hoping that Brusilov would be hiding in a hole in the ground like a rat. Instead, the bunker looked as well-lit and maintained as any Committee government building he had the misfortune of walking through. He could have been standing in the hallway the District Headquarters back home.

Soldiers rushed forward, staying close to the walls, their weapons up and at the ready. After a few steps they stopped and a single soldier moved forward slowly, their eyes darting around looking for tripwires or other signs of booby traps. Vincent stepped cautiously, expecting every concrete block in the ground to explode under his feet.

"Where the fuck are they?" Fiona hissed. There were doorways at regular intervals on both sides of the hallway and another one at the end of the hallway. Each one had a portrait of a high-ranking officer and a name plate underneath of it, denoting whose office it was. Vincent thought Brusilov's bunker would be a hive of military activity, but instead it looked as if they had invaded an office building.

"Probably behind these doors, waiting for us," he said. Skylar stepped forward.

"You heard the Consul, clear those damn rooms!" she barked. Her soldiers advanced. A soldier in a cut off t shirt and cargo shorts kicked the nearest door open, the name plate denoting it was the Office of one Major General Anton Strelka, and quickly spun out of the way. Another soldier stepped forward and began to spray automatic gunfire into the open door. He watched in awe as they continued this process for each door as they advanced down the hallway. Skylar walked down the hallway looking over her troops work with a look of disappointment plastered across her face. "They're empty!" she called out.

"If they didn't know we were here, they do now." Fiona sighed. As if on command, the door at the end of the hallway swung open and two Black Coats appeared. Rifle barrels poked out from doorway and raked the hallway with gunfire.

Three of Skylar's soldiers were cut down where they stood, painting the exploding hallway with blood as they fell bonelessly. Vincent through himself to the ground. Others jumped into the surrounding rooms. He crawled arm over arm into the nearest room, the concrete all around sparking and shattering with the impact of flying slugs.

Vincent found himself in an empty office, since destroyed by ganger gunfire. Committee propaganda posters hung from the wall above a wooden desk. It showed an EDF soldier with a chiseled jaw and jacked arms bravely standing watch over Lunar City, an Anarch fleet approaching him. He shared the small space with one of Pharos' Agents and Felicity.

"Hey!" Skylar yelled out, Vincent peaked his head out of the door and saw she was in the room across the hallway. "What should we do?" A slug slammed into the door frame by her face and peppered her cheek with shards of concrete. Bright red blood trickled down her pale face.

"Get some damn suppressing fire on the end of the hallway!" Vincent yelled. Skylar gave him a look of confusion and turned to talk to a few of her soldiers.

"Does she not know what suppressing fire is?" Felicity asked. Vincent shrugged.

"I assumed she figured all of that stuff out by now or she would be dead." When he turned back to the hallway, he saw a ganger with a homemade rocket launcher perched on his shoulder leaning out of the doorway. Vincent's stomach lurched.

"Get down!" he yelled. The ganger fired the rocket, shrouding the hallway in smoke and dust. The power of the rocket's motor pushed them out of the doorway as it flew by them. When it detonated on the far side of the hallway the bunker shook so violently it felt like the world was coming apart. The rocket had blackened the once grey walls and cracks spidered up the walls and debris tickled down on their head. The ganger fist pumped the air and hooted, Skylar slapped him on the back and cheered. Felicity waved her hand back and forth, trying in vain to clear away the smoke. The gunfire from the end of the hallway stopped.

"I guess that answers our question." She rolled her eyes. "She outranks me now by the way. Just thought I should throw that out there," Felicity added. Vincent felt his face get hot.

"You could have killed us!" he shouted. "That rocket could have brought this damn bunker down on our heads!"

"But it didn't." Skylar grinned. He was about to yell again when Pharos cut him off with a wave of his hand.

"It goes further down." The Spy Master was standing in the ruined doorway that the Black Coats had been firing from. Their words had silenced the chatter from the gangers and now Vincent could hear orders and curses being shouted from the floor below them. "We can expect further resistance," Pharos added. Zinvor stepped forward, a grenade in his hand.

"Good," he grunted. "Let us meet them." The stairwell was so narrow that if Zinvor went down he would cover the entire width of the space, each one of his broad shoulders touching the walls on either side.

He would act as a living shield for everyone behind him. Vincent was about to say something when Zinvor placed a hand on his shoulder and flashed a determined look at him. Zinvor knew it as well as Vincent did, and he knew there was nothing he could say to change his mind. Vincent already knew what he would say. He was a Tsarra. This was his mission. He was no longer asking for permission.

Zinvor primed the Grenade and tossed it down the stairs. They waited for what felt like an eternity for the small *thump* of a detonation. Zinvor rushed down the stairs, letting out a deep, guttural roar as he went. Vincent quickly ran after him, the rest of the assault force at his back. They were immediately greeted by a firestorm of slugs.

Zinvor's armor cracked and broke away as it was struck by incoming fire, but he did not slow down. His armor would not withstand the assault for long. Vincent was hit by wet flecks of blood as the Black Coat slugs found purchase in Zinvor's body. Still, the Tsarra did not slow. It was as if he did not notice he was being torn to shreds.

They hit the bottom of the stairs at a dead sprint and found themselves in something like a barracks. Rows of bunkbeds filled the room. Trunks of military supplies were overturned and repurposed as firing positions. Pointing directly up at the stairwell was a belt fed machine gun. Its two-person crew burning through hundreds of rounds of ammunition directly at them. Zinvor continued his suicidal charge directly towards them.

Vincent saw an opening and fired at them, forcing them to duck behind cover. Zinvor lumbered towards them, leaving a trail of blood in his wake. He shot one of them with his Riten and grabbed the machine gun by the barrel with his other hand. His hand sizzled on the red-hot barrel as he spun it around and fired a dozen rounds into the other soldier's chest. He turned and began to fire at the rest of the soldiers in the room, cutting through the paltry cover they dove behind. The ones who weren't killed immediately began to flee.

Vincent, Fiona, and Felicity took the opportunity to rush them. Fiona jumped on top of a crate and fired onto the soldiers hiding behind it. Vincent rounded around a trunk to find two

Black Coats frantically trying to reload their machine gun. He shot them both. Felicity dropped three of them as they ran for a door at the back of the barracks. The storm of violence only lasted a few seconds, but it left a dozen Black Coats dead.

Zinvor sat down heavily on a crate, his stolen machine gun slipping from his grip and clattering to the floor. His eyes lolled back and forth, and blood foamed out of a wound in his chest. Vincent ran over to him, putting his hand over the wound. He noticed blood coming from the corners of his mouth and the slits of his nose.

"You're going to be okay," he said, panicking. Vincent reached into his first aid kit and found a dressing and stuffed it into Zinvor's wound. He was covered in countless wounds, each oozing blood but the chest wound looked the worst. His armor had been mostly shot off of his body. Only scraps of black armor remained.

"Leave me," Zinvor wheezed, his breathing labored.

"No!" Vincent gasped. He felt the burning of tears in his real eye. "Get me a fucking Medic!" he demanded.

"We did not bring a medic with us," Pharos said. "There was no time—"

Vincent cut him off. "Skylar!" he called out. "Take your men and get Zinvor to the surface!"

"This is ill advised," Pharos said, matter-of-factly.

Zinvor's eyes began to close. His chest heaved and he began to slump. Vincent struggled to keep him upright.

"Do it!" he ordered. Skylar nodded and waved her people over.

"Of course, Boss," she said. Two gangers took Zinvor under the arms and began to drag him back up the stairs. Zinvor attempted to push them away, but he was too weak from his wounds to refuse their aide. Vincent attempted to gather himself and dabbed away the tears from his eye.

"How much further, Pharos?"

Pharos consulted a small display on the wrist of their uniform. "The next room is as far as the current scan goes." They nodded to the back of the room. That was where two large grey metal blast doors stood in their way. Above them hung an Eagle and Star flag, alongside the flag insignia of a field marshal: Four stars surrounded by a wreath. Brusilov's insignia.

"He's in there," Vincent said. "He has to be."

Fiona stepped forward and kicked the door.

"I hope you can hear us you mother fucker! We're coming for you!" she shouted.

Pharos stepped forward. They went over to the door control computer, which like the entry door showed red. Pharos placed his display on top of the computer and tapped the screen. After a few moments it beeped and flashed red. Pharos picked the device up and slipped it into a pocket.

"The encryption must be different on this door. I cannot override it."

"Looks like we get to do things my way this time." Fiona grinned. She turned and dropped her backpack off of her shoulder and began to rummage through it. She produced several small blocks of plastic explosive a spool of thick red wire.

"Where did you get that from?" Vincent asked.

"I'm not saying I stole it from Denta's ship but..." A smile spread across her face.

"You didn't steal it," Ezra corrected. "You *tactically acquired* it."

"Yeah, sure I did that."

"Do you even know how to use that?" Vincent asked.

"Nope," she said, shrugging.

Felicity sighed and stepped forward, grabbing the wire.

"You do?" Fiona asked.

"Of course. It's a part of Basic Officer's Academy," Felicity said.

"I'll make sure to check that out. You know, never," Fiona smirked.

Felicity rolled her eyes and began sticking the blocks of explosives on the hinges of the doors. She plugged the wires into each block, quickly connecting them all together as she unspooled the wire.

"How far back should we get?" Vincent asked.

"Uhh," Felicity thought out loud. "Back of the room behind some of those crates maybe?"

"Maybe?" Fiona asked. "I thought they taught you how to do this at that fancy officer's school?"

"Explosives is an inexact science!" Felicity shot back.

"Explosives is a very exact science," countered Pharos, as if her words were a challenge. Felicity huffed and continued to unspool the wire until she was at the back of the room. She kicked the corpse of a Black Coat out from behind a stack of metal boxes and set the spool down.

"This should be good enough," she said.

"*Good enough* doesn't really sound good enough in this scenario," Vincent said. He holstered his Riten and unslung his shotgun. "Everyone ready?"

Felicity threaded the wires into a handheld detonator and nodded towards him. "Blow the fucker."

A deafening explosion tore through the room sending bunk beds, crates, and dead bodies flying. A box crashed into the wall above their heads and broke apart, sending someone's personal clothes raining down on them. Foul smoke filled the room, the smell of chemical fire burning Vincent's nose. Fiona peeked her head over the crate they were hunkered behind and laughed. The double doors had been blown open, sending the right door cartwheeling back into the room behind it. The left door still stubbornly hung on.

"You only took out one of the doors! So much for your Academy!" Fiona heckled. Before Felicity could retort, gunfire erupted from the other side of the breached doors. Slugs smacked into the crate, one burst through the other side, slamming into an Agent's chest and exploding out his back. Bright Rhai blood spattered onto the group.

"Shit!" Vincent yelled. "Spread out!" They quickly got up and ran for it, another one of the Agent's twisted at an odd angle and dropped as a shot found purchase in its back. Everyone fired blindly as they scrambled for cover. Vincent tried to find a target, but the opening that Felicity had blown open was still shrouded with smoke from the blast, obscuring the defenders. He fired random shots into the opening.

Felicity stumbled and fell forward as an incoming round slammed into her leg. She hit the ground and rolled onto her back, giving Vincent a quick thumbs up. The bullet hole in her pant leg revealed it to be her Augmetic leg. He sighed in relief. Vincent fired into the swirling smoke and moved once again. He didn't make it more than a few feet before he came under fire and quickly dove behind the wreckage of a stack of ruined bunk beds.

He searched inside of a pocket and hand found a grenade. He ripped the out the pin and tossed it through the open door. Vincent waited for the telltale dull *thump* of the exploding hand grenade and the air filled with a chorus of screams. He pushed himself to his knees and began firing into the smoke. The screaming stopped. Blue lasers cut through the air as Pharos and his three surviving Agents swiftly advanced across the room to the doorway.

"We need to get into the room. Consul, can you cover us?" Pharos asked, their voice so calm they seemed to ignore the fact that they were in a gunfight. Vincent nodded. He reached into a pouch and found only a single shotgun shell. He cursed himself for not refilling his pouches when he had the chance. He slipped the shell into his gun and pumped it.

"Everyone move up!" he ordered. Ezra had dropped his shotgun for a discarded rifle and Fiona had done the same. Felicity had grabbed the machine gun that Zinvor had wreaked so much havoc with.

"I got your suppressing fire right here." She grinned. Felicity unfolded the bipod and set the gun up next to Vincent. He patted her on the shoulder and ran up to join Pharos, with Ezra on his heels. Pharos nodded at Felicity and she leaned heavily into the gun's stock.

Felicity let out a long burst through the door, her small frame struggling to keep the weapon under control. The lead Agent tapped the one behind it and it copied back through the line until they got to Pharos who was in the back. Pharos tapped the one in front of him on the shoulder and once again they copied this movement until it passed up to the Agent in the lead. Vincent had no idea what they were doing, but when they were finished with the second wave of taps, they moved out.

Silently, they peeled off into the room, leaving the humans to play catch up. The room they advanced into was a wreck. The explosion had sent furniture and several bookcases cartwheeling through the room, crushing people underneath of them. A few officers lay curled up, moaning from various wounds on the ground. Overhead lights had broken free and were dangling from sparking wires. A plush carpeted floor was smoldering, giving off noxious smoke.

The group spread out across the room, each of them looking down their weapons. A Black Coat wearing an officer's peaked cap jumped out from behind a toppled bookshelf, firing a pistol. An Agent quickly pivoted and fired two quick laser bolts into the center of the officer's chest. He shook and collapsed without a word. Another Agent shot a wounded man as he crawled for a rifle.

"Where is he?" growled Ezra. "Where is he?!"

"Show yourself you coward!" Fiona shouted. Vincent frantically began to look around the room for a door, a ladder, for any route of escape.

"I thought you did a planetary scan?" he asked Pharos. "You said this is as far down as the bunker went! Where the fuck is Brusilov!"

"You misunderstand me, Consul," Pharos said. "I did a scan of the EDF planetary intelligence we had on record. This room is the last one on the documented schematics we had."

"Shit!" He cursed himself for having something so important be lost in translation.

"There has got to be some passage around here somewhere." Fiona began to run her hands across the wall. "A rat hole for the goddamn rat."

Vincent nodded. "Spread out, let's find it before it's too late."

Vincent joined Fiona in desperately searching the walls for any hint of a door. Ezra was on the opposite wall, pounding on random areas with his fist.

"Hey!" Ezra called out. They turned to look at him. He was standing behind a desk and feeling along a wall. "It looks like there might be a door here." Pharos checked the wall, climbing down to his hands and knees. He pulled a small knife from his vest and probed along the area where the wall met the floor.

"It seems you are correct," Pharos said. "There does not seem to be a way to control the door from this side, however. Brusilov must have the only means of opening it on his person."

"Oh" Fiona began. "I have a means of opening that fucker." She produced another small block of explosive and tossed it to Felicity. "Light that shit up."

"But we have no idea what is behind the door. The walls around it might be load bearing or something. We don't know what will happen!" she said, panicking.

"Blow it," Vincent ordered. "If you kill all of us on accident, I forgive you." He gave her a smile.

"Maybe *he* will," Fiona grumbled.

Felicity stuck the single block over the crack that Ezra had found and stuck in a length of wire. They ducked behind a desk and she squeezed the detonator. A dull *crump* sent a wave of dust and debris into the room. Vincent coughed and tried to wave the polluting cloud away.

The Agents were already up and advancing through the breach. The hole that Felicity had blown was just big enough for the slender Agents to crawl through without any problems. The larger humans did not have such an easy time. One by one they squeezed through. Vincent and Fiona, clad in their Mawr armor, had to ditch their load bearing vest to fit. Once through, they found Pharos' team waiting for them, their black shimmering armor making them virtually invisible in the cloud of dark smoke.

Vincent heard a quiet humming noise, followed the sound of fans. The smoke began to fade and after a few minutes the air in the bunker was clearer than it was in Olympus.

"What was that?" he asked.

"Life support systems. It clears out smoke in case there is a fire and scrubs the air from chemical or biological weapons. Kind of like the air scrubbers on a ship" Ezra frowned. "It makes sure even if all hell breaks loose on the surface the Command Staff, Government, or whoever happens to make it down to the bunker survives long enough for the EDF to come rescue them." Fiona smiled.

"Well, all hell certainly broke loose."

The air scrubbers revealed another hallway in front of them. It was unadorned, unlike the entrance to the bunker. Crates of supplies lined the walls alongside shipping pallets piled high with replacement parts for ships or weapons. Instead of going further underground as Vincent assumed it would, the hallway slowly crept back up towards the surface. He began to worry if it was possible to get lost underground.

"We do not know what is ahead," Pharos warned.

"I advise caution going forward. We cannot sustain a prolonged fight with our current numbers and ammunition supply," Vincent agreed. The people who were still in the bunker would be fighting with their backs against the wall and he didn't want to walk into another attack like the one that had brought down Zinvor.

Ezra pushed passed the group and ignoring Pharos' warning, took off running down the hallway. Fiona chased after him, leaving Vincent and Felicity with the group of Agents. Vincent wasn't sure if he had ever heard a Rhai groan or curse before but the noise that came out of Pharos was pretty close.

"He leaves us no choice, Consul," Pharos said, before running after them. Vincent quickly caught up to Ezra and Fiona. Ezra was trying to run as fast as he could, but it was obvious that his age and recently acquired smoking habit had slowed him down.

"Do you hear that?" Fiona asked, running alongside him effortlessly. Vincent strained to hear anything over the sound of Ezra's pained wheezing.

"Hear what?" he asked.

"Engines!" Ezra gasped. "It sounds like ship engines!" Ezra found a second wind and broke into a sprint. The hallway opened into a large bay. A roof that had protected the facilities from the orbital bombardment had been retracted, opening the bunker to the red Martian sky. A Reaper was parked in the middle of the landing area, its engines winding up and ground crew circling around it doing last minute checks. Bored looking Black Coats stood around the ship, rifles in their hands.

A group of Black Coats escorted the hunched form of Brusilov towards the Reaper. He looked like he had aged another decade since Vincent had seen him last. He was leaning heavily on a cane and his skin was an ashen, almost sickly white. The guards around the ship snapped to attention and saluted him as he approached.

Vincent raised his shotgun and fired.

One of them was hit by Vincent's shot and pitched over. The rest of the guards quickly scattered as the group poured their fire onto them. Many dropped dead before they had a chance to bring their weapons to their shoulders. When the initial confusion subsided, the Agents began pushing forward. The guards jumped in front of Brusilov to protect him while others quickly pushed him aboard the Reaper and slammed the troop compartment door closed.

"No!" Ezra screamed, firing off bursts from his rifle. His shots sparked harmlessly off of the ship. Vincent dropped his shotgun and dropped a member of the ground crew with his Riten.

The Reaper began to lift off, severing the refueling hose and spraying toxic fuel through the air. The side of the Reaper slid open, revealing a soldier with a mounted machine gun. Before Vincent could react, Fiona shoved him to the ground and landed on top of him. A burst of machine gun fire swept through the attackers. A round slammed into the ground next to Fiona's face, peppering her with debris.

As the ship rose into the air it slowly spun around, firing another long burst down at them. Something slammed into Vincent's calf, sending a jolt of blinding pain throughout his body. He cried out and grit his teeth as his armor filled with hot blood. He rolled over and saw his calf had been blown away. What remained looked like stringy bits of raw meat with bits of armor were embedded inside. Waves of pain began to wash over him, and it felt as if his entire leg was on fire.

"I'm hit!" Vincent screamed through gritted teeth. Fiona was on him in a second, placing one hand over the wound in his calf and rummaging through her pockets with the other. She found a white first aide dressing and wrapped it around his leg, cinching it down tight. He yelled out in pain as she worked.

"Get back here you fucking asshole!" Ezra shouted, firing his rifle into the sky as Brusilov's Reaper floated out of view. Vincent saw Ezra's flight suit was stained red around his stomach. A large crimson patch spread further as he struggled to get to his feet.

"Ezra!" Vincent yelled. "You're bleeding!" He looked down and touched his stomach with his hand, looking at the blood, his eyes went wide.

"Son of a bitch!" he grimaced. His eyes welled up with tears. "I was so fucking close. So close."

"It is not over," Pharos said. Before Vincent could ask what he meant, another ship entered the open roof of the bunker. The *Shanna II*. The ship, a little more unsteady than usual, came through the bunker at breakneck speed and came to an unsteady hover in front of them. In the cockpit, alone, was Tyr.

"Get me on my feet," Vincent said. Fiona pulled him up effortlessly. When he tried to put weight on his left foot is entire body nearly doubled over in pain. His fall was stopped by Fiona who slung his arm over her shoulder. Ezra attempted to walk to his ship, but his wound had taken its toll and he dropped to his knees. Felicity grabbed him under his shoulder and pulled him back to his feet.

"Colonel Vorbeck, you must seek medical attention," Pharos said, walking behind him. "Your wound looks fatal."

"Cohort Leader Pharos, I need you to fly my ship," Ezra gasped.

"Yes, I can fly you to the *Mercy* immediately." Pharos nodded.

"No." Ezra seethed with rage. "Catch that damned ship. Catch Brusilov."

* * *

The now all-Rhai flight crew of the *Shanna II* piloted the ship through the thick Martian clouds. Ezra sat, his back against the wall as Felicity bandaged his wound. Within seconds the dressing she had put in place had completely soaked through with blood. His olive colored skin was growing pale as their flight progressed.

"You still hanging in there, buddy?" Vincent asked.

"I should ask you the same thing." Ezra smiled weakly.

"I already lost an eye." He forced a laugh. "What is a calf in the grand scheme of things?" Ezra laughed, wincing as he did so. "This is what you get for fighting on the ground with us."

"Yeah that was dumb. It is kind of dangerous down there, eh?" Ezra said.

"I'm starting to think so," Vincent agreed.

"The target is up ahead," called out Pharos.

"Requesting permission to engage," Tyr responded.

"Do it!" Ezra ordered.

Brusilov's Reaper came into view, climbing rapidly in an attempt to flee the planet. Missiles streaked out from underneath the *Shanna II* and Brusilov's ship quickly spun out of the way as clouds of chaff erupted from the rear of their ship, confusing the missile detection devices. The missiles spun off wildly and exploded uselessly in the distance. Brusilov's ship began to climb higher, forcing Pharos to give chase. The ship's engines screamed as the larger ship strained to keep up.

Tyr fired a burst from the ship's nose cannon, striking the rear of the Reaper. Smoke began to trail from its left engine.

"The enemy ship is slowing down," Pharos said. The Reaper began to slow, before both of its engines flamed out, stalling mid-flight. The *Shanna II* was going too fast to intercept it and they streaked by the stricken ship.

The ship rocked with an explosion. Sirens began to whine, and the cockpit lit up with various warning lights.

"Rocket impact," Tyr informed them. "It seems they stalled out to get behind us." Bullets punched through the rear of the ship. Oil and hydraulic fluid ruptured from overhead lines and sprayed down onto the people inside. Bright green liquid rained onto Vincent and Fiona who didn't bother to make an attempt to shield themselves from it. The air scrubbers kicked on in a vain attempt to preserve the ship's compromised atmosphere.

"Are we fucking crashing?" Fiona yelled. "*Again,*" she added.

"No," Ezra said. "Not yet."

"What do you mean *not yet?*" Felicity shrieked in panic.

A high-pitched warning claxon assaulted their ears from somewhere in the cockpit as Pharos and Tyr quickly fiddled with dials and switches trying to keep the dying ship in the air.

"Now," Ezra sighed. "Now, we are crashing." *Shanna's* engines rattled and died, coughing out a thick black cloud of smoke.

Pharos jammed the control stick to the side, swinging the ship in a full one-hundred eighty-degree arc. Vincent's stomach did cartwheels, and he felt vomit rise into his mouth.

"What are you doing?" Ezra asked. "If you don't bring us into a controlled glide we are going to crash!"

"I am catching that damn ship," said Pharos. Brusilov's Reaper was now flying straight towards them on a collision course.

"Fire," Pharos ordered. The cannon ripped off a burst so long it sounded as if the ship itself was groaning in pain. The *Shanna II* rattled violently as the cannon chewed through thousands of rounds in a second. The shots exploded into the cockpit of the enemy Reaper. A geyser of flame erupted from the windshield. As the cannon burst ceased, the *Shanna II* began to fall from the sky, the on-coming Reaper hurdled by, uncontrolled, toward the ground. "Prepare for a hard landing," Pharos said, buckling his seatbelt. Vincent quickly buckled himself in as did everyone around him.

The ship began to sway as Pharos attempted to guide it towards the ground at an angle that wouldn't kill them all on the spot. Fiona took his hand in hers, squeezing hard.

The ship hit the ground violently, jarring everyone in their seats. Everything that wasn't strapped down flew forward into the cockpit, a wayward rifle smacked into the back of Tyr's head. The grinding, screeching sound of metal scraping across the Martian surface assaulted their ears. Sparks leapt up into the crew compartment, causing Ezra to panic and attempt to snuff them out with his boots. When the ship finally came to a rest, the compartment doors had been jammed shut. Tyr and Pharos climbed out of the cockpit and forced the compartment doors open from the outside.

"Everyone okay?" Fiona asked.

"Never better," winced Ezra as he was helped to his feet by Felicity, looking around his ship. "You know I had the *Shanna* for fifteen years before I met you two?" Vincent and Fiona burst out into nervous laughter. Fiona helped Vincent to his feet, gritting his teeth through the pain. "Now I've done through two of them."

"I'll get you a new one." Vincent thought for a moment before adding. "Another new one I mean."

Fiona helped Vincent out of the stricken ship and out into Mars. The wind had died down, showing the clearest day he had yet seen on the planet. All around them for miles was flat, barren nothingness. And a crashed Reaper. Fiona screamed.

"Look!"

Brusilov's Reaper had come down on its side only a few hundred feet away from where the *Shanna II* had come to rest. Thick black smoke poured from the engines. Various colored fluids leaked from the ship into the Martian dust, turning the red into a bright orange. Flames lapped up from the cockpit where Tyr had scored the killing blow.

"Are they dead?" Vincent asked. Fiona scoffed loudly and unholstered her Riten. Vincent did the same.

"Cockroaches don't die that easily."

"Can't we just blast them with our cannon again?" Felicity asked.

"Our primary and secondary weapons systems cannot function without power from the engines," Tyr said. They motioned to the engines which were now on fire. Tyr grabbed a small carbine from under their seat and joined them.

The group limped towards Brusilov's downed Reaper when its troop compartment popped open. The door was forced off of its hinges and fell to the ground below, kicking up a cloud of red dust. Smoke belched from the compartment as Black Coats flung themselves out of the craft, gasping for fresh air. A cascade of incoming fire killed them before they could clear the smoke from their lungs.

The next Black Coat who came out, did so fighting. Wild rifle shots snapped over Vincent's head until Pharos fired an expert shot into the middle of the man's chest, dropping him back into the ship. Soon, the fight was out of them. Three more wounded Black Coats emerged from the ship with their hands in the air. Fiona shot them down in cold blood before they could plead for mercy.

"Brusilov!" Ezra roared. "Show yourself!"

First a hand a single trembling hand appeared. Then a second, at the lip of the door. Brusilov pulled himself up and slumped over the broken remains of his ship. After a few moments of struggling he flopped onto the ground, landing next to several of his dead followers. His once flawless dress uniform was torn and tattered. His legs were hanging at strange, horrid angles, and blood trickled from a cut above his eye.

The old man's eyes went wide as he saw them approaching. His hand reached for his sidearm, but Ezra's boot slammed down hard on his hand, pinning it in place.

"Don't even fucking think about it," Ezra growled, his decades of burning rage fueling him to push past the pain of his wound. Ezra bent down and took the sidearm from its holster. "Do you remember me?" he asked.

"Fuck you," Brusilov answered. His words were strong, but his voice was weak and wavering. Ezra twisted his foot, Vincent heard Brusilov's hand pop and crack. He howled in pain.

"I'll ask you again," said, mashing his foot down once again. "Do you remember me?"

"Of course I do!" Brusilov yelled. "Vorbeck."

"That's right." Ezra knelt down. His bandage had long soaked through with blood. His blood had seeped all of the way down to the pants of his flight suit. but he didn't seem to notice. "How about my family?"

"Why would I remember the family of some insubordinate little shit like you?" Brusilov sneered defiantly. Ezra brought the butt of the stolen pistol down onto the bridge of the old man's nose with a sickening crunch. Brusilov gurgled in pain as blood poured out of his shattered face. "You goddamn savages!" he cursed. "I thought your Great Traitor was supposed to be a man that followed the law! I heard your pleas for surrender." Brusilov spat blood. "What are you going to do now eh? Kill me?"

Vincent stepped forward with Fiona's aid.

"No, I'm not going to kill you, Brusilov." He shook his head. The old man leaned back and sighed. A momentary look of relief showed across his bloody face. "But," Vincent continued with a nod towards Ezra, "he probably will, though." Ezra's pistol barked and punched a round into Brusilov's shattered left leg. Brusilov screamed and cradled his leg with his good hand. His blood turned the Martian dirt a near black color.

"My ship sent out a distress beacon to the Chairman's army on the Moon. They'll be coming for you traitors! You can't escape!"

"Good," Ezra said. He pulled the trigger again, this time firing into Brusilov's chest. His eyes went wide with shock before rolling back, showing only whites. His head lolled back, and blood foamed from his mouth before going limp. Ezra fell onto the ground in a seated position, tears streaming down his face.

"Tyr can you patch us through to the *Mercy*, he needs a medic or he's going to die," Vincent said. Tyr nodded and ran back towards the *Shanna II*. "Fiona, can you bring me into their ship?"

"Why?"

"He said they were able to get a distress signal out. Maybe they still have an orbital radio that can talk to Lunar City." She lifted him up into the ship and as gently as she could dropped him into the nearest seat. He shoved a dead Black Coat out of the way and found a crew radio. It was damaged but he could still hear static coming over the speakers.

Vincent grabbed the hand mic and clicked it.

"Radio check?" It hissed back at him. He clicked it again. "This is the Military Governor of Mars. Radio check?

"Victoria base?" Asked a broken voice from the radio. It was a man's voice that was distorted and garbled from millions of miles of delay through space, but they sounded relieved. "What is your status? We have heard some wild rumors about the city."

"Brusilov is dead," Vincent responded. Again, a few seconds of static passed through the air as the message traveled to the other listener.

"Repeat last traffic?" The voice asked in disbelief. "Who am I speaking with?"

"My name is Vincent Solaris. The story you've been told is a lie. I fought against the Anarchs on Grawluck with our Fidayi allies to save Earth, side by side with hundreds of thousands of EDF soldiers such as yourselves. Just like the hundreds of thousands that were left to die on Ryklar without their families or the people of Earth ever being told what really happened to them. It was not the Soldiers of the EDF, the Warriors of the Fidayi, or I that destroyed our home. It was the traitorous acts of the EDF high command and Central Committee that just wanted to further their own power. Hundreds of thousands of your comrades saw what the Committee was doing and joined us in Liberating Mars from their tyranny. Wherever you stand now just know the animal Brusilov is dead and Mars is free. We, the allied forces of Elysian, the Union of Titan, and Free Mars will not suffer the Central Committee to live."

Vincent paused for a moment. Fiona smiled her devilish smile at him before reaching over and grabbing the mic from him. She clicked it and spoke calmly.

"We are coming."

ABOUT THE AUTHOR

Joseph Kassabian served eight years in the US Army and multiple tours in support of the Global War On Terror. After he got tired of getting yelled at for wearing the wrong hat, he exited the Army to pursue a career in writing. He has used the bitter, jaded, and sarcastic sense of humor that he learned in the ranks and turned it into books, articles, and a podcast. Joe spends his time with his dog in the Great Moist Northwest while screaming at a laptop screen.

Joseph is also the author of Hooligans of Kandahar, a memoir of his second tour in Afghanistan with the U.S. Army. Hooligans won the 2017 eLit Awards Gold Medal in Current Events and sat as a **#1 Bestseller** on Amazon in the Central Asian History category. You can find Hooligans of Kandahar at:

https://www.amazon.com/gp/product/B07D26JRXJ/

Connect with Joe on Twitter at https://www.twitter.com/jkass99

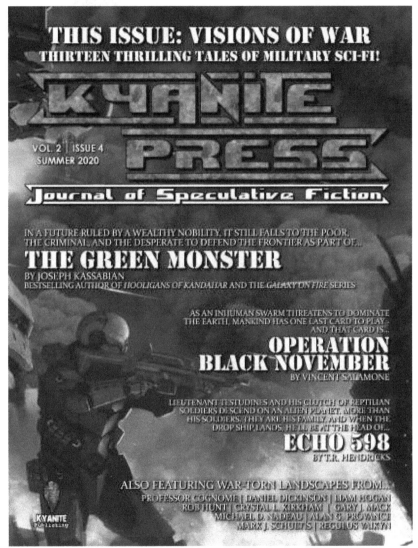

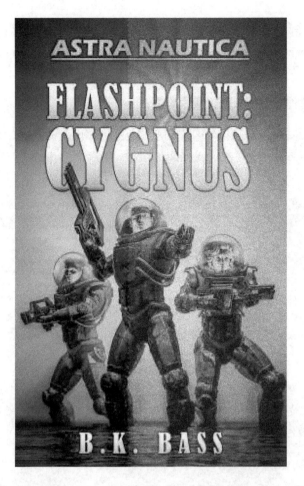

When Captain Fletcher Perry and the crew of the Terran Confederation frigate Falcata are sent to a backwater, independent colony in the Cygnus cluster, they expected to be overseeing a routine land rights dispute.

When they arrive, they find Marchovia embroiled in an all-out civil war.

As the frozen world becomes the focus of three stellar empires, Captain Perry and his crew find the only thing icier than the Marchovian landscape is the cold war they find themselves at the heart of.

COMING SOON FROM KYANITE PUBLISHING!

CPSIA information can be obtained
at www.ICGtesting.com
Printed in the USA
LVHW082141140820
663144LV00013B/149/J